DARK HAIR AND MATCHING EYES.

Perfectly proportioned.

No incidents on record. No signs of disobedience. The perfect submissive.

Multilingual. Fluent in current affairs. High aptitude for math.

I digested all the information as I memorized the portfolio laid out before me. After two years of searching, I'd finally found an ideal candidate, and just in time, too.

Item number seventeen, a twenty-two-year-old Caucasian female with striking features.

But her lack of rebellious instincts concerned me. Could I mold her into what I needed?

Any blood virgin I chose would require the same intense retraining. It might break a weaker mind, rendering my financial investment moot. But I had to try.

The brunette's photo glinted in the room's overhead lighting. All was revealed, including her supple breasts, slender waist, and feminine hips. Absolutely gorgeous. She would cost a small fortune.

I drew my thumb over my bottom lip. There was a fire in her near-ebony eyes that the others lacked. I'd use that to my advantage. Craft and mold her into the perfect poison.

The Blood Alliance would never anticipate it.

A hundred years of plotting, all culminating in the hands of a beautiful woman. She'd be the greatest weapon ever created and I would own her. Entirely.

Yes.

This was the one.

Hopefully, she wouldn't shatter under my command. If she did, I'd fix her. And start all over again. Until the endgame.

Which I would win.

At any cost.

Even if it meant sacrificing her life, in addition to mine.

Fuck the Blood Alliance.

Blood Alliance Series

Chastely Bitten

Royally Bitten

Regally Bitten

Blood Alliance

Volume One

USA Today Bestselling Author

Lexi C. Foss

Blood Alliance Volume One

Editing by: Outthink Editing, LLC

Cover Design: Manuela Serra

Model: Lucas & Evan

Photography: Wander Aguiar Photography

Published by: Ninja Newt Publishing, LLC

Print Edition

ISBN: 978-1-68530-083-8

Once upon a time,
humankind ruled the world while lycans and vampires lived in secret.

This is no longer that time.

Welcome to the future where the superior bloodlines make the rules.

PROCEED AT YOUR OWN RISK.

The Blood Alliance

International law supersedes all national governance and will be maintained by the Blood Alliance—a global council of equal parts lycan and vampire.

All resources are to be distributed evenly between lycan and vampire, including territory and blood slaves. Societal standing and wealth, however, will be at the discretion of the individual packs and houses.

To kill, harm, or provoke a superior being is punishable by immediate death. All disputes must be presented to the Blood Alliance for final judgment.

Sexual relationships between lycans and vampires are strictly prohibited. However, business partnerships, where fruitful and appropriate, are permitted.

Humans are hereby classified as property and do not carry any legal rights. Each will be tagged through a sorting system based on merit, intelligence, bloodline, ability, and beauty. Prioritization to be established at birth and finalized on Blood Day.

Twelve mortals per year will be selected to compete for immortal blood status at the discretion of the Blood Alliance. From this twelve, two will be bitten by immortality. The others will die. To create a lycan or vampire outside of this process is unlawful and punishable by immediate death.

All other laws are at the discretion of the packs and royals but must not defy the Blood Alliance.

Ghastly Bitten

Book One

Part One

Chastely Chosen

Darius

"ITEM SEVENTEEN IS A TWENTY-TWO-YEAR-OLD Caucasian female with mahogany hair and chocolate-colored eyes. Human is five foot seven, one hundred and thirty pounds, and speaks English, Spanish, Japanese, and German. Her other intellectual aptitudes are detailed on page nine of your guide."

I studied the brunette on the podium and recalled the qualities I memorized an hour earlier. Her profile suited my tastes and purpose—intelligent, multilingual, gorgeous, and innocent. Just what I needed.

The voracious gazes in the room confirmed this would be an expensive venture, but I enjoyed a challenge.

"Shall we start the bidding at one million?" The portly announcer seemed quite pleased with this amount.

I doubled it with a wave of my paddle.

Her sweet blood sang to my baser senses, which was entirely the point. She came from a rare breed of human who resembled ambrosia to my kind, and her virginity only enhanced the allure. The loss of her innocence would tamper the taste slightly, but not by much. Hence her value. I could keep her for days, months, years, or eternity, if I chose.

A beautiful pet to own and do with as I wished. And I would, just not in the way everyone anticipated.

I smiled as I raised my paddle again, tripling my neighbor's amount.

This woman would belong to me by the end of the night.

To fuck.

To eat.

To kill.

Whatever I wanted.

Poor thing. I almost felt sorry for her. But she seemed strong enough standing nude on the platform for all of us to examine her every attribute. I doubted she saw much beyond our legs, given the spotlight illuminating her gorgeous assets and face.

So pretty.

And so very much mine.

Chapter One

JULIET

SLEEK BLACK SHOES.

That's all I knew about my future.

No name, no face, just a vampire who bid the highest in the room for my body and blood.

"Remember your purpose," my matron murmured as she pulled a flimsy white dress over my head. It left me feeling more exposed than I had on the altar moments ago.

"Yes, Madam." The words burned against my dry throat. Standing naked on ceremony for a room full of society's most affluent monsters had nothing on what would come next.

Twenty-two years of training taught me what to expect and how to behave.

Bow.

Do not make eye contact.

Obey.

Three rules of etiquette all blood virgins followed. If I was lucky, he might let me live afterward.

My matron draped a deep-red cloak over my shoulders and tied it at the neck, hiding my sheer gown. A false sense of propriety that served as a way to preserve my innocence for my new master.

"You are ready, my child," my matron said as she secured the hood over my brown hair. The cape and gown were the only items I was permitted to keep outside these walls. I couldn't even take a pair of shoes.

"Thank you, Madam." An automatic reply brought on by years of strict discipline. If I performed as expected, I could one day become a matron too and instruct future blood virgins on proper protocol. But I had to endure and survive my own initiation first.

My palms heated as the doors of the ceremony room whispered open. Two vampires stood waiting in the stark white hallway. They weren't escorts, but guards meant to ensure my cooperation.

Running was never an option.

Neither was fighting.

Survival meant following procedure.

I swallowed the urge to scream. That never ended well. This would happen whether I agreed or not.

"Don't keep him waiting," my matron whispered, caution in her voice.

Part of the ritual was walking down that hallway willingly. Or so it would seem, anyway. Was it really consent when I didn't have a choice?

"Good day to you," I managed. My version of a goodbye to the only woman in my life I ever considered to be family. Not that I dared to tell her. Emotion equaled weakness when displayed outwardly, and I couldn't afford for anyone to consider me pathetic. Not if I wanted to live.

"And to you," she replied.

I inclined my head in a notion of respect before starting the path toward my future—to the male vampire I would call Sire.

My legs felt heavier with each step. I'd never ventured outside this compound. What existed beyond the front door other than a starless night?

The guards followed on either side, careful not to touch me. I belonged to someone else now. They were only permitted to handle me if I chose to fight, but I knew better.

My bare feet were silent against the pristine marble while the cloak rustled softly over my legs. I could feel the guards inspecting me. They had all seen me naked on that altar—like an animal put up for auction. Which was exactly how society perceived me.

An animal without rights.

I paused at the building's primary entrance and examined my destiny—a door handle. Once I twisted it, there would be no returning. Not without my Sire's permission.

But there isn't a choice.

I never had one.

My unique bloodline placed me here at birth.

The guards beside me shifted, an indication that my hesitation had not gone unnoticed. Any longer and I would be at risk of insubordination. I didn't want to end up there again.

My heart beat unsteadily as I pulled open the door to reveal the late hour of the night. A limo waited ominously in the driveway. No external lights.

Vampires preferred the dark. Only the hallway behind me illuminated the outside.

I stepped onto the porch and flinched as my feet touched the cold surface. The sensations grew with each move forward, then hurt as I found the cobblestone sidewalk that led to my fate.

The guards kept pace beside me, their gazes vigilant.

And then the back door of the limo opened.

I immediately fell to a bow, my knees touching the uneven stone as my forehead and palms met the ground. Vampires of status required complete and utter submission, especially a master. To greet him in any other manner would result in punishment, and I preferred to avoid that for my first night in his hands.

Expensive shoes appeared in my peripheral vision as a deep voice said, "I will take it from here."

"Of course," the guard to my right replied.

They disappeared on silent feet, leaving me at the mercy of my new owner.

Would he take me here? On the lawn? For all the others to see?

I trembled at the very real prospect.

He owns me.

I remained obedient, awaiting the inevitable. My matron prepared me for this moment. She taught me all the appropriate responses and platitudes to please my new master. But nothing could have equipped me for the reality.

What if I misspoke?

What if I couldn't handle the pain?

"Rise," he commanded.

Bile taunted my throat as I forced myself to comply. My eyes remained on his shoes as I stood gracefully with my hands clasped at my front.

Silence.

A test of my obedience? Vampires loved a good reason to invoke discipline, especially on the innocent.

Unfortunately for him, I excelled at these games. And I refused to break.

He circled me slowly, his steps soundless even in the still evening.

I focused on breathing steadily as he stopped right in front of me. Peppermint tickled my senses, as did a splash of something decidedly masculine. In the thickness of the night, I could barely discern his black suit, but he reeked of elegance and prestige. All vampires did.

He yanked the hood off my head so quickly my balance faltered, as did my pulse. I held my breath as he traced my jaw with the tip of his finger.

A male is touching me.

Forbidden.

Until now.

I knew to expect it, but the warmth of his touch was unlike anything I anticipated. Cold, harsh movements were what my matron told me to expect. Not this gentle exploration of my face. He paused at my chin and tilted my head upward and to each side, inspecting my neck.

"Have you been harmed in any way?" he asked, his voice softer now than before.

His word choice confused me until I translated his meaning. I swallowed twice before answering, "No one has touched me before you, Sire."

Only matrons were allowed in my quarters. The vampire guards could look, but not indulge, and their temptation was diluted anyway. Matrons satisfied guards as a form of training for the blood virgins. Some of those episodes would remain in my nightmares for years to come. Assuming I survived that long.

"I said harmed, not touched," he replied as he dropped my chin. "Get in the limo."

"Yes, Sire." I curtsied before adhering to his command.

I left my hood down since he didn't fix it and moved across the bench to allow him entry. He slid in beside me and closed the door with a finality.

Alone.

With a hungry vampire.

My stomach churned as the reason for my matron denying dinner tonight became obvious. She hadn't wanted me to throw up all over my new master.

I clasped my hands in my lap as the limo started to move and strived not to dig my nails into my palms. At least he hadn't taken me on the sidewalk. That had to be a positive sign. But now we were very much secluded and shrouded in darkness.

It felt more ominous this way.

His shifting did not help. Was he moving closer to me or farther away? The sifting of material suggested he was undressing.

Should I be removing my cloak as well? No. He would do that for me.

Oh, Goddess. We would do this now. I preferred the soft leather over the concrete outside, but—

"What is your given name?" he asked, interrupting my thoughts.

I swallowed the rocks in my throat, so I could force a response. "Whatever you desire it to be, Sire." Could he hear the raspy quality of my voice? The nerves escaping what should otherwise be steadfast control?

"Emotion will get you killed," my matron said more than once.

Pull it together.

"That is not what I requested," he replied, his voice holding an edge. "What is the name you were given at birth?"

I blinked. This did not follow proper protocol. Masters chose a blood virgin's identity. Who or what I was prior to meeting him no longer applied. Only my training mattered. But his tone left no room for disobedience. I would comply because I had to.

"Juliet."

More of that rustling occurred from his side of the car, followed by a snick of silk. Him removing his tie? Some of the guards did this when they wanted to play with a matron's pain tolerance. They would bind their hands or use the fabric as a blindfold. A chill swept down my spine. *What is he planning to do to me?*

"Juliet." It sounded as if he was tasting my name and found it to his liking. "I'm Darius."

I froze. This definitely broke protocol. A blood virgin always referred to her master as Sire. Never his name. My matron did not prepare me for such a twisted conversation. What sort of game was he playing?

No response felt appropriate, so I remained silent. His goading would not convince me to break decorum.

Light blazed around us, shocking my eyes. They shut automatically as I tried to quickly regain my composure, but he'd no doubt seen my startled reaction. His vampiric gaze wouldn't sting from the sudden brightness inside the limousine.

Something popped, but I couldn't see it.

My heart sang in my ears as I attempted to recover control of my wandering emotions. I felt sick and light-headed at the same time, and helpless.

Tears dampened my cheeks both from the abrupt brightness above and the terror building in my chest. I'd prepared for this. I knew what to expect. This should not be happening.

Stop reacting.

Focus.

Breathe.

My lungs refused as my hands fisted. All manner of punishments filled my thoughts. Not even ten minutes in and he'd managed to break right through my barriers and forced me to slip up.

By turning on the lights. Of all things to set me off…

"Here. This will help," he murmured as he nudged my hand with something cold and solid. "Drink."

I wrapped my quivering fingers around the thin stem and lifted the glass to my lips. Something sharp and fruity touched my tongue, causing my eyelids to spring open. The liquid sputtered from my mouth as I gasped.

"Well, that was graceful," he remarked as he bent to retrieve something from a cabinet near his feet.

He'd taken off his jacket and tie, leaving him clad in a black dress shirt that he'd unbuttoned at the neck to reveal a glimpse of olive skin.

My eyes moved of their own accord to catalog his handsome features.

Elegantly cropped dark hair.

Defined cheekbones.

Square jaw.

Striking green eyes framed with thick dark lashes.

Oh no.

I immediately dropped my gaze. In my moment of shock and confusion, I'd studied my master's face.

Could this go any more wrong? I knew the rules, yet it'd taken mere minutes to throw them all out the window.

"Forgive me, Sire," I whispered. "The alcohol startled me." It was expressly forbidden. Blood virgins did not imbibe. Ever. It tainted our bloodlines.

He plucked the drink from my shaking hand and draped a towel over my fingers. "Clean yourself up, Juliet."

My throat clogged with repressed emotion. To perform so poorly reflected not only on me, but also on my matron. He would seek her punishment in addition to mine.

How had I managed to mess this up so spectacularly?

I used the cloth to clean up my hand and cloak and started to kneel to wipe up the droplets on the floor, but his hand on my wrist held me in place. He said nothing for so long I wondered if he was struggling to determine how first to hurt me. Vampires were notorious in their cruelty. I'd witnessed so many executions, floggings, public rapes, and blood baths that I could too-well imagine his intentions for me.

He let go of my wrist to switch off the lights. I sat still in the shadows of the limo, waiting. My limbs shook with confusion and fear, too fierce to hide. Not that it mattered anymore. I'd more than earned my sentencing. A little emotion sprinkled on top would neither improve nor worsen my pending chastisement.

"You are forgiven, Juliet," he said quietly. "We will be traveling for some time. I recommend you sleep."

"You wish for me to sleep, Sire?" The waiver in my voice couldn't be helped. He claimed to forgive me, but vampires excelled at lying. I knew better than to let those words placate me.

"Yes. Rest."

"A-as you wish, Sire." Did he intend to wake me cruelly? Would that be my penalty for misbehaving? That seemed rather docile, but it depended on his methodology.

I closed my eyes in a false attempt to follow his command but knew my heartbeat gave me away. He would know the truth, but I had to try.

Anything to appease him.

My master.

It was my duty to obey. My duty to accept punishment. My duty to give my body and blood. Only to him. Until he no longer had use for me.

There was no escape.

Nowhere to run.

Follow the rules or die.

I didn't want to die.

Chapter Two

Juliet

"MISS." A sharp shake, followed by, "Please. You must wake up."

I blinked, startled by the unfamiliar voice. It didn't belong to my matron or any other woman in my history.

I sat upright in the foreign bed and took in my surroundings. Royal blues and golds flourished throughout the oversized room, all illuminated by candlelight. "Where am I?"

"Master Darius's home," a stout woman with graying hair informed. "He mentioned you may be drowsy from your long sleep, and also as a side effect of compulsion."

Perspiration dotted my brow and hands. The last thing I remembered was attempting to sleep, then nothing. I didn't even know how long we drove, or where he'd taken me.

"Master Darius requests you for dinner," the older woman said as she laid a revealing black gown over the bedsheets. "You are to wear this."

I studied her. "Are you my new matron?" Her age indicated her humanity, but I didn't recognize her as one of the blessed.

"Er, no, I'm one of Master Darius's housemaids. There are several of us, as well as other servants who maintain the manor." Her blue eyes crinkled. "You may call me Ida, love. Darius informed me to call you Juliet."

My brow furrowed. "He did?"

"Yes, is he wrong?"

"Oh, of course not. If he has chosen Juliet, then that is what I am to be called." How bizarre, though, that he would select my given name. Perhaps he liked it?

Ida looked me over with interest. "I've heard rumors of your kind. Master Darius is in for a treat."

I shivered at the underlying meaning of her words. My body would be his *treat* for *dinner.* I supposed that was better than the lawn outside the Coventus, or in his limousine.

"I shall prepare myself," I said quietly as I slid out of the silk sheets.

Someone had removed my cloak, leaving me in the sheer white gown from earlier. I pulled it over my head and traded it for the black dress. It was no less revealing than my previous outfit, with its sheer bodice and slitted skirt. Both my legs were exposed to the hip, and my breasts were pronounced beneath the translucent material. Typical blood virgin attire. Although, usually a woman in my position only wore darker colors after losing her virginity.

Unless…

Had he taken me while I slept?

Goose bumps filed down my arms at the very real prospect.

Perhaps that was the true purpose for knocking me out.

I spied a mirror in the corner near a door leading to tiled floors. *A bathroom.* One meant only for my use? *Not important.*

I moved on wooden legs, terrified of what I might see, but found my appearance to be normal with the exception of my sleep-nested hair. No visible marks on my neck, arms, or thighs. And I didn't feel sore anywhere. From what my matron told me, it would hurt, perhaps for days afterward. If he'd taken me, I should know.

"There is a brush and other essentials in there," Ida said, reminding me of her presence. She stood off to the side, hands folded before her, appearing curious. "Do you require any assistance?"

I cleared my throat. "No, Madam, but thank you."

She smiled. "I will wait for you by the door, then." She pointed to the large wood panel across the room and bowed her head slightly before leaving me by the bath area.

A human maid. How intriguing. I supposed vampires and lycans would employ them. My bloodline was too cherished and rare to be influenced by humanity. We were owned from birth and protected by vampire guards. Or perhaps *incarcerated* was the better word. Not that I could use it out loud.

I found a brush in the bathroom and went about fixing my brown hair into voluminous waves. My matron claimed it to be my best feature, so I would showcase it accordingly. Once finished, I brushed my teeth and added a few other feminine touches. I was already prepped and shaved from the auction, so it didn't take me long to return to Ida.

She smiled kindly, her eyes crinkling at the sides. "I wish we could all be so confident." She handed me a pair of four-inch heels with the words.

"I beg your pardon?" I asked, confused as I slid on the stilettos.

"Nothing, darling. Master Darius is waiting. He has two guests with him as well."

My heart sped up as we walked. "Guests?"

"Yes. Master Trevor and Master Ivan."

I swallowed the tremor bubbling up my throat. "Both are here for dinner?" *To enjoy me?*

"Yes," she replied as she escorted me down a very wide staircase leading to a grand foyer below.

Three vampires at once? I nearly missed a step at the thought. Surely Darius couldn't mean for them all to have me tonight. Unless he intended for me to die, in which case, he certainly did mean for this to happen.

"This way," Ida said as we reached the bottom step. My heels clacked against the marble tile, announcing our path. It reminded me of beating drums before an execution, or perhaps that was just my heart thumping an ominous rhythm.

Most blood virgins did not return to the Coventus. Our blood was so potent and addictive that vampires could hardly contain themselves and drank us dry.

Or so my matron warned.

I could do nothing to stop him if that's what he desired. Screaming only sweetened the moment. I was the equivalent of an expensive steak meant to be devoured, or savored, whichever my master preferred.

That thought used to bring tears to my eyes, but I learned long ago that fate would never change her path for me. At least my end would be quick.

Ida knocked on a dark-wood door.

"Enter." Darius's deep voice sent a flutter to my lower abdomen. I remembered the face that paired with the tone, and his bright-green eyes. I never should have looked.

"He means for you to enter, dear, not me," Ida murmured with an encouraging nod.

Of course she would prefer me to join the feast and not her. Clear self-preservation. I couldn't fault her for that.

"You've been very kind to me," I told her. "Thank you."

Her lips curled into a bemused grin. "A treat indeed." She shook her head. "Go now before he asks again."

I nodded. "Yes, of course." Vampires did not appreciate having to wait.

I pushed open the door to peek inside and found the room lit by more candles. A long mahogany table graced the center beneath a chandelier with enough chairs around it to seat an army. Expensive cutlery and plates adorned four place settings, and before them was an array of platters with scents that tickled my nose.

Master Darius stood against the wall just inside the door, flanked by his two suit-clad counterparts.

"Sire," I greeted as I assumed my position on the floor near his feet with my forehead touching the marble ground.

Their eyes felt like brands against my exposed skin, leaving marks as they admired my submissive position. They said nothing, yet I *felt* every unspoken word. Hunger and arousal thickened the air, churning my stomach as I waited for the first one of them to pounce.

This is my purpose, I reminded myself as I steadied my breathing.

In. One, two, three.

Out. One, two, three.

Focusing on my inhales and exhales did little to still my thundering heart. I couldn't hide the harsh sound from their predatory senses. It served as a beacon, alluring me to them more.

A tremor traversed my spine.

Three on one. I'd seen it done too many times. Would I be able to handle their penetrations? Would I die swiftly?

Goddess, I prayed, evoking the highest power on Earth. *Please end it quickly…*

Their shoes whispered over the floor as they circled me.

"She's exquisite," one of them murmured. "And there's no denying the temptation."

"Yes." The familiar masculine tone called to my training and demanded complete surrender. He owned me in every way.

"But can she be reprogrammed?" the third voice asked, his tone decidedly foreign.

"Time will tell," Master Darius replied as he crouched before me. "Are you going to do this every time you see me?" His finger found my chin as he forced me to meet his gaze. "Because I'm already annoyed by it."

"Sire?" I asked, confused as I tried to look anywhere except his face. To meet a master's stare was expressly forbidden. It suggested challenge, and I did not wish to engage him in that manner.

He pinched my chin hard, bringing tears to my eyes. "Look at me, Juliet." I swallowed and forced myself to comply. Those sharp green irises burned into mine. So hypnotically handsome, yet lethal. And so very old.

"You are not to bow in this manner unless I expressly request it. Do you understand?"

Not really… "May I seek clarification, Sire?" A bold question, one that could earn me additional punishment, but I needed more details to comply.

"You may," he replied, and I swore he sounded almost amused.

"How would you prefer me to bow?" I asked. "This is the way of my training, but as it displeases you, I will conform my methods."

"No bowing at all," he clarified.

"Shall I curtsy, then?"

"No." He dropped my chin and stood. "Rise, Juliet."

"Yes, Sire." I rose swiftly to my feet and averted my gaze once more to the floor.

Silence.

I didn't quite know what he wanted me to do with my hands, so I left them at my sides while the three of them admired my dress.

"She's truly lovely," one of the males murmured.

"Indeed," my master replied. "Shall we eat?"

My stomach churned at the casual words. No more platitudes or demands, just *dinner.*

"I'm famished."

"Likewise."

"Excellent," my master said as he moved into my personal space. I remained still as he placed a hand at the small of my back.

This was it.

My final moments.

If I complied, it would be less painful.

I pulled my hair over one shoulder, exposing my neck, and waited.

Please let it be quick.

Chapter Three

Darius

FUCK, SHE SMELLED AMAZING.

My maker—Cam—had once warned me of the temptation brought on by a blood virgin, but I'd never taken him seriously. However, after several hours in the limo beside Juliet, I finally understood.

The woman was irresistible.

My incisors ached with the need to taste her—even if for a second. Trevor and Ivan would feel it too, but propriety kept them from trying anything.

And Christ, the bowing. To put herself in such a submissive position aroused all my darker needs, which was obviously the point.

It had to stop. Everything she did, every word she said, were all express signs of submission ingrained in her from years of indoctrination. It shouldn't appeal to me, but damn if I wasn't aroused right now.

Ivan's amusement rolled off him in waves. Of course he was enjoying this. He'd been all for our royal friend's ridiculous idea that I purchase a blood virgin for status. Oh, it would work, assuming I could withstand the temptation of taking her too soon.

Juliet's pulse thrummed healthily in her exposed neck, taunting my instincts. I could devour her and she would do nothing to stop me—maybe even encourage me.

But it wouldn't be real.

All trained responses meant to please the highest bidder. Not that I blamed her. She was a victim of her bloodline.

I flexed my palm on her lower back to pull her slightly closer and lifted my opposite hand to curl around her nape. She leaned into the touch and closed her eyes, but her lips trembled slightly.

Fear.

It seemed no amount of preparation could properly ready her for this moment. Not surprising.

I flicked my thumb over her pulse and her jaw clenched.

Mmm, a fighter lurked beneath the surface. She wanted to live in a world where most humans preferred death. Fascinating.

I leaned in to inhale her addictive fragrance. So sweet, and alluring. Knowing I didn't have to resist only deepened my desire to taste her. To take her.

My lips found her pulse and kissed her neck coaxingly. She seemed to melt against me, her body recognizing its purpose. But her jaw remained tense.

I'd chosen well.

Very, very well.

I nibbled her tender skin, careful not to break the surface, before placing my lips at her ear. "Bow or curtsy in my presence again, and I will bite you next time, Juliet." I nuzzled her cheekbone as she shivered before pulling back to meet her gaze. "And I expect you to look at me when I'm talking to you."

She blinked, as if dazed. "But decorum states—"

I nipped her pulse, silencing her trained response.

"I don't care what decorum states, Juliet."

I laved the scratch created by my incisors and closed my eyes as a spec of her essence met my tongue. Fucking heaven. What I wouldn't give to sink my teeth into her vein and take my fill.

But I needed her alive, and I desired her acquiescence. It would make taking her all the sweeter. Because I would have her and her permission. Eventually.

I allowed myself one more taste as Trevor and Ivan watched with envy in their gazes. It wasn't just her blood that teased them, but this revealing dress. I'd chosen it to show them how lucrative she would be, and their expressions confirmed my every suspicion.

"I apologize for displeasing you, Sire," Juliet whispered.

I suppressed the urge to growl. My aristocratic brethren fancied this obedient behavior. Submission I understood and enjoyed, but her subservience was evoked by fear of harsh punishment. I preferred the pleasurable kind of reprimand, something Juliet would soon learn.

But I had a few walls to break down first.

And twenty-two years of ingrained etiquette.

"You are to do as I say, correct?"

"Yes, Sire."

"Then you will obey my requests not to bow or curtsy in my presence unless otherwise requested." I forced myself away from her neck and tilted her head in a way that made it impossible for her to avoid my gaze. "And you will make eye contact with me whenever we are speaking with one another. Do you understand?"

"I…" She swallowed visibly but held my stare warily. "Yes. Of course, Sire."

"Excellent." I released her nape and pulled her toward the table. "Take a seat."

"You always were gifted with the ladies, Darius," Trevor remarked, his humor evident.

"We should take notes," Ivan agreed.

"For when we buy our own fuck dolls?" Trevor asked, a smile in his voice.

"Absolutely. I want a redhead."

"Hmm, yeah, I'm craving a brunette right about now."

"I think we all are, mate."

"Enough," I growled as I helped Juliet into her chair. She sat very still and kept her focus on the table while I took a seat beside her. It seemed the eye contact thing would take some work.

Trevor and Ivan sat across from us, their expressions matching ones of amusement.

"Why did you both drop by, again?" I demanded.

"You know why," Ivan replied. "Trevor wanted to see your new toy."

I rolled my eyes. "She's not a toy."

"She's a walking fuck doll with delectable blood," Trevor murmured. "Definitely a toy."

Juliet didn't react to the crude description and remained outwardly complacent with her hands folded in her lap. That sort of control would come in handy later.

I reached for a platter of roasted duck and slid a few slices onto Juliet's plate before serving myself.

Trevor and Ivan followed suit, taking several sides and lathering their dishes with Gladice's fine cooking. They frequently tried to buy her from me, but I always refused. I had one of the best chefs in the region and did not plan to give her up anytime soon. All my servants were my own. I protected them fiercely, just as I would the beauty beside me.

She eyed the food I placed in front of her before shyly glancing around the table.

I grinned as understanding slithered through my thoughts. Juliet expected to be the main course. A definite temptation, one I might indulge another night when we were alone. Assuming she was willing.

My friends had obviously come to the same conclusion because they both smirked at her confusion.

Poor girl. She had no idea what I'd dragged her into, but she would soon learn.

I draped my arm over the back of her chair, crowding her personal space, and pressed my lips to her ear again. "Vampires eat food too, darling."

It was more of an unnecessary indulgence since we didn't require it to survive, but my taste buds appreciated the flavor.

"I know," she whispered. "Of course I know that." That last bit seemed more for her than for me, but I replied anyway.

"Good." I nipped her pulse and thought of something else. "You'll know when I intend to bite you, Juliet. Because I'll warn you before our first time."

She startled at my words, her perception clouded by what the Coventus had drilled into her pretty head. What she didn't realize was that not all vampires were created equal. And I prided myself on being a rebel.

"Eat," I told her as I righted myself. "You'll need your strength."

Juliet required a gradual introduction to my needs. If I rushed it, she'd die, and I needed her very much alive. I also required her trust, and that would be the trickiest emotion of them all. Because no sane human trusted a vampire.

Trevor lifted his wine glass in salute. "To new endeavors."

"To the future," Ivan added.

"To change," I replied, saluting them both with my glass.

Juliet was the only one who didn't indulge because she didn't yet understand. But she would. And soon.

I smiled as she picked up her fork to oblige my demand. That little obedient habit would come in handy over the coming months. She would do whatever I wanted, wherever I wanted.

Not a toy but an asset. With perfect breasts and the face of a goddess, no one would suspect her. And I owned every mouthwatering inch of her.

"Seems you'll have quite the training on your hands, Darius," Ivan said as he nodded to an apprehensive Juliet. She picked up a slice of meat and nibbled it gingerly before setting her fork down with a confused expression.

"Do they not allow duck in the Coventus?" I asked dryly.

She blinked big brown eyes up to mine and grimaced. "I… yes… but not quite like this."

"Like what?"

"Rich," she whispered. "It's decadent, Sire." She started to drop her gaze in submission but lifted them before I could comment on it. Yes, her obedience training would certainly suit my plans.

"You mean it's savory," I interpreted. "Let me guess; they forced you to live on the bare essentials and outlawed all foods with actual flavor?" Typical brainwashing technique. It also served to keep her figure in check, and they'd certainly accomplished that.

"My blood is pure, Sire."

"Pure." The word tasted sour on my tongue. Society meant to control her appearance to increase her worth, not strengthen her bloodline. She would taste the same no matter what she consumed, and her virginity wouldn't impact her natural flavor. "My brethren have molded you into the perfect woman, Juliet. Delectable, demure, gorgeous. I can assure you the eating habits ingrained in you only impact one of those traits, and it is not your blood."

I sampled the duck and found it cooked to perfection, as always, while Juliet frowned. Not her best look, but I preferred it to the fear radiating from her.

"Forgive me, Sire, but I do not understand your meaning. Is this a test of sorts?" She licked her lips. "I do not wish to fail you."

Trevor smirked as Ivan shook his head with a bemused smile. Both of them were enjoying this far too much. They knew my patience rarely upheld in these types of matters, but I could hardly fault the woman for what my kind had done to her.

I set my fork aside and wrapped my arm around her chair again. She stopped breathing as I traced the column of her neck with my index finger. "You denied my champagne in the limousine," I murmured. "Because alcohol is forbidden, yes?"

Her eyes—still holding mine as instructed—flared. So much for her terror level decreasing.

"Yes," she whispered. "I-I'm sorry, Sire."

It took me a moment to realize what she meant—spewing her drink all over the place after I demanded she take a sip. Most in my position would have punished the new pet for behaving impudently, but I saw her as something else entirely.

"I already forgave you," I reminded. "But I would like to teach you a lesson."

Her heart beat loudly, alluring all the vampires in the room, including me. Trevor and Ivan stopped eating, their focus shifting to the frightened blood virgin and her singing pulse.

"Of course, Sire." The words were so soft I nearly missed them.

My arm fell to her shoulders to hold her close as I said, "Give me your hand, Juliet."

She presented the one closest to me, as if her body was a puppet for me to command. I grasped her wrist with my free hand and brought it to my lips for a kiss.

Her body trembled, belying her stoic expression. I truly missed the days when human females provided at least a little bit of sass or fight. Perhaps I could instill some in this one, over time.

"You've been taught that alcohol and rich foods will tarnish your bloodline, yes?" I traced her pulse with my tongue and enjoyed the way it skipped beneath my touch. So lovely.

She nodded. "Yes, Sire."

"You've also been taught that keeping your blood pure is important to please your master?"

Another nod, this one firmer.

"Excellent, then this should be an easy lesson, darling." I nipped her tender skin, eliciting a tender blush across her hand. "I'm going to taste you now." I didn't wait for her compliance as it wasn't required. She knew her purpose.

My incisors pierced her vein with practiced ease, pulling just enough of her sweet essence to satisfy my curiosity and not excite the hunger within.

Heaven, my instincts murmured as my stomach clenched with the need for more.

It would be so easy to drag her into my lap and take everything from her. That dress left nothing to the imagination—a mere rip would remove it. And she would acquiesce to my every request.

Because she belongs to me.

Fuck. I never expected that to be so erotic. The art of owning a person was morally wrong, and yet, I couldn't bring myself to regret it.

One night and already my control threatened to slip from a single taste of her euphoric blood. I expected it to be alluring—addicting, even—but not this erotic inclination to take her completely.

She quivered as I allowed myself one more swallow, and her sweet arousal prickled the air. I had chosen unconsciously to introduce pleasure with my bite rather than pain. Her little trembles almost encouraged me to continue, but we had a lesson to finish. I released her vein—with considerable effort—and licked her wound while holding her drowsy stare.

"Try the wine," I told her with a hint of compulsion underlying my tone. "Now."

She lifted the glass with her free hand and brought it to her lips before realizing what I demanded. "Sire…"

"Now," I repeated.

Tears glistened in her gaze as she followed my command and sipped the red wine. Her throat convulsed around it as she swallowed, and her eyes closed. I didn't chastise her for the disobedience but instead laved at her wound and gently bit her again, this time a little deeper for my own personal enjoyment.

Her lips parted on a moan as I infused endorphins into the bite—my way of praising her for adhering to my demands. The crystal glass in her hand shook, and her head fell back against my arm.

No terror now, just pure, unadulterated bliss, and it was seductive as hell. If it weren't for our audience, I would have pushed her further. They'd more than received a show tonight—one that would only solidify my plans for her.

I eased her return to reality by slowly withdrawing my incisors and healing her marks with my tongue. Some of my kind preferred to leave the wounds open as a way of declaring ownership, but I wanted her healthy and unmarred. Her creamy skin was too beautiful to damage.

Her thick lashes fluttered as she opened her almond-shaped eyes and met my gaze again. *So well-behaved.*

"You're just as sweet now as you were moments ago, Juliet," I murmured. "The alcohol only alters your mental state and, in excess, could cause weight gain. But it holds no power over your delicious blood, love. I will taste you again tomorrow if you require more proof."

I kissed her pulse once more before returning her hand to her lap. "Now eat your dinner and stop fretting about rules that hold no meaning in this house. I will tell you what I expect and you will comply. Understood?"

Her pink cheeks deepened to an appealing crimson as she muddled her way through the cloud of desire. I imagined it was a foreign feeling, one her matron wouldn't have taught her because she wouldn't have known it existed.

As second-class citizens, humans were not promised the right to pleasure of any kind. Pain, certainly. Enjoyment, no. That didn't make my granting of gratification illegal, just not customary. Though, I suspected most of my kind allowed it in certain degrees, depending on our proclivities.

Her pink tongue darted out to wet her lips, then she nodded. "Yes, Sire."

"Then I consider this lesson closed," I replied as I removed my arm from her shoulders. "Enjoy your meal."

Because I certainly enjoyed mine, even if it barely qualified as an appetizer.

Chapter Four

JULIET

THE MOON SHONE BRIGHTLY OUTSIDE the balcony doors of my room. It lit up the courtyard and the thick cluster of unending trees surrounding the outskirts of the property.

I'd spent most of the early evening admiring the breathtaking view. Darius's home provided a false sense of calm that didn't exist in the walls surrounding the Coventus. Something new and quite… soothing.

Last night he had requested my presence for dinner, then excused me after dessert.

No proper feeding, nor did he offer me to his guests.

I didn't understand this game at all.

My matron had prepared me for every situation, or so I thought. But my Sire played by a foreign set of rules. He forced me to imbibe alcohol, something expressly prohibited. And yet, I enjoyed it. Perhaps too much.

Or maybe that was his bite.

My thighs clenched with the memory of his mouth on my skin. Never in my wildest dreams had I expected *that.*

It was unlike all of the scenes I'd witnessed between my matron and the vampires during my training. She usually cried silently as they took her however they craved. And when she screamed, they punished her more.

Silence was an important skill taught at a young age. Vampires preferred quiet pets who allowed them full access to whatever they desired. And I'd been prepared for that with Darius. I expected him to hurt me while sating his needs. Instead he granted me *sensation.*

My lips threatened to curl in a way they rarely did.

A trick, my mind whispered. *It's all a trick of some sort.*

Yes. A pleasurable one.

For now.

A knock startled my daydreaming. I blinked at the door, waiting for it to open.

"Juliet?" The deep voice ignited a flutter in my lower abdomen.

Why didn't he enter at will?

Another knock.

Odd.

I wandered over to open the unlocked door and revealed a suit-clad Darius waiting for me in the hallway.

"Sire," I murmured, my knees bending slightly on instinct. Remembering his command not to curtsy or bow, I straightened and caught his quirked brow. "It is a formal habit, Sire." Not that it was an excuse. My body should follow his every whim on instinct regardless of former training.

"May I come in?" he asked.

"Always." I stepped aside while forcing my eyes to remain on his face rather than averted. His chiseled jaw and sculpted cheekbones were easy to admire. It was his intense stare that I had to watch out for—I could easily lose myself in those green orbs.

"Ida informs me that you've been in your quarters all evening," he murmured. "Are you not hungry?"

Last night's feast offered me enough sustenance for a week. "I feel quite satisfied at present." I used the cup in the bathroom for water earlier when I required it.

"I see." He clasped his hands behind his back as he stared down at me. "You are free to wander the manor whenever you want."

"Sire?" That seemed… inappropriate.

He arched a brow. "Do you require a tour?"

"I…" Did I? "Would you like to give me a tour?"

He studied me for a long moment before saying, "This obedient habit is already trying my patience, Juliet. Change into something more appropriate, and I'll provide you with a new task."

"Of course, Sire." I fingered my robe. "What would you prefer me to wear?"

He smirked. "What would I prefer you wear?" He scratched his jaw before palming the back of his neck. "I'd prefer you in nothing, if I'm honest."

I untied the silk rope around my waist and allowed my robe to fall to the floor. "As you wish, Sire."

His grin slipped. "That…" He trailed off as his eyes dropped to my exposed breasts and continued lower to examine every inch of my body along the way.

Nudity didn't faze me, but I'd never stood this close to a male before without clothes. And this one could touch me at will.

That should have frightened me, yet my stomach seemed to tighten in a different manner entirely. Especially as his pupils dilated with unveiled hunger.

He wants to bite me again.

I think I want that too.

An unfamiliar warmth followed his stare, caressing all of my nerves and awakening a foreign sensation between my thighs. I fought to remain still and to maintain a calm demeanor as he met my gaze once more with a decidedly ravenous gleam.

"Sarcasm," he murmured as he stepped closer. He gathered my brown waves to one side, exposing my neck to his view. "But your literal interpretation is hardly something I can chastise."

His body brushed mine as he pressed his lips to my throat. "If I told you to please me orally—right now—would you drop to your knees?"

My mouth went dry at the prospect.

I'd witnessed fellatio countless times during my training, had even undergone oral exercises for practice, but I'd never performed the act on a real male—touching a member of the opposite sex prior to my auction was strictly prohibited. I hadn't minded, as I always thought the act would repulse me, but the idea of exploring Darius so intimately appealed in a dark way.

"Is that your wish, Sire?" I whispered.

"With a mouth like yours, I imagine it would be the desire of most men, Juliet." His teeth skimmed my pulse. I quivered at the sensual memory his mouth evoked and found myself longing for his bite.

None of this was what I expected. I anticipated harsh words, painful penetration, and the very real fate of death. Not this sensual play.

I opened my mouth to ask if he wanted me on my knees, but the words froze in my throat as he grasped my hips and pulled me flush against him. My heart skipped a beat at the very real proof of his arousal thickening against my belly.

A silent demand for me to act? I wasn't sure.

Perspiration dampened my palms as I lifted my fingers to trace the edge of his belt. He caught my wrist and whirled me around, pressing my back to his chest. My pulse skyrocketed at the fast, unexpected move, then stuttered as he flattened his hand against my lower abdomen, holding me in place.

I couldn't breathe, not with his lips tasting my neck.

Oh, Goddess…

His tongue traced a hypnotic pattern that left me delirious in his arms. A wave of heat rolled over me, centering in my stomach and spiraling outwards.

A whimper escaped me as I fought to understand all these sensations. Hot, cold, tension in every limb…

His palm started downward.

Slowly.

The breath caught in my throat, uncertain, as he explored the freshly groomed space between my hips. I'd been shaved everywhere prior to the auction, something my matron stated my new master would prefer.

"Time for a new lesson," he whispered.

"S-Sire?" I didn't—

My knees buckled as his fangs pierced my skin.

Intense.

Sudden.

And much harder than last night.

But also, really good.

He held me against him with one arm wrapped around my chest and a hand on my stomach. I shuddered at the possessive hold and the warmth swimming through my veins. Most vampires didn't infuse their bites with endorphins, but Darius did. And I was very thankful for it.

His name almost slipped from my lips as he drew my essence into his mouth. It burned in an intense way that caused my thighs to squeeze in response and my eyes to close.

This was my purpose, and it felt so right in his arms.

The fear I expected in this moment was replaced by a passion I never knew existed. Humans weren't meant to feel like this, or perhaps *allowed* was the more accurate term. The forbidden nature of our embrace only enhanced my enjoyment.

His hand ventured lower, to a place I didn't realize I wanted to be touched until now. I knew he belonged there and understood that he owned my body, but the reality far surpassed my assumptions.

I grabbed his forearm, needing something to hold on to as he parted my slick folds. My limbs shook as he slipped a finger inside me and penetrated me from above and below.

It was so overwhelming and powerful.

I didn't know how to think, couldn't remember how to breathe.

All I could do was feel.

His mouth.

His hand.

His heat.

I rocked against him wantonly, unable to stop myself from seeking more, *needing* more.

"Darius…" My legs trembled uncontrollably, his arm around my breasts the only thing keeping me upright.

I felt caged, protected, and owned.

He took a dangerous pull from my neck, so hard that I saw stars, while pumping more of that euphoria back into me, both with his bite and his fingers.

I couldn't move, so captivated by all the sensations that my entire body just seemed to freeze. And then I broke on a rapturous wave that left me panting and pleading and crying.

He'd ripped me in half.

Torn the air from my lungs.

Seared my skin and left me shaking wildly.

"That's it, Juliet," he whispered, his lips brushing my ear. "Feel."

I shuddered against him as my limbs refused to function. My mouth remained open on an unending moan as fire singed every nerve.

It seemed to take forever for the overwhelming sensations to subside.

And several more minutes afterwards for me to realize Darius had lifted me into his arms.

We were on my bed with me curled in his lap.

His mouth brushed my forehead and temple as he continued to whisper reassurances in my ear.

I blinked, dazed.

What just happened?

Darius tucked my hair behind my ear and cupped my cheek. "You orgasm beautifully, darling." He traced my lower lip with the pad of his finger while he spoke. "I look forward to feeling it when I'm inside you."

My pulse thrummed in my ears. Did he intend to do that now?

His finger slipped into my mouth, introducing me to a musky flavor I'd never experienced.

Me, I realized.

This was the hand he'd used to pleasure me.

My legs clamped together, arousing a quake from deep within.

His eyes smoldered as I sucked my essence from his skin. "I will very much enjoy having you on your knees," he whispered darkly as he outlined my lips again. "But not yet."

His mouth captured mine, shocking me to my core.

Vampires did not kiss humans.

But this one was definitely kissing me.

Darius's tongue slid through my defenses, coaxing me to respond. I'd never experienced anything like this but found it quite pleasing—especially the way his lips caressed mine.

I tentatively returned the movement, learning his preferences with each stroke. My essence mingled with his, thickening our kiss and creating an intoxicating atmosphere of addiction.

His fingers wound in my hair, holding me to him as he devoured my mouth, and I groaned with satisfaction. No one had ever touched me in this manner, as if I meant something.

Although I understood this was all a result of my temporary purpose here, a small part of me hoped that this could become my permanent reality.

Darius tore his mouth away from me and pressed his forehead to mine as our heavy breaths filled the air. Would he finish the task now and rid me of my maidenhead? Or did he have something else in mind?

I no longer knew what to expect from him.

He broke all the formalities.

And he fed without hurting me.

"Pleasure," Darius murmured. "You've now experienced it." He kissed me again, softer this time, before pulling back to hold my gaze. His irises had darkened to a forest green—so hypnotic and beautiful.

"Juliet." He uttered my name with an authority that required attention.

"Yes, Sire?" I thought perhaps I said his name out loud before, but couldn't remember. Another shattered rule.

"You are only to offer yourself to me when you crave pleasure, not because you wish to adhere to a command. Do you understand?"

I blinked at him. His words were clear, but the meaning behind them confused me. My duty was to provide blood and sex. Why would my desire play into our arrangement?

He arched a brow, waiting.

"Yes, Sire." The words were out before I could stop them as my training took over. *A displeased master was an angry master.*

"Good." He brushed his lips against my forehead and set me down to the side. "Now wear an outfit of your choice and meet me in the hallway. I want to show you something."

Chapter Five

Darius

THAT WENT WELL.

Shit.

I rubbed a hand over my face and used the wall for support while waiting for Juliet to join me in the hall. She had better put on some fucking clothes, or I would lose it.

When I heard she hadn't left her room all evening, I thought a conversation regarding expectations might be needed. I should have let Ida handle it. But no. I decided a tour would be a good way to warm Juliet to the idea of trusting me.

Instead I nearly fucked her.

"What would you prefer me to wear?"

I'd said the first thing that came to mind, and she took it quite literally.

Exquisite didn't even begin to describe a naked Juliet. Her subtle curves and creamy skin were designed with the male gender in mind.

And those lips... I meant what I said. I couldn't wait to have them wrapped around my cock. Which was hard as a rock in my pants right now.

So much for easing her into my needs.

The door creaked as Juliet turned the handle.

I held my breath.

What did a woman bred to model translucent gowns prefer to wear when given a choice? I'd left Ida in charge of Juliet's wardrobe. Who knew what she'd purchased.

"Is this acceptable, Sire?" Juliet asked softly as she joined me in the corridor.

I preferred when she called me Darius in the bedroom. It'd been the first slip in her polite façade, and I intended to continue down that path. Perhaps in the form of more orgasms.

Hiding my internal amusement at that promise, I turned to survey her outfit choice. A black strapless dress that ended just below her ass and hugged every curve. Great. Just what my dick requested.

At least it's not transparent.

I cleared my throat and nodded. "This is acceptable." I would have to find cause for her to bend over at some point just to see what she wore beneath it, as I bet she went without.

And now that thought would torture me throughout our tour. Fantastic.

Note to self: request Ida purchase a more appropriate wardrobe for Juliet.

"Shall we?" I didn't wait for her to agree as I started in the opposite direction from the staircase. Her bare feet moved quietly over the wood floor as she followed dutifully. The rumble in her stomach told me she either lied about her hunger or was just now realizing she needed food. I would address that matter after our first stop on the tour.

"This"—I gestured to the door closest to hers—"is the entrance to my quarters."

Her dark eyes rounded as I twisted the handle.

"Nervous?" I couldn't help the taunt as I entered the sitting area. Standing naked before me proved no issue, but showing her my private rooms stirred a fiery blush on her cheeks. Intriguing.

"Yes, Sire," she whispered as she paused beside me. Her succulent scent wrapped around me, causing my incisors to ache with need. The bite in her room had been about her—not me. I craved so much more, but I required her understanding first. Without it, everything would fail.

That didn't stop me from having a little fun with her, though.

I curled my palm around the back of her neck and stepped into her personal space. Her breasts brushed my chest on a sharp inhale. Surprise mingled with fear and something decidedly feminine in her gaze.

Desire.

I pressed my lips to her ear. "You're welcome to enter my room whenever you please, darling."

I nuzzled her neck, right over the spot I nipped her earlier. The skin had already healed thanks to my ministrations. One day, I would mark her as mine, assuming she met my expectations.

"But I should warn you," I added as I drew my teeth over her tender skin. "When you visit me here, I'll assume you're in need of pleasure, and I will require the favor to be returned." My tongue traced her escalating pulse to punctuate my warning.

I grinned as Juliet arched her neck in silent invitation. She had no idea what she was inviting out to play, but she would. Soon.

"Come, Juliet," I whispered. "We still have several stops on our tour." I placed a lingering kiss against her throat and skimmed my nose over her blushing collarbone.

Possessing her would be worth the wait.

I released her nape and left her standing in the center of my sitting room. She finally caught me at the staircase, her feet padding softly against the wood. I glanced at her flushed cheeks and fought a smile. The woman wore arousal beautifully.

"As I mentioned earlier, you're allowed to wander the estate as you desire," I murmured as we ascended to the foyer. "If I need you for a social engagement, I'll provide notice. And as for attempting to escape, I wouldn't recommend it."

Acres upon acres of land and trees surrounded the manor, and beyond it, small colonies of lycans. They would not be very kind to a wandering blood virgin.

"Escape?" Juliet repeated, her voice quiet. "Where would I go?"

"Where indeed," I agreed as I led her into the kitchen. Gladice had left a dinner plate on the counter for Juliet. I lifted the top to check the heat and decided it would do. "Eat something, then we will continue." I pulled out a stool and arched a brow, daring her to argue.

She studied the offering with a curious expression as she slid onto the cushioned seat. Her dress sat high on her thighs, not that she seemed to notice or care. I again wondered what she wore beneath. It would be so easy to find out, but the mystery almost entertained me more.

I secured a set of silverware from a drawer and handed them to her as I took the seat across from her at the kitchen island.

"Thank you," she murmured as she picked at the chicken on her plate.

I folded my arms on the marble countertop. "You never need to thank me for anything, Juliet." I meant it.

The world she knew didn't resemble the one I remembered. Juliet had been told her whole life that her sole purpose on Earth was to be fucked and bled. And while the predator in me understood this, the man in me was appalled.

Vampires and lycans were the superior race—no question—but with that status came a sense of responsibility that my brethren seemed to have forgotten. Even pets deserved rights.

She ate silently, but questions radiated from her gaze. I continued to break the formalities drilled into her head, yet she never argued. It hurt to see a woman so crippled by society's teachings, and Juliet not knowing or realizing her broken nature pained me even more.

Still, nothing compared to what I had to do next.

It was almost cruel, but I needed to shatter her bubble, and I only knew one way to do that.

By telling her the truth.

"I'm not well versed on your education, aside from the dossier I was provided during your auction. You speak several languages, your arithmetic skills are adequate, and you favor biology—all items I admire. What I don't know is, how well versed you are in history."

She finished chewing and set her fork against the half-eaten plate. Her eyes darted around, searching for something before landing on the sink.

Realizing what she needed, I stood and found a glass to fill with water. Her curious eyes held mine as I handed it to her. Another formality ruined; I'd served the servant.

Juliet took a longer than necessary drink before setting it aside. "Thank…" She bit her lip, halting the rest of the words I'd just told her weren't necessary moments ago.

"You're allowed to thank me," I clarified. "But it's not mandatory."

Her rounding eyes suggested we needed to start here rather than with the history lesson. Twenty-two years in the Coventus had molded her into the perfect pet by vampire standards. Obedient, subservient, and dutiful. I needed to rearrange her perception of the rules.

"Are you finished eating?" I asked before she could speak. She had consumed the same amount as the night before, but I wanted to be sure.

"Yes, Sire."

"Excellent." I pushed away from the counter. "Follow me."

She didn't wait to be told twice and trailed right behind me. "My education included a thorough understanding of the Blood Alliance. I am also well versed in geography, the vampire royal families, royal clans, and general government affairs."

I glanced over my shoulder. "Making you a perfect pet for someone of class." And exactly why I chose her. "But none of that is history, Juliet. Has no one taught you about the world prior to lycan and vampire rule?"

Her frown answered my inquiry.

"No, of course not," I murmured as we walked by the grand ballroom. "The Coventus wouldn't want you to know such things. It fortifies your training to believe this has always been the way."

"I… I don't know how to reply, Sire."

"I suspect you wouldn't." I paused outside a set of glass doors and turned to stare down at her. "You exist to serve and please vampire aristocrats. Your blood, specifically, is why you were chosen for this path. But life wasn't always that way, Juliet."

I pushed the doors open to the library and walked backwards, my gaze on hers. "Before I give you a task, I want to make a few things clear between us."

Her attention flickered to the floor-to-ceiling bookshelves surrounding every available wall in the room before spying the windows overlooking the vibrant garden patio behind me. She swallowed as she found her way back to me, her cheeks reddening with remorse. I held up a hand before she could apologize for being distracted. I understood; it was a magnificent sight. That's why I built it.

"Fear is a beautiful training mechanism. It's what my kind instills in humans to guarantee a certain behavior." I stepped into her personal space and grabbed her chin to tilt her head back. "I do not wish for you to be afraid of me, Juliet. While I appreciate your compliance, I also seek your willingness."

I brushed my thumb over her lips, silencing whatever programmed response she had planned.

"My rules are simple. I do not care for formalities in my home, and I expect you to look after yourself. You are free to roam my estate at your leisure, which includes anything and everything within my property lines. When I require you for something, I will inform you. Otherwise, your time is your own. Do you understand?"

She studied me, her pupils dilating with uncertainty. "I… I think so, Sire." The hesitancy in her tone coupled with those telling eyes did not leave me with great confidence in her comprehension.

Rather than explain more, I released her chin and turned toward a section of the library containing some of my favorite books. Tasks were something she could appreciate, and I had a horrible one for her.

I plucked a few older texts from the shelves and set them on a table near the fireplace. That would be enough to start her reeducation. When I turned to explain, I found her studying the item beside the fireplace near the oversized couch.

"A television," I explained from beside her. "This technology isn't created anymore, but humans used to love the cinema." Mine still worked with the attached media player. I only used it when my nostalgic side required it. "From what I understand, they are still quite popular with the lycan community."

"What does it do?" she asked, her head cocked to the side.

"It plays a movie, like a book come to life. Perhaps we will watch one sometime."

She blinked up at me. "Is this something that requires permission?" So I'd finally found something that intrigued her.

"No," I murmured. "But it does require a tutorial." One I had no patience for this evening. "I have a task for you first."

She eyed the books on the table. "You wish for me to read."

"Yes." I clasped my hands behind my back to keep from touching her. No amount of soothing on my part would soften my intentions for her. "You may know how the Blood Alliance operates today, but not about how it came into existence."

Juliet picked up the first text—a global history book. "There was a council before it?"

"There were many before it, including several human governments."

"Human governments?" she repeated, her eyebrows in her hairline.

"Read," I murmured. "When you're done, come find me, and we will discuss more." I made to leave her but paused as I passed another shelf and thought better of it. "When you finish with those, select a few books from this row. They should provide you with the evidence required to believe." The manuscripts contained various pictures, all of which depicted the various world wars and a few regarding the attempted purge of immortal bloodlines.

The humans failed. Miserably.

"I have no travel planned for the next three weeks, Juliet. Nor do we have any engagements. So, feel free to take your time and come to me when you're ready." I started toward the door, then paused again. "And you can read wherever you feel most comfortable, and do not forget to eat. Remember, you're allowed to explore my estate without an escort."

"Yes, Sire," she said, her focus on the book and not on me.

Let the retraining begin.

Chapter Six

Darius

"WHERE'S THE DOLL?" Ivan asked as he strolled through the glass doors.

I lowered myself to the ground and back up. "You mean Juliet?"

"*Doll* seems more appropriate, but yes." He came to stand beside me, his hands tucked into the pockets of his trousers.

I completed several more push-ups before hopping to my feet. Exercising wasn't necessary, but I needed the distraction today. "She's in the library. Reading."

Ivan snorted. "That's what you said last week."

"And she's still in there." I stretched my arms over my head and rolled my neck. "Want to go on a jog with me?"

My best friend looked me over and shook his head, bemused. "Why don't you just go fuck her? Isn't that why she's here?"

Leave it to Ivan to think with his cock over reason. "You know why she's here."

"Yeah, I do, and part of that requires fucking her." He waved a hand over my track pants. "I mean, this is absurd, mate. You don't even like to run."

True, but I needed a physical distraction to keep myself from seeking out the delectable scent calling to my every instinct.

Juliet had been in the library for ten days now, rarely leaving even to sleep. I had to stop myself several times from stalking in there to remind her to eat.

Fortunately, Ida had managed that part for me.

When I mentioned three weeks, I never anticipated Juliet taking that long. I merely meant for her to read a few books, then come to me with questions. But no, she just kept flipping through the pages without the slightest hint of concern. I had wanted to use the truth to fracture her conditioning, but it did not appear to be working at all.

Which meant I was starving myself for no reason.

I could walk in there and fuck her—as Ivan so eloquently put it—then compel her to do my bidding, and I would if it came to that.

Ivan folded his arms in that condescending way he favored. "Have you tried talking to her?"

"My words won't be enough, not with the training she's undergone." I ran my fingers through my hair and blew out a breath. "Blood virgins are broken at a very young age and servitude is ingrained in their psyche. That sort of brainwashing is not easily overcome."

"But you think a few textbooks will do it?"

"It provides Juliet with a historical context of what humans used to mean to this world and creates doubt." Once I had that, I could rearrange her thinking and spark a need for revenge. "But she's read over fifteen books now and hasn't asked for any clarification."

"Does she think it's all fiction?" Ivan wondered.

I'd considered that possibility as well. "If she does, I don't know how to convince her otherwise."

Vampires and lycans had completely restructured the world to hide all hints of humanity's rule. Hope no longer lived here. All of my textbooks were considered illegal propaganda, not that I had any intention of ever giving them up.

"Will you discard her for a new one?" Ivan's tone suggested he didn't give a damn, but I knew he cared deep down. "Assuming she's defective, I mean."

"If she proves untrainable, then we'll have to determine an alternative," I admitted. The new plan wouldn't require a replacement so much as a more drastic approach. "But my goal is for it not to come to that."

"Right, because you want her compliance, which I still say is a waste of time." His dark eyes glinted in the moonlight as he narrowed his gaze. "You have the means to complete this task, but you're refusing to do what needs to be done. Just force her to drink a few times and fuck her, Darius. Then she'll be your *Erosita,* and you can control her."

I palmed the back of my neck to keep myself from punching him. The bastard was right, of course. I could solve this problem in a handful of nights if I put my mind to it. But I craved her consent. I didn't require it—I owned her—but I wanted her to be a willing party, not a coerced one.

"You're playing a mind game when you don't have to," Ivan continued, "because you're bored."

"Or perhaps I want to be better than the men I intend to kill," I suggested as I rolled my neck again. "Seriously, I need to go for a run." Anything to distract myself from walking into that library and doing exactly as my friend suggested.

"No, you need to feed," Ivan growled. "I just enjoyed the company of a pretty little blood whore, and yet, my fangs are aching at the scent of your *Juliet*."

"Aww, you're worried about me. That's cute." I jogged away, knowing the dolt would choose to follow me. He always did.

"You're an ass," he muttered as he met my pace. "A fucking lunatic too."

"You curse too much."

"Fuck you."

I grinned. "Point taken and ignored."

"As if that shocks you." He rolled the sleeves of his expensive sweater to his elbows, more out of habit than necessity. "And you can run all you like, mate, but we both know what you need to do."

My hands fisted. "The coronation is in six months. I have plenty of time to reprogram her. It'll be fine."

"Fine," he repeated. "I'll admit, Juliet is gorgeous and smells divine, but she's a shell of a woman and nowhere near capable of what you need to get this done. You'll end up compelling her anyway."

I increased the pace and pounded my frustration into the ground.

Ivan wasn't saying anything I didn't already know. Juliet had the assets, but if I couldn't convince her to use them the way I needed, I'd have to force her. She was too expensive of an investment to just throw away, and purchasing a replacement would create speculation I couldn't afford.

I had to proceed with the process.

The first step was breaking her conditioning.

The second step would be convincing her to work with me.

And the third would be retraining all her instincts.

In six months.

Not the best timeline, but it could be done. Assuming I had picked the right blood virgin.

I ducked as I hit the trees lining the edge of the courtyard and found my preferred forest trail. Ivan cursed beside me about his shoes but didn't back down.

Neither of us required the workout. We were forever frozen in our thirties thanks to vampire genetics, but I still enjoyed a good bout of physical exertion. It expunged unnecessary energy and kept my reflexes in check.

"I swear you're part lycan," Ivan muttered as he jumped over an extended root. "Next thing I know, you'll fucking shift on me."

"You complain too much. Next time I'm calling Trevor."

"Oh, right, like he'll muddy his shoes for you."

True. Trevor would just wait at the forest edge for me to return. "At least it would be a quiet run."

"You didn't call me here for quiet."

And this was why I considered Ivan one of my best friends. He knew me almost as well as Cam had, once upon a time.

I ran in silence for a few minutes before admitting, "I want to talk about the secondary plan."

"No shit."

"I haven't given up on Juliet yet," I continued, ignoring his commentary. "But I've found the right scapegoat."

He jumped over a log and landed deftly on his feet. "Lycan or vampire?"

"Neither. A rogue." I maneuvered around a wide tree and started up a steep incline without breaking my stride. One of the many benefits to vampirism was increased speed and agility, and the ability to carry on a conversation while running.

"Making it a rogue hit takes the blame off of us and would free up the sovereign's seat again," I added.

"And keeps your name in the dark," Ivan pointed out. "Thereby defeating the purpose."

"Not necessarily." I jumped over a massive rock and used a hint of my enhanced vampiric speed to propel me onward faster. "It prolongs the game a bit, but there are other ways to work my name into the masses."

Ivan whistled. "You're talking years down the road, mate. Our royal friend wouldn't be happy about that, and neither would the others."

"It's a backup plan," I clarified. "To be used if Juliet doesn't come through." But I had every intention of winning her over. "She's still our best option."

"Which is why I say to just get it over with, so we can begin the training bit." He circled around a tree and met me on the other side. "Or give her to me, and I'll handle it for you."

A vivid image of Ivan *handling* Juliet blurred my vision. She wouldn't refuse him, may even enjoy it. Just as she did my bite while in her room…

Her body had moved sensuously against mine as she surrendered to the pleasures of my touch. I could still hear her little moans and the way she said my name while in the throes of climax. My cock twitched with the sensual memory, then died at the thought of Ivan's suggestion.

I could picture it clearly—his body taking hers while his fangs penetrated her creamy neck…

Fuck no.

Negative energy zipped through my veins, heating my blood and clouding my better judgment.

Mine.

No one, other than me, would touch Juliet's innocence.

I elbowed the jackass mid-stride, sending him cascading to the ground with a grunt.

To even think he had the right…

My hands fisted as I considered hitting him again, only harder. Part of my violent need was a result of bloodlust and unnecessary starvation. But the other part was all possession.

"She's mine, Mikhail," I warned, using his surname. "The only one handling Juliet will be me."

"Proprietorial ass," he grumbled as he pushed off the ground. "It was an offer, not a request."

"I refuse."

"Clearly." He shook some leaves from his hair. "Do you want to spar or continue running?"

Aggression tinted the air between us. Ivan had known full well how I would react to his "offer," suggesting the bastard was testing my possessive instincts on purpose. It seemed he wanted to fight. I could use the exertion, and he would provide a decent challenge.

"Both," I decided. I would kick his ass, then continue my run.

"Great. Hit me, then," he taunted. "Or try."

I smiled. "The last time you dared me like this, I rearranged that pretty face of yours."

He shrugged. "I healed."

"You cried."

"Bullshit." He fell into a fighter's stance. "Now I want to put you on your ass just to prove a point."

"Yeah? And what would that be?"

"That I'm well fed and you're starved. Maybe afterward you'll finally feed."

I snorted. "Even half-dead, I could best you."

"That's Trevor," he corrected. "You called me because you wanted an actual opponent, in addition to the pep talk."

I couldn't deny that. "Stop talking out your ass and hit me, Ivan."

He smirked. "Gladly."

Chapter Seven

Juliet

SEVENTEEN BOOKS WERE SPRAWLED out over the library floor—all describing a world where humans ruled.

Yet none of them mentioned lycans or vampires.

Except for the one in my hand.

I'd found it buried in the shelves, the masculine scrawl across the cover having caught my eye.

The Formation.

It seemed to be a notebook rather than a reference text, but as I flipped through the handwritten pages, I finally caught some words I recognized.

I curled into the oversized chair near the fireplace—it'd become my preferred spot over the last week and a half—and began flipping through the handwritten pages.

It started with a description of a world war between humans, something I'd read about five or six times now in the other textbooks. It's where most of the books ended, but this one began—another sign that I had picked something new.

I skimmed the familiar words concerning nuclear weapons and agreed with the stark comments regarding humans clearly wanting to destroy the world. Then I slowed as I read a new passage regarding lycans.

The Cyrus Clan outed us first. They were discovered in the late twenty-first century by a paramilitary unit searching for a missing woman from a nearby town. Apparently, the Alpha took a liking to the Governor's daughter and kidnapped her. So, truly, everything changed because of a woman.

This was definitely a journal.

I continued reading about how humans attempted to experiment with lycans in various ways, all of which resulted in failures to understand their biology. A few governments attempted to use their genetics for militaristic means, but failed.

Meanwhile, lycans and vampires met in secret to discuss the future of humanity. Several of the clansmen were furious about the treatment of the Cyrus Clan and demanded retribution, thus giving those who craved a reformed world a platform to stand upon. Hence, the Blood Alliance was formed.

The cadence of the words reminded me of Darius. Considering the notebook was stuffed in his shelves, it seemed appropriate for it to belong to him.

I turned the page, learning more about the uprising, where the superior species organized an attack that destroyed over half the human race and successfully took control of the world.

Humans were divided into camps to be tested. Spirit, strength, intelligence, beauty, and bloodline all contributed to the fate of each lesser being. Most were exterminated, leaving only 300,000 in existence for official sorting.

The Blood Alliance drafted legal requirements that suited both lycan and vampire and divided mortals into their requisite camps. All moral rights were removed, demoting humankind to property, and thus proclaiming them as objects to be owned and possessed as desired.

I shivered at the very real description of my purpose in this world. Vampires saw me as living food, to be enjoyed at will and otherwise ignored.

Although, Darius opened my eyes to a whole different regard of my kind. He allowed me to look at him, to talk to him, and he granted me pleasure.

But it could all be ripped out of my hands with a mere word from him.

I drew my nails down the page, considering the purpose. He asked me to review the textbooks, stating I should come to him when I finished reading the items on the floor and several from the shelves. I'd done as he requested,but still didn't understand why he gave me this task.

Did he mean to torture me with the history of my kind? How humans have been belittled to toys used for vampire and lycan enjoyment?

Or was it meant purely as informational, and a way to enhance my overall training?

I flipped to the next section defining the various mortal sectors. Blood farms, academies, immortal selection competitions, royal harems, clan breeding dens, human procreation camps—my eyes narrowed on a paragraph pertaining specifically to me.

Blood virgins are perhaps the most intriguing development. Their bloodlines are unique and considered to be almost lethally addictive. A special provision was made to allow for their genetic reproduction for the sole use of vampires, and in exchange lycans were given their own mortal line for full-moon games.

But what is truly fascinating is these blood virgins are being groomed for elite society. Both males and females exist in separate confines and are trained in the arts of intellectual affairs—unlike most humans—to better mingle with high society.

They are also groomed to be the perfect sexual pet, though most are only used once before being discarded. The lucky ones return to the Coventus to train future virgins, while the majority of them are sent into the breeding cycle to procreate, then eventually the farms.

My lips parted on that last line of the page.

Breeding cycle—to create more blood virgins.

My matron always said the majority returned to the Coventus. Darius's notes implied that wasn't the case, that my fate would be to fornicate until I no longer proved fruitful.

Ice drizzled down my spine.

I existed to serve my master by providing him unlimited access to my blood and body. That was the sole purpose for my being. I meant nothing otherwise; just a pet to be used however he desired.

And then I was to be thrown away to create more for future pleasure.

But these books depicted a history where humans used to rule—not well, considering all the battles and wars, but they at least *lived.* While all I did was serve.

I blinked tears from my eyes as confusion poked holes in my bubbled existence.

Why me?

Why was this my fate?

Because of my blood.

And as a curse, I would be forced to produce more of my kind. Then that child would be sent to the Coventus to be trained, just as I was, to serve a new master before continuing the cycle.

My stomach churned, reminding me that I had forgotten to eat again today. But what did it matter?

I tossed the journal to the ground and found the history book depicting a strong female leader—human. She didn't smile, but her eyes bespoke of intelligence and determination. Mine would never resemble hers. When I looked in the mirror, I saw a soulless being who knew nothing about life. Because I resided in a shell shaped by my vampire betters.

They were more powerful, stronger, and immortal. That granted them the ability to control everyone beneath them and to own a person like me.

Humans used to have rights.

Why would Darius require me to learn all of this?

It served no benefit other than to prove my place while removing all hope. Was that what he wanted to show me? In case I garnered any ideas about what we were doing here?

I preferred my state of ignorance where the Blood Alliance always existed as the superior power. Where humans were never in a position of authority.

Where I had no inkling of an optimistic future.

He'd taken all that from me with this library of books.

Why?

I set the female leader aside and stood, determined.

What did I have to lose? He intended to use me and throw me away anyway. I might as well demand an explanation. Maybe he would kill me as a result. That had to be better than forced breeding.

My hands curled into fists as I stomped out of the library and turned toward the foyer. He told me only to visit him in his quarters for pleasure. He also told me to find him when I finished. Well, I was more than done.

Damn the rules and etiquette.

I required answers, and I wanted them now.

"Juliet," Ida called as I reached the bottom of the staircase.

Normally, I responded to her with a demure smile or a polite greeting, but my mouth revolted against both actions as I turned to face her. If she noticed my lack of courtesy, she didn't show it.

"If you're looking for Master Darius, he is out back with Master Ivan." She winked and wandered away in that oddly chipper way of hers.

Darius obviously hadn't given her the same reading assignment as me, or she wouldn't be nearly as content with her fate.

Then again, she wasn't going to be sent to the breeding camps to produce more blood virgins.

My lips thinned.

Outside.

I'd yet to venture beyond the doors of this large home. Darius had given me permission to wander at will, but I feared it might be a test. Now I no longer cared if I passed or not.

Something sweet tickled my nose on my way through the kitchen to the dining area. A few of Darius's servants mingled around, giving me curious looks as I went straight for the glass doors that led to the oversized patio beyond it.

I hesitated. This could be exactly how he wanted me to react and might be out there waiting to punish me.

He also said to find him when I finished reading.

The hairs along my arms danced as I considered breaking the one rule my matron warned me never to breach. Demanding the audience of a vampire typically earned the human a harsh punishment, even death.

But he instructed me to locate him after I completed my task, and I was done with those books.

I'd rather die than be forced to breed.

And the farms?

I shuddered. The term alone painted a picture I didn't want in my head.

Not my future.

I refused.

Because you have a choice?

The human's eyes flashed in my mind again from the photo of the female leader who clearly *lived.* What would I look like if I stood up to Darius? A warrior? Or would I stare lifelessly up at the evening sky?

Would it even matter?

My lips flattened as I twisted the handle.

I had nothing to lose. No life to value living. Just rules that dictated my every action. Darius had shattered several already. What was one more?

The stone patio chilled my bare feet as I wandered outside. It took me several steps before I realized the gravity of what I'd just done.

The only other time I had ventured outdoors was when the guards escorted me to Darius's waiting limo. And yet I'd just walked outside as though it meant nothing.

No alarms.

No guards.

I blinked.

If I'd even managed to reach a door at the Coventus, I would have been surrounded as soon as I touched the handle. Not that I ever considered trying. It just wasn't done. Why would I escape? Where would I go?

The moonlight illuminated a path to the trees, almost beckoning me to follow. I knew from my window view that the forest went on and on, but it had to stop eventually. Where would it take me? To a worse fate? A better one?

I stepped forward and paused at the new texture below me.

Grass.

How… quaint.

I knelt to touch the cool blades when a whisper to the left jolted me upright.

"Juliet…" The murmur caressed my ear, announcing Darius's presence just as he materialized behind me. Heat enveloped my body as he pressed his chest to my back and wrapped his forearm around my lower abdomen.

"Hello, darling." He pressed a kiss to my neck just as Master Ivan appeared before me. I'd barely even considered running, and already two powerful vampires had trapped me between them.

Ivan stood close enough to touch but didn't. Lust shone bright in his brown gaze as he stared down at me with an arrogance I could never match. He knew he could overpower me with a flick of his wrist, and he thrived on that knowledge. His lips quirked up in a grin, drawing my attention to the blood glistening on the corner of his mouth. It lent a ravenous appeal to his otherwise handsome face.

"No bowing and eye contact," he mused. "Even with a guest. I'd call that progress, Darius."

His words dumped ice water over my head, freezing me in place. I hadn't meant to look at his face, or meet his gaze, but I'd fallen into a casual cadence after spending however many days in the library. I'd been lost in a haze of history and forgotten all my training.

Or perhaps I *chose* to forget it.

"Indeed." Darius's lips brushed my pulse with the single word. "Have you ventured outside to feed us, darling?"

"F-feed?" I repeated, my throat dry.

Ivan ran his fingers through his dark hair and appraised me thoroughly with his flaring pupils. "I think your Juliet had other intentions. Pity."

"Is Ivan right? Did you seek my audience for a different purpose, Juliet?" Darius pulled my curls to one side, exposing the full column of my throat while I fought to remember how to breathe. "Have you finished reading?" His teeth scraped my sensitive skin, causing my abdomen to clench.

I knew the sensations that accompanied his bite now, and a dark part of me craved another. It seemed like just yesterday he'd held me in my bedroom, but I knew that wasn't right. Maybe a week ago? I'd been—

"Juliet." He nipped my neck in warning, bringing me back into the moment. "Did you complete the task I gave you? Is that why you've joined us?"

I swallowed—or tried to, anyway. His warmth at my back dismantled my resolve. I'd wanted to demand answers, but the intention and inevitable recourse didn't resemble one another.

He could snap me like a twig.

Or send me away to create more humans…

"I read," I said slowly, my voice hoarse. "Blood virgins go into the breeding cycle prior to being sent to the farms." I swallowed again before adding, "That is my fate." A sour note crept into my tone, one I'd never heard before. He didn't give me time to contemplate it.

"Mmm, you found my journal." He whirled me in his arms with that lightning-fast speed and twined his fingers in my hair. The moonlight cast eerie shadows across his face while highlighting his green irises. They blazed with a hunger I could almost taste, and he appeared to have a fading bruise on his right cheek. It rather satisfied me to see it there, though I couldn't determine why.

"You sound displeased with your fate, Juliet," he continued. "Any particular reason why?"

"Displeased," I repeated, trying the word. "That I am to be forced to create more of my kind? That my progeny will be offered up to the highest bidder, then forced to continue the cycle? And that I will inevitably go to a farm?" Each word strengthened my voice, raising me from a whisper to a pitch I'd never heard from my mouth before. "After learning that humans used to have rights?"

Why would he teach me this?

Did he mean to torture me?

To poke fun at my fate?

To taunt the poor human girl with a false hope that no longer existed?

"I'd say she sounds displeased," Ivan remarked, a smile in his voice.

My hands curled into fists in response. A violent reaction I'd never before considered…

"It would seem that way," Darius agreed, grinning.

That smug amusement drove my nails into my palms. How cruel they were to pick on the weakling and laugh at my plight. I *never* had a choice.

I was more than *displeased.*

My head spun with an inferno of details that clouded my thoughts in a haze of red. Foreign emotions streamed through my conscious, heating my blood.

It consumed me.

Took hold of every nerve, demanding something I couldn't articulate.

My chest hummed with the need to scream.

And my fists clenched with the desire to hurt.

I couldn't do this. I couldn't breathe. Not with him so close.

I tried to dislodge myself from his hold, but he didn't budge. Instead he chuckled.

My eyes widened as a fire blossomed in my heart, causing my instincts to spiral out of control.

I wanted to hurt him.

Kick him.

Punch him.

Kill him.

All of them.

I'd never once even considered it an option, but knowing that humans had once fought for their lives against his kind encouraged all manner of thoughts.

"Yes," he murmured. "There's the emotion I wanted."

"Yeah, good luck taming it, mate," Ivan said as he started toward the back patio. "I don't envy you the task."

Chapter Eight

Darius

THE MOMENT JULIET'S SCENT HIT MY SENSES, I'd phased back to the estate with Ivan on my tail. I rarely used the teleportation-like ability, but I'd wanted to know what brought her outside.

And I couldn't be more delighted with the furious expression on her face now. It painted her cheeks a lovely shade of rose and deepened the allure of her plump lips. But it was the blaze in her dark eyes that intrigued me most.

This was the woman I wanted to invite out to play.

"What else did you read in my journal?" I wondered. "About the immortal bond?"

Her nose flared. "You intend to use me for my purpose and send me to a breeding camp."

I smirked. "That is the usual path, but tell me what else you read."

She tried to move away again, but I held her in place. "I do not wish to procreate!" she shouted, shocking me.

"Juliet—"

She squirmed violently, her body trembling with unsuppressed emotion as tears pricked her eyes.

Okay, the rage I enjoyed.

This, not so much.

I'd wanted to destroy her training, not the woman herself.

"Stop," I demanded, tightening my grip. "Juliet."

"No," she whispered brokenly. "I'd rather die." Her legs gave out, leaving her limp in my arms. I lifted her with ease, cradling her against my chest as she wept silently.

My resolve faltered at the sight of her training kicking in even as she mourned. Displays of strong emotion were punished by my kind, hence her attempt to mask her sobs by remaining quiet.

I shook my head. "You didn't read beyond the part about breeding, did you?"

Her lips moved, but no sound escaped.

I interpreted that as a confirmation that she'd not finished my notebook. She'd probably been too shocked to bother with the next page. A pity considering it would have given her a glimpse of the hope she so desperately needed.

Ivan had meandered into the house at the first sign of emotion and met me at the back door as I approached. He didn't say a word as I carried Juliet past him and the staff.

I considered taking her upstairs to her room but decided a detour to the library would benefit us both.

She didn't move or utter a sound as I walked through the threshold of the room she'd practically lived in these last ten days.

I wandered over to her bizarre arrangement of books on the floor. A familiar photo of a former female president glowered up at me, reminding me of a time where humans ruled unsuccessfully. Juliet must have found that fascinating since she left it on the chair for everyone to see.

Holding her with one arm, I bent to retrieve my notebook from the ground. "You didn't finish reading."

"I don't care," she managed on a choked whisper. "Punish me. Kill me. I don't care."

Those last few words were mouthed more than voiced, but I understood the resolve in her expression. She preferred death to her future. I couldn't blame her. Most would feel the same in her position.

I settled in the chaise lounge with her in my lap. "I have no desire to kill you, Juliet." It would be a waste of an exquisite blood virgin. I pushed the hair away from her pretty face with my free hand and held out my book with the other. "Finish reading."

She balked at the notebook and curled into my chest. "No." A pleading note colored her tone as she tucked her chin to hide her face.

"No?" I repeated, minutely impressed by her refusal.

She appeared to be both denying me and seeking comfort from me at the same time. An odd combination that stemmed from having her world turned upside down. I wouldn't apologize, but I could be lenient with her. To an extent.

"I'll read to you instead." And hopefully the additional explanation would help our situation.

I thumbed through the familiar pages, searching for my retelling of the sorting process.

This notebook had been my way of dealing with the formation of our new world.

As a former professor, I lived in a land of textbooks and research. Documentation came naturally, but I stopped writing when the Blood Alliance reached a status quo nearly a century ago. Their operation was seamless due to a hundred years of sharpening the edges and removing all those who opposed the movement—such as Cam.

Whispers of a revolution had died with my maker's proclaimed demise, leaving me with nothing new to document.

Until recently, anyway.

I found the section I wanted, ending with the line about the farms. Juliet hadn't confirmed it, but I felt certain this was where she had stopped reading, so I flipped to the next page.

"Then there are those select few who are gifted with an eternity of servitude. Some may consider death a preferable alternative beneath these new customs, as the ceremony that once required mutual agreement has now been tainted by enslavement. While society scoffs at the notion of bonded mates, it's still deemed an acceptable practice under the Blood Alliance laws."

I paused to ensure I had her attention and found her studying the book in my hand. Her shoulders still trembled, but the sobs had stopped. I took that as a sign to continue.

"Once a blood virgin—or any human for that matter—undergoes the ceremony, the human is considered valued property and is granted certain allowances. One such concession is the ability to attend social events with his or her master. Although elite society mocks the ritual, it is inevitably revered and garners a certain prestige that inspires envy from many. To touch another vampire's blood virgin, especially one granted ceremonial rights, is punishable by immediate death."

And that last bit was what intrigued me most. For some males couldn't resist the forbidden, particularly one of Juliet's caliber. Marking her as my *Erosita* would make her irresistible to my brethren, especially those who craved power.

I lowered the journal and focused on the gorgeous woman curled in my lap. She wore another one of those short dresses, causing me to wonder what Ida had purchased for her. Surely a pair of pants and a normal shirt?

"I…" Juliet licked her lips, her brow furrowed. "I don't understand what you're trying to tell me."

Yes, I supposed she wouldn't. Or perhaps she suspected but didn't wish to hope. I set the notebook on the side table and wrapped my arms around her waist to hold her close.

The comforting move likely confused her even more, but it was more for me than for her. I enjoyed the feel of holding a woman, specifically one who smelled decidedly edible.

"The purpose of reading all these books was to give you insight into the history of humanity." I glanced over her array of items on the floor. Everything from ancient mythology to the last of the world wars stared back at me. "Did you read all of these?"

"Yes," she whispered. "But I didn't finish the notebook."

I determined as much already. "You read more than enough to understand that lycans and vampires have not always ruled, and that the world has not always operated as it does today."

She nodded as some of that fire sparked in her alluring eyes.

Good. That's what I craved from her, that anger. It would help this conversation flow to my advantage.

"If you think the treatment of blood virgins is unjust, then you should witness a Blood Day." I gently rubbed my palms over her bare arms to help temper my yearning to possess her. Knowing that I could do whatever I wanted without retribution didn't help matters. But I knew her agreeing to help me would be so much sweeter than compelling her into action.

"So the purpose was to show me that my life could be worse?"

I grinned at the hint of irritation in her tone. "No, darling, the purpose was to give you context. You see, I have a proposition for you, and I couldn't offer it without the history lesson."

She twisted in my lap to fully meet my gaze. I'd required her to make eye contact whenever we spoke, but this felt different. Stronger, more confident—as though she felt she had the right to study me. It demonstrated a flaw in her conditioning, and that thrilled me.

"A proposition," she repeated, her brow pinched. "I'm yours to command, Sire. Why would you wish to offer me anything?"

I palmed the back of her neck and brushed my thumb over her steady pulse. She'd calmed down considerably since arriving in the library. Her flushed cheeks and puffy eyes remained, but her breathing had returned to normal.

"Hmm." She had the most alluring lips. I tried to ignore them, but being this close to her, with her supple body in my lap, I couldn't resist. "Your purpose has always been to serve a master, with the intention of it being temporary, yes?"

Juliet's heart rate escalated—just a little—but the usual fearful glint in her eye didn't appear as she nodded. *Intriguing.*

"From what I understand, they teach you to expect death." It served as a way to train the humans not to react to the inevitable. It also functioned as a brainwashing mechanism to remind them of their place at the bottom of the food chain. I observed her closely as I added, "I don't want your service to me to be temporary."

Her tongue darted out to dampen her lips as my words hit their mark. "You refer to… to the ceremony? From your journal?"

"Yes." I traced the column of her neck with my thumb and tracked the move with my eyes. "But I want something in return."

"What would you have from me?" she asked softly. "I'm already yours."

"Mmm, true." I threaded my fingers in her hair and pulled her closer, leaving a scant inch between our mouths. "I own your body and blood, but what I desire is your soul."

"You wish to kill me, Sire?" she breathed against my lips.

"No, darling, I wish to mold you into the perfect poison." I skimmed my nose along her blushing cheek before pressing a kiss to her throat.

Temptation personified.

My incisors ached to bite her. Ten days without her blood had been too long. I'd taken from some of the donors living in my estate, but it hadn't whetted my appetite in the slightest. If anything, I only craved her more.

She swallowed. "A poison?"

I smiled against her neck. "Yes. A lethal one."

"I'm not sure I follow, Sire."

"You're irresistible, Juliet," I breathed against her ear. "By making you mine through the ceremony, I'm creating a forbidden fruit that my kind will be unable to resist. And I will use that temptation to my advantage." She was the perfect poison, and I intended to exploit her accordingly.

"But how will you use me, Sire? What will be requested of me?" Arousal thickened her tone as her body instinctively responded to my unsuppressed yearnings. That kind of training could not be taught; it was all related to her bloodline and its natural response to my nearness. Some considered it a mating mechanism, while others a gift from the heavens. I thought of it as an opportunity.

"I could answer that in so many ways, darling." But I knew what she meant. "If you agree to the ceremony, I will use you to destroy my enemies. They'll never know what hit them. And I will most definitely use you to sate my every need as well." Because having her here and not enjoying the luxury of her company would be a waste of a perfectly good bedmate.

"I've only begun to demonstrate what I can offer you, Juliet." I placed an openmouthed kiss beneath her ear and grinned at her responding shiver. "And I believe I've shown that living here can be quite pleasurable for us both, yes?"

"Would…?" She cleared her throat. "Would this c-continue?"

"My seducing you?"

"And the other things?" she asked.

"You mean pleasure?"

She whimpered as I explored the column of her neck with my tongue. "Y-yes." I couldn't tell if she meant that as an invitation to continue or in response to my clarification. Perhaps both.

"As I mentioned during your tour of the estate, you're welcome in my room any time you desire more pleasure." I shifted to meet her gaze. "But tonight, I require it."

Her chest rose and fell in quick succession. So beautiful. I wanted to tug down her dress to reveal those gorgeous breasts and nibble every inch. This time I would take as well as give.

"My purpose is to sate your needs, whatever they may be," she said softly.

"Mmm, but I insist you give me everything, Juliet." I pulled away from the temptation of her blood to capture her hypnotic gaze. "You're trained to mingle with high society, to converse in various languages, and to seduce with a glance. All admirable traits, but what I desire to teach you is vastly different from what you already know."

She gazed up at me with an innocence I planned to destroy. I supposed that made me the villain in her story, or perhaps, her savior.

"Will you agree to learn more, Juliet?" I loosened my hold in her hair to run my fingers through her thick locks. "In exchange, I can offer you the initial ceremony. It will grant you unique privileges within society and mark you as mine, thus protecting you from any alternative future. And it will stop your aging." At least temporarily. The blood exchange had to be repeated several times prior to my claiming her body, but even the initial stages would gift her certain rights and strengths.

"Stop my aging?" she repeated.

"Yes. The bond between us will grant you immortality, darling."

Her pupils flared. "Immortality?" A note of awe touched her soft voice. She clearly hadn't understood my comment regarding eternal servitude from the journal. "And, er, what does the ceremony require?"

"Your willingness to meet my needs," I replied. "As for the ritual itself, you'll drink from me." *And I'll eventually fuck you to oblivion and back.*

Her eyes widened. "That's forbidden, Sire."

I smiled. "No, only the turning is outlawed. The ceremony is very legal. You'll understand after we attend our first social outing."

Several would ridicule my actions, but most would envy them. Blood virgins, especially one as tempting as Juliet, were rare and coveted. Purchasing her was the first step in drawing attention to my reemergence into society. Keeping her would be the second. Sometimes one had to play the game before destroying it.

I gathered her curls over one shoulder and forcibly relaxed into the chair. Touching her was an obsession, and I needed to focus.

"Immortality, pleasure, and safety, Juliet. That's what I offer. In return, I want your compliance and cooperation in everything I desire. It won't be easy, and you will do things for me that you will not enjoy, but I believe the benefits will outweigh the negatives in the end. The decision, however, is yours."

Chapter Nine

JULIET

"THE DECISION, HOWEVER, IS YOURS."

False. Nothing in my life was ever *my* decision. I existed to provide sex and sustenance to a master—something I always accepted. It wasn't a debate or an opinion, merely a fact of life.

Except the books sprawled out around us painted a different world, one where humans were given choices and allowed to live as they wanted.

That world no longer prevailed.

I had no rights here.

No choices.

I lived for Darius's pleasure for as long as he wanted me. My matron prepared me for the inevitability of being discarded, though she never mentioned the alternatives.

The notebook clarified everything. Blood virgins weren't necessarily killed by their masters, so much as sent elsewhere to procreate.

And a select few were offered the ceremony.

Darius didn't explain what all that entailed, but I inferred enough to understand his proposition.

If I refused him, he would return me to the Coventus or send me somewhere worse. Or maybe even kill me. He could, and no one would care.

Yet he claimed the decision was mine.

A lie.

Accepting the ceremony was the only option, even if it did require me to give him everything. But my very purpose was to please him, with or without the offer of immortality. That made his proposal more of a gift since he owed me nothing at all.

And living with him thus far hadn't been nearly as horrible as I originally expected. He provided pleasure where most elicited pain. Even now, his gaze held a voracious hunger that he controlled with admirable ease. The vampires of my limited acquaintance didn't wait, they took. Yet Darius possessed a patience I admired, and a touch I craved.

There was no choice.

I would accept.

Saying no earned me nothing, while agreeing granted me opportunity, even if temporary.

It would never truly be consent, not without any other feasible alternative. But humans didn't possess the right to decide; we merely did as we were told. Which made my response easy.

"I'll do anything you wish, Sire." *It's why I'm here.*

"Mmm." He tilted his head to the side and drew his thumb over his bottom lip. "You will, yes, but that's not entirely what I wanted." His pupils dilated as he studied me. "Well, I suppose it's a start. We can revisit my requirements after I teach you more about what I *wish* for you to do."

"Of course, Sire." I doubted it would convince me otherwise. Even if he chose to turn me into a poison—whatever that meant—I'd do whatever he requested. Because there was no other option, unless I wanted to breed or be sent to the farms. Hopefully, I wouldn't disappoint him.

"Then we'll initiate the ceremony," he murmured, his hands settling on my hips.

I swallowed. "Now?"

"Yes." He tightened his grasp. "Straddle me."

Electricity zipped down my spine as I shifted on his lap to place my legs on the outside of his thighs. It stretched the fabric of my dress, causing it to bunch closer to his fingers.

"You won't need to drink a lot from me." He ran his palms up and down my sides, creating a trail of fire through the thin fabric. "But I'll demand more of your blood in return, especially as I've not fed well in the last two weeks."

I studied the hollows beneath his eyes. Most vampires required daily nourishment, but the older and stronger ones could survive on little. That he hadn't come to me every day for a meal said a lot about his status. I'd not considered it until now.

But if he hadn't fed much, as he said, then he would indeed necessitate a lot from me. It would intensify his bite and, potentially, the pleasure that accompanied it. He did mention requiring the latter tonight.

A quiver worked its way over my limbs as I considered what that would entail. Surely he meant to deflower me as well.

It would hurt.

But I also might enjoy it.

There is something very wrong with me.

All the reading and unexpected conversations had derailed my being. I no longer knew what to anticipate, but one thing was certain.

"I'm ready, Sire." Pleasing him would not be a hardship, even if he did inflict pain. I gathered my hair to one side to expose my throat for easy access. It was my way of inviting him to feed, not that he needed it.

His hands fell to my exposed thighs as he relaxed into the chaise and gazed up at me with hooded eyes. All vampires were attractive, but my breath caught at the desire radiating from Darius's handsome features. He truly was one of the most beautiful men I'd ever seen.

No, this definitely would not be a hardship at all.

He traced the edge of my dress with his thumbs and inched the fabric upward. The hairs along my arms danced as he skirted the crease of my bottom.

I swallowed.

He's going to touch me again.

Pleasure…

Cool air met my intimate flesh, eliciting a tremble from deep within.

Yes.

"Mmm, as I thought," he murmured as the material gathered around my waist. "You're not wearing anything beneath this dress." His gaze fell to the apex between my thighs.

"I was instructed never to wear undergarments," I whispered.

"A rule that can remain," he said as his hand explored the zipper along my spine. It slowly loosened, bit by bit.

My breath hitched as he hit the base. I'd been naked in front of him before, but this felt different. My pulse didn't beat out of fear, but out of yearning.

Bite me, I nearly said, catching the words before they could escape on a groan.

He tugged the dress down, exposing my breasts. My nipples pebbled to painful peaks as I waited for whatever came next.

But he removed his hands and relaxed into the chair instead. "Gorgeous."

My skin heated beneath his slow visual inspection. Sensation stirred between my legs, begging me to find friction while I fought to remain still.

Oh, Goddess…

I wanted to squirm.

To lie against him.

Seek comfort.

Something. *Anything.*

"Sire," I managed, my voice sounding foreign to my ears.

"Yes, Juliet?" He folded his hands behind his head. "What do you desire?"

"I…" I licked my lips. "I wish to please you."

One eyebrow inched upward. "Do you?"

I nodded. "Yes." It would give me a distraction from the ache forming inside and also allow me to touch him—to explore him. "Oh, yes. Very much." The words flowed without my permission, but I couldn't take them back even if I wanted to. Amusement radiated from him.

"Very well. On your knees, Juliet." The command in his voice soothed me and provided the guidance I craved.

I slid from his lap to the floor and assumed a submissive position, as requested. This was the training I understood. He shifted to place his feet on either side of me, bracketing me between his strong thighs.

"You may please me in two ways," he murmured as he loosened his pants. They weren't his usual suit trousers, but of the athletic variety. I thought he meant to remove them, but he lifted his wrist to his mouth instead and bit down hard enough to draw blood. "Drink."

"For the ceremony," I breathed.

"Yes." He lowered the wound to my lips. "Now, before it closes."

"Yes, Sire." I couldn't refuse him, not when he used that tone. I grasped his hand and tentatively licked the area he desired.

His sweet essence touched my tongue, surprising me.

That… isn't horrible.

Actually, it's quite pleasant.

I closed my lips over the laceration and drew more into my mouth. His hand fisted in mine, as his opposite palm clasped the back of my head to hold me against him. I interpreted that as a sign to continue drinking and complied.

A humming simmered in my mind, causing my eyes to fall closed. It compelled me to take more, to suck harder. I responded instinctually, pulling more and more of his blood into my mouth and swallowing, until he threaded his fingers in my hair and yanked me away from his wrist.

My breaths came in pants as my body desired more, but he held me with ease.

"I want you to do that to my cock." His sharp tone snapped me from my daze and forced me into action. He released me to tug down his pants. My heart skipped a beat at the sight of his prominent erection. Not all men were created equal, and Darius put many of the others I'd seen to shame.

And he intends to put that inside me…

My thighs clenched in response.

"Your mouth, Juliet. Now."

"Yes, Sire," I managed roughly.

I can do this.

My matron taught me several techniques both through demonstration and by having me practice on similarly shaped items. But I'd never held a man in this manner.

I grasped the base and gave him a hesitant stroke.

So hot… I hadn't expected that, or the soft skin.

He pulsed in my palm, encouraging me to glide my hand over him again, this time with more pressure than before.

"Stop teasing and suck my cock," he demanded.

I leaned forward to take him deep into my mouth the way I knew he would enjoy. His head fell back on a groan of approval that I felt through every fiber of my being. I swallowed as much of him as I could before retreating and starting again.

"Fuck," he growled, his hands grabbing my head to help guide my ministrations.

An intense craving built between my legs as I pictured him entering my body as he did my mouth.

Oh, Goddess, I never thought I would want that, but I did.

My thighs clamped together as I moaned around his thick shaft.

"Do that again," he said, his voice hoarse. "Moan my name."

I did, not because he told me to, but because I *needed* to. "Darius" rolled off my tongue onto his bulbous head before I sucked him so hard he hit the back of my throat.

He fisted my hair on both sides and shoved himself into me even farther, making it impossible to breathe. I grabbed his hips for support as he began roughly plunging himself between my lips.

Darius grunted my name and a string of curses while I fought for air. Each harsh thrust taunted the ache throbbing inside me, stirring a yearning for him to take me in the same savage manner. It would hurt, but so did this, and I enjoyed it.

Tears stung my eyes as his fingers curled even more harshly, tugging at my strands. His movements sharpened in a sign I recognized.

"Breathe deep, Juliet," he rasped.

I inhaled as much as he allowed and relaxed my throat as best I could to accept his pleasure. He went impossibly deeper, forcing my lips to hit the base of his shaft as he emptied his seed with a possessive groan.

My legs trembled as I endeavored not to choke on his ruthless invasion. He loosened his hold just enough to give me room to gasp and swallow while remaining in my mouth.

I met his gaze as I finished, causing his lips to curl. "You're worth everything I paid for and more, darling." He combed his fingers through my hair as he slowly eased my mouth off of him. "But I still need to feed."

"Yes, Sire," I whispered through my aching windpipe.

He smiled. "Remove your dress."

I gathered the fabric at my waist and pulled it over my head to set on the floor while I remained kneeling before him. He stood and tucked himself back into his pants, only inches from my face.

His palm caressed my cheek as he stared down at me. "You looked so beautiful with my cock in your mouth. We will be doing that again very soon."

I was about to agree to his wishes, but Darius pressed his thumb to my lips, silencing me.

"Lie down on the chaise with your legs spread," he murmured. "On your back."

My knees protested as I tried to rise, and he held out his hand to help me from the ground. I accepted with a murmured "Thank you" before moving into the position he requested on the cushions.

He admired me for a moment, his gaze touching every exposed angle. "Slide farther up."

I moved until my head hit the upward cushion of the chair as he knelt on the bottom of the chaise. His palms clasped my calves before slipping higher to force my legs farther apart.

My shoulders hitched as he settled on his elbows between my thighs, placing his face directly above my dampening folds. "Mmm, you're glistening for me. I approve, darling."

I jolted as he placed an openmouthed kiss against my most sensitive area.

"Oh…" My nails dug into the cushions. "S-sire…" My pelvis bucked into his mouth as he suckled my intimate nub. "I…" I had no words.

It felt…

Amazing.

Hot and cold.

I shivered even as a fire blossomed inside. His fingers trailed up my inner thighs and joined his mouth to torture me more. Two digits entered me at once, causing me to yelp and moan simultaneously.

Never in my wildest dreams had I expected something quite like this.

His tongue… I didn't know they could move this way. Darius flattened and curled it, right where I desired him most. My legs trembled beneath his assault as my veins heated with some exuberant fluid.

His teeth scraped my delicate nerves, sending a shock through my system. He couldn't mean to bite me there. It would hurt far too much, and—

A scream caught in my throat as he pierced my skin just above, not enough to feed, but enough for me to bleed.

"D-Darius," I whimpered as flame overwhelmed every aspect of my being. He'd done something, sent some sort of wave of ecstasy through me with that nick, leaving every part of me throbbing uncontrollably.

"Embrace it, Juliet." The words vibrated my tender flesh, making me convulse. Then he suckled me hard into his mouth, and stars exploded behind my eyes.

I no longer cared how loud I yelled or that it was his name rolling through the air. He'd done something so incredible, so powerful, that I couldn't even begin to comprehend.

My soul detached from my body, returned, and escaped again. It left me shaking and moaning and crying. I couldn't stop. Wave after wave of euphoria hit me, and I barely even registered that Darius had moved from my center to my thigh. His thumb circled my inflamed nub while he drank directly from my femoral artery, weakening me by the minute.

But I couldn't focus enough to care.

I just felt.

And floated.

And luxuriated.

"Darius," I breathed as darkness dimmed the stars. Some part of me knew we were heading down a dangerous path. I struggled to emerge enough to warn him, to beg him…

"D…" My mouth felt dryer than it should. Heavy. I tried to lick my lips but couldn't move my tongue.

Everything felt so much cooler than moments ago.

Numb.

Darius.

Midnight consumed my vision as I blinked into a starless night.

So alone.

I always expected to die…

I never expected to want to live.

Until today.

Until Darius inspired hope.

Another cruel vampire joke.

I should have known—

Chapter Ten

Darius

"SLEEP," I whispered as I covered Juliet with a blanket. She looked so pale, but her heart beat healthily in my ears. The marks on her thighs had already healed. "My gorgeous Juliet."

I brushed the curls away from her face and bent to kiss her forehead. We'd only just begun the ceremonial process, but it would be enough for now. In the morning I would start her training. Perhaps after I fucked her beautiful mouth again.

Taking her virginity would have to wait. For now. I wanted to test her first, to determine just how far she would be willing to go to *please* me.

Regardless, I would keep her. She more than proved her worth on her knees, but if I could train her beyond the bedroom, her worth to me would be infinite.

"I'm impressed you've gotten this far," Ivan said. He leaned against the wall of my bedroom with his arms folded. "But you still have a way to go, mate. She's a beautiful doll, but looks are not everything for this job."

I ran my finger down her arm and back up. "She has spirit."

"Yes, but is it enough?"

"Only time will tell," I admitted. "But with the proper motivation, I think it will work."

Ivan scratched his jaw. "If you pull this off, you'll have earned that seat."

"We both know this is about more than power."

His brown eyes blazed. "Yes, but it's a side benefit."

"The side benefit," I repeated, my gaze falling on the beauty resting in my bed. "Will be watching our enemies fall at the hands of their very own creation."

It would be the sweetest revenge, and so very deserved.

"If anyone can pull this off, it's you," Ivan said as he pushed away from the wall. "You always did fancy the impossible."

I grinned. "I prefer to call it a challenge."

"Sure, mate." He left with a backward wave, leaving me alone with my future *Erosita.* Poor Juliet wanted to please me yet had no idea what I truly desired from her.

"You'll learn," I murmured as I ran my knuckles over her cheek. "And when I succeed, you'll be the most lethal weapon in my armory."

Both alluring and deadly.

And mine to train.

Fuck the Blood Alliance.

Part Two

Chastely Claimed

Chapter Eleven

Darius

Six Weeks Later…

"SHE'S NOT READY." Ivan pitched his voice low for my ears alone.

I sipped my bourbon while observing the room. "Yes, that's the point."

"You're risking her life, Darius."

"Which is my prerogative and choice, Ivan." Besides, she'd be well within my sight, and when she found herself in trouble, I'd save her. Tonight was about introducing Juliet to our future together, not harming her.

I fixed my tie while Ivan shook his head. "When does the show start?"

"As soon as Viktor expresses his interest," I replied.

"Well, considering he's [illegible]ting all over her, it won't take long."

I smirked, agreeing.

Juliet's translucent gown left nothing to the imagination, yet she wore it beautifully. It wasn't confidence so much as acceptance. Putting her body on display for a room full of vampires barely fazed her. She kept her dark eyes downcast, using her perceived obedience to her advantage.

And her blood…

Fuck, it aroused the entire room. Everyone would sense her chastity, as well as her purpose here—to entertain and provide sustenance.

And no one could touch her without my permission because she belonged to me.

To fuck.
To please.
To devour.
To share.
Anything I wanted.

Her dark gaze lifted to mine, then fell again. I suppressed a smile at her blatant show of defiance. To meet a master's stare without permission was expressly forbidden even though I allowed it at home. Here, however, was a risk to us both.

Maybe she would surprise me after all.

"He's interested," Ivan muttered beside me. "Lecherous prick."

I grinned against my glass tumbler. "You're just sour that I've taken on the task of killing him."

"No, I'm pissed that you're risking her life for a job I could do in my sleep," he retorted.

I snorted. He was right, of course, but there would be consequences involved if Ivan assassinated a prestigious member of the Blood Alliance. Juliet, however, afforded us a unique opportunity.

Touching another vampire's property without permission resulted in dire consequences. Harming the property enhanced the crime, making death a more than acceptable outcome. Even for high-ranking political members.

"Look at him," Ivan added darkly. "He'll have her on her back in seconds. She doesn't stand a chance."

I studied the blond male over the rim of my glass and shrugged. "I gave her a knife."

"That she barely knows how to use," Ivan countered.

Semantics. I demonstrated the key motions with her earlier. "All she needs to do is create a scene, maybe cut him in the process, and I'll take care of the rest."

"Because *that* will be easy for a woman with her history." Ivan shook his head. "You seriously overestimate her abilities."

"On the contrary, I'm well acquainted with her talents." Innuendo deepened my voice as I observed Juliet. I'd left her there to help the other human in the room hand out appetizers and drinks, something I had hoped would put her at ease. It also gave her a grander purpose, one that allowed her to mingle freely with the guests while being ogled to the fullest extent.

"None of which have anything to do with helping to assassinate a vampire," my oldest friend growled. "Let me handle this one."

"No." A flat command. One that few would be brave enough to dare contend. "I can't break her conditioning until I fully understand how it works. So you will not intervene. I have this handled."

Ivan's lips tightened just enough for me to notice. He clearly did not approve of my methods but remained quiet.

"Careful, old friend," I teased softly. "Or I'll start to think you might actually care about the girl."

He scoffed at that. "She's a fuck doll." Ivan and Trevor's favorite term for my pretty little toy. "I just think you're wasting a significant investment."

True. Juliet did cost a small fortune, but that was exactly the point. Owning her added to my prestige, something that gave me leverage in the political arena. Vampires admired wealth over all else because it equated to age and power, and I possessed all three traits in abundance.

"Darius," a deep voice spoke from the left. Not my mark for the evening, but an important society member.

"Sebastian." I held out my hand. "It's been a long time."

"It has," he agreed as he pressed his palm to mine. "I was beginning to think you'd decided to hibernate for eternity."

Ivan chuckled. "No, just a century."

I feigned amusement. "It's difficult to hibernate with Ivan constantly stopping by to irritate me."

"Cheers." Ivan knocked back the rest of his drink and set the glass to the side. "Someone had to ensure you were alive."

"Clearly, I'm fine," I replied dryly. "I've merely enjoyed my privacy of late."

"Yes, when I heard you had stepped out for the most recent auction, I thought for sure it to be a mistake." Sebastian eyed Juliet with interest across the room.

"As you can see, it's not," I replied. "I decided it was time to indulge more in the finer parts of society and desired something delectable to accompany me."

"I'd say you succeeded." Sebastian hadn't taken his eyes off her yet, something I couldn't entirely fault him for. That was her purpose, after all.

"Yes, I believe I did," I murmured, pleased with his assessment.

"It's good to have you back." Sebastian's tone held no hint of a lie and neither did his gaze as he finally refocused on me. "At least, I assume that is the purpose of your attendance tonight?"

"I'm easing into it slowly." I finished my bourbon and placed the tumbler on the table beside Ivan's discarded glass. "This seemed a reasonable event in which to socialize. Maybe I'll attend the coronation later this year as well." The absolute truth considering I intended to be crowned the new sovereign of this region. Not that anyone outside of my circle knew that—yet.

Sebastian's eyebrows lifted. "You mean to involve yourself in politics?"

I allowed myself a small grin. "*Involve* is such a strong word. Let's just say, I'm interested in mingling with old friends." And winning over their favor in the process. Starting with tonight. Viktor was one of the candidates up for consideration, and I intended to rectify that by using Juliet as bait.

"Hmm, well, should you decide you want to play, be sure to talk to me. I think the alliance could benefit from a man with your skill set."

I hid my resulting smile. Sebastian carried significant weight in the political arena. Having him on my side would certainly be a benefit, and exactly the kind of support I intended to recruit.

"I appreciate the vote of confidence," I replied smoothly. "And I will take your suggestions under advisement."

"Do," he encouraged, handing me his card. "We should catch up formally, perhaps over dinner sometime this week?" His gaze shifted to Juliet as he spoke, his underlying request clear.

"Of course," I murmured, pleased. Already Juliet was serving her purpose in helping me recruit allies. And all she needed to do was exist. "I'll give you a call to arrange."

"Brilliant." He held out his hand and I accepted it. "I've missed you."

"Likewise," I lied.

Ivan stood silently beside me as Sebastian took his leave, then asked, "Am I invisible?"

I grinned. "Only to a man of status."

"You're a man of status and you seem to notice me just fine."

"Because you refuse to leave my side." Like an irritating gnat who buzzed permanently around my personal space. Except I actually liked him.

"Jackass," he muttered, causing me to smile. Very few would dare to call me such a name, but Ivan did it with a skill I greatly admired. It was why I'd selected him as a best friend.

"You seem to be getting on well," Trevor said as he joined us in the corner. "And your little fuck doll is causing quite the stir."

"Is she?" I mused, following his gaze to Juliet. She stood beside the bar, holding a tray of drinks, all of which were laced with blood. "I hadn't noticed."

Trevor chuckled. "Liar. You'll have her naked over your lap the second you depart."

True. "She does wear that dress rather well."

"Is that what it's called?" Ivan asked. "Because it reminds me of lingerie."

"It flows to the ground," I pointed out. "It just happens to be translucent and slit up to her hip on both sides. Easier access to the femoral artery that way."

I snapped my fingers and her head lifted immediately, her dark eyes catching mine for a split second before she started toward us with the tray. No one tried to stop her, but several of my kind observed her ambulation across the room.

When she reached me, she curtsied. "Sire."

"Are you all right, darling?" I asked softly as I took a flute from her tray. Ivan and Trevor followed suit.

"Yes, Sire," she whispered.

"Then you're ready?" I pressed, already knowing she wasn't anywhere near prepared for the task at hand.

But she nodded anyway. "It's what you wish, Sire. So yes."

Ivan rolled his eyes beside me while Trevor grinned wickedly. He was clearly looking forward to Viktor's future demise. I met my mark's gaze and read the inquiry in his expression.

"It seems he's ready too," I murmured as I inclined my head discreetly toward the door beside me. Beyond it lay a hallway that led to several private quarters. I'd already informed Juliet which one I intended for her to use. Viktor would be able to find her on scent alone.

I pressed a kiss to her temple as I passed her tray to Ivan.

"Don't fail me, Juliet," I whispered against her ear. To Viktor, it would appear that I'd just given her a command while the rest of the room merely witnessed me conversing with my pet. This was all a very delicate dance. If anyone caught the subtle exchange between me and Viktor, the plan would fail.

Which was why I had Trevor and Ivan there to observe. They both gave me understated nods of approval, confirming no one had noticed.

"Y-yes, Sire."

"Remember my warning," I added, my lips brushing her pulse. "Now go."

"Sire." She curtsied again before disappearing through the door.

I fixed my tie and smiled good-naturedly at my closest friends. "Punishing her failure later will be fun."

Ivan swirled the contents in his flute, his gaze hard. "You're a sadistic ass, D."

"More like a genius," Trevor corrected.

"Don't worry, Ivan. I'll ensure she enjoys it too." Or I would try, anyway. It depended on just how badly she fucked this up.

Viktor approached, his gaze darkening with ravenous hunger. My smile fell slightly as I considered what I was about to unleash on Juliet. If that look was anything to go by, then it would take significant effort not to act too soon on her behalf.

"Thank you," he whispered as he passed me on his way toward the exit.

I lifted an eyebrow as he wandered through it, both an act for the room and in response to his perceived rudeness. "His conversational skills leave a lot to be desired."

"He appears to be in a hurry for something," Trevor replied, playing his role perfectly. His voice was pitched just high enough for a few to overhear, but not too high that it was obvious.

"Rude," Ivan agreed, sipping his flute casually.

I joined him in enjoying my own flute of bubbly liquid, feigning an ease I didn't quite feel. My senses were tied to Juliet's, waiting for any ounce of panic to ripple through our tentative bond. The ceremony linked us initially, just enough for me to feel her emotions. Such as the rising panic and self-doubt spiking through our connection.

Yes, it seemed she would fail miserably.

Oh, my darling Juliet.

I slowly finished my drink and set it on a nearby table. Then I made a show of loosening my tie and eyeing the door Juliet and Viktor had escaped through. "If you gentlemen will excuse me, I'm in need of a different kind of refreshment."

Ivan smirked. "I knew you wouldn't be able to last the night without indulging in a little foreplay."

"Can you blame him?" Trevor asked.

"I certainly can't," a male commented from nearby, his lips curled in amusement.

"Neither can I," his companion said. "She smells fantastic."

"Well, I'm glad you all approve," I remarked dryly as I started for the door. *Because you're all in for quite a show.*

Let the games begin.

Chapter Twelve

JULIET

BREATHE IN.

Breathe out.

My hands shook.

You can do this.

There was no other choice. Darius commanded it, therefore I would complete the task. Even if it meant taking a life.

My lips curled in an inviting smile while my insides turned to ice.

"Well, you are a tempting morsel, aren't you?" The deep tenor sent a shiver down my spine, and not the good kind. I demurely stared at the vampire's shoes, as was the etiquette by one in my position.

A blood virgin. A possession. A human without rights.

"So pretty…" The male's smoke-laced breath lingered over my lips as he traced a finger along the deep V-neck of my sheer black dress. Darius had chosen the outfit and piled my dark hair up on my head to better expose my throat. I wore nothing beneath the thin, see-through fabric—something the vampire touching me appreciated thoroughly.

"How generous of your master to share you with me," he continued with a sharp pinch to my nipple. I bit my tongue to hold in the yelp his touch inspired.

The blade strapped to my inner thigh begged me to act, but my instincts held me steady.

Not yet, I whispered to myself.

Coward, my conscious replied. *You're not ready for this.*

"Straddle me," the vampire demanded.

My body moved of its own accord, adhering to his will as if I were a puppet. All the while my brain rebelled, dared my new learnings to override the old, but my every action felt entranced by his command.

Humans obey.

Then obey your master's command.

My eyes threatened to close as a war raged through my heart and mind.

To harm a vampire was strictly forbidden. As was to disobey a master. Either way, I broke a cardinal rule.

The vampire's palms ran up my sides as I slid onto his lap on autopilot. His arousal settled between my legs—a hot invitation I had no desire to accept. But if he took me, I'd have to comply.

Master Darius put me here.

To challenge the being beneath me.

Not to pleasure him.

A test.

One I would fail if I didn't slide my fingers beneath the fabric of my dress, find the dagger, and plunge it into this vampire.

Oh, Goddess… How had this become my life? The auction seemed like a lifetime ago. I was meant to be a new master's blood virgin—to provide sustenance and sex—not to become an accomplice to murder.

My stomach revolted as the vampire drew his fangs across my collarbone and up the column of my neck. It felt wrong. Only my master—Darius—was allowed to touch me there. Except he had given me to this blond male without a name and left me with a single demand to create a scene.

Use the blade.

Goose bumps pebbled across my flesh.

No. It's only there for protection.

Hot air seeped into my skin, the vampire readying my pulse for his bite. Darius had told me not to let the male strike, to defend myself as needed…

Grab the knife.

Oh, Darius would be so angry with me if I failed. I'd yet to earn his wrath and punishment, but it would ensue if I didn't pull the weapon out and wield it.

What if I missed?

What if I wasn't fast enough?

What if someone caught me?

Hot and cold fused in my blood, paralyzing me. Then the prick of a fang pierced my skin, and I fell victim to the compulsion to obey.

Twenty-two years with the Coventus overruled my master's two-month tutorial. Muscle memory was a powerful tool.

Succumb.

Allow.

Yield.

Pain flickered through the fog of my mind as the vampire deepened his lethal kiss. Darius was the only other ever to taste my blood, and he always infused it with euphoria… This was not Darius.

My lips parted on a scream I forcibly swallowed. Showing signs of pain only encouraged them. I knew this from observation during my many lessons.

Rough hands went to my dress, ripping the fabric from my chest to my waist. His mouth followed, clamping onto my breast in a cruel bite that scalded my insides.

No pleasure.

Only excruciating pain.

A preference most vampires seemed to share.

Not Darius…

My hands scrambled for the knife, but the vampire took too much too fast. My limbs had gone cold in a matter of seconds, leaving me helpless on his lap.

And very, very alone.

One command.

To reject the male's feeding by screaming or fighting back. Something, *anything*, to garner attention, and now I could barely scream, let alone yell.

I'd failed.

Hadn't even removed the dagger from its sheath around my thigh.

And this would be my punishment—to endure the fate I always feared—death by overzealous vampire. My blood was intoxicating, and from the fanatic way the male suckled at me now, he'd definitely fallen beneath the spell.

No one would care.

Not even Darius.

I was property. A broken toy my master had failed to retrain. It didn't matter that he'd essentially thrown me into the fire with no experience. I should have done better. He would most certainly allow me to succumb to this death.

Splinters fractured along my chest, whether from the pain of failure or the vampire, I couldn't tell.

Everything hurt.

Warm liquid seeped over my skin, drenching me in the life being cruelly sucked from my body.

A knock to my head caused light to flicker behind my eyes—the vampire trying to bring me back to lucidity, no doubt to admire his handiwork.

Or to deflower me.

Because Darius never had, and now I'd failed him.

He would start over with another.

Replace me at a new auction.

I never meant anything to him.

Don't let that hurt, I chastised. *You know better.*

But he was a kind master, far better than I ever anticipated, even with his intention of molding me into his personal poison.

"Juliet," Darius's voice traveled over me in a warm caress that nearly pulled me from my reverie.

Even post-death he would haunt me.

"Juliet." Harsher now, followed by a shake that confused my senses. I felt heavy. Covered in a warm muddy substance that weighed down my chest. It hurt to breathe.

"I'd say it's justified," a male voice advised. Flat. Unfamiliar.

What's justified? I wondered.

"Clearly," Darius snapped. "As if there was any question."

"Hmm. Well. I do hope she's not thoroughly defiled. Would be a shame." Same flat male voice.

My eyelids fluttered but remained unseeing.

Too much… something.

"If she is, I'll be seeking retribution on his entire line," Darius growled.

"Fair enough." Fabric shifted—suit pants, maybe?—as the voice grew fainter. "I'll provide my report of events to the alliance. You won't be held accountable."

"I'll do the same," another man declared. It reminded me of Trevor…

"Me too." And that was Ivan.

Where am I?

"Thank you all," Darius replied, sounding somewhat mollified. "Now, if you wouldn't mind, I'd like to tend to my future *Erosita.*"

Erosita? Had I heard that right? What did it mean?

"Of course," the cool voice said. "If you need anything, you know where to find us."

"Noted," my master murmured, his fingers on my neck.

Everything seemed to shift around me. Savory foods and liquor melted into the crisp evening air. Then leather. New or freshly cleaned.

My head swam.

Something warm touched my lips.

Decadent.

Liquid.

Addicting.

Gone.

My world continued to change, floating in a haze of foreign sensations and scents, until silence overtook the buzzing in my ears.

"Ah, Juliet," Darius whispered. "I had hoped for better, but at least I know where to begin." His lips feathered over mine. "Now. Wake up." The command in his voice pulled at all my nerve endings, forcing my eyes to open.

Even in the subdued lighting of the limo, I could discern the stern lines of his handsome face. High cheekbones. Long, dark lashes. Lush, brown hair. Square, masculine jaw. Smoldering green irises.

"What the fuck happened, Juliet?"

I swallowed. "I…" My mouth reminded me of sandpaper. Not because of my brush with death, but because of his intense expression. "I couldn't kill him."

"Meaning you disobeyed my command," he replied as he gripped my chin to hold my gaze. "What happens when a blood virgin disobeys her master, Juliet?"

"Punishment," I whispered.

"Louder, darling. I want to ensure you understand the ramifications of what you've done."

My throat bobbed as I struggled to repeat myself. "Punishment." It still came out raspy.

"Hmm." His palm slid to my throat and squeezed just enough to threaten. "What will I do with you?"

Only then did I realize he'd seated me over his lap, my legs dangling off to one side as he held me steady with one arm around my lower back. Normally, I wouldn't mind being this close to him, but danger lurked in his tense form.

"Whatever you wish, Sire," I replied softly, meaning it. He owned me. Mind, body, and soul. My purpose was to appease him and I'd failed. I deserved to be punished.

"Indeed." His thumb traced my jawline, his voice silky and menacing. "He bit you, Juliet. Do you know how that makes me feel?"

Lead rocks weighed down my insides. Since I'd broken the number one rule, I had no doubt he was… "Angry."

"Possessive," he corrected. "He touched what's mine, and why? Because you failed to act as I instructed."

I licked my suddenly dry lips. "I—I'm sorry, Sire."

"Are you?" he asked in that same velvety tone. His hand slipped over my exposed chest. My pulse jumped as he pinched the stiffening peak between his thumb and forefinger. "He had his mouth here. Drinking the essence that belongs to me."

I bit back a pained moan as Darius harshly squeezed my tender skin. Normally, his touch elicited pleasure. This was not meant to please—not entirely, anyway.

"Darius," I breathed as he twisted his hold.

"Do you know what it does to a vampire to see his possession caressed by another?" More agony shot through my breast at the subtle hold. Goddess, how did his forefinger and thumb *do* that? "And all because you allowed it. Why, Juliet? Why did you allow it? I warned you what would happen if you let another bite you, didn't I?"

I nodded, and he slapped my breast so sharply I gasped. *Holy…*

"Words, Juliet. Give them to me."

"Yes!" I cried, shaking both from his tone and the odd sensations his touch inspired. Agony… mingled with arousal?

What is wrong with my body?

"More," he growled, his fingers switching to my unabused nipple. "*Why* did you allow it?"

"Habit," I admitted as he applied pressure. "I… I'm trained… Submission."

"And reason is not enough to break the binds to the Coventus?"

Too much… It hurt too much… "It's not that easy," I said, tears in my eyes. "I don't… The rules… I can't."

My whole body thrummed beneath his touch. It burned between my legs, and heated my bare skin, even as numbness tingled along my chest.

"Darius, please…" I begged, not knowing what I wanted. Him to stop? To continue? "I'm sorry I failed you!" Anguish rippled through my voice—a convoluted response to this sensual torture coupled with his obvious irritation.

I'd never fought anyone before, nor had I ever desired it.

Even knowing that vampires and lycans had destroyed humanity, relegated humans to specific factions, removed all our rights, and essentially created my bloodline specifically for vampire enjoyment…

"I'm not a fighter, Darius," I whispered, my eyes closing. "I can't do it."

Chapter Thirteen

Darius

"THAT'S WHERE YOU'RE WRONG, JULIET." A warrior lurked beneath her skin; I just had to coax her out to play.

Testing her tonight was the first step.

Her punishment would be the second.

I released Juliet's breast and suppressed a smile as she squirmed in my lap. Even pained, she still sought to please.

Perfect.

Gorgeous.

Mine.

Yet, despite all my warnings, she'd readily allowed another to bite her. Had I not been waiting for Viktor to lose control, she would have died.

I caught the exact moment when her indoctrinated thoughts took over, forcing her to succumb to Viktor's needs. I could have stopped the feeding then, but I needed his aggression to stage the scene properly. Which wouldn't have been needed had she merely reacted the way I instructed her to.

Killing a vampire without appropriate cause created a mountain of unnecessary paperwork. Having Juliet nearly bleed out in my arms gave me a just reason to act. I did so swiftly, severing Viktor's head from his body even while he continued feeding. A gory scene, sure, but strong messages were best served bloody.

But not even assassinating Viktor could chill the burn inside of me after seeing him maul Juliet. Worse, she'd simply accepted her fate.

I pinched the bridge of my nose.

This beautiful creature was crafted and molded into the perfect temptress. She could speak several languages, hold intelligent conversation on a variety of subjects, walk naked through a room of men without breaking her stride, and she had the mouth of a goddess.

And she was a submissive in every manner of the word.

With a snap of my fingers, she would fall to her knees and suck my cock for as long as I desired. She'd please whomever I gave her to, including a complete stranger, all because the Coventus ingrained this sense of duty into her pretty little head.

I fucking hated them and loved them at the same time.

Such a conundrum. I wanted her to think for herself, yet my sinister side luxuriated in all the ways her body could please mine. Over and over again.

My dick throbbed beneath her, begging to be allowed out to play. But now wasn't the time. Her life relied on her ability to follow my orders to the fullest extent.

If she couldn't fight, she was worthless to me outside the bedroom.

I slid my fingers into her long, nearly black hair and wrapped the strands around my fist. She yelped as I tugged, hard, forcing her gaze once again to mine.

"I gave you my blood, Juliet. That's the only reason you're alive right now." My immortality healed her quickly and efficiently, but that belied the whole point of this exercise. "You would have happily died beneath his fangs. Pleasing another master. How disloyal of you."

"No!" Her dark eyes flared as they met mine, the first spark of challenge flashing in their depths.

I cocked a brow when she didn't continue. "No?"

"You gave me to him." The breathy, slightly sullen quality of her voice suggested her wavering resolve, but the words were clear.

"To fight. Not to fuck and feed." She'd been naked in the vampire's lap, her breasts exposed to his mouth, and she'd not even screamed for him to stop.

Because she expected it. Accepted it. Embraced it.

Fucking Coventus.

It had been a miracle that Viktor hadn't seen the knife strapped to her thigh. It'd been the first item I had grabbed before killing him. The whole scene was a nightmare.

"I'm a blood virgin," she whispered brokenly. "That's our purpose."

"That's not *your* purpose, Juliet." I loosened my grip slightly. "But if all you wish to do is please me, then get on your knees."

She stiffened. "Now?"

"Yes." My cock would enjoy the attention while I taught her a lesson. I released her completely and raised a brow. "Are you going to make me wait?"

"No, Sire." She scrambled off my lap to the floor and placed her shaking palms on my thighs.

Having her like this between my legs helped tamper some of the fury rioting inside me. I meant what I said about possessive instincts. She belonged to me. No one else. And that vampire had touched her in places only meant for my hands and lips.

We would be rectifying that error right now.

"Do your job, Juliet." Cruel words, but effective.

"Yes, Sire." Her blood-coated chest heaved with a deep breath as she trailed her fingers up to my belt. The clasp came undone beneath her expert touch, followed swiftly by the button and zipper. My dick practically leapt out to meet her, but I withheld all emotion from my face. This lesson was not meant to be enjoyable.

Her tongue darted out to dampen her lips as she stroked my shaft from head to base. I relaxed into the leather seat, not giving her the satisfaction of a response, other than the one she held in her palm. If she wanted this to be her sole purpose, I'd make her work for it. The lack of lighting in the limousine aided my plight. She wouldn't be able to see me nearly as well as I could see her.

"Deeper, Juliet." She knew what I liked after several weeks of providing oral pleasure. I'd yet to take her fully because I desired her true consent, not the compliance her Coventus had instilled in her.

My cock hit the back of her throat as she sucked hard. I nearly growled, but I swallowed it at the last minute. Fuck, the woman possessed the most talented mouth I'd ever experienced. No gag reflex. No hesitation. Just pure, unadulterated understanding of exactly what I craved.

It took considerable effort to remain relaxed and unfazed on the surface, especially when my blood started to boil from her ministrations.

So perfect.

So hot.

So damn amazing.

Electricity hummed through my veins, heightened by her constant eye contact. Yearning brightened her gaze, giving her a goddess-like appeal. The woman was gorgeous even when covered in another man's blood.

Shit.

I focused all my energy into remaining neutral even as my groin throbbed. Maybe Juliet truly did belong on her knees, servicing me. Because fuck if I wanted her anywhere else.

My fingers itched to curl in her hair, to force her to take me to the hilt, hard, over and over again. I would come powerfully down her beautiful throat. And she'd swallow every drop, just as she always did.

Mine.

She was crafted for my pleasure.

Trained in all the arts of sex, including the darkest desires.

I couldn't wait to explore them all. In time. Soon.

Now.

I gave in to one of my urges, threading my fingers through her hair and shoving myself all the way down her throat without warning. Her eyes widened a fraction, but she didn't fight me. Just waited for me to let her breathe again.

Submissive to her core.

Trusting.

Not wavering.

Tears gathered at the edges of her irises, the only indication she needed air.

But still no other reaction, not even a plea. Such a turn-on, and yet, so infuriating. How could I break one so obviously broken?

By putting the pieces back together in a new pattern.

One befitting a warrior.

I allowed myself one thrust out and back in again before yanking her off me completely. My other hand wrapped around my shaft, giving it a violent pump as my balls tightened at the pending explosion.

"You're mine," I growled. "No one else touches you."

"Yes, Sire," she agreed, her pupils enlarged as I glowered down at her. With one final jerk of my cock, I unloaded onto her chest while gripping her hair in a way that forced her to watch.

Her name teased my tongue but didn't meet the air. I refused to indulge her when I felt so fucking unsatisfied.

"Rub it into your skin," I demanded as soon as I finished. I wanted it to erase the other man's presence. To mark her in the most degrading way as *my* property.

But she didn't move or respond.

I tugged sharply on her hair. Not enough to hurt, but enough to capture her attention. "Now, Juliet."

Her palms flattened against her breasts, massaging and smearing my essence all over her skin. I observed beneath my hooded gaze, watching as my cum branded her.

"Don't stop." It came out sharp and a little gruff, causing her fingers to move faster over her nipples. She obviously understood my desire since that was the spot Viktor had bitten her. Each swipe of her thumb reaffirmed my place there, my ownership.

Such a good little blood virgin.

I yanked Juliet forward and her mouth opened without my command, her tongue darting out to lick the liquid coating my slit. She hummed in approval before taking me deep into her mouth and drawing every last drop from my shaft.

My grip didn't loosen. If anything, it tightened as she devoured my cock in a manner few others could fathom.

Her hands continued to massage her breasts while she sucked me off, but slowly and more intensely now.

She had adopted an erotic rhythm, one that intensified her arousal.

I stole a deep breath, luxuriating in her intoxicating scent.

Mmm... So, so good.

Damp heat radiated from her, no doubt dripping down her thighs.

She relished in this—my owning her body. My dominance.

And now my darling little Juliet wanted to come.

Perfect.

I let her continue, reveling in the slight squirm of her hips as she fought for the friction she needed. Her nipples were hard little peaks now, begging for my touch, and her pupils overshadowed her irises.

"You enjoyed that," I murmured.

"Yes, Sire." The words were spoken around my still-solid erection. Her attentions had only taken the edge off. I craved so much more from her, but not until she learned her lesson.

"Zip me up, Juliet." We had reached the manor a few minutes ago, but I'd allowed our moment to extend just long enough to ensure her sensitive state. If she spread her legs, I'd no doubt find a very swollen, wet, and ready pussy to sink into.

Not yet.

Her fingers didn't fumble as she secured my hard-on into my pants. I'd tend to it later.

The door opened not a second later, my driver clearly sensing my next move, and I stepped out into the night with a hand for Juliet. She pressed her palm to mine even as her brow furrowed in confusion. Every time we indulged in these types of activities, I returned the pleasure.

But not tonight.

Unless she requested it.

I tucked her arm into mine after she stood. Her bare feet probably didn't appreciate the cobblestone, but that was the point. I wanted her hot, bothered, and uncomfortable.

She moved at my side without flinching, following me into the house and upstairs, and not seeming to mind at all that she wore nothing but semen-laced blood. Her confidence, at least, was intact.

I pushed open the door to her quarters and her nostrils flared as excitement tinged the air. She thought I meant to devour her on the bed. Poor darling. No. That was not the game we were playing tonight.

Instead, I led her to the bathroom, and flipped on the shower.

"You have my permission to bathe, Juliet. I suggest you use the opportunity while it's offered to thoroughly clean yourself." I let that insinuation hang for a moment before continuing. "Then get some sleep. We have a long day tomorrow."

"Y-yes, Sire," she said, her lips curling downward.

"Unless there is something else you require?" I prompted, one eyebrow raised.

She blinked. Frowned. Shook her head. "N-no, Sire. I will bathe and sleep."

Hmm. Disappointing. "Good," I said instead. "See you tomorrow."

I turned and left without looking at her, and ignored the hitch in her breath, too.

The rules in this house were clear. Juliet had an open invitation to join me in my bedroom whenever she desired pleasure. Given the way her arousal taunted my nostrils as I left her room, it was a safe bet to assume she yearned for me tonight. Badly. It would be up to her if she chose to seek me out.

Hence, tonight's primary lesson: living.

A gift not many humans received in this world, but one I happily bestowed upon her. Unfortunately, I couldn't force her to accept it.

Twenty-two years of training to accept fate regardless of personal satisfaction was a difficult mentality to alter.

I needed the fighter hidden beneath her skin to surface and play. Once I coaxed her out, we could well and truly begin the retraining.

Until then, I really only had a shell of a woman to work with, and I desired so much more.

"Join me, Juliet," I whispered into the empty hallway. "Please."

Chapter Fourteen

Juliet

MY BODY WAS ON FIRE.

Not literally, but it burned so fiercely I couldn't sleep under the bedcovers. And the fan above did little to cool my hot skin.

I could still feel Darius on me, even after the shower. His essence scorched my very being, imprinting on my soul.

He well and truly owned me. I knew that from the beginning, but to feel it in such a way was intoxicating. Addicting. Frustratingly arousing.

I kicked the remainder of the blankets off of the bed and huffed in irritation.

How had I gone from expecting to be used within an inch of my life to anticipating Darius's pleasurable attentions?

I was here for his needs, not my own. Yet, he'd always returned the favor.

Except tonight.

Why? Because I'd failed him. Was this his version of punishment?

I bolted upright. The Coventus introduced me to various methods of reprimand, all of which resulted in severe pain and sometimes death. None of those applied here.

A test, then?

"For what?" I whispered to myself. "What do you want?"

I examined our ceremonial bond, curious to see if I could sense anything from him.

It was there—a psychic connection shrouded in darkness—as if we were on the verge of linking our thoughts, but not quite.

Darius had mentioned it wasn't yet complete, that it would require several more rounds of exchanging blood to hold. Perhaps that's what he meant?

Still, I *knew* he was awake as if he were a part of me already. But his emotions were shut off.

He's waiting.

I frowned at the thought. A guess or an instinct?

Does it matter?

He told me I could enter his room whenever I pleased.

"But I should warn you," he had said. *"When you visit me here, I'll assume you're in need of pleasure, and I will require the favor to be returned."*

I shivered at the vivid memory of his incisors brushing my pulse with those words. A promise and a threat rolled up into one.

My sex pulsed with craving, urging me to take him up on the standing offer. If this ache between my thighs was meant to be a punishment, would he send me back to my room unfulfilled? Or reward me for asking him to care for my needs?

I bit my lip, considering. There was only one way to find out.

You're insane, a small voice whispered. *He can kill you with a flick of his wrist, or worse.*

True.

However, in our nearly two months of knowing each other, he'd never truly hurt me. His version of pain always mingled with pleasure. My core ached with the memory of the limo. Some of it had hurt, but it had also created an inferno inside of me that still burned.

I moaned as my nipples hardened against my flimsy nightgown. Even silk felt too heavy right now. I hadn't bothered with underwear. There was a whole drawer of untouched undergarments I chose not to use, likely because they were forbidden at the Coventus. The only ones I even considered were the sexy pieces. Darius would like those.

My eyebrows lifted.

If I went to his quarters wearing one of those sets, he might be more inclined to indulge me.

Maybe.

I pushed off the bed to look for the most enticing lingerie in the drawer. Darius seemed to prefer darker colors. A black negligee caught my eye with its translucent material. I swapped my silk shirt for the thin fabric and shivered as it tickled the top of my thighs.

A pair of matching panties completed the set, but they suffocated my aroused center to the point of discomfort. I tore them off, gasping at the relief that small action afforded me.

My legs quivered as desire overwhelmed my being. Goose bumps filed down my arms despite the heat boiling within, and a moan parted my lips.

I could handle this on my own, or try to, anyway, but I coveted Darius's expert skill. Only he would be able to truly relieve me of this incessant throbbing. His touch was an addiction my body now required. Without it, I would continue to burn.

A pair of four-inch heels and a silk robe completed my outfit. I'd lose the latter as soon as I stepped into his room, assuming he granted me entry.

With a deep, steadying breath, I started down the hallway toward his quarters. The words he spoke during my initial tour bolstered my steps, reminding me that I had an open invitation to seek him out for this very reason.

He might still be displeased with me for earlier, but he never told me I had to stay in my room.

Just bathe and sleep.

Which might have been a command…

Stop. We're doing this.

I paused before his door, hand raised and ready.

Knock.

Run.

Introduce your fist to his door. Softly.

Go back to your room.

You were a coward once tonight; don't do it again.

Choose sanity.

Choose pleasure.

My knuckles tentatively tapped the wood as my thighs clenched. I needed this—him. Strength infused my muscles as I solidified my resolve and knocked with slightly more force.

"Come in." His voice carried through the door and seemed to caress every fiber of my being.

I twisted the handle and stepped inside. He sat shirtless with a notebook in his lap, his back pressed against the pillows and the headboard of his oversized bed.

"Juliet," he murmured, setting his pen down. "What can I do for you?"

I quietly closed the door and moved into the soft light streaming down from his high ceilings. "I can't sleep," I admitted, dropping my robe. "I'm… I *need*."

His green eyes trailed over my form, taking everything in before meeting my gaze. "What do you need, darling? Tell me."

"Pleasure," I whispered.

He arched a brow in challenge. "Louder, darling."

"Pleasure," I repeated, my throat dry and my thighs trembling. "Please, Sire. I'm so hot it hurts."

"Are you wet for me?"

"Yes." It came out on a moan as I clamped my legs together. Any more and I would surely collapse in agony.

"Show me." His low voice coupled with the request stirred a volcano of sensation inside me. It was so intense I couldn't breathe. Couldn't move. Couldn't think.

His muscles flexed as he moved the notebook from his lap to the nightstand and resettled onto his back.

"I'm waiting, Juliet," he murmured, hands tucked behind his head. He resembled a dark angel, his gaze devious and his lips inviting.

The meaning of his request slammed into my gut, forcing my feet to move before the words caught up with my brain. By then, it was already too late.

I knelt beside him on the bed, lifting the lace for his inspection.

"Closer, love." His tone was an erotic caress that tantalized every nerve. My body succumbed to his every wish, doing exactly as he required without question.

The pillows beneath his head dipped as I pressed my knees into them and positioned the hottest part of me directly over his face. His palms slid up beneath the translucent lingerie to grab my hips while I gripped the headboard for balance.

"Mmm, you're so aroused you're swollen." His breath teased my damp flesh, stirring a groan from my throat that sounded nothing like me.

"Please, Sire," I begged. "Please."

"Only because you asked so sweetly." His grasp tightened as he guided my core to his mouth. The first touch of his tongue against my clit elicited a guttural scream from me that resembled his name.

My body shook uncontrollably above him, his hold the only thing keeping me steady.

I needed this, craved it.

Oh, Goddess…

His mouth was pure magic. Just the right pressure.

"Darius," I breathed, my legs quaking violently.

His headboard creaked beneath my palms. It was almost too much, but I couldn't stop the pleasurable assault. Not when it consumed me so completely.

Fire churned inside my lower belly, shooting sparks through my limbs. My indecent position above him only heightened the sensation. It gave me a false sense of power, some semblance of control never before experienced. His hands anchored me, his lips possessed me, and I felt like a queen.

His queen.

Molten heat pooled between my legs, frying my insides and creating a cyclone of energy focused on one single point.

"Oh," I moaned, my body screaming for release. Something sharp—Darius's incisors—skimmed the center of my pleasure, piercing me ever so slightly and vaulting me into a sea of dark bliss.

His name rent the air, sounding suspiciously like a growl, as I came undone. Every sensor exploded at once, my body breaking on a crash of such extreme ecstasy that I could no longer think.

My forehead hit something hard.

My hands squeezed impossibly tighter.

Savage spasms shot through me over and over.

"Darius," I managed, my brain shattered, my heart in tatters, and my soul crushed.

How could something so phenomenal hurt?

"Shh," he murmured, coaxing me back to him, to reality.

I still straddled his face, my shoulders curled in torturous pleasure, and my head pressed against the cool headboard. Light slowly filtered into my vision. The heat of his palms registered against my thighs. His mouth against my intimate flesh.

"Beautiful." Praise deepened his voice, sending a shiver down my spine. His hands skimmed my legs all the way to my ankles where he deftly removed my heels. The pads of his fingers massaged the bottom of my feet, sending tingles up my calves.

So, so good…

"What did I tell you about coming in here?" he asked softly.

My dry throat convulsed as I tried to swallow. "Reciprocation," I rasped.

"Good girl." His irises darkened to a forest green as he smiled. "Slide down. I want to feel your arousal against mine."

It took far too long for me to adhere to his command, but he didn't push me. His hands acted as a guide as I shuffled backward across his body to his bare waist and lower.

He's not just shirtless; he's naked.

I'd yet to see Darius nude. He always kept his clothes on, even when I serviced him. My palms went to his abdomen for balance and also to *touch* him. Solid muscle. Gorgeous. Sleek. A predator encased in hot, tan skin.

All vampires were good-looking, but Darius redefined the meaning of the word. He perfected it. All lean, exquisite lines, handsome face, athletic figure, and beautifully proportioned. His erection was no different. It slipped between my damp folds, molding flawlessly to my body as if we'd been created for each other.

"Fuck," he whispered, his back arching slightly off the bed. "Ride me, Juliet. I want you to soak every inch of me."

We'd not done this yet. It felt intimate, right, and slightly terrifying. His hard member would more than fill me. It would rip through my maidenhead and definitely cause discomfort.

I had to be ready for him, especially if he intended to finally take me tonight. My body belonged to him, to be fucked as he required, and I would allow it. Whatever he wanted.

My hips shifted, drenching him as he commanded, spreading all of my subsequent pleasure over him and dampening his hot arousal. Every time his head met my cleft, I flinched. He'd left me too sensitive, too used, but I had to give him what he desired. His fingers danced up my sides, beneath my negligee, and wandered to my breasts.

"You're so perfect." A note of reverence touched his voice, granting me immense satisfaction. His lower body moved with mine, the friction intensifying with every thrust. I half expected him to reposition me and force his cock inside, but he seemed lost in our movements.

My lingerie disappeared with a rip, and I found my hair wrapped in his fist as he forcibly pulled me down to ravage my mouth with his. I forgot how to breathe beneath the onslaught and lost all touch with reality as he rolled me onto my back.

This is it, I thought, terrified and aroused.

He kissed me hard, his shaft continuing to slide through my damp folds with sharper thrusts. My clit throbbed from the abuse of his bulbous head, but I no longer flinched. No. I was starting to feel hot again.

I bowed off the bed as his fangs pierced my neck.

I hadn't even felt him move. He just struck, his vampiric kiss claiming my essence as his.

"Darius," I whispered, threading my fingers in his hair.

"Mine," he growled as he lowered to my breast and bit me in the same place the other vampire had just hours before. It occurred to me then that he'd done the same to my throat.

He's remarking me.

Except this bite didn't hurt.

Electricity surged down my spine, centering in the place where our arousals connected, heightening the sensations.

Then his member disappeared, his hips lifting slightly as he grabbed my wrist and forced my hand lower. "Stroke me, Juliet. I want to come all over your clit."

I wrapped my fingers around his thick arousal. The effects of my orgasm had drenched his skin, just as he had desired, enabling me to easily fondle him. Up and down, applying pressure where I knew he enjoyed it. My opposite palm joined the action, cupping his heavy balls as I worked his throbbing member with purposeful pumps.

"More," he demanded, his teeth scraping my nipple. I shuddered as he pierced me again, drinking my blood as I massaged him intimately below.

He was close. I could feel it as his sack tightened in my palm, and the way his cock grew impossibly larger. The temptation to put him at my entrance slammed into my gut, forcing my hand to angle his head toward my weeping slit.

It would be so easy.

One thrust.

But it wasn't what he requested.

I continued my task, moving in a way I knew he couldn't resist, and grinned when I felt his growl against my breast. Hot spurts of semen met my intimate flesh, striking me with the force of his orgasm and branding me indefinitely as his.

My hips rose to meet his of their own accord, desiring more, wishing he was inside me and not just hovering above. His scorching essence blended with mine, creating spasms of delight. I squeezed out every drop with my hand, relishing the feel of him.

Darius lifted onto his knees, his gaze between my spread legs. He swiped his thumb through my slick folds to my clit and then back again. "You look amazing like this, drenched in my seed."

I shivered from both his touch and the view of his very naked body crouched so close to mine. Muscle and strength radiated from him, as did an aura of danger. Darius wasn't just a vampire, but an old one too.

He smeared his essence around my entrance, awakening a hunger deep within me. Then he pressed inside, introducing his pleasure to mine and mating them in the world's oldest dance.

"Soon," he whispered darkly. "But not yet."

Why? I wanted to ask, but only a moan escaped instead. He applied just the right amount of pressure to my sensitive nub, massaging our combined euphoria into my flesh.

Lava slithered into the pit of my stomach, growing with each swipe of his thumb. Darius played my body with such expertise, his gaze always attentive and his focus on my reactions. He pinched me, kneaded me, and teased my nerves. I shook beneath him, completely lost to his will.

One hand.

That's all he used.

And I was already coming undone.

When he leaned down to capture my nipple with his mouth, I bucked against him. My breathing stopped. The whole world blacked out around me. Everything focused on Darius.

"My seed owns you now," he whispered. "And soon, so will my cock."

His words increased the intensity building inside me, cresting the volcano threatening to erupt. I trembled from the potency of it all, my mind losing its grip on reality.

"So close." He nibbled my breast. "I can feel it bubbling beneath the surface, awaiting my command. Your body is so beautifully trained, Juliet." He trailed kisses up to my collarbone and along my jaw.

My nerves were linked to a live wire, sizzling with energy and waiting to combust. I felt imprisoned, frozen in time—a slave to my master's desire.

"Please," I whispered, aching from the force of it. "Please, Sire."

He grinned against my throat, his tongue tracing my pulse. "You beg so prettily, darling."

My nails dug into my palms as waves of excruciating need rolled over my being. I was gasping his name, writhing beneath his attentions, dying for the release he held in reserve.

His lips brushed my ear, his exhale heavy and intoxicating. "Come for me."

Agony coupled with gratification exploded inside me, destroying my ability to move and think.

Flashes of light.

Fractures of my consciousness.

A world of discomfort and euphoria.

My lungs burned from my screams while my limbs melted into a puddle of repletion.

"Glorious," Darius murmured, his lips against mine. "Fucking perfection."

I trailed my fingers up his strong arms to hold on to him while he kissed me. He tasted sweet, with a hint of sex, his tongue masterful as he explored my mouth almost tenderly.

"Sleep, Juliet." He nuzzled his nose against mine. "We'll continue your training tomorrow."

Chapter Fifteen

Juliet

I STRETCHED MY ARMS OVER MY HEAD and sighed in contentment at the warmth flowing through my veins. A foreign feeling, one I wished to enjoy for a few minutes more.

Most nights were so cold that I awoke to the feeling of ice drizzling over my flesh. It numbed me before the day began, helping me to endure whatever new trial the Coventus threw at me.

Waking with Darius was different.

New.

Intoxicating.

His lips were on my neck, his bare chest pressed to my back, as he slowly coaxed me from my dream state. I wiggled my hips, loving the sensation of his hot erection pressed into my backside.

"Careful," he murmured. "Or I'll accept that invitation, darling."

I might enjoy that, I thought. But I stopped moving for the sake of my sore body.

Darius had used me so completely last night that I felt exhausted today despite the decent sleep. When he took me for the first time, he wouldn't be gentle. No vampire ever was, and Darius had more than shown his penchant for rough sex. I expected it to hurt. A lot.

He caressed my chin and tilted my head back to meet his kiss.

Mmm. Long, fluid strokes of his tongue against mine.

I could become addicted to this treatment. So gentle, caring, almost reverent.

"Good morning," he whispered when he finished. "Or I suppose I should say 'evening' since it's well after midnight."

Yes, a typical vampire schedule. The sunlight didn't particularly bother them; they just preferred the night. Lycans, however, embraced the day. Or so I'd been told. I'd yet to meet one.

"Hi," I managed, my throat sore.

He nudged me onto my back to lie beneath him and smiled down at me. "I'm proud of you, Juliet."

I blinked. "Me? Why?"

His mouth brushed mine. "Because you came to me last night and told me what you needed. I want that to happen more often."

So, it was a test.

Or rather, a lesson of some kind.

Everything Darius did seemed to have some sort of motive.

He kissed me again, this time with slightly more force as his erection pulsed between my legs. I dampened for him automatically, had probably slept in that state most of the night on instinct alone.

"Mmm, hold that thought." He pressed his palms into the pillow on either side of my head and lifted himself up while holding my gaze. "We need to discuss your comments about not being a fighter."

Ice slithered through my veins, freezing me beneath him. "I'm not."

"I agree that you're not," he replied. "Yet." He rolled off of me and held out his hand. "Come with me."

His tone brooked no argument. My palm met his as he assisted me from the bed. Rather than head toward the hallway, he directed me to his oversized marble bathroom and flipped on the shower. I stood beneath the already warm water, awaiting his instructions.

"Your survival instincts have been beaten out of you," he murmured as he ran his fingers through my dampening hair. "I'm going to help you find your spirit and resolve." He selected a bottle and poured some of the clear liquid into his palm.

"Vampires and lycans are superior beings," he continued as he massaged the shampoo into my hair. "There is no question on that front, but that does not mean all humans are weak. With the right training and mindset, you have the capability to be my lethal counterpart. The Coventus taught you how to tempt. I will teach you to fight."

Darius pushed me under the water, his hands running over my damp strands until the last of the bubbles went down the drain. Then he started over with the conditioner.

"We have four months until the coronation." His voice lowered with the words. "I need you to help me eliminate the competition."

My eyes widened both at his words and the inherent trust underlining them.

Not once had he mentioned *why* he wanted my cooperation. "You intend to run," I realized.

"No, I intend to win." He fondled a stray piece of my hair that had fallen over my breast. "The best way to defeat an enemy is to become the enemy."

"You refer to the alliance?" I pitched my voice low, uncertain.

"Yes." He nudged me beneath the water again and repeated his actions from before. Then rotated us so he stood closer to the showerhead. "The vampire you helped me assassinate last night was Viktor Armintrov." He ducked beneath the spray while my jaw dropped.

"He's aristocracy." It came out on a shocked whisper that of course Darius heard.

"Yes and an utter bastard who deserved his fate." He shook the droplets from his dark hair and stepped forward. "His favorite establishment is the whorehouse. I'm sure your Coventus explained that to you?"

Yes. The vampires in charge had used it as a potential threat should anyone misbehave. "It's a place where humans with less worthy bloodlines are sent," I said, quoting my texts. "The average age of death is twenty-five."

"Because of men like Viktor," Darius replied as he lathered his head with shampoo. "Trust me when I say he deserved a far worse fate than beheading."

I considered that while he rinsed and applied conditioner. "Why do you wish to join the alliance?" I wondered out loud. "You do not strike me as having political motivations." Perhaps that was out of turn for me to say, but given all of my learnings, Darius did not fit the mold.

His lips curled into a dangerous smile. "I want to destroy it and reinstate our rightful leader."

All the breath left my lungs. He'd mentioned the tidbit about enemies, but this...

The alliance was the glue that held our society together. Without it, lycans and vampires would go to war, leaving the humans as collateral damage.

Everything would collapse.

Darius pressed a bar of soap to my breast and began massaging it in small circles.

"Tell me, Juliet, are you happy?" he asked softly. "With this life, I mean. Do you enjoy being relegated to slavery? To being a source of food and pleasure for my kind?"

My mouth opened and closed, no sound escaping. They weren't questions I knew the answers to as I'd never even considered them. My purpose was defined at birth. I never had a choice. What other means of happiness was there for a blood virgin?

"Humans used to have a higher place in society." His hand moved south as he lathered more soap into my skin. "I showed you the history books when you first arrived so you would understand. It's not something the Coventus teaches. The information is considered irrelevant, which is really a fancy way of classifying it as illegal."

He turned me away from him and lifted my hair over one shoulder to better access my back while he continued speaking.

"There are those who disagree with the way our government works today. It favors the old aristocracy and degrades those of lesser bloodlines. Ivan and Trevor are two examples—they don't qualify for a judicial position merely because they were born into the lower class as humans. It bars them from certain career paths as well, disqualifies them from events such as your blood virgin auction, and even prevents them from entering certain social circles without a representative."

Darius's palm ran down my thigh as he kneeled behind me.

"As you've no doubt ascertained, blood is very important in vampiric hierarchy. And it's the foundation of the alliance. Turn."

I did as he asked, placing my most sensitive body part before his eyes. He placed a kiss on my shaved mound before gently washing the area of his attentions from last night.

"How much do you know about lycans?" he asked, his green irises meeting mine.

"Bloodlines are important to them as well," I replied. "They have royal houses and hierarchy in their packs."

"A crude assessment, but true," he agreed. "The alpha males control everything, including the females in their territories. Property can be exchanged for a woman of choice, and they very much believe in forced breeding. And as that's how they treat their own kind, you can imagine humans have it far worse."

I shivered. Lycans were never the predator I had to worry about, so I hadn't spent much time studying them, but I knew their kind to be violent. There were rumors about what happened to humans chosen for the full moon. None of them survived.

"My point is that our system is flawed and there are those—myself included—who do not agree with how everything is run, and we wish to fix it." He stood. "Rinse."

I stepped beneath the water again as he soaped himself off in a far more efficient manner and then traded positions when he was ready to wash away the suds. They pooled at our feet, creating a swirling motion over the drain as I observed numbly.

Of all the masters, I had been selected by the one who desired change.

A world without the alliance. I couldn't even begin to imagine what that would look like.

Darius lifted my chin, his gaze capturing mine. "My bloodline is purely aristocratic, identifying me as an ideal candidate for ascension."

"What happened to the former sovereign? Adrian Loughton?" The name was a guess based on his comment regarding Viktor. I remembered his region from my studies and knew he resided beneath Adrian.

"I'm impressed," Darius praised. "And to answer your question, Mister Loughton met an unfortunate end at the hands of a few misguided lycans.

Tragic."

He didn't sound all that upset about it. "You orchestrated it." Another guess, one I knew was correct by the gleam in his green eyes.

"As I said, tragic." He turned off the water and pulled an oversized towel from the rack. The warm cotton covered me from my shoulders to my knees. "There are several in this region who qualify to replace him, myself being one of those candidates. But I've avoided politics for nearly a century, choosing instead to live alone."

"Why?" I asked, curious.

His smile was sad. "A story for another day, darling. We have other activities to tend to that take precedence, including a dinner with Ivan and Trevor."

"Dinner?" I repeated.

"Mmm." He wrapped a towel around his waist. "Yes. It'll be a practice run for later this week."

"What's happening later this week?" The words were out before I could stop them, an indication of an error in my conditioning. To question a master was wrong, not that Darius seemed to mind. If anything, he appeared amused.

"An engagement with Sebastian Cromwell."

My eyes rounded. "The Regent?" He was second in command to a sovereign and notoriously powerful. That couldn't be the vampire he meant…

"The very one," he replied. "He requested it."

"Why?" I just couldn't seem to stop my mouth from moving or speaking.

Some of his amusement dissipated as he stepped closer, forcing me to back up against the wall behind me. He placed his palms on the marble on either side of my head, caging me between his muscular arms.

"A ceremony is rare, Juliet. So rare that the last one on record occurred over five decades ago. And while ours isn't complete yet, the initial stages have begun, which has inspired a certain amount of curiosity among my brethren."

"Meaning he's coming because of me," I inferred.

"Yes." He let that response settle between us, his expression patient as though waiting for an additional inquiry, but he'd finally silenced me. "Do you know what purpose a mated blood virgin typically serves at a dinner party?"

I recalled all my texts and came up blank. None of them had ever discussed the ceremony, let alone the etiquette that followed it. "No, Sire."

"Sharing," he murmured.

My brow furrowed, not understanding. "Sharing what?"

"You, darling. Sebastian wishes for me to share *you,* and given my innate response to Viktor last night, I need to practice my patience where that is concerned. So, we'll begin with Ivan and Trevor. Today."

"YOU TOLD HER ABOUT THE ENDGAME?" Despite his elegant suit and tie, Ivan appeared ready for a fist match, with my face being his primary target.

"Yes." I didn't elaborate because what was the point?

Sharing my desires with Juliet suited the moment. Her understanding my objective was crucial to her training.

"Yes," Ivan repeated, pacing. "That's it, is it?"

"Yes." That time I said it to piss him off, and it worked. My old friend rounded on me, his nose inches from mine.

"She could go to the fucking alliance and have you slayed. You do realize that, right?" His anger was founded in his concern for me, which was the only reason I didn't respond outwardly to his physical proximity. "Fuck, where is that damn royal when I need him? If anyone could talk some sense into you, it'd be *him*."

I ran my fingers over my tie and held his gaze unwaveringly. "No one would believe a blood virgin's babbling over a vampire of my status, not that she would ever have access to anyone of aristocracy to inform them. Above all of that, she is mine and she will not repeat a word to anyone." As for his comment about "the royal," he'd understand as my oldest friend and ally. After all, most of this was his idea. *For Cam.*

Ivan's eyebrows popped up to meet his dark hairline. "You trust her?"

"I own her," I clarified. "Trust isn't required with property." A harsh statement, but true nonetheless.

"I don't like it."

"You don't have to like it to accept it."

He picked up his glass of bourbon and downed the contents before slamming it on my desk. "Fine. But if she ends up endangering you, don't expect any pity from me."

I chuckled. "Duly noted. Now, where's Trevor?"

"Probably sating himself in some redhead," Ivan muttered.

"When I offered him my blood virgin for the night?"

"*Because* you offered her."

I smiled. Trevor clearly worried he might lose control. Well, that wouldn't be an issue, because I planned to be in charge of every detail. No one would harm my Juliet.

"Is she terrified?" Ivan asked.

"Yes." I'd scented her terror when I mentioned sharing her earlier and again when I dismissed her to ready herself for dinner. The outfit I'd requested she wear didn't help matters. Rather than black, I'd opted for a dark red tonight. It would look beautiful against her pale skin.

"Then you clearly didn't tell her how this is going to go."

I snorted. "Of course not. What would be the fun in that?"

"Still a jackass, I see."

"Why would that ever change?" I asked, smirking. "Now, shall we go have a little fun?"

"You're an evil man, Darius."

"Another fact that will never change," I pointed out as I led the way to the foyer. Juliet's scent had grown stronger—indicating she'd left her room—and I wanted to observe her reactions as she descended the grand staircase. Her glittery dress caught the light from the chandelier above, illuminating her curves as she paused at the top.

"Shit," Ivan growled beside me. "I fucking hate you."

"We both know that's not true," I replied softly as Juliet started toward us on her four-inch stiletto heels. Never once did she falter despite her obvious nerves over what dinner would entail.

Her breasts swayed with each step, making me quite pleased that I had chosen this dress for her to wear tonight. Thin gold chains held the fabric up on her shoulders, and the neck split to her belly button. There was no back, the slits on her skirt went up to midthigh, and, as with everything else she wore, the sheer fabric revealed everything beneath.

"Juliet," I murmured, kissing her cheek as she joined us. "We're going to pretend this is a traditional affair—just for dinner—to practice for future events. So I'll need you to bow as you normally would as I properly introduce you to Ivan."

They'd already met on a few occasions, but tonight was about preparing for our meal with Sebastian. And to do that, we needed to pretend a little.

Her dark eyes slipped from mine, her subservience immediately taking over. "Yes, Sire."

I lifted her chin, wanting to hold her gaze for a moment longer. "I'll be here the entire time, love. And I'll coach you through it, all right?"

She swallowed. "Yes, Sire."

I cupped her cheek and kissed her on the mouth. "I won't let anything happen to you that you won't enjoy," I whispered against her lips. "You'll see."

"All right." She didn't appear all that convinced, but I would prove my point by the end of the meal.

I released her and took a step back. "As much as it pains me to say, please bow for Ivan." Such a ridiculous formality, but humans were considered to be the lowest echelons of society. They ranked on the same level as cattle.

Juliet lowered to the ground with a practiced ease, her gaze again on our shoes. She wouldn't stand again until I granted permission.

"When Sebastian arrives later this week, you will descend the staircase with the same confidence and bow as soon as you reach the foyer."

"Yes, Sire." Her voice held no hint of fear, this type of formality no doubt being typical for her.

"Ivan," I prompted.

He gave me a look that expressed his irritation before eyeing Juliet's submissive form. With his hands in his pockets, he circled her, eyeing every asset on display while purposely brushing against her as he moved. She didn't flinch, her posture perfect the entire time.

"She's lovely, Darius." He stopped behind her. "May I?"

My instincts rioted while I replied, "Of course."

I could handle this.

I had to.

"Kneel for Master Ivan," I instructed.

Juliet sat up onto her heels, palms on her thighs, head still bowed respectfully. My cock hardened at the now familiar position. She truly was a gorgeous woman.

Ivan brushed his knuckles over her cheek before trailing them down her neck to the gold chains gracing her shoulders. I monitored her heart rate as he continued his exploration and admired the steady rhythm, especially as he moved to press his legs to her exposed back.

He gripped her chin to force her head back, meeting her gaze with a smoldering one of his own, and smiled seductively. "Hello, pet."

"Master Ivan," she greeted. "Welcome."

Such a natural. No trembling or hiding, just utter compliance in a dangerous situation. The Coventus had certainly done their job well. Too bad I had to undo all their hard work.

Oh, on the surface she would remain the same, but not beneath. And her reactions today proved it all to be possible. Juliet had questioned me openly without fear—a leap forward in our arrangement whether she realized it or not.

Ivan drew his thumb over her lips, tracing them slowly and thoroughly. "You have quite the fuckable mouth. Perhaps your Sire will allow me to experience it later."

I swallowed my choice response to that statement and maintained my air of indifference. An improvement from the Viktor situation.

"Oh, I've missed the introductions." Trevor's voice carried through the foyer as he entered my home without knocking—an indication of our friendship. Very few could do that without risking their lives.

"You're just in time," Ivan replied, his palm on Juliet's cheek. "Come meet Darius's pet."

Trevor wandered over in a black tailored suit and stood in front of Juliet while Ivan continued to slowly stroke her jaw. Trevor trailed his gaze slowly over her low-cut neckline to her waist, down to her slightly parted thighs, and back up.

"She's delectable, Darius," Trevor praised, playing his part appropriately.

"Would you like to touch her?" I offered.

"Mmm, yes, I would. With your permission." His blue-green eyes lifted to mine in polite question.

"It's given." The words tasted sour in my mouth but sounded normal. An indicator that I might be able to complete this evening without killing one of my best friends. Of course, this was the easy part.

Trevor touched her shoulder before tracing the line of her dress down over the swell of her breasts and back up again. "So soft," he mused, his attention focused on her hardening nipples. "And responsive."

Her body reacting to a vampire's touch—yet another impulse driven into her through years of conditioning. Was that why she submitted to me so easily? Or was it something else?

Does it matter?

Yes.

"Shall we move to the dining room?" My steady voice sounded nothing like the one rioting in my head.

"I'm certainly famished." Ivan released Juliet but didn't move away from her. "Your pet is exquisite."

Meanwhile, Trevor continued his exploration, moving from her collarbone to her jawline. "May I escort her?" he asked with a glance my way.

I forced a smile. "Absolutely."

"Excellent." He held out his hand, palm up. "Beautiful?"

Her eyebrows lifted a little in surprise at the nickname he'd bestowed upon her while Ivan smirked at the clear social mishap. Not that Trevor cared. He more than embraced being snubbed by aristocracy.

Juliet accepted his help up from the ground and slid her arm through his as he offered it to her. "A pleasure, little one."

"Thank you, Master Trevor."

He chuckled. "Oh, how I do enjoy hearing those words from a woman's mouth, especially one as gorgeous as yours."

"I doubt Sebastian will be nearly this good-natured," Ivan drawled as he followed the couple down the hall. I remained a few steps behind, my goal to show trust and respect.

Trevor snorted. "Certainly not. The man has a dick up his ass."

"Stick," Ivan corrected.

"No, I definitely meant a dick." Trevor led the way to the dining room, a grin on his face the whole way while I shook my head.

"I told you he wouldn't last more than five minutes," Ivan said conversationally. "Do you think perhaps it's the blond hair? Bleached it too much during his surfing days?"

"Seriously, a blond joke?" Trevor tossed back. "I suppose I shouldn't expect much from a former Brit."

"Poor Mister America doesn't understand our dry sarcasm, D," Ivan murmured. "Do you think it's because his former political system didn't value education the way ours did?"

"Absolutely," I agreed, even though I didn't grow up in the same era. Both of my friends were born much, much later than me.

"What do the nicknames mean?" Juliet asked, her gaze meeting mine unexpectedly in the dining room.

Everyone stopped smiling, the air cooling to a frigid level. Juliet's eyes grew wide as she realized her social faux pas, her lower lip trembling.

Hmm. If Sebastian were here, I'd have no choice but to publicly punish her for such an outburst. However, since Trevor had already broken all formalities, I could let this slide.

Besides, this was the type of behavior I desired—a fracture in her conditioning that I could exploit.

Trevor stepped away as I moved forward, and Juliet immediately fell into a formal bow. I bit my tongue to keep from chastising her for it. She thought we were still practicing, which meant I'd enforce her penalty now. But no. I had no desire to reprimand her for showing curiosity.

Both Ivan and Trevor gaped as I knelt before her, my palms going to her face to lift her gaze. "America is a former country and technically where we live now. Brit is short for British, which relates to Great Britain or the United Kingdom. They disappeared with the fall of humanity. Now everything is divided into regions."

Her brown eyes gazed deeply into mine. "I read about those in the history books. So many wars."

I hid a smile. "Yes, they participated in several, but most humans did throughout the centuries. Remind me to let you read about the Crusades some time." A devastating period that I did not enjoy living through.

"You are British?" she asked softly.

"Actually, no." I smiled as I stood and held out my hand for her to join me.

"I was born in the Gaul region, which later became Western Europe. I'll show you on a map later, but my ancestry is Roman. I later moved to the Britannia province when it was otherwise known as Roman Britain."

"What he's trying to say is that he's fucking old," Trevor translated.

I ignored him and focused once again on Juliet. "Nearly three millennia, to be precise."

She didn't appear shocked by that information in the slightest, suggesting she'd either anticipated it or been numbed to eternal beings. Likely both. "You look very good for your age," she replied, shocking me yet again.

"Was that…?" Ivan trailed off.

"A joke," Trevor finished. "Oh, I knew I liked her."

"You keep calling her a fuck doll."

"Which she is, but a clever one."

"Enough," I snapped, tired of the side conversation interrupting the moment.

Juliet flinched, her gaze falling. "I'm sorry, Sire. I meant it as a compliment."

"I know," I whispered. No way had she suddenly adopted a sense of humor. "Thank you." I kissed her forehead and folded my arms around her in a hug. Ivan and Trevor both gaped at me as if I'd grown a second head.

"What? You fucked up the practice round back in the foyer, Trevor. We'll start again in a moment." It wasn't like they cared about decorum. We never followed it here.

I kissed Juliet soundly on the mouth to display my pleasure at her breaking the confines of her training. So beautifully disobedient. I wanted to see more of it, but only in the confines of our home.

"You can't act like this around society members, Juliet." I held her gaze, ensuring she understood the importance of my words. "Only here."

"Yes, Sire." She frowned. "I didn't mean to speak out of turn; I'm not quite sure why I did."

"Because you're learning how to live," I advised softly. "Now go take the middle chair. Trevor and Ivan will sit on either side of you, and I'll be across the table."

We were nowhere near done yet.

I still had to share her.

Physically and sexually.

Chapter Seventeen

JULIET

"OPEN," Trevor demanded.

I parted my lips while keeping my eyes closed, as instructed. Something warm and decadent slid over my tongue, and I fought a responding moan.

They told me not to speak or utter a sound—a demand they seemed to be testing through a game of feeding me sweet desserts. Breaking the rules resulted in punishment, and these men clearly wanted me to disobey their commands.

"I think she likes it," Ivan mused. "Give her another bite."

Ohhhh, I sighed mentally. I was so full already. After years of eating food only of nutritional value, it was hard to enjoy meals in the way Darius and his friends did. My stomach couldn't tolerate the rich flavors.

"Only one more," Darius advised, voice flat.

"Spoilsport," Trevor grumbled.

"Here, love, open," Ivan said as the edges of a spoon met my mouth.

I obeyed dutifully. Another sweet slice of heaven tortured my underdeveloped taste buds as I forced myself to chew and swallow.

"Gorgeous," Trevor praised as someone trailed a gooey substance along my collarbone. I almost glanced at it but remembered their order for me to shut my eyes.

Something wet—a tongue—met my skin as one of them laved up whatever had just been applied to my body. They'd done this a few times during dinner, their hands and mouths finding one reason or another to touch me. But never beneath the dress, and always with Darius's permission.

"Mmm, I'm craving something else for dessert." Ivan's words flowed over and through me, the insinuation in his voice punctuated by his palm sliding over my thigh. "Darius?"

"Yes." The sound of a chair scraping over wood, then footsteps.

My heart skipped a beat.

The stroking and licking throughout dinner hadn't bothered me nearly as much as I expected because Darius sat close by. They were all busy eating as well, lost to their conversations in politics while using my body as a side amusement.

But now I was under the spotlight.

I felt it with every fiber of my being, all three gazes on me—voracious.

Oh, Goddess.

It was like the first night in Darius's home, when I thought they'd all intended to devour me. Except this time, I *knew* that was the plan.

To share.

Three men.

Can I manage it?

I could barely handle Darius…

A warm palm slid beneath my hair, curling around the back of my neck as Darius's familiar scent overwhelmed me. "You've done so well, darling. But now it's time for the real test." His thumb stroked my thrumming pulse. "Stand."

Finding my footing while blind wasn't easy, but I managed. The chair disappeared as Darius pressed his chest to my back.

His hands found my hips. "Open your eyes."

I did and found nothing had changed. Trevor and Ivan both sat in the same chairs, their expressions predatory.

"Gentlemen, you've ensured Juliet's appetite is well sated. Would you like her to return the favor?" Darius asked, his tone dark and sensual.

My heart fluttered. *Return the favor…*

Ivan stood and ran his hand over his tie, his caramel-colored irises a thin line around his oversized pupils. He looked hungry. Very, very hungry. "I would adore that."

"Me too," Trevor added, standing.

"Excellent." Darius pressed a kiss to my neck—a show of open possession—and splayed his fingers along my sides. "Shall we adjourn to the great room?"

Ivan's heated gaze danced over me, his lips quirking. "I suppose that would be more comfortable."

Trevor smirked and turned to lead the way, Ivan right behind him.

"Follow them," Darius whispered when my feet refused to move.

I swallowed, my throat dry. "Yes, Sire."

It took a moment for my legs to work, my limbs frozen with trepidation.

The Coventus had well prepared me for what came next. While I'd never experienced it for myself, I'd witnessed several threesomes and foursomes throughout my training days. So much blood, and not all mortals survived.

Darius needs me alive. Or that's what he had said, anyway. Hopefully, he and his friends remembered that.

Trevor and Ivan stopped on either side of an oversized chaise lounge in the mansion's ornate living area. Plush chairs and couches decorated the immense room, leaving multiple other options for seating, suggesting they chose this spot with purpose. It provided ample angles for devouring their dessert—me.

I refrained from the urge to wipe my clammy palms against my dress and stood with my eyes downcast, awaiting Darius's instructions. His fingers lightly traced my arms, eliciting a row of goose bumps in their wake as his hands settled on my shoulders.

Trevor slid out of his jacket and draped it over the back of a chair. "What was the name of tonight's wine?" he asked while rolling up the sleeves of his crisp white dress shirt.

"An old French wine that isn't made anymore." Darius's thumbs brushed my collarbone while his fingers toyed with the gold chains of my dress.

Ivan mimed Trevor's movements as he murmured, "That's a shame."

"Indeed." Darius drew the metal across my shoulder slowly, his lips near my neck. "Shall I reveal your dessert?"

My heart slammed a chaotic rhythm against my ribs. They could already see right through my dress, minimizing the impact of my pending nudity. Yet, the idea of Darius removing the only barrier between me and these three men—

"Yes." No hesitation from Ivan, not that I expected any.

"Absolutely," Trevor added, his tone taking on a low growl that rippled across my skin.

Darius chuckled darkly as he drew the straps down my arms, exposing my breasts inch by inch. My nipples pebbled in reaction to both the cool air and the sexual tension igniting throughout the room.

"Gorgeous," Ivan murmured as the fabric reached my stomach. I could *feel* their gazes on me, memorizing my flesh, or more likely, determining where to bite me first.

My blood heated and cooled, my body at war with how to respond. Darius's vampiric kiss always elicited pleasure, but I knew that wasn't how most of his kind fed. How would Trevor and Ivan feel? Would it hurt? Would I like it?

Darius's thumbs skimmed my hips, the dress following his lead and slowly slipping from my body to pool at my feet.

"Leave the heels on," Ivan said, his tone laced with yearning. "Please."

"Of course. Just one thing first." Darius twisted me in his grasp so fast that I would have fallen if his arm hadn't wrapped around my lower back. His opposite hand lifted to grab a fist full of my hair. A sharp tug forced my gaze to his—two smoldering orbs of the deepest green.

His mouth sealed over mine in a punishing kiss that left me wondering what

I'd done wrong. Had it been the goose bumps? My thundering pulse? Both were considered mortal faults. The Coventus tried to break my kind of those instinctual reactions through hours of forced observation. Alas, I never managed to master the art of hiding my body's responses. Just as I couldn't deny the heat Darius provoked in me now with the dominating swipes of his tongue against mine.

I gripped his jacket for balance as he deepened his claim. My head stung from how tightly he held my hair, while my stiff nipples luxuriated in the feel of his fine wool jacket abrading my bare skin. It evoked pleasure and pain simultaneously, leaving me off-kilter. I didn't know whether to scream or to moan, and that convoluted swarm of emotions only worsened as blood filled our mouths.

My breaths came in pants against him, uncertain of this possession. The sticky essence coated my tongue and throat, causing me to gag. That only seemed to spur him on more, his arm squeezing me tighter as the fingers knotted in my hair loosened to trace my face.

"Take a deep breath," he instructed, causing my heart to jump.

Why? I wondered even while I complied. Then he gripped my nose while resealing his lips over mine.

My eyes flew open.

I couldn't breathe.

More blood filled my mouth, drowning me, forcing me to swallow in heavy gulps while my lungs burned with the need for air.

Tears flooded my vision, my body aching, my heart beating a mile a minute.

Why? I blinked. *What did I do wrong?*

My nails dug into his jacket while I gulped the thick substance lining my throat. I didn't dare inhale, but I would be forced to soon if he didn't release me.

Domination.

Darius owned me. Each subtle sweep of his tongue over mine confirmed his power, and the erection against my lower belly said he enjoyed his dominion. I was his to do with as he pleased—to fuck, to bleed, to suffocate, to kill. That notion of complete and utter control calmed me despite the inferno etching a path through my lungs.

He'll let me breathe.

The confident thought pierced my haze of fear and stirred a quiver deep in my belly. So contrary to the act at hand. I should be screaming and fighting; instead I relaxed. My body yielding to his desires and trusting him in the most crucial of ways.

I'm broken. Shattered. His. Just as the Coventus trained me to be. A human toy.

Darius's lips slipped from mine as his hand drifted to my hair again, his grip far gentler than before.

The unexpected reprieve sent a jolt through my system, shooting electricity to my nerve endings and heating me to my very core. I inhaled deeply, completely, my body shaking uncontrollably from fright and a lethal need for *more*. Fire laced my veins, setting my skin ablaze with conflicting messages while my lungs wept with joy.

Arousal deepened Darius's irises to a dangerous forest-green color as he studied me intently. "You enjoyed that."

I shuddered, my body enflamed from his touch and kiss. *What did he just do to me?*

He brushed his mouth against mine and smiled. "Yes, you definitely enjoyed that."

I licked the blood from my lips and shuddered again as I swallowed. *So sweet. So addicting. Like life in liquid form.*

My eyebrows drew down at those errant thoughts and shot upward as understanding dawned.

Not my blood.

Darius had forced me to swallow *his* essence, not mine. "Why?" I mouthed. Would this further the ceremonial bond between us? He mentioned after the first time that we would have to consume each other again.

"Protection," he whispered, brushing his knuckles over my cheek. "Now go lay on the chaise and spread your legs for us."

Chapter Eighteen

Darius

JULIET RESEMBLED A GODDESS with her dark hair fanned out against the lounge pillows. Her perfect breasts rose and fell with each breath, her pulse a constant thrum in my ears.

She behaved so beautifully—so submissively. Her long, creamy legs were parted just as I requested, revealing every intimate inch of her to our gazes. Hunger radiated from Trevor and Ivan, their stances predatory. One signal from me and they would pounce, but not a second before. I controlled this moment, this room, this woman.

My blood sang as my essence settled inside her, coating her in yet another layer of immortality that deepened our bond. I could have asked her to feed from my wrist, but it seemed too chaste. The possessive man in me demanded a show, a declaration to those in the room that I owned her. That regardless of what would transpire in the coming minutes, Juliet was *mine.*

I removed my jacket and added it to the pile on top of the chair. "This is going to hurt, Juliet." A warning she likely didn't need. The look Ivan flashed me also said it went against protocol. So did my eternal kiss. Fuck if I cared. This was a test run for a reason.

"Yes, Sire." Her pulse sang an entirely different tune from her tone.

I knelt beside her and kissed her temple. "Your fear is intoxicating, darling." I nuzzled her jawline, her neck, and nipped her thundering pulse. *Mmm, divine temptation.* I glanced at my friends. "Ivan, Trevor, care to join me?"

Fuck you, Ivan seemed to say with his brown gaze. "I thought you'd never ask."

Oh, I definitely considered that option, I thought, grinning. "Be my guest. Please."

With an arrogant lift of his brow, he lowered himself to the chaise and settled between Juliet's splayed thighs. Far too close for my liking, but we'd already agreed that he could feed from her femoral artery.

Trevor remained standing, his focus on Juliet's breasts. Her breath hitched as he drew his finger between them. "Jumpy," he murmured.

"Something to work on before Sebastian's visit." Ivan grasped her thighs, his attention shifting to her shaved mound. "Although, her arousal will please him." He dropped a kiss to her hip, then slightly lower, and smiled at her responding shiver. "Oh, yes, it'll please him very much indeed."

I fought the urge to punch my best friend and instead focused on Juliet's breathing, her heartbeat, her dilated pupils. She inhaled sharply as Trevor palmed her breast, then exhaled slowly. He pinched her nipple—hard from the looks of it—and smiled when she didn't outwardly react.

"That's better, gorgeous," he praised while settling beside her. His blue-green eyes met mine, seeking permission to explore more. It was his way of deferring to his elder and superior before playing with the delectable toy.

If I told them to leave, they wouldn't hesitate. Of course, Ivan would give me hell later for it, but my dominance in this room was absolute. Both males were waiting for me to give them permission to continue.

We reviewed the ground rules in depth while discussing this exercise, and I trusted them not to cross the boundaries I set. That's why they were here. I would entrust Juliet with no one else. Not yet. Perhaps not ever.

I circled Juliet's throat with my palm, my thumb resting against her artery, and squeezed. "Look at me."

She complied immediately, her big brown eyes locking on mine with a relieved expression. Had she craved my gaze this entire time? Pride blossomed inside me at the prospect—another crack in her conditioning.

"Sire," she breathed, her cheeks flushing.

I lifted my opposite hand and drew my fingers through her thick hair. The thudding against my thumb slowed, her body surrendering to my will. We were developing trust, an important component to our future plans. I held her gaze for a moment longer before shifting my attention to Ivan and Trevor.

"You may proceed," I said quietly.

Juliet didn't tense or make a sound as both men bent to run their mouths and hands over her exposed skin—Trevor at her breasts, Ivan near her femoral artery.

I held her gaze, my grip on her neck tightening a fraction to keep her in the present. My friends wouldn't be gentle. It was the only way to ensure she understood the future expectations of my counterparts. I couldn't afford for her to react negatively to Sebastian or anyone else.

Her lips parted, her expression clouding with a mixture of pleasure and pain.

I brushed my thumb over her pulse again before glancing down her naked body to my feasting friends. Trevor had her nipple in his mouth, his fangs firmly lodged into her skin. A deep flush crept its way across her chest, leading back to her neck and up into her cheeks. My Juliet enjoyed a little roughness in the bedroom. Whether that was truly her or a result of her upbringing, I would never know.

She gasped as Ivan's incisors pierced her femoral artery, his mouth pulling hard and sharp. A typical vampiric kiss providing no ecstasy for the victim, only for the predator. My kind notoriously thrived on cruelty, luxuriated in the agony of others. Fear was intoxicating to a predator, sometimes more so than a being writhing in the pleasure of climax.

Tears glistened in Juliet's gaze, but her body remained relaxed, her breathing even. Such an impressive pain tolerance.

Her lips trembled. I caught her bottom one with my teeth, hiding her reaction from my friends.

Juliet could not show any weakness in front of my brethren. Kept humans were used to excruciating games, blood play, harsh sex, and domination. To be fazed by a mere bite would raise questions regarding our relationship that we couldn't afford.

Part of this exercise was for me to learn how to help her survive in my world. Mated blood virgins were rare for a reason, and I fully intended to keep mine alive.

I traced her tongue with my own, wiped the tear from her cheek, and tightened my grip around her throat. It wasn't meant as a punishment, but as a reminder of my presence—a way to hold her here with me and provide comfort. Despite the two males feeding from her breast and thigh, I was the one in control of her fate, and hopefully by now, she realized I had no intention of losing her.

She returned my kiss with graceful strokes, her body melting beneath my command.

Very good, sweetheart, I praised with my mouth. Her heart rate accelerated for an entirely different reason now, her blood singing an alluring song that prompted a delicious idea. I smiled against her lips, more pleased with her than words could express, and trailed my mouth along her jaw to her ear.

"Needy little pet." I nipped the tender lobe in mock reprimand. She shivered in response, her throat working beneath my palm. "Mmm, I can taste your arousal, Juliet." It sweetened the air, taunting my carnivorous senses. "Naughty darling," I whispered before tracing my lips down her neck to the breast closest to me.

Trevor had moved to her opposite nipple, his fangs imbedded deep into her skin. Two puncture marks highlighted her rosy peak, both dribbling blood thanks to my friend's clumsy bite. But that was typical, the lack of care for a human.

I sliced my tongue across my own lengthening incisor—just as I had earlier before kissing Juliet—and licked each abrasion to help her heal faster. Her eyes held mine, her pupils two round black points of desire. I smiled and licked her again while my hand left her neck and traveled down to cup her sex.

Mine, I told her with a look that brought a flush to her cheeks. She wasn't thinking about Trevor or Ivan anymore. Only me. I wanted to reward her for it, for letting go, for her perfect submission.

I slid a finger through her slick folds while kissing a path up to her neck. She remained perfectly still beneath my touch, but the heat radiating from her skin confirmed her yearning.

Fuck this test. My age and stature in this society dictated I could do whatever the hell I desired, however the fuck I wanted. And I *needed* her to come.

My incisors struck her deep, pulling her intoxicating essence into my mouth and coating my aching throat with her life. More decadent than any other food, the most delicious of blood, and it was all mine. The art of sharing was an old-world practice, one that solidified relationships and sealed business arrangements. Fine. I could handle that, but it would be under my terms.

Her moan was music to my ears. It fractured the rules, playing her into my hands and my game the way I preferred, and as her back arched, I heard the hiss of frustration from Ivan. I ignored him, my fingers sliding into her waiting heat while my thumb circled her clit. Her inner walls clenched around me, causing my cock to ache with want.

Soon, I promised.

I kept my penetration shallow, not wanting to disturb her innocence—yet—and sucked hard from her neck. Three vampires feeding from her delicate body would steal her consciousness quickly, but damn if I wouldn't provide her with a little ecstasy to inspire her dreams. For that was the only place she was safe from me, this world, and the nightmares surrounding us. It was the least I could do—a thank-you she more than deserved.

Her tension intensified, her groans growing in length. A glance downward showed why—Trevor and Ivan had joined the game. They weren't touching her outside their designated areas. Rather, they'd chosen to fill their bite with euphoria while continuing to drink.

Sweat glistened across her over-sensitized skin, her body shaking with restraint. She caught her lip between her teeth and bit down so hard she drew blood. I released her neck and lifted to lick the droplet away, then nuzzled her flushed cheek.

"You look so beautiful like this," I praised. "Waiting for my command." She knew better than to let go completely without my permission. I hadn't even needed to say it or warn her; she already understood.

So fucking perfect.

Her dark eyes simmered with yearning, her body so tight I knew she would scream if I allowed it. I applied pressure to her clit and she bit her lip again, her expression one of pure agony and bliss tied up in a gorgeous box of desire.

"Come for us, Juliet," I demanded, my dick eager to join her. "And don't hold back."

My name left her lips on a scream I felt all the way to my very soul as she shattered.

So. Fucking. Hot. I doubted I'd ever tire of that rapturous expression on her face or the way she trembled beneath the pleasurable assault.

Waves of electricity radiated through our bond, her body grasping at my immortality to pull much-needed life into her being. Trevor and Ivan had begun drinking in earnest now, yanking from her reserves while she writhed in the throes of a climax that seemed unending in its brutality and ecstasy.

I stroked her through it, my touch varying between gentle and harsh while her eyelids grew heavy from the fierce sensations. Gone was the pinkness of her cheeks as her blood flowed elsewhere into the greedy mouths of the men feeding from her addictive essence.

Blue touched her lips next, even while she trembled beneath the astounding shroud of hedonism. Her pupils flared at the last instant, her brain triggering some fight-or-survival mechanism far too late, and a tear leaked from the corner of her beautiful eyes. I caught it with my tongue and pressed a kiss to her closing lids.

A few lasting sparks ignited between us as the magic of my being swept over her, encasing her in a protective shell.

Her breathing thinned, and her heart slowed.

My forehead fell to hers as a painful ache stirred inside my chest. Foreign in its intensity, unwelcome in its presence.

I hate this. These rules, these practices, this monstrous side to our tendencies. Isn't this act exactly what I wanted to stop?

I sighed. Changing the system took time, something I had on an infinite loop. This would be a long gambit, a harsh one, and there would be unpleasant sacrifices on both sides.

She never had a choice, my conscience chided.

Neither did I, I reminded on a growl.

"Enough," I said out loud, unable to bear the shuddering gasps spilling from her purple lips as she struggled to breathe.

They'd nearly sucked her dry, which was the plan. An unmated mortal would die—no, she would've died already—but my old blood thrived inside Juliet while her agony ripped at my heart.

I could *feel* her fear, her sorrow, her confusion. She thought I meant to kill her and didn't understand why. Then a hint of self-assurance chased that notion, reminding her that I needed her alive.

To see inside her soul, inside her thoughts, was part of our connection. It would increase as I deepened our eternal link, to a point where we would be able to sense everything inside each other. My determination, my craving for revenge, my frustration at the current state of affairs—all of it would become evident. This was why I'd already begun confiding in her. She would know eventually anyway. Telling her up front merely solidified our partnership, helped encourage trust, and would hopefully recruit her desire to help the cause.

"You royally fucked that up," Ivan said, his voice a low snarl. "But you already know that and don't care."

I took in every detail of her immobile form, including the lack of bite marks. My friends had already healed her. Good. I added my blood to the incisions on her neck before kissing her on the cheek. Now she just needed rest. Tomorrow she would be fine.

"Grab that blanket behind you, Trevor." I gestured to the couch with my chin.

He snatched the fleece material, arousal simmering in his gaze. "You're totally fucked."

"Thank you," I said, both for pointing out the obvious and for handing me the item I requested. I wrapped it around Juliet before lifting her in my arms. "Join me for a cigar." It wasn't a request but a demand. I didn't bother looking to see if they followed me through the manor to the seating area outside. I already knew they would.

Several plush chairs were situated around an already glowing fire—my servants knew us too well. They'd even left a package of cigars on the table, prepped and ready. Trevor lifted the bottle of aged bourbon beside it and poured himself a drink before collapsing in his usual spot. Ivan selected a cigar instead and joined him, his brown eyes smoldering from the dancing flames as I settled into a chair with Juliet in my lap. I refused to leave her alone until her skin regained its creamy color.

"She comes beautifully, Darius," Ivan remarked before taking a puff. He blew out his breath slowly, expression thoughtful. "I can see the appeal, but others won't. Especially not the Regent."

I considered his words while stroking Juliet's jaw. The icy quality left an unpleasant sensation against my fingers, leading straight to my chest. "Perhaps not," I agreed. "Perhaps, I don't care."

"Clearly." Trevor knocked back the contents of his drink. "Pretty sure that won't help you win the sovereign's seat."

"Or maybe it will." Ivan scratched his chin. "It's all a show of arrogance and prestige, yes? Darius breaking from decorum will shock them and inspire intrigue. It's one way to ensure his name hits the masses."

"Says the former politician," Trevor muttered.

"I was a political advisor," Ivan corrected, tone irritated. "Far more useful than a shitty surfer."

"Back to that again. One of these decades, you'll get more creative."

"And perhaps you'll grow a brain. We all can dream."

"Enough," I cut in, not needing to witness another of their bickering matches right now. Sometimes I wondered why I chose them as my best friends. "I will figure out our strategy for the Regent's visit. A lot of our brethren seduce their unwilling victims. Perhaps I'll play into that lifestyle notion."

"By telling him you enjoy forcing orgasms from her?" Ivan asked, gaze astute. "That might actually work."

"Or you could tell him the truth." Trevor shrugged. "Not all of us prefer resistant partners."

"No, only the old ones," I replied, sighing at the reminder of why I indulged this friendship with Trevor and Ivan.

The ancient of my kind had given in to their harsher selves ages ago, choosing to embrace the darker parts of our nature and thrive at the top of the food chain. Trevor and Ivan still remembered what it was like to be human. They preferred consensual sex, not that it really existed anymore. One of the many aspects of this world I desired to change.

I traced Juliet's cool lips with my thumb. Testing my resolve was the primary reason for tonight's interaction. Juliet behaved admirably. I did not, at least not according to the rules governing higher society. But I was older than most, a direct descendant of the royal bloodline, and therefore a power in my own right.

"The Regent may hold a position higher than me now, but if I win the sovereign's seat, he'll bow to me." I uttered the words out loud despite them mostly being for myself. "Why should I bend to his will?"

"He has the trust of numerous sovereigns and royals. Winning him over will ensure your election." Ivan—the constant political voice of reason. "And, to be blunt, there is the matter of your ties to Cam."

My blood cooled at the familiar topic. "Severed ties," I corrected flatly. "And I have support from other royals." Including the one who desired me as his new sovereign.

"True. However, your rivals will point out the direct lineage, which means you can't afford to have anyone question your treatment of Juliet. Not if you want them to believe this charade."

"Any other obvious points you'd like to mention, Ivan?" I asked, bored.

We had discussed this part a thousand times. Cam met his *Erosita* by chance and fell in love. By contrast, I bought my future *Erosita* through the proper channels and treated her as everyone expected in social situations. Very different approaches.

"I've done everything to prove I'm willing to play by their rules, including denounce my blood ties," I added bitterly. "Even as Cam's sole progeny, they have no reason to suspect me of being a sympathizer."

"Right, because you resolved the issue by denying his royal throne a century ago," Trevor added, waving his hand theatrically. "I'm with Darius here, mate. Move along, puppet master, so I can enjoy my blood high."

Ivan narrowed his eyes at the blond. "Political mastermind."

Trevor's lips twitched. "Sure."

"I'm working with children," I muttered, my focus shifting to the gorgeous woman in my lap. Juliet's heart beat steadily against my palm, the only indication of the life thriving inside her. I drew a line across her collarbone with my thumb. So delicate and beautiful, and far too fragile for the games ahead.

Fewer than four months to coronation…

Ivan cleared his throat. "You've done everything right so far by purchasing a docile, obedient slave. She behaved admirably at the event over the weekend, at least in terms of their standards. But that brings us to the matter of sharing, specifically with the Regent. I don't think you'll have to, at least not yet."

Hmm, words I wanted to hear. I met his knowing gaze. "Keep talking."

His lips twitched. "She's still a virgin. Use that to your advantage. It shows a restraint very few possess—"

"I certainly would have fucked her by now," Trevor interjected, his electric gaze on the woman in my arms. "Probably killed her by accident too."

Ivan snorted. "Crudely accurate, and honestly, I'd do the same. Regardless, tell the Regent you're savoring her, perhaps offer to pour him a drink yourself, or give him a wrist. She's not afraid to dance naked, so give him a show, but keep his fangs off her. If anything, it'll encourage him to come back for more, thereby giving you cause to develop that relationship."

"A clever plan," I murmured, considering. "It'll also grant me time to feel out his proclivities and human interests." Something I did with everyone in my acquaintance, for the desire for change expanded well beyond Trevor, Ivan, and me. I just happened to be the first pawn to move into place after decades of preparation, and we would need at least another ten to twenty years to move the rest into their respective positions, if not longer.

"Well, at least this wasn't a complete waste of time." Trevor relaxed with a yawn, his eyes fluttering closed. "I don't regret tasting your delicious little fuck toy. At all."

Ivan chuckled. "I don't normally agree with the idiot, but on this matter, I certainly do."

"You're both assholes." I couldn't help the growl in my voice. They both deserved it and worse.

"And you're far too protective of your property," Ivan tossed back. "Should probably work on that, mate."

"'Cause it's only going to get worse," Trevor added softly, his eyes closed in contentment from his recent feed. "Especially after the mating."

I admired the gorgeous woman in my arms. "Yes. I know."

Ivan cocked a brow, his gaze assessing. "The man brings up a good point, Darius. All it takes is a good fucking now."

I feigned a boredom I didn't quite feel, not with the pleasant weight settled across my lap. "Any other comments or questions about our trial run?" I asked, ready to move on from this conversation.

"Yeah." Ivan puffed his cigar and relaxed with a sigh. "Juliet's blood is fucking heaven, mate."

"Mm-hmm." Trevor looked half-lost to sleep, the glass of bourbon loosely held in his hand. "Starting to understand the whole cost thing."

"Right?" Ivan chuckled, his eyes shifting upward to the starry night. "We might have to crash here, D."

"You already have rooms waiting for you." My staff had prepared them knowing they would need a place to sleep during daylight.

Juliet's blood served as both an aphrodisiac and a drug, especially in younger vampires without any tolerance. Trevor and Ivan were only a few centuries old. Their tastes and temperance were still being refined—as was currently evident by Trevor chuckling at whatever he saw dancing behind his closed eyes. Ivan joined him, making them resemble a pair of drunken lunatics who would no longer provide any meaningful discussion tonight.

Fair enough. There wasn't anything left for us to deliberate anyway.

"I'll leave you both to your… personal fascinations." I stood, holding Juliet close to my chest.

"So you can go luxuriate in your own?" Ivan asked without opening his eyes.

"Fuck toy," Trevor added, grinning. "Go get laid."

I didn't bother pointing out that she was still half-dead. "Good night, lightweights."

"Fuck you," Ivan growled. "Ancient one."

Trevor laughed. "So fucking old."

I shook my head. "You're both high as kites."

"And not sorry at all," Trevor replied. "Maybe next time I can play with the fuck doll more. Her tits are fantastic."

"Her pussy is even better." Ivan sounded almost wistful. I walked away as he started detailing all the things he wanted to do to Juliet. If I stayed, he'd probably die.

Because no one would be touching her except for me.

"Mine," I whispered as she snuggled into my chest, her body naturally seeking my warmth. "I'll never share you again, Juliet."

A forbidden promise, one that felt far too right leaving my lips.

Societal obligations. The words ghosted through my thoughts, leaving a trail of doubt across my mind. I pushed it back, refusing to acknowledge the threat.

"Rest well, darling," I told her as I placed her in my bed. "Tomorrow we'll start your physical conditioning, and I won't be going easy on you."

Chapter Nineteen

Juliet

"AGAIN." Darius's voice rumbled through me like a bad dream.

I hated him.

Or rather, my body did.

Yet my aching legs moved on his command, my feet hurtling over the ground outside as I forced myself to complete another lap around the grounds.

Every evening this week had started with a light breakfast and some stretching, followed by this insane series of activities Darius referred to as "conditioning." It went on for hours, until dinner. We only stopped when I needed water or food. Three days of training, and I was already done with it. Especially the running.

Sweat beaded against my skin, my breath labored from the endless trials. I thought the Coventus had been hard on me. Darius was slowly disabusing me of that notion.

"Twenty push-ups," he said as I completed the circle. "Now."

I collapsed to the ground and considered just lying there. What would he do? Bite me? My blood heated at the prospect. He hadn't touched me since Trevor and Ivan's visit. I'd woken alone in Darius's bed with a note that said to get ready and meet him at the dining table. Then I spent the last two sleeps in my own room while he rested elsewhere. Despite spending most of our nights together exercising, I missed him.

"Push-ups, Juliet."

My gaze flicked up to his as a denial tickled my lips, but the threat in his gaze sent me into motion. Vampires loved to punish, and Darius was no different. Although, I usually enjoyed his brand of castigation.

How would he react if I refused? He couldn't force me to run. Well, not entirely true. He could compel me. That might hurt more than operating at my own pace. Still, it could be fun to deny him.

Listen to yourself! a logical part of me chastised. *You've clearly lost your mind if you think challenging a vampire is a good idea.*

Not a vampire, but Darius…

"What are you doing?" he asked, his voice holding a touch of irritation.

"Um..." I started doing push-ups again. "Sorry, Sire."

"Twenty more," he growled.

I narrowed my gaze at the ground and fell back to my knees to stare up at him. "Why? What purpose does this serve?"

His eyebrows shot upward. "Are you questioning my command?"

"No, I'm requesting a purpose." I could hear the obedient version of myself screaming in my head, but I ignored her. "I want to know why we're doing this."

He crouched before me in his jeans, elbows braced on his knees. "You're defying me."

"I'm…" I swallowed from both his nearness and the intensity smoldering in his green irises. "No, Sire. I—"

He grabbed my ponytail—something he insisted I wear—and yanked me to him. "You're. Defying. Me."

I trembled at the lethality lurking in his tone. *Oh, Goddess.* I'd managed to anger him, and on the night of the Regent's pending visit. What had I been thinking? "I-I'm sorry. I-I, it won't—"

His lips touched mine gently, silencing me. "Very good, Juliet. You're learning."

I blinked. "S-sire?"

He kissed me again, his tongue parting my lips as he pushed me back onto the grass, his body stretching out over mine. My short-clad thighs parted automatically to embrace him, even though I didn't understand. Was this my punishment for acting out? Because it felt more like a reward.

"I like you defiant." He tugged my bottom lip into his mouth, sucking lightly, before reclaiming me with his tongue. I moaned as he pressed his erection against me in the place meant only for him. "I like it very much."

His lips trailed fire over my cheeks, my neck, my collarbone. I arched as he bit my nipple through the material of the sports bra, my heart beating rapidly. "D-Darius?"

"Yes, pet?"

"I'm confused," I admitted as I grasped his bare shoulders. "Am I in trouble?"

He chuckled darkly against my breast. "No, darling. You're learning."

I swallowed. "I'm not sure I understand."

His fangs pierced my cleavage so unexpectedly that I yelped. He took a deep pull and groaned. Adrenaline mingled with bliss shot through my veins, all inspired by his bite and the way he felt on top of me.

"Darius," I whispered, running my palms over his bare back. His muscles flexed and moved beneath my touch, stirring desires in the base of my soul.

When had this attraction grown so deep? Just moments ago I'd fantasized about killing him by forcing him to run to death. Now I wanted him to pleasure me with his tongue, his body, his hands.

He took my mouth with a ferocity that left me breathless, my breasts heaving from exertion. Trickles of warm blood flowed across my skin from the bite he'd left unsealed, and a small part of me hoped that meant he intended to return. Instead, his essence spilled down my throat, causing me to cough and sputter, as he forced me to drink from him like he did the other day.

I clung to his shoulders, accepting his immortal gift with heady swallows. It warmed me from the inside, sending tingles of energy to my limbs and fingertips. His possession washed over me, coupled with his need to keep me safe. He wanted me stronger, more athletic—a fighter. The thoughts overwhelmed me while simultaneously explaining his behavior this week.

Darius was training me to be his partner. His blood strengthened me, made me faster, less breakable, harder to kill. But not all of it was tied to his need for me to help him win the sovereign's seat.

A flicker of something else—an emotion he kept buried—spurred his need as well. I reached for it, needing to know more.

The link severed abruptly, causing my eyes to water.

What just happened? How was that even possible?

I had *felt* him inside me, connected in a way I couldn't explain. Like I knew him better than I knew myself. His intentions, his desires, his feelings—they were all clear. And now gone with a snap that ached inside my heart.

"Fuck." Darius moved back onto his knees, his breathing harsher than usual, his gaze simmering. I couldn't tell if he wanted to devour me or hurt me. Maybe both.

"Sire," I whispered, uncertain. Did he want an apology? Had I done something wrong?

He wiped his hand over his face and exhaled slowly. "I think that's enough for now. We should prepare for the Regent's visit."

"O-okay." I swallowed. "Um. Is there anything I need to do?" We had yet to discuss our trial night with Ivan and Trevor, leaving me uncertain as to whether or not my behavior was acceptable. They would have told me if it wasn't, right?

"Just get ready as usual, Juliet. I'll handle the rest." He stood and turned toward the house. "Your dress is on your bed."

I went to my elbows, my mouth opening before I could stop it. "Darius?"

He stopped but didn't turn. "Yes?"

"Am I…" I cleared my throat. "Are you sharing me with him? Like Master Trevor and Master Ivan?" I shivered at the memory, not entirely convinced I wanted to repeat it.

The pleasure had been intense, almost painfully so. I'd floated through a cloud of ecstasy while my life had slipped through my fingers, Darius's eyes the last memory I possessed before everything had gone black. I hadn't known if I would survive, and that fear nearly suffocated me in my last seconds before death overwhelmed me. Then I had awoken in Darius's bed feeling renewed and full of life again.

How many times could someone survive such an experience?

He glanced over his shoulder. "Would you like me to share you with Regent Sebastian?"

I stared at Darius. Was this another test? His way of gauging my submission after acting out earlier?

My training kicked in, my response automatic. "If it is your wish, then yes."

His darkening expression told me that was the wrong answer. "Then it shall be my wish, Juliet." The words sounded cruel on his tongue, as did the way he narrowed his gaze. "Try not to disappoint me again."

Again? "Y-yes, Sire."

He turned on his heel and disappeared into the house, leaving me even more confused.

"When did I disappoint you the first time?" I whispered, my lips trembling. I looked down, spying the blood trickling over my sports bra.

Darius hadn't closed the wound.

Another translucent dress—this one royal blue with a slit up both legs to midthigh. The silver chains on my shoulders held up the fabric while the deep V-line revealed my breasts all the way to my nipple.

Darius's bite stared back at me in the mirror, almost as a taunt to remind me to behave. I still didn't understand what I did to displease him, but I would do everything I could tonight to make it up to him.

Ida knocked on my door as she entered, her motherly grin firmly in place. "Master Darius asked me to bring you some shoes." She held up a pair of silver heels that matched the adornments of my dress.

I pulled my hair over one shoulder and walked over to accept them. "Thank you."

She frowned, her brow pulling down ever so slightly. "Are you all right, dear?"

"Yes." I slipped on the four-inch stilettos. "No. I've done something to upset Master Darius." I covered my mouth, startled by my brazen reply. I knew better than to admit that out loud.

What has gotten into me? I felt undone, a tad out of control, as if I couldn't rely on the rules any longer.

"Oh, Goddess," I mumbled beneath my hand. "I'm sorry, Ida. I…" I had nothing else to say. Here I was about to meet the Regent and speaking out of turn.

I'm going to die tonight. Painfully.

"Darling girl, you have nothing to apologize for." She picked up a comb to fuss with my hair, her eyes far too kind. "If you upset Master Darius, it was probably his own doing. He's a stubborn old vampire, but there's a good man underneath. Surely you've seen that side of him by now?"

"I—yes. Yes, of course I've seen it. But earlier, I did something. He said I disappointed him."

"Ah," she murmured, gently brushing my long, dark strands. "Well, I'm sure he will forgive you, dear. He seems quite fond of you." Her eyes twinkled with the words.

"But he didn't tell me why I disappointed him," I whispered, confiding in her.

"Then ask him," she replied, making it sound so easy to defy a master by demanding explanations.

Except, hadn't I done that during the push-up session? Demanded to know why he wanted twenty more on top of however many I'd already done?

And he had rewarded me with a kiss, saying he enjoyed my defiance. Then when I asked about the sharing, he requested my input, and I yielded the decision back to him.

Darius enjoyed my defiance.

He didn't like me deferring to him on the subject of sharing.

He wanted to know how I felt about it.

I blinked. Why would Darius care? Or perhaps "care" wasn't the right word, insomuch as he wanted me to voice my opinion. To make a decision and ask questions. To be defiant.

"I see," I said, frowning. "I see." Why I felt the need to voice that twice was beyond me. Nor did I truly *see* anything, but I sort of understood. Darius craved my disobedience, not because he wished to punish me, but because he wanted to crack my shell of deference. It took me one step closer to becoming his poison—submissive on the outside, defiant on the inside.

Fine. However, what about my desires? My needs? My aspirations? Did he care nothing of those? What if I didn't want to be the weapon he used to lure his enemies into a trap?

I stopped at the door of my room, my eyes widening. Since when did I ever consider *those* questions? Never once had I possessed a dream for myself. All I ever craved was survival.

Oh, Darius, what have you awakened inside me?

An ache caressed my heart, sending spasms to my lungs and prickling tears behind my eyes. *What is this madness? How do I stop it?*

"Juliet?" Ida prompted behind me.

I cleared my throat and blinked several times to clear my vision. "My apologies. I lost my way for a moment." *Understatement of the century*. I swallowed the remains of my emotions, forcing them back into the confines of my chest, locking them away hopefully for eternity. "Is the Regent here?"

"He and Master Darius are waiting for you in the foyer, yes."

I nodded, expecting as much. "All right. Thank you, Ida."

Time to meet my fate.

Chapter Twenty

Darius

JULIET'S CONFLICTING EMOTIONS flickered through our bond while I listened to Sebastian Cromwell prattle on about the most recent royal scandal.

Confusion and hurt poured through our connection, Juliet's thoughts a rolling wave through my head. I hadn't been fair with her earlier when I allowed my frustration to get the better of me, but her brainwashing was just so damn frustrating.

We finally had a breakthrough when she questioned my authority, demanding a reason for all the physical training. My rewarding response had been automatic—a kiss laced in blood. Except I gave her too much, granting her access to my mind without meaning to, and had abruptly cut Juliet off when I felt her prodding for more.

Her intrusion hadn't upset me. Not really. Just startled me.

It was her subservient response regarding sharing that infuriated me.

I asked her what she wanted and she gave me a practiced response. No trust, no truth, just a colossal step backward in our work together.

Fuck. Even now I wanted to punch a hole through the wall, but instead I grinned at Sebastian and nodded along with his words. Something about Kylan killing his entire human harem out of boredom. Typical behavior for a member of the royal family.

"He requested the next Blood Day be brought forward so he can replenish what he lost, which, of course, the Goddess denied."

"An intelligent move," I replied, my eyes on the stairs. "Breaking from protocol would set a poor precedent. Besides, he can borrow from the others or seek out a whorehouse in the interim." For the right price, they would probably loan him a new harem while he waited for his replacements.

Sebastian's eyes twinkled. "My thoughts exactly. Well, not the borrowing aspect, as the royals are quite possessive of their harems, but same principle."

True. Royals didn't mind occasionally sharing but only only temporarily.

"He's going to decimate the incoming flock," I added, hands tucked into the pockets of my trousers.

Sebastian shrugged. "Most don't survive the trials anyway, but I suspect the Goddess will select extras from this year's crop to join the harem camps."

I nodded. "Likely." This was what my kind had reduced themselves to—discussing humans like sheep.

Blood Day was an atrocious ritual where humans of a certain age graduated into their futures. They competed for their positions, all hoping for the coveted immortal cup where twelve mortals fought for immortality. Only two won—one became vampire, the other lycan—the rest died.

It was a brilliant system, really, pitting humans against humans. Only the fastest, brightest, and most gorgeous, were awarded the top honor of killing each other in the name of a future. The rest were sent to battle in other ways.

Some went to the harem camps, where they vied for a royal's attention with the hopes of prolonging their very short lives. A select few with useful skills went back to human camps to procreate—thus providing the next generation—and perform menial tasks. The list of factions went on, all divided equally between lycan and vampire needs. I personally pitied those who were relegated to the moon harvest.

A shimmer of light appeared at the top of the stairs as Juliet stepped into view, her sapphire gown dazzling beneath the chandelier. Her dark eyes captured mine briefly before she descended, her head bowed in reverence as expected.

"I thought I smelled something sweet," Sebastian said, his gaze taking in every inch of the gorgeous woman descending the stairs.

"She is quite delectable," I murmured.

Juliet's apprehension trickled through our mental link, but her steps remained steady, her body deceptively relaxed. It was almost fascinating to feel the truth emanating behind her flawless facade, providing a glimpse of the woman within. My Juliet—a jewel I intended to unearth, polish, and shine. Unless she continued to bury herself and hide.

I'll dig deeper, darling. So deep that you'll glisten and burn when I'm finished with you. Only then will I make you well and truly mine.

The mental vow stirred something ancient and dark inside me—a possessive instinct as old as time itself.

Juliet folded onto the floor in a graceful bow as soon as she reached the bottom, her body frozen and awaiting my command to rise.

"Allow me to formally introduce my future *Erosita,* Juliet." A note of wonder traveled through my mental chain to Juliet. I'd never explained that term to her, nor had I ever used it in her presence while she was awake.

"I'm impressed by your restraint," Sebastian replied, his hazel eyes lifting to mine. "Some might assume your actions, or lack thereof, boast a certain purpose."

I smiled. "Aspirations are wicked dreams, are they not?"

He returned my amusement. "Indeed they are."

Word games always bored me, but vampires adored them, especially the political ones. It would be so much easier to admit that I was undeniably refraining from fucking my blood virgin to prove I possessed superior age, skill, and the control necessary to lead. Alas, we chose riddles instead.

"May I familiarize myself with your Juliet?" he asked, his pupils dilating with barely restrained hunger. To deny him would be an insult of the highest degree. I needed to impress him, not piss him off, but that didn't stop me from imagining what his face might look like beneath my leather shoe.

"You may." I waved him forward and tucked my hand back into my pocket. In a fist. That I badly wanted to introduce to his jaw.

Off to a great start, D, I imagined Ivan saying.

I didn't kill him was my reply. Because I certainly wanted to with the way Sebastian circled Juliet now, his expression predatory. He crouched before her, drew his fingers through her thick hair before tracing his thumb along her jaw to her chin. "Let me see your face, sweetheart."

Her mental wince told me he'd pinched her, his hand too impatient for his words. She lifted her head, meeting his gaze in a bold way that caused my lips to twitch. No fear in those dark depths, something Sebastian seemed to take as a challenge.

Tendrils of hesitation threatened her mental resolve as the Regent leaned in to nuzzle her cheek and throat, but beneath her fear was a sense of comfort. I followed that train of thought, curious, and found the source of her solace.

Me.

Juliet knew I would protect her. Her absolute faith in me caressed my heart in shocking waves, my mind instantly opening up to hers.

You're safe, I whispered to her.

I know, she replied, her heart rate steady as Sebastian kissed her pulse.

"Remarkable," he marveled, his voice one of utter respect. "The Coventus has either perfected their training or you have found yourself a rare blood virgin, Darius. I've never seen one so calm. So trusting." He stood and held out his hand. "Stand, young one. I must learn more about you."

Juliet glanced at me, her expression inquiring. "Do as he says, Juliet."

"Sire," she replied, bowing slightly as she accepted Sebastian's help up from the ground.

"No, no." Sebastian placed two fingers beneath her chin. "You're too beautiful to hide." He held her there, his eyes on hers, and smiled. "Such fire, Darius. My admiration for you continues to grow by the second."

This riddle was slightly less clear. Did he admire me more for not fucking my blood virgin yet, or was there a hidden meaning to his words? Perhaps something tied to my treatment of her? Maintaining eye contact with a vampire clearly didn't faze Juliet, thanks to our time together. Sebastian wouldn't be blind to that fact, might even wonder at it, but instead he appeared to be praising me for it.

He chuckled, his hand lifting to stroke her hair. "I adore her," he said as one would about a pet. "You're going to help your master in more ways than you realize, sweetheart. Let's chat more over dinner?"

"Of course, Regent Sebastian." Her steady voice matched the confidence in her expression, eliciting a joyful laugh from our guest.

"Utterly delightful," he praised, his hazel eyes sparkling at me. "I'm positively envious."

Age and experience had taught me how to read my competitors, search for traces of a lie, uncertainty, and manipulation. All of Sebastian's cues confirmed his sincerity and enjoyment. Something new—a fascination—had piqued his interest in the best way possible. All in the form of my beautiful Juliet.

"She's very special," I agreed, pleased with her performance. "And probably starving after the workout I gave her earlier."

Sebastian's focus shifted to the bite marks on her cleavage, his lips tilting. "I'm certain she enjoyed it."

I captured her gaze and smirked. "I'm not quite sure she did."

The subtle flattening of her lips confirmed my words and provoked another laugh from the Regent. I was referring to the running—something she knew—but Sebastian mistook it as something else.

Another word game, one my opponent unknowingly lost.

"Shall we?" I gestured toward the main hall that led to the dining area.

"We shall," Sebastian agreed, extending his arm to Juliet. "If you would lead the way, sweetheart."

"Thank you, Regent," she murmured, her steps sure as she escorted our guest. I admired her pert little ass in the translucent sapphire fabric. My cock stirred at the sight, irritated that I'd ignored my needs all week. Alas, she had needed her strength after the way Trevor and Ivan had fed from her a few days ago. And now, she definitely required the energy to handle Sebastian. He would not go easy on her, might even kill her if I didn't monitor him carefully.

We entered the dining area—a room I was beginning to dislike—and Juliet guided Sebastian to the chair Ivan had sat in earlier this week. Rather than sit down, the Regent assisted her into the seat and smiled up at me. "May I join her, Darius?"

Okay, yeah, I really fucking hated this room now. "Please, be our guest," I said waving at the space meant for Juliet.

Sebastian flashed a pair of dimples that gave him a young appeal as he settled beside my blood virgin. She didn't move as he draped a napkin over her lap, then one over his own, and eyed me as I took over the space across from them.

Raquel, one of Gladice's cooking aides, entered with a tray of salads, her head bowed in reverence. Decorum. Something I rarely expected in my home, but had to be engaged because of our guest. Another aspect of society I would love to change, but I was getting ahead of myself.

Sebastian placed his palm on Juliet's thigh. "Tell me about your education, darling girl. What are your strongest attributes?"

She flicked her gaze at me, again seeking my guidance, and I gave her a subtle nod. Her pink tongue swept over her lower lip, her shoulders squaring as she looked directly at our guest and recited her portfolio. It reminded me of the auction when the Coventus's auctioneer listed all her traits and aptitudes. High marks in linguistics, history, logic puzzles, memory games, and government affairs. All the makings of a perfect blood virgin.

"What about the arts?" Sebastian asked in fluent German—one of the languages Juliet spoke fluently.

She replied with a flawless accent, studiously recalling her scores in dance, music, and choir. Sebastian ate his salad while she spoke, his other hand still firmly affixed to her thigh. I busied myself with my own food to refrain from the desire to break his arm.

"And sexual prospects?" he prompted, his eyes darkening with curiosity.

Juliet swallowed, the only indication of her discomfort. All those years of brainwashing kept her calm and collected as she detailed every aspect of her sexual education from throat training to observation courses to female-on-female instruction. I knew all of this, but to hear it outlined so openly, to realize why she sucked cock so incredibly well, enraged my sensibilities.

And yet, compared with so many others, Juliet's experience was considered easy. No vampire could touch her in the Coventus, not as a blood virgin. She had to witness unthinkable actions around her, but never *to* her. Only the mortal matrons could touch their charges.

"Fascinating," Sebastian said, his gaze appraising. "You'll forgive me for my questions, but you're quite rare, Juliet. While blood virgins are trained for such affairs as this, very few actually graduate to this level."

Because most of them were fucked to death, sent to breeding farms, or returned to the Coventus to train the next generation. I set down my fork, finished with my wilting salad. "Eat, Juliet," I said, asserting my authority in the room.

"Yes, Sire." She immediately complied.

Sebastian smiled. "Beautifully obedient." He finally removed his palm from Juliet's thigh and relaxed into his chair, his salad long gone. "She's perfect for your platform, Darius. The royals will love her."

"Platform?" I repeated, arching a brow.

"Enough with the posturing." He waved an errant hand. "We both know you want the sovereign's seat. No point denying it."

"And here I thought we might play a few more word games," I said, amused and slightly relieved. I expected at least another hour of posturing and pontificating before we reached this point. Thankfully, it seemed my guest was done with the formalities and ready to progress to business. "Your frank summarization means you have an opinion. What is it?"

"I want you to run." No hesitation, no hint of a lie, not even a smile.

I lifted my glass of wine—a dark red laced with blood—and swirled the contents. "Why?"

The Regent smiled. "Because you're Cam's only blood heir."

A surge of shock traveled down the connection, the only indication Juliet recognized the name. Her gaze remained on her plate, her mouth slowly chewing, although she clearly understood the implication of Sebastian's statement.

"You wish for me to assume a position because of my blood ties," I mused and took a sip of the fortifying liquid.

"You're essentially royalty, Darius, and by far the most powerful of our kind in this region. There are a few who will challenge you on the basis of your century of disappearance—"

"And Cam's treason," I interjected, the bitter note in my voice coming easily after decades of practice. "Can't forget that major detail."

Raquel returned, switching our salads for the main course of roasted chicken, mashed potatoes, and a melody of vegetables. Juliet picked at those first, her old habits of eating healthily overriding her taste buds.

Sebastian murmured a few words of appreciation about the meal and suggested we eat before continuing our discussion. I maintained an air of nonchalance, as if I didn't have a care in the world, and indulged in the rich food while memories whirred through my thoughts.

Cam. My maker. A royal and the rightful heir to the Goddess's throne.

"I'm sorry to lay this burden on you, Darius, but it's the only way. You must continue what I started, or all of this will be for naught. My death will mean nothing. My sacrifice will be in vain. Do you understand? You're humanity's protector now. You're the future's only hope."

His strong hands had gripped my shoulders so hard they nearly broke. Then he hugged me for the last time and disappeared into the night.

The next time I saw him, he existed inside of an urn.

I denounced him that day. Poured gasoline over his ashes, lit a match, and watched him disappear with dry eyes. The hardest fucking charade of my very long life.

"That was delightful," Sebastian said, patting his stomach.

Juliet was only halfway through her plate and slowing down. I let her off the hook for tonight but decided a bigger breakfast would be in order tomorrow.

I finished my last bite and set down my fork, dreading what I had to offer next.

"They're calling it a harmonious future, saying it's the only way for lycan and vampire to

live in peace—by enslaving humankind. But it's a classist system meant to benefit the royals and alpha packs. It's a game of power and blood and death. We are the superior race; of that I harbor no doubts. But that doesn't mean we must be cruel and torture our food."

Cam's vehement words scoured my soul, leaving a bitter taste in my mouth.

"Play the game, my son. Move all the pieces into place and strike from within. You know the chessboard better than anyone, including me. Use it. Embrace it. Own it."

I fought the urge to clench my fists. Cam gave up everything for this future. Decades of planning since and it was finally time to make my move. I couldn't afford to falter, not even for her. My darling Juliet.

I sipped my wine, collecting my thoughts and easing my insides. Then smiled indulgently. "Can I interest you in any dessert, Sebastian?"

Desire lit the Regent's features as he shifted his focus to Juliet. She pushed aside her plate, her throat working to swallow her last bite.

"Yes," he replied. "You most certainly can."

Chapter Twenty-One

Juliet

THE CHICKEN TURNED OVER IN MY STOMACH. I knew this was the plan, yet a deep pain echoed in my heart upon hearing Darius's words.

Can I interest you in any dessert, Sebastian?

My instincts rioted, hating the idea of letting yet another man bite me.

And yet, that's always been your purpose, my logical side reminded. *Why would that ever change?*

Because Darius asked me if I wanted to be shared.

And you never told him no.

I wanted to growl in frustration at that pliant voice, the one always spouting reason and reminding me to obey. Why now, of all times, I didn't know. Maybe it was exhaustion. Or perhaps I'd hit a limit of some kind. An impenetrable wall lined with foreign words detailing a past where humans had rights, where vampires didn't use my kind solely for food and sexual gratification.

Impossible.

Go away.

You're going to die. Do as you're told.

I'll die anyway.

A finger trailed down my neck to the chains of my dress, fondling the metal. "Do you have a preference, sweet girl?" Sebastian asked, his voice indulgent.

I'd like to drive a stake through your dead heart.

The foreign thought popped through my head so suddenly that I nearly gasped. To think about killing a vampire was tantamount to treason.

What is wrong with me?

Ice cubes danced along my spine.

Pull it together. Obey. Or die.

Would that be so bad?

Yes!

The sound of a chair scraping over the floor followed by Darius's familiar footsteps had me glancing up at him. His scowl told me that was the absolute wrong thing to do. He grabbed me by my hair, yanked my head back, and captured my gaze.

"Is something wrong, darling?" he asked, a growl in his voice. "Did you not hear the Regent?"

Had I missed something? "I…" I swallowed the oversized rock clawing at my throat. Or I tried to, anyway. "N-no, Sire."

His brow furrowed, his grip loosening slightly. "Are you feeling all right?"

Say no, Darius whispered through our connection, his voice clear in my mind. *Tell me you're unwell. Do it now.*

The command in his tone made me flinch. "I'm not feeling well, Sire. My apologies."

He tilted my head to the side, ran his finger over my pulse. "Hmm. Did I work you too hard earlier, darling? I noticed you barely touched your food."

I'd only eaten about half of it because of the rich quality. It upset my stomach to eat too much. "I'm sorry, Sire."

He shook his head in reproach, his irritation evident. "She's still new to this, doesn't realize that she needs to tell me when I've drained her too thoroughly." He tugged on my hair, making me flinch, and cast an apologetic look at Sebastian. "Clearly, I have some work to do with her."

I couldn't see the Regent, but I heard the smile in his voice as he replied, "Discipline is important."

"Indeed. I have half a mind to let you drain her dry right now for her impudence, but then I wouldn't be able to apply my own brand of punishment later." He sighed, long and hard. "What would you do, Sebastian?"

"Spank her ass raw, fuck her, and then drain her." The words sent a tremor through me. I'd seen that particular brand of discipline administered on my own matron more than once. It usually took her days to recover.

Darius chuckled. "A delightful idea, but it would take up much of our remaining time together before dawn. And we still have a discussion to finish." His thumb brushed my pulse while he spoke, applying a subtle pressure that felt more like a brand. Ownership. Possession. A way of marking me as his in the most basic of ways.

"Too true," Sebastian said, standing beside us. "I suspect there will be more dinners in our future. Perhaps I will indulge in your offer of dessert then."

"She'll be more experienced," Darius responded. "In all ways." The implication churned my stomach. He was offering more than my blood.

Experienced. In all ways.

He meant sexually.

As in, he would share my body in the future to make up for this transgression.

My mouth went dry, my heart hammering against my ribs. Darius intended to share me beyond drinking.

I no longer needed to fake feeling ill because now I truly did.

A foreign touch drifted up and down my arm, shooting ice through my veins. "I've always enjoyed a good game of delayed gratification," Sebastian murmured. "Gives me more to look forward to on my next visit."

"I promise she'll be better behaved as well," Darius replied, his grip tightening on my hair. It pulled so harshly my eyes started to water. Or maybe that was the deep sense of betrayal simmering beneath my skin.

I trusted you.

Because you're a stupid, naive little girl. Trusting a vampire. What were you thinking?

Another tug forced me to my feet.

"Go to my room, Juliet." His growl pierced the haze of my mind, settling across my shoulders. "Wait for me. Naked."

"Y-yes, Sire." It came out raspy, twined with fear.

He truly meant to punish me this time. I could feel it in the angry lines of his body, the way he shoved me away from him as if I were nothing but a piece of meat, and the dismissive way he turned his back on me.

Try not to disappoint me again.

I had failed miserably, yet I didn't understand what I'd done wrong. My heels clacked over the marble, dragging me toward his room with heavy steps of dread. At least he would be with the Regent for a while longer discussing their future plans. Politics. Cam.

The name sliced through the fog of my shame and terror, sending a jolt of confusion through my thoughts.

Everyone knew Cam—the treacherous royal who tried to assassinate the Goddess. *He* was Darius's maker? Regent Sebastian had referred to Darius as Cam's only heir, another term for progeny. That essentially made Darius royalty—the next in line.

Why does he live here? I took in the ornate fixtures on the walls, the oil paintings, fancy chandeliers, handwoven rugs. They screamed wealth and privilege, as did everything else about Darius. His age, his control, his prestige.

I reached the door to his room and blew out a breath.

What awaited me in here? What would he do? Nothing good, not with the way he vibrated fury downstairs. I'd never felt him so furious. He always maintained an air of calm, his countenance patient to the extreme. Well, I'd apparently crossed a line. I just didn't understand how. I did everything he asked. I ran. I learned how to play with knives—not well, but I tried. He'd forced me to fire a gun just yesterday. I never complained, not once, even when

I felt like running those laps would kill me.

Well, I did question him today. But he kissed me afterward. That meant I did well, right?

"I don't understand," I mumbled to the door. "None of this makes any bloody sense!" I slammed my fist against the wood and jumped at my own outburst. The sound bounced off the walls, no doubt reaching the vampires downstairs.

Oh no.

Oh no, no no.

I slid into the room, needing to hide. Maybe they would assume it was someone else, a servant accidentally dropping something. I flicked the chains of my dress from my shoulders, allowing the garment to pool on the ground and slipped beneath the comfort of Darius's sheets.

Protection, my soul sighed.

A lie, my mind replied. *You're not safe anywhere.*

I winced and cocooned myself even deeper within the blankets. My shiver had nothing to do with the temperature and everything to do with the immediate future.

My eyes refused to close even as my body relaxed into the comfort of the plush mattress. Darius could enter at any minute, enraged, and demanding penance.

For what?

My sins. My wrongdoings. My disrespect.

I shuddered, my vision blurring.

"I hate this," I whispered.

For over two decades, I simply accepted my fate, bowed to the will of the vampires around me, did as I was told to survive. And for what? To live in constant fear? To be bitten and drained to within an inch of my life over and over again? To be forced to sexually please whomever my master demanded?

That wasn't living.

It was walking death.

I had it wrong this whole time. The rules, the decorum, the constant obeying. I followed them all to placate the superior beings and to keep them from killing me. What I should have been doing was rebelling to encourage them into ending my misery.

"I'm such a fool," I marveled. It was death I needed to court, not life. To put an end to it all.

Yes, a dark part of me whispered. *Tonight…*

I nodded, feeling suddenly relieved.

No more pain, confusion, or turmoil.

No more pleasing a master I couldn't understand.

No more false promises of a changed future and poison nonsense.

No more anything.

My body relaxed, my eyes falling closed.

The future was blissful.
Quiet.
Death.

Chapter Twenty-Two

Darius

I CLOSED THE DOOR after watching Sebastian depart.

"Thank. Fuck." I ran a hand over my face, blowing out a breath.

Our conversation had gone well, his support clear and true as he endorsed me for the position of sovereign. Another chess piece moved into place, shifting me into the perfect position for ascension.

I smoothed my hand down my tie and pulled out my phone. Ivan answered on the first ring.

"Good. You lived through the meeting."

I snorted. "You forget that Sebastian is half my age and of nonroyal blood." To kill him would have been as easy as flicking my wrist, and I had considered it more than once tonight.

"Ah, but he's the Regent. He carries the power of the law." His mocking tone made my lips twitch.

"Yes, which only means the paperwork and consequences would be mildly irritating. And, admittedly, keeping him alive also serves a more useful purpose."

A beat of silence as Ivan read between the lines. "He's agreed to back your candidacy."

"Better," I replied. "He's agreed to nominate me formally at the Parliament Gala in a few weeks."

"Well, shit. That went better than expected. What did you do, let him fuck

Juliet?"

My amusement died on a growl. "No." I hadn't even been able to let him feed on her, let alone touch her. Fortunately, she seemed to have received my message to feign illness and did so spectacularly. I would be rewarding her once I joined her upstairs.

He chuckled. "I'm sure her blood was enough, then."

I didn't bother correcting him and started toward my room, eager to reconnect with Juliet. Focusing on Sebastian had required cutting off her thoughts, and, oddly, I rather missed having her in my head.

"I need you and Trevor to make the appropriate preparations for the gala," I said as I reached the top of the stairs. "Also, message our royal friend with an update. He'll approve of this outcome."

"Considering it removes him completely from the scheme, I agree. As for the gala, options A and B, correct?"

"Yes." Option A, my opponent balked and withdrew his interest in becoming the new sovereign. Option B, a lethal accident lurked in his future. I preferred the latter. Gaston was a sadistic ass who preferred his blood young, as in under the age of ten.

"On it. Anything else?"

"Not yet."

"Sweet. Go play with your fuck toy to celebrate."

I stood just outside my bedroom and couldn't fight the smile his words evoked. "I intend to."

"Not jealous at all," he replied and hung up.

My lips twitched again. Ivan would be extremely jealous if he knew what I had planned for my sweet Juliet.

I twisted the handle and slipped inside the dimly lit room. *So quiet.* I closed the door softly, my footsteps silent against the carpeted floor.

Juliet's small form was curled into a ball in the center of my bed, her hair spilling seductively over my silk pillows. She didn't stir as I approached, her slender shoulders rising and falling in soft, peaceful breaths.

Gorgeous, I thought, loosening my tie. I should request she sleep here every night. Naked. Wrapped up in my sheets.

Warmth touched my chest. The only reason she slept elsewhere this week was to protect her from my harsher needs. She required rest. I required sex. The two did not mix, but I couldn't go without her any longer.

I slipped the knot from my neck and let the ends hang on either side. Juliet still had no idea I stood behind her, lost to her dreams.

I shrugged out of my jacket, laid it over the chair beside the bed, and unfastened my cuff links. They dropped to the nightstand with a clink that resonated through the room. My darling blood virgin, however, remained soft and unbothered, like an unknowing mouse resting in the middle of a viper's den. She didn't seem to hear me slip out of my shoes or unfasten my belt, her body peacefully still in slumber.

Hmm, how should I wake her? With a kiss? Lightly tracing her spine? I considered my options while moving around the foot of the bed, needing to see her face. My fingers busied themselves with unbuttoning my still-tucked-in shirt. Juliet would remove my pants for me. Preferably with her teeth.

Except as I reached her again, I frowned. Dark circles rimmed her eyes, her skin pink with exhaustion.

No, not exhaustion. Devastation.

I brushed my thumb across the damp stains on her cheeks. Her lashes fluttered open, two pinpoints of pain staring at me with abject fear lacing their depths. She jolted back, pulling the covers as she went, her body curling into the fetal position.

"Juliet," I murmured. "It's just me. Sebastian's gone."

Her pulse spiked, calling to my predatory instincts. *Terror.*

She smelled delicious, but I preferred my lovers aroused, not petrified. I left my shirt partially unbuttoned and sat on the bed beside her, my hand catching her shoulder as she tried to roll away.

My brow furrowed. "What's wrong, Juliet? Are you hurt?"

Her breath shuddered out of her on a harsh sound that suspiciously resembled a laugh. "No. Yes." The hoarse quality of her voice coupled with the wet stains of her abandoned pillow confirmed she'd been crying.

I lay down next to her on top of the comforter. "Look at me, Juliet."

"Why?" she mumbled sullenly.

"Because I told you to."

She tugged her lip between her teeth and tightly closed her eyes. A tremble worked its way through her limbs, beneath my palm, until she gasped for breath and finally met my gaze. The fire in her pupils shrouded in agony was an intoxicating combination.

"I hate you," she whispered. "I hate you more than breathing."

"That's quite a statement," I replied, surprised and a little turned on by her furious outburst. "May I ask why?"

"Why?" she repeated. "Why?" Louder now. "I have no choice. No freedom. No reason to live other than to survive, which means little when my life—however short it may be—is spent slaving away for you and your kind. Being used to the point of death, revived, and used again! And it goes beyond just sharing my blood. You intend to require sex. My body isn't even my own. My mind sure as hell isn't my own. Nothing, Darius. Nothing belongs to me!"

She let out a cry and flung my hand from her as she rolled to her back, the heel of her palms digging into her eye sockets.

"Death would be easier. Kinder. If you possess any humanity inside you, you'll kill me. But I know you won't. I'm too expensive of an investment, and even now, I feel compelled to beg for your forgiveness for an outburst even an animal would proclaim in my position. And I'll accept my punishment because that's what a good blood virgin does."

Her hands curled into fists above her head, lifting and crashing downward.

I caught her wrists before she could harm herself, my knees going on either side of her hips in the process. She growled beneath me, bucking like a wildcat, her gaze crazed with fury and fear.

"Juliet," I soothed, my voice calm as I restrained her as gently as I could.

"I hate you!" she yelled. "I want to die!"

Fuck.

She'd finally shattered. All the mind control indoctrinated into her through years of harsh conditioning had finally subsided to the reality of our situation.

"Kill me," she begged, her words slicing my heart. "I want to die. Please kill me." Fresh tears spilled from her eyes, the fight leaving her body on a whoosh of air that sounded so painful I felt it deep inside.

This was the moment I had most desired and dreaded. The moment where she broke so completely, so utterly, that emotionally she had nowhere to go but up.

I shifted off of her prone form, my back going to the headboard as I pulled her quivering body onto my lap. "Juliet," I murmured, my arms holding her close. "You're safe with me."

Another of those harsh laughs left her, fractured by a sob. "Safe," she mumbled. "You plan to share me with Sebastian, let him spank me and fuck me raw."

Her use of his earlier words simmered in my blood, but I swallowed back the fury. "Never, Juliet. He'll never touch you."

She shook her head sadly. "He will."

"No, Juliet. He will not." I pinched her chin, forcing her gaze upward. "You are mine, and I will not share you with him."

"You already said you would." It came out soft and defeated, and suddenly, I understood what had pushed her over the edge. I'd destroyed her faith in me with a few carefully worded phrases. It went beyond that, of course, her background having paved the way to this unavoidable end, but my statements tonight cracked what remained of her glass walls.

"Oh, darling." I sighed and kissed the top of her head. "I only *implied* a future experience to satisfy him tonight."

"Experienced. In all ways." She uttered the words on a shaky exhale and trembled violently, her disgust and revulsion written clearly across her rounded shoulders. It seemed my earlier proclamations had struck a nerve. Considering them from her point of view, I could see why.

"It's true that you will be more experienced—in every way—the next time we have him over for a meal." I lifted her chin again, catching her focus. "Because I don't plan to entertain him again until after I'm crowned sovereign." I let those words sink in, but only torment stared back at me. Her emotional haze was clouding her logic. She needed more information to understand. Specific words. Comfort. Trust.

"Juliet." I traced my thumb over her quivering bottom lip. "It is considered quite unbecoming for one in a lower position—such as a regent—to request anything of a sovereign. Especially, favors involving something as precious as an *Erosita*."

She blinked those big brown eyes up at me. "*Erosita?*"

I smiled. "Yes. The formal term for a human bonded in the ceremonies. It's a title of sorts that carries great respect among my kind." And a hell of a lot of envy. "You will be my *Erosita* once we complete the ritual."

"More blood," she mumbled.

"Yes, and the communion of our souls." *Mind, body, and soul.* We would share everything then—our blood, our passion, our thoughts. I nuzzled her hair, my chest tight.

"I'm sorry for earlier, darling." The apology escaped me without preamble. I wasn't even sure what I meant to ask forgiveness for, but the words felt right. They felt needed. None of this was fair to her. All her irate comments, her accusations and statements, were founded in truth. She never asked for any of this; none of her kind did.

"I want to understand," she whispered. "I *need* to understand."

My gaze fell to hers, the yearning swimming in her chocolate depths a palpable thing. "You need to see," I replied, agreeing. That had always been part of the plan, but not until she could truly appreciate what I had to show her. "You're right, Juliet. It's finally time." Tomorrow I would make the arrangements. Now that she had broken free from the shackles of her brainwashing, I could move to the next phase of her training.

A firm introduction to reality. Not the one painted in her books, texts, and presentations given by the Coventus. But the real world and what had become of it outside the confines of wealthy vampire society.

I kissed her hair, holding her tight.

This was just the beginning of her reeducation. Poor darling. If she thought tonight's truth hurt, she had a lot more pain coming.

Chapter Twenty-Three

JULIET

WE'RE FLYING.

On a jet.

In the starry night.

Never in my wildest dreams had I imagined such an experience.

The nearly full moon painted the dark sky in shades of alluring colors. I took in every detail, memorizing the scene in case I never saw it again.

"Midnight," Darius said, his phone at his ear. He sat beside me in a pair of black trousers and a cream-colored pullover that offset his darker features. I wore jeans, a deep-red sweater, and boots. It was by far the most suffocating outfit of my existence. No part of me was on display except for the hint of my breasts at the V-neck collar.

"Main courses for six," he continued, pausing to listen. "No, room for one. The others will handle their own accommodations." He reached out to grab my hand, pulling it into his lap to rest against his thigh. "Yes, that would be acceptable."

My attention drifted to the stars again. Darius had dimmed all the lights, granting us an undisturbed view of the exquisite scenery.

Amazing…

"That is correct. Thank you." Darius ended the call and relaxed beside me, his thumb lightly brushing my hand. "We should be landing in about an hour."

I nodded mindlessly, unable to truly focus with the giant, distracting orb outside my window. The stars beyond it twinkled in the midnight sky, soothing my soul.

"I can feel your fascination burning through our connection, Juliet," he murmured. "It's such an unusual sensation. Very little intrigues me these days." He lifted my hand to his lips and nibbled my wrist, causing my belly to flutter.

"Where are you taking me?" I asked, my lips moving before I realized what I intended to say. My heart faltered for a beat at the bold inquiry, but my mouth refused to retract it or apologize.

I wanted to know.

No, I *deserved* to know.

"Chicago," Darius replied.

I blinked, surprised at his easy acquiescence. *Of course he replied. Why wouldn't he?* I shook my head.

If last night taught me anything, it was that I didn't understand Darius at all. I expected a beating—or worse—for my behavior, and instead he spoke to me in calming tones while holding me all night.

He promised never to share me. He didn't yell at me when I ranted incoherently. He let me cry. He even kissed away my tears.

And now he answered my question without hesitation.

"Chicago," I repeated. The name struck a familiar chord, but not from my studies at the Coventus. "That was a popular city in the former United States, right?" It came up numerous times in his history books. "Does it still exist?"

"Everything still exists. The question you mean to ask is, what has the city become?" He lowered our joined hands to his thigh and sighed. "You know it as Lilith City."

My gaze finally left the window, my heart in my stomach.

Lilith City? That was the heart of the vampire world. The Goddess herself lived inside those notorious walls, maintaining law and order among her kind. Blood virgins only visited for political functions or to undergo a trial and execution.

Did Darius intend to hand me over to the vampire court for punishment? To have me put to death for insubordination? To make a public example of me?

Goddess, I deserved it. Especially after last night. I'd broken every rule, allowed emotion to control my behavior, acted poorly in front of the Regent, and considered death a better alternative to fate. The list of my transgressions was endless.

Am I going to die?

Would that be so bad?

Darius leaned into my space, pressing his lips to mine. My thoughts melted into a warm puddle as his tongue slipped inside my mouth, binding me to the present.

Safe, my soul whispered. An instinctual trust that surpassed logic. He could be flying me to my death, or worse, and I couldn't stop myself from returning his kiss.

"Relax, Juliet," he said softly. "I have no desire to punish you. Not for doing exactly what I wanted." He kissed me again, this one slower, more intimate. His hand still held mine, his thumb drawing languid circles against my wrist.

"Darius," I whispered, finding my nerve.

"Yes, darling?"

"Tell me why we're going to Lilith City." It came out bolder than I expected, the request sounding more like a demand.

He smiled against my mouth. "Hmm, I knew you were the right one." His alluring eyes brimmed with approval as he held my gaze. "What did the Coventus teach you about Lilith City?"

"It's the revered home of the Goddess and the vampire governance board." The words sounded textbook to my ears, but accurate.

"Revered home of the Goddess," he repeated with a snort. "Let me guess; you were forced to pray to her, right?"

I nodded. "She is the supreme being."

"More like a supreme bitch." He shook his head. "I've known Lilith for over two thousand years. Goddess, she most definitely is not. Just a very old royal vampire with a penchant for power."

My mouth hung open in utter shock at his easy candor. He had just insulted the highest-ranking official in our world—the Goddess herself—while maintaining a sardonic tone.

"You could be killed for such a statement," I whispered, dismayed.

They're always listening, my matron had warned. *Never take* Her *name in vain.*

Darius chuckled. "Sheep scare so easily." He squeezed my hand. "Don't fret, darling. Lilith may desire to kill me, but it won't be for belittling her precious title. None of my brethren consider her a supreme being, merely a royal queen. Humans are the ones taught to worship her, mostly because she finds it amusing."

I frowned. That couldn't be right.

Except, well, maybe it was… Why would he lie?

The Coventus had held rituals where blood virgins read passages from ancient Latin texts thanking the Goddess for gifting us all life. All the ceremonies were led by the matrons, not the vampires. They merely lurked along the sidelines, serving as guards to keep us all in line.

"The vampires never kneeled or paid homage to her during the rituals," I said, realizing the truth as I spoke the words. "Your kind doesn't worship her."

"No. However, there are many who respect her leadership." The way he said it suggested he was not among those who did.

"Whom do vampires revere?" I wondered out loud, curious now.

"Ourselves, mostly." He drew his thumb over my knuckles, his voice thoughtful. "The Coventus preaches propaganda to keep humans in line. Having a higher power to pray to gives you all a false sense of hope that is easily manipulated. It's actually quite brilliant in terms of a control mechanism, and also terribly sad."

Control mechanism—an accurate summation of my life. I never had a choice, not once, and until Darius came into my life, I never desired one.

"We are the predators; humans are the prey," he continued softly. "And my kind has always enjoyed playing with our food." His gaze dropped to my neck while he spoke, warming my blood.

Yes, please, my body whispered. *Bite me.*

"And you?" I asked breathily. "Do you enjoy playing with your food too?" *Do you enjoy playing with me?*

His lips curled. "Stand," he said, releasing my hand.

My breathing slowed, his demand heating me from the inside out. *Dare I refuse him?* More importantly, did I even want to?

The answer came as I rose, my legs sure. Even after my convictions last night, I still desired to please him. Not the vampire. Not society. But Darius himself.

Because I enjoy *satisfying him.*

"Straddle me, Juliet."

I slid onto his lap, my thighs parting intimately over his as my hands fell to his flat abdomen. "You still haven't told me why we're going to Lilith City."

"I know." He wrapped his palm around my nape, his other hand going to my hip. "It's a quick stop on the way to our true destination, one that allows me to reveal the truth of our world to you." His thumb stroked my pulse. "I want to show you what the Coventus has hidden."

"Why?"

"You'll see when we get there." His nose stroked my cheek as he slowly inhaled, his touch a featherlight caress. "You smell amazing," he murmured, his grip tightening around my nape. "My own version of heaven."

His lips skimmed my jaw, causing goose bumps to prickle my arms. I loved the feeling of his mouth on me, the way it whispered over my skin, leaving a smattering of heat in its wake.

"You asked if I enjoy playing with my food," he said softly against my ear. "Was that an invitation, darling?" He nuzzled my neck, his teeth skating over my sensitive skin. "Because it certainly sounded like one."

My throat went dry, my eyes falling closed.

Please…

Darius's fangs taunted the vulnerable place below my ear, sending a tremble down my spine. Not of fear, but of temptation. I craved his vampiric kiss, his possession, the feel of him absorbing my essence and *owning* every intimate piece of me.

Think, Juliet.

There was something I wanted to know.

Several somethings, actually.

But, *ohhh*, maybe they weren't that important. Not with Darius's mouth against my pulse, lightly nibbling.

"Answer me, Juliet," he demanded in a deceptively soothing tone. "Tell me if that's what you meant."

Was it? I couldn't remember. Not with the way his hand felt splayed against my hip, the other holding my nape, and the hint of his incisors teasing my sensitive skin.

"Bite me," I begged, my voice husky with yearning. "Please."

He chuckled. "Do you desire pleasure, sweetheart? Is that it?" He pulled me closer, up his thighs, placing my center against his unmistakable arousal. I arched into him on a moan, thirsting for more.

Who am I?

Who cares.

I pulled at my sweater, needing to remove it. So hot and restricting, and—

Darius grabbed the hem, holding it against my stomach. "Clothing remains on," he said, his voice low and commanding.

I groaned and met his heated gaze. "Why?"

"Because we're landing soon." He nipped my lip hard enough to draw blood. It hurt rather than pleased—a punishment for being too eager? "Because you're tempting enough as it is, and my control isn't infallible." His tongue lightly traced the wound, sending a shot of ecstasy to my core and chasing away the residual pain of seconds ago. "Because I intend to devour you properly later, once our work is done."

"Properly?" I repeated, my mind foggy from the delirious sensation of his mouth teasing mine. "Do you intend to finally deflower me?" A thrill went through me at the prospect, followed by a shadow of concern.

Would it hurt?

Would he still want me afterward?

Would I survive?

The last thought gave me pause, my pupils fully focusing on Darius's handsome face. His smoldering gaze ignited a flurry of butterflies in my lower belly. Oh, it would hurt—no question—but Darius never gave me pain without pleasure.

"Claiming your body is the final phase of the ceremony, Juliet." His hand slid beneath my sweater, his touch soft against my bare skin. "It will make you mine. Indefinitely."

"Isn't that the point?" I asked, breathless. "Or are you waiting until I've proven myself in some way?"

His thumb glided up my side, tracing my ribs. "You have nothing left to prove to me. I know you're perfect for my needs."

"Oh." I licked my lips, considering. "Then… tonight?"

Amusement touched his gaze. "So eager for me to fuck you, darling?"

"I… I just don't understand why you haven't yet." I cleared my throat. "My matron prepared me for the night of my purchase, but—"

"I hardly touched you," he finished, his palm slipping up to caress my breast. "No bra. Does this mean you are without panties as well?"

I pressed into his touch, desiring more. "You told me the 'no undergarment' rule still applied."

His lips twitched. "Indeed I did." He thumbed my nipple, exciting a tingling sensation between my thighs. "Not fucking you has been a challenge, but it serves two purposes. First, showing restraint is considered a strength among my kind, an important consideration when vying for a position of sovereign. Second, the ceremony only works when blood is exchanged at least three times prior to the claiming."

I frowned. "So if you had deflowered me before I drank from you…?"

"We could never be connected."

"And if someone else had deflowered me?"

"We could never be connected," he repeated. "Even now, if another vampire were to take you, it would destroy the process."

"Because I would be bound to a new master?"

"No, you would merely be ruined." He pinched my stiff peak, then massaged the hurt with his clever fingers. I fought back a moan while trying to process everything he just said, but it was difficult with his hand branding my tender skin.

"So." I cleared my throat, my attention shifting between arousal and information. "Um, does the ceremony only apply to blood virgins?"

"Not blood virgins, but virgins in general. And the human must remain untouched in all ways. Meaning, if you had drunk from another of my kind or been deflowered by anyone prior to me, we would not have been able to initiate the ceremony. Also, sharing your blood doesn't disrupt the ritual, nor do sexual acts without penetration, but anything tied to the bond—sex and vampire blood—can shatter everything we've built."

His hand dropped from my breast to lift my sweater, his gaze falling to my teased nipple. I didn't bother pointing out that he'd just demanded I keep my clothes on, not with the soothing air rushing across my skin. He bent to nibble my breast, his stubble chafing my stiff peak.

"From the moment you imbibed my essence, Juliet, you were forever bound to me and no one else."

"Unless someone else takes me before you," I breathed, referring to his previous comment about the potential for someone to interfere with our bonding process. That seemed to be a solid argument for him to take me sooner rather than later.

Darius captured my taut bud between his teeth and bit down. Hard. His name left my lips on a hiss as tears glistened behind my eyes. There was no pleasure in this vampiric kiss, just a harsh tugging of my essence into his mouth and a branding of my flesh. My nails curled into his shirt as I fought the scream building in my throat.

A wave of euphoria shocked my system, tightening my skin to a painful degree.

Oh, Goddess, what is he trying to do to me? My thighs clenched as another ripple of rapture pulsed through my bloodstream.

"Darius," I breathed, grasping his shoulders. The weight of his erection against my tender core licked fire across my skin. I writhed wantonly in his lap, desiring more friction, more something. More *him.*

"No one else will take you, Juliet," he vowed darkly against my abused skin, his grip on my neck tightening. "Ever."

I panted against him, my heart pounding. "But you told the Regent—"

"Enough," he growled, raising his head to capture my gaze. "I insinuated to Sebastian that you would be more experienced, allowing him to assume I meant to share you more indulgently in the future. That was his mistake because I have no desire to ever allow another to touch you, let alone feed from you. Anyone who tries without my consent will die. Do you understand?"

The vehemence in his tone sent a jolt to my chest, derailing the rhythm. "Y-yes, Sire. I understand."

He sighed and pulled me closer, his lips meeting my forehead as he wrapped his arms around me. "Juliet, the ceremony binds us until either I die or another being claims your body." He paused, letting the information settle between us.

"Meaning only you can take me to bed," I said slowly, translating his words. "Now and forever, or the connection breaks."

"Yes, which would render you mortal again, causing you to age normally." He pressed his mouth to my hair, sighing. "This is why *Erositas* are so coveted among my kind. They are quite literally forbidden fruit. It only takes one intimate touch to shatter the eternal bond. Why would I jeopardize something so sacred for the likes of Sebastian?"

I stilled against him. "But, but you told me sharing is a requirement for my position at your side. That was the point of the training with Master Ivan and Master Trevor."

"Yes, *Erositas*—especially ones with your precious blood type—are expected to offer sustenance to guests under our current political structure. It's a way to belittle the relationship, to remind humans who is in charge, and also serves as a punishment to vampires who choose the ceremony."

"A punishment?" He loosened his hold, allowing me to shift backward. "Why?"

"The world we live in is all about power and control, Juliet. Forcing a vampire to share his mate is the ultimate form of dominance." He drew his thumb over the wound on my breast and brought the blood to his lips, licking it slowly while holding my gaze.

"Is that what I am? Your mate?" I couldn't help the note of wonder in my voice. All this time, I thought the ceremony was merely a way of binding me permanently to his side as a blood slave whom he shared and enjoyed for eternity. It granted me protection without freedom. Not that I had minded, as my purpose was to please.

Until Darius introduced me to the notion of choice…

His pupils dilated as he sliced open a wound of his own and lowered his healing essence to my nipple. My skin hummed with electricity, mending beneath his touch.

"Yes, you will be mine in all ways," he confirmed softly.

"And you will be mine?" The words were out before I could stop them, and they seemed to amuse him.

"Are you demanding exclusivity, darling?"

"I—I don't know," I answered honestly. "You said I can't be intimate or it fractures our connection. What happens if you take another to bed?"

"The ceremony binds you to me, not the other way around. I could take several blood virgins, if I wanted, without harming our connection."

I frowned. Darius could take other lovers, while I had to remain faithful. It meant I only had to sleep with him—a positive—but I disliked the notion of him pleasuring another. A knot formed in my stomach as I realized that Darius might have already taken other lovers while performing the ceremony with me.

He hadn't drunk my blood in several days, other than the medial sip. Hadn't shared my bed for two nights in a row either. Had he been indulging in another? Or several others? Was that how Darius refrained from deflowering me, by obtaining gratification elsewhere?

"This is unfair," I blurted out, my heart hammering painfully in my chest. I didn't want to share Darius. Nor did I want him to share me. It felt wrong. Cruel. Unjust.

He's mine.

"It's nature, darling." He slipped my sweater back into place, his hands falling to my hips with a gentle squeeze. "Now, I need you to buckle up. We're about to land."

Chapter Twenty-Four

Juliet

DARIUS ESCORTED ME down the stairs of the private jet to the black car waiting for us. He exchanged a few short words with the driver, shook his hand, and helped me into the back, where he settled beside me.

Lights unlike any I'd ever witnessed paved the way, leading to a horde of skyscrapers in the distance. So very different from Darius's isolated estate and the bare walls of the Coventus.

He reached over for my hand as the car left the airport behind, driving us toward what appeared to be a barricade of sorts in the middle of the otherwise vacant road. I peered through the windows, studying the odd formation.

No, not a barricade. A line of soldiers dressed in black, holding guns. *Just like the Coventus.*

I froze. *They are here for me, to take me back, to—*

"It's border patrol," Darius murmured, squeezing my hand and pulling me closer. "Their job is to keep everyone inside the city limits."

We slowed to a crawl, then stopped as the uniformed men surrounded the car. Darius rolled down his window, his expression bored. "Evening, gentlemen."

"Sire," a deep voice replied.

He's human, I realized with a start. *How?*

His deep-blue eyes met mine briefly before he glanced down at the clipboard in his hands. "How long are you visiting?" he asked.

"As long as I want," Darius replied, his voice underlined with authority. "I own several properties here."

The male flipped through his documents, nodding. "Right. Yes. Of course." He raised a hand, waving to someone. The soldiers surrounding the car immediately stepped back. "Have a good evening, Sire. Apologies for the intrusion."

Darius didn't reply, merely rolled up the window and relaxed as the car began to move.

"Human guards," I whispered, glancing over my shoulder at them. There were at least fifty, likely more.

"Yes, it's a coveted position among your kind because of the benefits."

"Benefits?" I repeated, shifting forward again.

"Yes. Sex, decent food, reasonable living conditions. The Vigils—as they are called—are given these luxuries in return for their service at the borders, where their primary job is to catch anyone trying to escape." His green irises flared as he met my gaze. "You will see them all over the city. They maintain law and order and are allowed to administer punishments within reason."

"Humans," I said, astounded. "Working for the vampires?" I thought most were enslaved or in various camps. Those soldiers were wandering free. With guns.

"The Vigils serve the lycans too. As I said, it's a desired placement. Not many are selected, making it rather competitive." He brought my hand to his lips, kissing my wrist. "Force the masses to contend for a coveted position in society so they don't band together and rebel. It's a textbook control mechanism, and flawlessly executed. Essentially, humans regulate themselves without the higher beings having to put in any effort."

I opened my mouth, closed it, then opened it again. But I had nothing. No words. Not even a question.

He smiled sadly and brushed his lips against mine, lingering. "The Coventus taught you all about vampire political affairs, but nothing about Blood Day or the factions. And, likely, very little about lycans." Another kiss, this one longer, his tongue dipping in to taste mine. "Mmm, that's going to change, darling. I want you aware and knowledgeable, not sheltered and docile."

His mouth captured mine, silencing any sort of response I might have desired to voice. Not that I had one. My mind was still reeling from trying to comprehend the Vigils. *Humans policing humans. Vying for positions. Regulating ourselves.*

Darius grabbed my hips and pulled me onto his lap, forcing me to straddle him like I had on the jet. A whirring sounded behind me—a privacy screen being deployed?—as my sweater disappeared over my head, dropping to the seat beside us.

"I need to feed," Darius murmured, his lips dropping to my neck. "I wanted to on the plane, but now is more appropriate." He nuzzled my collarbone, breathing deeply. "Touch me."

My palms went to his shoulders, obeying him instantly.

"Lower, Juliet."

"Yes, Sire." I trailed my fingers down his sweater to the bulge growing beneath his trousers.

He gathered my hair into one of his hands at the back of my neck, exposing my throat. "Unfasten my pants," he whispered, his lips at my pulse. "Pull out my cock." His incisors pierced my skin on the last word. Hard. Sharp. Fast.

My eyes threatened to close even as I loosened his belt, popped the button, and slid the zipper down. His arousal—all hot, silky male—met my palm on an eager pulse. I ran my grip over him the way I knew he desired, and he rewarded me by palming my breast.

"Darius," I moaned, the ecstasy of his bite spiraling downward to the sensitive spot between my legs. He shifted my weight on his lap, moving me off-center until my core met his strong thigh. My head fell forward on a sigh, but he used his grasp on my hair to tug me back up, keeping my throat exposed to his voracious mouth.

I increased my rhythm, moving my hand over his shaft in the way my lower body craved. If the pants didn't exist, I would have been tempted to press my damp center against his erection.

Oh, Goddess, yes…

I wanted him inside me.

To seal the bond. Make me his in every way. Claim him as mine.

Except he wouldn't be. Not really.

A lie, my soul whispered. *He's mine.*

Electricity hummed across my skin, his essence mingling with mine as he drank his fill. I gave myself to him completely. Trusted him to know when to stop. Luxuriated in the ecstasy his mouth evoked. Slid my hand up and down and imagined him repeating the same motions inside me.

I wantonly pressed my aching core against his leg, requiring friction. Needing more. Needing *him.*

The hand on my hip slipped lower, his thumb unerringly finding that special place through the fabric of my jeans. A single expert press sent me flying over the edge, my scream unencumbered as his name rolled off my tongue in waves.

It was always like this—explosive.

Intense.

Overwhelming.

Insanity.

My body shook, my limbs refusing to function, my hand grasping him far too tightly. He groaned against my neck, his fangs leaving my skin. Another shock wave slammed into me, sending me spiraling even deeper. A second orgasm? A continuation? Oh, I didn't know, didn't care, just lost myself to the sensations. Hot and cold, light and dark, sound and silence.

I hardly registered Darius pushing me to my knees, his cock finding my mouth and lodging deep. Swallowing was my only option. Every salty, warm drop went straight down my throat. My own euphoria still trembling through me as my lungs burned with the need to breathe.

"Fucking perfection," Darius praised, his fingers combing through my hair. I met his gaze through the black spots dancing in my vision. "Hmm, you look gorgeous like this, Juliet—waiting so patiently for me to allow you to breathe again." He brushed his knuckles over my cheek, collecting the tears I'd unknowingly shed, and brought them to his lips. He licked them slowly, prolonging the moment while my vision clouded into a haze of black.

My eyes opened and closed several times, clearing my foggy vision to reveal a city skyline filled with twinkling lights. I blinked again. And again. But the floor-to-ceiling windows remained showcasing a night filled with activity.

"Darius?" I whispered.

No response.

I rolled onto my back—the mattress beneath me molding to my body—and took in the high ceilings. A fan rotated overhead, doing little to cool my clammy skin. The sweater and jeans were not helping.

Why had Darius redressed me? No, better still, why did he leave me here?

I stretched my arms and legs and slid off the fluffy white comforter. The silver and black adornments of the room were very masculine and clean, but the air lacked the familiar scent I craved.

A walk-in bathroom with marble furnishings and an oversized shower stood off to the left with a closed door beside it. I twisted the handle slowly and found a hallway bathed in light.

Voices floated to my ears—a female. Followed by a deep laugh that made my stomach flip.

Darius.

With another woman?

I started walking before I could stop myself and found him in the middle of an oversized living area with his arm spread along the back of a couch. A gorgeous blonde sat in the chair beside him, her legs crossed and angled toward Darius and her lips creased into a charming smile. Her bright-blue eyes found mine and widened for a moment, as though shocked to see me.

The feeling was mutual. Even more so considering I'd just pleasured Darius before arriving here. He had no need for another, and I was not sharing. If he required more blood, he could have mine. And my body. And my mouth.

He glanced up as I approached, the ankle resting on his knee shifting to the ground just in time for me to plant myself on his lap.

Mine.

I made sure my expression conveyed that while meeting the blonde's gaze. Her response was another one of those tinkling laughs.

Darius's arms came around my waist, tightening slightly. "What happened to bowing for our guests?" he asked softly.

My spine went rigid. *Bowing. Guests. Formalities.* We were in the middle of Lilith City, and I had just forgotten the most fundamental of rules. Clearly, the death wish from last night still remained because I was going to get myself killed for behaving this way.

I needed to apologize. To grovel. To… to… oh, Goddess, I had no idea what to do to fix it. Formalities weren't required with Darius, but everything changed with guests.

I tried to move, to fall to the ground, but he held me against him, his arms thick bands of solid muscle. Tears flooded my vision. "Sire, I—I—"

"Oh, stop torturing the poor girl, Darius," the blonde said, her tone chastising. "You know I hate all this submissive shit."

He chuckled, his lips caressing my neck. "Juliet, this is Mira." He nipped my pulse. "She's an old friend."

My nostrils flared. An old friend, as in a former lover? Or someone he still enjoyed intimately?

Another of those too-happy giggles from the blonde. "She reminds me of Izzy." Her eyes twinkled as she met my gaze. "So possessive."

I dug my nails into Darius's arms, not at all amused by this female and her joviality. But the man beneath me seemed quite entertained as he chuckled again. "It's a rather new development, Mira. I kind of like it."

"Liar. We both know you love it," she replied, smiling indulgently before fixating on me again. "You can put your claws away, sweetheart. I'm not interested in your future mate. I already have one of my own."

I gaped at her. "You're an *Erosita*?"

She laughed so hard that tears leaked from her eyes. Apparently, everything in this world was humorous to this woman.

Maybe she's not quite right in the head?

"Mira is a lycan," Darius said, his lips grazing my ear. "She's mated to the alpha of her pack."

"A lycan." I blinked. "Oh." I'd never met one before, had always expected them to be more animalistic than human. But in her cream-colored dress, tousled curls, and perfect manicure, she appeared quite human. "Nice to meet you," I added awkwardly.

"The pleasure is all mine," she replied, her focus shifting to Darius. "Now that she's up, you should get ready."

"Indeed." Darius slid his palms to my hips and squeezed. "I just need Juliet to let me up first."

"I believe she's claimed you," Mira murmured, eyes twinkling again.

"It would appear that way," he replied, his hands gently guiding me off his lap.

I slid to my feet and turned as he stood, my lips parting without sound. *What did I want to say?*

He wrapped his palm around the back of my neck and tugged me into a kiss that ruined my train of thought. Not that I had one anyway. I hardly recognized myself anymore.

She's claimed you.

Yes. Yes, I had. Which was wrong. Humans had no rights of possession, and yet, I wanted Darius to be mine. I showed him that with my mouth, dueled with his tongue for balance and demand, and felt him grin against my lips.

"You make me so proud, Juliet," he whispered, his thumb stroking my pulse. "But I need you to be on your best behavior for dinner. My presence always attracts attention, and being rumored as a sovereign candidate in the Jace Region is only adding to the excitement of my presence here tonight. It is imperative that I be seen as accepting of our current affairs, which may include saying or doing things you won't like."

Mira snorted. "Don't forget about the live-meal entertainment and tastefully decorated waitstaff."

He ignored her and focused on me. "I need you to play the part of submissive blood virgin, or questions will be raised, and those dining with us tonight are not beings you want to intrigue. Do you understand?"

He continued to trace patterns against my throat, distracting me only slightly from his request. "Another dinner."

Darius smiled. "Yes."

"And you wish for me to maintain formalities as taught by my matron."

"Yes," he repeated.

"Such as bowing."

"Unfortunately, yes."

To adhere to my training and the codes set forth by my matron. Why did that suddenly feel like an impossible task?

Because you know better now. But surely I could maintain decorum for a dinner. Unless… "Will there be sharing?"

"No." An emphatic response. "You will be silent unless spoken to, eyes downcast, the picture of subservience, and you will refer to me as your Sire, not Darius. But absolutely no sharing." His grip tightened, his mouth brushing mine. "The only tasting allowed will be my lips on your skin, Juliet. If I request a drink, you obey. If anyone else asks, I shall handle it. Understood?"

I swallowed. *No sharing.* I could accept that. Submission came naturally. Not having to talk would be a blessing. I would observe and nothing more. "Will this be our future?" I asked softly. "Events that require my silence and subservience?"

"Once I am named sovereign, yes. This will become a common outing when inside Lilith City for political affairs." He tucked my hair behind my ear and palmed my cheek. "We're dining tonight with several influential vampires. They are powerful, they are mean, and they believe me to be on their side."

"With one exception, which—"

"Isn't relevant," he interjected, silencing Mira. "Juliet, the rumors of my purchasing you have spread, and it is vital that we be seen as a proper master-and-blood-virgin couple. If anyone suspects otherwise, there will be punishments, such as the one I mentioned earlier."

"Sharing," I whispered.

He nodded. "I don't want to share you, but I need them to think I wouldn't care. It lessens the amusement." He kissed my forehead and sighed. "Consider this an introduction to the roles we will play. I need you to be the perfect submissive, just as the Coventus taught you. All right, sweetheart? Can you do that for me?"

A request, not a demand. Although, we both knew I had no choice. I couldn't refuse him, not when this was my entire purpose for being.

It would be far easier for him to compel me into subservience, but Darius desired my compliance. Just as I craved the opportunity to please him. My chest warmed at the prospect of making him happy, to hear him praise me again as he had moments ago.

You make me so proud, Juliet.

Energy sizzled across my skin, his words repeating in my thoughts. I needed him to say those words once more, hopefully later tonight.

"Okay," I agreed, my heart smiling. "I will be who I am meant to be at your side. In public."

He kissed me tenderly. "Sweet Juliet, my perfect poison." Another kiss, this one longer and punctuated by his tongue. I chased the euphoria his mouth offered and fought the urge to growl when Mira cleared her throat.

Darius sighed. "There's a dress waiting for you in the closet beside my suit." He nibbled my lower lip. "I'll help you change."

"Worried she might hate you later?" Mira asked with a sardonic twist of her mouth.

"We both know she will," he replied. The words he added next were in a language I didn't speak, but they sparked a hint of sadness in his eyes. "Just remember this is all a charade, Juliet. Please."

Chapter Twenty-Five

Juliet

DEATH STARED AT ME FROM ACROSS the dining table in the form of two glassy eyes. She seemed almost at peace with her blue lips curled at the edges, as if she'd been in on a secret the rest of the world knew nothing about.

The other naked female wasn't dead, yet. Her quiet whimpers taunted my ears while I forced myself to swallow another bite of my pasta. A smattering of tomato sauce hid the splatters of blood that had landed in my dinner from the gluttonous vampire to my left, but its concealed color didn't stop me from tasting the rusty essence.

"A little tangy for a B positive," the vampire opposite me said as he lifted his dark head from between the dying brunette's thighs. "But not horrible."

Darius shrugged. "My tastes of late are too rich for comparison." His palm rested against the back of my neck, his thumb stroking my pulse possessively.

I took another bite, ignoring the bile rolling in my stomach.

A charade, Darius had called it.

Looks pretty real to me, I thought as the woman took her last breath. It stuttered through the air with a finality, followed by a sigh from a redheaded female vampire. *Veronica*, Darius had called her.

Their names weren't ones I recognized, but I gathered from their statures that they were old and powerful. Darius, however, was the highest-ranking member at the table. It showed in his easy candor and the way he handled the waitstaff while the others observed.

He lifted the hand not caressing my neck, signaling something to the restaurant waitstaff. Probably his way of indicating that their dinner was dead.

I suppressed a shudder. They killed so easily and without a hint of remorse. Even Darius had sipped from the woman as if she meant nothing.

A trio of humans adorned in nothing but various metal piercings appeared to handle the corpses. They moved silently while the vampires eyed them with a predatory gleam.

I coerced another forkful of pasta down my throat. It tasted bitter and wrong, but I had no choice or I would end up like the women on the table. There were several others in this room, all being devoured in a similar manner, most of them silent. I refused to be the next one.

Pick. Up. The. Fork.

The vampire beside me—Brent—started fondling the chains hanging from one of the staff member's breasts.

Ignore him. Swallow the food.

"So pretty," he mused, tugging sharply. The metal ripped from her skin, causing her to flinch without yelping. Blood poured from the wound, some of it landing on my plate.

I almost dropped the fork, but Darius's grip tightened beneath my hair, his hand grounding me in the present.

Don't vomit, I told myself, breathing deeply through my nose and out through my mouth. *It'll only make matters worse.*

The female yelped as Brent yanked her into his lap, his mouth fastening over the wound. No one jumped in to stop him, not even the other waitstaff. They continued cleaning up the table as if nothing were out of the ordinary.

Because this happened every day.

Everywhere.

Act normal. Darius's voice in my head heated my blood. Whether it was him or my imagination, I didn't know. Didn't care. I latched onto our link, drowned in his power, and listened for further instruction. *Set your fork down.*

I did.

Good, darling.

The woman whimpered as Brent moved her to the table, her body replacing the two already removed by the other waitstaff.

Juliet, pretend to be finished with your meal. Wipe your mouth with the napkin. Say nothing.

A chill threatened to sweep down my spine, yet somehow I complied. Dabbing my lips, folding the fabric primly over my plate, eyes still averted while the human's breathing shallowed.

They were all feeding from her except Darius. His focus was on me, his thumb gently stroking the column of my throat.

"Darius," a deep voice said from directly behind me.

The hand at my neck disappeared as Darius stood. "Well, this is a surprise."

"I've said the same phrase about you several times lately," the newcomer replied, a note of amusement underlining his tone. "When Sebastian mentioned your interest in becoming my new sovereign, I thought surely he had misunderstood. Yet, here you are with your delicious new blood virgin. Fascinating."

Icy droplets froze my veins, sending a spasm to my heart.

My new sovereign.

A royal was behind me. *Jace*, my memory supplied based on my knowledge of the seventeen territories. Sebastian resided in his area, meaning the sovereign position Darius sought also existed under Jace.

"Mind if I join you?" the royal vampire asked.

"Please," Darius replied, his demeanor unfazed. The rest of the table had gone still upon Jace's arrival, leaving the human on the table barely breathing, but alive.

Fingers trailed down my arm. "Stand." The command didn't come from my master but from the royal vampire.

I couldn't say no to any of them, and especially not him. I did as he requested and fell into a bow, my head touching the ground in a severe sign of respect.

His resulting chuckle was alluringly masculine, warming my skin. "She's lovely, Darius, if a little too eager to please."

"I consider that a benefit," my master replied. "But do what you wish."

My breath caught on an inhale, my heart stuttering to a halt.

Sharing.

He promised that wouldn't happen. Yet, his words implied otherwise. An act to show nonchalance? To take away the fun of a potential punishment? Because this was the one vampire in the room Darius couldn't refuse? The royals were gods, the oldest of their kind, and revered by all. Only the Goddess stood alone at the top.

Jace slid into my vacated seat. "Come, young one. You may sit on my lap."

I hesitated, unsure if he meant me or another.

Who else could he be talking to?

Right.

I rose onto my stilettos, head lowered, and accepted the hand he held in my direction. His thighs were solid muscle, reminding me of Darius.

"Now, let's have a proper look at what all this fuss is about," he murmured while collecting my hair at the base of my scalp with one hand. With a sharp yank, my head came up, my gaze landing on his striking silver-blue eyes. They narrowed before trailing over my features, as though inspecting a new purchase. "Lovely shape and bone structure."

"Fuckable mouth," one of the others supplied helpfully.

He ignored the comment, his focus shifting to the cut of my maroon dress. The finger of his free hand traced my collarbone to the center and down to where the fabric met my belly button. My nipples pebbled beneath his touch—a sign of arousal derived from fear. His pupils dilated at the sight, his touch drifting up to reveal my reaction to the table.

"Beautiful breasts," he murmured, fondling my flesh and pinching my stiff peak. "Responds wonderfully as well."

If Darius minded, he didn't voice it. "You see why I've decided to keep her, then."

"I do," Jace replied, still stroking my skin. "She's going to be quite popular at future functions." His striking eyes met mine again. "Perhaps you and I can discuss that future—in private—while I acquaint myself with your new asset."

A sharp, invisible spear pricked my side, leaving a mark inside my heart.

Darius couldn't say no. I knew this, understood why, and still hated it when he said, "Absolutely. Just let me know when."

"Now would be lovely." Jace pressed his nose to my neck, inhaling deeply. "I'm quite famished, and nothing else on the menu has whet my appetite."

"That's why I ordered a few desserts for later." Darius sounded bored. "Actually, they should be about ready in the room."

"Excellent." Jace lifted his head and smiled. "Tell me your name, beautiful."

I swallowed and somehow managed to say, "Juliet."

"Lovely." He kissed me on the cheek. "Stand again and escort me to your room."

"Of course, Your Highness." I slipped from his lap, his hand in mine.

Jace chuckled. "She's well educated."

"Indeed." Darius pushed away from the table, saying a polite goodbye to his friends. They must have understood that he had no choice but to leave, not with a royal requesting his attention. He added a comment to the waitstaff on our way out, saying to add whatever other "items" they ordered to his bill.

How many humans would they devour in one sitting?

Don't think about it, I told myself. *You're in far bigger trouble.*

The hand holding mine squeezed as I selected the button to our floor. Darius joined my other side, his posture aloof. I kept my gaze averted and focused on not screaming. Or running. Or crying. Or demanding they add me to the menu downstairs so maybe I could join that smiling woman on the table.

Maybe I'll die from the voracious royal instead.

But I don't really want to die, do I?

Conflict warred in my heart and mind, an innate part of me wanting something more from this life. An option, a choice, *something*.

It's all just a charade, I reminded myself. *Right?*

Darius had warned me tonight would be hard, that he would do and say things to maintain his status. Was this one of those things?

No, surely not. He hadn't expected Jace—a royal—to crash our dinner party. This wasn't part of Darius's plan at all.

The bell dinged, indicating our level. I led the way as requested, my steps far steadier than my heart.

Darius promised not to share, but he had no choice. He couldn't refuse a royal.

If Jace wanted me, he would have me. The ceremony would shatter. I wouldn't be bound any longer, nor would I ever be bound again. Wasn't that what Darius had said? That once taken, I was forever soiled? A human destined for the breeding camps, or worse, the dining hall downstairs.

My knees shook as Darius slipped his key into the lock. The doors slid open to reveal three naked women, all kneeling with their heads bowed.

"Your dessert specials?" Jace asked.

"As you said, the menu downstairs was distasteful."

Jace chuckled, his chest warming my back. "One might think you knew to expect me, Darius."

"Perhaps I did," he replied stepping inside and shrugging out of his jacket. "Come on in and join the fun. I'll even give you first dibs."

"How generous." Jace's hands fell to my hips as he pushed me through the threshold. "I choose Juliet."

Darius smirked. "Excellent choice. Would you like her in here or the bedroom?"

"The bedroom," he replied, the door closing behind us, sealing off my only chance for escape.

Trapped.

The word rattled around in my head, shooting energy to my limbs. I couldn't do this. I refused. I didn't want anyone else. Only Darius. And maybe not even him.

This world… this life… I refused.

It wasn't right.

I needed to escape. To run. To *scream.*

My mouth opened, my lungs ready, but a hand covered my lips before I had a chance to voice a sound. An arm—solid as steel—clamped around my abdomen and yanked my back into a hard chest.

Jace.

The royal knew my intentions and had stopped me before I even thought to act.

He tsked in my ear. "Oh, darling." He nipped my neck, and it felt so wrong to feel his mouth there that I couldn't help the cringe ricocheting up my spine. "Are you trying to deny me?"

I squirmed against him, tears popping into my eyes. *No!* I wouldn't do this. Not without trying to at least fight.

No more rules.

No more decorum.

No more formalities.

Death was a better fate.

Jace chuckled darkly, his mouth at my ear. "I'm going to enjoy this far more than I care to admit, Juliet." He lifted me and I kicked back at him, but my resistance only earned more amusement from his chest.

"Don't hurt her too badly." The nonchalance in Darius's tone hurt.

He didn't care. Perhaps he never did. Was everything a lie? Had he already gotten what he needed from me?

Did I mean nothing to him?

No. I refused to believe that. Darius confided in me. Told me his plans, introduced me to this new world. Why would he disgrace me now? This had to be a ruse, just like with Sebastian.

I sought Darius's gaze and his mind, my eyes brimming with tears. He merely stared back, unfazed, and kept his thoughts locked up tight. No communication. No advice. Nothing but silence.

This couldn't be happening. It had to be an act. He couldn't just leave me to this fate, not after everything—

"It'll only hurt for a second," Jace murmured, his incisors grazing my neck.

Darius, I pleaded, my heart shattering beneath his indifferent gaze. *Please don't do this to me.*

No reply. Not even a grimace.

I could see it then, the monster lurking beneath the veneer. I was a means to an end. He never needed me to win a position of power, just the favor of a royal. The one at my back.

Hatred poured out of me. Betrayal. Fury unlike any I'd ever known.

I *trusted* him. Cherished him. Wanted to be everything for him. And he threw me away like a piece of trash at the first sign of victory.

My chest fractured as pain unlike anything I'd ever experienced scored my soul. Tears leaked from my eyes, falling to the floor, my pupils locking on my executioner.

He did this to me. Chose me for this deranged project. Tricked me into believing in another version of this world, with possibilities and choices.

I'll never forgive you, I told him with my eyes. Not that he seemed remotely bothered. Pure indifference. He never cared. It was all a lie. The only charade that existed here was between us.

My determination and strength vanished. There wasn't any point. This had always been my fate, just more prolonged than I had anticipated. I was never meant to live.

More tears fell, dampening my skin, my spirit, my heart.

Hope and desire died inside me, leaving a shell of a woman crafted by vampire kind. *Take me. Use me. I no longer care.*

Jace's mouth sealed around my pulse, his teeth puncturing deep. I didn't fight him. Didn't whimper. Didn't even move. Just held Darius's gaze, allowing him to see the woman he had broken.

Congratulations, I thought bitterly. *You'll make an excellent sovereign.*

Chapter Twenty-Six

Darius

ENOUGH.

I sent a blast through the connection to Juliet, forcing her to lose consciousness. Jace caught her without preamble and flashed me an irritated glance at being cut off in the middle of his scene.

If you hadn't gone off script, that wouldn't have been necessary, I told him with a glower. *Asshole.*

He glanced pointedly at the indents in her neck. *That could have been a hell of a lot worse*, he seemed to be saying. Likely because his fangs had been lodged inside her skin when I knocked her out.

You weren't supposed to bite her, I returned. Not that he could actually hear me, but my glare conveyed my feelings well enough.

He rolled his eyes. "Hold her while I decide which of your desserts I want to enjoy with your Juliet." His voice lacked the annoyance clearly written in his features.

"Of course," I replied, sounding just as nonchalant despite wanting to introduce my fist to his face.

Jace handed Juliet to me with great care before moving to the humans on the other side of the room. I sliced my tongue and dabbed it against the two shallow puncture wounds on her neck. It wasn't really necessary from a healing perspective. I just didn't appreciate Jace leaving marks on her.

My Juliet. I nuzzled her warm cheek and withheld a sigh. The hatred in her expression had nearly broken my composure. I expected it, but I wasn't prepared to *feel* it.

Jace touched the humans, describing their physical attributes as he guided each of them to the floor into a deep slumber. When the blonde hit the ground, he asked if I had a preference.

Mira appeared from the bedroom, her steps silent over the ground while I engaged in the script we had decided upon earlier.

We commented on their blood types and personal preferences while Mira skimmed each of the humans with her fancy scanner. Her technology overrode the listening devices buried in their arms. They doubled as trackers in case the mortal somehow escaped. Juliet had come equipped with a similar one that I removed after knocking her out in the limo on our first night. I'd left it somewhere in the formally called country of Italy—where the Coventus also happened to be located.

"Perhaps we should see who screams the loudest?" Jace suggested upon Mira lifting her fingers into the five-second countdown.

"Sounds delightful," I replied on cue.

Mira's hand closed. "Clear."

"Thank fuck," Jace said, sweeping his hand down his face. "I thought Darius might actually try to kill me."

"You weren't supposed to bite her," I growled, finally able to say the words out loud. The script had called for scaring her, not tasting her.

"If it makes you feel any better, mate, I didn't swallow."

I took a step toward him—ready to show my oldest friend how much that didn't improve matters—when Mira moved between us.

"You two can hit each other later. We need to move if you want to reach Majestic Clan by sunrise." Mira nailed me with her icy blue eyes, the alpha inside her lying just under the surface. "Wake her up and dress her for the drive. You have ten minutes."

I didn't bother arguing, my feet already moving to the bedroom. If the look Juliet had given me before passing out was anything to go by, she'd wake up fighting.

"Juliet," I murmured softly while laying her on the soft white comforter. "Open your eyes, darling."

Her lids fluttered, her cheeks a soft pink. So beautiful and innocent. Stirring her from slumber was a luxury I could enjoy for a lifetime.

"Darius?" she breathed, her pupils narrowing as her brain caught up with the moment. "You!" Her palm sliced through the air, and I caught it before it could connect with my face. She tried again with her other hand, and I pinned both of her wrists above her head.

"Juliet." I kept my voice low and calm. "I need you to listen to me."

"I hate you!" she shouted, squirming beneath me and trying futilely to escape my hold. More words of disdain fell from her mouth, some of it surprising me. Either she truly craved death or she felt comfortable enough around me to say these things. Because no human yelled like this at a vampire.

"Settle. Down." Threat and command underlined my tone, requiring her submission. If anyone overheard her, there would be hell to pay, and I wanted to be the only one to ever make her bleed.

I collected her wrists with one hand and used my other to cover her mouth while stretching out on top of her. My cock lengthened, excited by the prospect of more, despite my brain's focus on the long night of travel ahead. Her fighting me had been such a turn-on, one I wanted to both punish and please her for—a sexy contradiction. One to take up later.

"I'm sorry Jace bit you," I said in as soft a voice as I could muster with my arousal heating my blood. "It wasn't part of the plan."

Her eyes narrowed, an indication that she still desired a piece of my flesh. Or worse.

I sighed. "Juliet, I told you this was a short stop on the way to our true destination. We're leaving in a few minutes and I need you prepared. You can hate me later, but right now, I need you to trust me and do as I say."

Her expression didn't falter.

"Consider everything I've told you, darling. I warned you tonight would be a charade, and yes, I promised no sharing. I'm sorry—"

"It wasn't his fault," Jace said, interrupting my explanation. I glared over my shoulder at the pompous ass leaning against the doorway. "Don't look at me like that. You're the one taking forever in here."

"Because you scared the life out of her." *And pissed her the fuck off in the process.* Not that I could entirely complain about that last part. I had wanted her to grow a backbone and leave the subservient bullshit behind. It seemed my wish had finally been granted in the form of a seething female.

"I had to make it look believable, Darius. I have a reputation to uphold and all that."

I shook my head, annoyed, and met Juliet's confused gaze. "He's an old friend—my oldest, actually—and a prick."

"Yeah, well, this 'prick' saved you from having to dine with those imbeciles downstairs for another hour. You're welcome for that, by the way. Remind me *not* to help next time, if this is the thanks I'll get."

"You're both children," Mira growled. "Why isn't she dressed yet?"

"Because Jace interrupted," I replied, again glaring over my shoulder. "Both of you—out. Give me five minutes and she'll be ready."

"She better be," Mira replied, completely unfazed by my tone. "You"—she pointed to Jace and then the door—"out."

"I love when you go all alpha on me, baby. It's adorable."

"Yeah?" She batted her long eyelashes at him. "I'll be sure to mention it to Luka."

Jace chuckled as he left. "I'm not afraid of your alpha mate, Mira, darling."

"What about my claws?" she asked, following him.

Fucking flirt. Royal vampire or not, Jace was going to get himself killed one of these days for pissing off the wrong lycan.

I concentrated on the task at hand and found a much calmer version of Juliet beneath me. "I'm going to let you speak now."

She blinked in response.

My palm slid to her throat, circling it possessively. Her pupils flared, her tongue darting out to lick her lips. Now wasn't the time, but I wanted her. No, I *needed* her.

Before she could move or voice her denial, my mouth claimed hers. I unleashed all my pent-up frustration from the evening with my tongue, brutally coercing her to accept my apology and comply.

She didn't move at first, didn't react, but slowly she yielded to my kiss and returned it with a moan I felt deep within.

Mine.

I hated that Jace had touched her. Had put his mouth on her. I needed to erase him and everyone else, remind myself that she belonged to me. I kissed her jaw, her neck, the spot where Jace had dared to mark her, and sank my teeth into her throat. She arched into me on a cry of pleasure, her body shaking beneath mine. This wasn't about blood or needing to feed, but about reaffirming her place at my side.

"No one else," I whispered, more to myself than to her. "I'll kill anyone who touches you." I released her hands, my fingers trailing down her arms to her dress. I ripped it off of her in one pull, leaving her exposed. "Fuck, I need to claim you, Juliet. I need you to be only mine."

She threaded her fingers in my hair, yanking my head upward. "I won't share you."

I smiled at her proprietorial tone. The ceremony was so rare, so few vampires choosing to take a mate, but I knew of one similar to this where the female felt just as covetous as the male.

Ismerelda.

The name was the splash of cold water I needed to break the moment, a severe reminder of our mission.

I kissed Juliet soundly, promising her with my lips that we would revisit this discussion soon. "We need to get ready," I said, pulling away from her. "I'm taking you somewhere very special to me, Juliet. But it's very, very dangerous. You'll need to do exactly as I say."

"It's not another dinner, is it?" she asked warily.

I chuckled and helped her up from the bed. "No, only a few minutes have passed since the last one."

"Oh." She glanced at her ruined dress on the bed. "I didn't pass out from blood loss?"

"No, I compelled you to sleep." I brushed my knuckles down her cheek. "You were only out for the few minutes it took to organize the humans in the other room."

"Organize?" she repeated.

"Yes." I found her clothes from earlier—jeans and a sweater—and handed them to her. "Mira has a way to alter the devices implanted in their arms. Anyone listening in is hearing a lot of screaming and male grunts right now. It'll calm during the daytime hours and pick up again in the evening."

She pulled on the pants first. "Why?"

I helped with her sweater, combing my fingers through her thick hair as it fell over her back. "It provides an explanation for my absence, as well as Jace's." We did this every time we visited Lilith City together. It helped us maintain our reputations while granting us the freedom to visit our obligations up north. "Mira has a friend who keeps the humans sedated and healthy in our absence. But we only have roughly seventy-two hours at our disposal, which is why we're in a rush."

Her brow crumpled. "Why would you need to pretend to be here?"

There were too many answers to that question. I cupped her cheek and gave her the most straightforward response I could. "We're going somewhere vampires typically avoid."

"Will you tell me where we're really going?"

I smiled at her boldness and pressed my lips to her ear. "Majestic Clan headquarters, where Mira is from."

She gasped. "Lycan territory?"

"Yes, darling." I nuzzled her neck, licking the mark I left there. "You'll understand when we arrive. But can you trust me and follow my lead?"

Juliet met my gaze, her expression concerned. "Is Jace going to bite me again?"

I snorted. "Not if he values his life."

Her pupils widened. "But he's a royal, right? Don't you have to obey him?"

"Yes, Darius. Perhaps you should bow more? Kiss my hand? Pray to me?"

My eyes lifted to the ceiling. *Prick*. "Have you forgotten how to knock?"

"I heard my name from your sweet human's mouth and hoped she desired more teasing." He sauntered to my side, his silver eyes gleaming with mirth as he extended a hand. "Sorry for the theatrics earlier, Juliet. I'm Jace and delighted to officially meet you."

She grabbed my arm, her nails digging into my shirt. The fighter I awoke only moments ago had lost herself again behind a sea of doubt.

I pulled Juliet close, kissing her forehead. "You don't need to fear him. He's a royal jackass, but also a friend."

"Love you too, mate." Jace clapped me on the back with the hand she rejected. "And it's Mira we should fear because she's pacing in the other room. If we don't start moving, she might go wolfish on us."

My lips twitched despite the severity of the moment. "One of these days she's going to kill you."

Jace shrugged, unconcerned. "She's welcome to try. Now, shall we? I'm eager to get this show started."

That made two of us. "Juliet?" I asked, rubbing a hand down her back. "Can you trust me?"

She didn't move, her gorgeous eyes transfixed on Jace, her body rigid.

His expression softened. "I'm sorry for the fright, darling. I barely had my fangs in you before Darius knocked you out." His pupils narrowed up at me. "And it's a bloody good thing I caught her, by the way, or I could have ripped her throat out by accident."

"Don't blame me. You're the one who bit her without permission."

"And you're never going to let me live it down, are you?"

"Not anytime soon," I admitted. "Now apologize to Juliet again."

Her eyes widened at my demand, her lips parting on soundless words.

Jace merely gave her his most charming smile. "I'm so very sorry, sweetheart. Will you please forgive me so Darius can stop acting like an ass?"

Her jaw completely unhinged, all signs of composure gone as she remained frozen at my side.

"I've done as you requested, but she doesn't seem keen on accepting." Jace frowned. "Is it because I'm a royal that she expects such horrid things of me?"

"The Coventus definitely enjoys its propaganda," I muttered.

"Clearly." Jace smoothed his hand down his tie. His jacket had disappeared in the living area somewhere. "Shall we go, then? Perhaps I can make amends in another fashion."

"Juliet?" I prompted softly, rubbing her back. "I need to know you'll follow my lead outside this room. Please?"

She blinked those gorgeous eyes up at me. "I have a choice?" It came out hoarse, but it was better than her remaining silent.

Best to admit the truth, not lie. "Not really, no."

She didn't appear at all fazed by that blunt reply. Her gaze—now curious instead of petrified—flickered to Jace and then back to me. "You trust him?"

"With my life," I replied, meaning it. "He's my oldest friend."

Jace smirked. "For what it's worth, I trust him too."

She glanced between us again. "All right. Then we should go."

I pressed my lips to hers. "You'll understand everything soon. I promise."

And then I'll claim you as mine. Completely. In every way. Forever.

Chapter Twenty-Seven

Juliet

DARIUS'S HAND FIRMLY GRIPPED MINE while we descended the stairs, Mira in the front, Jace at the back. They didn't move quickly, just casually, as though they didn't have a care in the world.

A royal is working with Darius. Does he dislike the alliance as well?

I resisted the urge to check my neck, to feel for Jace's marks.

He never drank from me.

My certainty of that fact increased with every step. My body felt refreshed, not weakened, and I couldn't actually recall him sucking on my neck. I vaguely remembered the prick of his fangs as he had initiated his bite, then everything went black.

I glanced over my shoulder at him now, and he met my gaze with a smile in his silver-blue eyes. He didn't resemble the terrifying royal from dinner at all now, just a regular male with an incredibly attractive face. No mistaking his vampire roots, not with a bone structure like that.

Darius pulled my attention back to the stairs as we rounded yet another corner. The tennis shoes he'd given me felt foreign on my feet. They were so flat I almost felt unstable. Somehow I managed to move alongside him without stumbling, but I missed my heels.

Mira held some sort of device that seemed to be directing us. When we reached the bottom, she paused, hit a few buttons, and led us through a door into a dull corridor. No one spoke, but I sensed Darius's alertness.

Majestic Clan. Lycan territory. What reason could he possibly have to go there? Vampires and lycans worked together as the supreme world leaders but notoriously stayed within their own domains. That didn't mean they couldn't cross borders; they just preferred not to. And yet, this visit was of a clandestine nature. Why?

We stopped at a steel entryway, Mira playing with the item in her hand again. The metal hissed open after a moment to reveal a garage full of cars.

She moved with purpose toward a large black vehicle and smiled as another female slipped into view. They embraced with a hug and kiss on each cheek but didn't say anything. Jace followed suit, while Darius merely nodded.

The back doors opened to reveal two males waiting inside dressed in jeans and T-shirts. They signaled for us to move. Darius lifted me into their waiting hands and hopped up on his own to join us. They gestured to a boxlike compartment swathed in black. Darius lay down inside it first, then held out his arms for me to join him.

A very different way to travel, but all right.

I pressed myself lengthwise against him and jolted when something warm and hard met my back. A glance over my shoulder displayed a smirking Jace, his hand falling to my hip.

A drum kick-started in my chest, sending goose bumps down my limbs.

Why is this happening?

Darius's finger found my lips, silencing my ability to ask for an explanation. His gaze burned with warning.

Shh, he hushed through my mind. *There are listening devices everywhere.*

Would have been nice to know that before we started, I thought back at him. His twitching lips suggested he either heard me or understood my look.

A swathe of dark fabric covered our bodies, followed by a case clicking into place over our heads. I shivered despite the two warm males pressed up against me.

It's so dark…

I know, darling. Darius's murmur sent a shiver of delight down my spine. His mental presence felt so intimate, as though he belonged there. *It's only until we breach the city limits undetected,* he added.

That part I still didn't quite understand. They were going through a lot of effort to conceal this visit, just to avoid some questions. *Are you not allowed to visit the lycans?*

Oh, we're allowed, but it's uncommon and raises questions. Questions, Juliet, that we cannot afford. So I need you to remain calm and quiet for me, okay?

The vehicle started to move, our bodies knocking into each other in the confined space. Jace inhaled deeply, reminding me of his presence. Not that I had forgotten with his hips pressed against my backside and his nose in my hair.

Calm. Yeah, that wouldn't be an issue at all.

Hmm, I have an idea for how to pass the time. Darius tilted my chin up and captured my mouth. His tongue slid inside to slowly caress mine, shooting my heart rate up a notch.

Jace nuzzled the back of my neck, his palm a brand against my hip.

Oh, Goddess, what are you doing to me? I was trapped in a confined space between two vampires—one I adored and the other a stranger.

Darius's palm slid beneath my sweater, traveling up to cup my breast. I arched into him, my blood heating at the sensation of his erection meeting my lower belly. He pushed back, forcing me into the aroused male behind me.

Jace remained still, apart from his thumb gently tracing the top of my jeans.

This is wrong. He shouldn't be here.

Embrace it, Darius replied, massaging my nipple. *Jace won't hurt you.*

Whatever I could have said back to that was swept up in another soul-binding kiss that left me breathless against him. Jace's lips were in my hair, his breath hot against my nape.

Darius, I—

He tugged my lower lip into his mouth, biting down gently. *Stop thinking, Juliet.*

I did. My brain shutting down and allowing him full control as he devoured me from the inside out, possessing my every breath.

Jace remained a solid warmth at my back, shielding me from the world. I should have been afraid, terrified even, but I felt oddly protected between them. Maybe because, despite their clear desires, they didn't push me. Jace never strayed from my hip, his mouth staying in my hair and not touching my skin, while Darius kissed me soundly, his caress gentle against my breast.

When the car rolled to a sudden stop, their grips tightened, but their embrace didn't end. If anything, it intensified with Darius's mouth moving more urgently against mine and Jace's palm sliding up and down my thigh.

I fought the urge to moan, some sane part of me knowing I had to be quiet. It just felt so good, so *hot*, that I could hardly contain my need for more.

Pleasure me, I begged. *Please, Darius.*

The vehicle lurched forward, knocking me against him and back into Jace and fracturing my mind from the lust-induced fog surrounding me. I shuddered, my body begging for more while logic threatened to pull me into the present.

Darius's tongue continued to coax mine, his touch searing my skin. I fell into his embrace again, my heart beating in time with his, my core aching with need. It overwhelmed my senses, making me oblivious to our surroundings.

Until we halted again.

Jace chuckled behind me, the first sound to grace the air in longer than I could remember. "That's one way to keep her quiet, Darius."

The mouth against mine curled. "I thought you might approve of that."

"I'd approve more if you let me properly indulge in her."

"Not a chance in hell," Darius replied, his nose skimming the flame dancing along my cheek.

"In the nearly three thousand years we've known one another, you've never turned down the opportunity to share." Jace kissed the back of my head. "You chose well, mate."

"I know." Darius's hand slid out of my shirt and up to cup my face. "Stay calm for me."

I didn't get a chance to reply before a pale light slithered into our black cavern. Jace disappeared, exposing me to the chilly night air. Darius nudged me onto my back and rolled over me, then extended a hand to help me out of our former safe haven.

"There we are," he murmured as my feet touched the paved ground.

A few masculine chuckles had me jumping to his side. Over a dozen pairs of yellow eyes glowed in the night, the moon overhead our only illumination. Darius stroked his palm down my spine as a white wolf approached and sniffed my hand. My pulse beat erratically in response, but I forced myself to stay still.

He—I assumed the wolf was male because of his size and stature—growled low in his throat and took a few steps back.

Um…

"You should know that fear is an aphrodisiac to a predator," a feminine voice warned from the darkness. A woman stepped through the trees alongside the road with a pair of white wolves on either side of her. The moon highlighted her pale skin and ash-blonde hair, giving her an almost ethereal appeal as she walked over the pavement. "Although, I'm sure Darius doesn't mind."

"Ismerelda," he murmured, a fond note in his voice. "You shouldn't be this close to the border."

She tsked. "When Luka told me you'd initiated emergency protocols for an unexpected visit, I knew there had to be an important reason. Now I see why." She walked up to him and kissed both his cheeks, her intimate knowledge of him clear in the way she hugged him. "I've missed you, sweetheart."

"I've missed you too," he replied softly, holding her for too long of a second.

The hairs along my arms rose in retaliation, displeased with this development. How dare he bring me here to meet with a former lover? I made to step away, when his arm came around my waist, keeping me beside him.

"Juliet, I'd like you to meet a very old friend of mine, Ismerelda."

She smiled warmly. "That's a name I only ever hear when you pay a visit, Darius. Everyone else calls me Izzy now, even Jace."

"It's shorter," Jace replied, as though that explained everything.

Izzy laughed, her gorgeous face lighting up beneath the moon. Her light-green eyes met mine and crinkled at the side. "Welcome to Majestic Clan."

Darius squeezed my side. "This is who I wanted you to meet, Juliet," he murmured. "Not only is Ismerelda human, she's also an *Erosita*."

My lips parted. *An* Erosita*? In the woods? Surrounded by wolves?*

Someone who understood my fate? Could tell me the truth about what awaited me at Darius's side?

It was almost too good to be true. A trick of some kind. *If she's an* Erosita, *where's her Sire?*

"It's true. Cam is my mate." Her smile was sad. "You may know him as Darius's maker, or perhaps as Jace's cousin."

I knew him as both, but wait… *Is? Present tense?* My brow furrowed. Cam's betrayal and subsequent death was well known. The Coventus had described him as a corrupt vampire who unsuccessfully tried to take over the alliance and was killed for his attempt.

But if she's his Erosita, then she should be dead too, right?

Darius's words from the plane slipped through my mind. *"Juliet, the ceremony binds us until either I die, or another being claims your body."*

If Izzy was Cam's mate, then his death would have broken their bond and returned her to a human status several decades ago. Yet, she didn't appear a day over thirty, suggesting her immortality was firmly in place.

"He's still alive," Darius confirmed softly. "But no one knows where."

"We've all been led to believe that Cam's dead, but Izzy's existence proves he's not," Jace added. "And one day, we will free him."

Izzy smiled, but it didn't quite reach her eyes. "Well, now that introductions are finished, perhaps I can accompany Juliet back to the compound while you two ride in the back? It'll be dawn before we reach our destination at this point."

Darius kissed my temple, his voice low as he asked, "Are you comfortable with riding up front next to Ismerelda?" *It is your choice, Juliet,* he whispered through my thoughts. *She won't be offended if you refuse.*

I didn't need to think about it, my decision made the moment I realized who and what she was. "Yes. I would like to talk to her."

Darius hugged my side. "I thought you might." Another brush of his lips. "I'll be right behind you if you need me, at least until sunrise."

"What happens then?" I asked, suddenly concerned. Sunlight couldn't kill a vampire, but it severely weakened them. Hence the reason they preferred to roam at night.

"I'll go back in the trunk coffin with Jace where it's safe." His lips curled. "You're welcome to join us again."

A wolf howled in the distance, causing everyone to lift their heads and stare in the direction of the sound. When a second howl graced the night air, the lycans began to move.

"We need to go," Darius said, propelling me toward the front of the car and Izzy. She grabbed my hand and guided me to the middle seat between her and the driver while Jace and Darius settled behind us. The rest of the lycans disappeared in wolf form or on motorcycles.

"Nothing to worry about," Izzy murmured. "Just a warning of human scouts on the horizon. They sometimes like to prowl along the border, usually because they're bored. But they won't venture too far into the territory, not without repercussions from our own patrol."

"You mean the Vigils?" I asked, recalling the formal term Darius had used.

"Yes, the human vigilantes who prey on their own kind to earn favors from vampires and lycans." She scoffed. "Walking scum, if you ask me."

"Opportunists," the driver beside me said, his voice rough and low. Definitely a lycan.

"Sure." She snorted. "Anyway, you must be very overwhelmed."

I considered her statement while Jace and Darius spoke softly to one another behind us. Their words were too quiet for me to hear, but I knew they would have no trouble understanding me even if I whispered. "Am I allowed to speak freely?" I asked, more to the beings in the back seat than those in the front.

"You may say whatever you want, Juliet," Darius replied, confirming my suspicion that he was listening. "In fact, I encourage you to."

"How nice of you," Izzy deadpanned.

"She comes from a different world than you, Ismerelda. She asks permission because the requirement has been instilled into her through years of torment." He sounded irritated, reminding me of the time he told me to stop bowing.

"Fucking vampires," she grumbled.

"Lycans are not any better, sweetheart," Jace said. "No offense, Hunter."

The lycan beside me grunted. "None taken."

"Ignore all of them and talk to me," Izzy encouraged. "How do you feel?"

How do I feel? I suddenly had the urge to giggle. The last ten, twelve, twenty-four, however many hours, had been an emotional whirlwind . Had dinner with Sebastian only been the night before? Now I sat beside an *Erosita* and a lycan, with a royal vampire and Darius behind me.

Dear Goddess, I was losing my ever-loving mind.

I had gone from wanting to die to not knowing up from down.

One kiss from Darius confused my entire world, a touch from Jace had me wanting to scream one minute and moan the next, and to top it all off, we snuck out of a city of vampires to visit a lycan clan.

My lips curled despite my mind rattling with thoughts, and the giggle threatening my throat exploded through my mouth on a laugh. It was either that or cry. No, wait, tears were leaking from my eyes too.

And I couldn't stop, the burst of energy filling the quiet car with a sound I rarely ever heard, let alone made.

"She's losing it, mate." Jace's voice barely pierced my thoughts because I didn't care. It felt too good to just let the emotion fly free.

I could laugh here. Cry. Scream. Whatever I wanted. With no punishment.

Safe, I realized. Darius had brought me somewhere *safe*. I met his concerned gaze in the mirror. This was what he wanted me to see—life outside the confines of vampire society. And I had no idea what to do next.

Chapter Twenty-Eight

Darius

JULIET'S LAUGH WENT STRAIGHT TO MY HEART. It was so laden in emotion, so broken, all I wanted to do was drag her into my arms. But a sharp look from Ismerelda kept me in my seat.

"Tell me what happened to Viktor," Jace said, helping me shift focus back to our primary objective.

"He tried to touch my blood virgin, so I killed him."

Jace smiled. "That's what Sebastian reported, but what really happened?"

I shrugged. "I may have discreetly indicated that he had permission to fondle my property while no one else was looking."

He chuckled. "Brilliant. And how do you plan to handle Gaston?"

I loosened my tie, slipping the knot from my neck. Formal wear grew tiresome after a while. "My hope is this impromptu rendezvous with you in Lilith City reaches his ears and he backs down when Sebastian nominates me at the Parliament Gala. If he doesn't, then he may experience a fatal demise. Purely coincidental, of course."

"Like my former sovereign, Adrian?" he asked, amused.

"Pity those rogue lycans got ahold of him." A snort from the driver's seat followed my words, bringing a smile to my lips. Hunter was an excellent marksman, one I valued having on my side.

"Pity," Jace agreed, sounding the least bit saddened by it. Which, of course, he wasn't since the whole bloody plan had been his brilliant idea. Jace was the first pawn put in place as a royal with inherited standing.

When he took over the former Northwestern United States, I chose to live at my estate in Washington under his rule, waiting for the next step. Over a century later, he orchestrated the plan of bringing me on as one of his two sovereigns, granting me power and authority over his land and vampires.

There were other pieces in play elsewhere, all strategically lining up to eventually overthrow the alliance. My ascension was only the beginning—a sign to the others that the game had begun.

And all the while, we searched for Cam's whereabouts. He was the rightful king among our kind. Not Lilith, the queen bitch who stole his crown.

"A thousand years ago?" Juliet gasped from the front, her laughter long gone thanks to Ismerelda's storytelling. She was deep in to the history of how she met Cam, her voice hinting at a much happier time in her life. I couldn't begin to imagine what it must be like for her to know her love existed in a place she couldn't find.

Their mental bond had fractured—an indication that he had cut her off—likely to hide her from whatever torment our kind was inflicting upon him. Not to mention, it protected her existence.

The royals thought Cam had killed his *Erosita* before the supernatural uprising, a scene he had strategically orchestrated to protect her from the inevitable future of human enslavement. He hid her among the Majestic Clan, some of our only lycan allies, knowing the vampires would never think to look for her there.

And then he had been caught and tried for treason. Not because of the treason Lilith claimed he had committed, but because of his potential threat to her power.

A note of awe entered Juliet's voice as she asked Ismerelda about her relationship with Cam. She wanted to know about possessiveness and if vampires typically took more than one mate.

"I think she wants your fidelity," Jace murmured, listening.

"It would seem that way," I smiled. "She's grown quite proprietorial, but I don't think she understands why."

"The bond."

I nodded. "She's channeling my emotions for her." I had to keep all my instincts locked away out of fear someone might test them, and it seemed by doing so, I'd shoved some of them into her through our connection.

"I think there might be more to it." He cocked his head to the side, listening as Juliet quietly spoke about our relationship progression. "She likes you."

"Because she has no alternative."

He lifted a shoulder. "I provided one in the coffin and she barely knew I was there, something we both know never happens to me."

With his dark hair, silver eyes, and striking face, no one ever denied him. Hell, some of the humans we ordered for sharing had actually appeared relieved to be chosen by him. Not to mention, the majority of those sent to the royal sex-training camps desired his harem above all others.

"She's afraid of you," I pointed out. "The Coventus taught her to fear all royals and influential vampires."

"Yet, she doesn't fear you," he mused. "Fascinating considering you are one of the most powerful of our kind. You have Cam's essence flowing through your veins, marking you as a true prince."

"Something she doesn't understand."

"Oh, I beg to differ. She senses it plenty, but trusts you despite her instincts because her emotions are telling her you're safe."

I considered her in the mirror, her flushed cheeks and thoughtful eyes. She was deep in conversation with Ismerelda, completely unaware of us discussing her in the back seat. They were going over the benefits of being mated, the immortality, the mental connection we'd only begun to explore, and the pleasures shared between vampire and *Erosita*. Juliet blushed at that, her voice dropping to a whisper as she asked if Cam had waited a long time before deflowering Ismerelda.

I smiled, sensing Juliet's frustration at my delay in culminating our own bond. Now that she knew everything, I would be able to provide her with a proper choice, something I hadn't considered in the beginning but now desired. Having her at my side would prove beneficial so long as she actually wanted to be there. If she didn't, then she could live the rest of her days here among the lycans and other humans they kept safe.

There was a whole clan of mortals living mostly as they once did with freedom and families, hidden among the trees by the lycans who controlled this territory. No one thought to scout the forests for stray humans, assuming them all rounded up or dead. Besides, what lycan would allow fresh meat to roam free? That's what the others thought, thereby marking this as the safest territory for mortals. And my Juliet, should she choose to stay.

"How are Ivan and Trevor?" Jace asked, refocusing me on the present.

I provided him a brief update, including Ivan's thoughts on current political affairs and who we might want to consider for our side. Jace listened to every word, nodding in agreement and adding his own ideas to the mix. We rarely had an opportunity to chat freely about our plans and used the time to our advantage. Jace caught me up on the royals and their antics, even mentioned Kylan killing his entire harem out of boredom.

"Is he falling into an immortal insanity?" I wondered out loud, curious. Some of the oldest of our kind lost touch completely with life and started dabbling in death to pass the time. It seemed Kylan might be heading in that direction.

"His motives remain unclear, but something isn't quite right. He's secluded himself for the time being, stating he requires time to mourn."

"Sebastian said he tried to move up the Blood Day ritual to replenish his harem."

Jace scratched his chin. "He did, but it lacked heart. I'm still trying to figure out what's happened. Regardless, he's lost the plot and clearly doesn't mind killing for sport."

"A summary of most of our kind."

"True." He glanced out the window, taking in the last vestiges of the night. "Sometimes I wonder if we'll ever be able to right all these wrongs."

"We won't," I replied quietly. "But we can try to improve the future." *By returning Cam to his rightful throne and treating humans better than cattle.*

Vampires and lycans would always rule, our preternatural nature placing us at the top of the food chain for a reason, but that didn't mean we had to relegate humans to camps. They were our source of life. We needed them more than they needed us, something the alliance had forgotten when nearly wiping humans out of existence.

"Yes," Jace agreed. "We can try."

The horizon began to lighten, indicating the coming day. "Time for a nap," I drawled. Not that we needed to at our age, but old habits and all that. Besides, I wanted to be rested and alert when Juliet joined me later. There was an important discussion in our near future, and I needed to be prepared for whatever she had to say.

Chapter Twenty-Nine

JULIET

"THIS IS WHERE DARIUS USUALLY STAYS," Izzy said, flipping on the lights to a bedroom decorated in shades of brown.

We had spent the entire drive here talking about her life, Cam, what it was like being a vampire's mate, and her view on the current affairs. My mind spun with thousands of additional questions, but my body required rest after all the traveling and stress.

"This is lovely," I told her, touching the wooden door frame. "May I sleep here?"

She smiled. "I don't imagine Darius would like you sleeping anywhere else."

"You always were an intelligent woman." Darius's voice came from down the hall, his saunter sure and confident as he strode toward us. I'd never seen him up and about during daylight hours. He didn't appear any different, not even as he kissed Izzy on the cheek. "Thank you, love. I can take it from here."

"Now you be nice to her, Darius." She gave him a stern look. "I like her."

He smiled, his green eyes meeting mine. "Don't worry, Ismerelda. I like her too."

My heart fluttered at the sincerity of his tone, my cheeks heating. He never spoke about me in that manner to anyone, not even Trevor and Ivan.

"Good," Ismerelda replied, satisfied. "Cam would approve too." The last was spoken a little wistfully as she patted Darius on the arm and walked away, leaving us standing alone in the threshold.

"Are you all right?" he asked softly, his expression softening. "I imagine this is all a bit overwhelming."

A bit overwhelming? I wanted to laugh, or perhaps cry.

There were free humans outside. Wandering. Laughing. *Living.* We had passed them on our way to this oversized log cabin. They'd all watched us curiously; some had even waved.

And beyond them had been lycans, some in clothing, others in wolf form.

"Welcome to the heart of Majestic Clan," Ismerelda had said.

After everything she'd told me on our way here, I shouldn't have been surprised. But seeing her reality was far different than hearing about it.

"I want to explore later," I said. "Please." My brow furrowed. I didn't know how to behave here, around him. Did decorum still apply? "Am I allowed to explore?"

Darius tucked a strand of hair behind my ear and cupped my cheek. "You can do whatever you want here, Juliet. No permission required."

I leaned into his touch, seeking his intimacy and warmth. His other arm came around me, pulling me into the hug I didn't realize I needed. He held me for a long moment, one foot inside the bedroom, the other in the hallway, and said nothing.

"I'm not sure how to act," I admitted in a whisper. "We went from a dinner horror show to, well, this, and I don't know what you expect from me." Moisture welled in my eyes with the words. "Tell me what to do. Please." I needed his guidance, his understanding, his words.

I needed *him.*

"Shh, it's all right." He ushered me into the bedroom and closed the door, then took me in his arms again, holding me tightly. His strength enveloped me, lending a sense of security and familiarity that I craved.

"It's all so much to take in. I never even dreamed… never thought to consider… Darius, there are humans outside. Living with lycans. Is it this way with all the clans? Can I stay here?" The words were clumsy and rushed, tears streaming down my cheeks.

I hadn't realized just how exhausted and overwhelmed I felt until now. My legs threatened to give out, my heart hammering in my ribs. Everything crashed over me at once—Sebastian, the lethal dinner in Lilith City, Izzy, this log cabin filled with fresh air and happiness…

"Darius." I clung to him for support, and he lifted me off the floor.

"I have you," he murmured, carrying me to the bed and holding me on his lap.

I curled into him and stopped fighting the onslaught of sensation desecrating my being.

Too much. It was all too much.

The conversation with Izzy had been enlightening and terrifying, and so, so *sad.* She chose this life. She chose Cam. I never had that, had never even *hoped* for it. And then to see her life here—even a glimpse of it—the freedom, happiness, humans *smiling*, while I lived in a world controlled by vampires… I shuddered. Darius had shown me such an existence what felt like years ago, by having me read all those books and walk through the history of human nature.

It had felt like fiction at the time, but now, *now*, I understood it. Had witnessed the differences in a few short hours, seeing Izzy laugh and tease supernaturals—as a human.

I would never have that. This was a visit, not my life. And even if it was, I didn't belong here. How would I ever fit into a world with choice? I couldn't even ask to wander without permission, and worse, I didn't *want* to explore without Darius's blessing. Because a part of me lived to serve him.

Even as I asked if I could stay here, I knew I didn't really want to. My mind rioted at the insanity of it all, smearing my vision and sending violent spasms down my spine.

Crying was a weakness. Forbidden. Not tolerated by vampires. And yet, *my* vampire held me through it all. He whispered foreign words in my ear, in a lyrical and sweet language. They soothed my aching heart, distracting me from the commotion in my mind.

"What are you saying?" I asked against his chest, his dress shirt ruined by my tears.

"I'm reciting an old poem." He drew his fingers through my hair and down my back. Again and again. "It's about forgiveness and compassion, but has no true translation. The language is too old."

I sniffled, my eyelashes still damp. "Why are you so different from the others?"

"You mean my brethren, like Sebastian and Brent?"

"Yes. You can be so cold—like them—yet, also warm. Why?"

He shifted, his legs stretching out to cross at the ankles as he repositioned me on his lap. I pressed my cheek to his shoulder, my gaze on the dark-wood wall.

"The coldness is natural, a product of age. However, unlike most of my kind, I haven't lost my sense of humanity. Vampires and lycans are the superior races, but humans are the source of our life force. Without your blood, vampires would die. Without your ability to procreate, lycans would also die." He rubbed my back while he spoke, his touch peaceful and right, lulling me into a state of comfort I'd experienced with no one else.

"There has to be a way for us all to live in harmony without relegating your kind to camps and torture," he continued. "We managed it for several thousand years, which, of course, changed after humans discovered our existence. Still, the solution put in place—today's society—wasn't the only option. That's Cam's belief, and there are many among us who agree with him. Including me."

"And Jace."

"Yes. Trevor and Ivan as well, and several others you've not met yet. We've been positioning ourselves appropriately throughout the world for the last several decades in hopes of staging a coup d'état. My becoming a sovereign beneath Jace is the signal to the others that we're ready to begin shuffling the pieces on the board."

"Why now?" I wondered. "Did something happen to prompt the change?"

He shook his head. "Not exactly. We had hoped to have a better idea of Cam's location before we began, but it's become increasingly clear that we need more positions in power to find him. The changes we seek won't happen overnight, or even within the next few decades. This is a long game we are playing, one that started a century ago and continues today."

I blinked, my vision blurry. "So humans will continue to suffer."

"Unfortunately, yes." He hugged me to him. "But it's not only humans, Juliet. The nomad lands are terrifying and desperate and far worse than even the lowest of supernatural classes. Our society today is based on aristocracy and power, and it's grossly inadequate for all parties involved. Only the most powerful and ancient of our kind—the royals, for example—benefit. The rest are left to their own devices, or to starve."

I hadn't seen that aspect of our world. The Coventus's teachings centered around the influential lifestyle because that was always my future—to be the slave of a wealthy vampire. Like Darius.

My focus slid to the man holding me, to his handsome face, alluring gaze, and full mouth. "Why did you pick me?"

His palm slid up to my neck, beneath my hair, to grasp my nape. "When one in my position is interested in procuring a blood virgin, we are sent portfolios of all the candidates. I requested my first set two years ago and received a monthly dossier, but none of them piqued my interest. I had almost given up on the idea, as we were running out of time, but then your profile crossed my desk." His thumb stroked the side of my throat, skimming my pulse.

"Your intellectual aptitude and affinity for languages were the first marks in your favor. But it was your eyes"—his irises sizzled with green fire—"that sealed your fate. I knew you would be able to bring my enemies to their knees with a glance, and become my own perfect, intelligent, gorgeous weapon."

I licked my suddenly dry lips. "The Coventus taught me to do whatever my master desires, meaning I would try to help you with anything you asked of me regardless of the ceremony. So why bother with the ritual? Is it because you need me to be immortal like Izzy?"

"The ceremony affords us a deeper connection and a way to communicate should we need to. And yes, your immortality carried an important purpose. I needed you less breakable for the situations I had originally intended for you, which is also why I started training you about weapons and self-defense." The hand not on my neck fell to my thigh, his fingers splaying possessively across my jeans. "But those plans have proven impossible."

I swallowed. "What do you mean?"

"I can't put you in a situation again like I did with Viktor. Hell, I can't even share you." Those last five words were spoken with a hint of frustration. "I've tried, even managed to a little with Ivan and Trevor, but when Sebastian visited,

I couldn't do it. That's why I sent you upstairs."

I frowned. "But I thought I displeased you. I went to your room expecting your punishment."

"Oh, darling, no." He pressed his lips to my forehead, his arms folding around me. "Any frustration you felt was directed at Sebastian, not you. My words were all part of the charade we must play to survive. I had intended to pleasure you until you couldn't walk, but instead found you devastated." He pulled back, his gaze again meeting mine. "Was that because you thought I intended to harm you?"

"I—I, yes. You said I disappointed you earlier in the night, and I thought I had again with Sebastian." My throat worked over the words, my emotions surfacing again. "I expected pain."

He sighed, his forehead falling to my shoulder. "I've never desired to hurt you, darling. Not cruelly, anyway." He kissed my neck, my ear. "I much prefer sexual games to punishing ones."

"I don't understand how to act anymore," I admitted. "You asked if I wanted to be shared with Sebastian, and I didn't, but I'm trained to do as you wish. Then with our last dinner, you promised not to share me, but Jace bit me. I'm so confused, Darius. I don't know how to please you or what you want from me. I keep making mistakes, but I promise to do—"

His lips sealed over mine, silencing my despair. He kissed me softly, his mouth gently gliding against my own. I slid my fingers into his hair, holding on to him, desperate for him, breathing him like air.

I need you, I told him. *Please, Darius.*

He responded by shifting my legs until I straddled him, his hands seizing my hips as he deepened our embrace. My tongue parted his lips, demanding more. He didn't smile or react, but let me take what I desired, exploring his mouth as he always did my own. And I tasted every inch of him, claiming him as he did me and marking him as mine.

I won't share you, I warned him. *Izzy was Cam's only mate, so don't tell me it's not possible. I won't believe you.*

He broke the kiss, green flames dancing in his gaze. "You're demanding my fidelity." Not a question, but a statement.

I didn't hesitate, my heart and soul refusing to back down from this. "Yes. You said vampires can take more than one *Erosita*, but that's not acceptable to me. If I am to remain loyal to you, then I expect the same."

"And now you're giving me an ultimatum." He rolled me off of him and onto my back, his body caging me against the mattress. "Have you forgotten who is the master here, Juliet?"

I shivered beneath him, his position and tone reasserting his dominance. Not that I ever denied it.

"If you take another, I'll kill her." I realized as I said it how true that statement was. Darius had taught me enough self-defense with weapons that, paired with my proprietorial emotions, I could kill. "I won't share you," I repeated, this time out loud. "I refuse."

He chuckled, his lips falling to my neck. "Fuck, Juliet." He pressed his erection into my hip, his body all brute strength above me. "I don't know if you're just saying these things because of my possessiveness influencing you through our bond, but it's arousing as hell." He slid between my legs and settled his hardness at the apex between my thighs. "You're mine too, Juliet. But society will force me to share you. It's why I brought you here—not just to learn, but to offer you an escape."

I stilled beneath him despite the fire scalding my veins. "What?"

"You can stay here if you want. Humans, even blood virgins, go missing every day. No one would suspect anything after my taking you up to the suite with Jace. If anything, they'll be shocked you survived." His lips met my neck, his kisses filled with reverence. "You've already done what I needed by assisting me with my reemergence into society. I've acquired the requisite results, which means you've upheld your side of our arrangement."

His breath shuddered across my skin, trailing goose bumps across my flesh.

"What are you saying?" I asked, my breath catching in my lungs.

"I'm saying that you could have a real life here, Juliet. No one would be surprised by our short-lived bond; they would just assume I grew tired of you as my kind is wont to do."

My eyes narrowed at his words. "Short-lived?" I grabbed his shoulders and shoved, needing to see his face. "You're suggesting our ceremony be *short-lived*?" Hadn't he promised me immortality in exchange for my agreement to help him destroy his competition? Or had he only meant to provide me temporary immortality through the election process, and not beyond it? "Are we not completing the bond?"

He stared down at me. "You no longer desire the ceremony?"

That was not at all what I'd just said. I shook my head, confused and conflicted. What was the point in initiating the bond only to leave me here? I thought Darius wanted eternity, to train me to be his perfect poison always, not *temporarily*. I pushed him again, this time intending to shove him off of me, but the hard vampire didn't move.

"Juliet, are you rejecting my bond?"

My eyebrows jumped up. "Rejecting the bond?" Was he joking? "I just told you I don't ever want to share you, and you replied by informing me that my purpose in your life is essentially done!" I couldn't help raising my voice. All of this was complete and utter madness. "You required my acceptance of our deal, stating I would gain immortality, then you tell me vampires can have more than one *Erosita*, and now, you intend to leave me here. Alone. In a world I don't understand because you no longer need me and our bond can be short-lived."

I officially hated that term. I officially hated him. I officially hated everything. This life. This world. This situation. I wanted to scream—an act forbidden by vampires. But why did I care? What purpose did it serve to always be in perfect order? *To please my master.* I almost laughed, but instead another sound parted my lips.

A screech filled with all the emotions and hatred I felt for everything and everyone. My world shattering beneath a veil of hurt and torment.

No more.

Darius wanted to leave me here? Fine. But not without him realizing just how much he'd broken me first.

Chapter Thirty

Juliet

"FUCK!" Darius's palm covered my mouth, the complete opposite of what I desired. I squirmed beneath him, fighting with everything I had to dislodge his much bigger body, to no avail. "Stop!" he demanded.

"No!" My shout came out muffled behind his hand. Tears burned my eyes as I glowered up at him. He could silence my mouth, but not my mind.

I hate you! Why even bother with the ceremony if you didn't intend to see it through? To just leave me here? Alone? Without you? I tried futilely to throw him off me again and screamed internally in frustration when he didn't even budge.

You should have just compelled me to help you without all the extra requirements! That would have been a better fate than forcing this temporary bond between us just to shatter it once I completed my purpose. Or is that how you play with your food, vampire? Promise her eternity just to steal it away and leave her in a place with complete strangers while you go off and find a new mate?

He held me down, his gaze smoldering with unveiled fury as I trembled angrily beneath him. *Let. Me. Go!*

Both of my hands were locked over my head in one of his while his thighs pinned mine to the bed, his other palm still covering my mouth. "You have completely misunderstood my intentions," he growled.

I snorted. *I've misunderstood everything all along because you prefer to talk in riddles than to actually explain yourself.*

His eyebrows rose. "You want a full explanation, Juliet? Then I'll give you one." His hand slid from my lips only to be replaced by his mouth. I bit his tongue in response, eliciting a deep snarl from him. But he didn't stop despite the blood pouring from the wound, his lips devouring mine in a punishing kiss that stole my breath.

Walls crashed down around us, an influx of sounds and voices piercing my ears.

The assault left me dizzy and floating in a consciousness that didn't belong to me.

Darius.

His mind surrounded me, encasing me in his memories, his thoughts, his feelings and intentions. I gasped, my lungs enflamed with the need to inhale, but all I absorbed were more words and emotions.

Tenderness, fear, possession, hurt.

Taking her here is the right thing to do, even if it kills me to leave her.

I can't keep her. Not in this world.

I'm losing focus.

Fuck, she's amazing. So broken, so beautiful, so mine.

Breaking her is going to be the most fulfilling and devastating act I've ever committed.

This world is too dangerous for her.

I'll kill anyone who touches her, even though I shouldn't.

Cam is counting on me. But all I can think about is her.

She'll be safe with the Majestic Clan, even more so than with me, but I'll rarely see her. A sacrifice I have to make—for her.

I'll be miserable without her, but how can I be so selfish?

What if she remained at my side? It would hurt her even more, society would make so many demands… I can't do that to her.

What about the original plan? Have I forgotten everything?

This could never be short-lived, not between us.

Oxygen burned my insides as he released me, his mouth a hairsbreadth away from mine as I panted from the onslaught of his invasion. Two orbs of liquid emeralds seethed down at me, his cheeks pink from the exertion of allowing me into his mind.

"Darius," I breathed. I had nothing else to say, only my lips on his mattered now.

I closed the gap between us, kissing him with a fervor that was amplified by his thoughts. He had left the door to his mind wide open, showing me everything. His unhinged desire, the restraint it took for him not to claim my body, the anger he felt at society, his possessive instincts, his heart…

I arched into him, needing more. His hand slid to my hip and then up beneath my sweater to palm my breast. I moaned in encouragement. My exhaustion no longer mattered, nor did all my tortured emotions. *Only him.*

"Take me," I whispered. "Complete us."

He groaned against my mouth, his grip on my wrists tightening. "It'll hurt, Juliet. Especially like this."

"It'll hurt more if you don't." I rubbed against his arousal, my thighs straining beneath his. "Claim me, Darius. *Please.*"

His mouth dominated mine with a brutality I felt to my very soul. I fell into his kiss headfirst, my brain no longer functioning, my heart no longer beating, my lungs pumping mindlessly.

Darius was everywhere. *Everything.* My obsession, my reason for being, my life.

He sat up, pulling me with him, and yanked my sweater over my head while I tore through the buttons of his shirt, leaving our chests bare against each other, as our mouths continued to destroy one another. My jeans were next, my shoes vanishing along the way, and then he lowered me to the bed, naked for his perusal.

"I will never tire of seeing you like this." His voice held a note of awe, his eyes simmering with unrestrained yearning as he discarded the remains of his shirt. My pulse spiked in response, begging for his bite. I wanted everything he had to offer. All of it. Always. He slid his belt through the buckle slowly, tauntingly, then let the leather fall to his side. "I should make you unbutton my pants with your teeth."

I shifted onto my elbows, eager to try, but he'd already popped them loose, the zipper inching down to reveal his engorged cock. Moisture beaded at the top, so deliciously alluring. I loved tasting him, was addicted to his flavor and pleasure.

His pupils dilated. "You're eyeing me as though you want to devour me, sweetheart."

"I do," I moaned, my nipples tightening to painful points.

He grinned. "Soon." He slid his pants down his strong thighs, then kicked them off onto the floor along with the rest of our clothes.

I fell from my elbows to my back and met his ravenous gaze. A shiver of longing cascaded goose bumps down my arms. *Darius is finally going to claim me.* A maelstrom of fire and ice swirled in my lower belly at the thought. I wanted this, craved it, and feared it all at the same time.

"Are you wet for me, Juliet?" he asked, his body hovering above mine on his hands and knees, trapping me against the bed.

"Yes," I whispered.

He sat back onto his heels between my splayed thighs. "Show me."

I parted my legs wider for him, displaying my intimate flesh.

"Use your fingers." A quiet command, not a request. "Dip them into your sweet cunt and bring the moisture to my lips."

A hot flush swept over me at the wanton directive, even as my hand dipped down to touch my shaved mound and lower. I arched into my palm, desperate for the friction. It felt so good, yet not nearly good enough. I whimpered at the contradiction, my lip caught between my teeth. Tension curled in my limbs. *So close…*

I slid two fingers inside my tight channel, hoping for sweet relief, but all it did was worsen the ache pulsing between my thighs.

"Go deep for me," he urged, his eyes on my hand.

"Yes, Sire." My touch did little to alleviate the need clawing at my insides. If anything, it only magnified the torment, sending a fresh surge of warmth to my already weeping core.

"That looks delicious, darling." His thumbs skimmed my inner thighs so close to where I desired him most, eliciting a guttural sound from my throat. He bent to press a kiss to my working hand. "Give me a taste, love."

I shuddered and lifted my fingers to his waiting lips. He groaned as he took them into his mouth with strong, luxurious strokes of his tongue. I wanted him to do that to my clit, to drive me to that place he'd introduced me to, the one where I let go of all my thoughts and only *felt.*

"Darius, please…"

He grinned. "Mmm, I do love when you beg." He lowered my palm to the bed and pressed a kiss to my aching center. "Is this what you need?"

"Yes," I hissed, my lungs forgetting how to function.

"Do not come," he warned, sending a flush of heat up my abdomen to my breasts. My nipples hardened to excruciating points, his mouth hovering against the heart of my desire, breathing me in.

"I…" No words followed. I was strung so tight with anticipation I couldn't tell if I wanted to yell or to cry. No longer knew how to beg. No longer understood words…

And then his tongue parted my folds.

I fisted the comforter on either side of my hips, his name renting the air on a scream. One stroke against my sensitive nub had me teetering on the edge of an explosion. But his tongue went in the wrong direction, drawing a path up my body to my breasts, where he nibbled my tender peaks.

"Darius," I panted, my body demanding release. All of the emotional upheaval, the teasing in the car, the insight into his mind… "I feel like I'm on fire…"

"Good," he murmured against my nipple. "That's exactly where I need you."

I opened my mouth to ask what he meant, when the head of his arousal nudged my entrance. His hands went to my hips, holding me down, his mouth still on my breast.

"You have permission to scream, Juliet." His fangs pierced my areola, blasting ecstasy through my bloodstream, centering in the ache between my thighs. I cried out—confused and *hot*—and he thrust forward.

I forgot how to breathe, my body too shocked and pained by the invasion to function. Tears glistened in my vision, my body frozen in time.

This was the act I feared for so many years—the act of being ripped in half for a vampire. And I'd craved this from Darius.

His palms traced my sides, his lower body still as my walls shuddered around his harsh intrusion. I barely registered my stinging nipple or the way his tongue traced the rivulets of blood trickling down my breast.

"Deep breaths," he instructed softly, his hips flexing subtly.

I winced, not ready. His hands gripped my waist, his fingers bruising my skin, as though he had to fight to stop himself from seeking more friction. His mouth moved to my neck, his lengthened incisors skimming my pulse.

"I need to move," he whispered, his voice agonized. "I need to fuck you, Juliet."

My throat worked over the words I needed to say, but no sound escaped my lips. I wanted to ask for another minute, to beg him to go easy on me.

"Fuck," he groaned, his teeth sinking into my flesh.

I flinched, startled.

It hurt, but, oh, that felt rather interesting.

I tilted my hips again, his hardness rubbing some place deep inside that shot adrenaline through my veins. "Darius," I breathed.

He slid out of me and back in—hard—and I moaned in appreciation. He repeated the action, his own groan adding to mine. Heat spiraled from where our bodies joined, rekindling a flush of excitement. His mouth remained on my throat, his fangs teasing my blood.

I tilted my head, granting him full access, inviting him to drink his fill. "I'm ready, Darius. Make me yours."

"Oh, darling," he whispered. "Don't you realize? You've been mine from the start." His incisors pierced my skin again as his lower body began to truly move. He'd been teasing before, testing my boundaries. Now he no longer cared, his body taking mine the way he needed.

His hands were on my breasts, my hips, and my breasts again, his sanity a loose thread in his thoughts.

Mine.

Finally.

So fucking tight.

So good.

More…

I screamed as he powered into me, his hungry thoughts and the sensations his body created, spiraling me over the edge into oblivion.

My nails dug into his back, holding on as he owned me in the way only Darius could. His hips driving violently into mine, his mouth dragging the life essence from my body into his, and his hands possessing every inch of my skin.

I cried out beneath him, the brutality of his assault exactly what I anticipated and yet so much better. He took me with a ferocity renowned for his kind, but hot emotions overshadowed the cloud of hunger. His mind remained opened to mine, his thoughts and feelings heightening our union.

Gripping my cock so tightly, I barely fit… Fuck, I can't stop. I'll never stop.

He picked me up, my legs going around his waist. I rode him, forcing him even deeper, as his thighs drove each thrust.

"Darius," I moaned, my body fracturing beneath the onslaught of pleasure and pain. He'd already pushed me through one climax and another was already building.

"Drink from me," he demanded, lifting his wrist. He sliced his fangs across his flesh, blood welling from the wound. "Finish the ceremony."

A choice. If I chose not to imbibe, the connection would falter. I only understood because he showed me with his mind how the process worked. His body claiming mine with a savage need to finish this, to complete the bond, but not without my final consent.

I was never going to refuse.

I accepted his wrist, my mouth latching onto the laceration and sucking deep. His sweet blood pooled into my mouth, his resulting growl filling my ears.

Mine, I heard him shout. Whether out loud or not, I couldn't tell, too lost in the feeling of our bodies, minds, and spirits marrying one another in an eternal promise.

His pace quickened, my hips bruising from his punishing grip and harsh assault, but pleasure mounted deep inside with each upward stroke. I released his wrist, my mouth finding his while his arm wrapped around my back. His other hand dropped to my waist, his grip firm as he propelled himself into my body.

Fucking me. Loving me. Annihilating me.

I returned the pressure in kind, meeting him move for move, needing to stake my claim too, and I felt him smile against my mouth.

"The perfect mate," he said, capturing my tongue with a bold strike of his own. "You feel fucking amazing."

"More," I begged. "Give me more."

He flattened me on the bed, his cock lodged deep inside me. "Hold on to me."

I wrapped my arms around his neck, holding on for dear life as he took me to a new level of existence. My heart raced, sweat trickling down my brow, the pain almost too much to bear.

But it also felt so, so good. Better than I ever imagined.

My body shook, the fire in my veins reaching a melting point. And still, I needed more. Of what, I didn't know. I was lost to his movements, his speed. He rotated his hips in a way that stroked my clit, but it wasn't enough.

So hot.

No, too *hot.*

Oh, Darius.

He owned me. My entire being existed for this joining of souls and flesh. It burned, searing every nerve, singeing my heart. I couldn't breathe, my body trapped in the throes of an impending spasm that refused me.

It hurts…

"Come for me, Juliet," Darius demanded harshly against my lips. "*Now.*"

I pulled my mouth away from his on a savage exhale, his name the only one gracing my tongue as I shattered beneath his command.

His resulting growl rumbled through my chest, clawing its way to my heart and soul. It wrecked me from the inside out, solidifying his claim and my own while my body shook violently in the blissful agony of our addictive passion.

"*Mine.*" Darius's fierce proclamation rattled the walls as he followed me into delicious oblivion, his rapture scorching through our connection and stirring another explosion from within.

Black and white lights danced behind my eyes, my world flipping upside down in an instant. I lost consciousness, too absorbed in the bliss of my soul lifting to a new plane of existence to remain among the living.

This is what it feels like to fly…

I floated higher, happier than I'd ever been, and found myself staring up into Darius's grinning green eyes. His thick cock pulsed inside me, hot and very hard. "Are you ready to continue?" he asked softly. "Or do you need another minute?"

"There's more?" I asked, dazed.

"Oh, Juliet." His lips curled into a dazzling smile. "That was just the beginning."

Chapter Thirty-One

Darius

JULIET SLEPT SO PEACEFULLY that I hated to wake her. We were well into the evening hours after having spent much of the day fucking. She was an excellent student, taking my direction without hesitation and relying on her instincts.

I smiled, thinking about how she'd knelt for me, her hands on the headboard while I drove into her from behind. My cock throbbed for more against her firm ass.

Not yet.

She needed to recover from earlier before we ventured into that territory. Her immortality was firmly established, her life force thriving inside me, but she still required sustenance to stay healthy.

I nibbled her neck gently, my tongue gliding over her pulse. She groaned, her backside pressing into my eager groin as she stretched and yawned. "Darius?" she murmured, her voice groggy with sleep.

"Juliet." I kissed her bare shoulder. "It's after midnight."

"Mmm." Another stretch that had me growling low in my throat.

"Keep doing that, and we won't be leaving this room today."

She stilled, then repeated the action.

Little rebel. I flipped her onto her back and knelt between her spread thighs. "Juliet, do I come off as the joking type to you?" I had meant my threat. She could go a day without food, especially with my blood running through her veins.

"Erm, no." She licked her lips, her brown gaze falling to the arousal between my legs. Her cheeks flushed, her pupils dilating with hunger.

"Don't look at me like that unless you plan to do something about it." I grasped my cock and gave it a firm stroke, my muscles clenching with need.

She shivered visibly, lifting to her elbows. "I, uh…" Her stomach growled on cue, causing my lips to twitch.

"Yes?" I cocked my head. "Are you desiring an appetizer, darling?"

She groaned and fell back onto the bed, covering her head with a pillow. Her hardening nipples and glistening pussy told me exactly how she felt about my offer. I placed a kiss at the apex between her thighs. "You can't hide from me, Juliet."

Goose bumps pebbled along her flesh, her lust thickening the air. I gave her a long, deep lick before crawling over her and caging her with my arms. She jolted as my erection prodded her slick entrance.

"Are you sore?" I asked softly.

Her mumble was unintelligible behind the pillow. I removed the barrier with a flick of my wrist and gazed down at her flushed face. So beautiful and turned on, but another gentle stroke against her folds confirmed my suspicions.

"I should fuck you to prove a point." I nipped her lower lip. "You need to tell me when I push you too far."

She swallowed. "H-how?"

"Just open up your mind," I murmured. "I'll listen."

Her brow rose, her doubt filtering through the bond.

My lips curled, amused. "I didn't say I'd stop, but I'll listen."

I slid into her slowly, her sweet heat enveloping my cock in a sheath of damp arousal. Her cheeks reddened to a deep, luscious shade. I ran my nose along her soft skin, inhaling the sweet aroma while setting a luxurious pace. Her eyes rolled into the back of her head on a moan, all earlier hesitation gone.

I kissed her neck, her jaw, the sensitive spot below her ear. "It doesn't always have to be hard, love." Another kiss to her temple. "I can be tender, too."

Her palms slid up my arms, her fingers gripping my shoulders. "I think I prefer rough."

"I know you do." I lifted to my elbows again to find her gaze. "But you need more energy before I take you like that again. I want a partner in the bedroom, not an unconscious doll."

Her hips rose to meet mine, driving me deeper. "I'm coming back with you." She spoke the words on a groan, her pupils engulfing her alluring brown irises.

"Are you?" My soft question didn't match the hard thrust of my hips as I tested her pain tolerance.

She bit her lip, her back arching. "I am," she gasped out. "You're not leaving me here."

"You'll be safe." An important factor considering my political agenda. "And if you chose to remain faithful, we could be together in the future."

Her nails dug into my skin. Hard. "You're mine."

I smiled at her ferocity. "I know, darling. But you have a choice."

She lifted into me again, guiding my erection to the place she desired inside. "No, Darius. I'm going with you." Her eyes fluttered closed, her expression the perfect picture of agonized pleasure.

"It hurts, doesn't it?" I asked, keeping myself sheathed inside her.

"Yes," she whispered. "But I want more."

"Harder?"

"Yes," she repeated. "And tell me I can come with you. Stay with you." Her gaze pierced mine on those last three words. "Say it, Darius. Please."

I released the answer in a kiss, allowing her to *feel* my emotions and punctuating them with my increased momentum. Her heart beat rapidly against my chest, her breathing erratic. It wouldn't take long for her to come, and the thought of that alone brought me one step closer to climax. Feeling her walls grip my shaft was one of the most amazing experiences of my very long life. I would never tire of it, would never tire of *her*.

"Oh, Juliet," I whispered against her swollen lips. "Don't you understand what it means to be my mate?" My weight fell to one elbow while I used my other hand to angle her hips for a more intense connection.

A guttural sound parted her lips, her approval evident in the way her back bowed off the bed.

"It would hurt like hell to leave you here," I continued, my voice darkening from my mounting need. "But I would do whatever you asked, whatever you wanted." My tongue found hers, yearning to prove my point, to claim what I owned and to reciprocate in kind. She shook beneath me, her pleasure cresting at its peak, awaiting my approval and final touch.

"Fuck, your body is perfect," I said, awed. "*You* are perfect."

"Darius," she breathed, a hint of urgency in her voice. "*Please*..."

I drew out the moment, plunging into her with a frenzy, enjoying the freezing of her limbs as she fought to hold on to her sanity. A light sheen of sweat decorated her skin, her eyes closed so tightly she had to be seeing stars.

Gorgeous.

"I'll take you wherever you want to go, Juliet," I vowed. "So long as you take me with you." I kissed her deep, her limbs violently trembling around me. "Come for me, sweetheart. Embrace me."

Her scream pierced the night, my heart, and my soul, and I followed her over the cliff with a mind-blowing orgasm that put all the others to shame.

Fuck.

I growled her name, my seed filling her so deep, staking my claim. My arms shook from the effort to remain hovering above her, my legs actually weak from the force with which I took her body. Her pleasure contracted around me, squeezing every last drop into her greedy little cunt.

My forehead fell to her neck, my eyes glistening with tears at the impact. I would never desire another, not after Juliet. All those years of doubting the

Erosita bond, wondering why Cam would ever choose to engage in it, and I finally understood.

Juliet's the other half of my soul. It could be the bond talking, some magical twist of fate, but I doubted it. Not with the way my body and mind reacted to her presence. She did everything I wanted, fought me when I needed it, submitted when I required it, and still wanted to remain at my side.

"I'll never leave you anywhere you don't want to be," I murmured. "And if being by my side proves too much, I will find a way to return you here. To safety."

She cupped my cheek, lifting me from her neck to gaze dazedly into my eyes. "Your world terrifies me, but I can survive it with you."

I shifted to kiss her palm and rested my face against her hand. "It won't be easy. Lilith City was just the beginning."

"I know, and that would have been more bearable had you told me what was happening."

"I needed your reactions to be genuine."

"Then trust me to know how to act, Darius." Her eyes burned into mine. "I spent twenty-two years learning about vampire politics and decorum. You want me to be your weapon, right? Use me, but communicate. I can do this if you believe in me."

So fiercely intelligent, my Juliet. "I don't deserve you." Not in this life, but perhaps an older one. "But I'm keeping you anyway."

Her eyes glimmered with a happiness that touched my heart. Then her stomach rumbled, reminding me of her needs.

I smiled. "I did promise you an appetizer, hmm?" I pulled out of her slowly and knelt between her thighs. "Your pussy looks so good with my cum dripping out of it," I told her, dragging my finger through her tender folds. "Open."

She parted her lips, accepting my sex-drenched finger. Her pupils flared as she sucked my skin clean.

"I want you to do that to my cock," I said, awed.

"Yes, Sire," she replied, voice husky. Her legs bent as she repositioned herself onto her knees and grasped my hips.

I groaned as she bent to take me into her mouth, her head a tangle of dark curls mussed from our lovemaking.

"Fuck," I growled, tangling my fingers in her hair to force her lips to the base. Her tongue worked me over thoroughly, licking up every drop. My dick practically shone when she finished, her mouth puffy from my forceful attentions.

I tightened my grip on her dark strands, giving it a sharp yank to tilt her head back for my rewarding kiss. She deserved so much more, but first, she required proper sustenance. As much as I would love for her to live on my cum alone, that seemed improbable and a bit cruel.

Her breaths came in pants as I pulled back, her pupils large and overwhelmed. "I'm definitely going to fuck you again," I promised. "After we eat."

Something akin to disappointment flashed in her eyes. "Another dinner."

I laughed, my chest light with humor. Of course she would dread everything to do with food after the last week. "It won't be anything like the others, love." I slipped from the bed and gathered her into my arms. "Shower first." The hot water would be good for her muscles, as would some explicit care to her more sensitive regions.

She didn't argue, her body caving to my will while I bathed and clothed her. Only her eyes told me she didn't much care for her outfit. "It feels hot," she muttered.

"That's the purpose of a sweater." I tugged on the hem. Ismerelda had arranged for some clothes to be delivered during daylight hours, the sizes perfect for Juliet. My clothes were already in the room, where I kept them indefinitely. We would have to add a wardrobe for Juliet for the rare occasions we were able to visit.

I pulled a navy long-sleeved shirt over my head and paired it with jeans that matched Juliet's ensemble. Her eyes ran over me with interest, and I cocked a brow. "Yes?"

"Nothing, it's just, well, I like this look on you."

I wrapped my palm around the back of her neck, beneath her damp hair. "Mmm, the feeling is mutual, Juliet." I kissed her for a second longer than was necessary. "Let's go find food so I can strip you again later."

Her expression softened. "So, that's the point of the clothes."

I chuckled. "No, but we can pretend it is if that makes you feel better." No woman I'd ever met preferred to wander around naked. I wanted to fault the Coventus for that, I really did, but my heart just wasn't in it. My mate wandering around nude for a lifetime would not upset me. Not in the least.

My fingers linked with hers as I guided her down the hall toward the kitchen. Jace stood just inside, his head bent over a blonde lycan's shoulder, his lips at her ear. Whatever he said painted her cheeks a deep red, her arousal and excitement more than evident.

Spying us in the doorway, she giggled and darted out of the room, leaving Jace smirking after her. "That'll be fun to chase later."

I shook my head. "You seriously have a death wish."

He pressed a palm to his chest. "What? She's not a mated lycan and definitely of age to make her own decisions."

"She's the alpha's daughter," I reminded, opening a cabinet to pull out two bowls while Juliet rested against the counter. "Surely he has some political arrangement in place for her."

Jace waved a dismissive hand. "Not for another few years. It's fine."

"Lycans prefer virgin mates."

"There are things I can do to her that maintain her virginity," he drawled. "Surely you discovered a few of them with Juliet?"

She cleared her throat beside me, her face flushing a delectable shade of crimson. I brushed my knuckles over her cheek before opening the fridge. "How do you feel about soup?" I asked, spying a vat of chicken noodle on the top shelf. *Comfort food.*

"Okay," she said, her eyes still on Jace.

He had a curious gleam in his eyes as he glanced between us. Then his lips curled. "You two had a good day. Sleep much?"

"Stop embarrassing her," I chided, pouring the liquid into the bowls. "I want to keep her, not scare her."

"Does that mean she'll be coming back with us?" he asked, fully aware of my thoughts about leaving her here.

"Yes," Juliet replied before I could. "I can play my role as required."

My lips twitched at the certainty in her tone as I glanced at Jace. "She's requested I communicate more."

"Fancy that." Jace smiled. "Well, then on that subject, I have an idea to run by you both."

I put the bowls in the microwave and turned around. "Regarding?"

"Gaston," he replied. "I think I know a way to make him step down and to ensure your victory without further bloodshed. It will also solve your sharing problem."

My eyebrows rose. "All right, you have my attention. What's your idea?"

Chapter Thirty-Two

Darius

A Few Weeks Later…

THIS WAS A HORRIBLE PLAN. Killing Gaston would have been so much easier, and far more pleasurable.

"Relax," Ivan murmured beside me. "Or you're going to shatter that glass."

"I'm going to shatter something," I muttered. *Such as Jace's face if he kisses Juliet one more time.*

I'm fine, Darius, she replied, her voice soothing. She sat across the room in Jace's lap wearing a black gown cut to her belly button. His arm was around her shoulders, his opposite hand tucked beneath the slit of her dress to rest on her bare thigh.

I agreed to do this, she reminded. *It's the best way and also my purpose as your mate. Trust me to play my role.*

My grip loosened, her calm tone relaxing my bonded-male instincts. Jace had suggested this scene as a way to demonstrate to society my lack of affection and care toward my blood virgin.

"Removing the forbidden allure will take away all of their fun," he had said. "And it also serves as a way for you to show me favor, something the masses will more than appreciate in this political game. Gaston won't stand a chance because he has nothing of interest to offer me, and he knows it."

I finished my drink and set it on a nearby tray. Word of my nomination had already spread, Sebastian making a point to tell everyone in the room that he was the one to thank for my newfound political aspiration. I would enjoy killing him some day, once his usefulness no longer applied.

"Looks like Gaston has just received the news," Ivan informed, his chin nodding at the vampire in question. His bald head glistened in the chandelier lights as he spoke to Sebastian, his face paling.

"He looks thrilled," Trevor said, handing me a replacement flute. "Don't break this."

I snorted. "I'm in control."

"Sure." He grinned. "Keep telling yourself that."

"She's had you by the balls since you brought her home." Ivan sounded far too amused. "It's been entertaining as hell to watch."

I sighed, secretly thankful for their distraction. "Why am I always surrounded by children?"

"Because you're so fucking old?" Trevor suggested. "Just a thought."

Ivan chuckled. "And true." His lips twitched. "You're being summoned, Darius."

I glanced at Jace's table, noting his raised brow. "Hmm. This should be fun. If you'll excuse me." *I'm going to kiss you, Juliet,* I told her as I approached. *Prepare yourself for it.*

Why does that sound like a threat?

Because you know me well. I took another sip of my champagne before passing it off to a human servant without a word.

"Your Highness," I greeted formally, my fingers knotting in Juliet's long strands. "One moment." I tugged her back and kissed her as I promised, my teeth scraping possessively over her tongue. Her sweet essence filled my mouth. "Mmm, that's better," I murmured, releasing her as suddenly as I had grabbed her.

Jace chuckled, his fingers combing through her now tangled strands. "Was that an invitation to taste her again, Darius?" A brilliant reference to our time in Lilith City for the benefit of the room. Some days I suspected Jace knew how to play this game better than me, perhaps because of his experience on the royal court.

I lifted a shoulder, feigning nonchalance. "You're welcome to do whatever you'd like to her." Cold words that I could only utter because I trusted him. Maybe this was a good plan after all.

His silver gaze glimmered. "I may just take you up on that offer later."

I brushed my knuckles down Juliet's exposed arm, eliciting goose bumps in my wake. "She would be happy to oblige in whatever you have in mind."

Jace kissed her throbbing pulse and then her cheek. "I look forward to it." He sighed, relaxing into his chair. "Join us, Darius." He gestured to the chair beside him. "Gloria can share with Lisa."

Gloria's expression remained stoic as she stood and moved to the chair on his other side, silently sitting on Lisa's lap. Both humans were members of Jace's royal harem. They were alluringly dressed in navy lingerie, but their collective beauty was nothing compared to my Juliet.

"Thank you," I murmured, sitting beside him.

The symbolism was not lost on the room. Inviting me to sit at his side indicated his favoritism in my accepting the position as his new sovereign. I met Gaston's fuming gaze across the room. *Message definitely received.* Sebastian stood beside him, his lips curled in triumph. The power-hungry vampire assumed I would benefit him somehow. He would be sorely disappointed.

"I was just telling Benedict how thrilled I am by your interest in finally joining my political council," Jace said conversationally. "Adrian left a rather large gap in my team, and it will be nice to have someone competent at my side to replace him."

"Hopefully, I can live up to your expectations." A scripted response that he knew was intended to be sarcastic despite my respectful tone.

"Oh, I believe you already have." Another stroke through Juliet's hair trailing all the way down to her waist. "I've never understood the allure of procuring a blood virgin—perhaps because I have my own harem—but I haven't been able to stop thinking about your Juliet's blood for weeks."

I allowed myself a smile. "She is quite addictive."

"Which I imagine is why you chose her as an *Erosita*," Jace added thoughtfully. "Another aspect I've never comprehended, but can definitely respect where she is concerned." He smirked at the other aristocrats seated around us. "She screams beautifully."

Their lust-driven expressions said they desired a taste themselves, but no way in hell was that happening.

"Your Highness," a familiar voice said from behind us. "May I have a brief word?"

Jace waited a beat before turning. "Gaston. Of course." He trailed a finger down Juliet's throat. "Go back to your master like a good pet."

"Yes, Your Highness," she murmured dutifully, sliding from his lap to mine. I wrapped an arm around her exposed lower back and splayed my hand along her side. Her hair fell to one side as she taunted me with the column of her neck.

Desiring a bite, darling?

Only from you, she replied.

I kissed her pulse and nibbled the tender skin. *I'll take your femoral artery later.*

She shivered. *Yes, please.*

"How can I help you, Gaston?" Jace asked, his body angled toward the older vampire. Fury flashed through my opponent's eyes at the blatant disrespect of his position. Most of our brethren would stand in his presence, but a royal could get away with remaining seated. And Jace took full advantage of that right while also delivering a very clear message. *I don't support you.*

Gaston cleared his throat. "As you may know, I've put my name forward for the position of your sovereign."

"Yes, I'm aware." Jace kept his voice politely curious, his charade flawless.

"In light of recent events, I believe it best that I withdraw my candidacy." It sounded like those words hurt Gaston to say, but he delivered them appropriately. "Darius is far more suitable for the position." He couldn't conceal his grimace as he spoke the words. I hid my grin against Juliet's hair.

"On that, Gaston, we agree," Jace replied. "I accept your withdrawal. Is that all you needed?" The quick dismissal had a few heads turning our way, their gazes curious. Royals were commonly rude to their constituents, but to be rude to one as old as Gaston would certainly reach the gossip circuit.

"Yes, Your Highness. That's all I have to say."

"Excellent. Nice speaking with you, Gaston." Jace turned around before the male could reply. "Now, where were we? Oh yes, discussions of later and the things I want to do to your Juliet…"

I slid into the limo beside Juliet and captured her hand in mine. She said nothing as Jace joined us, his expression impassive for those watching our departure. The two members of his harem were riding with his driver and following us back to my estate.

"Well, that went as predicted," Jace said as soon as the door closed. "But we'll need to keep an eye on him."

"Yes, your blatant rejection definitely wounded his ego a bit."

Jase shrugged. "Anyone who preys on children deserves to be taken down a peg or two."

I couldn't agree more with that statement. Juliet relaxed into my side as the limo lurched forward, her arm wrapping around my abdomen. A very different reaction from all those months ago when I procured her from the auction.

"Tired, darling?" I asked softly, fondling her hair.

She nodded.

"That's too bad," I murmured. "I have plans for you later."

Arousal slithered through our bond, heating my blood and hers. Clearly, she wasn't *that* tired.

"While I've always enjoyed voyeurism, we need to discuss your ascension."

I sighed. "And so my life in politics begins."

It didn't matter that the coronation wouldn't take place for another three months. Those who mattered had been in attendance tonight at the Parliament Gala, and they were all in favor of my placement as Jace's new sovereign. There would be no contest to my accepting the position.

The dinner invitations had already started, as well as the high society events. My schedule had quickly gone from quiet to busy in a matter of hours.

I'll be with you, Juliet whispered, my thoughts completely open to her.

I squeezed her hand. *I know.*

Jace started discussing the future, his ideas, how we could work together, and also commented on the ongoing charade with Juliet. So long as our brethren thought I openly shared her with him, no one would bother asking for a taste. She was used goods, thus making her not nearly as exciting. More like a pretty ornament that smelled delectable.

Is he staying at the estate tonight? she wondered.

Yes, with his harem, and possibly for a few days.

To solidify his support of you as the new sovereign?

That, and to hide for a few days. There were very few others Jace could be himself around. It helped that my home was also listening-device-free, allowing him to say and do whatever the fuck he wanted.

That will be nice, she admitted, her mental voice soft.

My lips curled. *You like him, don't you?*

I sensed her mental shrug. *He's growing on me.*

So long as you're not inviting him into our bed later, I'm okay with that.

Never. Only you, Darius.

For eternity, I reminded her.

For eternity.

I closed my eyes while Jace droned on about the Blood Alliance, listing names of those he thought we could sway to our side and why. Soon others would begin to join the ranks, their identities only known by a few.

My ascension served as the signal that the fun was about to begin.

For the king had stepped onto the chessboard accompanied by his queen.

It's time to play.

Epilogue

JULIET

Blood Day

DARIUS'S HAND TIGHTENED AROUND MINE, his body rigid as the rituals began.

Chants and prayers from the humans lined up in rows across the field littered the air, the Goddess herself sitting high on the platform. We sat behind her, beside Jace, and all the other royals, sovereigns, and regents. Vampire high society, a group we were officially members of after Darius's formal acceptance of the sovereign position last week.

Lycan clan leaders—including Mira and Luka—filled up the other platform, their expressions bored as they watched the proceedings.

Latin words echoed around us, the humans pledging their undying devotion to Lilith. I'd never seen her in person, but she was just as gorgeous as I imagined. Long, flowing, ash-blonde hair, pale skin, sharp green eyes.

She didn't sit with any others, her throne situated highest on the stage. "My children," she murmured, a smile in her voice. "Today marks our one hundred and seventeenth Blood Day. As with those before you, twelve lucky souls have been chosen to compete for immortal blood status. Of these twelve, two will be chosen for immortality."

Silence fell over the crowd, the eagerness to know those names clear in their anticipatory stances and expressions.

This was what Darius explained, the art of pitting humans against one another. By forcing them to compete, they failed to work together. And it showed in the way they all appeared separated from one another, not a single human attempting to comfort another.

"The rest of you will be sent to your respective factions," she continued, her voice far too kind for a vampire. "Now, may the ceremony officially begin. Magistrate?"

A dark-haired lycan cloaked in royal-blue robes stood, a large book in his hand.

The human classifications, Darius explained. *He's going to call them up one at a time to inform them of their fate. Prepare yourself, Juliet. This is going to become ugly quickly.*

I swallowed. *Yes, Sire.*

A nervous hush fell over the crowd as he positioned himself behind a podium, opening his book to begin.

I glanced over all their downturned faces and the army of Vigils surrounding them with guns, a chill creeping down my spine.

For twenty-two years, I understood my fate. I knew my future before it ever began, was trained to be the perfect blood virgin, and had feared my turn on the auction block.

While observing these humans awaiting their own futures, I realized how much better I had it. At least I knew what to expect. These poor beings had no idea where they were going, and worse, no choice. It was all dictated by a book, a magistrate, and a fake goddess.

We'll seek justice for them all, Darius vowed, sensing the direction of my thoughts.

Yes, I agreed as the first name was called.

Heels clicked up the stone stairs as the first lamb approached her impending slaughter. Her nightmare was about to begin. I'd survived mine. If only she could be so lucky. But I knew she wouldn't. None of these humans would.

I yearned to cry for them, but instead I held my position—a servant at Darius's side. One day I would be allowed to fight, and when that day came, I would be ready.

To the future, Darius murmured.

To the future, I echoed.

Royally Bitten

Book Two

BLOOD DAY.

Humans lined up like cattle at the slaughter, all awaiting their fates at the hands of a vampire queen they considered to be a goddess.

A few would try to run, others would cry, and several would meekly accept their fate.

I sighed. These mortals were the lucky ones—the top five percent of their twenty-second year. All the other humans were on their way to the blood farms or were being held for the monthly moon chases.

Every ceremony, the same. A power play meant to keep the little lambs in line. As if they required it.

I skimmed the electronic records on my phone, eyeing the attributes of this year's harem selection. Nothing extraordinary. Of course, mortals couldn't necessarily flourish under these conditions.

"See any that intrigue you?" Robyn asked, her manicured fingers trailing up my suit-clad arm.

I glanced sideways at the blonde beauty in her little black gown. "Aside from you, darling?"

Her red lips curled, interest flashing in her blue eyes. "Shall we pick one together?"

Ah, this game. We played it so many times. Pleasurable, yes. Bloody, too. And mind-numbingly boring. Still, I had a reputation to uphold in this dance, one I couldn't afford to tarnish. Not with recent events blackening my good name.

"Did you have one in mind?" I asked, feigning intrigue.

"There's a brunette with promise. Prospect One Hundred and Eight."

I thumbed through the nude images on the screen, searching for her pick. A female with a slender waist, no curves, and dead eyes. Definitely Robyn's type. She loved torturing the broken ones.

"I'll consider her," I murmured, forcing a grin. "Anyone else?"

She shrugged. "Two thirty-eight isn't bad, but he's a bit scrawny."

As was to be expected when society forced the mortals to live on minimal sustenance. A glance at the profile showcased an emaciated boy who did not capture my fancy in the slightest.

"You always did have an eye for beauty," I praised, not meaning a word of it.

"Yes," she agreed, drawing her nails up my bicep. "I do."

"Flirting?" I teased, knowing her far too well.

She pinched my arm. "Flirting implies necessity. We both know I could have you on your knees with a glance, Kylan."

I leaned into her, my lips finding her ear. "The only one who will be kneeling is you, sweetheart." I nipped her neck hard enough to bleed. She knew better than to try to dominate me. "I'm not one of your toys, Robyn."

She licked her lips, her arousal darkening her eyes to a sapphire shade. "Then we'll pick one that submits to us both."

"An arrangement I accept," I murmured, relaxing as Lilith approached her throne. "You best find your seat, darling. It looks as though our queen is ready to shine." Or was she a goddess now? Hmm. Political affairs always did bore me.

"I'll see you after, lover." Robyn kissed me on the cheek and slid from her chair, leaving me blissfully alone.

Other royals glanced my way, none of them brave enough to approach.

Yes, consider me mad, I encouraged, not smiling. *I did kill my harem for sport, after all, right?*

That's what they all assumed, and yet, society intended to reward me with more humans to slaughter. Because that's how this world worked.

A total mindfuck. Boring and necessary and horribly old.

Chants rolled through the air, welcoming Lilith to her murderous stage.

Poor little lambs.

Let the Blood Day—or bloodbath—begin.

Chapter One

RAE

THE WHITE SILK GOWN CLUNG to my clammy skin despite the cool air. My legs shook, my muscles tense, as yet another sentence was delivered from the podium before us.

Willow stood frozen at the verdict, her fate assigned. *The breeding camp.*

My empty stomach clenched, my mouth going dry. *Please don't send me there, Goddess. Please.*

I'd spent my life preparing for this moment. My test scores were among some of the best in my graduating class, but so were Willow's.

Good stock, the Magistrate had murmured.

What if he said the same about me?

I swallowed. *Don't panic. They'll smell your fear.*

"Go on, then," the Magistrate urged, gesturing to the area in the field where those destined to procreate the future human race were gathering.

Willow managed to hobble off the stage, her face ashen.

I'd never see her again.

Her bright eyes met mine, blinking once before she dutifully followed the Vigil guard down the row. We'd said our goodbyes on the bus a few hours before, but seeing her depart now made this more real.

I could be sent to the blood farms, caged for a moon chase, or sentenced to a short life of servitude.

My fingers threatened to curl into fists. There were no options. Nowhere to run. Nowhere to hide. Face my fate or die.

Several had already been punished for their inappropriate reactions. Colleen's remains littered the side of the stage, her head situated near the stairs like a morbid trophy for all to see. *Act like her and pay the price.*

Just breathe, I told myself. *This will all be over soon.*

Or begin.

"Prospect Seven Hundred and Two, Year One Hundred Seventeen," the Magistrate called. Silas brushed his knuckles against mine, wishing me farewell, before starting the walk to his fate.

I'm next.

The words reverberated in my head, clouding my vision. This was it. My final moments before everything changed. No more classes. No more training. Only my future position in society remained. Where would they send me?

"The Immortal Cup," the Magistrate announced.

My lips parted.

Holy shit.

Silas actually did it.

He got in.

We'd spent the better part of the last decade working toward that goal, hoping one of us—Willow, Silas, or me—would make it.

My eyes glazed. Goddess, this meant he may live a full life. A happy one. An immortal one. But it also meant I stood no chance.

"Only two spots remain," the Magistrate murmured, sounding amused. But of course he would be entertained. The lycans and vampires adored the Immortal Cup. I grew up watching them annually, preparing, wishing for a chance.

Tension lined the ranks, everyone feeling their chances slipping from our grasps. Only twelve were gifted the opportunity to fight for immortality. My scores qualified me to be among them, but the same could have been said about Willow.

They're going to breed me…

Stop. You don't know that yet.

"Prospect Seven Hundred and Three, Year One Hundred Seventeen." The familiar designation sent a chill down my spine. It was my turn to face my fate. All the focus fell to me as I started up the path, my gaze averted in reverence. Blood splatters painted the fresh grass, the bodies of those who had disobeyed long gone. Except for Colleen's head, her dead eyes watching me as I ascended the stairs.

Breathe.

I inhaled slowly, exhaled, and repeated, my heels clacking over the stage. The silky gown swished against my legs, the front gaping just enough to reveal that I wore nothing beneath—a requirement for all graduates.

I kneeled before the Magistrate, head bowed in reverence. He ignored me in favor of his book, his clawed finger dragging loudly over the page with a patience I didn't feel.

"Interesting." He cleared his throat, the verdict hanging between us. "Prospect seven hundred and three is also destined for the Immortal Cup."

My heart stopped beating.

What?

Had I heard him right? The Immortal Cup?

Am I dreaming?

"That leaves only one available position," the Magistrate continued, his voice drawing me back to the present.

Not a dream.

Reality.

I stood, my limbs tense from shock. *I'm going to battle for immortality. With Silas.*

My legs gained strength with each step toward the waiting Vigil. He didn't bother with intimidating posturing, merely wandering along beside me with carefree strides. No one would run from this opportunity, even knowing only two would survive.

Silas stood on the sidelines, hands loose at his sides, but I sensed his elation at my joining him. Because I felt the same about him. Two of us had made it to the top.

Oh, but Willow. Fuck. This had to hurt her more than being sent to the breeding camp. Our test scores were the same, our appearances graded as well-above average, and our physiques acceptable.

Something about her genetics must have predetermined her aptitude toward breeding.

Silas's knuckles touched mine as I took the open position beside him. I didn't dare glance at him, nor did I acknowledge the affection in that simple graze. But I understood it.

I'm so glad you're here, he was saying. *And I'm sorry for Willow, too.*

The three of us were inseparable and known for our competitive standards. I used to hate Silas for always besting me. My lips threatened to curl at the memory of all the times Willow and I plotted on ways to bring him down. Then he caught us midsession and our lives changed forever.

Another brush of his fingers near mine, his subtle way of telling me to focus. Always coaching me, even now.

I swallowed my emotions. Willow's fate was out of our hands.

I'll remember you always, I vowed. *I'm sorry.*

The word wove a web into my heart, forever locked away with the memories of our lives together.

Today, I was reborn.

No longer would I be known as Prospect Seven Hundred and Three of Class One Hundred Seventeen.

My name was now Immortal Cup Contestant Eleven, Year One Hundred Seventeen.

And if I won, I'd be known as Rae—my chosen name.

Electricity hummed over my arms, through my chest, down my limbs. The real competition would begin immediately following the ceremony. Only ten would move into the next phase. I would be among those ten.

The Magistrate continued his roll call, assigning fates.

"Royal harem."

"Vigils training."

"Breeding camp."

"Lycan mating."

"Lilith City service industry."

"Clan harem."

Each designation made me feel more and more relieved. The Vigils had been my second choice. None of the others had appealed, but were all better fates than the blood farms or the moon chase.

Being hunted for sport by lycans during a full moon… I shuddered. *No, thank you.*

"Prospect one thousand," the Magistrate finally called, designating the final human to be sorted. "Clemente Clan service industry."

My stomach tightened at the familiar name. The Clementes were renowned as the most powerful lycan clan. Their alpha was on the verge of retiring, his son—Edon—taking the reins. Whoever won this year's Immortal Cup would either join his clan or Jace's vampire ranks. The eligibility shifted annually, and our class was their pick.

Jace Region would be my preference, not that I'd be the one choosing.

"This concludes our annual Blood Day," the Goddess announced, taking over the stage. We knelt in respect, our heads bowed. "Vigils, if you would please escort your respective teams to their exits. The harem prospects and Immortal Cup participants shall remain."

It's beginning.

This was the part they never explained—the initial selection. While twelve were gifted the opportunity to compete, only ten contestants survived to see the first competition. No one knew how the numbers were reduced.

I'm about to find out.

"Rise, my children," the Goddess cooed, her voice as beautiful as it sounded on film. This was my first time in her regal presence. Her formfitting red gown was cut to her belly button, her long blonde hair flowing to her waist. Despite my high scores in physical appeal, my auburn hair and pale features fell flat in comparison. Another designation of her higher status and my lowly human one.

That is going to change when I win.

I stood with the others, my eyes lowered as I considered my opponents. Three-quarters of them were strangers from other schools. But I knew Silas, Clarence, and Daniella. Silas's weaknesses weren't ones I would use. The same could not be said about my other former classmates.

Silence fell as the last of the humans left with their Vigil escorts.

Goodbye, Willow, I thought, my eyes closing briefly. *Forever friends. Never forgotten.*

The rustle of clothing had my lids flashing open, my limbs tensing.

Vampires and lycans were surrounding us—the royals and pack alphas. Their elegant attires boasted wealth and status, their silence meant to intimidate. Years of studying helped me identify them by their emblems alone. Each wore a symbol of their territory or clan, usually in a ring, but some on a necklace or a bracelet.

Jace.

Robyn.

Clemente Clan Alpha.

Hazel.

Stella Clan Alpha.

I steadied my pulse by focusing on my breathing. They merely wanted a good look at the potential humans to join their ranks. That's all.

Claude.

Kylan.

Ernest Clan Alpha and his mate.

Naomi.

They kept moving, their steps soundless over the gravel. Some were behind me, some in front, all circling, admiring, but not touching. Silas remained absolutely still beside me. I focused on him, on our potential future, the destiny we desired. Immortality.

"Thoughts?" the Goddess asked, the crowd shifting to allow her entry. She stopped a few feet away from us, her delicate fingers clasped before her.

"These are the best?" a gruff male demanded, the snarl in his voice denoting him as lycan.

"Come now, Walter. You must see at least some potential?" She sounded hopeful, but a hint of chastisement underlined her tone. A miraculous combination that secured her position as head of the hierarchy.

The Clemente Alpha, Walter, snorted in reply. "Let's get on with it, Lilith. I'm tired of this game and it's my last round."

My breath caught in my throat at the use of the Goddess's given name, not her formal address. A human would be killed for such insolence. Would she punish a lycan, let alone an alpha, for the offense?

"In a hurry to claim your harem?" she teased, her voice filled with humor. "But of course you are. You all are. Vigils, please bring the prospects forward to join those selected for the Immortal Cup."

My brow threatened to furrow, but I quickly smoothed out the lines. Showing emotion was a weakness I couldn't afford. Not now. Not ever.

The lycans and vampires moved back, allowing the humans designated to the harems to join us on each side, forming a U-shaped crowd of white.

"Excellent," the Goddess murmured. "Now, we may begin the true selection process. All of you standing before us are the cream of the crop, receiving the highest aptitude scores in all the categories we value. That is why we offer you the gift of being in the presence of our most esteemed."

I forced myself to swallow. *This sounds ominous…*

"Those selected for the harems will enter a two month training course to learn how best to serve our physical needs. But a handful of chosen ones will be gifted with the opportunity to study under a royal or alpha exclusively. Or under their existing harem, if that's the preference." The smile in her voice did not match the implication of her words.

Was she implying that the royals and alphas were going to choose candidates to serve them—*now*—without any training? We received sexual instruction in school, but nothing at the level they would require.

This applies to the harems, not to—

"We have a history of selecting the best for our Immortal Cup, something that is a bit of a disappointment when only two of you survive to the end. As it's a waste of potential, all of you are to be considered during this round to help ensure our royals and alphas don't miss an otherwise desired opportunity. Well"—she clapped her hands—"Vigils? Please help the candidates disrobe."

My heart skipped a beat.

This was how they decreased the number to ten? Not through a battle or a death match, but by giving the royals and alphas the option to add one of us to their harems?

A Vigil stepped before me, his hands ripping the gown from my shoulders.

I didn't fight him. Didn't yelp or point out that I would have removed it on my own had he given me a moment to process. Instead I let the fabric fall and kicked it away with my heel before he had a chance to touch my legs.

Silas tossed his to the ground beside mine, his muscular form putting the others to shame. I'd seen him nude on countless occasions and had partnered with him in various class demonstrations. To say we knew each other well would be an understatement.

He remained close, his body heat a comfort I couldn't deny. With our gazes still downcast, the vampires and lycans moved closer, lining up in front of us.

"Kylan, the floor is yours," the Goddess said, deferring to the eldest of the living royals. His name sent a chill down my spine. The royals were essentially gods who led divided territories, and each of them was renowned for something.

For Kylan, it was cruelty.

He stepped forward in an all-black suit with matching tie. With my gaze lowered, I couldn't see his face, but I knew his features well—dark hair, matching eyes, sharp cheekbones, and a harsh jawline dusted in stubble. Gorgeous, as all vampires were, and brutal in nature.

"Hmm, and I'm only allowed one?" he mused, wandering slowly, perusing his choices.

"Killing your harem doesn't mean you're entitled to more of this year's crop," a female replied, her disdain clear. "Try not to harm them before we get a taste."

"I've always enjoyed your candor, Naomi." His tone held a touch of amusement that died as he continued. "But as your elder, I advise you to remember who it is you're addressing."

Even the royals had a hierarchy, and Kylan sat at the top. A chill frosted the air, the implication in his admonishment carrying its expected weight.

Fuck with me. I dare you, he seemed to be saying.

And from the shuffles backward, no one wanted to take him up on the offer.

"Apologies," Naomi gritted out.

"Accepted." Kylan moved closer to the vampire harem, his hand lifting and disappearing beyond my field of vision. "She's pretty." The female yelped in response to whatever he did, causing him to tsk. "Well, that certainly won't do."

He repeated the action with several more, all of them reacting similarly. Kylan sighed dramatically, stepping our way. He muttered several words in an old language that had a few of his brethren chuckling.

His palm slid over a woman near me, causing her to flinch. I almost rolled my eyes. If she couldn't handle the touch of a royal vampire, then she stood no chance in these games.

When Kylan finally reached me, I forced my limbs to relax and kept my breathing even. *Move on, vampire. Nothing to see here.*

His gaze burned a trail over my exposed skin, scattering smatters of heat in his wake. I fought a resulting shiver, my body overriding my mind.

Don't attract him, I told myself. *Just feign indifference.*

He brushed my hip with his knuckles, almost as if he'd heard me and wanted to test my resolve. I didn't move. Didn't react.

Focus.

Just inhale, then exhale.

Repeat.

Kylan grabbed my chin and forced my attention upward, his dark brown eyes capturing mine. A spark shot through me, knocking me off-kilter. I grabbed his arm, needing something stable to ground me. Eye contact with a vampire was forbidden, a show of disobedience. Yet he'd just forced me to meet his gaze, and he held me there, scant inches from his face.

He tilted his head slightly to the side, his expression curious.

I swallowed, uncertain. Was he trying to force me into misbehaving? To give him a reason to punish me?

No. I wouldn't be tricked this easily.

My nails dug into his jacket, my forearm tensing, ready to react, push, *something.*

Wait… I'm touching *him.*

Oh, shit…

My hand locked in place and refused to loosen, reacting the absolute wrong way in this situation. I opened my mouth, an apology ready, when his lips covered mine.

I stood frozen, unable to process.

He's kissing me.

Why the fuck is he kissing me?

His tongue slid inside, exploring.

Oh, no. This wasn't good. I couldn't afford for Kylan to be interested, not with immortality dancing at my fingertips.

You can't want me, I thought.

But how did I convey that?

I… I…

Do something!

My jaw clenched in frustration, not knowing how to stop this—*him*. His grip on my chin tightened painfully, his growl vibrating my chest. It took me too long to realize why, to realize what I'd done.

His tongue was trapped between my teeth.

I'd just bitten him.

I'd just bitten a royal vampire.

And not just any royal vampire, but Kylan, the oldest royal in existence.

Chapter Two

KYLAN

SHE *BIT* ME.

From the alarm radiating from her ice-blue eyes, the reaction had shocked her almost as much as it had me. Yet her nails continued to dig into my suit jacket.

A fighter. Courageous. Just what I needed.

My penchant for picking from the lycan harem—just to piss off the wolves—disappeared in a flash.

I wrapped my palm around the back of the redhead's neck and squeezed. "That was a mistake, little lamb," I whispered darkly. Because now I wanted her. Badly.

Her lips parted, but no sound escaped. Not even an apology.

Oh, I'd enjoy this one.

I stepped backward, pulling her with me. "If I kill her before the selection is through, can I select a replacement?" I asked Lilith without breaking eye contact from my chosen conquest.

"Considering her insolent display, I'll most certainly allow it." The irritation in Lilith's tone nearly had my lips curling. Of course she would wish to punish the girl for her reaction. That just made the auburn-haired beauty all the more perfect.

I nipped at her trembling lower lip and tightened my grip on her nape as I dragged her with me back into the circle of royals. They gave us room, no one wanting to risk any residual blood splatter.

The things they expected me to do.

Pity I wouldn't be obliging them in a show.

"I should force you to your knees, make you beg me for forgiveness," I growled. "But I'm not sure I trust that mouth of yours."

"Walter, if you please," Lilith said, signaling the Clemente Alpha for his turn. We would alternate for the next hour or so as everyone selected their initial prize. Then the Immortal Cup candidates would be reshuffled to meet the requisite ten.

What the lamb didn't know was that I'd just saved her life. Because had I not chosen her, one of the lycans would have. She was far too beautiful to be wasted on the Immortal Cup, with her fiery red hair, light blue eyes, and creamy skin. And her curves were mouthwateringly perfect as well.

She didn't look away, her defiance written in the lines of her flattened mouth. Because I'd threatened to force her to her knees? Or because I'd pulled her from the competition? Maybe both.

I brushed my lips over hers again and smiled when she clenched her jaw. "Oh, you do have a death wish, young one," I murmured. "I may just keep you for the fun of breaking you." The words were spoken for those around us more than for her.

She didn't reply, but the fire in her blue eyes told me everything I desired to know. This one had spirit. Such a rarity these days. Most of the humans were broken by the time I met them, their minds fractured from decades of harsh treatment or mental reform. But she possessed a fire I wanted to play with, not smother.

"What shall I call you, little lamb?" I asked against her lips.

Her gaze narrowed, delighting me more. She stood against me, clad in nothing but a pair of heels, her life very much in my hands, and she *glowered* at me.

A scream from the field confirmed Walter's choice. I ignored the howls of approval and focused on my prize. How had I missed her profile? Too busy skimming to care, I supposed.

"Jace," Lilith called, referring to the second oldest of the royals.

The name soured my mood considerably. Someone was fucking with me, and I strongly suspected the outwardly fun-loving, carefree royal to be the culprit. His recent appointing of Darius to sovereign only solidified my suspicion.

A shiver shook the woman in my arms, the midnight air chilling her bare skin. It seemed some of her bravado had worn off and the elements were touching her now.

I released her to shrug out of my suit jacket. Humans were so frail and easily susceptible to disease. I couldn't have her weakening on me too soon.

Her eyebrows rose as I wrapped the handcrafted material around her shoulders.

"What? Surprised I want to keep the sole member of my harem alive?" I asked softly, my lips twitching. I pulled the lapels of the coat over her breasts, tugging her to me. "I have plans for you, sweetheart. You'll need your strength."

She swallowed, her gaze finally leaving mine to drop to my lips before drifting upward again.

Jace made his selection while I watched my new pet, and Lilith called on the next alpha. His choice resulted in an earsplitting scream that didn't faze my little lamb in the slightest. She continued to hold my gaze unflinchingly through the next several rounds, surprising the hell out of me. Any other human would have looked away in deference or subservience after mere seconds. But not her.

"Tell me your name," I demanded, my words for her alone.

Another shriek sounded as one of the lycans familiarized himself with his new toy in the most ancient of ways. I could do the same, bend this woman over on the ground and fuck her until she answered me, but that wasn't my style.

"Your name," I repeated, yanking on my jacket. "Or I will find another, more creative way to make you talk."

The grunts sounding to our left punctuated my threat. She swallowed, her icy gaze thawing the slightest bit with the first signs of discomfort. Fate was finally making her presence known. I almost pitied the woman, yet couldn't. Humans existed to serve their superiors, and she would serve me as required.

And she would enjoy it, too.

I slid my fingers into her hair to twine with her thick strands. "You're trying my patience, little lamb. I suggest you work with me before you see the results of my impatience."

"Why? So you can change my name before killing me?"

Fuck, the female oozed sex in every way. In her gaze, her full lips, those delectable curves hidden beneath my jacket, and in the sultry quality of her voice. I didn't even care that she'd still avoided my question. Just hearing her speak was enough to calm the most turbulent storm.

I tightened my grasp in her hair, pulling until she winced. "Keep pushing." Both a threat and a request tied up into two darkly whispered words.

Fight me.

Submit to me.

Give me everything.

My hand on the jacket slipped beneath the lapels to her bare hip. Her palms flattened on my abdomen as I forced her closer. My lips grazed her cheek before settling at her ear. "I want to know what name to growl later when I'm inside of you."

Her resulting shiver had nothing to do with the cold and everything to do with my lethal promise. And yet she remained tense, as if ready to hit me.

Fascinating.

"Prospect Seven Hundred and Three, Year One Hundred Seventeen," she gritted out. "Have fun with that."

A laugh escaped me—loud and enjoyable—causing several of the others to glance our way. I ignored them all in favor of the defiant female before me. "You're adorable."

Frost coated her blue irises as she remained infuriatingly silent again.

My already hard cock throbbed at the obvious display of resistance. This one would not break easily. No fear, no shame, no willingness to lie down and take it. I didn't realize humans like this still existed.

"We're going to have a lot of fun together, little lamb," I whispered, my lips brushing hers with each word. "And you will give me your name." Because I knew she had one. They all did, our records just didn't bother tracking them.

Challenge poured from her in waves, exciting me.

Fuck, I'd missed this. A woman who could actually hold her own, who refused to bow down to me because of my social status.

Even surrounded by predators, she didn't flinch. Because she would rather I kill her than take her home, perhaps? Hmm, a disappointing thought. One I wouldn't be obliging. My question to Lilith about selecting another had been all about maintaining my image. No, this feisty female I intended to keep, and her warrior tendencies may just keep her alive in this dangerous game called life.

The perfect bait.

I spun her in my arms, placing her back to my chest, and caged her with my forearms. "Watch." I spoke the word against her ear. "See what your fate could become." Royals and alphas traded harem members all the time. Not that I ever participated, but she didn't need to know that.

The remaining humans still up for selection had huddled closer together. Most of my brethren had already made their choices. Robyn had gone with the scrawny male over the brunette. He knelt at her feet while she combed her fingers through his hair as one would a dog.

Jace's pick was the beautiful brunette I'd fondled first. She didn't appear as skittish now that he'd wrapped her up in his jacket. He met my gaze with a cocked brow, daring me to comment on his similar actions. I didn't bite and instead followed my pet's stare to the blond human male standing among those selected for the Immortal Cup.

I recognized him from the files. He was off-limits for this round, marked as a prospect both Jace and Walter had agreed would make a fitting immortal. The way he held his shoulders back, his strong legs spread, his expression bored, I had to agree with the designation. Six of the humans were favored, and of them, he clearly held the most promise.

But what had my lamb so entranced?

His focus never wavered, even as Naomi drew a nail down his sternum to his groin. She loved fucking with the recruits. If she weren't such a bitch, I might like her.

Then again, probably not.

My lamb tensed as Naomi pressed her lips to the male's ear to whisper a taunt. His lips curled in response, intriguing me, but not nearly as much as my pet's unsteady breath. She didn't relax until Naomi moved on to the next victim.

"Ah, a weakness," I whispered against her ear, low enough that no one else would hear except her. Not that anyone was paying us any attention. They were all too busy entertaining their new playthings or salivating over the remaining crop.

Her shoulders stiffened again, causing me to smile against her neck.

"Oh, yes, a definite weakness." I nibbled the tender skin covering her thundering pulse. "If I kill you, I could pick him instead. I've always found males to be more skilled at certain activities than females." I skimmed my nose along her jaw. "What do you think, little lamb? Should I dispose of you and request his company instead? Or perhaps you have something that might entice me otherwise?"

A cruel threat, one that left her quivering against me. I almost hated to do it, but I couldn't pass up the opportunity to reaffirm my dominion here. My brethren would have killed her the second she bit them. I didn't expect gratitude or groveling, but I did want her name. And I would push her until she gave it to me.

"Tick tock," I taunted, nuzzling her throat. "Your silence is boring me."

She grabbed my forearm, squeezing it as her body trembled. It was the second time tonight she'd used me for support without realizing it. The first time had intrigued me so much I hadn't been able to step away. Then she sealed her fate with that kiss.

"Rae." The word barely reached my ears over the animalistic groans coming from the sidelines. Jenkins, the Winter Clan Alpha, had given his new human pet to his son to play with, and the young lycan had wasted no time in becoming acquainted.

My female tried to turn, surprising me. I clasped her hips and allowed her to move, then met her infuriated gaze.

"My name," she said slowly, her voice a throaty purr that intrigued my male senses. "My name is Rae."

"Rae," I repeated, tasting the single syllable on my tongue. "Hmm." I liked it, but it seemed too weak for her. Too quick. *How about*… "Raelyn."

She shook her head. "No, it's Rae."

"I like Raelyn more."

Her gaze narrowed yet again. "If you were just going to rename me, then why ask for my name to begin with?"

"Because I wanted to hear you speak."

"Like a dog."

"Exactly."

She stared me down with such passion that I couldn't stop my lips from curling at the sides. I rather enjoyed her voice, but mmm, I would so enjoy evoking that look from her in bed.

"Your secret is safe with me, little lamb," I promised.

Her brow furrowed. "What secret?"

I pressed my lips to her ear, not wanting anyone to hear. "Whatever secret you share with that human male." I nibbled on her lobe, exhaling slowly and wrapping my arms around her. "But whatever it was, it's over. Because you're mine now, Raelyn."

Chapter Three

RAE

MY TONGUE FELT THICK IN MY MOUTH, as if it had been Kylan who bit me and not the other way around. His hard body held mine, his lips at my ear breathing words I didn't want to hear.

Because you're mine now, Raelyn.

How had this become my fate?

One minute, I was destined for the Immortal Cup. Now, a royal owned me. All because I couldn't keep my body in check. After Kylan had suggested killing me to the Goddess, I'd stopped trying. Because what did it matter? If he was going to slaughter me anyway, I might as well go down with my dignity intact.

Except then he'd threatened Silas. My weakness. The one place Kylan could hit me to force me to behave. Because I couldn't let my behavior lead to Silas's demise. Not after everything we'd been through together. He deserved a chance. I would do anything to see that through. Including playing nice with the royal I'd rather kill than fuck.

Kylan had ruined everything.

No, that wasn't true. I'd ruined it by biting him. By reacting to him.

He pressed an openmouthed kiss to my neck. "Has anyone ever bitten you, Raelyn?"

I clenched my teeth at his use of that ridiculous name. "Does it matter?" I countered, avoiding his question. "You're just going to bite me anyway." And use my body for his physical enjoyment.

Of all the royals to pick me, it had to be the one with a fondness for violence. The recent slaughtering of his harem had been a popular discussion amongst my vampire professors. No one had actually cared about the lives lost, just the wasted blood and the very real possibility that Kylan was going insane.

And now he owned me.

His incisors skated over my pulse in warning. "When I ask you a question, I expect an answer. Have you been bitten?"

My nails dug into his flat abdomen.

For Silas, I reminded myself. *Do it to save him. Then, when he's on his way to the next stage, you can push back.*

Because no way in hell was I going to willingly lie with this royal vampire. Gorgeous or not, I'd rather die. And I would go down fighting.

"No," I forced myself to say. "I have not."

He smiled against my neck. "Mmm, another point in your favor." He kissed my throat, then my jaw, and returned his dark eyes to mine. "Keep intriguing me, Raelyn, and I may just let you live." He tucked my hair behind my ear before palming my nape. "How were your test scores in sexual studies?"

He would ask that because that's all a man in his position cared about. Yet, I felt compelled to correct him on that score. "My ratings in all subjects were at the top of my class."

"I imagine they would be to qualify you for the Immortal Cup," he murmured. "But I want your sexual arts scores in detail. What acts do you excel in, and what techniques require more"—his gaze dropped to the jacket covering my breasts—"training?"

"Kylan?" the Goddess called, causing him to shift his focus to where she stood. "Have you made a decision? The others are finished."

"Hmm." He glanced down at me, his cruel gaze unreadable. "Answer me, Raelyn." The *or else* remained unsaid.

I swallowed. *They're just test results like any other course.* "I'm rated as excelling in oral activities, and my pain tolerance is well above average. The only area I ever received a somewhat negative score in was submissive play, but I still ranked above average compared to my class." And the only reason I received that negative score was because I had a hard time giving up control when Silas led our exercises together. It just felt wrong to submit to him, regardless of how talented he was in the art of foreplay.

Kylan's lips curled. "Thank you, Raelyn." He whirled me in his arms, placing my back to his chest again, his hand at my throat while his opposite arm wrapped around my lower abdomen.

Silas's blue gaze flashed to mine, fear radiating from their depths.

I'll be fine, I tried to tell him. *Don't show them you care.*

The silence stretched, Kylan's grip tightening.

I will not cry.

I will not beg.

I will remain calm.

Black spots danced before my eyes, but not before I caught the pain in Silas's features.

Goddess, I hoped Kylan didn't pick him. But I knew he would. This had all been a cruel game to force me to speak, to make an example of my behavior.

It had all gone so wrong. So horribly wrong.

I'm sorry, Silas. I'm so fucking sorry.

Kylan's thumb brushed my weakening pulse, his touch a brand against my skin. "It seems breath play may be something to explore later," he whispered against my ear. He lessened his hold just enough to allow air to flow back into my lungs. I sucked it in greedily, my gaze blurring from the humiliation of my body's necessary reaction.

A weakness.

I hated him in that moment more than any other.

He was fucking with me.

Pretending to kill me, just to drive home how easy it would be, and he'd made Silas watch.

"I think I'll enjoy breaking this one, Lilith," Kylan said, a smile in his voice. "Thank you for granting me the opportunity to keep her."

"If you're sure," she replied. "Seems more work than it's worth."

"Oh, I could use the amusement." He stroked the column of my neck while keeping his palm tight against my throat. I could breathe, but only barely, and the arm banded around my lower stomach wasn't helping.

"Well then, that concludes our selection process. Now there's just the matter of evening the ranks left of our Immortal Cup participants."

I counted the remaining members and found only six left. All the others had been selected. Two of them were on the ground, their chests unmoving and lower halves… I looked away, unable to process what had been done to them. One body was formerly Daniella.

That could have been me…

Kylan's grip loosened a bit more, his lips brushing my temple as if sensing the direction of my thoughts.

But no. That was impossible. If he could read minds, I'd be a dead woman because he'd see all the ways in which I'd love to kill him. Vampires couldn't die—or so they said—but I'd love to find a way to take him down. Make *him* beg *me* to breathe.

"Jace, Walter, please." The Goddess made a gesture as if to say, *Fix it.*

Jace handed his new harem member to the vampire beside him—a dark-haired male I didn't recognize as a royal. Beside him stood a woman with dark hair and matching eyes, wearing a formal gown made of translucent material. Her gaze was on the ground.

A human. But not from the selection. I'd missed her before, as well as her Sire, who was now looking directly at me with striking green eyes. I lowered my gaze with a flinch.

Have I completely lost my mind today?

No, just my life.

"She's a blood virgin," Kylan said softly against my ear. "And she's recently mated to Darius, Jace's new sovereign."

I blinked. Did he just explain something to me?

And what the hell was a blood virgin?

I glanced at the woman again. Gorgeous, well groomed, and no sign of fear. She appeared bored, like her master, who had refocused on the events unfolding before us. Jace had selected two humans, his palms on their shoulders. Walter had one and seemed to be struggling to find a second.

Silas hadn't moved, his posture confident while his gaze remained averted. *Good luck*, I wanted to tell him. *Not that you need it.*

Kylan's palm slid up to my chin, forcing my head back at an angle that met his gaze. "What did I say about it being over, Raelyn?" he asked softly, his pupils flaring in the moonlight.

My neck ached from the uncomfortable position coupled with the pain of having been nearly strangled. I tried to reply and couldn't, my throat raw. Tears gathered behind my eyes again, making me hate him more. I never cried. Never begged. Never complained. Yet, not even an hour in his presence and I wanted to weep.

I want to kill you, I told him with my eyes since my voice refused me.

He smiled before releasing me, his hands falling to my hips to keep me against him. His erection pressed into my backside, confirming the hatred between us was not mutual.

Fucking him would be my worst nightmare come to life. Because while my mind despised him, my body would react favorably.

His strength and power served as an aphrodisiac, and his face was crafted by the heavens. A gorgeous male encased in muscle and experience—I couldn't deny the physical appeal. And from what I understood, a vampire's bite possessed an ecstasy unlike anything a human could give to another.

He would take from me what he wanted, and a sick part of me would enjoy it while the rest of me loathed him.

His lips traced my neck again, his breath hot against my skin. "I'm going to destroy you, little lamb," he whispered darkly. "You'll never think of him again when we're done."

A chill swept down my spine. Because he was right. Once he fractured my soul, I'd no longer have cause to think about anyone, let alone Silas.

I lowered my gaze, a feeling of defeat settling inside of me.

So many I knew desired this destiny, to live in a life of luxury with the royals or alphas. But seeing the field around me, the already broken bodies, feeling the aroused male at my back threatening my fate, I realized it was all just a glamour. A false sense of hope instilled in us at birth to keep us in line. And for what? The minute chance at immortality?

Was it worth it?

Silas would say yes. I hoped.

"These are the prospects you wish to add?" the Goddess asked, her voice filled with surprise.

"They won't survive, nor are they lycan material. Send them for the chance." Walter sounded disgusted as he shoved the humans he selected toward the Immortal Cup selection.

I would have survived, I thought with a mental growl. The two he picked were meek and broken already. At least Jace's selections held merit, even if they stood no chance against Silas, or even me.

But I'm no longer competing.

To have the fate I desired for so long ripped from my fingers after only minutes of experiencing the potential glory was a cruel act indeed. Yet, so very fitting.

Vampires and lycans loved to play with their food and their pets.

This was no different.

Kylan's arms circled me again, his touch holding a hint of comfort I immediately rejected. He was no better than the rest of them. In fact, he was worse.

Words rolled through the air, the Goddess commending those chosen for the Immortal Cup, something about harem training, and a dismissal that all blurred together in my mind. I no longer cared. There wasn't any point.

Silas met my gaze, his holding a mixture of excitement and sorrow that broke my heart.

Kill them all, I told him with mine. *Rise, my friend.*

He gave me a subtle nod before turning to disappear, and Kylan sighed. "If you can't ignore a simple command to forget, then how will I ever train you to serve?"

I bit my tongue. *Don't react yet. Wait until Silas is safe.*

"Follow me, pet," he demanded, releasing me.

My feet threatened to do the opposite, to stand and stare at him in defiance. But my mind pushed me to obey.

He led us past the other royals, who all gave him a wide berth, their discomfort at his presence evident. The rumors claimed him to be going mad, an ancient who was losing his mind to immortality.

I considered that as we walked. His control over me and our situation suggested his mental state to be healthy and clear, strong even. He could just be toying with me, especially since he had suggested killing me a short while ago.

Does it matter? I wondered. *He's going to destroy you, remember?*

A shiver traversed my spine at the thought. He could mean so many things by that statement.

Kylan led me to a small black car with two doors. A beep sounded as he clicked a button, and the door rose. "In you go, little lamb."

Several humans stood near waiting cars, the other royals and alphas slowly making their way toward us. It appeared Kylan had led the pack.

He cocked a brow at my hesitation. "Disobeying me again?"

Always, I very nearly replied. Instead, I slid into the bucket seat and stared straight ahead. His chuckle was stilted by the closing of the door, but he still wore a grin as he climbed into the driver's seat beside me.

"Seat belt," he said, leaning over me to grab the item in question. "Safety first."

Alone in a car with a sadistic vampire. Yep. Very safe.

"Silence," he said, buckling himself in as well. "You're boring me again, Raelyn."

"Would you prefer I sing and dance?" I asked as Jace strolled by our car with his arm around the female Kylan had called a blood virgin. Darius moved behind them with the new harem member at his side. "You don't have any sovereigns," I said, recalling my studies about Kylan's territory. "I've always found that odd."

The engine purred to life, the throaty sound powerful like its master. "Sovereigns are trusted minions," Kylan replied as he pulled out of his spot. "And I trust no one."

A female appeared in front of our car, hands on her hips, causing Kylan to come to an abrupt stop before exiting the parking lot.

The royal female cocked her head to the side, causing him to sigh.

"Right." He put the car in park but didn't turn off the engine. "Don't touch anything or I'll be forced to punish you." He flashed me a look that said he meant the threat. "Now stay like a good little pet."

Chapter Four

RAE

MY PALMS ACHED FROM HOW HARD I dug my nails into my skin. Vampires and lycans had spoken down to me all my life, but never quite so condescendingly.

Kylan stepped out of the car without a backward glance before meeting the woman—Robyn—in front of me. He wrapped his hand around her neck and pulled her into a kiss that left me feeling sick to my stomach.

Vampires were always affectionate. These two were no different, but the way he handled her denoted a history I wanted to know nothing about.

Robyn's hands went to his sides before sliding up his black dress shirt to his shoulders, feeling him as if she owned him. He smiled against her mouth before catching her wrists in his free hand. Whatever he said to her in reprimand created a smile that was all female satisfaction.

I rolled my eyes and looked for her recent acquisition. He knelt on the ground—still naked—with his head bowed. She'd put a metal collar around his neck and connected it to a leash she'd dropped in favor of touching Kylan.

Whatever he said to her next had her lips flattening into a scowl. Then she looked directly at me in the passenger seat. Barbarity lurked in her eyes, making me reconsider Kylan's reputation as the cruel one. Because that look left nothing to the imagination as to what she wanted to do to me.

Kylan wanted to destroy me.

This woman wanted to shred me.

I should look away, but to what purpose? My fate was already sealed and in the hands of a monster.

Robyn started toward the car, but Kylan caught her by the elbow and yanked her back to him, his elegant expression morphing into the powerful predator lurking beneath the fancy clothes.

I couldn't hear them, but the conversation was clearly not in her favor. She scowled at him but lowered her gaze in submission. He kissed her on the head, as if praising a pet. Whatever platitudes he whispered seemed to calm her slightly, but her hands remained fisted as he walked away.

"I'll see you again soon, Robyn," he said as he opened the door.

"Yes," the woman replied as she retrieved the leash. She yanked the human toward her with so much force he skidded across the gravel.

I flinched at the display, my lips parting as she forced the male to crawl after her as she walked away at a clipped pace.

Kylan navigated us away from the scene, leaving me quite relieved despite not knowing our future destination. He'd given me his jacket and treated me somewhat humanely compared to the others. My neck still ached from his attentions, but I preferred that over a leash and collar.

And the sexual exploits in the field… I shivered. Kylan could have done much worse. So why didn't he?

Silence settled between us, both comforting and ominous, as he pulled onto a vacant road with the moonlight illuminating our path. Nothing existed out here apart from farmland. No buildings or other structures, no signs of the city, just the stars in a black sky. It was actually sort of peaceful, unlike the surroundings of my former university. Snipers, guards, cement walls lined with barbwire, and sky lights were the primary scenery.

Hmm, I wished there were trees here. I'd never seen one, but the grassy landscape, even in the night, was gorgeous.

"Robyn relishes in breaking her toys," Kylan said, his voice soft.

I glanced away from the serenity around us to eye the devil beside me. "And you?" I asked, unable to help myself. "What do you prefer?" *I'm going to destroy you,* his words from earlier whispered through my thoughts, taunting me.

"I adore submission," he murmured, his lips curling. "But I love a fighter."

Our surroundings whipped by us as he accelerated, my stomach churning both from the unfamiliar momentum and his reply. He wanted me to oppose him, to say no. That was why he chose me—because he knew I wouldn't submit easily.

He wants to force me to accept him physically. To hurt me in the harshest of ways, by taking my body whether I liked it or not.

A tremble I couldn't hide shook me to my core. I'd seen this done countless times, had heard the screams, had even witnessed it tonight on the field. But to know he craved it, that he was taking me home with every intention of injuring me, caused bile to rise in my throat.

He's going to kill me, but only after he fucks me.

And there's nothing I can do to stop him.

"Ah, there it is, the fear that's been missing all evening," he mused. "You were one of the few who didn't display an ounce of it during the selection. It's what drew me to you."

He turned without slowing, causing my insides to twist violently. I pressed the back of my hand to my lips, refusing to be sick. Not here. Not yet. Not this easily.

Lights appeared in the distance, bright and white, with a few red dots spaced between. It grew as we approached, highlighting a wider road on the other side of a wired fence. Beyond it sat an item I'd only ever seen in my books.

A plane.

My lips parted in awe. It was so much bigger than I expected. Several bodies stood around, all dressed in black, a few of them guarding the gate Kylan navigated us toward at a much steadier pace.

"Your Highness," a human greeted, his gaze briefly looking me over in Kylan's jacket. "Everything is ready."

"Thank you, Jackson," Kylan replied, surprising me.

He knows the human's name?

Most vampires didn't acknowledge mortals, even Vigils.

Kylan drove around to the back of the aircraft to a ramp and maneuvered onto it with minimal direction from the humans standing guard. After pulling all the way inside, he shut off the engine and waited as the ramp lifted behind us, sealing us in the belly of the plane.

His dark eyes slid to mine, studying, saying nothing. I didn't dare look away, needing to know what he planned. He unfastened his seat belt and slowly leaned toward me.

My palms dampened. *This is it. He's going to hurt me now and expect me to struggle against him.*

Could I?

Would I?

It might be less painful if

The click of my belt startled me from my thoughts. He smirked and exited the car, then walked around to open my door, his palm waiting to assist me.

I frowned at him and stood on my own.

"It's considered quite rude to ignore a formal gesture from a superior." He nudged the door closed with a finality that shook my spine. "I'm beginning to question your schooling and how you've survived this long."

So am I. Because I never acted like this in school. While rebellious thoughts often occurred, I never acted on them. I knew better. But with Kylan? I wanted nothing more than to punch him in the face.

And now that Silas was safe, I could.

Kylan caught my wrist before I lifted it and whirled me in his arms, placing my back to his front. He tsked against my ear. "I want a challenge in the bedroom, not in the garage, darling."

"Well, this looks fun," a male voice announced from behind us.

"You have no idea," Kylan replied, his thickening groin pressing into my backside. "Raelyn, this is Mikael, my blood virgin. Mikael, meet my new toy, Raelyn." He pushed me forward, causing me to stumble as I tried to regain my balance on my heels. I spun to face them both.

Mikael walked down a set of stairs to stand at Kylan's side, his blond hair long and brushing his broad shoulders. He wore a black suit that matched his master's, minus the tie, leaving his collar open at the neck.

"She's pretty," he murmured appraisingly, his light gaze running over me. "I like the added touch of dressing her in your clothes, Your Highness."

Kylan smirked. "Yes, she does wear my jacket rather well, doesn't she?"

"Mmm."

"Shall I ask her to remove it for you?"

Mikael scratched the stubble on his jaw, his gaze heating. "I would enjoy seeing the full package, yes."

"Raelyn?" Kylan asked, cocking a brow.

He wanted me to strip for his pet human? "No." If he wanted me to remove the jacket, he could do it himself.

Mikael's blond brows shot up as Kylan chuckled. "Isn't she fantastic?"

"Did she just deny you?"

"She did." Kylan cocked his head to the side, a smile playing over his lips. "Shall we try to entice her into stripping for us?"

"We could," Mikael replied, sounding perplexed. "But we've never had to in the past."

Kylan shrugged. "Perhaps I should explain how this is going to work."

"Can we do it upstairs in the lounge? The pilots are waiting to take off and won't while we're in the undercarriage." The human spoke with Kylan so casually, as if they were friends, that it shocked me into silence.

"Of course." Kylan held out a hand. "Come, Raelyn."

And my shock melted into irritation. "Woof. Woof."

Kylan chuckled again. "Do you require a collar, darling? Like the one Robyn gave her new pet? I do think I'd enjoy watching you crawl."

The image of the royal with that poor male was still fresh and flashed with precision behind my eyes. I shuddered at the memory.

"I didn't think so," Kylan murmured, his fingers waving impatiently. "Come here, Raelyn, or I'll drag you by your hair."

"I'd listen to him," Mikael added, turning toward the stairs. "The man doesn't bluff."

I gritted my teeth and strode forward, ignoring Kylan's hand. He grabbed me by the elbow and yanked me backward so hard I lost my balance and fell into him.

"That's two times you've ignored a polite gesture from me. Would you prefer me to be harsher with you?" he asked, his hands gripping my arms painfully as he kept me standing. "Because I can be, Raelyn."

I winced from his tightening grasp but refused to give him the satisfaction of an apology. "Silas is no longer here for you to use against me. I have nothing left."

His lips twitched. "Silas. An intriguing name for a prospect." He pulled me closer, his lightheartedness disappearing beneath a shadow of darkness. "Just because *Silas* isn't here doesn't mean I can't hurt him. He's in the tournament now. All it takes is a message to the organizers and your former lover will experience an accident he'll never recover from."

My heart skipped a beat. "You'd hurt him to tame me?"

"I'd do a lot more than hurt him, darling." The promise in his words pierced my chest, stirring up the nausea from the car again.

My stomach rolled, my throat working. *Don't throw up. Don't do it.* I swallowed, but the burn of acid brought tears to my eyes. Or maybe that was brought on by the heaviness settling over me.

Silas's life is in my hands.

One wrong move and Kylan would carry out his threat. How could I resist him, knowing the repercussions?

My shoulders sagged. There was no choice. "I'll do whatever you want."

Kylan's brows rose. "For a male you'll never see again?"

I didn't bother replying. My loyalty to Silas was none of his concern. "Do you still wish for me to remove the jacket?" Because I would. And I'd crawl, if he so desired it.

His grip loosened, his eyes narrowing. "He's a human you'll never see again, Raelyn. And if he wins, he'll forget all about you. Why give up your fire for him?"

I met his gaze with a sigh, my body more exhausted than it had been in a long time. "Because he at least has a chance at a future. I wouldn't jeopardize that for anything in the world, even my own dignity." I moved out of his grip and let the jacket fall from my shoulders. "I'll do whatever you want, Your Highness," I repeated more formally.

Defeated, I turned toward the stairs, ready to face my fate.

Kylan wanted a fighter in the bedroom.

Well, he'd just extinguished my flames.

Hopefully, he'd settle for a submissive instead.

Chapter Five

KYLAN

I WATCHED RAELYN ASCEND THE STAIRS to where Mikael stood waiting at the top platform. He raised a brow in question and I nodded, knowing what he intended to do.

The girl needed a shower, clothes, and food. Mikael, being human, would be able to handle all of that better than me. He always took care of my harem, and in return, most of them usually cared for him. We established the relationship after I purchased him from an auction a decade ago. Sometimes we shared the females, but only when they preferred it.

Raelyn assumed a great many things that I should have clarified in the car but chose not to. Sometimes actions spoke louder than words. And in time, she would realize I had no intention of forcing her to do anything with me. I preferred my partners willing, and when I mentioned loving a woman with courage, I meant a female who could challenge me in the bedroom, not lie there and take it.

Rape was for the weak.

I was not weak.

If Raelyn preferred isolation, I'd allow it. Her relationship with the human—Silas—went deeper than I had originally realized. When I used him against her, it was merely a tool to keep her in line so the others wouldn't kill her. And my words just now were only meant to taunt her but had the completely wrong effect.

Killing her spirit was never my intention. I needed her strong to face the trials to come. Because someone was framing me by painting me as an immortal gone mad with age. They destroyed my harem, leaving me with the choice of claiming the massacre or admitting that someone had breached my territory. Neither was acceptable, both suggesting a weakness. But I'd rather be known as a mad immortal than an inadequate one.

With a sigh, I retrieved my jacket and trailed after Mikael and Raelyn.

Mikael was one of very few who knew the truth. He'd been with me long enough to know I'd never harm my harem, even out of boredom. And we'd mourned their loss together.

I'd chosen Raelyn for her resilience, knowing I needed a replacement who could stand up for herself. Yet, now, I wasn't as certain in my choice. She loved another male, something I could tolerate even if it did have me considering ways to destroy him, and she was willing to sacrifice herself for him.

Mikael met me in the hallway near the jet's only bedroom, a glass of champagne laced with blood in his hand. I traded him my coat for the flute. "You always bring me the best gifts."

He grinned as he hung my jacket in the closet beside us. "You looked like you could use it after that display downstairs."

I snorted and sipped the bubbly liquid with a sigh. "Yeah, I think I messed that up."

"Just a bit," he agreed, his dimples flashing. "But we'll fix it. She's lying down, though, and refusing to shower or eat. To use her words, she just wants to get it over with."

My lips twitched. "Poor darling expects a quick performance."

"Apparently."

"I'll prove her wrong, but not tonight." She was nowhere near ready for me. I'd rather have her begging me to fuck her than taking her in a dull state. "Can you let the pilots know we're ready for takeoff? I'm more than ready to go home."

"Only if you go talk to her in the interim." He pointed at the door. "Explain the rules, at a minimum."

I set the glass aside. "You're always such a spoilsport."

"And you're an ass," he returned, not at all afraid to voice his opinion. "Go show her who you really are so she stops pouting. It's unbecoming."

"Unbecoming," I repeated, shaking my head. "You would use that term."

"Stop stalling or I'll withhold blood."

I raised a brow. "Now you're attempting to be in charge? What the fuck is happening to the world today?"

He chuckled and tried to move past me, but I grabbed his hip, pulling him to me. I brushed my lips over his pulse, his essence singing to my instincts. Blood virgins were rare and delectable and addictive, but I always paced myself with Mikael. I'd chosen a male because, while I had no problem drinking from him, he wasn't my preference sexually. Which meant I never lost control with him, even when he encouraged me to.

"You can't deny me anything," I whispered, my tongue teasing his vein.

He shuddered against me, his hands going to my sides. "I would never want to."

I pierced his neck, just enough for a taste and to tease him with my endorphins. His cock hardened against mine, his body always receptive to whatever I wanted to give him and more. Sharing women with him was easy as a result. We both enjoyed it, and each other, but never engaged in acts alone with just the two of us. It wasn't my preference, nor his.

He groaned as I pulled away, and I smiled. "What was that about withholding blood?"

"Fuck you," he growled, his light eyes aroused. "Go talk to her."

I shrugged. "Only because I want to."

"I bet." He ran his fingers through his long hair and wandered off down the hall toward the main seating area. "I'm borrowing Zelda for a bit. Don't come looking for us."

I smirked. "Is that why you brought my favorite chef along for the journey?"

"No, I knew the girl would need food, but now I'm going to use Zelda to feed something else." He glanced over his shoulder with a smolder. "So I hope you're not hungry, because we'll be busy for a while."

I chuckled. "We'll fend for ourselves." As I assumed he or Zelda had already left food in the bedroom. I hadn't eaten much with tonight's festivities, and they would know that.

"You always do," Mikael replied with another flash of those dimples and disappeared toward the front of the jet.

With a shake of my head, I knocked on the bedroom door. Raelyn didn't respond. I took her silence as permission to enter and found her curled up on the edge of the bed, staring at the wall. Her high heels were on the floor, tucked against the wall, leaving her completely nude.

I loosened my tie and removed my cuff links to roll my sleeves to the elbows. Raelyn shifted her toned legs but remained infuriatingly silent. My taunts regarding the boy had clearly pushed her too far. Such a pity. I had hoped it would take a lot more than that to subdue the courageous spirit inside of her.

Humans were fragile beings, most of them shattering with a mere glance. But this one held promise. I'd just have to coax her defiant side back out to play.

I placed my shoes beside hers and stood before her, hand on my belt. "Shall we test your oral skills first?" Just the idea of it had me hardening, but I had no intention of following through. I merely wanted a reaction.

Her lips flattening was all she gave me.

I sighed and moved to the opposite side of the bed to lie down beside her. "You're boring me again, Raelyn."

Nothing. Not even a flinch.

"Do I need to bring up Silas to make you cooperate?" I asked, curious. "Is that how I provoke the reaction I desire?"

"What do you want from me?" she demanded, rolling to face me. "You want me to suck your cock? To prove my high marks?" Her hand went to my belt. "Because I can do that if it's what you want. Just tell me so I can get it over with."

I let her get as far as unfastening the buckle before I grabbed her wrist to still her movements. "Your skills in foreplay and pillow talk clearly require development."

I pressed her hand into the pillow beside her head and nudged her onto her back, my thigh sliding between her legs as I settled over her.

She grabbed my shoulder with her free hand, pushing. I tsked and captured both of her wrists beneath one of my palms over her head while my opposite hand went to her throat. The bruise blossoming over her skin confirmed I'd been too rough with her earlier. I'd meant it as a demonstration to my brethren, to show I had her well under control, but seeing the mark now left me uneasy.

"Are you sore?"

"Because you care?" she growled, causing me to smile.

"You know nothing about me, little lamb," I whispered. "Only what society has shown you."

"I think the last few hours, or however long it's been, in your presence have shown me what I need to know."

"Is that so?" I tilted my head, holding her gaze. "And what do you know, Raelyn?"

Those gorgeous baby blues narrowed at me, thrilling me. *There you are, darling. Come play with me. Intrigue me.*

"I offered you my jacket when you were cold," I murmured, recounting the evening. "I didn't just bend you over and fuck you the way several of the others did to their new toys, and I didn't let Robyn punish you after you boldly stared her down from the car. I also allowed you to live when few others would never have tolerated your disobedience. So, tell me, darling, what all does that say about me?"

The bed rumbled beneath us as the jet picked up speed, causing her gaze to fly to the nearby window. I allowed her the moment and released her hands, expecting she may want to grab on to the headboard or bed. She latched onto my shoulders instead, her expression filled with a mixture of wonder and concern as we accelerated into the air.

Most humans had never flown, at least not consciously. It was far easier to drug them and stow them away on a massive cargo plane, like one would cattle. Her lips parted, her eyes widening.

"Would you like to look out the window?" I asked, amused.

Her gaze flew to mine. "I, no, I…" She swallowed, her brow furrowing. "I've never, I mean—"

"I know." I tucked a strand of hair behind her ear while balancing on my elbows on either side of her head. "If you want to look out the window, you can, but be careful." I started to roll off her, but her grip tightened, fear tinging the air.

Flying scared her, but my lips near her neck did not.

I almost laughed. Society had deadened her to the obvious threat who happened to be lying on top of her. No wonder most of the humans came to me broken.

She started to relax as the plane stabilized, her brow smoothing out on a sigh. It wasn't until she met my gaze again that she realized she'd basically clung to me the entire time, but rather than let go, she froze.

"Tell me again what you know about me?" I taunted, unable to help myself. I pressed my lips to her throat—gently—and nuzzled her jaw. "Mikael wants me to tell you the rules. Sometimes he fancies himself in charge, but he's not."

It had taken a year to unleash the personality he kept hidden beneath the Coventus's indoctrinated training. He barely resembled the male I purchased from that dreadful auction. Mikael was much stronger now and not afraid to call me on my shit, making him a good friend and an even better partner.

"That's my first rule," I continued. "This is my territory, Raelyn. You are now mine and you will do as I say, which includes allowing Mikael to care for you." I considered that the second rule. "So if he tells you to shower and put on clothes, you shower and put on clothes."

Her gaze narrowed. "You're the one who told me to remove the jacket."

My lips twitched. "No, I asked if you wanted to remove it. You were the one who chose to drop the jacket."

"No, that's not—"

I pressed my mouth to hers, silencing the argument.

She'd inferred my comment as a demand, which I may have done on purpose, but the fact remained that I'd never actually commanded she drop my coat. Her lips remained flat beneath mine, not yielding or receptive, which brought us to my next rule.

Forcing a woman in the bedroom held little appeal.

However, seducing an unwilling woman, I very much enjoyed. Especially one who didn't want to be attracted to me.

This was my unspoken rule, one that Mikael understood, that I would never voice out loud. What would be the fun in putting Raelyn at ease? I much preferred her defiant and hating me. Her submission would taste so much sweeter as a result.

I rolled us so I lay beneath her, her legs straddling my hips, and tucked my hands beneath my head. She sat up, her palms on my abdomen for balance, her chest heaving from the shock of our rapid movement.

"You have gorgeous breasts," I praised, admiring the rosy peaks and the firmness of her tits. The subtle curve of her waist led to the shaved apex between her thighs. Whoever forced her to remove those beautiful red curls needed a good beating because I bet she was gorgeous when properly groomed.

I slowly returned my gaze to hers and found her cheeks flushed to a delectable pink shade. Mmm, yes, I enjoyed that almost as much as the glowering.

"I don't… What do you want from me, Kylan?"

My name in her throaty purr of a voice went straight to my groin. Humans rarely addressed superior beings by their given names, and the way her hand covered her mouth now said she'd just realized her error. Her blue eyes widened. "I… I… I didn't—"

"You may call me Kylan when we're alone. In fact, I prefer it." Mikael always used my formal title of *Your Highness*. It could be kinky, but it grew old when everyone referred to me as such.

Her shoulders relaxed, her palm falling to my abdomen. She didn't seem fazed at all by her nudity—a conditioning my brethren had ingrained in her. I should feel bad about that, but I really couldn't.

"What do you want from me?" she asked—again—her voice barely a whisper.

"What don't I want from you, darling?" I reached for her, wrapped my palm around the back of her neck, and dragged her over me, placing her mouth a scant inch from mine. "What do you think I want from you?"

"T-to challenge you."

I nipped her bottom lip. "Good girl." I kissed her again—because I could and I wanted to—and smiled when she growled.

"I'm not a dog."

"No, you're definitely not," I murmured, licking the seam of her mouth. "Open for me, princess."

"I don't—"

My tongue interrupted her, my yearning to really kiss her taking over. The exploration on the field was just the beginning. I craved more, needed to properly taste her, to *know* her.

She grabbed my biceps, her arms tensing to push away. I tightened my hold on her nape and grabbed her hip to rotate us again, placing her back against the mattress and settling myself between her splayed thighs. Her nails dug into my shirt, causing me to smile. "That's it, Raelyn," I whispered. "Keep protesting. We both know you don't mean it."

"I hate you," she panted, her hips arching into mine in direct contrast to her words.

"I know." I would hate me, too. This world. This life. What current society had demeaned her to. There wasn't a damn thing I could do to stop it, but that didn't mean I accepted it. Mikael was proof of that. My treatment of her, even now, also a testament to my core beliefs. I recognized my position of power over her—a right my kind earned by being the superior species. But did that make it right? A question I often pondered.

She groaned into my mouth, her palm sliding up my arm to my neck, her fingers digging into my hair as her tongue finally responded to mine.

Because she wanted this? Or because she wanted to trick me into stopping?

Clever girl knew I wanted a challenge and giving in was the opposite of that request. Although, the arousal dampening my trousers suggested it might be a mixture of both defiance and lust. An intoxicating invitation that I accepted by deepening our kiss, taking command of our mouths and teaching her what I preferred. She reciprocated in kind, her nipples hardening into alluring little points against my chest.

Oh, she approved, even though I knew she didn't want to.

I pressed my erection against her welcoming heat, coating my pants in the evidence of her mutual appreciation. My lips brushed her cheek, sliding to her ear. "You're making quite a mess for someone who supposedly hates me." Her breath hitched at my words, causing me to smile. "I should make you lick my trousers clean in punishment for lying, darling. Teach you a lesson in humility and truth."

"My body might approve," she said on a sharp exhale. "But my mind never will."

Yes, there was the challenge I coveted. I nuzzled her neck, luxuriating in her escalating pulse. "Just give me time, little lamb. I'll conquer your mind just as easily as your body."

"Never."

"Maybe I'll go for your heart too," I whispered darkly. "Steal it from Silas." Just saying the human's name cooled my ardor. Having a pet who fancied another certainly did not appeal. At all. "How did you two manage to hide your relationship?" It was unlawful for humans to engage in affairs. Bonding could lead to uprisings, and Lilith certainly didn't want anything to impact her queendom.

Raelyn stilled beneath me, her breathing all but stopping.

I pulled back to meet her gaze. "Worried I'll tell someone? Ruin his chances at immortality?" Because it would. One breathed word about their forbidden connection would have him killed. A human with a weakness was not worthy of immortality by most standards.

Her lower lip trembled as tears marred her beautiful gaze. "What do you need me to do?" she asked, her voice broken. "I don't… Please don't…"

Ah, there was that sacrifice again, her willingness to do whatever I wanted just to protect a mortal boy she'd never see again. Such a human reaction. Impractical and contrary to a warrior's mentality. Silas truly meant a lot to her, but from experience, I knew the male wouldn't reciprocate her loyalty. Survivors did whatever they needed to remain alive, something she would do well to remember.

I pushed away from her before I did something truly catastrophic. Like make a phone call while she listened and request the male be strangled and killed on live video. I had more than enough cause to convict him, Immortal Cup status or not.

"Kylan," she pleaded, her voice breaking.

Definitely not the kind of begging I preferred in the bedroom.

I'd give her this moment, this night, to get over it. Blood Day was intimidating and emotional, and having her recruited to my bed likely hadn't been at the top of her selection list.

But she needed to realize there were a lot of worse places she could have gone.

My reputation paled in comparison to some of the others, a fact she would soon learn. Especially if Robyn followed up on her request to visit.

"Get some sleep, Raelyn. You're going to need your strength if you intend to remain alive in this world." I wove compulsion into my words, knowing she'd ignore me otherwise. We had a long flight ahead of us. She may as well use it to rest.

I paused at the door, my hand on the knob.

Fuck.

I couldn't help the glance over my shoulder. Raelyn had succumbed to slumber as I willed her to, but not before allowing those tears to fall. They streaked over her delicate features, destroying her warrior mask.

"Such wasted promise," I said, sighing.

I almost left her but couldn't. If she slept in that position, her neck would be worse in the morning, and I'd already done enough damage.

She felt frail in my arms as I shifted her in the bed, sliding her legs and torso beneath the covers. Her red hair spilled across the pillows, reminding me of fresh blood. My thumb drifted over her steadying pulse as I wondered if the colors would match.

"We'll try again tomorrow, Raelyn." She couldn't hear me, but the words were for me more than her.

Normally, I would hand her over to Mikael and leave him to groom her. But as my sole harem member, I felt obligated to keep her safe. There was a target on her back, not because of anything she did, but because someone wanted to portray me as insane. Until I resolved that issue, her life, quite literally, rested at my feet.

I always fiercely protected my territory, and Raelyn would be no different. It meant we'd be spending more time together than I usually did with my humans. We'd have to make it fun, which would be difficult if she only lived to protect another.

There had to be more to her existence than a boy. I just had to find what made her tick. Good thing I enjoyed challenges.

I tucked the blankets around her shoulders and brushed a kiss against her temple. "Sweet dreams, little lamb."

Chapter Six

RAE

LIGHT SURROUNDED ME. Dull, white, and foreign.

I blinked, my gaze on the floor-to-ceiling windows and the whiteness beyond it.

Mountains, my mind supplied. *Real mountains.*

"No fucking way," I breathed, rolling out of the flannel blankets and bounding toward the closed doors of a balcony. A twist of the handle allowed a cold burst of air into the room, but I didn't care.

There. Were. Mountains. Outside.

And trees.

Real. Trees.

I stepped through the threshold and flinched as my bare feet touched the cold texture below.

Snow.

My mouth fell open as I dropped to my knees, my hands going into the fluffy whiteness and coming away frigid. "Oh!" That was so cold, but so beautiful. I repeated the action, thrilled by the phenomenon I'd only read about in books.

The moon vibrantly displayed the grounds, illuminating every silvery detail. That was the cause of the foreign brightness—the clear night sky and nearly full moon bouncing off the wintry landscape.

My lips parted in awe even as my limbs began to shiver. "It's so beautiful,"

I marveled to myself, shocked.

"Yes," a deep male voice replied.

I jolted backward into something—someone—hard. Warm arms came around me, immediately dispelling the coolness from outside. Only then did I realize someone had clothed me in pajama pants and a shirt.

Kylan.

"Welcome to my home, Raelyn."

I blinked. This was his home. His room. Because he owned me. Because I'd been selected for his harem, to be fucked however he pleased until I died.

This was now my life.

My excitement died on an exhale. There would be no exploring or enjoying the scenery. Only submitting to the royal behind me.

"You need to eat," he murmured, his lips against my neck.

My stomach grumbled in agreement, reminding me that it'd been hours, maybe even days, since I'd last eaten. Mikael had tried on the plane, gesturing to a plate of food on the nightstand. I hadn't bothered, not wanting to be sick when Kylan touched me afterward.

But now, I had no choice. Not eating would only weaken me, and I couldn't afford that in Kylan's presence. That I'd slept as long as I had said a lot about my debilitating state already.

"More silence," he said on a sigh. "How repetitive." He spun me, my feet slipping over the cool ground. His hands caught my face, his dark eyes smoldering. "You will eat."

"I never said I wouldn't," I retorted, irritated that he was already manhandling me. "And if you'd given me more than two seconds to acclimate, I would have replied."

His eyebrows lifted as though impressed. "Much better."

I almost rolled my eyes. Almost. "You must lead a very boring existence if this is entertaining to you." I couldn't believe I was saying these words out loud. It had to be this location overwhelming my senses, because I knew better than to speak to a vampire, let alone a royal, in this manner. But damn, the man was infuriating.

His mouth curled into a feral grin. "You have no idea, sweetheart."

And I had no desire to know. "I thought you wanted me to eat."

"I do."

"Then why are you holding me like this?"

"Because I want to." He tightened his grip. "And I can."

"Fine," I snapped.

"Fine," he snapped back.

We stared each other down, his dark eyes on my light ones, my feet freezing in the snow. I desperately wanted to turn back around to gawk at the mountains once more, but his thumbs held my chin in place. The ice spread from my toes to my limbs, sending a shiver up my spine. While the snow was very pretty, it was also extremely cold. My teeth started to chatter, causing me to clench my jaw in protest.

Kylan dropped his hands to my hips and lifted me before nudging the door closed with his boot. He sported jeans and a black turtleneck sweater that I begrudgingly had to admit looked good on him.

He set me down inside a walk-in closet filled with clothes. "Let's get you properly dressed, and I'll take you outside after you eat."

"For a walk?" I asked, a hint of sarcasm in my voice.

His grin was wolfish. "Yes, little pet. For a nice, long walk. Would you like me to grab a collar and leash as well?"

I gave him my best curtsy. "If that's what you want, *Your Highness*."

He laughed out loud and shook his head. "If sleeping makes you this feisty, I'll be forcing you to dream often."

"Forcing me…" My jaw clenched as the realization of why I'd slept so well became abundantly clear. "You compelled me to sleep."

He gave me a sardonic look. "I did a lot more than that." He grabbed my shoulders and spun me toward a rack of feminine outfits. "Pick something."

"Why? You seem to dress me just fine."

"Then you'll go naked."

I shrugged, not caring at all. "If that's your choice."

"You'll freeze outside."

I shrugged again. "That'll hurt you more than me."

"Oh?" He wrapped his arms around my waist, his chin falling to my shoulder. "Do explain your logic."

"A frozen toy is a dead toy." *What the hell is wrong with me?* I was essentially taunting a monster with the idea of making me freeze to death outdoors.

His resulting chuckle vibrated my back. "Oh, Raelyn, you truly are a treat."

Well, while on a roll, I might as well say, "Rae." I spun in his arms, my gaze narrowed. "Raelyn is a ridiculous name."

"The same could be said about Rae."

"Well, that's what I respond to. Either deal with it or expect me to ignore you."

His eyebrows rose. "Where has this bout of confidence come from, my darling lamb?"

"I don't know. Maybe I realized I have nothing to lose, and before you even say it, no. You won't use Silas to taunt me anymore." The words spilled from my mouth as my mind pieced together a crucial piece of our fated puzzle. It just clicked, as things often did, and I couldn't help the smile that followed. "You can't."

Kylan looked far too amused. "Oh, I can't? And why is that?"

"Because you can't," I repeated, feeling elated by my self-discovery.

He wrapped a hand around my neck to walk me backward into the wall beside the clothes. "That is not a satisfactory explanation, Raelyn. Try again."

I refused to let him intimidate me. "If you get rid of Silas, you'll have no more leverage over me, Kylan. I'll be a shell, a broken toy, and then what?"

He'd no longer have any interest in me, and the way he stared down at me now proved it.

A shadow of respect lurked in his shrewd gaze. "How have you survived so long in this world?"

"By being the best in my class." And understanding my opponents better than they understood themselves.

"Because you desired immortality."

"Or to become a Vigil."

He cocked his head to the side, his expression almost evil. "Yet, you ended up in my lair instead."

I tried not to let that last point hurt, but it did. "Only because you picked me."

"If I hadn't, another would have."

"You don't know that."

"Oh, but I do know that. You were marked as fair game. One of the lycans would have selected you in a heartbeat, and that valiant spirit of yours would have been smothered and killed on that field for all to witness." He released me so suddenly that I nearly fell. "It's a cruel play, Raelyn, but you were never meant to fight for immortality. The ceremony was just crafted to make you believe it for a second, to give you that false sense of hope and rip it away for our regal enjoyment. That's how our society works."

He turned and started going through the clothing rack while I gaped at him.

To give you that false sense of hope and rip it away for our regal enjoyment. Was he implying that everything had been staged? That I'd never actually been selected to compete? Just a human pet to be led on and mentally tortured for the cruel entertainment of others?

It matched what I knew of vampires and lycans. And Kylan telling me now only added to the torment.

"Here." He held out a crimson V-neck sweater and a pair of jeans. "These should fit."

I didn't accept them. "I was never meant for the Immortal Cup."

His sinful gaze grabbed mine. "No, you were destined for my bed, which is precisely where I'll put you if you don't start changing clothes."

"And Silas?"

His pupils flared. "The damn human again. How many times have I told you to forget him now? Three, four maybe?"

"Tell me what will happen to him," I demanded, ignoring the annoyance in Kylan's tone. "Is it all just a mind game for him too?"

Kylan dropped the clothes and pushed me up against the wall again, his hands on either side of my head. "You are trying my patience, which, I should warn you, has been extended only for your benefit. Do not push me."

"Then tell me what will happen to him." I grabbed his waist, his silky sweater soft against my palms. "I need to know he has a chance."

"None of you have a chance."

"No." I shook my head, refusing to believe that. "He has one. Tell me he has one."

His brown eyes simmered with violence. He'd kept the predator veiled, but now he peeked at me with unconcealed fury. I would have taken a step back if I weren't already pushed up against the wall.

This is the real Kylan.

The oldest royal in existence.

And I'd just infuriated him.

I swallowed, my mouth trying to form an apology while my heart refused. I had a right to know, didn't I? If this was all just a ruse meant to torment my oldest friend, me, all of us, then I wanted him to admit it. I *needed* him to tell me.

His cheekbones tensed into brutal lines as he growled, "I am not your friend, nor am I someone you have a right to question or command, Raelyn."

He would never tell me. Because he saw me as a pet. A human without rights.

None of us were worthy.

I bowed my head in deference.

For too long a moment I'd forgotten who stood before me. Not a man, not a person, but a royal vampire with a very long history of slaughtering those beneath him.

And right now, it seemed he wanted to kill me.

I'd well and truly lost myself. Standing up to a superior… *Who am I?* I'd been verbally sparring with him the way I would Silas or Willow. I knew better. This was not a human but a supernatural being who could kill me with a flick of his wrist and no one would care.

Because I have no one.

No friends.

No allies.

No choices.

Kylan *owned* me, and I'd dared to stand up to him. No, I'd demanded something from him, had refused from him the comfort of clothes, had rejected his every common courtesy. Why? Because I blamed him for stealing my chances at immortality.

I never had a chance.

What had he called me? Fair game? It had all been a mental device meant to entertain. *Look at the mortal who thinks she's worthy; how adorable is she?*

All my courses, all my scores, none of it mattered. It just groomed me to be his glorified pet for as long as he wanted to play with me.

"He's one of the preferred candidates," Kylan said, his voice laced with annoyance. "If your former lover wins, he'll become an immortal and he will forget you, Raelyn. But it seems you'll die remembering him."

He pushed away, his steps silent.

"He's not my lover," I whispered, unsure of why I bothered clarifying. "Just my best friend, like Willow."

I closed my eyes, suppressing the tears that threatened to fall. We always knew our fates would divide, that upon our twenty-second year, we'd never see each other again. But the reality of it *hurt*.

My knees shook, my body exhausted all over again. I really did need food. But what did it matter? I thought I wanted to be strong before Kylan, but I'd more than proven that to be impossible. A few quarrelsome words were nothing compared to his brute strength and power.

I would spend my remaining days serving him and die when he grew tired of me, or be relegated to a member of his staff so he could take on younger, newer lovers.

A passing amusement.

What a legacy.

His palm cradled my face, his thumb brushing away a tear I hadn't realized had fallen. I hadn't even heard him come back to stand before me. "It's a savage time," he whispered, his lips against my forehead. "Take a moment for yourself, Raelyn. Have a shower, get dressed, and meet me in the hallway. We'll eat and I'll give you a tour of the estate."

Chapter Seven

KYLAN

JUST MY BEST FRIEND.

Her words had doused my ire in an instant, leaving me more than a little perplexed. Why had I been so infuriated to begin with? Because she had a human lover? Who the fuck cared? Yes, she belonged to me now, but why should I be bothered by her past or current feelings?

I ran my hand over my face.

"You need to shave," Mikael said by way of greeting, his gaze pointedly on my three-day-old stubble. "Or I really will withhold my blood."

"Why do all the humans in my home think they are in charge?" First Raelyn, now my blood virgin. "I'm starting to think I just need to fuck some sense into all of you."

Mikael's gaze brightened. "Please do."

I snorted. He would immediately accept the offer. The man preferred women but wouldn't turn me down if I desired a change. Unfortunately for him, it rarely appealed. His mouth, however, I rather enjoyed.

Except I was craving something a little more feminine and feisty at the moment.

Shutting Raelyn up by shoving my cock down her throat… Mmm, yes, now that did sound divine.

Mikael leaned against the wall beside me, his blue-green eyes alight with curiosity. He'd tied his hair back into a low ponytail today, leaving his neck exposed, just the way I liked it. "You let her sleep in your room."

"Yes."

"That's new."

"Yes," I repeated. The harem had their own wing. That was where I fucked them, never in my private quarters. "Current circumstances warranted the change."

"You're worried someone will get to her."

"Can you blame me?" I glanced at him sideways. "You know she's a target."

He nodded. "Killing her would further harm your image."

"They won't just kill her, Mikael. They'll make a scene of it." After her defiance during Blood Day, no one would truly blame me for administering a death sentence. Which meant, to imply my insanity, the murder would have to be spectacular and public.

"Have you gotten any closer to identifying the culprit?"

I shook my head. "No, but I have a list of suspects I intend to invite for a visit now that I've acquired a new consort to dangle before them as bait."

Jace was at the top of my list.

His recent appointment of a new sovereign provided the perfect opportunity. I knew Darius already, but arranging a formal introduction to a royal's new regional leader was perfectly in line with vampire politics.

And, as Jace Region bordered mine, it seemed obvious that he or one of his minions might be the culprit for my harem's demise. Because, if I were proven incapable of leading, Darius—as the heir of a former royal—could feasibly inherit my entire territory.

That put Jace at the top of my list of suspects. The conniving royal was up to something. I sensed it every time I saw him.

"Sounds draining," Mikael said, his lips curling at the pun.

I leaned into him, my hand going to his hip. "You're mine to share or not to share."

Yearning deepened his irises to a harsher shade of turquoise. Such a beautiful man, with those sharpened cheekbones and delicate jaw. As if I'd let anyone touch him without my permission.

"I know," he murmured, his palm lifting to my cheek. "You always take care of me."

"And that's never going to change," I vowed softly just as the door opened.

Rather than acknowledge Raelyn, I pulled Mikael closer to brush my lips over his. He returned the kiss, his body molding to mine in a familiar way that left me feeling like a king. I slid my tongue into his mouth and relished in his resulting groan.

Dominating a male—especially one as strong as Mikael—was a rush unlike any other. I loved the feeling of establishing my dominion, stamping my claim, and bending him to my will.

This was what I wanted from Raelyn, the complete faith Mikael laid at my feet as I devoured him. His fingers slid into my hair, holding me to him as my grip tightened against his hip in warning. He loved to push my boundaries, to try to take what wasn't his, to challenge me in every way.

I shoved him against the wall, my lips leaving his in favor of his neck and piercing his vein without warning. Raelyn had put me in a mood with all her talk of that human. Fortunately, Mikael could handle the consequences on her behalf. He loved my brand of pain, even when I pushed him too far.

"More," he moaned, his body quivering from the pleasure I unleashed with my bite.

Making him come would be cruel, especially in front of Raelyn. It would be so easy—just increase the endorphins and send them straight to his groin. The curse leaving his lips said it was working, that I was taking him to a point of no return without so much as stroking him. Oh, he'd loathe that more—my forcing him to explode without offering the kindness of my touch.

But the worst torture of all would be to leave him high and dry, to make him seek out one of the maids, or Zelda again, for relief.

His sweet essence burned in my throat, reminding me why I'd paid so much for him. Blood virgins were bred for their rare blood, hence their significant cost. Most were fucked once and discarded, but I chose to keep mine for companionship, and frankly, because I liked him.

"You're killing me," he hissed, referring not to my drinking but to the ecstasy flooding his veins.

I chuckled but continued to swallow as he rubbed his hard cock against my hip.

"Fuck, Kylan," he growled.

His use of my name told me how far gone he was to my bite, causing me to smile against his neck. "And you wanted to withhold your blood." I licked the wound closed and met his smoldering gaze. "You can't even last a day."

"Asshole," he said, his voice low and pissed off, and tinged with arousal.

I palmed his erection. "I was trying to save you the embarrassment in front of Raelyn."

"Still an asshole."

I smiled, rubbing him in the way I knew he preferred—the way I enjoyed as well. "Shall I finish it, or would you prefer Zelda?"

He grabbed my wrist, his orgasm clearly close. "I hate when you do this."

"I know."

"Yet you do it anyway."

"Yes." I nipped his bottom lip hard enough to bleed and licked the wound, causing him to spasm once more.

"Kylan," he growled.

"Tell me you want more."

"You know I do."

I glanced at a very flushed Raelyn, her lips parted as she fought to steady her breathing. "Would you like to see him come? It's really quite glorious." I applied more pressure, causing him to groan louder and grab my arms for support.

"Well, Raelyn? Shall I let him come? For you?"

Her eyes rounded, her face deepening to a darker crimson.

"I'm not sure she's ready, Mikael," I murmured, my eyes still on her as I massaged him torturously through his jeans.

His head fell to my shoulder, a curse slipping from his lips. "Fuck…"

"I'm not sure she's ready for that either." I tilted my head to the side. "Raelyn?"

She licked her lips, her pupils darting from me to Mikael and back. She must have seen the agony in Mikael's expression or posture because, slowly, she nodded.

"Say it," I encouraged.

"Yes," she whispered.

Mikael shuddered against me, his relief palpable. He knew if she had refused, I'd have refused him too.

I unfastened his jeans and drew down the zipper to relieve his engorged shaft. He jerked as it landed against my palm, his breathing heavy as I stroked him from base to tip with harsh, swift movements. He always preferred me to be rough instead of soft, his desire to be mastered only evident in moments like this.

Rather than force him to wait—as I usually preferred—I gave him what he craved and pierced his neck once more.

He came on a guttural yell, his body exploding from my bite and my touch. I wrapped my arm around him, holding him through his violent spasms. The sensations would both hurt and please, the force of his orgasm doubled by my fangs in his neck. He whispered my name as a curse and a plea, his muscles bunching and twitching against me.

So much strength for a human.

So much beauty.

I drank my fill, satisfying my thirst, and gently closed the marks on his neck. Raelyn stood to the side, her breathing loud in the hallway, her sexual interest more than evident. Gone was the broken female in the closet, and in her place a woman realizing the potential of her situation.

Because this could be her in my arms, and I let her see that with my eyes.

Mikael's head rested against my shoulder as he fought to regain his control, his pants from exertion heady and intoxicating.

I held her gaze, letting her feel the passion of the moment. From the way she clenched her thighs, I knew she enjoyed the show, maybe even wanted to join us.

But she wasn't ready for any of that yet.

I brushed my lips against Mikael's temple as I eased him away, his spent cock still hard in my palm. He'd made a mess of my sweater, as well as his own, but his satisfied expression said he harbored no regrets.

"Thank you," he whispered.

"I think you needed that." Especially considering he'd spent just last night with Zelda.

"You know I did," he replied, gazing up at me from beneath hooded eyes. "I'd return the favor, but that's not what you really want."

Sometimes he knew me too well. Rather than acknowledge it, I pulled my sweater over my head and handed it to him. "Have that cleaned."

He pressed it to his groin and used it to wipe himself off. "Sure."

Raelyn's deepening arousal tinged the air, causing my eyes to find hers. They were firmly affixed to my bare abdomen. "I think she approves, Mikael."

"She'd have to be blind not to," he returned, glancing over his shoulder with a smirk. "Be a good pet and maybe he'll let you touch him."

I would be allowing her to do far more than that. "Don't go anywhere, Raelyn. I need another sweater."

She nodded mutely, her focus having fallen to my groin. Her silence now didn't bother me nearly as much as earlier. She wet her lips, causing my cock to pulse behind my zipper.

We'd definitely be testing those oral skills—soon.

I ran my fingers through my hair and entered my suite. Several black sweaters lined my racks, making my choice easy. I pulled another turtleneck over my head and grabbed a scarf for Raelyn to wear when we ventured outside.

"It's a unique bloodline," Mikael was explaining. "Blood virgins don't attend universities like you did. We are raised in the Coventus and auctioned during our twenty-second year."

"Auctioned?" she repeated, sounding intrigued. "Similar to a Blood Day?"

"No, not really. The Magistrate reads your fate. Wealthy vampires buy mine, and fortunately, Kylan found me worthy enough for the highest bid."

Fortunately, I thought, nearly rolling my eyes. He wasn't wrong, but he wasn't right either.

"So he bought you."

"Yes."

"And how long have you lived with him?"

"Over a decade."

I chose that moment to rejoin them, mostly because I wanted to see her expression, and she didn't disappoint. Her jaw was on the floor. "And don't you look surprised, darling," I teased, closing the door. "Mikael is an example of what happens when I like a human. I let him live. Fancy that?"

Mikael narrowed his gaze. "Stop being an ass."

"As you've pointed out several times tonight, that's my specialty."

He just shook his head. "I give up trying to help you."

"One might think you owe me."

"I paid my debt in blood," he retorted, turning away with a pointed look. "Have a good outing. I'm going to take a nap."

I smiled at his backside. "Something exhaust you, Mikael?"

He held up a one-finger salute in response, making me laugh. Heavens, he was so much more fun now than when we first met. All those old movies and television shows had taught him how to be a proper human, equipped with a filthy vocabulary and all.

Raelyn stared after him with a perplexed expression. "I don't understand what that means."

Of course she wouldn't. Most of my kind despised crude behavior and language. "He's telling me to fuck off."

Her gaze widened. "And you allow it?"

"You cursed in my presence earlier without any reprimand. Why would he be any different?" Which inspired a good question. "Who taught you that language?"

She frowned. "What language?"

"Fuck."

"Are you kidding? The lycans use that word all the time."

Ah, yes, they would. "That makes sense."

"Would you prefer me not to use it?"

"On the contrary, I hope you do." I stepped closer, crowding her against the wall. "Especially in the bedroom. The phrase 'Fuck me' is a personal favorite. Feel free to use it anytime." I wrapped the scarf around her reddening neck and slowly draped the long end between her breasts. "Mmm, that is a gorgeous color on you."

She swallowed, her blue irises heating. "Th-thank you."

I nearly kissed her again when her stomach rumbled just loud enough to remind me of her mortal needs.

Food.

Yes.

Then a walk outside to entertain my pet. My lips curled at the reminder of her reaction earlier. While I hadn't appreciated her comments about Silas, I had enjoyed her banter.

I brushed my knuckles against her cheek, down the column of her neck, and over her breast, then linked my fingers with hers. I brought her wrist up to my lips. "Time for mortal sustenance."

Chapter Eight

RAE

I'D WITNESSED VAMPIRES take humans several times over the years, but nothing compared to Kylan and Mikael. Normally, the screams were of pain, not pleasure. But Mikael had clearly enjoyed Kylan's attentions.

My thighs tensed just thinking about it.

"You all right, pet?" Kylan asked, a devious twinkle in his gaze. He could probably smell my arousal.

"I'm fine." I forced myself to take another bite of the food he'd given me. Some sort of creamy pasta with far too much flavor. When I'd asked for protein and greens, he'd laughed and handed me this instead, calling it a treat. All I sensed was that I would be very ill later.

I pushed the half-eaten bowl away. Kylan smirked and plucked the spoon from my hand to take his own bite. "The richness, right?" he asked after swallowing. "The universities, as you call them, only provide you with basic nutrition. But don't worry, I'll retrain your taste buds in time, and you'll thank me for it later."

"Why?" I asked. "Food is meant to give you energy. Nothing else."

"Oh, darling." He gave me a look. "Food provides pleasure. Trust me."

"How?"

"Remind me to introduce you to chocolate later." He finished my bowl and placed it in the sink. "We'll eat more after our walk."

I touched my stomach and shook my head. "I don't think I can handle that."

"Believe me. You will." He grabbed my hand and pulled me from my perch on the counter. "Come, little lamb. Time to go outside and play."

"You really want me to punch you," I muttered.

"I'd love for you to try, yes." His attention fell to my feet as he frowned. "You need shoes."

I hadn't known what he wanted me to wear with the pants, so I'd not chosen any footwear. Most of my wardrobe at school had been heels and dresses—the proper wardrobe of females. I only deviated from the norm during physical training, where I typically wore nothing.

"Right," he muttered, releasing my hand and disappearing in a blink.

A literal blink.

Like he phased before my eyes.

I'd seen vampires do that at the university, but nothing quite that impressive.

He really is ancient. Over five thousand years old, if the textbooks were right. But he didn't act the way I expected. He was almost… playful.

"Here," Kylan said, appearing before me again, boots and socks in hand. "Put these on. Now."

He said it as if he expected me to argue. I accepted them with a sweet smile and donned them without a word, just to prove him wrong.

I stood and batted my eyes at him. "I'm ready to play outside, Your Highness."

Amusement lightened his near-black eyes to a luscious brown shade. "So you can behave like a good little pet. I'll remember that later."

He pulled a knitted hat over my head and ears before I could mutter a retort and led me through the oversized dining area toward a set of glass doors.

All my irritation fled at the gorgeous sight ahead of us.

Mountains. Snow. Trees.

My heart skipped a beat, my lips parting in awe. Not even the blast of cool air could dispel my fascination. I stepped through the open threshold, my attention on the mountains in the distance.

Gorgeous.

I wanted to get closer, to explore. I started to run, eager to—

My feet tripped over one another, sending me forward into a bank of snow. I pushed upward, confused, and slipped onto my side with an "Omph" before rolling onto my back to stare up at the stars.

Or perhaps those were just the lights flickering behind my eyes.

Ow.

"Well, that was graceful." Kylan appeared, his expression amused as he held out a hand. "How about we try that again, but instead of trying to jog on top of the snow, you learn how to walk through it."

I blinked, my teeth beginning to chatter from the cold seeping through my clothes to my bare skin beneath. He waggled his fingers and I grabbed them, not knowing how else to move. With a tug, he had me standing again, his palms brushing the fluffy white flakes from my arms.

"Take a step," he urged.

I did and nearly fell again, his arm around my waist the only thing keeping me upright. I grabbed his sweater, pulling him closer for balance.

This was not nearly as fun as I expected.

He chuckled, his hands falling to my hips. "I suddenly have the urge to take you skiing, just to see how you handle it."

My brow furrowed. "What?"

"It's a sport and one of my favorites. I'll show you sometime."

A sport? "Like a game?"

He shook his head, his expression saddening. "While I understand the shifting of balance and power, I will never agree with the destruction of your culture."

I stared at him. "What do you mean?"

"You believe the world to have always been led in this way, but it's a lie, little lamb. Humans ruled once while the rest of us hid." He palmed my cheek. "It all changed after a lycan took the wrong female. Your kind tried to weaponize his pack, and we retaliated."

My breath quickened. *Humans ruled once?* What? How was that even possible?

"You outnumbered us," he added as he wrapped his arm around my waist and gave me a nudge. I took a step only because he forced me to, and another after he nudged me again. "There you go," he praised, coaxing me alongside him. "It's about nine inches deep here. If you keep a steady pace, you'll be fine."

Somehow I doubted that. While the snow gave way with each of my movements, it also threatened to trap my limbs by clinging to my boots.

"Anyway, back to what I was saying. You outnumbered us quite significantly, but a flock of sheep pales in comparison to a pissed-off wolf. And exterminating ninety percent of your race, give or take, made controlling you all the easier."

My legs moved—slowly—with his while my mind fought to process his words. Humans were fragile with shortened life spans. How could we have ever led these superior beings? Why would they bother to hide?

Kylan picked up our pace, his arm a band around my lower back.

"It's the one hundred and seventeenth year of this new world, Raelyn." His sigh mingled with the night air, denoting the cooler weather. I marveled at it and his words. All my years were shrouded in humid nights or the occasional cool evening, never this crisp air littered in wintry delight.

This is my new life.

It wasn't perfect, far from it.

But it could be worse.

"I miss the old world," he continued, his voice soft. "More often than I should."

I gazed up at him, curious. "What do you miss about it?"

His eyes were on the stars as we walked, his expression distant. "I've always preferred my peace and quiet, but I could always count on humans to provide some form of entertainment. It evolved over the centuries, changing from generation to generation, always a new shift in cultural evolution. Until we destroyed those with determined souls and left only the meek alive to be retrained and bred for our personal diversions."

A shiver traversed my spine at the harsh statement.

"There's no hunt anymore," he murmured. "No excitement. An hour drive to Kylan City will place me in the center of a metropolis where I can have whatever I want, whenever I want, without so much as batting an eye. How is that enjoyable?" He finally looked away from the sky, his gaze returning to mine. "Humans don't argue or fight anymore. You just bend over and take it. I miss the challenge, Raelyn."

We stopped walking, the tree line of the forest before us and the estate at our back. His pupils pulsed, the predator inside him lurking in wait. I should submit, glance down, anywhere other than directly at him, but I found myself hypnotized by his beauty.

Seeing him in his true form with Mikael had awoken something inside of me, something hungry. Which had, of course, been the point. I was smart enough to realize that. But I couldn't deny his enigmatic appeal.

"How have you survived?" he marveled, repeating his question from earlier. "You should be a shell of a woman, just like the others, but there isn't an ounce of fear in you. How did your professors not notice your potential?"

"Do you want me to fear you?" Because a logical part of me did. Yet something about him inspired me to bite back instead of yield.

He wrapped his palm around the back of my neck, beneath my hair, and pulled me against him. "I want to know why you don't when everyone else does, how you've managed to go undetected in a society where even the slightest hint of rebellion gets you sent to the blood farms."

I trembled at the mention of the infamous factories where humans were sent to be bled to death. So many of my classmates had been sent there throughout the years, and several more just this week instead of attending the Blood Day ceremonies.

Only a thousand were chosen across the world.

Out of how many, I didn't know.

"Even now, you don't jump to reply as you should," he whispered. "I could kill you without blinking, Raelyn, yet you trust me not to."

"Maybe I'm not afraid to die," I whispered back at him.

His grip tightened. "Don't lie to me. You want to live. Why else would you have desired immortality?"

He had me there. "I should be afraid of you."

"You should," he agreed.

"But I'm not."

"I know. Now tell me why."

"I can't." *Because I don't know why.*

He cocked a brow. "Perhaps I need to inspire a better reply."

"That—"

His lips silenced mine as he walked me backward. Something hard hit my back—a tree, maybe?—causing the air to whoosh from my lungs. I clung to his sweater, needing his strength to ground me. His palm moved to my throat, holding me where he wanted me as his tongue slid into my mouth, taunting me to retaliate.

But I couldn't.

Not after what I'd seen.

Not after how my body responded to his.

I practically melted against him instead, my resolve tarnished and destroyed in less than twenty-four hours in his presence. I didn't want to be attracted to him, to desire him, to *need* him. Yet, I did, more than anyone I could recall ever yearning for before. Was it his age? His experience? Being the head of a bloodline?

Warmth caressed my veins despite our frigid surroundings, his tongue unleashing endorphins I'd never knew existed.

Goddess, I'd never felt anything like this, as if he'd lit my soul on fire from within. Why him? Why now? Why here?

It couldn't last. It wouldn't. I'd die in a blink of his lifetime, gone and forgotten.

But at least my life would have purpose and fulfillment.

Would it, though?

His hips rocked into mine, derailing my thoughts. So demanding, so *big*. I shuddered against him, both terrified of his potential and excited. The palm around my throat slid downward to my breast. A jolt hit me dead center at the contact.

Oh, I like that…

Silas had touched me there previously, but only in a classroom setting. I'd been his subject for an exam. He was being measured by how fast he could bring me to orgasm, of which I helped him by faking it. He had returned the favor an hour later for my own test.

But Kylan's touch was different, rawer, more real and intense. He tweaked my nipple through the fabric, causing me to moan.

I couldn't remember the point of this demonstration anymore, or why he'd started, but I didn't want it to end.

He lifted me up, causing my legs to wrap around his waist as he balanced me against the hard surface behind me. Then he began kissing me in earnest. Before was just a taste of what he could do, an introduction, a test. And I must have passed because he unleashed everything now, dominating me down to my very core.

My head spun.

This was the predator.

The animal.

The male who wanted to devour me.

And all I could do was accept him.

My arms circled his neck, my mouth opening even more for his sensual assault, my tongue not daring to defy his. He wanted me, so he would have me.

Obey or die.

He was right.

I didn't want to die.

But I also didn't mind living… for this.

"Fuck," he whispered. "I can't remember the last time I wanted someone like this."

His words startled me almost as much as his fangs sinking into my lower lip. I yelped, then moaned.

"Oh…" I liked that far too much—his tongue against the open wound. I trembled violently, the pleasure overwhelming all my senses. "What…?" I couldn't finish, my legs tightening around him. "Kylan," I breathed, unsure of what was happening.

His groin moved against the sensitive juncture between my thighs, heightening the sensation. I whimpered, my head falling to his shoulder.

What are you doing to me?

A knot formed inside me, twisting and pulling, shooting electricity to every nerve.

"Give in," he whispered, his hardness stroking my clit through the jeans.

How?

Why?

I'd been touched there before, but never like this. I usually squirmed, but he elicited a demand for more.

"Now, Raelyn." He captured my chin, pulling my mouth back up to his, and bit me again. I could hardly feel the sting through the euphoria that followed.

And then I was falling.

Tumbling.

Darkness consuming my vision, followed by bright lights.

A scream I hardly recognized as my own.

And a satisfied chuckle that was all Kylan.

The explosion went on and on, my limbs shaking uncontrollably as pleasure overwhelmed every sensor.

An orgasm. A real one.

I thought I'd experienced them before, but no. Nothing compared to this, to Kylan, to the way he so masterfully owned mine.

No wonder Mikael had been so exhausted. I could barely continue kissing Kylan, let alone pull away. If his arms weren't holding me upright, I would have fallen.

"I stand corrected," he murmured against my lips. "*That* was glorious." He took my mouth again, harsher now, his body rock hard against mine.

It took me a moment to follow his reference, to remember his words about Mikael coming earlier.

"Would you like to see him come? It's really quite glorious."

I wondered how that worked, the relationship between them. It was clearly sexual in nature, but Kylan hadn't taken any pleasure. Did he expect me to reciprocate now on both our behalves? An image of taking him in my mouth flashed behind my eyes. I knew the mechanics, could perform them well. Was I to offer now? To kneel in the snow? Unzip his pants and swallow his cock?

"Still not afraid," he said, smiling against my mouth. "It's amazing."

His pupils engulfed his irises, a startling sight in the night, especially with me being the focus of his unveiled lust. "Why would I fear you after that?" I asked.

He chuckled darkly and drew his nose across my cheek. "Why indeed." The words were low, seductive, and eerily controlled. "I could destroy you, Raelyn."

"You already said you would."

"Yes," he whispered, his lips sliding to my neck. "I did. And yet, you cling to me as if I'm your source of life."

"Because you are," I replied, arching into him. "You own me."

He stilled, his mouth hovering over my pulse. "Do I?"

"Yes." I felt exhausted despite barely doing anything today, my body replete in the strangest of ways.

"And you don't fear me." Not a question, but a statement.

"I should, but no, I don't." Not really, anyway. Not the way I should. "If I'm going to die, I'll die with my dignity intact." He only derailed that resolve for a second with his threats against Silas, but now that no longer applied.

I would die when Kylan deemed it time.

I wouldn't beg for a different fate, nor would I just lie on my back and accept it.

But to fear the inevitable no longer seemed rational. What would happen, would happen, with or without my compliance.

"Why obey when the end result will never change?" I asked, drawing back to meet his sheltered gaze. No sign of emotion dwelled in his expression. No anger. No curiosity. Just Kylan inscrutably observing me.

"The end result being?"

"My death."

"I see." He tilted his head, his hands falling to my hips. "You assume so quickly that death is all I have planned for you."

"Don't you? That's your method, isn't it? Fuck the harem, then kill them?"

I regretted the words as soon as I said them. They were abrasive and challenging, and they simmered in his gaze as he stared back at me. I'd struck a nerve, one that shrouded us in ominous silence for far too long.

Was he reliving the moments in his mind? Relishing in what he'd done? Envisioning how he would eventually slaughter me? Because his darkening expression suggested he wanted to now, as did the way his grip tightened almost painfully.

"You should be careful, Raelyn," he said, his voice low. "I'm understanding to a point, but speaking of actions you know nothing about is liable to earn you a punishment you won't appreciate."

He lifted me off him, forcing me to stand, then released me so suddenly that I nearly fell.

The loss of his body heat coupled with the frost coating his features sent a chill down my spine. "This has been enlight—" He spun with a growl as a dark-skinned female ran across the grounds at incredible speed.

A vampire.

No, not just any vampire.

Angelica.

The human who won the Immortal Cup when I was fifteen. She'd been an inspiration to me, proof that females could win immortality just as well as males.

I gaped as she fell to her knees in the snow at Kylan's feet, her brown hair splaying around her. "Y-your Highness. I came as s-soon as I could."

"What is it?" Kylan knelt beside her, his hand going to her sweater.

Blood, I realized. She was covered in it.

"What's happened?" he demanded when she didn't immediately respond.

"T-Tremayne," she whispered, her shoulders shaking.

"What about Tremayne?" he asked, clearly recognizing the name whereas I didn't. My studies focused on the royals, not their constituents. "What did he do?"

Angelica trembled, her fear palpable as he forced her to lift her head and meet his gaze.

She's terrified—not of the situation, but of him, I realized.

Kylan palmed her cheek, his voice softening. "I won't discipline you for his actions, Angelica. Now tell me what he's done."

She swallowed, doubt radiating from her expression. Kylan was renowned for his wicked punishments, his reign not a kind one. Yet he'd been mostly gentle with me, even when I'd clearly pushed him over the edge.

Which version is the real Kylan?

"He killed them all, Your Highness," Angelica whispered.

"All of them," he repeated. "All of whom?"

"Every single human under his employment at Tremayne Tower." Her pupils widened. "It was a bloodbath. I came here to tell you, to warn you, that he's in Kylan City now and I think he's going to do the same at K Hotel. He's saying…" She shuddered, her expression falling. "He's telling everyone that you executed the order."

Chapter Nine

Rae

KYLAN WENT EERILY STILL.

Angelica whimpered, returning her head to the ground while I stood frozen behind them.

He's telling everyone that you executed the order.

To slaughter humans as he did his harem?

It seemed something he would do, based on his reputation, but the rigidness in his spine suggested otherwise.

He rose slowly, his hands fisted at his sides. When he turned toward me, I saw the royal in full display—regal brow, tightened jaw, cold eyes.

His expression required submission.

I tried to bow, to yield to his dominance, but my knees refused to bend. Even my neck protested the notion.

You don't fear me. His words from earlier taunted my mind, trying and failing to inspire reason.

I should. I know I should. But you're right; I don't and I have no idea why.

He took in my disobedient form with a sweep of his gaze before refocusing on the other woman.

"Rise, Angelica," he demanded. "We have work to do." He glanced at me again. "I need you upstairs in my suite. Now."

I didn't argue, not with the barely contained anger simmering in his dark eyes. He looked ready to kill, and I didn't want to be the target of that rage.

I pulled my jacket closed and scurried into the house, up the stairs, and directly to his room.

Now what? I wondered, chewing my lip. Did he want me naked again? Was he planning to join me at all? Had I just been dismissed for the rest of the evening?

I toed off my boots, setting them on the mat inside the closet. Then I removed my jacket and hung it on a nearby hook to dry. What next? My clothes?

The door opened before I had a chance to disrobe, Kylan's sudden presence behind me ominous. I turned slowly, terrified of what I would find in his expression, but needing to know all the same.

He merely stared at me, his dark eyes hiding every detail.

Does he not care?

Is he just bored?

But as I studied him, a glimmer of something flashed in the depths of his gaze. It was there and gone so quickly that I almost missed it, could have easily just made it up. But no. It was definitely there.

Devastation.

"We need to take a trip to Kylan City," he said flatly, stepping closer. He pinched my chin between his thumb and his forefinger, his gaze intensifying. "I need you on your best behavior, Raelyn, which means bowing and engaging in all the formalities." His chest met mine as he backed me into the wall. "If you disobey, I will be forced to punish you publicly, and you do not want me to have to do that."

The promise in his words sent a chill down my spine. No, I definitely didn't want that. "I understand," I whispered, swallowing.

"This is not how I wanted to spend our first week together, but Tremayne has left me no choice. If I could leave you here, I would." He almost sounded apologetic, which made no sense. Royals took their favored harem members with them everywhere. Being his only consort at the moment left him little choice. "I mean it, Raelyn. I need you to behave."

"I said I understood," I replied, then quickly added, "Your Highness," to lessen the tone of my words.

He shook his head disapprovingly. "Not off to a good start, Raelyn."

"We're not in the city yet," I muttered.

He raised both brows, his patience clearly nonexistent. "I love your courage, but now is not the time unless you want me to beat your ass red and then fuck it in front of a room full of my constituents. And if you're really disobedient, I'll be forced to let them enjoy you as well. Is that what you want?"

My lips parted, shocked by his brash description and the furious way he said it, as if even the notion of it all infuriated him. I cleared my throat, searching for the nerve to respond. "I... No. Of course I don't want that." Who the hell would?

His grip on my chin tightened, his gaze narrowing. "My reputation is what keeps this territory alive. You may not fear me, but others do, and I need it to stay that way. Do you understand?"

I blinked.

Had he just… confided in me? Explained why he needed me to behave? Essentially admitted that the mask he wore was for the public alone? Because that fit what I'd seen so far, that the Kylan of my textbooks did not match the Kylan standing before me now.

The royal I'd read about would have no issue with fucking me in public—including during Blood Day—and would do so again now without caring at all about the report Angelica had just delivered.

But he did care.

Enough to necessitate a trip to Kylan City.

Which meant he never gave the order for those human deaths.

I studied him, his darkening gaze, the tight line of his lips, the tension in his cheekbones, and his strained posture as he continued to hold my chin firmly between his thumb and forefinger.

He wanted me to understand not only his request but also the importance behind it. He needed me to comply. "You don't want to punish me." The words weren't the ones he was waiting for me to say, but they were the first my mouth allowed me to voice.

"Not in the way our society requires, no," he agreed. "But I will if you do something that necessitates it."

"Like argue with you in public." Something I never thought I'd consider saying out loud, let alone do, but my reactions to Kylan hadn't been sane since the moment he stood in front of me on that field.

"Yes, or anyone else," he replied. "I need your fear, Raelyn."

"And if I can't give you that?"

"Then I'll be forced to make you fear me."

The words alone caused me to tremble. "I don't want that."

"I don't either."

"Why maintain an image of torment when you don't enjoy it?" I asked, genuinely curious.

"Because it keeps the peace. Someone has to be the bad guy, Raelyn. It's a burden I've carried for centuries, and my people thrive beneath it—or they have, anyway—until recently."

"Until recently?" I repeated.

He shook his head. "I've already said more than I intended to say." He stepped back, releasing my jaw to rub his own and allowing me a brief glimpse at the exhausted male behind the charade. The male who led under a cloud of brutality because he believed it to be the best governing method, and maybe he was right. This society thrived on violence, and he was the notorious king—the eldest of them all, save the Goddess herself.

"Tell me you'll behave, Raelyn."

I essentially already did, I wanted to say, but he clearly needed to hear the words to believe them. So I did the only thing I could to pacify him. I kneeled, my head bowing to the floor as I gave him the highest form of respect a human could give a superior by leaving myself exposed and completely at his mercy.

"Yes, My Prince," I said, refusing to move or look up until he released me.

He said nothing for so long I thought he might be testing me, but then he crouched before me and used his finger to lift my chin. "I like you in this position, Raelyn," he murmured. "It could only be improved by you being naked."

Good luck with that, I wanted to say. Instead I whispered, "Whatever you wish, Your Highness."

His lips quirked. "I almost believe that, Raelyn. But your eyes imply otherwise." He brushed his thumb over my mouth and stood again. "You're going to need a new outfit. I'll ask Mikael to arrange it." He glanced at me. "I'd be lying if I apologized, so I won't, because I'll definitely be enjoying every minute of it."

My brow furrowed.

What kind of outfit will I be wearing?

* * *

Lace.

That's what Kylan meant when he mentioned my need for new apparel. The deep-red translucent dress—if it could be called that—left everything exposed beneath and ended at the tops of my thighs. Kylan had wrapped his suit jacket around my shoulders for the journey, but I knew it would disappear as soon as we arrived.

He sat beside me in the back of the limousine, his palm on my thigh while he gazed out the window at the growing city lights. Mikael was across from us in a black dress shirt and pants, sipping a glass of red wine, his face hidden ominously in the shadows.

The moon illuminated the snowy landscape, which ended against a harsh blockade coated in floodlights. A chill crept down my spine at the familiar structures dotting the perimeters—watchtowers. Vigils maintained those huts, all serving the sole purpose of keeping humans in line. I'd wanted to join their ranks because they were afforded certain privileges where others were not. Such as decent sleeping quarters and food.

Most would say ending up in a royal harem or clan harem was an even better fate because of the luxuries provided to those who served their masters sexually. After hearing the way some of the mortal consorts were treated on Blood Day, I strongly begged to differ.

But Kylan had been good to me. So far.

His palm tightened on my thigh as the limousine slowed, approaching the city's primary gates. "Remove the jacket and straddle me, Raelyn." Not a request, but a command.

Arguing wasn't an option, not with the perimeter of military-clad men and women waiting for a reason to hurt a defiant slave. They were trained to capture, not to kill, for a reason.

Vampires and lycans loved to punish errant humans.

I had no desire to join their list of insubordinates.

The wool slipped from my shoulders as I slid onto Kylan's lap, my too-short dress bunching at my hips. Mikael gave an appreciative noise, my ass clearly on display.

"She's beautiful, isn't she?" Kylan murmured, his palm wrapping around the back of my neck.

"Gorgeous," Mikael agreed.

"She tastes amazing, too." Kylan spoke the words against my mouth. "Open, Raelyn."

I parted my lips for his tongue and shivered as he dipped inside to mark his territory in the hottest of ways.

Damn, I didn't want to like him, but the man knew how to kiss. He wasn't my first, but he was certainly my best. So much passion, experience, and heat wrapped up into a technique that made my toes curl.

He pulled me closer to rest the rigid length of his erection right against my sensitive flesh. One upward stroke had me damp and ready despite his pants between us. I almost hated his ability to convince my body to take him even when my mind resisted, but I couldn't muster enough anger to care when he pressed into me again.

To be desired by such a powerful man, to be handled with such confidence, was an intoxicatingly addictive sensation.

I shouldn't love this.

Shouldn't enjoy it.

But fuck if I could stop myself from moaning in approval.

His incisors pierced my lower lip sharply, whether in reprimand or excitement, I didn't know. It stung, bringing tears to my eyes as he pulled away to examine his inflicted wound.

The window whirred down beside us, but his focus never left my mouth. "Yes?" he asked, his voice holding an edge I never wanted to hear directed at me.

"Forgive me, Your Highness. We were not expecting your arrival and—"

"Do I require an invitation to my own city?" he demanded.

"N-no, My—"

The window closed before the human could finish. Kylan traced the blood oozing down my chin with his tongue and followed it up to my mouth. His murmur of approval went straight to my heart, sending it into a chaotic rhythm against my rib cage. He'd lightly bitten me earlier, but this was different, more intimate, more purposeful.

A marking.

He kissed me with purpose, his lips dominating mine and leaving no room for questions or arguments. I belonged to him, to kiss, to fuck, to do whatever he wished with, and he wanted everyone—including me—to know it.

My head spun from the onslaught of sensations and emotions pummeling me at once. I didn't understand what he'd just done, or how he'd done it, but it forced me to bow to his will.

His gaze glittered as he released my mouth, his pupils dilated with unrestrained hunger. "You may just survive this yet, little lamb."

Chapter Ten

KYLAN

I HATED THE CITY, especially at midnight. Vampires littered the sidewalks and roads, running errands or grabbing a bite to eat on their work breaks. Several wore managerial robes designating their roles in overseeing the city's various human employees. No one wanted to do the necessary grunt work to keep our society alive, hence the mortal purpose.

A cruel world, but a practical one.

Money flowed as it always had, just in different currencies now and to purchase more useful items—like blood.

And I sat at the top of the food chain in this territory, which necessitated certain protocols. Such as keeping Mikael's presence a secret.

I kept Raelyn on my lap in case we were stopped again and also because I enjoyed her there. She held on to my shoulders, her red hair falling around us as I kissed her again, softly this time.

Whether she realized it or not, she was already learning my tastes and preferences. Her lips parted for my tongue, accepting what I desired and granting me unhindered access.

My fingers knotted in her silky strands, holding her where I wanted her as my driver gave an indication of our arrival by flipping the locks. Raelyn didn't notice, too lost to our embrace, her sweet arousal singing to my cock and begging me to do more than just kiss her.

In time, I would.

But not now.

I eased her away with a gentle tug on her hair. She blinked at me as if lost in a daze, causing my lips to curl. "I barely fed from you and you're already passion-drunk."

That little bite of my fangs against her bottom lip had been enough to mark her as my possession, but not nearly enough for a proper taste. Yet, she clearly enjoyed the introduction.

I rapped my knuckles against the window, indicating it was safe to disturb me now.

Judith wasted no time, greeting me with a formal bow before she finished opening the door. "My Prince."

Gavin and Karl joined her on their knees, waiting for me to allow them to rise.

The three of them were among the most trusted on my security team, Judith being their superior.

I lifted Raelyn off my lap to place her on the seat beside me as I slid out of the car. "Come, little lamb." I held out a hand for her to join me and brushed my lips against her temple as she obeyed without argument.

She shivered, the heated garage around us doing little to protect her exposed skin from the wintry elements outside. I fixed her dress, pulling it down to her upper thighs again, and sighed at seeing my three security members still kneeling. "Stand," I said. "Status, Judith?"

My favorite lieutenant straightened her spine, meeting my gaze. "We're safe here, Your Highness. I've already turned the security feeds on a loop all the way up to the suite."

I smiled. "Excellent. Mikael, would you like to join us?"

"Of course, Your Highness," he murmured, exiting the back seat with a grin for my security detail. "Judith."

A faint blush tinged her cheeks as she replied, "Mikael."

My blood virgin charmed everyone in his path, proving him more than worth my time and investment. Hence my reason for hiding him. The target on his back was almost as wide as mine, everyone knowing what he meant to me. I never announced his whereabouts. This trip was no different.

I retrieved my suit jacket from the limousine and wrapped it around Raelyn's trembling shoulders. "Lead the way, Judith."

She inclined her blonde head and turned with Mikael beside her. I followed, my palm against Raelyn's back to keep her with me, while Gavin and Karl trailed behind us. The elevator ride up went by in a flash and deposited us in one of my favorite homes—a lavish penthouse boasting seven bedrooms with en-suite bathrooms, two kitchens, several lounges, and floor-to-ceiling windows overlooking the city.

Perfection, opulence, home.

Zelda appeared in the hallway, blue eyes downcast, and a smile tilting her lips. Some of my human staff had arrived before us to prepare the space. It seemed wasteful to employ different help at all my homes, so I required them to travel with me.

"Midnight lunch is ready," she announced while curtsying.

Mikael wasted no time in following my blonde chef, while Raelyn remained dutifully beside me. She could be herself here without fear of punishment, but I refrained from telling her that. This was our practice round. If she passed, I would take her with me to visit Tremayne. If she failed, I'd keep her here with Mikael under Judith's protection.

There were very few I trusted with my valuable possessions, and Judith was among them.

I removed my jacket from Raelyn's shoulders and handed it off to Gavin. "Are you hungry, little lamb?" I asked her. She hadn't eaten anything since the pasta from the house, and that was hours ago.

"Yes, Your Highness," she replied, her voice low and sultry.

So far, so good. "Then let's follow Mikael, hmm?" I nudged her lower back with my palm, sending her in the direction Zelda had come from.

Raelyn's steps were steady, but her heart rate raced in my ears. It seemed far longer than twenty-four hours since I selected her for my harem, which was odd. Life spans usually passed quickly, not slowly, but I seemed to be savoring my time with her as if a year passed with each minute.

Mikael glanced up as I entered, his expression not contrite in the slightest for being caught standing between Zelda's open legs. She was hoisted up on the counter, her cheeks red, her lips parted.

"I see you had another meal in mind," I murmured, Raelyn freezing at my side.

My blood virgin shrugged. "After that show in the limousine, can you blame me?"

I arched a brow. "Are you implying I didn't handle you thoroughly enough earlier?"

His dimples peeked at me. "That was before my nap."

"Insatiable," I said, returning his smile before focusing on the tense woman beside me. "Raelyn, eat something and wear whatever Mikael gives you. We leave in an hour." I turned, then glanced back at my blood virgin with a pointed look. "Mikael, don't make a mess in my kitchen."

His responding snort trailed after me as I went straight to my office to make the requisite calls.

By now, my presence in the city would be known, as word traveled quickly. No one enjoyed my surprise visits, which was precisely why I chose to make them.

Judith joined me, phone in hand. "Where are you headed, Your Highness?"

I smiled at my always prepared lieutenant. She would help dismantle the security feeds. "You may want to sit down, Judith. I have a list of arrangements for this visit." We would be staying for a few weeks to clean up this mess, and while here, I might as well invite a few royals.

What better way to narrow down the list of suspects than by throwing a party? Alcohol loosened tongues and provided a breeding ground for suspicious behavior. It would also afford me the opportunity to reassert my place as the eldest living being of the royal lines.

Yes, vampire politics was a devious dance I'd mastered through the ages.

Raelyn would be my bait.

And the culprit would attempt to bite.

Welcome to Kylan City. I dare you to come out and play.

* * *

"Mmm, you look positively edible, little lamb."

Raelyn stood in the foyer wearing a black gown, her auburn hair pulled back to expose her neck. Lace bled into silk, leaving her seductively covered in all the right places. I traced the plunging neckline with my finger. Her nipples beaded in response, the rosy color concealed, but the shape outlined perfectly.

The slits up both her legs made removing the dress unnecessary, but I very likely would indulge in the pleasantness of it later.

I kissed her thundering pulse and skimmed my nose up her throat to her ear. "Mikael tells me you've been the picture of obedience." I'd stopped by his room on my way to meeting her in the foyer. "Unfortunately, rather than reward you, I need you to accompany me on what is likely going to be an unpleasant visit."

I tilted her chin, forcing her gaze to mine.

"I realize your university training has equipped you with the proper protocols, but this meeting pales in comparison to your meager preparation. As such, I'm inclined to gift you with a safe word. If, at any time, you feel you're about to break decorum, refer to me as 'Your Highness' and I will do what I can to improve the situation. Otherwise, continue to address me as 'My Prince' to let me know you're all right. Do you understand?"

It was the only leniency I could grant her, and even then, it didn't guarantee I could help her. Vampire society maintained certain requirements for humans, and while I may not admire them all, I understood them.

Humans were inferior beings, their place at the bottom of the food chain well established. But unlike many of my kind, I chose to remember how we started—as mortal.

Raelyn swallowed, her pupils flaring. "I understand, My Prince."

"Kylan," I corrected. "When in private, you call me Kylan."

"Kylan," she repeated. "I'm trying to obey," she added, a slight edge to her tone that forced my lips to twitch.

"There's my spirited female," I murmured, drawing my thumb over the mark I'd left on her lip. "Don't lose her tonight, Raelyn. I'm hoping to play more with her later."

"You want me to obey one moment, then rebel the next." Her gaze narrowed. "Would I be punished for calling you mercurial, Kylan?"

I laughed.

I'd certainly been called far worse.

"Oh, little lamb, we're just getting started." She hadn't seen my cruel mask yet, but she was about to. "Let's go."

Chapter Eleven

Rae

KYLAN'S PALM BURNED AGAINST MY LOWER BACK as he handed his car keys to a human. He'd insisted on driving himself, taking a sleek black two-seater from the garage that resembled the vehicle we rode in after the Blood Day selection.

Was that just last night?

It felt like a decade ago.

A female dressed in a tailored suit opened the door for us with a low bow, her shudder evident.

Kylan guided us through the threshold, ignoring the woman, his steps sure.

Several vampires milled inside, some sitting on leather couches, others in the lounge near a bar boasting oversized televisions, and a handful standing in line before a long wooden welcoming desk.

I followed Kylan's movements as he led me to an elevator bank near the back, his thumbprint calling the car down as a human appeared.

"May I help you, Sire?"

The palm against my lower back tensed as Kylan addressed the man. "Do you have any idea whom you are speaking to?"

A shiver traversed my spine at the lethality lurking in Kylan's tone. Referring to a royal as anything other than *My Prince* or *Your Highness* was a grave offense, especially for a human.

"I-I… no… Y-your—"

Heels clacked loudly over the marble floors, approaching us from the left and silencing the poor human boy who had fallen to his knees. "Your Highness, I apologize. I hadn't expected your presence, or I would have properly informed my employees. Please forgive me." A woman knelt beside the male, her dark head bowed.

The elevator chose that moment to arrive.

Silence fell around us, everyone waiting for a response. Kylan had finally been noticed and recognized.

Rather than grant them a show, he guided me through the threshold, punched a button, and allowed the doors to close. I didn't dare speak or ask for an explanation. The boy had insulted his position; that had to burn. All humans were taught to recognize royals at a young age. How that human failed to realize the one in charge of his own region was beyond me.

Kylan pressed his thumb into my back, massaging gentle circles.

Is he trying to reassure me? Calm me?

A ding announced our arrival, and the motion against my back stopped.

The doors whirred open to reveal two suited men with guns, both aimed our way. I forced my gaze to the floor, not wanting to encourage retaliation, but it wasn't needed. They dropped to their knees with murmurs of apology upon recognizing Kylan.

He ignored them and escorted me into an ornate suite with windows overlooking the city—much like his own home. It took effort to keep from studying my surroundings with the elegant furnishings glittering beneath the lights.

Gold, I realized.

It lined the floor as well, weaving its way between the marble stones, exuding squandered wealth.

Kylan didn't seem fazed or impressed, his palm steady at my back as he led us down a few steps into a living area filled with plush couches circled around an oversized metal—*gold*—table.

Two human females lay atop it, naked, pleasuring each other.

Kylan released me to circle them, leaving me alone and cold.

"Your Highness," a male greeted as he entered the room while buttoning his dress shirt.

The lack of shoes and socks suggested he'd dressed in a hurry. He bowed his blond head but didn't kneel like the others, indicating his higher ranking in society. I averted my gaze, knowing better than to make eye contact.

"To what do I owe the honor?"

"I hear you had quite the eventful evening, Tremayne." Kylan drew his finger down the spine of the female who lay on top of the other, his voice intrigued. "I stopped by to learn more and brought my new pet along for a potential lesson."

That's why he gave me a safe word.

My stomach clenched with the realization, my palms suddenly clammy.

If he asked me to join those women on the table… Oh Goddess, I couldn't even process the notion. That sort of training had been an optional course in school that I ignored in favor of a fencing class. My oral sex qualifications were for males alone.

"She's beautiful," Tremayne said, the sensation of his gaze crawling over my skin. "A rare redhead. Blood type?"

"B positive." Kylan returned to my side and stepped behind me, his hands on my shoulders. "Would you care for a closer look?"

"Always."

Kylan hooked his thumbs beneath the straps of my dress and slid them from my shoulders, down my biceps and lower, exposing my breasts. My nipples pebbled in the cool air, an army of goose bumps stampeding down my arms to where his hand stilled just below my elbow.

"Responsive," Tremayne praised, his voice lowering to an octave that churned my insides. He stepped close enough for me to smell his alcohol-laced breath. "Rosy, too. Remarkable choice, as always, My Prince."

Kylan kissed my nape and drew up my sleeves, re-covering my chest. "I agree," he murmured, his hands falling to my hips. "Now, tell me what happened earlier." He pulled me backward and sat on the couch, his hands guiding me onto the cushion beside him.

Tremayne took a seat across from us, leaving the women on the table between us. "I assume you are referring to my purging of useless staff members?"

"I am." Kylan teased the slit of my dress while he spoke, his palm sliding inside to rest against my bare thigh. "Did they wrong you in some way?"

"They bored me." His tone suggested that alone justified the extermination. Kylan must have given him a look that said he required additional details because Tremayne sighed dramatically. "I desired a change of pace, new flesh to play with. These two are auditioning for a replacement role in my household, as are the three I left in my bedroom."

"The winner gains employment," Kylan translated, his hand branding my skin. "And the loser?"

"Doesn't deserve to live." Tremayne slapped the ass of the female on top. "This one's currently winning, having made the bitch below her orgasm twice so far. But honestly, I'm not all that impressed with either of them, which is why I'd left them out here to practice with each other. The universities clearly require better instructors, Your Highness."

Kylan didn't reply immediately, his touch sliding farther up my leg to reach the apex between my thighs. "Is that true, Raelyn? Do you feel inadequately prepared to service me orally?"

His fingers brushed my intimate flesh, sending a jolt through my system.

I didn't want to like that.

Not here.

Not now.

But my body seemed hell-bent on denying reason, the memory of his touch earlier rekindling a flame meant only for him.

I swallowed, subduing the sensations and focusing on his question. "My studies"—I started slowly, considering each word before I uttered them—"groomed me to sexually satisfy males, My Prince. As a result, I feel confident in my oral abilities." Something he already knew after asking me about my highest marks.

He lightly traced the seam of my sex. "Having only owned Raelyn a day, I've not yet experienced the pleasure of her mouth, but her marks were quite high. Shall we put your theory to the test, Tremayne? See if Raelyn lives up to my standards? Because I assure you, they are quite high."

Here?

In front of Tremayne?

My palms dampened despite the ice grazing my spine. *What if I failed?*

"If I'm proven right?" Tremayne asked.

"Then I'll look into the matter personally with Raelyn as my star pupil for demonstration purposes." He slid a finger inside me, punctuating his point and sending my heart into a chaotic rhythm. I hadn't known what to expect from this visit, didn't have a clue where he intended to take me, and that was all entirely the point.

He owned me.

To do whatever he wanted, including finger-fucking me in front of a vampire subordinate.

I had no choice.

No argument.

No will.

No rights.

I'm Kylan's property.

The realization slammed into me so fast my breathing hitched. I'd been lying to myself for the last twenty-four hours, pretending to have a chance against a royal when none existed. I'd literally lost my mind, failed to remember my position in this world, and Kylan was effortlessly putting me back in my place.

His kiss during the selection ceremony had jarred my mind.

No, my unintentionally biting him had sent me down this path. That accidental clench of my jaw had flipped a defiant gene hidden deep inside me—the unmistakable urge to fight. I had wanted to die with my dignity intact.

My greatest error was believing Kylan would kill me immediately in response.

But of course he wouldn't. That'd be too easy.

No, he wanted to snuff out the light inside me before granting me death.

There would be no dignity left when he finished with me.

Another mental trick, just like the Immortal Cup selection.

Another way to break the human spirit.

That explained his mercurial behavior. He wanted me to oppose him because it prolonged his entertainment, but he also needed me to follow his orders to prove his power over me. Except no one would ever question his superiority, not even me.

"But if she proves you wrong," he continued, his voice lowering. "Then we will have a very serious conversation on human potential and how to properly dispose of undesired employees."

"Properly dispose?" Tremayne repeated, snorting. "I burned them, just as you did your harem."

The reminder had my legs tensing, which resulted in Kylan sliding a second finger inside me—deep. A punishment for reacting? I clenched around him, my muscles unused to the intrusion. My training included superficial penetration, a way of keeping my innocence intact, something he was dangerously close to discovering.

Some humans chose to go through more in-depth erotic training, including intercourse, mostly because they desired to be in a harem.

I had never wanted to be in a harem or to be used for sexual gratification.

Becoming a Vigil or competing in the Immortal Cup had been my chosen path.

"Did I?" Kylan asked, his voice holding an edge. "I don't recall—"

A moan from the table cut him off as the female on the bottom began to convulse. Both men admired the show, making bile inch its way up my throat.

Tremayne smacked the ass of the human on top again, reddening her skin. "That's three, babe. Keep going."

The woman on the bottom squirmed, her moans turning to noises of protest, her body clearly not ready for more.

"Do you see my issue?" Tremayne asked, standing. "Switch positions. Now."

A pair of panicked green eyes met mine as the humans jumped to obey. It took considerable effort not to react. Not wanting to join them was a good motivator to remain still.

Kylan continued fondling me as if nothing had happened, as if the woman now lying on top didn't have red lines marring her skin from lying on the hard surface.

Tremayne pushed her bottom half down onto the other woman, causing her to whine in protest. His hand cracked across her ass so hard even I flinched.

"Do your job, slut," he growled, punctuating it with another slap.

Kylan chuckled.

Fucking laughed.

But of course he would. This was his playground, only a scaled-down version of it. He favored pain. Punishment. Hurt.

"Raelyn comes beautifully, something I learned earlier this evening." The motion between my legs shifted, his thumb sliding upward to stroke my clit. "Perhaps she should give a demonstration of how to properly display pleasure. Then she can return the favor by proving her oral worth. Assuming you're interested in the offer to test your previous theory, of course."

"I want to join you in investigating the universities."

"A bold request."

"It was my finding," he pressed.

Kylan's touch stilled, his thumb resting over my sensitive nub. "All right. If Raelyn proves unsatisfactory, then we'll approach the universities together. But I have a requirement of my own, Tremayne."

"Go on."

"If she proves herself valiant, then we will not only discuss the disposal of employees, but you will tell me why everyone in this city is under the impression that I issued an extermination edict."

Chapter Twelve

RAE

THE AIR IN THE ROOM CHILLED CONSIDERABLY.

Disapproval emanated from Kylan, the hand between my legs unflinching.

"You… you didn't issue an edict?" Tremayne asked, the first hint of unease entering his tone.

"No, I did not." He removed his touch, lifting his hand to my mouth. "Open, Raelyn."

I parted my lips, allowing his fingers to dip inside and coat my tongue in my own arousal. A new flavor I'd never experienced, one that sent a fresh rush of heat between my thighs despite the tension building around us.

"Don't play the fool, Tremayne," Kylan said, sounding bored. "I don't issue edicts indirectly, something you are more than aware of, so you know what I think?" He withdrew from my mouth to glide his damp fingers across my cheek and down my neck. "I think you've been spreading rumors based on assumption. Prove me wrong." He folded his leg over the other and dropped his arm over my shoulders.

Tremayne stood. "If you'll allow me a moment, I need my phone."

Kylan gave him a dismissive gesture with his hand. "I'm waiting."

"Your Highness." He bowed before scurrying out of the room, leaving us alone with the still-performing females. They had to be exhausted, and from the lack of moans, they were clearly not enjoying themselves.

"On your knees, Raelyn," Kylan murmured. "Between my legs."

My heart skipped a beat.

He didn't mean…

He couldn't really want me to…

Not after…

His arm shifted, his palm going to my nape and squeezing. "Now, Raelyn."

"Yes, My Prince," I managed, my throat dry.

I shifted to the floor, my knees immediately disapproving of the marble tile. With my head bowed, I placed my palms on his thighs, waiting for his next command.

"Prove your worth, little lamb. Show me how you earned those test scores." Challenge underlined his words.

Did he not believe my academic records?

Or was this because of Tremayne's comments regarding the universities?

A combination of both?

I drew my nails up his strong thighs to his belt and unfastened it without hesitation. If he wanted me to demonstrate my skills, to validate my education, then so be it.

Tests were something I excelled at.

This would be no different.

Unbutton.

Done.

Now, the zipper.

I swallowed as my ministrations revealed his more-than-impressive cock. Silas was my only comparison, and I didn't remember him being quite so… pronounced.

Kylan relaxed, his arms spreading across the back of the couch. "I'm already bored, Raelyn. Perhaps Tremayne is right, hmm? Do I need to leave you here to learn with his other toys since I don't have a harem of my own to properly teach you?"

My eyes narrowed. No. I absolutely did not want to be left here. Nor would that be necessary.

Unless I mess this up.

Which I'm not going to.

I hope.

Just do it, Rae. Pretend it's Silas.

Except this was most definitely *not* Silas. Not in size, stature, or power.

No, Kylan was bigger, longer, and far more intimidating.

I wrapped my hand around his shaft. *This is not going to fit inside me.*

It will. It has to.

My thighs clenched at the notion of him penetrating my innocence, a foreign ache burning in my lower belly that made me feel a little dizzy.

He would be harsh. Demanding. Maybe even cruel.

As if sensing my thoughts, he threaded his fingers through my hair and harshly tugged my head back to meet his smoldering gaze.

"Am I not being clear?" he asked, his grip tightening. "Suck my cock, Raelyn."

"Yes, My Prince." The hoarse quality of my voice betrayed my nerves, and the arch of his brow confirmed he'd heard it as well. Or, more likely, that was his way of expressing irritation.

What is wrong with you? You know how to do this.

But it's Kylan…

Just fucking do it!

I stroked his shaft, learning the silky feel of him. So long, soft, *hard*. I bent and traced the path of my palm with my tongue—from base to head. His fingers knotted even tighter in my hair, his impatience clear. My lips parted over the tip of him, sliding down as far as my throat allowed and sucking as I went.

"Your Highness, my phone," Tremayne said, appearing beside me.

I started to pull away, but Kylan pushed me right back down, causing his cock to go even deeper than before. My training kept my gag reflex at bay, allowing me to take the harsh thrust, but my breathing faltered.

He extended his opposite hand. "What am I looking for?" he asked, sounding completely unfazed.

My throat worked as I tried to inhale and failed. His palm held me in place, refusing my attempt to move.

Does he realize I can't breathe?

I couldn't use the safe word to tell him, not that I expected him to listen anyway.

"The second item," Tremayne said. "It shows you as the sender."

My eyes flicked up to Kylan's face, but he was too busy studying the device to notice. Tears clouded my vision, my lungs burning with the need for air. I swallowed—or tried—causing my throat to constrict around him. His grasp shifted just enough to grant me an inhale that instantly cooled my insides.

"Hmm, I see," he murmured, his hold loosening even more. "Continue, Raelyn," he said softly, his focus still on the item in his other hand.

I sucked him deep again—to the point of near pain—and hollowed my cheeks around him. His lack of an outward reaction almost irked me. He seemed too consumed by whatever he was doing with Tremayne's device to even notice my efforts below. I tried again, grasping his base with my palm and swallowing him all the way down to my hand.

The slight pressure on my head, the twitch of his fingers, confirmed it was working, despite his steady expression.

Again, I decided, perfecting the move and adding a swirl of my tongue to the tip. A hint of his salty essence leaked from the crown, fueling me onward.

His grip in my hair tightened again, his thighs tensing.

"I'll be keeping this." He tucked Tremayne's phone into his pocket and slid that palm to the back of my neck. "My technician needs to trace that message, as it was not sent by me."

"I didn't know, Your Highness. I thought—"

"No, Tremayne," he growled, his palm squeezing my nape as he took control of my rhythm. "You want to know why I won't name you sovereign? It's because you don't fucking think. You never fucking think." Kylan's head fell back on the couch. "Good God, she's proving you wrong right now."

I almost smiled, but he shoved himself down my throat again.

"That message came from you," Tremayne snapped. "How the fuck should I have known it wasn't real?"

"Because a good subordinate knows his royal," Kylan replied on a sharp exhale, his legs straining around me. "*Fuck*, Raelyn."

Heat blossomed inside me at hearing him lose control because of *me*. This powerful male was lost to my mouth, the subtle sweeps of my tongue against his sensitive head, the way I sucked him deep when he reached the right point in my throat.

"Your assessment of the university…" He trailed off on a low growl, the predatory sound searing my being. "Is inaccurate." My scalp ached with how hard he held me while my heart thudded loudly in my ears.

I'd always seen this as an act meant solely for the man, but it was just as much for me. Seeing his jaw go rigid, feeling his hands clutch me tighter, and sensing the orgasm coiling within him—it was a heady intoxication I could easily become addicted to.

He may own my body, but in this moment, I owned his.

"Your Highness—"

"Enough." Kylan's cock pulsed inside my mouth, his fingers clenching in my hair. "Swallow, Raelyn. All of it." He shoved me down, forcing me to take his seed directly into my throat as his pleasure erupted on a groan.

I consumed his salty essence without flinching. My eyes were on his face, memorizing every inch of his ecstasy.

Such a beautiful male.

I'd noticed before, but it was even more evident now. His full lips were parted, his aristocratic features somehow less severe, and his dark eyes had turned a molten brown with desire and approval swimming in their depths. He stared down at me, a smirk playing over the edge of his mouth.

It took me a moment to realize why.

I was staring at him without permission

And I'd completely forgotten my need to breathe.

His grip loosened as I pulled back, sucking as I went to ensure I had every last drop of him, and I dropped my gaze to his still-erect cock.

Even that part of him was beautiful.

Of course. Because all vampires were gorgeous.

"Oh, darling, you certainly earned your high marks." Kylan stroked his thumb against my pulse, his palm still against my nape while the other had fallen to his abdomen. "Your theory could not be more incorrect, Tremayne. Which means, we now get to discuss your inappropriate disposal of human property."

Tremayne snorted. "Why do you think I believed that edict, Kylan?" His familiar use of the name had Kylan freezing beneath me. "You slaughtered your harem. Why can't we do the same? They're just humans."

A squeal from the table ended in a scream as something warm and slick landed against my back. Gurgling filled the air, the sound of someone struggling to breathe, followed by violent slurping.

Kylan didn't move or react, his posture relaxing as he lifted his palm from my neck to my head to begin gently stroking my hair.

Another shriek sounded, causing me to flinch.

He's ripping them apart.

I couldn't see, but I could *feel* it.

That's blood oozing down my back.

Blood from the women.

And Kylan's doing nothing to stop it.

"Are you done throwing your tantrum, Tremayne?" he asked after a beat, his tone bored.

"Isn't that how you killed your humans?" he retorted. "Why don't you demonstrate with the new one? Show me how you prefer it to be done since clearly you feel I'm doing it wrong."

My shoulders tensed, my heart stuttering.

He won't.

He might.

Kylan kept petting me, his fingers running through my strands. Then he sighed. "Stand up, Raelyn."

Rocks settled firmly in my throat, making swallowing impossible. *What's he going to do? Slaughter me? Give me to Tremayne?*

I closed my eyes, refusing to let him see the tears threatening my vision, and slowly climbed to my feet. Not even the ache in my knees could distract me from the pounding in my ears.

Kylan stood as well, his body heat doing little to dispel the chill engulfing my being.

The sound of him zipping up his pants and fixing his belt had me chewing on my lower lip, my eyelids refusing to open. Then he palmed my cheek and placed a kiss against my forehead.

"Why would I kill a female with such fantastic oral skills, Tremayne?" he asked against my skin. "I've not nearly enjoyed her to the fullest extent."

I almost sagged in his arms, relieved, but he was already setting me off to the side.

"That's what you fail to grasp," he continued, stepping away from me and toward the other male. I peeked at the ground.

Blood splattered against gold.

Human blood.

From the two women.

Their corpses were both lying on the table, their throats ripped wide open, their expressions frozen forever in terror.

My stomach rebelled, threatening to expel my earlier meal. I clamped down my jaw, refusing, causing my body to shake from the effort.

"You just don't understand," Kylan continued, tucking his hands into his pockets. "A human may no longer have a use to you, but that doesn't render the mortal useless to others. You can buy and sell property, Tremayne. I have explained this to you several times."

"Who would want to buy used goods?" he retorted, his posture bordering on aggressive. "Isn't that why you killed your harem? Because they lacked profit?"

Kylan slipped out of his jacket and set it on the couch.

"Another thing you fail to understand, Tremayne, is that all property within this region belongs to me. That includes all the possessions—material or otherwise—of the vampires under my care. Which means, those humans you just slaughtered—the ones who were auditioning and not even your property yet—were mine. As were all the others you murdered earlier today."

He scoffed. "You're seriously going to chastise me over a few mortal lives after the example you've set? That's rich."

"And lastly." Kylan paused to begin slowly rolling up the sleeves of his dress shirt. "You seem completely unapologetic about your actions."

"You want me to apologize for committing the same acts as you." Tremayne actually laughed, sounding genuinely amused. "So, what, only royal Kylan is allowed to kill slaves when he tires of them? The rest of us have to ask for permission?"

"Humans may be property, but their lives are what keep us thriving. To kill them without purpose is unacceptable and will not be tolerated in my territory."

"So your harem was killed with purpose?"

"Indeed." Kylan's forearms were exposed as his hands returned to his sides. "But you're mistaken on a key element to all of this, Tremayne."

"Yeah? And what's that, *Your Highness*?" he asked, mocking the formal name.

"I didn't kill my harem."

Kylan's arm moved with impeccable speed as he punched Tremayne in the face, following up with another hit to the male's abdomen and a third to his chest, all in the blink of an eye. Meanwhile, his words rattled around in my head.

I didn't kill my harem.

Tremayne lunged at Kylan with a furious roar, but the royal was too fast for him. Security rushed into the room, but a look from Kylan kept them all at bay.

My hand flew to my mouth as Tremayne used the distraction to his advantage, his fist connecting with Kylan's jaw.

The royal chuckled and shook his head.

"You might be one of the eldest in my region, Tremayne, but I still have nearly two thousand years on you."

A flash of a blade followed his words, glinting in the light as it sailed into Tremayne's skull. He fell to the ground with a thud, only to be picked up by

Kylan and carried to the windows.

"You're hereby excommunicated until such a time that I allow you back into my territory. Enjoy the fall."

Crash.

My jaw dropped.

He'd just thrown Tremayne through the window.

From the top floor of the hotel tower.

Chapter Thirteen

KYLAN

RAELYN'S GASP DISAPPEARED beneath the wind roaring in through the broken glass. I brushed the debris from my shirt, unrolling the fabric from my elbows as well, and retrieved my jacket from the couch.

She stood gaping at the destruction, her shoulders locked and coated in blood thanks to Tremayne's ridiculous show of aggression. This outcome had been a long time coming. He frequently tested my boundaries, always looking for a way to outdo me.

Whoever impersonated me sent that edict to him with purpose, knowing he would jump at the opportunity. Which meant it was someone with knowledge of my territory. That still suggested Jace, considering our close proximity, unless the culprit was working with someone from within.

I'd give the phone to Judith and have her team do some digging and also determine if anyone else received a similar note.

From what Angelica had said, it sounded like Tremayne had started the rumor of my supposed declaration. Well, that would be fixed. Right now.

"Come, Raelyn," I called over the wind, extending my hand. She carefully maneuvered around the blood on the floor, her arms covered in goose bumps.

We turned, facing half a dozen armed guards all kneeling with their heads bowed, waiting for my directive.

Right.

Tremayne's former staff.

"Clean up this mess," I demanded. "You'll have a new supervisor soon. Make sure the girls in the bedroom are alive and get them some food and clothes. Harm them in any way and I'll kill you myself."

There'd been enough meaningless death in this building tonight. I would not be adding those females to the list, even if they preferred to die after whatever Tremayne had done to them.

Sick fuck.

"Yes, My Prince," the leader of them said, head still bowed.

Having nothing left to say, I pulled Raelyn along with me to the elevators and pushed her inside as soon as it arrived. Her back hit the wall, her lips trembling as she kept her head bowed.

Please don't be broken.

I selected the Hold button with my fingerprint, forcing the car to stay in place after the doors hissed closed.

Raelyn didn't move as I approached, didn't flinch as I aligned my body with hers—thigh to thigh, pelvis to pelvis—and gripped her chin between my thumb and forefinger. I tilted her head back to properly search her eyes.

Bright blue irises focused on me right back, her pupils flaring.

I smiled. The trembling had been from the cold.

Good.

"There's a camera over my shoulder, but it doesn't have sound. You may speak freely, Raelyn."

"And say what?" she asked, her voice hoarse from the way I'd fucked her throat raw. Mmm, I needed to fix that.

"Whatever you want," I breathed, brushing my lips against hers. "But first…" I sliced my tongue against my incisor and slipped it inside her mouth. She jolted, her palms clasping my biceps as I deepened the kiss, sending my blood down her pretty, talented throat.

After the tentative way she'd stroked my dick, my expectations of her oral skills had decreased drastically. But the female had surprised me. No, she'd floored me. It'd been a long time since someone had learned my preferences that quickly and applied them, and under pressure as well.

Fucking perfection.

I thanked her with my mouth, worshiped her with my tongue, and vowed to return the favor later—thoroughly.

She moaned, losing herself to the endorphins of my essence.

Blood exchange with mortals was a rare activity, typically reserved for those with promise whom a vampire desired to protect. It granted increased healing and strength and enhanced their senses. Temporary powers, so to speak, that could easily become addictive. But if this was how Raelyn reacted—by rubbing her body against mine—then she could drink from me whenever she pleased.

I licked her bottom lip, the mark I'd left earlier healing now, thanks to my blood. Mmm, it didn't matter. Any vampires who scented her would smell my essence all over her.

Mine.

And I was not sharing.

I admired her lust-fused gaze, nuzzling my nose against hers. "Feeling better?"

"What did you just do to me?" she asked, awed.

"Rekindled your spirit with a little immortal flare." I kissed her again, loving the taste of her mingled with my essence—both blood and sex. A hint of fear trickled through the air, a sign that my brethren were beginning to react to the message I'd delivered to the sidewalk down below.

They would want to know why.

And I would explain in my own way.

"We're not finished yet," I warned, pulling my mouth from hers. "I have more work to do here."

She blinked up at me. "Okay."

I studied her expression for signs of terror. The initial stirrings of it had escalated her pulse several times, particularly when Tremayne crudely suggested I kill her. But she merely gazed back at me now, her heartbeat steady and strong, her cheeks tinted with pink. "You're still not afraid of me," I marveled.

"You'll have to do better than throwing an asshole through a window to frighten me," she whispered. Then her eyes rounded upon realizing what she'd just admitted out loud. "I mean—"

I chuckled, pressing a finger to her lips. "You're always free to speak openly in private with me, Raelyn, especially if it includes calling Tremayne an asshole, which he is."

"Is?" she repeated, frowning. "Meaning, he's not…?"

"Dead?" I finished for her. "No, he'll live. It takes a lot more than a fall to kill a vampire, but it's going to take him a while to heal. Primarily because I'm going to forbid anyone from helping him. He's earned his agony and excommunication. Let him pick up his own pieces without bringing anyone else down."

Cruel, maybe, but necessary to make a statement. I would not tolerate mindless killing in this territory, even if they believed my behavior to be an example.

I pressed my forehead to hers. "Which brings us to the next task of the evening. Ready?"

"Do you really need my permission?"

"No."

"Then why ask?"

"I'm allowed to care at least a little bit, Raelyn," I said, turning to select the bottom floor. The car began to move while I kept her crowded against the wall. "I didn't kill them."

She swallowed, her gaze holding mine. "Then who did?"

"That's what I'm trying to find out, and until I do, you're accompanying me everywhere. Because I suspect whoever did this will want to make a violent example out of you."

Her pulse finally faltered. "W-what?"

The elevator dinged, announcing our swift arrival. Raelyn remained frozen, her face paling.

Well, at least her reactions would be appropriate now.

Even if it was a bit cruel to give her the truth so bluntly.

I held her chin as the doors opened. "Don't leave my side, and remember decorum." I brushed my lips against hers and released her. "Come."

My ire weaved an ominous cloud through the air with every step. The vampires under my protection would be able to feel my fury, even as I observed them all with a carefully blank expression. Several stopped speaking and fell to their knees. Others—the oldest in the room—bowed their heads in respect while the humans whimpered and fell to the stone floor in supplication, passively begging for their lives.

I moved slowly, hands in my pockets, surveying them all. Raelyn followed at my side, her gaze downcast, her skin still pale.

Good. That's the way a harem member should act after seeing what transpired upstairs.

Myers burst in through the lobby doors. "He's a fucking…" The long-haired vampire trailed off upon seeing me in the center of the room, his knees immediately bending and taking him to the floor.

"Finish your statement, Myers," I prompted, curious. "He's a fucking what?"

The male's tan skin whitened, his terror palpable. "Mess, Your Highness."

"Who?"

His throat bobbed as he managed to reply, "Lord Tremayne."

"Lord?" I repeated, chuckling. "No, surely not. He is, however, exiled until I say otherwise. Any vampire found assisting him in any manner will answer to me. Do you understand?"

A chorus of "Yes, My Prince" and "Yes, Your Highness" sounded throughout the room, no one daring to argue or look me in the eye.

"For those wondering, the crime that earned him this sentence was the spreading of false information. I have not and will not condone killing mortals indiscriminately in this territory. If you're craving a bloodbath, order a human from the food service or entertainment industry."

I waved my hand toward the dining area of the hotel designated for that explicit reason. Several humans adorned in chains were on the tables, some dead, others barely breathing. That was their purpose. To feed a vampire's hunger. Whether or not I agreed with it was a moot point. We were vampires. Humans were food.

No one dared comment or raise a question, so I continued.

"Tremayne required the reminder that everything in this region belongs to me, including your humans. Do not meaninglessly harm my property just because you're bored. It is unacceptable and prohibited."

More silence, but a hint of discontent underlined their inclined acceptance.

"Tremayne argued that killing my harem served as an indication that you all can do the same. I will only address two points. First, harem members are sexual servants who provide entertainment. Enjoying them to their fullest extent is acceptable, just as you are allowed to indulge in your entertainment purchases. Second, as my property, it is my prerogative to do whatever the fuck I please. If anyone disagrees with these points, speak now."

Of course no one did. And that hint of discontent disappeared as well.

No, I am not losing my mind to immortal age.

Yes, I am still your royal.

And this is my fucking territory. If you don't like how I run things, leave.

"Well, hearing no questions, I have an announcement to make. Rise."

The vampires in the room quickly abided my command while the humans remained on the floor, leaving Raelyn as the only standing mortal. I wondered if she realized the symbolism in that, that there were perks to being in a royal's harem. This was one of them.

"The K Hotel Enterprise CEO position is officially open. I will be accepting applications throughout the week and will make a decision in a month." Whomever I selected would inherit not only this hotel but also several like it across the territory, including one in the heart of Lilith City. The competition for the position would be an entertaining one, as several vampires in this region were old enough to take over Tremayne's former empire.

"Spread the word," I demanded, referring to my warnings in addition to the employment opportunity.

Chatter spread as my constituents did as requested, sending messages to their contacts and murmuring expectations amongst each other. Some of the names mentioned were ones I would be contacting directly.

"Your Highness." Cherise curtsied with the greeting, her head low and her interruption insufferable. Had she not learned her lesson when I closed the elevator in her face? "About earlier, I wanted—"

I silenced her with a slice of my hand through the air. "What did you do with the human who failed to recognize me?"

The voices around us quieted, waiting.

She swallowed. "I-I gave him to the kitchen staff to add to the menu."

Well, I supposed that was better than killing him herself. "That punishment implies you blame him for his failure, yes?"

"He should know his prince, Your Highness." She lifted her chin, her position on the matter clearly resolute.

"I agree. And who do you believe is responsible for teaching them, Cherise?"

Her nostrils flared. "The universities, My Prince."

"Initially, yes. But who is responsible for maintaining that knowledge and preparing the humans for face-to-face interactions with their royals?"

A tendril of fear sweetened the air, her cheeks losing color.

Too little, too late, Cherise. You brought it up again.

"Their s-superiors, Your Highness."

"Meaning *you* as the reception manager in this case," I translated. I would have let this go, having more important matters requiring my attention. Alas, Cherise had to say something to remind me of the earlier altercation. In front of the room, no less. "You sent the human to the kitchens for slaughter. That's Maeve's department." I searched for the blonde vampire and found her leaning against a wall, expression impassive. "Join us."

She didn't hesitate, her leather boots clacking against the stone with each step. The jeans and sweater were very last century, denoting her younger vampire age. Most from that generation chose comfort over style.

"My Prince," she greeted, bowing instead of curtsying.

"Is the human still alive?"

She pointed a red nail to the brown-haired male on a table in the dining area, his nude form in a fetal position and shaking.

So yes, still breathing and untouched, from the looks of it.

Excellent.

"How do you feel about reception management, Maeve?"

Her hazel eyes glittered. "It would be a desired change from overseeing the kitchen, My Prince."

"I just so happen to have a new opening, if you're interested. But I have a requirement."

Cherise sputtered. "Your High—"

"Was I talking to you?" I demanded, sending her my best glower. "Kneel, Cherise, and do not dare stand or speak again until I say otherwise."

Raelyn's pulse jumped at my tone, reminding me of her presence beside me. I palmed her lower back and pressed a kiss to her neck out of habit more than necessity, earning me a few raised eyebrows from the room. Apparently, showing affection to my harem was unexpected. Good.

"As I was saying, I have a requirement and it involves the male. I want you to take him off that table and retrain him. Consider it an audition for the role. I'll return later in the week to assess his improvement. If he passes, you can keep the job. If he doesn't, you'll go back to the kitchen with the boy."

Her lips curled. "Thank you for this opportunity, My Prince. I won't let you down."

No, I suspected she wouldn't. "Excellent. Please retrieve the human and start tonight."

"Your Highness." She bowed and moved with purpose toward the dining hall.

Now to handle the vampire at my feet. I sighed, my thumb drawing little circles against Raelyn's back. "Cherise, I'm disappointed not only in your lack of leadership but also in your lack of candor and respect. Perhaps a new role in kitchen management will help refresh your outlook on life, hmm? Make the arrangements to switch roles with Maeve, and when I check in with her in a week, I better not hear of any issues."

She said nothing, her head still bowed.

Very good. She'd taken my instructions regarding standing and speaking seriously. There was hope for her yet.

"Go on, then." I gestured for her to leave. "I'm tired of your presence."

I wrapped my arms around Raelyn and kissed her softly. The move effectively told the room I considered my consort more important than Cherise because I dismissed her in favor of a human. It also showed everyone that I could be tender with my property when I desired it.

Raelyn's mouth opened for mine, allowing me to take her as I craved. I ignored Cherise's movements and words as she left, ignored everyone watching us, and reveled in her addictive taste.

My cock hardened against her lower belly, needing more.

I could force her to give everyone a show, to demonstrate just how skilled she was with her tongue, but that seemed more of a punishment than a reward. And my darling, obedient little lamb had earned my praise, not my wrath.

"The valet better have my keys ready," I murmured against her lips. I kissed her soundly once before addressing the room. "Enjoy the dawning hours and expect an invitation shortly for a gathering at Kylan Tower later this month."

A few grins flashed, the idea of a party exciting the audience. There were enough vampires here to initiate the rumor mill, but Judith would assist in sending formal memos to my constituents in the early evening. There were close to five thousand in my region, one of the largest in the world. Only fifty or so appeared to be here tonight, which didn't shock me. This was a hotel, not a residence, nor had anyone expected my arrival.

I guided Raelyn toward the waiting valet and plucked my keys from his hand without acknowledging him. The passenger door opened, and as I helped Raelyn inside, I noticed Tremayne's splatter all over the paved sidewalk and hotel furnishings.

"Myers," I called.

The lanky male immediately joined me outside, his hazel eyes downcast. "My Prince."

"See that this mess is cleaned up, and ship Tremayne's remains east toward the border with the Calgary Clan. Do not help him in any way."

Myers bowed his head, his lips curling at having been given a task. "Yes, Your Highness. Thank you."

I left him with a nod and joined Raelyn in the warm interior of my two-seater. Not the best for snowy roads, but the engineered tires helped with handling the slick concrete. And the humans did a reasonable job plowing and shoveling.

Reaching over, I buckled Raelyn in before pulling away from the hotel. "You may be yourself again, darling lamb."

She remained quiet for a beat. "I'm not sure I know what that means."

I chuckled. "We're alone, which means punishment is far less likely."

"But still a possibility."

"Always, yes." I had standards. If she broke them, she'd know. I shifted into a higher gear to pick up speed, wanting to make it difficult for anyone to follow us. Owning half the city made guessing my whereabouts difficult. I preferred it that way. The underground tunnels would help. My engineers had crafted them into mazelike patterns while transforming the destroyed city formerly known as Vancouver into Kylan City.

I navigated onto a ramp leading us downward into the stone-crafted caverns and placed my palm on Raelyn's thigh. "You were remarkable this evening, little lamb. Proof that somewhere inside you is a properly trained human."

"I know the rules, have followed them all my life. Until you kissed me." She sounded frustrated by that.

My lips curled. "Do you think it was the stress of the moment?"

"Maybe. I just didn't want you to pick me, and, well, I bit you."

"Most humans want to be selected for a harem, thinking they'll be granted access to the finer luxuries in life." What they failed to consider was the cost. Several of the royals and alphas preferred pain to pleasure. I preferred a mix of both.

"I wanted to go into the tournament."

"Yes, I know, my immortality-craving lamb." I squeezed her thigh as I turned off the car lights to hide our trail.

She tensed, her mortal eyes not granting her the same sight as my night vision. I accelerated for fun, enjoying the way it escalated her heartbeat.

"Lilith dangles immortality before you all as a controlling measure. Rather than work together, you squabble with each other over the minute possibility of a better future. Although, it does seem you bonded a bit with Silas." Something I suspected contributed to her spirited responses to me. "Did you ever banter with him?"

She snorted. "We started as academic rivals and fought all the time, but Willow brought us together. She pointed out that we were essentially the same person, just in female and male form." A hint of nostalgia entered her voice, her fondness of her old life clear.

"Where was Willow sent?" I didn't know any of her class by name, apart from Raelyn and Silas. My kind preferred numbers. Easier to manage and remember.

"The breeding farms," she whispered.

Ah, yes, that was a sad fate. Forced human procreation. It was necessary to keep the numbers high, and we only wanted those with quality bloodlines to continue. "She must have had significant test scores."

"The same as mine."

I nodded. "Likely, yes." Because Raelyn would also make good breeding stock, but luck of the draw had sent her to the final selection rounds instead. The Magistrate pretended to have everything down to a science. Realistically, he put a bunch of scores into his computer and randomized the results for those in a certain breed and class.

Silas had been meant for the Immortal Cup, selected years ago for his potential by Jace and Walter, just as I had selected a handful a decade prior. The top of the class were followed and reviewed frequently, their skills and attributes setting them apart from others.

I turned into another tunnel, winding our way beneath the city and using the technology built into my car to disrupt the video feeds.

Judith was magical.

"What will happen to her?" Raelyn asked softly.

"Do you really want me to answer that?"

She was quiet for a long moment, her pulse slowing as she breathed deep and exhaled. "How many children will she bear?"

"It depends on her biology. She can only safely have one pregnancy a year, sometimes even fewer. Our scientists have learned how to move the process along, but Mother Nature refuses to fully cooperate. And as human life is actually sacred to our kind, as your lives are necessary to our survival, we do what we can to keep the breeding stock healthy until they are no longer of use."

"And then?"

"They go to the blood farms or into the service industry." Zelda was an example of someone previously used for breeding who now worked in a household. She'd been sent to Vilheim's property in the city to help in the kitchen, and I'd quickly learned about her skills through her superior and Vilheim. "Some of them end up in reasonable accommodations."

"But not all."

Not most. I squeezed her leg once more before returning my hand to the shifter. An apology threatened my tongue, something that rarely happened. *A wolf does not apologize to a lamb; he simply eats it.*

I cleared my throat and changed the subject to something safer. "We'll be staying in the city for several weeks, perhaps months. Also, the party I mentioned will have other royals in attendance, which means I need to escalate your sexual training. They'll expect you to be on a level similar to their own consorts, and should I have to share you with one, I'll need you properly prepared."

Her pulse stuttered at the mention of sharing. Not surprising. She probably assumed I'd give her to Robyn. Not a chance in hell I'd allow that to happen without supervising. I wasn't even sure I intended to share Raelyn at all—given the potential threat to her life—but I had to instruct her on the rules regardless.

"We'll begin immediately." Why waste any time when the sun wouldn't rise for another two hours?

God, I loved winter.

Long nights, short days, and endless hours to play in bed.

Which we would.

Starting tonight.

Chapter Fourteen

RAE

"UNDRESS." Kylan wasted no time after guiding me through the threshold of his bedroom suite, his single-worded demand a warm caress against my ear.

Sexual training.

For the purpose of sharing me with other royals.

Royals like Robyn.

My stomach twisted in protest. I didn't want a collar or a leash, or to be hauled across the concrete.

Were there others like her? Were they worse?

Does it matter? I have to survive Kylan first.

I shivered, recalling the way he handled Tremayne and then the others downstairs. That had been the Kylan everyone feared, the one who exuded power and authority and did not take disobedience lightly.

Yet, he'd treated me—

"Raelyn." The slight hint of admonishment in his tone said he didn't appreciate my hesitation.

Right, I needed to focus.

And undress.

I pushed the thin strap off my shoulders and let the gown fall to my feet, leaving me naked except for my heels. I bent to remove them, but his palm on my nape pulled me back up.

"Those can stay." He nipped my ear, pressing his suit-clad chest to my bare back. "Get on the bed and spread your legs. I want to see you, Raelyn, and explore every inch of your sexy little cunt."

Heat pooled between my thighs at his vulgar words.

Goddess, what is he going to do to me?

Was it really only earlier this evening that he'd pushed me up against that tree? And just last night that he selected me?

No wonder my limbs shook as I climbed up onto the oversized bed. This had been the longest twenty-four hours of my life, even with the rest on the plane.

Or maybe it was his blood coursing through my body. I'd felt more alive, more alert, since he kissed me in the elevator. As if my very being had been lit on fire from within. My senses were more acute, my body more aware. I could almost *feel* Kylan's desire from his predatory gaze alone as I lay back on the bed.

Pure, unadulterated hunger.

I swallowed.

That was the look of a male who either craved sex or violence, or perhaps a mixture of both.

My legs trembled as I slid them apart, revealing my intimate flesh for his perusal. His focus shifted downward—slowly—searing a path along the way before centering between my thighs.

That heated look stirred something inside of me. Something hot and intense and foreign.

I shuddered, the desire to close my legs almost overriding my mind. *He wants them open. But oh, I need… I need…*

Kylan slipped out of his jacket, laying it over a chair beside the bed. His tie was next. He stepped closer, his nimble fingers plucking at the buttons of his shirt one by one to slowly reveal the muscle beneath.

I'd seen him shirtless earlier, knew what to expect, but him undressing with the intent of touching me intensified the experience.

Vampires were all perfect. It seemed to be a requirement of their immortality.

But Kylan? He redefined the meaning of perfection.

All hard, clean lines wrapped up in smooth skin.

My mouth watered just looking at him.

His lips curled as he dropped his shirt on top of his jacket. "Your arousal is intoxicating, Raelyn," he murmured, prowling toward me. My limbs tensed as he crawled onto the bed between my legs, his intent clear.

He gave me less than a second to react—not even that—before licking a path up my sex. I gasped, my fingers curling into the covers on either side of my hips.

Fuck…

Silas had done this more than once, but it never felt anything like *this.*

Kylan repeated the action, this time applying more pressure, causing my body to convulse uncontrollably. He smiled against my clit, his teeth touching the sensitive nub and shooting even more spasms up and down my spine.

"You swallowed me so beautifully earlier, little lamb. Allow me to return the favor."

Wha—

Oh Goddess…

I arched off the bed on a groan, only to be pushed back down by his palm on my abdomen. His opposite hand went to my hip to hold me in place while he devoured me with his tongue.

Fierce waves of energy rippled over me—through me—consuming me completely. I couldn't breathe, couldn't think, couldn't move; I could only feel.

I had no idea this type of pleasure was even possible. It almost hurt in its severity, burning through my veins to singe each nerve ending.

"Kylan," I whimpered, unsure of whether to push him away or grab his hair. "It… it…"

His incisor skimmed my sensitive flesh.

He wouldn't—

I screamed, the pleasure too much. My body shook, my lips trembling incoherently while Kylan obliterated my senses.

He'd bitten me.

Down there.

Or maybe he'd only nicked me. It didn't matter. He'd set my essence on fire.

But, Goddess, that shouldn't be allowed. Ecstasy mingled with pain as he laved the wound with his tongue. Sucking, nipping, pulling me under a cloud of insanity that lacked reason and focused primarily on feeling.

My limbs tingled.

My heart raced.

My lungs fought for air.

"You're denying it," he murmured, approval in his voice. "But you won't win, sweetheart." Another lick that sizzled through my veins. "Give in, Raelyn. Submit to the sensation. Submit to me, love."

He scraped me again, and I grabbed his shoulders, my nails digging into his skin.

"Kylan." It was both a plea and a curse, a desire for more and a need for him to stop. I couldn't stop shaking, the flames burning inside me close to ripping me apart.

This was nothing like what he did to me against that tree. That had barely qualified as an introduction.

"Raelyn." His growl vibrated my core, shooting sparks up my spine. "I want to feel you come on my tongue." I quivered, my entire being lost to his will and the movements of his mouth. "Now."

His command hummed through me, reaching the depths of my soul and forcing my compliance. The world shattered around me, painting my vision in shades of black and white. Kylan's name rolled off my tongue with disjointed words chasing after it.

I felt destroyed.

Misplaced.

Liquid.

My chest burned as euphoria vibrated my limbs.

"Your pleasure is addictive, Raelyn," Kylan murmured against my wet flesh. "I need more." His tongue speared me deep and sent me over another cliff of oblivion.

How was that even possible?

Was it because I'd imbibed his blood?

Oh, it didn't matter. Not with his ability to do *that.*

I squirmed against his mouth, his nips and licks sending me into a fog of disoriented bliss. My mind fractured, thought no longer possible.

Just sensation.

Heat.

Sex.

Fuck.

I barely registered Kylan removing his pants, too consumed by the starry abyss swimming before my eyes. My shoes had disappeared too.

How?

When?

What had he just done to me?

His cock pressed against me—there. My clit throbbed and protested as his thick head rubbed against it, his heat obliterating my senses.

"Kylan," I whispered.

I've never—

His lips captured mine, silencing what I needed to say, his shaft sliding purposely through my arousal. I quivered beneath him, terrified and excited, all at the same time. But rather than push into me, he merely slipped through my slick folds, coating his hardness in my damp heat.

"Open," he murmured, his tongue tracing my lips.

I complied, granting him access to every part of me. He continued to saturate himself in my essence while coating my mouth in the aftermath of my orgasm.

"Do you taste yourself?" he asked softly. "Your sweet pussy wept all over my tongue, sweetheart." He punctuated the point by kissing me again, deeper this time, his ownership abundantly clear. "Some of my kind no longer enjoy giving pleasure, but I find that, when done right, it's very gratifying." His cock slid lower, the head finding my entrance.

I tensed, waiting.

It would hurt.

A lot.

But I had to take it.

That was his right as my owner.

"Mmm, a virgin." He smiled. "That inspires several intriguing possibilities, little lamb."

I shivered as he sat back on his heels between my knees, his hand wrapping around his shaft.

"Fuck, your arousal feels divine against my cock, Raelyn." He ran his palm up and down, his grip harsh and hypnotic. His abdominal muscles flexed with the movements, pulling taut as his tempo increased.

I licked my lips, going up onto my elbows to see more, fascinated.

Wasn't that my job?

And what did he mean by "intriguing possibilities"?

Better yet, how did he know I was a virgin?

"Stay just like that for me," he said, his voice low and deep.

He slid forward, straddling my hips with his knees, providing an even better view of his ministrations. The stirrings of that addictive sensation began again, pulsing and tensing in my lower belly.

I wasn't anywhere near ready for another wave of pleasure, but watching him stroke himself was undeniably stimulating. His forearm flexed.

"Open your mouth, Raelyn." The command was underlined with a growl that went straight to the ache between my thighs.

I parted my lips, holding his gaze.

"Fuck." He grabbed a fistful of my hair with his free hand, tugging me forward. His orgasm erupted onto my tongue in hot, thick spurts that slid into the back of my throat, forcing me to swallow.

His face contorted in such beautiful agony that I couldn't help memorizing every detail—his tightened jaw, the fan of his long lashes against his cheekbone, the way my name fell from his beautiful lips.

"Suck me clean," he demanded, his grip in my hair yanking me forward.

I took him as deep as my throat allowed, the remainder of his ecstasy mingling with mine against my tongue. His grasp only tightened, holding me in place as I hollowed my cheeks around him.

"Every last drop, Raelyn. I want you full of my cum, my essence, so everyone knows you're mine."

I shuddered at the possession in his tone. Vampires and lycans were notoriously proprietorial.

Yet, he plans to share me with other royals.

I ignored that thought, refocusing myself on the task. Kylan's hold eventually loosened, his fingers combing through my hair as he stared down at me with a look of almost wonder.

"You look gorgeous like this," he murmured, his other hand going to my jaw. "Your mouth wrapped around my cock." He pushed himself farther, a devious twinkle in his gaze. "Your lack of a gag reflex confirms your throat training—an advanced course—yet you've never been fucked. That's fascinating."

I swallowed around him, my eyes beginning to water from the harsh intrusion. He slid back, the head slipping from my mouth with a satisfying pop.

He glanced down, a smirk playing over his lips. "Spotless. Beautiful, Raelyn."

His mouth captured mine before I could reply, his body flattening mine against the bed. He placed his elbows on either side of my head and settled his groin against the soft spot between my thighs.

"I could kiss you for hours," he whispered. "Fuck you for even longer. Dine between your thighs for a century." He nuzzled my nose. "But I can sense your exhaustion. It's been a very long evening, and you'll need rest for your next set of trials."

"Trials?" I repeated.

"Sexual training." He kissed my jaw, his lips trailing a path to my ear. "We'll need to be inventive now that I know you're a virgin. That's a playing card I intend to use during the right situation."

I swallowed, uncertain of what he meant by that.

Did he intend to gift my innocence to another? In exchange for something of higher value to him?

While proprietorial, vampires were also practical and notorious for trading property. It kept them from becoming too attached. By swapping items frequently, their possessive instincts remained only on the surface.

Very few kept a human long-term.

But he's held on to Mikael for a decade…

"We'll discuss this more later." He kissed me softly, his tongue coaxing me into responding. "I'm very pleased with you, darling lamb. You'll make a fine consort."

An ache formed in my chest at the reminder of who I was to him.

For a moment, I'd almost forgotten, too lost in the sensations he'd evoked.

But this was all temporary.

A pleasure he would enjoy and forget in the blink of an eye.

While for me, it would be my entire existence. Born only to serve in the bedroom of a royal vampire. And soon there would be others as he expanded his harem, forgetting me, moving on to the others…

That shouldn't hurt.

It *couldn't* hurt.

Emotions were for the weak, and I wasn't weak.

My name is Rae and I will survive this.

There was no other choice, no other option, no other way.

Live or die.

My choice will always be life.

Chapter Fifteen

KYLAN

I COMBED MY FINGERS through Raelyn's red strands. The color was such a beautiful contrast to her creamy skin.

Such a gorgeous human.

Skilled, too.

And definitely a virgin.

The way she'd tensed had suggested her innocence, and her file confirmed it.

She never took an intercourse class. Fascinating. Most humans did, but she'd opted for physical sports instead. Likely because of her Vigil inclinations. Hmm, that path would have suited her. But so did the path to my bed.

I stroked her neck while skimming through her university notes with my free hand, reading about her curriculum choices.

The beginning years were the same for all humans—indoctrination courses meant to provide a stern introduction to society's requirements. Those who passed moved on to the next level, which included basic academics. The elite scores of that round, of which Raelyn's were impressive, were given certain liberties to advance their studies.

That's where the choices came into play.

Humans were allowed to pick their paths, but it was all a clever test—a way of observing their natural inclinations. Raelyn's record indicated varied interests, her coursework not identifiably specialized.

Fencing.

French.

A political science course surveying clan leadership throughout the last century.

Religion.

That last one made me snort. Lilith certainly did enjoy forcing the humans to worship her. If they only knew she was just a vampire like the rest of us and actually younger than me.

Cam was the eldest of our kind.

I sighed up at the ceiling, wondering for the thousandth time what actually happened to him. Lilith claimed him to be dead, but I knew her better than that. She had the old vampire locked up somewhere. The same place I would end up if anyone managed to prove me insane with immortal age.

Which wasn't going to happen.

I'd left Tremayne's phone with Judith and expected to hear from her any minute now. But I couldn't bring myself to leave Raelyn just yet. She intrigued me—her innocence, her defiance, her submission.

She's a virgin.

My lips curled in triumph. It provided me with the perfect angle and opportunity to manipulate the royals. They would desire her even more, and with a little training, she'd become the perfect bait for whoever had dared to make me an immortal enemy.

Typically, I would expect my other consorts to explain the formal procedures to Raelyn, to provide her with warnings and properly initiate her into the royal harem world. But they no longer existed.

That left Mikael as the only available teacher.

His experiences were similar, and he'd been with me long enough to understand my usual protocols when it came to sharing.

Yes. He would do well.

That task I would assign to him while I handled festivity arrangements. Personal invitations would be required, and I needed to ensure certain accommodations.

I sighed. Entertaining others was one of my least favorite activities, but it was the best play. Put them all under the same roof, set up Raelyn as bait, and see who pounced.

My phone buzzed, Judith summoning me from the bed.

I'm in the living area, she wrote.

I'll be there in five.

I wasn't quite ready to leave Raelyn yet. She'd snuggled into me to use my chest as a pillow, thus my arm being around her shoulders and my fingers in her hair. The female fit so perfectly, her legs scissored with mine.

Amazing what sleep revealed—her body already trusted mine. A dangerous proclamation considering what I could do to her, but the woman lacked fear. It had to be a result of her illegal friendships with Willow and Silas, a fact her files neither proved nor disputed.

There were, however, several videos of her oral exams with the male where she'd clearly faked her orgasm. That alone confirmed her lack of sexual feelings for the male, something that pleased me far more than it should.

I liked her. And her file only endeared her to me more. My feisty little lamb would make an excellent consort and may very well prove to be a favorite.

She stirred against me as I set my phone on the nightstand.

I kissed her forehead as I gently rearranged her on the pillows. "Sleep, darling. I'll have Mikael bring you evening breakfast in bed." He'd enjoy finding her naked. My gift to him.

Dressed in a pair of sweatpants and nothing else, I met him and Judith in the living area. Mikael handed me a cup of coffee—black and laced with his blood.

"You do love me," I murmured before taking a sip. "I left you something in the bedroom as well. She needs training on royal seduction and general expectations. I assume you're up to the task?"

His blond brows lifted. "Is that your way of saying she didn't live up to your expectations last night? Because her screams suggested otherwise."

My lips twitched. "On the contrary, she's quite gifted. But I need her properly informed on certain society requirements, which may necessitate a few hands-on tutorials."

His light gaze glimmered. "You're giving me permission to play."

"I'm giving you permission to teach," I replied, grinning around the rim of my coffee mug. "Enjoy."

"She'll need food first." He started toward the kitchen. "Then we'll get to work, Your Highness."

"I expect results," I called after him, settling onto the sofa beside a straight-faced Judith. Her severe blonde bun and white pantsuit deeply contrasted with my casual attire. I placed my ankle on my knee and relaxed into the leather cushion. "Tell me you found something, Judith."

"I did." Her gray eyes met mine. "You're not going to like it."

I took another sip of the coffee and set it off to the side. "I'm listening."

She handed me a tablet, the screen showcasing a series of lines and numbers. "The message went through a series of coordinates, but after an hour, I finally pinpointed the origin and original send time." Her index finger swiped along the screen. "It originated from your plane, Your Highness. During the Blood Day ceremony."

The proof glared at me from the device. "How is that possible?"

"I have a few theories, the strongest being that someone hacked into your systems while sharing airport space. There were other jets close enough to do so, and once hacked, it would be easy to send an email from one of the many devices you had on board."

"You've just suggested your team isn't handling my security properly," I noted dryly.

"Which is why I've already begun an investigation into the apparent breach."

The woman was constantly proving her worth and loyalty. "Good."

"I also put together a list of the royals and alphas who used the same airport and had planes in the same vicinity as yours." She pushed something on the screen that populated a series of names. "They're in order of closest to farthest, although that detail isn't important. Any of them could have accessed the plane's systems given their proximity."

Naomi.

Walter from the Clemente Clan.

Niklas from the Stella Clan.

Robyn.

Claude.

"Jace isn't on the list," I noted.

"No, they didn't have a plane. He stayed in Hazel City for a few days with Darius and Darius's new *Erosita* before driving in for the ceremony. All the surveillance confirms he returned to Hazel City after the Blood Day selections and is still there now."

"Meaning he didn't fly home."

"Not yet."

"But he could be working with someone." Of course, that would imply more than one royal was out to destroy my name. Or, perhaps, a clan leader. "Where were Brandt and Luka?" I shared borders with the Calgary Clan and the Majestic Clan. They would be ideal partners in this game, sharing equal desires to possess my land.

She took her tablet and began skimming through notes, her lips twisted to the side. Mikael chose that moment to appear with two plates—one of which he handed to me.

"Eat," he demanded.

My brow arched. "You humans seem to have a penchant for commanding me."

"I wouldn't dream of it, Your Highness." He gave a mock bow before heading toward the master suite with a skip in his step.

Raelyn would be either thrilled or mortified.

"They both landed on the other side of the ceremony site," Judith said, tapping the screen. "Unless they sent some lycans in stealth mode, it's highly unlikely they infiltrated your systems."

I plucked a piece of bacon from the plate and enjoyed the savory flavor while considering this new information. "Paints Jace in an innocent light."

"Which could be precisely what he wants," she murmured, still playing with her tablet. "Although, if that's the case, he's doing a great job of it. There's absolutely nothing to suggest he's the culprit."

I nodded. "True." He was in Naomi City when someone massacred my harem. "Of course, he could be hiring others to carry out his missions." I ate another slice of bacon while pondering. "Have there been any suspicious breaches on my property?"

Judith had installed several additional security measures after the incident. I'd grown comfortable in my leadership, assuming no one would be foolish enough to attack me on my own turf.

It was a mistake I would not be making again anytime soon.

She shook her head. "Nothing, and while impossible, all signs still point to there not being a break-in to begin with."

"Yes, because whoever killed my consorts wanted to make it look like it was me."

"And they did an excellent job," she muttered.

I couldn't agree more. "Well, what fun would this game be if the culprit was obvious?"

"Game," she repeated with a snort.

"What else would you have me call it?"

"A suicide mission?" she suggested.

"Well, there is that," I agreed. Because whoever challenged me to this duel would die. Of that I was certain. "Invite them all to the party, including Jace, Brandt, and Luka."

Their schedules and behavior may indicate innocence, but my gut still told me Jace was hiding something. I'd known the royal a very long time. He played the political arena almost as well as I did. Which meant, if it wasn't him, he might be able to aid me in my search.

"Actually, I'll call Jace personally."

Her eyebrows rose. "You will?"

"I will." I'd invite him to visit early with his new sovereign and give them both an opportunity to interact with Raelyn. Their reactions would either prove them innocent or increase my suspicion. I took another bite from my plate and set it on the table. "Anything else, Judith?"

"Yes." She hit a few buttons on her screen before showing me two identical messages. "Zion and Vilheim also received copies of your supposed edict."

I arched my eyebrows. "And you didn't think to lead with that?"

"They're both being monitored. Neither has acted on the message."

"Yet," I added flatly. Well, it seemed visiting two of the oldest vampires in my region had just been escalated to my top tasks of the day. I'd have to call Jace from the car. Priorities and all that. "Is there anything more you need to tell me?"

"Only a final logistical clarification, My Prince. I assume we're hosting the party at K Hotel?"

I nodded. "Seems appropriate. I'd like Tremayne's former quarters completely renovated as well."

"That project has already been assigned to Bethany."

"Brilliant." The woman possessed an eye for detail and had decorated several of my properties. I stood, then remembered a final item. "I need you to promote Angelica."

The young vampire had risked her life and position by visiting my compound uninvited, and she'd somehow managed to circumvent my security to reach me. All impressive, if a little suicidal. However, she'd shown great loyalty by not only informing me of Tremayne's affairs but also knowing I'd never send that message.

Very few would question the edict. That Angelica did made her valuable.

Judith's gray eyes flashed up to mine. "The freshling?"

"That freshling, as you call her, is the one who warned me about Tremayne's behavior. She might be the youngest vampire in my region, but she has potential, Judith. I want to see that potential cultivated and rewarded."

She held my gaze for a long moment and nodded. "I'll add her to your detail."

"Good." I didn't trust her implicitly yet, but it would give me an opportunity to properly judge her value. "Thank you, as always, for your due diligence, Judith."

"My Prince." She bowed her head as I stood.

Zion and Vilheim would make for a tiring evening. Both wanted to be promoted to senior leadership positions due to their age and power. Zion was the only one I'd even consider, yet he hadn't bothered calling me after receiving my supposed edict. That alone disqualified him.

I sighed, heading back to my bedroom to change.

Raelyn's pleasant tones greeted my ears, causing my lips to curl.

The fun had begun.

Too bad I couldn't stay to play.

Chapter Sixteen

RAE

"RAELYN." The male voice drifted over me—somewhat familiar. "I brought you evening breakfast."

I rolled in the cloud of blankets, my red hair covering my face. A warm hand helped brush the strands from my eyes, allowing me to see Mikael smiling down at me. I sat up and nearly knocked the plate from his hand.

His gaze fell to my breasts, causing me to frown.

I'm naked.

Right.

I yanked the blanket up and moved backward until I hit the headboard. My knees bent to my chest, acting as a shield.

His lips twitched. "You'll challenge Kylan but run from me. That's fascinating, Raelyn."

"It's Rae, and I barely know you."

"You don't really know Kylan either," he pointed out. "I brought you unsalted eggs, steamed broccoli, and a donut."

I eyed the items, my brow furrowing. "A donut?"

"Hmm, one of my favorite breakfast foods. I thought you might want to share one." He sat on the bed, the plate in his lap. "It's plain since your taste buds aren't ready for more, but it'll provide a good introduction nonetheless." He picked up a round, bready-looking food and held it out for my inspection. "Try it."

"I'd rather not."

"Suit yourself." He took a bite and set the plate beside me with a fork. "Go ahead and eat."

The broccoli was familiar, but the eggs were unlike any I'd ever seen.

"They're over medium instead of that scrambled packaged crap. Trust me, you'll appreciate the difference." He nudged the food closer. "Now, eat, *Rae*."

He'd actually used *my* name. The shock must have crossed my expression because he chuckled.

"I may have been trained through the Coventus, but I'm just as human as you are, Rae. I provide blood and you provide sex. Both items meant to satisfy His Royal Highness and no one else." He shrugged and savored another piece of his donut. "My fate was just slightly more defined than yours; that's all."

He had a good point.

Another human—only, male. Like Silas.

I lifted the plate and balanced it on my knees. Eggs and broccoli. Normal items. I could eat these. Besides, I needed the energy after last night. Kylan's blood had waned and left me feeling off somehow. Not exhausted so much as down. Or maybe that was waking up to find another man in the room, not him.

The broccoli provided nutrients my body required, whereas the eggs were a bit rich. I ate them slowly while Mikael watched, his donut long gone.

"Zelda comes from the universities as well," he murmured. "She knows what humans are used to and how to slowly introduce you to new flavors. You'll see. She's fantastic in the kitchen."

I'd met the blonde briefly last night, her cheeks bright red after being caught with Mikael. She'd seemed pleasant enough.

"How did last night go?" Mikael asked. "At the hotel?"

I swallowed the bite of egg in my mouth. "What part?"

"In general, I mean. Were there any issues? Anything you didn't know how to handle?" He cocked his head to the side. "Kylan says you need training, and I want to know where I'm starting."

I set the fork down. "Y-you're training me?" I hated that it came out unsteady, but Kylan hadn't mentioned Mikael being the one to train me. I thought he meant to continue my sexual instruction exclusively. Not invite his human pet to play, too.

"That's Kylan's directive, yes." His light gaze held mine. "It can be hands-on or hands-off, Rae. I'm here to coach you, not force you."

I frowned. "How can you properly instruct me without touching me?"

"Not all education requires physical contact, Raelyn." Kylan entered the bedroom wearing nothing but a pair of sweatpants sitting low on his hips. His muscles flexed as he moved, drawing my eyes downward to the impressive bulge below. My mouth watered with the memory of his orgasm. I shouldn't be craving him. Not like this. But I couldn't help it. Just being near him had my legs clenching with a need for *more*.

What has he done to me?

It had to be his blood. I thought it was out of my system, but clearly, it wasn't.

His lips curled. "She's just as insatiable as you, Mikael. Perhaps you two can work out an arrangement." He brushed a kiss against my temple that shot ice through my veins.

Such a casual statement about sharing. Would it really mean nothing to him for another male to touch me?

But of course it wouldn't. Kylan would have a harem in a few months, or sooner, and I'd just be one of a few. A toy to pass around to his royal friends, like Robyn.

This is my life.

How had it taken me this long to realize it?

Shock?

Hope for something more?

A wish to trade places with Silas?

I could be Willow. The thought had me shuddering. *It could be worse.*

Kylan pinched my chin and lifted my eyes to his. Whatever he saw made him frown. "Start with the formalities, Mikael. Detail your experiences as well so she knows what to expect."

"Yes, Your Highness."

"I have two items that require my immediate attention." He threaded his fingers through my hair and yanked me upward to my knees, causing the plate to fall as well as the blankets. "When I return, I'll provide the hands-on part of your training."

He brushed his lips over mine, rekindling the flames inside me with an ease that almost frightened me. Almost.

His bare chest seared mine, causing my nipples to pebble to painful points.

I knew my body would betray me, would adore worshiping his, but I never expected to *enjoy* it.

Kylan had warned me that he intended to destroy me. I had accepted that fate, assuming he meant physically.

No.

This being would *shatter* me before he was finished.

He's going to demolish my very soul.

"I want you wet and ready for me the moment I walk through that door, Raelyn." Kylan ran his nose over my cheek, his inhale heady and intoxicating. "Don't disappoint me." He pressed a kiss to my thundering pulse. "Most evenings, I'll expect you to join me in the shower on your knees. Alas, pressing matters supersede the pleasures of life. You'll make it up to me later."

The bulge in his pants was noticeably more pronounced as he stepped away, leaving me cold and naked and kneeling.

"She's exquisite, isn't she?" he asked.

"Indeed," Mikael replied, his voice deeper.

He's staring at me—at my breasts.

I swallowed.

I've been naked in front of men before.

This isn't any different.

Yeah, no, it's extremely different because I actually want *one of them.*

Kylan's mouth curved. "Yes, little lamb. Wet and waiting, just like you are now. I'll be back to taste you soon." He winked and left for the bathroom, leaving me staring after him with a hint of discomfort between my thighs. I slowly sat on my heels, my breathing somewhat erratic.

"He's addictive, isn't he?" Mikael sounded almost sad, his voice soft. "Try not to fall in love with him, Rae. Remembering who and what he is helps. At least a little."

I met his light gaze and caught a glimpse of the male lurking behind his confident mask.

Pain.

He blinked it away, his lips curling again. "Well, shall we begin by going through the invite list? I can ask Judith for a copy, and we can review each of their kinks."

"You've been with them all?"

He lifted a shoulder. "Several, but not all."

"Because Kylan shared you."

A glimmer of sadness filled his expression again. "I do whatever pleases him, just as you will too."

I stared at him, finally *seeing* him.

He's like me.

He'd said as much earlier about his body being used for blood and mine for sex, but now I *saw* it.

An ally.

"Does it hurt?" I whispered.

"Depends on the task," he answered quietly. Then his gaze lit up, his eyes crinkling at the side. "I know. How about you throw on a robe, and we'll take a walk around the penthouse. It's big with a lot of rooms filled with surprises you won't believe until I show you."

"Like what?"

Mikael shook his head, sliding off the bed and taking my plate with him. "Follow me to find out." A pair of adorable dimples followed that pronouncement. "But get dressed first. I'll meet you in the hallway. Going to get rid of the dish and let the maids know to change the bedding after Kylan departs." He waved over his shoulder. "There are robes in the bathroom or clothes in the closet."

Both of which required me to go near Kylan in the shower.

Great.

Mikael left without another word, leaving me with a decision. Either I waited for Kylan to come out or I braved his presence in the bathroom.

Neither option appealed.

Both provided the same results—seeing Kylan again.

At least one option left me with clothes.

Decision made, I rolled off the bed. If I hurried, maybe Kylan would still be—

His hard, wet chest met my face as I turned the corner directly into him.

He caught my hips, holding me in place when I would have bounced backward.

"Couldn't wait until I returned, hmm?" he teased, his dark eyes capturing mine.

"I, uh, no. I, well, I need clothes." Why did I sound like an ineloquent dolt all of a sudden?

His lips quirked up. "I beg to differ, Raelyn. I very much prefer you without clothes." He slid his palm to my lower back, holding me against him. Only a towel separated us, his impressive arousal hot through the fabric. "I expect you naked and in my bed every night until I say otherwise." His mouth hovered over mine. "Understood?"

"Yes," I whispered.

"Good." He kissed me softly. "The shower is all yours if you need it."

Mikael just told me to find something to wear, but washing off sounded better. I'd be quick. Then he could show me whatever had excited him enough to bring out his dimples.

Chapter Seventeen

RAE

A TELEVISION.

But not just any television, one that showed *humans*.

I'd only ever used these to watch clips from the Immortal Cup or a televised broadcast from the Goddess.

Never anything like this.

Every day this week, Mikael took me into the theater and showed me a new film. Today's was some crazy film about a human traveling through portals into other realms.

Mikael handed me a bucket of popcorn, a new food I could only stomach in moderation. I took the requisite three bites and gave it back to him. We'd spent the early evening reviewing the royals and alphas again. He picked two each day to go over, telling me about his personal experiences with each, their preferences in the bedroom, and their potential requests.

Today had been Robyn and Luka. The latter was happily mated and therefore not a threat. Robyn, however, enjoyed females and males and would very likely request a night with me. Mikael explained her proclivities in detail, confirming his intimate familiarity with the sadistic female.

I shivered.

Kylan had been demanding each evening, his passions in bed seeming to escalate each time he touched me, but he'd not done anything like what Mikael described.

Robyn favored pain, something I had initially expected from Kylan given his cruel reputation. Yet, he seemed more intent to please me than to hurt me.

I'd never felt so replete and exhausted in my life, and there were courses in school meant to kill my kind—literally. But nothing compared to the way the royal mastered my body.

I orgasmed five times last night.

Five.

That shouldn't even be possible, but Kylan forced them from me, refusing to stop tonguing my clit until tears streaked down my cheeks.

Then he'd healed me with his blood again, something that was expressly forbidden between humans and vampires. Yet, Kylan continued to force me to drink from him in small amounts.

He was clearly a rule breaker.

And a fierce lover.

A crash on the screen returned my focus to the movie. Mikael chuckled and said the words out loud with the human on the screen.

Actors, he'd explained.

From a previous world.

One where humans ruled.

Apparently, these films were outlawed, but Kylan had kept them anyway. *Yeah, definitely not one to adhere to or follow rules.*

I sipped my water and selected another kernel from the bucket. Mikael had added more butter to this one, his goal to gradually warm me up to more savory foods. I finally gave in and tried a donut today. The sweetness limited me to two bites, but I begrudgingly approved. Tomorrow we were supposed to try chocolate.

The door opened, Kylan appearing in a suit, his gaze searching.

My lips parted. *He's early.*

We'd fallen into a routine: Kylan disappearing before evening breakfast to handle work-related items, leaving Mikael in charge of my royal and alpha tutorials. After midnight lunch we watched a movie, and Kylan always returned during dinner, or rather, *for* dinner.

Mikael glanced at Kylan. "I'm introducing her to pop culture."

"I see that." He shut the door behind him and removed his black jacket, his gaze going to the screen. "This is a favorite of mine."

"I know."

Kylan folded his suit coat over the back of the couch and settled onto the cushion beside me. "Come here." He pulled me into his lap, his arm wrapping around my back for support. "I'm disappointed to find you clothed."

"I wasn't expecting you yet," I admitted.

He tsked. "You should be waiting for me," he whispered against my ear. His palm slid up my thigh, pushing between my legs to force them apart. "And you could have at least worn a skirt for me."

"She prefers jeans." Mikael held out the popcorn. "Want any?"

"Why do you think I'm here?" He nuzzled my neck.

"I meant the popcorn."

"I meant Raelyn."

"And you call me insatiable." Mikael held a kernel up to my lips, and I accepted it with my teeth. "She likes it."

"She likes a lot of things," Kylan replied, his lips against my pulse. His thumb traced up my center to unfasten the button of my pants. "I want these off, Raelyn." He drew the zipper down with the words, exposing my intimate flesh.

There were no undergarments in the wardrobe he'd assigned to me, not that I wore them to begin with. Vampires and lycans had a preference for mortal nudity.

"Off," he repeated, tugging harshly.

Mikael snorted and shook his head. "So impatient."

Kylan grabbed Mikael by the collar of his dress shirt, yanking him closer. "No, Mikael. *This* is impatient." He struck so fast I yelped, his fangs sinking deep into Mikael's neck, causing popcorn to scatter over the floor.

Mikael groaned, his eyes rolling into the back of his head. Kylan had left one hand on my jeans and gave them another sharp jerk. I scrambled to pull them off, his hot palm against my freshly exposed skin not making it any easier.

My feet helped, kicking the fabric from my legs.

Kylan's fingers trailed over my mound and lower, piercing me two at once.

Shit. I stole a deep breath through my nose, out through my mouth. He normally eased me into this, but something restless lurked beneath his skin tonight. I could feel it in the tense lines of his body, the way his forearm aligned with my lower body, holding me in place.

Was he angry about finding us in the theater instead of studying?

We had two weeks left before the party, and I'd reviewed almost all the portfolios, as well as endured the nightly sexual training.

What else did he want?

"Kylan," Mikael breathed, his nails digging into the cushion. "Fuck!"

"You're in need of a long-overdue reminder, Mikael," Kylan growled against his neck. "You serve me."

"Yes, My Prince." His face contorted into agonizing lines, his eyes falling closed. "Always."

"And in return, I take care of you," Kylan continued, his tongue tracing the column of Mikael's throat. "Don't I?"

"Yes," he agreed, voice soft. "You do."

"I do." Kylan released me. "Stand, Raelyn. Now."

My legs shook as I complied. The movie still played behind me, casting shadows oddly throughout the room. It gave Kylan a darker, more sinister glow that revealed his true nature.

Predator.

Vampire.

Old.

I swallowed. He was unreadable and highly unpredictable. What did he want from me now? Was this another lesson? A punishment? Playtime?

Kylan settled his ankle over his knee, his arm going over the back of the couch behind a lust-drunk Mikael. "Remove your sweater for us, Raelyn."

A shiver worked its way down my spine. I licked my lips, his ominous gaze tracking the movements while he waited.

He cocked a brow. "Is there a problem, Raelyn?"

With both of them seeing me naked? No, not really, except I hadn't really done anything like this in front of Mikael yet. He'd more or less become a friend over the week. But we were never meant to be platonic with each other, not when we both existed in Kylan's sexual playground.

It's just a sweater, I told myself. *Nudity is the easy part.*

I pulled the fabric over my head, my nipples hardening from the cooler air.

Mikael seemed to relax, his light eyes slowly tracing my form while Kylan toyed with a lock of his blond hair. "Isn't that better?" Kylan asked conversationally as he used the remote to pause the movie.

"Than the jeans?" Mikael smirked. "Yes."

"I should have them removed from her wardrobe, just give her short dresses from now on to showcase her legs." His focus shifted to the apex between my thighs. "Maybe some lingerie, too."

"Red," Mikael added.

"Absolutely. I'll discuss it with Taylor. Raelyn requires additional outfits for future dinners anyway." He continued stroking Mikael's blond hair while speaking, his expression inscrutable. "Or maybe she should attend naked."

I'd seen worse, such as mortals dressed in metal piercings and chains. *Collars, spikes, covered in blood.* I shuddered. *No, thank you.*

"Nervous, little lamb?" His dark eyes glimmered. "Because this is exactly what I'll do to you with my fellow royals. Let them see you, pet you, maybe even fuck you."

My stomach churned with those last two words. *Fuck you.* He hadn't done anything other than take my mouth all week. Would he truly allow someone else to take my innocence?

A playing card, he'd called it.

I still didn't know what that meant.

"Isn't this more entertaining than an old movie?" Kylan asked.

Mikael glanced sideways at him. "Is that why you're doing this? You're dissatisfied with my training methods and felt the need to make a scene?" His tone earned him a sharp tug on his hair that didn't even make him flinch.

"On the contrary, I'm quite pleased. I merely feel it's time to introduce Raelyn to the next level. She pleases me amazingly well, but I wonder, how does she do with others?" He bent to lick the wound on Mikael's neck, slowly, purposely. "Would you like her to touch your cock, Mikael?" he asked softly, his tongue drawing a wet path up his skin. "To get down on her knees and suck you off with that pretty mouth of hers?"

My lips parted, my throat going dry.

Kylan wanted me to pleasure Mikael.

While he watched.

Was this what he would do with his royal friends? Tell me to get on my knees and orally please them while he observed?

Mikael had explained that the harem members went through training for two months, and would be fully experienced in the sexual arts before joining Kylan's harem.

It was Kylan's job to provide me that same training.

And Mikael's, too.

His light eyes lifted to mine, his pupils eerily glowing in the dull light behind me. Knowledge and understanding colored his expression. He knew this wouldn't be easy for me but also understood that I had no choice.

This was life with Kylan. Life with a royal. Life with a vampire.

We both existed to serve, and this was what our superior required.

He gave me a small nod, a shared moment of compassion before saying, "I want her mouth."

Kylan smiled. "An excellent choice. Raelyn, I believe you're familiar with this requirement?" He cocked a brow.

"I am, My Prince." Not *Your Highness* just in case our safe word remained. Because I could do this. It was just Mikael.

Something akin to approval passed through his features. Because I didn't argue? Could I even try to debate him in this mood? "Good, little lamb. On your knees, then." He continued combing through Mikael's hair, his dark gaze on me while I knelt between his blood virgin's sprawled legs. "You know what to do."

I gingerly placed my palms on Mikael's thighs, gliding them upward to the bulge growing beneath his zipper. My fingers threatened to tremble at the wrongness of touching a male that wasn't Kylan.

It's okay. He wants me to.

But I don't want to.

What you want doesn't matter. This is for him, *not you.*

As if sensing my hesitation, he brushed his knuckles down my cheek, reminding me of his presence. His desire. His command.

Pausing like this with another royal would earn me a death sentence.

They would expect confidence and seductive skill, not a trembling mess after barely touching another man's thighs.

I am not the right woman for this.

Yes, you are. You're a survivor.

"I think she needs proper motivation," Kylan murmured, his lips against Mikael's neck again and trailing to his mouth. Their resulting kiss had my heart skipping a beat.

Primal heat singed the air.

So virile.

So erotic.

So intoxicating.

My own lips parted, my tongue darting out to dampen them as if I were the one being kissed.

I'd seen them embrace before, but not quite like this—all hunger and raw energy and *need.* Kylan reached for my palm and placed it over Mikael's arousal, forcing me to stroke him through his black pants. I could barely focus, my attention on their devouring of each other, the dueling of their tongues.

I want that…

The devotion.

The intensity.

The trust.

Mikael gave in to Kylan completely, his body a puppet for his master to play.

What did Kylan and I look like together? As fitting? As sexual? As savage?

The pressure against my hand intensified, the order clear. I unfastened the pants, allowing Mikael's arousal to spring free. Kylan guided my fingers, wrapping them around the base and guiding my stroke upward and back, his instruction thorough and unmistakable.

I followed his lead, letting him direct the pace. Mikael groaned, his arousal pulsing as Kylan nipped his lip hard enough to bleed.

"Asshole," he growled.

Kylan tightened his grasp around my hand, causing me to squeeze Mikael's shaft. "Careful. She might be the one touching you, but I'm very much in control."

"You're always in control."

"Yes, I am." Kylan took his mouth again with an intensity that stole my breath. He didn't stop guiding my hand, his movements sure and experienced, his lips even more practiced.

I pressed my thighs together, the ache building between them almost unbearable.

I wanted Kylan to kiss me like that while Mikael knelt between my thighs.

To be between them.

To share them.

To let them share me.

The foreign thoughts roused a flame in my center, spreading warmth through my veins, touching my nerves, and bringing my core to life.

I moved my hand in earnest now, no longer requiring Kylan's expert touch. His hand brushed my cheek, sliding upward into my hair, and urged me downward toward Mikael's cock.

He wasn't as long as Kylan, his head slightly rounder, but equally as proportioned and beautiful. I traced his throbbing vein with my tongue, smiling as he jolted, and slipped his crown between my lips.

"Fuck," Mikael growled, his muscles tensing as I swallowed him down to my fist and sucked upward.

"I told you she's skilled," Kylan murmured, his fingers knotting with my hair and pushing me to take Mikael deeper. "I hope you're ready to swallow, Raelyn. I expect you to take everything he gives you and more."

My eyes began to water from his grip in my hair and the cock hitting the back of my throat. Mikael may not have been as well endowed, but he was certainly long enough.

I met his heavy-lidded gaze. All signs of apology and understanding were gone and replaced by a male deep in the throes of passion. Kylan moved to his neck, his bite eliciting a soft curse from his blood virgin. The violent pulls into Kylan's mouth sent shock waves of energy through Mikael, his body tensing and spasming beneath my touch and his cock surging in my mouth.

He'd grown impossibly larger.

My throat constricted, my lungs protesting.

Air…

Kylan didn't relent, his grasp in my hair not allowing me to move.

"Fuck!" Mikael groaned, his orgasm ripping through him and spilling into my throat with a force that would have sent me backward if Kylan hadn't been holding me in place. I swallowed because there was no other option, his seed hot and plentiful as it slid down my tongue.

It didn't stop.

A second round of ecstasy tore a yell from him as he came again. My nails bit into his thighs as my vision began to blur behind black dots. I couldn't… I needed… But fuck, I consumed him anyway, his essence, forcing it down as my lungs ached.

Kylan pulled me back a fraction, opening my airway, and I breathed in greedily. I craved more, a break, but as soon as I filled my lungs, he'd shoved me down again in time for another explosion.

"Kylan…" The name left Mikael on an exhale, drawing my blurry vision upward again. He'd gone pale, his lips turning a shade of blue that didn't look right.

Because of my eyes?

The force of his rapture lacked the heat and power from earlier, his body notably less tense, almost relaxed.

"Please," he whispered, his palm going to Kylan's leg. "I…" He cut off on a whimper, his eyes flashing open. "Kylan…"

No.

He wouldn't…?

His hand remained in my hair, but the rapture had fled, replaced by a cooling skin that had my heart dropping to my stomach.

I froze on my knees, unable to speak, to move, to react.

Mikael grew colder, his skin paling to a deathly shade I knew all too well.

His light eyes flicked to mine, real pain staring back at me.

And then his lids closed.

A tear escaped the corner of my eye.

I barely knew him, but he'd been so kind to me. How could I just sit here and watch this happen? Why would Kylan do this to him? To me? To us?

I pushed away, Mikael's erection long gone, but Kylan held my hair, forcing me to remain between the dying man's legs as he continued to feed.

"Try not to fall in love with him, Rae. Remembering who and what he is helps. At least a little."

Mikael's words rattled in my thoughts as an ominous reminder.

I'd not heeded his warning nearly enough.

Because, for a minute, I had started to trust Kylan. To maybe even like him a little.

This was the royal I had feared.

The one I'd read about.

The cruel master who killed meaninglessly.

The one who claimed to have not massacred his harem.

A liar.

A vampire.

A monster.

Chapter Eighteen

KYLAN

MIKAEL'S HEARTBEAT FALTERED, the final draws of his mortality calling to me in warning.

I released him, sealing the wound with my tongue, but not immediately pulling back.

Raelyn's mounting fear called to the predator inside me, begging me to pounce. If I looked at her now, I'd take her—harshly. And she wasn't ready for that yet.

"You're evil," she whispered, hatred pouring off her in waves.

My eyebrows rose. "Excuse me?"

"You heard me." The raspy quality of her voice intrigued me. I'd love to hear her yell my name in that voice, especially as I made her come. "He trusted you."

"I know." It was one of Mikael's biggest flaws, and a trait I adored. He loved pushing my boundaries as a result, never afraid of what I could do to him. Fortunately for him, he'd never pushed me too far. I finally met Raelyn's blue eyes, then dropped my focus to admire her swollen lips. "You did such a good job, little lamb. I owe you a reward."

I tried to pull her up onto the couch, but she protested, her head yanking from my grasp at the expense of a few red hairs. She stood and scrambled backward until her back hit the theater wall. "I don't want anything from you, *Your Highness.*"

My heart faltered at the use of her safe word. I held my palms up and relaxed into the couch, confused as hell. "Talk to me, Raelyn. Tell me what pushed you too far."

"Are you fucking kidding me?" She sounded furious, her tone unlike anything I'd heard from her to date, and incredibly disrespectful.

"Have you forgotten who I am?" I wondered, shocked.

She laughed without humor. "Oh, apparently I did, but thank you for the bloody reminder. I'll never forget again. That's for damn sure."

I blinked. What the hell was she going on about?

"Is that how you killed your harem?" she demanded, pointing at Mikael. "Or did you just rip their throats out like the monster you are?"

"I didn't kill my harem, Raelyn." Something she already knew. "Why are you acting like this? What did I do?"

She gaped at me. "What did you do?" The shrill quality of her tone prickled my ears. "That!" She pointed at Mikael again. "You killed him while making me… Goddess, he trusted you and you killed him. Bled him to death, as if he meant nothing to you, which, of course, he didn't. None of us do. You're all a bunch of fucking monsters who prey on the weak and force us, force us…" She trailed off, her legs giving out and sending her to the ground on a sob.

Something fractured inside me, a sensation I hadn't felt in a very long time. *Regret.*

I'd unintentionally hurt this beautiful, warrior soul.

"Raelyn," I whispered, moving to her side on the floor. She pulled her knees in close, trying to squirm away, but I lifted her with ease into my lap. "Raelyn."

"I hate you." Her fist connected with my jaw with more strength than I expected, sending a shock wave down my spine. She scrambled off me and threw another punch that I caught before it could connect with my nose.

"Raelyn," I repeated with more force, pushing her hand away. "*Stop.*"

"No!" She started to struggle in earnest, tears pouring from her eyes as she attempted to hit me again. Her fist met my palm, but her other one managed a jab at my side. It fucking hurt.

"That's enough!" I snapped, done with this foolishness. I flattened her on the ground, trapping her wrists in one of my hands over her head as she bucked her hips futilely beneath mine. I'd have enjoyed it a lot more if she wasn't spitting angrily in my face.

"Kill me!" she shouted, still trying to fight despite my impenetrable hold. "I'd rather die than be here with you another moment. I'll bite you, scream at you, I'll—"

"Fuck, Raelyn, he's not dead," I growled. As if I would ever kill Mikael. I adored the male. "He's just drained." Rather literally. But the blood I'd slipped into his mouth would heal him back to normal.

She finally stilled, her breathing erratic. "W-what?"

"He'll wake up in a few days with a hangover and have a few choice words for me but will otherwise be fine." I wiped the spittle away from my jaw with my free hand. Not appealing. "I needed him incapacitated to protect him."

Her watery eyes locked on mine. "I don't… I don't understand."

"Jace will be arriving tomorrow with Darius and Darius's new *Erosita*. Mikael being indisposed reaffirms my reputation and marks his blood as off-limits." While I'd kept Mikael's whereabouts a secret originally, everyone would expect him to be with me now. That meant the visiting royals could request a bite, something I refused to allow.

Territorial behavior was seen as a weakness among my kind. And I couldn't afford to be seen as weak. Not with the rumors of immortal insanity hanging over my head.

"You don't want to share him," she said softly.

No point in lying to her. "No, I do not."

"But you'll share me."

I shrugged. "Well, it's customary to swap consorts." Although, I didn't really want to share her. I'd almost enjoyed incapacitating Mikael, something that had never been the case before. I usually gave him a warning and drained him slowly, but watching him benefit from Raelyn's attentions had set my blood on fire. Which was strange considering I always shared my harem with him and others.

But Raelyn, well, I hadn't enjoyed watching her service him. At all.

Our circumstances were different, a result of the madness of these last few months. She slept with me every night, a pleasure I'd never preferred. I typically met my consorts in their own rooms and varied my visits between them, never really having a favorite. Sometimes I even went a month without seeing any of them.

And I never used a consort multiple nights in a row.

Until Raelyn.

She'd kept me entertained all week, and I still desired more from her. Her virginity was only part of the draw. I looked forward to seeing her, to finding that flame in her gaze that seemed to ignite in my presence.

My fearless little vixen.

She'd landed not one but two hits. An impossible feat for a human, even with shock on her side. Her daily regimen of imbibing my blood may have helped her too, but I was still impressed by her nimble movements.

"You do realize punching a vampire, let alone a royal, is grounds for death, yes?" I asked, amused.

Her gaze narrowed even as pain radiated from her blue depths. "I'm not sorry."

"No, you're not." I cocked my head to the side. "And you're still angry with me."

She bit her lip, saying nothing.

"The silent treatment again?" My brow lifted. "Surely you can be more inventive than that."

"I'd hit you again, but you have my hands secured."

"Tell me why you're angry."

"Because I hate you."

"More words, Raelyn. I want an explanation."

"Why?" she retorted. "It's not like you care."

I laughed. "If I didn't care, I wouldn't ask." I learned long ago not to bother voicing an opinion or wasting words over useless drivel.

She still said nothing.

"I've told you Mikael will be fine." A slight ache formed in my gut with the words. Did she truly adore him this much already? They weren't romantically involved from what I'd witnessed, just friends. But clearly, the thought of his death bothered her immensely. Or was it that I'd so carelessly disposed of him? "Talk to me, Raelyn."

"Fine. What will you have me do with Jace?"

Of all the things I expected her to say, *that* was not even a consideration in my mind. "You'll follow decorum, as always."

"I mean, as your consort." She spoke the words with such disdain I nearly cringed. None of my consorts had ever acted like this, even the ones I'd selected and groomed myself. They were always eager to please me or others.

"Be blunt, Raelyn. What is it you want to know?"

"Blunt," she repeated, a flash of fury igniting her gaze to a gorgeous azure color. "Are you going to make me fuck Jace?"

The question slapped me across the face.

Would I allow her to fuck Jace? No, *make* her, was her phrasing.

I nearly laughed.

Like hell would I grant him—or anyone else—such a valuable opportunity.

"You're mine, Raelyn."

She had the audacity to roll her eyes. "Yes, I'm aware. I'm yours to share and all that. The least you could do is give me an idea of what to expect when Jace arrives—or any of the others, for that matter. But no, you can't even afford to give me, the lowly human, the courtesy of knowing how you plan to... What was the phrase you used? Oh, right, use my virginity as a playing card." She tried to maneuver out from beneath me again and huffed when I didn't move. "*Fine.*"

I hadn't heard a human female mutter that word—in *that* tone—in ages. Clearly, allowing Mikael to introduce her to the cinema had rubbed off on her, and in only a week's time, no less.

"You want to know how I plan to take your innocence?" I asked, bemused. "And you're angry that I haven't told you?"

She merely glared at me in response.

"Has it occurred to you that I haven't decided yet?"

More silence.

"Would you like me to take it now?" I settled more firmly between her thighs, allowing her to feel my thickening arousal. "Because I'll gladly fuck you, Raelyn, if that's what you desire from me."

Her nostrils flared. "Fuck you."

"That is the topic at hand, yes." I ran my nose over her flushing cheeks. *Delectable.* I was well fed, but her blood tempted me to bite. "Would you hate me less if I fucked you, Raelyn? Because I suspect you'd hate me more. Especially since it would mark you as a consort with every option available."

I nibbled her thundering pulse, reveling in her heady scent. Fear mingled with desire and anger, creating an aroma I could hardly turn down. My incisors begged me to truly taste her. She wouldn't satisfy my cravings in the same way Mikael's blood did, but oh, how I longed to devour her entirely.

"Every option available?" she repeated, her voice pitched low in a whisper.

"Mmm, yes." I skimmed my incisors across her sensitive skin. So easy. So tempting. "Once I've fucked you, everyone else can request you. Is that what you want, Raelyn?"

Because I didn't. I wanted to savor her and keep her as my own for as long as I could. No royal or alpha would be interested in just her mouth. They'd want the entire package, which was off-limits until I sampled her for myself.

"They can't… until…?" She swallowed, falling quiet.

I pulled back to meet her conflicted gaze. "You thought I meant to share you before I've had you?" I tsked. "Darling lamb, that's never going to happen."

She searched my face. "But you called it a playing card."

"Because it is." I released her wrists and went to my elbows on either side of her head. "One I can play against my opponents. Not by offering your innocence, but by protecting it. Unless you'd prefer I take it now?" The offer was still on the table, and I'd happily oblige.

It would put her in danger.

Or not.

Only a fool would kill a royal's property while on loan.

No, my adversary was smarter than that. She or he would strike when I least expected it.

Still, I didn't want to risk Raelyn being accidentally harmed.

You don't want to share her, my darker side whispered. *She's ours.*

It was that same side who took over at the end, adding a hint of pain to my bite as I pushed Mikael over the edge into unconsciousness. A subtle punishment for indulging in *my* female.

Spending all week with her was fucking with my head.

I needed a fresh perspective, a break.

Or maybe I just need to fuck her to get her out of my system.

My cock hardened at the prospect, nudging against her tender flesh. It would be so easy with her already naked and wet beneath me.

"N-no," she said, shaking her head. "I… I don't want to be shared."

Her words slid over me on an icy wave, cooling my ardor. "You don't want to be shared?"

She shook her head again. "I… no. I really don't."

I just told her I wouldn't share her yet. Did she require a reminder already?

Or was I not clear? "I won't be sharing you until I've had you myself, Raelyn."

She bit her lip. "B-but I don't..." She seemed to be reconsidering what she wanted to say, causing my brow to furrow.

"Are you saying you never want to be shared, Raelyn?"

She was silent for a long moment, a war battling behind her eyes, as if she couldn't decide how to properly respond. "Y-yes."

I nearly laughed. "But you're my consort and that's your purpose—to fuck whomever I tell you to fuck." Did she not understand the design of a harem? "Surely the university explained this to you."

She trembled, some of the fire dying in her eyes. So fragile and broken and hurt.

That was the look Robyn's pets wore, not mine.

The fuck just happened?

"Yes, My Prince," Raelyn whispered, her gaze falling from mine.

Her submission sliced my heart and stirred a maelstrom of emotions inside me. At the forefront was extreme disappointment.

"Is it that easy to break you?" I demanded. "How very unfortunate." I expected at least a flare of disapproval or a frustrated snort, not outright acceptance. I pushed off of her, standing. "Get dressed, Raelyn."

She didn't move.

I shook my head, not able to handle this foolishness any longer. If she wanted to shatter beneath the truth of her station, so be it.

"If you want to fuck me, then do it." The unadulterated rage in her voice caused me to pause with my hand on the doorknob. "If you want to give me to one of your royal friends, then do it. But don't ask me what I want and put me down after I give you the truth."

I turned, curious, and found Raelyn standing with her hands on her hips, her cheeks red from her exertion.

"You can do whatever you want to my body, but my mind is my own, Kylan. So fuck off."

My eyebrows rose. Did she learn that phrasing from a movie or from a foulmouthed lycan? Maybe Mikael had mentioned it to her.

Either way, she should not be using those words on a royal, least of all me.

And worse, I absolutely should not have enjoyed hearing it nearly as much as I did.

I stalked forward, backing her up into the wall, my palm circling her throat as she stared me down. "And what if I desire your mind, little lamb?" I asked softly, my thumb stroking her escalating pulse. "What if I demand it?"

"You'll never have it."

I squeezed, just enough to threaten. "Oh, but I own all of you, darling. Or did you forget that detail?"

"No." Her voice shook with a mixture of fear and anger. "I own my mind, my heart, and my spirit. All you have is my body, and I refuse to give you anything else. It's my right to choose."

"You have no rights."

"Not anymore." Her gaze narrowed. "But I used to."

I smiled and it was almost sad. "No, love. You never did."

"Humans did."

"In the past," I agreed, pressing my hips to hers. "We live in the present, where your liberties are forfeit and belong to me. You're mine, Raelyn."

"To fuck, to touch, to command." Her pupils contracted, allowing more of that pretty blue flame to shine through. "You can try to manipulate my mind all you want, Kylan, but I will never give in to you. I refuse."

"Whom are you trying to convince here, sweetheart? Me or you?" Because it sounded as if it was she who needed the pep talk, not me. "Because I've not even begun to manipulate your mind."

She scoffed at that, her courage bright and palpable despite being trapped naked against the wall. "I tell you I don't want to be shared, and you hastily remind me that it's my purpose. You want me meek one moment and strong the next. You told me I was never destined for the Immortal Cup, saying it was all just a cruel play, but the only one playing here is you, Kylan. And I'm done participating."

My grip loosened, startled by her far too accurate assessment. I'd been toying with her as one would an intriguing pet. It was never my intention, but when summarized so bluntly, I couldn't deny the validity of her words.

I desired a warrior and required a submissive. Two very different objectives, both correct.

For the first time in centuries, I lacked a retort. The woman had outwitted me, leaving me only one thing to say. "You're right." I released her and took a step back. An apology threatened my tongue, shocking me more.

I never apologized.

Ever.

"I… What?"

"You're right," I repeated. "Do not make me say it a third time." I couldn't even believe I'd admitted it twice. But I supposed it was the least I could do.

"You've been playing with me."

"That's what you said, isn't it?"

"And you admitted it."

I folded my arms. "This has just become boring again."

She laughed, the sound near hysterical in nature. "How is this my life? Why is it my life?" She ran her fingers through her hair and laughed again, but it lacked joy. "Was everything you said about my virginity a lie too? A way to give me confidence just to shatter it when you hand me over to someone else?"

A growl built in my chest. "Absolutely not." My hands fisted at my sides. "No one touches you except me."

She gave me a disbelieving look. "Okay, Kylan." The dismissive way she said it set my blood on fire.

"I've never lied to you, Raelyn, and I do not take lightly to the accusation."

Her hands went to her hips again. "No, you've just been fucking with my head."

"I prefer to call it 'providing conflicting priorities,' which does not equate to dishonesty." I stepped toward her again and she held her ground. "I have been more honest with you than with any other consort."

"Easy to do since you killed them all."

I didn't bother correcting her. She knew the truth. "Are you trying to provoke me into hurting you, Raelyn? Because I would not advise continuing down this path."

"What more could you do?" she countered with another of those humorless laughs. She threw her arms out to the sides. "Do your worst, Kylan. I dare you."

"You dare me?" I raised a brow. "That's a dangerous proposition for someone who believes me capable of mass murder."

"You're a vampire, Kylan." She pointed at Mikael's prone form on the couch. "And you're clearly capable of hurting people."

"I've taken care of him for a decade. Try again."

"You just drained him while forcing me to suck him off and didn't bother to tell either of us your intention. That's harmful."

Back to that again, then. "Mikael knew my intentions the second he tasted my blood. He didn't protest, so we proceeded."

She arched a brow. "Then why did he beg at the end?"

I sighed, running my fingers through my hair. Why was I even indulging this tomfoolery? I had far more important tasks to complete today.

Two more minutes, I told myself. *That's all she gets.*

What had she asked?

Right, she wanted to know why Mikael had sounded so betrayed before losing consciousness. "I withdrew the pleasure at the end, causing him to feel a hint of pain."

"And why did you do that if you didn't mean to hurt him?" she demanded.

"Because I didn't like seeing you between his legs, Raelyn. And I hated how much he enjoyed it." The words were out before I could stop them, surprising us both.

Why did this woman constantly force the truth from me?

Her lips parted, her cheeks reddening. "But… but you made me…"

All right, two minutes were up. "Meaning I only have myself to blame, yes?" I'd thought it would be a good introduction to expectations, but it'd backfired in my face. My territorial drive to take her for myself was far too strong for sharing, something I needed to get over, and quickly.

Once I fucked her, it would be fine.

But I couldn't yet. Not until after the party.

Unless I wanted to risk another royal or alpha taking her.

"I have work to do," I said, turning away from her. "I'll find someone to carry Mikael back to his room. Go to bed early, Raelyn. You'll need your rest before Jace arrives tomorrow."

I didn't wait for her reply, just slammed the door behind me and headed to my office. The damn woman accused me of playing mind games with her? Well, it seemed she was doing the same to me.

But I would win.

I always did.

Chapter Nineteen

RAE

I WOKE UP ALONE, Kylan's side of the bed as pristine as it was when I went to sleep.

He never joined me last night.

That should have pleased me, but my lips curled downward instead of upward.

Because I didn't like seeing you between his legs.

His words had stayed with me throughout the night, carrying over into my dreams. What did they mean? He kept harping on my purpose to serve yet said he disliked it when I did. Another mind game? Kylan seemed to favor them, but he'd sounded so earnest when he had spoken those words.

He claimed to be honest with me.

Truth or a lie?

I couldn't tell, and I hated him for that. He lived in riddles, constantly requesting one thing while demanding the opposite. I'd lost it last night and given him a piece of my mind.

And he never retaliated.

My behavior would have earned a severe punishment at the university. I'd witnessed death sentences handed out to those who behaved far better than I had last night. Yet, Kylan merely walked away.

Did he have something worse planned today? To make an example of me?

I sat up, my head foggy with too much sleep. Worrying over Kylan and his intentions would drive me insane. Nothing was predictable with that man. Nothing.

A soft knock on the door had me pulling the covers up to conceal my bare chest. I'd slept naked, expecting Kylan to join me. Which, of course, he hadn't.

My frown curled downward more as Angelica's head appeared. Her dark eyes met mine, and surprise at seeing her again held me captive in the bed. "K-Kylan isn't here," I said, unsure of what she needed. I hadn't seen her since the incident at his home.

Her lips twitched. "I know. He's on a business call but asked me to tend to you."

Uh, and that means...? "Oh, uh, okay," I mumbled.

She entered with a plate in one hand and shut the door behind her.

"Spinach eggs," she said as she moved closer. "I ate a lot of these growing up, figured you probably did the same." She set the food on the nightstand and pinched her lips to the side. "Kylan has requested I assist you with your wardrobe. Jace and Darius are expected to arrive within the hour."

My lips parted. "Oh." I didn't know what else to say. Mikael had been the one to guide me around all week, but of course, he couldn't do that today. Not after what Kylan did to him.

"Yeah, so, uh, you eat that"—she pointed to the plate—"and I'll go find you a suitable outfit." She walked away muttering, "Because apparently feeding and dressing up humans is my job now."

"I can do that on my own," I offered. "If, I mean, you don't..." I trailed off, biting my lip as she faced me with a surprised expression. Right. Decorum completely broken. It was bad enough that I constantly challenged Kylan. To speak out of turn to others, to even look them in the eye, broke so many protocols.

I clearly have a death wish.

And worse, I'd acted this way in front of Angelica, a freshly turned vampire who *knew* the rules just as well as I did, if not better than me.

"F-forgive me," I whispered, lowering my gaze.

She laughed, the sound churning my stomach.

Angelica couldn't kill me—not without Kylan's consent—but she could reprimand me. Maybe.

I frowned. *No one touches you except me.* Did he mean that? Did it apply to discipline as well?

A shiver shook my spine at the thought of Kylan's version of a punishment. He'd yet to chastise me in any way aside from a few verbal threats. And I'd more than earned it by constantly challenging him.

Except that's what he wanted—a challenge in the bedroom and an obedient dog in public.

Technically, I was still in the bedroom.

"Do you have any idea how long it's been since I've been around an unbroken human?" Angelica asked, collapsing on the bed beside me. "Fuck, it's been ages." She fell backward on a huff. "Everyone bows and refuses to look at me, as if I'm some scary monster. But I was human less than a decade ago."

I waited for her to say more, but silence fell between us, oddly peaceful.

"What's it like?" I asked softly. "Transitioning from, well, human state to a vampire?"

She rolled to her side, her brown eyes meeting mine. "Not nearly as glorious as one might expect. They start you at the very bottom, with minimal income and bare essentials, and force you to work your way up. I'm only here because Kylan requested it, something Judith made very clear when promoting me to his security team. His decision is going to cost me, I think. Everyone wants to be closer to him, to his power, and I'm the youngest and most worthless of them all."

"If Kylan promoted you, then he sees potential in you." The words left my mouth without thought. They just sounded right.

Angelica remained quiet for a long moment, her lips pinched to the side. "I hope you're right."

"She is," Kylan murmured from the shadows, his body seeming to materialize before our eyes as he stepped into the light cast by the windows. "Why are you not eating, Raelyn?"

My jaw had dropped at his unexpected appearance, my voice forgotten.

Angelica leapt off the bed with a strangled sound, falling to her knees. "Forgive me, My Prince. It's my fault for—"

"I highly doubt it's your fault at all," he replied. "Raelyn?"

Rather than reply, I picked up the plate and shoveled a giant bite into my mouth. He cocked a brow, his lips twitching at the sides, and shook his head.

"Angelica, please find Raelyn a suitable dress. Jace's plane just landed, making him early."

"Of course, My Prince." She rose and went straight to the bathroom suite, her head bowed the entire way.

I consumed a forkful as he approached, my heart thundering in my chest. "Shall I punish her?" he asked quietly. "For chitchatting with you instead of following through on my demands to feed and dress you?"

I narrowed my gaze, swallowing the half-chewed food in my mouth. "I'm perfectly capable of feeding and dressing myself without a supervisor."

He tilted his head. "Is that what you told her?"

"No, I asked her what it's like to be a vampire." Which went against protocol, but was the truth.

"Because you want to become one?"

"What's the point in desiring an impossibility?" I countered, setting the plate down despite eating only half the contents. My appetite was nonexistent.

"Everyone has dreams, Raelyn." He tucked a strand of hair behind my ear and leaned in to brush his lips over mine. "Even gorgeous pets."

"Dreaming is for the weak."

"It used to be for the spirited."

"Well, as you pointed out just last night, we live in a very different time, don't we?"

"Indeed we do." He kissed me again, lingering. "But you remind me of a time I preferred, Raelyn." He straightened and turned as Angelica returned.

"Does this suit, My Prince?" She held up a deep-red silk gown that would barely cover my breasts. At least the skirt fell to the ground.

"It does," he replied, holding out his hand for the dress. "I can take it from here. Please inform Judith that I've changed my mind and will be entertaining Jace here instead of at K Hotel."

Angelica noticeably paled. "O-of course, Your Highness." She bowed and retreated quickly, leaving me alone with Kylan.

He laid the dress over the bed and began unbuttoning his shirt. "We have time for a quick rinse. Go turn on the water and wait for me there."

Part of me wanted to refuse just to irritate him, but the dangerous glint in his gaze forced me from the bed and into the bathroom.

The shower had just started to warm when Kylan appeared—naked—behind me.

Tracing, I realized. Only the oldest of vampires possessed that ability. They couldn't teleport long distances, only a few miles or so, but it was as if he disappeared and reappeared before my eyes.

He kissed my shoulder, his hands on my hips and guiding me forward beneath the spray. This was the first time he'd followed through on his comment about wanting me in the shower with him every evening.

I waited for the demand to kneel, to satisfy the prominent erection resting against my ass, but the words never came. He combed my dampening strands, spreading the moisture evenly.

His lips met my temple as he reached around me for the shampoo. He continued his ministrations, creating suds on top of my head before rinsing me clean, and repeated the action with the conditioner.

"Turn," he said softly, picking up the soap.

I swallowed and did as directed, facing his immortal beauty.

This was a far cry from a punishment.

Unless he meant to tease me to death.

Each stroke of his warm palm over my skin excited my hormones, stirring an inferno in my lower belly that spread through my veins. His touch slid over my abdomen, lower to the tops of my thighs, and up my side, missing all the areas I desired him most.

A groan fought its way up my throat, but I caught it with my teeth, clamping down so tightly something cracked.

Kylan chuckled, his hand moving to my shoulder and down my arm. "Your determination is admirable, Raelyn. But I'll win."

"Win what?" I managed to say through my teeth.

"You," he replied simply, the soap returning to my sternum to slide between my breasts.

My breath hitched as he continued down to my belly button and lower, brushing the top of my mound. "Y-you already own me."

"I do," he agreed. "But according to you, it's your body I own and nothing else." He dipped between my legs, causing my heart to stop completely. "But I want more, Raelyn."

It took serious effort to concentrate on his words and not his hypnotic touch. Because, Goddess, that felt amazing. A single night without him had ignited an overwhelming need, one only Kylan could satisfy.

"I want to possess all of you," he added, his silky voice a deep caress against my ear.

A tremble licked across my skin, trailing goose bumps along the way despite the hot water. "That's never going to happen," I managed on an exhale.

"I disagree," he whispered, his lips flitting across my cheek to hover over my mouth as he pulled me against him. "I'm going to start with your mind, not by playing a game but by telling you the truth."

Another shiver shook my being, teasing my nipples into sharp points against his too-hot chest. "The truth," I repeated, trying with all my might to focus on the conversation and not on his hand between my legs. The soap had switched to his other palm, gliding up my side.

So much sensation.

So much *heat.*

"Yes." He tugged on my lip, sucking it into his mouth. "Turn around, Raelyn."

My feet moved before my mind could even process the demand.

"Put your hands on the wall."

I did.

He trailed the soap down my spine. "Spread your legs."

That was the opposite of what I wanted. My core ached for friction, something he'd taken away when he forced me to rotate. But I followed his order, sliding my thighs apart and widening my stance.

"Beautiful." He pulled my hair over my shoulder, exposing all of my back to him, and began massaging me in slow circles, the floral scent tickling my nostrils.

No one had ever done this to me before. I felt almost cherished, worshiped, which couldn't be his intention.

"Now, as for the truth." He kissed my nape and nipped the tender skin, shooting sparks to all of my nerve endings. "Jace is arriving early because I asked him to. Despite evidence to the contrary, I think he's behind the attack on my character."

I blinked. *What?* "Jace?" *Why?*

"His territory borders mine, and his new sovereign would be next in line to inherit my region, providing them both a motive and an opportunity." Kylan's palm slid downward, slipping between my cheeks and shooting a shock up across my skin.

He couldn't mean to—

His incisors pierced my neck, sending euphoria through my bloodstream. I quivered against him, my legs threatening to collapse.

"Kylan," I breathed, arching back into him. The soap disappeared, his arm circling my waist to hold me in place while his opposite hand remained against my ass—considering, prodding, testing my boundaries.

I'd never been touched *there.*

Until now.

Flames ignited across my flesh at the forbidden nature of his exploration. The university had offered courses on this. I'd avoided them, not knowing why anyone would favor such an act. But oh, maybe, just maybe, I'd been wrong.

Ecstasy pooled between my legs, Kylan's bite exciting all my senses. And his finger—no, fingers—were doing wicked things to my insides.

My nails scraped the tiles, my arms shaking from holding my position.

Too much sensation.

The hot water trickling over us only added to my misery, overriding my being with a foreign elation that rattled me to my core.

Only my body, I vowed. *Only this.*

But, *fuck!*

My head fell forward on a harsh exhale. He'd intensified the pleasure, ripping me in two, his intrusion below overwhelming my being. The hold around my waist was all that kept me standing, my legs no longer functioning.

"I, oh…" I trailed off on a hiss, his resulting chuckle sliding over my senses.

"Too much?" he asked softly, my neck throbbing with desire.

So that's what it feels like to be bitten.

No wonder Mikael enjoyed it.

My limbs vibrated, my palms barely balanced against the wall. He was destroying me. Slowly. Fully. Completely.

But not my mind.

His hold shifted, his palm sliding down to cup my sex while he continued to penetrate me from behind with his opposite hand.

"K-Kylan…" I didn't know whether to beg him to stop or demand more.

He kissed my pulse, his tongue lapping at the wound he'd left open on my skin. Each swipe sent another tremor through my body, centering in my core. His finger circled my clit, deepening the moment, shooting off stars behind my eyes.

So close.

But not enough.

I *needed…* Oh, I didn't even know.

His name fell from my lips once more, his teeth moving to my earlobe to nibble instead. "I can't wait to fuck you, Raelyn. In all ways. Your pussy, your ass." His fingers plunged into me with the words, stoking my inner flames. "I will own all of you. Including your mind."

I shook my head, swallowing. "No."

"Yes." Another thrust, this time from the front and the back. I moaned in reply, my heart thudding in my ears. My muscles had pulled tight, my abdomen curling with that familiar ache only Kylan could relieve. "Your heart, too, princess. Your spirit. I want it all."

"No," I repeated, my nails threatening to break against the wall from how hard I dug into the hard surface. "Never."

He nuzzled the sensitive spot below my ear. "Are you on fire, little lamb? Feeling as if you might explode?"

I groaned as he increased the pace, stimulating my orgasm without giving me that extra push my body required. "Y-yes," I whispered. "I don't… I can't…" It was right there. So close. So fierce. And refusing my embrace. A frustrated scream built up in my throat, my body begging for the edge that eluded me.

"That's your mind, Raelyn," he whispered. "Waiting for my command, refusing to let you come without my permission." He licked my throat again, showering wildfire across my being, piercing my very soul.

"Kylan," I whimpered, no longer able to process anything other than the passionate spell weaving a binding pattern beneath my skin, forever labeling me as *his*.

"Your mind longs for my approval. Beg me, sweetheart, and I'll let you shatter." The words were a dark promise against my ear.

I quivered, unable to deny his power. "Please." My body clenched around him, urging him to finish it, to grant me the release I so desperately craved. "Please, Kylan."

His amusement trickled over me, his fingers fucking me in earnest. "More."

"What do you want?" I asked, water prickling my eyes from the insanity throbbing within me. "I can't give you all of me. Anything else, but not that."

"Don't you see?" His lips were against my ear. "I already *own* you, Raelyn."

"No." I shook my head, tears falling freely. "No."

"Oh, yes," he murmured, pushing deep. "Come for me, princess." He punctuated the demand by sinking his incisors into my skin.

I screamed as my world came undone.

Everything shook.

The ground.

The air.

My very being.

Devastated.

Broken beyond repair.

He owns me.

The words reverberated in my thoughts as his name left my mouth as a curse and a prayer.

It hurt. It overwhelmed. It destroyed.

And I wanted him to do it all over again, to take me to this place of oblivion that only existed with Kylan. Only existed in his arms, beneath his touch, with his *permission.*

Fuck, I hated him.

I adored him.

I wanted to kill him.

To fuck him.

To hit him.

My knees gave out from the onslaught of emotions and feelings, my body incapable of such a divine experience. Kylan caught me, lifting me into his arms with the ease of a much stronger being. His lips whispered over my cheek, his tongue tasting my tears.

He'd obliterated me.

I couldn't even open my eyes.

"I'm becoming addicted to the way you say my name in the throes of passion, Raelyn." He held me beneath the water to wash away the soap. The warmth prickled my too-sensitive skin, eliciting tremors from my lower body.

He kissed a path to my mouth, his tongue dipping inside with ease to fill my mouth with his blood. I choked, not ready, but he was relentless, forcing me to swallow or risk inhaling his essence.

My insides tingled, welcoming the energetic boost and healing properties of his being into mine. The heady fluid wrapped me in a euphoric cocoon, one I craved far more than I should.

Kylan was creating an addiction, one only he alone could satisfy. I longed to fight it but couldn't, not when it left me feeling so blissfully complete.

Mine, a foreign voice whispered through my thoughts. *My world. My place. My purpose.*

I blocked the seductive chant from my mind, refusing to let it guide me. I would not—could not—fall into Kylan's web.

Too late…

No.

The water shut off, and Kylan stepped out with me still in his arms. When had we stopped kissing? Was he even clean?

He enveloped me in a towel, my feet somehow sturdy on the ground despite the fog clouding my mind.

What had he done to me?

Who am I?

"Jace will be here soon," Kylan said, his palms rubbing my arms with the cotton fabric. His erection stood proud between us, a firm reminder of my lack of reciprocation.

Would he push me to my knees now?

My legs started to bend, anticipating his demand, but his grip on my biceps kept me upright.

"Later, Raelyn. Jace is our priority right now. I need you to listen to me."

I blinked at the water droplets dancing along the planes of his chest. *Male perfection.* I bent to trace the line with my tongue, loving the taste of him. One of his hands went to my hair, his fingers knotting in my strands.

Now he would force—

"Raelyn." He yanked me back to meet his gaze. "I need you to focus."

I just smiled. "Then you shouldn't have showered with me."

He chuckled and shook his head. "You're blood-drunk."

I shrugged. Or I tried to. My shoulders just seemed to flop. "Okay."

With a smirk, he wrapped a towel around his waist and picked me up to carry me into the bedroom. "You need more food." He dropped me unceremoniously onto the bed and handed me the half-eaten plate of eggs. "I want those gone by the time I'm finished talking."

My nose crinkled, but I forced a forkful of cold eggs into my mouth and chewed.

"Good, little lamb." He patted me on the head.

I narrowed my gaze, which only caused his lips to curl in response. "Jackass," I grumbled, recalling the term from a movie earlier this week. It seemed to be an appropriate nickname for Kylan.

His laugh startled me. It was full of life and humor and nothing like his usual low chuckles. His face crinkled into lines I'd never seen, his enjoyment almost palpable.

He grabbed me and kissed me so hard I almost forgot how to breathe. Kylan released me just as suddenly, his smile still firmly in place. "Careful, darling, or I'll keep you forever."

I snorted. "Not likely."

His eyebrows rose. "Excuse me?"

Oh, had I said that out loud? Hmm. I ate another bite of egg and just stared at him. We both knew he couldn't keep me forever, so why even discuss it?

He sat beside me on the bed, his palm going to my cheek.

"Truth," he murmured. "I don't trust Jace, and I'm concerned he may try to hurt you. Not directly, but indirectly, to cause a scene. Assuming he's the one framing me for insanity, I mean. So I need you to stay by my side all night, and I need you to behave for me."

I swallowed the last bit from the plate and set it on the nightstand beside me.

"You really think he's the one who killed your harem?" Because it didn't match the Jace I'd studied in school, the Jace who was a political mastermind and nearly as brilliant as Kylan.

"I think he has the best motive."

"Which makes him too obvious."

He tilted his head to the side. "Meaning?"

"Meaning he's too obvious," I repeated. "Would you do something so conspicuous?"

He snorted. "No, for several reasons, the primary one being I'm more strategic than that."

"And Jace isn't strategic?"

"He is, which explains the lack of evidence and his perfect alibis. It's exactly as I would play it."

"Minus the obvious part," I pointed out.

He opened his mouth, then closed it, his dark eyes glimmering with appreciation. "Fascinating," he murmured. "You're the first person brave enough to counter my opinion."

My brow furrowed. "There's nothing brave about logic." And it seemed too easy for Jace to be the culprit.

"There is when it's contrary to a royal's thoughts on the matter. You'd be surprised how many of my constituents are afraid to debate with me."

"I'm not debating." Or that hadn't been my intention, anyway.

"No, you're forcing me to see beyond a millennia-old rivalry and acknowledge reason." He drew his thumb over my bottom lip. "This meeting with Jace may just prove even more enlightening than I originally anticipated. Thank you."

"I didn't really do anything."

"On the contrary, little lamb." He kissed me softly, his tongue playing over my lips. "You did more than you realize." He nudged me onto my back and settled his hips between my legs, the towels the only fabric separating us. "Jace will be here in twenty minutes. I'm going to spend ten of those minutes kissing you. Then you're going to ready yourself to help me greet him."

"O-okay," I whispered, swallowing.

"I won't be sharing you, Raelyn," he vowed against my mouth. "As a royal and his elder, it's my birthright. Besides, as you may have learned, I'm not particularly fond of rules."

I nodded. "Yes."

"Good. Now open your mouth."

Chapter Twenty

KYLAN

MY LIPS TINGLED. Actually *tingled.*

I resisted the urge to touch them.

Raelyn made me feel… young. Alive. Oddly at peace.

I hadn't meant to go to her, but after hearing the comments about Angelica's promotion, I couldn't stop myself from appearing. That was my consequence for eavesdropping.

Raelyn had asked about the transition to becoming a vampire, a clear breaking of the rules, and Angelica had replied. Both of them should be punished, but how could I discipline them when my lips had lifted in response? Sending Angelica to Judith with news that I'd changed meeting locations was penalty enough.

My phone buzzed with a message from my most trusted lieutenant. *Jace has arrived.*

Send him upstairs, I replied, knowing full well she hated this plan. Of course, she said nothing. No one ever questioned me.

Except Raelyn.

She wore the red silk gown perfectly, her breasts barely contained by the low-cut fabric. Her luscious red locks were pulled up on top of her head in a messy array I'd assembled myself. The only problem was my blood had healed her mark.

Something I should fix.

I grabbed her hip and yanked her against me. She wobbled on her heels, her hands going to my biceps for balance.

"I love this dress." The slits went up both sides to the tops of her thighs, and her back was completely exposed. "Removing it later will be a great joy."

She shivered, her blue eyes lifting to mine. "You wear a suit nicely."

My eyebrows lifted. "Did you just give me a compliment?"

Her lips twitched. "Maybe."

She'd surprised me. Again.

"Who are you?" I marveled softly. The woman constantly shocked me, from the very first bite on my tongue. I wrapped my palm around her neck and debated where to mark her. The pulse point was too easy. I wanted something more intimate, more scandalous.

"Rae," she replied, a defiant flash in her gaze that went straight to my chest. It had not escaped my notice that Mikael had called her that name all week.

"Raelyn," I corrected.

I didn't give her time for a reply, my need to bite her too strong.

My incisors met the flesh of her breast, right next to her silky dress, striking deep and fast and eliciting a yelp from her. Her nails bit into my jacket, her breath hitching as I sucked hard, ensuring my claim remained even with my blood thriving inside her. It would partly heal, enough to stop her bleeding, but the blemish would be fresh for introductions. Especially with the elevator announcing Jace's impending arrival.

Ignoring the sound of steps over the marble, I continued feeding, Raelyn's moans music to my ears. She'd lost herself to me, unaware of our audience, and I adored it too much to stop. Not right away.

I gave it a long moment, easing her out of the oblivion before righting her again and smiling down at her. "Say your name," I whispered.

"Rae," she replied, her gaze drowsy.

I shook my head and smiled. "Defiant until the end, hmm?" I turned to face Jace and his new sovereign. "What do you do when a pet misbehaves, Jace?"

Raelyn froze beside me, finally realizing our company had arrived.

"It depends on the infraction," he replied coolly.

"Failing to remember her given name." I cocked a brow. "What would you do?"

"Make her repeat the name while I fucked her mouth. And I wouldn't stop until I was convinced she remembered it."

I smiled and wrapped my arm around Raelyn's lower back. "A sound idea. Raelyn?"

She bit her lip, her gaze on the floor. "As you wish, My Prince." It came out soft but sure. I kept her upright when she started to bend her legs and pulled her tight to my side.

"A punishment for later," I whispered against her ear. One I may or may not indulge in. It would depend on the rest of the evening. "Ah, well, welcome, Jace. Darius." I held out a hand to them both, shaking firmly while holding

Raelyn at my side. They both noted the fresh marks on her breast, but neither remarked on it.

"We appreciate the invitation," Jace murmured, following formalities. "Darius, introduce Juliet."

"With pleasure." He guided the striking brunette forward with a palm against her lower back. "This is my blood virgin and *Erosita*, Juliet." She curtsied low, her translucent gown displaying all her assets and two sets of fresh bite marks. Had Jace and Darius shared her on the way here?

Whatever they had going between them should have fascinated me a hell of a lot more than it actually did. Having Raelyn at my side, her aroused screams still fresh in my ears, dulled me to Juliet's charm.

"She's beautiful," I murmured. "I can see why you kept her, Darius." She remained in a low bow, waiting to be released, her training abundantly clear. "She's welcome to stand."

Darius returned his hand to her back as she obeyed, her focus on the floor, just like Raelyn's.

"Did you leave your consorts at home?" I asked Jace, noticing his lack of an entourage.

"They weren't needed." A smooth reply. "Not when I have access to Juliet's finer attributes. You should hear her scream. It's a lovely sound."

I considered that with a smile. It seemed a clever excuse for keeping his harem from me, which suggested he feared what I might do to them. Because he believed me insane, or because he expected retribution? Time would tell.

"Well, this is my Raelyn." I nuzzled her throat. "She, too, screams beautifully. Care for a demonstration?" Her pulse escalated at the suggestion, a hint of excitement underlying the alluring rhythm.

"I may enjoy that later," Jace murmured. "Juliet would be happy to reciprocate, right, Darius?"

"Of course." He seemed almost cold, his posture stiff, aloof. The rumors stated he had only taken an *Erosita* to prove his wealth and power and kept her because Jace enjoyed the benefits. His bored expression and light touch against the female's back confirmed the speculation. No outward signs of possession apart from the mark on her neck and she certainly didn't seem all that inclined to him.

But it's too perfect, my instincts whispered. It was exactly how I would act should I ever take a mate. Which would never happen. Not even with…

Raelyn.

I glanced at her, realization slamming me in the gut.

She was an untouched virgin.

Never bitten.

Until me.

I'd unknowingly initiated the ceremony between us by exchanging blood.

Fascinating. No wonder I felt so connected to her.

Well, I certainly needed to fix that problem, and quickly.

But first, our guests. I returned my gaze to Jace and grinned. "Can I interest you in a drink before dinner?" Zelda probably needed another hour to prepare considering I'd switched the meeting location at the last minute.

"Wine?" my fellow royal suggested, his lips kicking up at the sides.

I tightened my grip on Raelyn. "With a splash of blood to top it off?"

"It's as if you read my mind, Kylan." He glanced at Juliet, the indication clear. "Speaking of decadent items, where's your favorite pet?"

"Ah, Mikael is feeling a bit drained at the moment." I led the way to the seating area while adding, "He had a little too much fun playing with Raelyn yesterday."

Jace chuckled and settled into an oversized chair. "I bet." He held out a hand that Juliet accepted and assisted her into his lap. Darius took a seat beside them on the sofa.

An intriguing dynamic, one that came off as natural but struck me as intentional.

Protective, even.

Because they feared I might ask for a bite? Or something else?

"Raelyn, would you mind asking Zelda to help us with the wine? Tell her a French red will do nicely; she'll understand." I had a cabinet of favorites that she kept well stocked.

"Of course, My Prince." She curtsied beautifully and strolled off with a confidence I admired. Her dress revealed her curves without putting them on display like Juliet's gown.

"I'm glad you didn't kill her," Jace remarked, his silver-blue eyes on Raelyn's ass. "Would be a shame to waste such gorgeous talent."

I welcomed the jibe and reference to my former harem. "Yes, she's rather disobedient. Very different from my previous consorts."

He smirked, giving nothing away. "Then hopefully you'll keep her around for a while."

My lips curled. "You mean, as opposed to what was done to my deceased harem?"

"Yes, some may refer to that as a misuse of resources." Jace pulled Juliet's hair over one shoulder while speaking and kissed her neck. Her pulse remained admirably steady, her familiarity with Jace evident. "I prefer to reallocate my pets when I grow bored of them," he added, his focus on Juliet. "But to each his own."

Perfectly played, as always.

He didn't admonish my behavior yet managed to offer his opinion—disapproval. Was it all a ploy because he orchestrated the deaths himself? Or did he truly feel that way?

Obvious, Raelyn had said. *All right, little lamb. Let's see if you're right.*

I took up the opposite end of the sofa from Darius and folded my ankle over my knee. "Congratulations on your new position."

"Thank you," he replied, confidence and age radiating from him. "It's an intriguing change."

"I bet." I considered him carefully. Darius was old enough to be a royal, had the bloodline in him as well. And his maker, Cam, had been one of the best chess players I'd ever known. Which labeled Darius as a fierce competitor even without Jace seated beside him.

"So what sparked your interest in joining the political arena after all this time?" I asked, genuinely curious.

Raelyn and Zelda returned with the wine, but Darius's focus remained on me. "Mainly, I didn't feel there was anyone else better qualified in Jace Region to run. And secondly, I'm tired of being governed by vampires half my age."

A fair statement, one I could respect.

I accepted the glass Raelyn handed me and pulled her into my lap, leaving Zelda to pass out wine to the others. She finished and left without a word, her focus on dinner.

"But why now?" I asked Darius. "Because of Adrian Loughton's untimely demise?" Mauled by a pack of rogue lycans, if my sources were correct. But I suspected the lycans were actually hired. That's how I would have played it, anyway.

"His passing afforded me a new opportunity." He snapped his fingers, and Juliet raised her wrist. No tremble. No fear. Merely a soft scent of arousal.

Well, now *that* was fascinating.

She liked him.

And the slight twitch in her lips proved it.

An *Erosita* could communicate telepathically with her master. Were they speaking to one another right now? Darius kissed her wrist before sinking his fangs into her delicate skin. She didn't flinch, not even as he squeezed to force droplets of her addictive essence into his glass. Jace shook his head in polite—yet odd—refusal.

What kind of vampire turned down the offering of a blood virgin? Especially after suggesting it in the foyer.

One with a secret up his sleeve.

I didn't follow suit with Raelyn, having enjoyed my fill earlier.

Darius sealed Juliet's wound and her lips twitched again, her arousal piquing.

Oh, they were most definitely communicating.

I met Jace's penetrating gaze, noting the protective quality lurking in those silver depths. Of Darius, Juliet, or both?

"I wonder," I said slowly, determining my phrasing. "How far will your new political aspirations take you, Darius?"

He relaxed into the sofa, leaving Juliet on Jace's lap, where she relaxed far more than a human should. Even Raelyn's shoulders were lined with tension, her pulse beating seductively in my ears.

"I'm quite content with my new title," he replied smoothly.

"Of course." I slid my palm up and down Raelyn's arm in an attempt to smooth the goose bumps pebbling her creamy skin. "But what of the future?

You're of royal blood—Cam's line—and could qualify for a region of your own should one become available. Surely that's a consideration?"

He chuckled, sharing a glance with Jace. "No. I've never had—nor will I ever have—a desire for my own territory."

Truth or a lie.

I sipped my wine while continuing to stroke Raelyn with my opposite hand, her body slowly easing into mine. She must have expected me to bleed her into my glass. Poor little lamb, always guessing. I kissed her shoulder softly. "Would you like a sip, little lamb?" I asked, holding the wine before her.

She glanced back at me with wide blue eyes, then dropped them. "No, thank you, My Prince."

Her breach in decorum had me grinning. "What color are Juliet's eyes?" I wondered out loud, refocusing on Jace and Darius. "I mean, does it bother you at all that they are constantly lowered?"

"You would prefer her to be more direct?" Darius asked, his eyebrow lifting.

I shrugged. "I would prefer to admire her beautiful face, not have her hide beneath a veneer of dark hair." My grip shifted to Raelyn's neck and up into her messy array of red strands, gently pulling her upward. "My consort has gorgeous blue eyes that she constantly hides. Wouldn't you rather see them?" I glanced between our guests, waiting.

"Are you offering a closer look?" Jace asked, his heated gaze traveling over Raelyn suggestively.

An irrational urge to growl tempted my throat. *Never.*

"Not tonight," was my response instead. It came out slightly deeper than intended, my instincts rioting against even the possibility of sharing her.

That's new.

It's the bond…

I studied Darius, Juliet, and Jace, an idea forming and solidifying, an answer to a question I hadn't even realized I'd asked.

But I had to be sure.

I took a long sip, debating my next play. Yes. The rules. I released Raelyn to stroke my thumb over her cheek, appreciating the delightful blush blossoming beneath the skin. "I'm just wondering why we force such beautiful women to hide their best features," I murmured, feigning curiosity in the trivial statement.

"Decorum," Darius replied simply.

"Yes," I agreed. "Lilith's version of it, anyway."

I waited and caught the surprise I expected in Jace's features. Darius did a better job controlling himself, but the flare in his pupils confirmed my suspicions.

"What? Don't tell me you prefer all her ridiculous rules too?" *Because I can tell you don't.* I sighed and waved it off as a flippant comment. "Well, if you prefer they hide, they can hide. But I am curious about something."

Jace affixed a bored expression, his part in this play almost perfect. Almost. "Regarding?"

I finished my glass and set it aside, taking my time and drawing out the moment. Darius's responses were too perfect, and Jace's body language was too practiced.

The perfect facade.

And if anyone could see through such a charade, it was me.

I'd suspected for months that Jace was up to something and had assumed it revolved around plots to obtain my territory. But Raelyn's commentary earlier forced me to see beyond the rivalry I'd quietly enjoyed with Jace for millennia.

Oh, he possessed a secret all right, but it had nothing to do with me and everything to do with the female on his lap.

She was too calm.

Because his touch remained mostly neutral. She wore a practically nonexistent dress, and his hand remained on her upper thigh.

He didn't kiss her.

He denied her blood.

And Darius remained completely at ease while having his *Erosita*—his mate—on the lap of another male.

I'd barely engaged in the ceremony with Raelyn, and I already felt the stirrings of possession, hence my cruelty with Mikael just last night. Just the mere thought of sharing her now with either of these men had my blood boiling.

No.

There was absolutely no way Darius would approve of Juliet being manhandled by another male, even his royal and superior, unless they had an arrangement.

I wrapped my arms around Raelyn, pulling her close, but also having a hold on her in case I needed to remove her quickly.

"You might be wondering why I invited you both here this evening," I said.

"You're not one to engage in political platitudes," Jace replied, his shrewd gaze narrowing. "So yes, I am. Are we finally going to arrive at the point?"

Ah, there was the royal who reminded me too much of myself—my rival for good reason. "I thought, perhaps, you were responsible for killing my harem, but I see now that's not the case at all."

His gaze widened a fraction, the only indication of shock he displayed. Darius, however, had gone eerily still, his green eyes focused with the predatory senses of a male detecting a threat—not to himself, but to his female.

I smiled. "Yes, that's what I thought," I continued. "But that's not the case at all, is it?"

"If I wanted your territory, Kylan, I wouldn't frame you for mental insanity," Jace said flatly. "Which I assume is what you suspected of me."

Yes, my rival indeed. And also a potential ally.

"It was, until about an hour ago when Raelyn mentioned it was too obvious." I kissed her temple, proud of her instincts.

His dark brows shot upward. "You're taking advice from your consort?"

"You're surprised?" I tilted my head, my lips threatening to twitch. "That's intriguing considering you're playing some sort of game with Darius. I mean, you are in fact only pretending to enjoy his *Erosita,* yes?"

Chapter Twenty-One

KYLAN

SILENCE.

Tension thickened the air as Juliet's breath finally faltered.

Yes. I'd definitely read the situation accurately. "You don't want anyone to know because having a mate is perceived as a weakness and you refuse to share."

Darius neither confirmed nor denied it, merely waited.

"Prove me wrong," I encouraged. "Put on a show for me, Jace, with Juliet." I waved at the table. "It's not like I haven't seen you fuck a woman before." We'd shared plenty of females together once upon a time.

Jace's jaw tightened. "What do you really want, Kylan?"

"Oh, I already achieved my goal for the evening by confirming you're not the one framing me for immortal insanity. This is merely fun."

"So you didn't kill your harem." He removed Juliet from his lap and handed her over to Darius, who gladly accepted her into his arms. "But someone managed to get through your defenses and frame you."

"Indeed."

"Which explains why you're hosting a party in two weeks. You intend to draw out the guilty party by using your new consort as bait. They'll want to make it a grand show, after all." He set his barely touched wine aside. "Clever."

"Yes, well, you are—or were—at the top of my suspect list."

"I'm both flattered and insulted."

Yes, I'd feel the same if the roles were reversed. "Could it be Brandt or Luka?"

Jace snorted. "No. Luka has no desire to be near water, and Brandt is abrasive, not strategic. If he wanted your land, you'd know."

That'd been my assessment as well. "Any suggestions?"

"Off the top of my head?" Jace rubbed the back of his neck, his gaze traveling upward. "Naomi's hatred of you is no secret, and she has the resources to pull it off."

"Yes, I suppose she would be quite satisfied by my removal." But she wouldn't gain anything else. My land was nowhere near her region in what was formerly known as South Africa. "If I consider all those with personal vendettas, essentially everyone would be a suspect."

Jace smirked. "You do have a penchant for pissing off the lycans."

"Vampires, too," I pointed out. "But it has to go beyond mere revenge for something petty. Whoever it is sent someone into my house to kill my property. That takes a level of skill and planning that not many possess."

"Unless it's someone who's bored and craving a diversion," Darius said while combing his fingers through Juliet's hair. She'd relaxed against him, her head on his shoulder and her dark eyes on Raelyn. It seemed decorum had gone out the window, fucking finally.

I shifted Raelyn to my side in an attempt to make her more comfortable and wrapped my arm around her shoulders. "That begs the question: who would be both brave and foolish enough to challenge me?"

"Another royal," Darius suggested. "Someone who wants to knock you off the top of the ladder."

"That would place Jace at the top." I arched a brow at him. "And we just decided it's not you."

"Which implies that I would be the next target," he inferred. "Hazel would be next, but it's not her."

"No, it's not," I agreed. It wasn't her style. When Hazel wanted something, she was blunt and direct. She'd never been the game-playing type.

"Which brings us back to the diversion potential," Darius murmured.

It was an angle I hadn't considered. "Any ideas?"

"Robyn," Jace said, chuckling. "That bitch always wants to play."

I laughed. "She knows better than to fuck with me."

Jace shrugged. "True. But I wouldn't rule anyone out."

"Except you," I replied dryly.

"If I wanted your territory, Kylan, I wouldn't try to discredit you; I would kill you." A blunt statement, not a threat. "I know better than to leave you alive after engaging in such a game."

Because he knew I would come after him and return the favor tenfold. "Touché." I felt the same way about him. "Well, how would you like to move forward? I've expressed a weakness by admitting I didn't kill my harem, and you're clearly hiding a weakness of your own." I looked pointedly at Juliet.

Jace considered, his silver eyes blazing with intelligence. "We've spent a thousand years or so working against each other when we used to work quite well together."

It was true. Our rivalry had begun over a conflict of interest in properties. We always enjoyed similar luxuries, and it became almost a game of chess as to who could acquire the most the fastest. None of it really mattered now, not in this new world.

"Do you miss it? The way things used to be?" I drew my thumb up and down Raelyn's shoulder, considering my own questions. "Because I do. I miss the challenge and the lack of responsibility for anyone other than myself."

Running a territory of vampires was a necessity more than a choice. They required justice and order. It was the only way to control the population, to maintain proper blood supplies, and to ensure the survival of the human race.

"Cam always thought we could coexist with humans differently," Darius admitted.

"Yes, Lilith clearly didn't agree." Since she'd put the eldest of our kind on a public trial that ended in his death sentence, except I never actually saw her carry it out. "Do you suppose Cam is alive somewhere?" It was considered treason to speculate or discuss the past, but Lilith and her army of enthusiasts didn't scare me.

Jace's pupils flared. "Why would you suspect that?"

"It's something I've wondered and thought you might know. If anyone was invited to his execution, it would be his only living relatives, yes?" Darius as his only progeny and Jace as his cousin.

"You think he might be alive?" Darius asked.

"Did you see him die?" I countered.

He remained silent for a long beat before saying, "No."

"Then." I waved my hand, signifying my point as made. "So where is he and who has him?"

"I thought we were here to discuss the issue of you being framed," Jace said slowly. "How did we switch to Cam?"

"Darius brought him up after I asked about former times." I narrowed my gaze. "But it's interesting that you want to avoid the topic."

More silence fell, the tension of earlier returning.

Ah, so there was more to his secrets, something to do with Cam. "Do you know where he is?" I wondered, fascinated.

His nostrils flared, but still he remained quiet.

"Then you don't, but you want to know." I glanced between him and Darius and noted the way Juliet had avoided his gaze. Even she was in on the ploy. "Oh, now I'm fascinated. You've been holding out on me, Jace."

"We're not friends, Kylan. We're not even allies."

"But we used to be," I reminded him.

"A long time ago."

I gestured around us, to Juliet, to Raelyn, to the floor-to-ceiling windows overlooking Kylan City. "It's a new world, Jace, filled with fresh beginnings."

"You invited me over tonight because you thought I was trying to steal your territory," he growled.

"Which you've proven isn't the case and have instead brought me a wealth of intriguing information." I eyed the blood virgin again before meeting Jace's gaze directly. "If I can see through your charade, how many others will?"

"How many will believe you've gone mad?" he countered.

I snorted. "Several, and I welcome the accusation. I'm more than capable of holding my own."

"As am I."

"But together we would be formidable, and no one would ever expect an alliance between us."

That gave Jace pause, his jaw tightening. He knew I was right. Our notorious rivalry painted us on opposite sides of the playing field. Working together would be the last thing anyone would anticipate, something I could use to help solve my current problem and something he could use to his advantage in whatever scheme he had going.

"What are your terms?" he asked slowly.

"For starters, I would appreciate your assistance at my social engagement in two weeks. Someone may say something to you, or near you, assuming you would never pass the information on to me. In return, I can offer assistance in hiding Darius's, shall we call them, affections?"

Darius arched a brow. "And how do you propose to do that?"

"The same way Jace is helping you now. You'll be staying in my city for the weeks prior to the party. We'll let assumptions be made about *how* you spent your time here."

"Wouldn't that imply a partnership of some kind?"

I smiled. "Not if we spin the gossip appropriately." Something Judith excelled at greatly. "Perhaps I took a liking to your *Erosita* and proposed a temporary trade. Being your elder, you can hardly refuse."

"And what will actually be occurring?" he pressed, his grip around Juliet tightening possessively.

"You and Juliet can remain here, and I'll take Raelyn to my estate north of here." That would give me plenty of time to fix this accidental bond I'd created while also offering Darius and Juliet a moment of solitude disguised as something far darker. Two birds, one stone. "Everyone will believe we made an arrangement, one you could negatively discuss during the festivities."

"The part of a disgruntled houseguest," Jace translated. "Sharing is fine, but the least Kylan could have done was respect Darius's property. Some of the marks were a little too deep, almost as if he'd lost himself to the moment."

"All signs of immortal insanity," Darius added. "Coupled with how he slaughtered his harem, I'll admit that I'm concerned."

"Rightly so." Jace picked up his wine again, his gaze meeting mine. "He's certainly lost the plot."

I chuckled and shook my head. "You're nearly as old as I am."

"Yes, but I wear my age far better than you do."

I snorted. "The key is being realistic, not going off on fantasy tangents."

"We'll handle it just fine," he murmured, swirling the contents of his glass. "Am I to stay here as well? Because that would be less believable."

"You had business to attend to and left me behind to keep an eye on Kylan, worried that his recent behavior may impact the borders to your territory. I agreed and used Juliet as my bargaining chip to procure an invitation." Darius kissed her neck, causing her lips to curl. "The party is the first time we've had a chance to connect, hence our resulting conversation over Kylan's antics."

"Brilliant," Jace replied. "I knew I promoted you for a reason."

Darius smirked. "More than one."

Their easy camaraderie revealed a true friendship, one I knew existed but hadn't seen in over a century. All the formalities Lilith insisted upon in society had removed all semblance of humanity, even among ourselves. Everything was about law and order, running a smooth region, following protocols, and respecting the elders of the species.

Being at the top afforded me opportunities very few would ever see. That's what Angelica had mentioned to Raelyn—being a vampire wasn't nearly as glamorous as humans were led to believe. The youngest immortals started with nothing unless their royal or alpha decreed otherwise.

"We'll do this for you," Jace said, drawing me back to the conversation at hand. "If all goes according to plan, then we should discuss the notion of an alliance more in depth."

A test.

He meant to see how this all played out before deciding to trust me.

"That's fair." Because I, too, wanted to see how he and Darius handled themselves. I had no doubt they weren't the culprits, but we'd shared surface-level secrets this evening that could easily be used against one another.

"Then we have an agreement." He stood.

I joined him, extending my hand. "We do."

Zelda entered with her blonde head bowed as we shook on the tentative partnership. "Dinner is ready, My Prince," she informed me, curtsying again and leaving us as quickly as she'd appeared.

"Dinner," I repeated. "Shall we, then?"

"One thought before we do," Jace murmured, releasing my hand. "I imagine you've already looked into this, but as the attack happened at your estate, you should be searching for accomplices, perhaps within your own staff."

"You're right. I've already vetted them all." I trusted my team implicitly and kept them happy in order to secure their loyalty. "That said, I'm always listening and watching."

"I would expect no less, as I would do the same." He nodded. "Well, I'm famished and I believe Juliet is as well, aren't you, darling?" His gaze sparkled as he grinned down at her. "You can speak freely."

"I am hungry, yes," she admitted softly.

Darius chuckled and nuzzled her neck affectionately. "She's learning the joys of real food."

I glanced at a stunned Raelyn and held my hand out to her. "Raelyn still desires spinach and broccoli with her eggs for evening breakfast. Come, little lamb. Perhaps Juliet can demonstrate how to properly enjoy food."

Raelyn's nose crinkled as she joined me.

I lifted her chin with my index finger. "You can stop hiding now. Jace and Darius won't bite." Not Raelyn, anyway. "Come out and play. I miss you."

Her icy blue eyes glittered up at me. "I've been sitting beside you for the last thirty minutes."

My lips quirked up. "As my obedient slave, yes, and I'm quite proud of you for it. But I want my defiant princess."

"Another mind game?"

"Just the truth." I tapped her head softly. "You know what I want."

"It's never going to happen."

"It's already started." I kissed her nose. "And now we have a week at home to deepen my hold."

The party preparations were well underway and didn't require my involvement. All the vampires interested in Tremayne's former role had submitted their candidacies, and my meeting with Jace was complete.

"I'm looking forward to spending time with you, Raelyn." *And fixing this bond between us.* That was more important than keeping her virginity intact. I couldn't afford to have an emotional connection. Not now, not ever.

She scowled at me. "A week isn't going to change anything."

"On the contrary, darling, a week alone together will change everything."

Chapter Twenty-Two

RAE

DINNER WAS NOT WHAT I EXPECTED. It turned into a reminiscence between the vampires, filled with laughter and references I didn't understand. Juliet had appeared just as lost as I had, her dark eyes finding mine several times throughout the meal and her eyebrows lifting.

I wished we could have spoken so I could have asked about her unique relationship with Darius, but Kylan had been eager to leave once we finished eating.

He drove, using the tunnels and evading the city's security on the perimeter. Judith followed with Mikael and some of the staff, her displeasure at us moving locations evident by the look she'd given Kylan before we left. If it fazed him, he didn't show it.

The snowy landscape enveloped the world outside of the city, causing my heart to race at the picturesque views. They'd been hidden behind the buildings, the streets freshly cleared, leaving little traces of the gorgeous wintry mix.

Kylan squeezed my thigh, his touch hot through the thin silk of my dress. "You want to explore again, don't you?"

"It's just so beautiful," I whispered, awed by the moonlight illuminating the snow-dusted trees.

"You prefer this to the city." Not a question, but a statement.

Still, I felt compelled to say, "Yes."

"Me too." He drove in silence a few minutes longer, the hum of his engine the only sound in the still night. "There's still plenty of time before dawn. How would you feel about a hike when we get back?"

I blinked. "With you?" The question left before I could swallow it, my shock at his request evident in the way my voice squeaked at the end.

He chuckled. "Yes, with me, Raelyn."

A hike. With Kylan. I'd never been on one before, let alone through the snow. I glanced at my dress, my lips pinching to the side. "Can I change first?"

His chuckle turned into a laugh and he shook his head. "You're adorable."

"That's not an answer."

"You're right. It's not. As much as I'd enjoy watching you try, you can't hike in heels, little lamb. Last I saw, you could hardly walk through the snow in boots."

My brow furrowed. "I figured it out."

"Yes, you did." His palm disappeared from my leg as he turned off the main road. "We'll venture into the trees where the snow is less thick. The trees more or less protect the ground."

His estate came into view, framed by the mountains behind it, taking my breath away. I definitely preferred this to the city.

The outer gate opened as we approached, granting us entry. Kylan maneuvered down the path with expert ease, pulling us up to the front of the manor where two of his staff members waited to open our doors. He greeted them by name, handing the tallest human the keys.

Most of Kylan's staff were mortals of varying ages, something I noticed more and more throughout the week. Judith was one of the few on his staff of vampire origin.

She parked behind him, exiting without assistance, Angelica in the passenger side wearing an ashen expression.

That must have been an uncomfortable car ride.

"Raelyn and I are going hiking," Kylan informed her, taking my hand. "Get settled and enjoy the rest of your evening, Judith."

"Do you think that's wise, Your Highness?" she asked, glancing around pointedly.

His lips twitched. "I am more than capable of handling myself and protecting Raelyn, unless you meant to suggest otherwise?"

She stilled, her jaw tightening. "Of course not, My Prince."

"Then what are you trying to imply, Judith?" His thumb brushed my pulse, his expression expectant.

"That it may not be safe," she admitted. "But I know you can handle yourself."

"Yes, I can." He turned, pulling me with him. "Good night, Judith."

Her response—if she made one—was lost to the winter elements as Kylan guided me into the foyer, past more staff, toward the grand staircase. "All right, little lamb. Time to bundle you up for the weather."

* * *

I couldn't feel anything.

Not the ground beneath my boots.

Not the air separating my red strands.

Not the snow in my gloved hand.

And I hated it.

I glowered at Kylan dressed only in jeans and a sweater, his dark hair windswept and gorgeous. "This is ridiculous," I mumbled from behind the scarf he'd wrapped around my face.

His dark eyes glittered with mirth as he looked me over. "I think you look adorable."

I patted the puffy jacket with my oversized gloves and snorted. Or attempted to, anyway. It was barely heard over the thick layer of wool swathing my head.

He caught my hand and pulled me forward with a chuckle. "It was this or risk frostbite."

"I'm going to melt to death instead," I grumbled. At least my legs were mobile in the jeans and boots.

"I'll strip you before that happens," he promised, a dark note underlining his words. "Come along, little lamb. Time to explore."

"Yes, master," I deadpanned, causing him to laugh. I'd learned that little quip from Mikael after watching a movie featuring a sarcastic female. She was my kind of human.

"Fuck, I adore you." He yanked me to him and kissed my scarf-covered nose. "Now try to keep up."

He led us to a nearby forest path shrouded in tree cover, the snow more scattered and shallower inside. I followed, my jacket snagging on the branches as we went, our path darkening with each step.

The distance between us grew as we moved, his long strides far more efficient than my short, careful ones. Another tree caught my arm, jerking me back. I shifted, trying to untangle myself, only to find myself worse off.

"Dress warm," I grumbled, repeating Kylan's words from earlier to myself. "It'll protect you from the elements." It seemed nature disagreed.

I yanked my arm away from the sticky needles with so much force my feet slid over the ground, sending me tumbling to the forest floor.

"Protect indeed," I wheezed, my head and back aching from the collision.

Kylan appeared above me, his face shadowed in the night. "Not very graceful, Raelyn."

I just stared at him, unable to reply. Because what could I say? He was right. The tree definitely won.

He held out his hand. It took me a moment to focus enough to grab it, my mind protesting from the jarring fall. I finally managed to accept his help up, my mittened hands grabbing his biceps for balance.

"Can I please take these off?" I asked, irritated by my forced clumsiness.

He flicked the top of my zipper with a smirk. "Not used to wearing so many clothes, hmm?"

"I keep getting stuck on the branches."

"Is that your excuse?" He slowly drew down the metal clasp, exposing my sweater beneath. "Because I think you just want me to undress you." He reached my lower abdomen, the coat falling open. "I think you prefer to be naked in my presence."

A shiver slipped up my spine, not from the weather but from his words. "It's just the jacket," I whispered.

"Uh-huh." He pushed the puffy material from my shoulders, causing it to fall to the ground behind me. Cool air weaved through my wool sweater, taunting the heated skin beneath.

I sighed in relief, my forehead falling to his shoulder. "So much better." I'd felt suffocated by it, my upper body protesting the additional weight and layers. My arms felt freer, lighter now. "I'm ready."

"Oh, I know, but not yet." He tugged on my scarf and stepped away, his grasp on the wool around my neck forcing me to follow. "No more excuses, little lamb." He gave the fabric another pull, causing my eyes to go round.

He'd fashioned my scarf into a leash.

A fucking leash.

Like a dog.

And he was now walking us through the forest as one would a pet.

I tried to unravel myself, but another yank compelled me forward. "Kylan," I growled.

"Yes, pet?"

"This isn't funny."

"On the contrary, I find myself very amused." Another tug. "Pick up the pace, darling lamb." He leapt over a log that I nearly tripped on, but by some miracle, I managed to mimic his action.

He moved slower, but not by much, his long legs far more accustomed to this activity than mine. I tried futilely to loosen the suffocating item from my neck, except each way I went only seemed to tighten the knot.

Why had I let him dress me?

I ignored the scenery—not that I could see it in the dark anyway—and focused on not falling while trying to keep up with him.

A glimmer of light caught my eye a few yards before us, the temporary whiteness blinding me and causing me to stumble into his back. He chuckled. "Eager, hmm?"

"To kill you?" I asked. "Yes." Not that I ever could.

"Oh, love, that would be a fun game indeed. Perhaps we can try fencing sometime. Your marks in the sport were quite high." He started moving again, leaving me only two options: follow or strangle myself.

Damn vampire.

He could see in the dark, allowing him to move freely while I had to watch every step, which was exceedingly difficult when leashed. Not that he seemed to care.

I threw one of my gloves at him because I had nothing else to throw. He laughed, earning him a second glove to the head.

"You'll regret that later, little lamb."

Yeah, yeah. I had pockets. I'd be fine.

The light grew before us, replacing some of my fury with curiosity. It seemed brighter than the courtyard by his house, as if the moon was reflecting off a stronger source.

Kylan stepped through the last of the trees and turned, blocking my view of what lay beyond him. I thought he meant to tease when he pressed a finger to my lips, his body tense with warning.

What? I wondered. *What is it?*

Be very still, he replied in my head, nearly sending me backward.

His hand found my hip, holding me upright while my eyebrows reached my hairline. *How are you in my head?* Vampires weren't telepaths. Unless my books and professors failed to mention that part.

It's temporary, he said. *Just don't move.*

Why?

Shh. He released me slowly and turned, his broad shoulders hiding the scene beyond him. "You know me," he said out loud, his voice low and growly.

My brows furrowed. Did he expect me to reply to that?

"Come," he added, extending his arm. "You know who I am."

I frowned at his back, baffled. *What—*

Shh.

I almost growled at him but froze when something *did* growl.

"Oh, that's how it's going to be tonight?" He tsked. "Gone a few weeks and you forget your alpha."

The creature responded with a snarl, raising goose bumps along my arm. I gripped Kylan's sweater. He no longer held my scarf, giving me freedom, and I found I wanted to be attached to him even more now.

"She's harmless and mine," he snapped. "Stop snarling."

A grumble was the reply.

Silence fell over the forest, the sound of rushing water overwhelming my ears. What was happening? Had a rogue lycan found its way onto Kylan's land? Was this the threat? The monster lying in wait?

Something nudged Kylan, his leg bumping into mine. I glanced down to see a white tail wrapping around his thigh. My nails curled into his wool sweater, my heart thudding wildly.

The wolf grumbled again, causing Kylan to chuckle. "Yeah, her fear is intoxicating; I agree." He squatted, leaving me awkwardly hanging on to his sweater while almost falling over him. Bright yellow eyes met mine, causing me to scramble backward into a tree. The wolf rubbed his giant white muzzle against Kylan's face and licked his cheek.

"A lycan," I whispered.

Kylan snorted. "No, this is a proper wolf. The alpha of his pack." He gestured with his chin to the scene beyond—a frozen lake spreading into the distance and framed by mountains. At the water's edge were several wolves, all standing, alert, their eyes on us.

"W-we should go."

"Nonsense." He stood, patting the alpha's head. "They're old friends. Just irritated with me for disappearing for a few weeks." He scratched the wolf's ear, earning him another kiss on the hand before he trotted back to his pack, who noticeably relaxed. His lips twitched at finding me glued to the tree behind me. "Showing fear makes you smell like dinner to them and to me. I suggest lowering it a notch."

"They're wolves."

"Yes."

"Real wolves."

"Yes." He cocked his head to the side. "You fear them and not me? Because I assure you, I'm the bigger predator here." He prowled forward, wrapping his hand around my scarf again. "And I have every intention of eating you, little lamb."

"You have pet wolves," I whispered, swallowing.

"I wouldn't call them pets," he replied, brushing his knuckles over my cheek. "That term implies a certain level of obedience and submission that they lack. Consider them wild friends who understand my animalistic side."

He stepped closer, his hips pinning mine.

"This is one of my favorite places, Raelyn," he murmured, his mouth scant inches from mine. "I come here when I need to be alone and think."

My brow furrowed. Why bring me here if he wanted to be by himself? "But you're not alone."

"Indeed I'm not." He kissed me softly, his grip on my scarf tightening. "I wanted to share this with you as a thank-you for being honest with me earlier and pointing out the obvious nature of my accusation."

I started. "You're thanking me?"

His lips curled. "I am, by sharing a special place with you. It's magical out here. Let me show you."

"I…" Words failed me. He was rewarding me for pointing out the obvious? No, for being brave enough to poke a hole in his assessment. For being defiant. For having a brain and using it. For being *me.*

I blinked.

He likes me.

I do, he whispered back at me, his dark eyes glimmering. *Come play with me, little lamb. I'll make it worth your while.*

"How are you doing that?"

Amusement teased his features. "It wasn't intentional, I promise, and I'll fix it, but let's enjoy the moment while it lasts. Please?"

Okay, now I'd seen everything. "You're begging."

"I prefer the term *urging*. And besides, this so much more pleasant than forcing."

"You own me."

"I do," he agreed.

"So you don't need my permission to do anything with me."

He tilted his head. "True, but perhaps I desire it."

"Why?"

"Because having you at my mercy willingly is far sexier than demanding your compliance." He nipped my lower lip. "You're already out here. Let me show you the beauty of it, and maybe the wolves will let you return."

I glanced around him at the pile of white fur by the shoreline, all lazing about without a care in the world. Much better than the growling from earlier.

Kylan kissed me again, his tongue dipping inside for a taste that was all too brief.

"Let me reward you, Raelyn," he murmured. "I promise you'll enjoy it."

My blood heated at the underlining prospect of his words. He meant to do more than hike and sightsee.

I have every intention of eating you, little lamb, he'd said.

Oh…

"Yes," he mouthed, still listening to my thoughts. "I'm going to devour you until you implore me to stop." *And I'll continue even then,* he added, the words a caress against my thoughts.

I quivered, my thighs clenching.

Having him *inside* me, whispering to me, increased the intimacy, heightening the sensations.

He desired my mind.

He'd won.

I waited for bleakness to fall, to take me under a shadow of depression, but curiosity consumed me. If Kylan had entered my thoughts, then maybe I possessed the ability to reach his as well. I could turn this around and beat him at his own game.

"Okay," I said, wanting to explore this more. To be inside Kylan's reasoning, to learn his true musings and his goals? That was a priceless opportunity.

I could understand him—the man behind the regal mask, beyond the fondness for games.

I would finally know the real Kylan.

Chapter Twenty-Three

RAE

"WELCOME TO MY VERSION OF PARADISE." Kylan led me down the path to the edge of the glistening lake surrounded by snow-covered trees with mountains in the distance.

My breath caught, the winter wonderland something I never thought to experience. "It's gorgeous," I whispered, spinning to take it all in.

The echoes of moonlight lent a hypnotic glow to the air while the stars painted a picturesque sky. I'd never seen anything like it, not even in my textbooks.

Something prodded my thigh, causing me to freeze midstep. I glanced downward to find a pair of yellow eyes gazing up at me.

"Kylan," I mouthed. *Kylan!*

His chuckle infiltrated my thoughts. "Well, I wouldn't suggest running, or you'll excite his prey drive." Kylan relaxed on a log near the water's edge, his dark eyes sparkling in the night.

Another poke.

What does he want?

"Give him your hand," he replied. "He'll smell my essence on you and back off."

I swallowed. *My hand. All right.* I slowly extended it toward the muzzle filled with very sharp teeth and waited. The wolf gave it a sniff and nuzzled it forcefully until my palm landed on his head.

Kylan chuckled. "Well, now he wants you to give him a good scratch."

"H-he wants me to pet him?" I slowly stroked his fur, surprised by the soft texture. It felt… nice. "Oh." I drew my nails over his head, down to his nape, and back up again, repeating the action over and over, awed. "He's beautiful."

"Yeah, just don't let his mate hear you talk like that." Kylan gestured to a lean wolf watching me with keen eyes. "She's possessive."

The wolf beside me sat, leaning against my legs and almost toppling me into the snow. I shifted for balance while supporting him, my hand still on his head.

"Ah, he likes you," Kylan murmured, approval in his voice. "He's validating you to the others and showing trust."

"He barely knows me."

"Wolves, like most predators, rely on their instincts." His gaze intensified. "And sometimes you just know."

"Is that how you judge most people? By your initial impression?"

"Always, but I also constantly evaluate." He looked me over slowly, thoroughly, his irises deepening to a molten shade along the way.

I shivered, feeling naked despite my abundance of clothes. "And what do you see when you evaluate me?" I asked, my voice dropping to a husky whisper by the end, my fingers curling into the wolf's fur.

"Mmm." Kylan relaxed, his palms resting on the log beneath him, his legs stretched out and crossed at the ankles. "A warrior spirit I long to tame for my own use, a body I desire in my bed more than I probably should, and a mind filled with an intelligence I feared was lost among the human race centuries ago."

"You see all that?" I managed, my throat suddenly tight.

"I do." He leaned forward. "And while you claim you're not afraid of me, deep down, I know you fear what I might do to you. Even more, you're terrified that you might enjoy it." His eyes locked and held mine. "I guarantee you won't just enjoy it, Raelyn, you'll love it."

I swallowed, my hand stilling against the wolf.

"You were made for my brand of ownership, little lamb." The dark words slithered over my senses, heating my blood. "I will possess you, mind, body, and soul." His lethal promise lanced my being, marking me as his even while I protested.

I'll own you, too. The thought rose unbidden, coming from a secret place deep within me. If he made me his, he'd be mine too.

He smiled. *You can try, princess.*

I followed his taunt to the source, piercing his psyche—such a natural reaction, a defense to being teased. And found the truth lurking behind the fog, the realization that he'd never initiated a link of this nature with anyone prior to me.

Mine, the predator before me whispered. *Finish it.*

What happened then?

I took a step toward him, craving more.

The connection.

The binding.

The proper insight into his mind.

He wasn't good for me, would destroy me, but it seemed I could do the same to him. I sensed a note of panic within him, an unease his expression and words didn't otherwise show. He didn't want to let me in, to show me more, but a part of him demanded it.

I straddled him on the log, my body moving as if controlled by an energy I couldn't contain.

More.

He cocked his head, his dark eyes radiating an intoxicating mix of need and confidence. But I felt the concern resting within him, the worry that we might connect completely, providing me the deepest insights to his soul.

And in return, he would have mine.

A mutual binding.

A promise.

My lips brushed his, my yearning to learn more overruling all logic and thought. I wanted to be inside him, to *know* him on the most basic level. This was the way to that goal.

I wrapped my arms around his neck, holding him to me as I kissed him in earnest, my tongue parting his lips to explore the cavern of his mouth. He always led, always dictated our pace, but he gave me this, allowed me the moment of learning I so craved.

He remained utterly still, his muscles clenched.

My seconds were numbered before he took control. I refused to waste it by thinking and gave in to feeling him, memorizing every detail, reveling in his masculinity and power, the way his tongue felt against mine.

Kylan, I breathed into his mind. *Give me more.*

I didn't want to play. I wanted *him*. All of him.

He growled, low and deep, his fingers knotting in my hair while his other hand caught the end of my scarf and gave it a sharp tug. My nails bit into his biceps, reacting to the sudden tightness around my neck.

"Careful, little lamb." The fabric tightened even more, restricting my airway. He drew his tongue over my bottom lip, his dark eyes holding mine. "I give the commands here, not the other way around."

"Yes, My Prince," I mouthed, unable to draw in oxygen.

His pupils flared. "Mmm, I like that, Raelyn. You at my mercy and still obeying." He kissed me softly. "It's arousing." Another kiss. "Addictive." Harder this time. "Invigorating." The scarf loosened but his grip in my hair strengthened, forcing me to remain against him while he devoured my mouth. I melted on top of him, my body his for the taking.

I want you, I whispered.

I know. The cloth around my neck pulled tight again, cutting off my ability to inhale. "Are you wet for me, Raelyn?"

A whimper caught in my throat, unable to pass. I nodded, my thighs clenching around his.

"Even in the woods, surrounded by wolves," he whispered against my lips. "Fuck, you're perfect." He released my scarf, his palm falling to my hip. "And so fucking mine."

Kylan took possession of my mouth, stealing my breath and forcing me to survive on him alone. I clutched his arms, holding on while he devoured me. Bound me. Owned me. Worshiped me.

He unraveled the wool from my neck, his other hand sliding up my abdomen beneath the sweater to palm my bare breast. I arched into him, moaning against his tongue.

More, I begged.

He tweaked my hard nipple, his touch rough and all Kylan, and exactly what I needed.

So demanding tonight. His mental voice caressed my thoughts, stirring a quiver deep within. I liked him there far too much. Something to consider later. Right now I could only care about his hand, his mouth, his hard arousal pressing into the apex between my thighs.

"Kylan." I yanked my sweater over my head, feeling brazen and alive, and much too hot despite the cold air.

"Fuck, Raelyn," he hissed, his mouth going to my neck and lower. He palmed my ass, forcing me to my knees to provide him easier access to my breasts.

I loved having his mouth on me, his tongue lashing my skin, his breath warming my being. Each caress was a brand, each scrape of his teeth a reminder of his possession, his right, his claim.

His touch slid to the front of my jeans, his clever thumb unfastening them with dexterous skill. I dug my fingers into his hair, holding on, requiring more, yearning for his bite.

He skimmed my peak with his incisors, taunting, playing, cascading goose bumps across my flesh before pulling away. "Stand up."

I swallowed, my limbs trembling as I complied.

My boots disappeared.

My pants.

Leaving me naked in the snow and not the least bit cold. I only burned for him more, his gaze blazing hot paths down my body. He removed his sweater, laying it on the ground near mine, and stood. "Take off my jeans."

I licked my lips, my fingers trembling as I worked his button and zipper. He grabbed my wrists, my palms on his hips.

"Kneel, Raelyn." The command shivered down my spine, coiling between my legs.

"Yes, My Prince." I lowered to the ground, his sweater protecting my bare shins and knees from the snow.

He released me. "Finish the job."

I tugged on his jeans, freeing his engorged cock and revealing his strong thighs. His gaze glittered with intent, his arousal seeping from the thick head and enticing my instincts. I leaned forward, desire fueling my movements, and took him into my mouth, sucking the precum from his tip.

His fingers threaded through my hair, holding me there, his growl echoing around us. I pulled his pants down to his ankles, and he kicked them off with his shoes.

"Look at me," he demanded, his voice low and menacing.

I met his gaze as he forced me to take more of him, his head hitting the back of my throat.

"Did I ask you to suck my cock?"

I tried to shake my head but couldn't. *No.*

That's cheating, Raelyn. Use your voice.

"No," I mumbled, his shaft preventing me from being coherent.

"Try again."

I did, but it came out just as garbled.

He tsked. "Now I have to discipline you."

I narrowed my eyes and swallowed more of him in response. *You can't punish me for doing something you enjoy, Kylan.*

His lips twitched. "Defiant even on your knees."

I sucked hard in response, my nails biting into his thighs.

"Fuck," he muttered, his fingers clenching in my hair.

I repeated the action.

He hissed and tugged me off of him and onto the makeshift bed of clothing and snow.

My thighs fell wide as he settled between them, his mouth hovering over my clit. "You need a firm reminder of who is in charge here, darling." His tongue teased my already aching bud, causing my hips to buck against him. "Mmm, I'm going to enjoy this far too much."

"Ky…" I trailed off on a scream, his bite shocking me senseless.

I couldn't move. Couldn't think. Could only feel and endure.

And, oh my Goddess, was it something to endure.

Sensation unlike anything I'd ever felt rocked my core, slicing my being in two, splintering my ability to breathe. It hurt so good. My vision blackened, whitened, the stars overhead spinning in a cloud of ecstasy I could taste on my tongue. He lit my veins on fire, my blood rushing to meet his mouth while he replaced my essence with pure euphoria.

My throat ached from chanting—yelling—his name.

Time froze.

Unfroze.

Froze again.

Mine. His voice echoed through my mind, lancing my soul.

Yours, I agreed, unable to process, to remember why I didn't want to agree. But anything to end this sweet, blissful agony destroying my body. *It's too much.*

You'll take it, Raelyn. His growl vibrated every part of me, his dominance taking hold of me in every way. I couldn't fight him, didn't even want to.

Yes, I whispered. *Anything.*

Everything, he replied, his dark mind blossoming to mine. So many secrets wrapped up in complicated webs of reasoning established over thousands of years.

Ancient, powerful, sophisticated.

I pushed my way inside, only to be stopped by a wall.

"Kylan," I breathed, begged, craved. I writhed beneath him, my orgasm endless and capitulating. "Please."

His fingers were *there*, his throat still swallowing, my body drifting into an odd, cooler state.

Was he drinking me dry?

Numbing me?

Snow started to fall around us, or were those the stars? I couldn't distinguish.

Another wave crashed over me, shaking my limbs and causing my back to bow. Kylan's palm against my belly held me down, his touch literally grounding me when my soul threatened to fly.

I can't take anymore…

You can, he replied. *You will.*

A sob escaped me, equal parts needy and devastated. *You're destroying me.*

I'm owning you, he clarified.

I want to own you, too. And I did. In every way. He couldn't take all of this from me without giving some of himself in return. *Please, Kylan. I'm begging you.*

He growled, releasing me from his bite. "This bond is going to kill me."

Bond?

"Yes." He laved my clit once more, sending a shock wave of pleasure through me. Was he healing me? Oh, fuck, I didn't care. I just wanted him. To know him as he did me. To be with him.

"I need you," I whispered, my veins cooling without his bite, or maybe from his bite.

"I know," he whispered, crawling over me. "I'm here, Raelyn."

His mouth captured mine, my arousal tinged with his blood gracing my senses. I quivered beneath him, overwhelmed and exhausted and titillated all over again.

Kylan threatened to destroy me.

I understood what he meant now.

Because I was completely bewitched, ready to do whatever he desired for just another taste.

His cock nudged my weeping heat. *Yes…* Not that he needed my consent. It was already given, acquired, owned.

"Tell me you're mine." His lips whispered over mine. "Tell me you want this."

"I want *you*," I replied, wrapping my legs around his waist. They shook from the cold, but I didn't care. "I'm yours, Kylan." *And you're mine.*

He sighed, his tongue dipping into my mouth, providing me more of his essence. Each swallow burned in the most delicious of ways.

His hands grabbed my hips, holding me in place. "You're so fucking wet." He sounded almost distraught, his voice breaking at the end. "Fuck, Raelyn. I can't. I shouldn't, but I can't stop."

"What—"

Unexpected pain cut off my words, silencing my voice. I grabbed his arms, my body freezing beneath his.

He's inside me, I realized. And fuck, it *hurt.*

"I can't remember the last time I wanted someone like this," he whispered, his mouth brushing mine. "It has to stop."

My brow furrowed, his words not making sense. "I don't…"

"Shh…" He kissed me again, his tongue tender and coaxing, his body still over mine. "Focus on the sensations, Raelyn. Focus on me. My cock deep inside you, stretching you, filling you, owning you."

His words warmed me in a foreign way, igniting a flame in my lower belly. He shifted, causing me to flinch, anticipating pain. But nothing followed, only a tiny shudder that tingled through my legs. He repeated the action, this time with more force, and my body jolted in response.

I moaned, the fire increasing, heating me inside and out.

A thrust—harsher and sharper—had my nails scoring his back, my jaw threatening to clench around his tongue.

"Mmm, that's it," he praised. "Hang on to me, princess. Enjoy, feel, scream. I want everyone to hear you, to know who is fucking you, to know whom you belong to."

I opened my mouth to protest, to demand the same, but my words cut off on a harsh exhale as he truly started to move. He'd been kind before, easing me into the movements.

Now the predator had come out to claim his prize. To dominate me. To destroy me for every other man.

"Kylan," I groaned, an inferno coursing through me, consuming me from head to toe. He'd already taken me to unspeakable levels of bliss. There couldn't be more. I wouldn't survive another dose, let alone a headier one.

But fuck, he wasn't stopping.

His cock hit me deep, pressing a euphoric part of me that paralyzed my being.

I was a slave to his ministrations, lost to his will.

"So fucking good," he growled, his mouth against my neck. "You're hugging my cock, owning me with your little cunt." His teeth slid into my skin, forcing rapture into my bloodstream and sending me spiraling over the edge of oblivion.

Again.

No warning.

No buildup.

Just shattering.

And my body succumbed to him without preamble.

It almost hurt.

"Fuck, Raelyn." The guttural curse against my throat sounded almost pained.

Energy hummed between us, his shoulders and arms tightening. My name fell from his lips once more, the invocation in his tone so agonizingly beautiful it brought tears to my eyes.

His orgasm poured into me, sending me to the stars with him, my mind departing my body and gracing the heavens above. I'd never felt anything like it, this electricity zipping between us, binding us, forcing me to a plane of existence I never knew was possible, with Kylan at my side.

Such beauty.

Such intensity.

Such torment.

...not the way...

...break it...

I can't be bonded to her!

Not like this.

Too much.

I need to end it.

There's only one way...

A vision slammed into my heart of Kylan giving me away, to be taken by another. Fucked. Fed on. *Used.*

No choice, his voice drifted through my thoughts.

I clawed deeper, trying to understand. More words, ceremonial chants, *Erosita*, the binding between a virgin human and a vampire, the connection of our minds, bodies, and souls.

Kylan had bound me to him in an ancient ceremony meant for mates.

And he wanted to break it.

More visions, his plans, his obligations, all striking my chest, lashing at my heart and soul.

A mistake. Those two words burned. *I never meant to do this.*

More thoughts—his thoughts—filled my head. Some old. Some new. All wrapped up in the same truth.

I have to kill the obsession.

Once I do, it'll be fine.

Back to normal.

Good.

Yes.

Just have to share...

I tore my mouth away from his, not even aware that we'd been kissing, my eyes blazing with tears. "You're going to give me to another royal?" I demanded, my voice hoarse from all the screams, the pain, the pleasure, the rapture we'd just shared that meant nothing to him other than to be a means to an end.

He stared down at me, a mixture of agony and dismay in his gaze. "Raelyn…"

"This was all… all…" I couldn't think of the right word, my heart breaking.

I wasn't supposed to fall for him.

I wasn't even supposed to like him.

My mind. My heart. My soul.

When had he slipped through? How?

My hands curled into fists, my nails biting into my palms.

Fuck, how ridiculous was I? Letting hope possess me. For just a moment, I thought there might be something special between us. A unique bond. A relationship. A connection. Something.

He called it a mistake.

An obsession he had to dismantle.

My heart.

That's what he would destroy.

Oh, how wrong I'd been. It was never my body he wished to shatter, but the fundamental part of me. My spirit.

To link us in such a passionate way, to give me insight into his mind, to take full control of my own, all to just sever it with a demand. To fuck another.

"But you're my consort and that's your purpose—to fuck whomever I tell you to fuck."

A sob caught in my throat, my soul withering up inside of me. "It was all just a game," I whispered. "A mental ploy to lower my guard."

He never cared.

Just a vampire playing with his new toy.

And it only took him a little over a week to break me.

"Raelyn." He cupped my cheek, but I looked away.

"Stop, Kylan," I begged. "Just stop." There wasn't a point. Not anymore. "You won." The words were barely a whisper, my fight deflated.

He said he would own me.

I'd naively thought—hoped—I could own him too.

What a fool I'd been.

There were no happy endings in my world.

Only pain and suffering.

And Kylan had just delivered the worst punishment of them all.

A soulless life, forever serving at his side.

I closed my eyes. "Just leave me here to die."

Chapter Twenty-Four

KYLAN

SPEECHLESS.

Raelyn had rendered me frozen, immobile, unable to comprehend how such a beautiful moment could shatter so catastrophically.

I hadn't expected her to enter my mind so easily, to see the truth of my intent. But it'd been at the forefront of my thoughts, my frustration over our situation.

I had to share her to break the bond.

But I didn't want to share her.

I possessed a newfound respect for Darius and his allowances with Jace because even the notion of letting someone touch Raelyn had me wanting to commit murder. It was a weakness I couldn't allow, one I knew would be removed by letting another fuck her.

A growl caught in my throat, the agony of the plan searing me inside.

I can't let this consume me.

I was stronger than this.

Raelyn lay utterly still, her eyes taking on a lifeless quality that nearly broke my resolve. She'd be okay. She had to be. My fighter would return. She just needed some space to see that this was the best solution. Her emotions were just as tied up as mine, the bond to blame. We'd work through it.

I pulled away from her, noting the discoloration in her limbs. Sex in the snow was not the best idea for a mortal, but now that my immortality ran fresh through her veins, she'd heal quickly.

Immortality I plan to take away from her.

Because it's the only solution.

I ran my fingers through my hair, irritated with my own uncertainty. Decisions were easy. I made them daily, quickly, and efficiently. This woman—Raelyn—had changed everything.

No, the bond had.

Fucking ceremony.

Why hadn't I realized that was happening? I never gave consorts my blood. Only Mikael and only because he required substantial healing.

I rubbed my jaw while Raelyn lay motionless on the ground, a tear streaking across her cheek.

I sighed, hating that I'd hurt her. "This wasn't my intention. It just sort of happened." Probably the lamest excuse in the history of time. And why was I explaining myself to her? She wasn't my equal. Just a human—a *consort* I'd indulged in a little too heavily.

A few days apart would fix this.

I'd let her heal, then find a proper candidate—my jaw clenched—to break this bond. There was no other choice.

"We need to get inside," I told her, noting the horizon. We'd been out here far longer than I originally anticipated.

This female was toxic for my routine and common sense.

"Raelyn."

No response. Not even a flinch.

So that's how this was going to go.

I palmed the back of my neck. "Do you want me to compel you to follow me inside?"

Do whatever you want, she replied, her mental voice solemn. *I'm yours.*

The two words prickled at my heart. I'd enjoyed hearing them earlier, but now they sounded dull and broken, as if she were accepting the inevitable, not vowing herself to me for eternity.

She looked so fragmented and abused, lying there with her legs spread, naked on the blanket of clothes, her eyes unfocused and unseeing.

I hated seeing her like this, hated that I'd *made* her like this.

"It's the bond," I told her softly. "Once it's broken, you'll understand." We'd be free of this complicated web, able to feel normal again.

She said nothing, her expression void of emotion save that single tear frozen to her cheek. Like a distorted macabre doll. Forever damaged.

No. She'd come back from it. She had to.

I bundled her up in the clothes and lifted her in my arms. The least I could do was carry her back to the house. I left our shoes—I'd grab them later—and phased through the forest to the back door. Much faster than walking. If it bothered Raelyn, she didn't show it, her eyes having fallen closed as if asleep.

She remained in the same state as I entered our bedroom, her breathing slow as I laid her on the bed. "Do you need anything?" I asked softly. "Water? Food?"

Raelyn curled into a ball. No response.

The silent treatment almost had me entering her mind, but I refrained. She deserved peace after the hell I'd accidentally introduced her to.

Ugh, but I couldn't leave her like this.

How had this become so complicated? She was meant as a diversion, a passing entertainment in my very long existence. Yet, she'd come to mean so much more.

I brushed a damp strand of hair from her face, her blank gaze on the glass windows.

We would stay here a few more days and relax before I'd tackle the task of finding someone to fix this for us. It couldn't be Mikael. I didn't trust myself not to kill him in the process. No, I needed a stronger vampire, someone who could defend himself.

My hand curled into a fist. *Or I could keep her.*

No.

That wasn't an option. She was a risk—a weakness—I couldn't afford. And there were too many who would happily hold her against me. Society labeled the ceremony as taboo, but it was really a product of envy. *Erositas* were rare, and none of the royals had one. Well, except Cam, but he killed his before the Goddess took him into custody.

I rolled my neck, exhaustion hitting me hard in the gut.

This shouldn't be so difficult.

Raelyn blinked, her soulless eyes unfocused. She needed rest. We could discuss more in the evening. I removed the scattered clothes I'd used to bundle her and guided her beneath the covers. She didn't fight me, but she didn't help either, her limbs heavy.

"Raelyn," I whispered, agonized. "I'm sorry." I didn't know what I was apologizing for exactly. The unexpected bond, accidentally letting her into my mind, taking her virginity so roughly on the ground, all of the above.

I shook my head.

"Just get some sleep," I told her, not that she seemed to be listening.

I slid into the sheets beside her, yearning to hold her but knowing she needed her space.

Maybe she'd be more herself in the evening.

* * *

Raelyn wasn't more herself in the evening.

Or the next day.

She barely moved from the bed. Zelda had to bring her food, something that only happened because I demanded it. And even then, Raelyn only ate a few bites before lying down again. When I tried to talk to her, she ignored me.

At first, it concerned me.

Now, I was irritated.

I missed my fighter, which only pissed me off more. Fucking her should have killed this obsession, but all I craved was more. All because of this damn bond.

Every vampire I considered for the task of helping me break the connection was immediately vetoed. Either I liked the male too much to risk his life or I hated him too much to let him near something so precious.

"Fuck," I growled, dragging my fingers through my hair. I couldn't even focus on the work I needed to sort through. Messages from constituents, all requesting one thing or another. Some wanted money. Some desired more land. Others expressed needs for promotion.

And then I had the pile of letters of intent to go through for Tremayne's position.

This was why royals had sovereigns. I usually didn't mind all the tasks, preferring the way they passed the time, but I couldn't stop thinking about a certain redhead in my bedroom.

A knock at my door had hope sprouting in my chest, only to be squashed as Angelica appeared.

"My Prince," she greeted, bowing slightly.

Right. I'd summoned her. "I have a task for you."

She entered with her hands at her sides, expression curious. "Yes, My Prince?"

"I need you to accompany Raelyn outside. Try to get her moving around a bit." The two seemed to get on all right in Kylan City. Maybe Raelyn would confide in her, or enjoy the female company.

"O-of course," Angelica replied, her expression conveying doubt.

"She's feeling unwell, but she really likes the snow." My lips twitched at the memory of her awe over the windows that first day, her little trip out onto the balcony. "Make sure she dresses warm, please."

Angelica nodded, her brow slightly wrinkled. "I will."

"And try to get her to eat something more than broccoli and unseasoned chicken." I really wanted to introduce her to chocolate, but the moment hadn't arrived yet. "Oh, and maybe a movie after. Something with humor." I gave her a few titles I knew were in the old movie collection.

"Uh, yes, I'll figure that out," she said slowly. Right, being so new to immortality, she wouldn't be familiar with the old entertainment systems. The only programs on television now were those sanctioned by Lilith and the few lycan-made films.

"Mikael can give you a tutorial." He was awake, but only barely recovered, and apparently not speaking to me either. When I saw him earlier this evening, he'd scowled at me and went back to his room. It seemed all the humans in the house hated me right now. Even Zelda had given me a touch of attitude in the kitchen.

"Okay." Angelica's bemused expression would have been comical if it wasn't so accurate. "Anything else, Your Highness?"

"Yes. Guard her," I demanded with more force than necessary.

She swallowed. "I understand."

"Good. That's all."

"Thank you, My Prince." She bowed, excusing herself.

I blew out a breath, uncertain if this would work, but hopeful. If it didn't, I'd have to enter Raelyn's conscious to search for a solution. When I'd told her I wanted her mind, I hadn't meant like this. I wanted her trust, which I clearly botched. And if I pushed through the thin barriers between us to read her, I'd cause even more damage.

My lips flattened. Why was that even a consideration? I never cared what others thought. If she didn't trust me, I'd make her. That's how I operated. And if she refused, I'd work around it.

Yet, I couldn't bridge the gap between us.

It was as if my soul refused, terrified of hurting her more.

"This fucking bond is going to kill me," I growled. I'd only finalized it to be the first to taste her, knowing full well I'd have to share her.

And now I couldn't fathom the idea of letting another touch her.

I stood.

All right.

Time to take my own advice and get the hell out of here. Beat something up. Wrestle with the wolves. Anything to stop thinking about my predicament with Raelyn.

It was driving me insane.

Or, perhaps, I'd reached that stage in my immortality long ago.

I stripped out of my jacket and dress shirt.

A run.

Yes.

That's what I needed.

And a good fucking.

With Raelyn.

I snorted. Like that was going to happen again anytime soon. I was all for seducing a woman, but that task felt impossible now.

Get it together, I told myself.

Over five thousand years old and a human of twenty-two years had me tied up in knots. Ridiculous.

Maybe I really am going mad.

Chapter Twenty-Five

RAE

THE SNOW ON THE BALCONY was thicker tonight. I'd watched it grow the last two evenings, the mountains in the distance my only solace.

I felt dead to the world.

Numbed.

Foolish for falling into a vampiric trap.

I kept waiting for the inevitable, a male of Kylan's choosing to arrive to *fix* our problem. The bond he never wanted to create.

His mind remained closed off, not that I wanted to venture inside that cruelty again. I'd seen enough for my lifetime.

He only fucked me so he could be first, his goal to rid himself of me as soon as possible and pass me off to someone else.

I hated him.

Hated myself.

Hated this life.

But worst of all, I hated how I couldn't motivate myself to do something about it. I felt lost, alone, hopeless. Like a black swirl had consumed me and refused to let go.

Silas would be so disappointed. Willow, too.

How are you? I wondered, my heart stuttering. *Where are you?*

Was Silas still alive?

Was Willow worse off than me?

I shivered, knowing the truth. Of course she was worse off. Kylan would share me, but he owned me exclusively. Willow…

A sob caught in my throat, a dark part of me preferring her fate to mine. Sex, I could handle. But Kylan played with more than my body.

My eyes narrowed, fury bubbling to the surface, followed by a wave of silence.

What could I do? Yell at him? That would only impress him. He wanted to destroy me. He did. The end.

I pressed my palms to my face, a groan slipping through my lips. The same thoughts and impressions kept spinning through my head, pushing me deeper into a place I hated.

A dark abyss with inky claws shredding my soul piece by piece.

My future.

My fate.

My new world.

But I didn't want to exist here. I wanted to live, to breathe, to see the sky, to fly. *And go where?* I almost laughed. The snarky tone sounded too much like Kylan.

I hate you, I growled at him.

A scream built in my chest, demanding release, but the one I wanted to yell at wasn't here. And he would only laugh.

Oh, but just for two seconds to shock him with my fury might be worth the mockery.

I sat up.

Where are you? I demanded.

Nothing.

The wall between our minds locked tight from the other side.

Of course he wanted to keep me out. He was probably working on a list of people for me to fuck.

I flopped backward, my eyes narrowed up at the ceiling. *Asshole.*

He used me. Which was the whole point, wasn't it? But just for a moment, I hoped…

I rolled to my side, refusing to continue that train of thought. It was dangerous. It hurt. It only led to agony.

"Raelyn?" a feminine voice called, followed by a knock.

My eyes fell closed automatically, my desire to be left alone forever overriding the need to acknowledge the vampire. Why bother with decorum anymore? I'd prefer death to this entrapment.

I flinched at the dark notion. It wasn't entirely true. There were reasons to stay alive. I just had to find them.

"Raelyn?" Angelica was next to the bed now. "I know you're awake. I'm supposed to take you outside."

I started to laugh, but it came out as a choked, deranged sound. The urge to bark hit me hard, causing more of that weird noise to spill from my lips.

Outside.

Like a dog.

I fucking hate you, Kylan, I said to him.

Still no reply.

Because of course not. The prick couldn't even acknowledge this bond he'd forced on me. He just wanted to rip it away now that he'd fucked me. No more fun for him. Just a broken toy to eventually kill. After he gave me to all his friends.

That was my purpose, after all, right?

I snorted half-heartedly, a tear prickling my eye.

Goddess, I was tired of crying. Of wallowing in my pain. Of lying in this bed that reeked of Kylan.

Maybe I should go outside. Find an icicle sharp enough to drill into Kylan's skull and pay him a visit.

Oh, I liked that idea.

I'd have to find him, but maybe Angelica knew where he was hiding.

Or I could bring the ice stake back here and wait for him. It would stay cold on the balcony.

Yes.

A sound plan.

Murder by ice.

How touching considering our last interlude in the snow.

I giggled at the hysterical idea, knowing it would never work. Kylan had driven me to madness. Seemed fitting given he owned my mind now.

Angelica cleared her throat. "I don't know what happened between you and Kylan, but he was very specific about accompanying you outside."

"I bet he was," I grumbled.

"I suggest we both obey him," she added, her tone laced with warning. "I have no intention of being on the receiving end of his disappointment."

Part of me wanted to tell her to go away. She could send Kylan in here to punish me, for all I cared. The saner, more practical side of me knew he would discipline not just me for the behavior but Angelica too. And she didn't deserve that. She'd been almost nice to me before; even now she stood by patiently, waiting for my compliance. Most vampires would have reacted violently by now.

I swallowed. "Give me twenty minutes, please." I needed to shower. Find clothes. Try to brush my hair. General things.

"Only if you promise to dress warm," she replied. "Because he also required that."

"Yeah, he pretends to care," I grumbled, sliding out from between the sheets, naked. Might as well get used to walking around without clothes on amongst vampires. Kylan likely had a parade of them coming my way soon.

Less than twenty minutes later, I had my wet hair pulled up in a bun on top of my head, a sweater and jeans on, and boots covering my feet. Angelica handed me a hat and scarf, which I begrudgingly added, and I followed her downstairs.

Zelda passed us along the way, her surprise at seeing us together evident. She immediately dropped her gaze and continued without a word.

Angelica's lips twitched as she shook her head. "You asked me what it's like the other day. Well, the whole submissive thing is really hard to get used to. I was a human less than a decade ago. It puts me on the outside of humanity while marking me as inferior to all the others. I'm in this in-between zone where no one will talk to me unless they need something."

"Like taking me outside," I said, walking through the door she held open.

"Exactly." She followed me onto the back patio, the snow deep and untouched. "They make you think life will be so much grander, and maybe it will be eventually, but that's not been my experience yet." She kicked some snow. "The only reason I'm not living on the street is because Kylan offered me decent employment. Most royals delegate position assignments for new vampires to the sovereigns or regents."

I followed her into the yard, considering that. "So… did he make you?" No one ever spoke about the task of turning another into an immortal, the conversation essentially forbidden among humans. But I'd already given up all pretenses of decorum with Angelica. Seemed ridiculous to abide by them now.

Her dark eyes flashed, meeting my gaze, but her lips twitched. "You're far braver than I am," she murmured. "I see why he likes you."

My brow furrowed. "Who?"

"You know who."

"Kylan?" I laughed outright. "Yeah, no, he's made it quite clear how he feels about me. And *like* is not the word I'd use to describe that feeling." Lust, maybe. Obsession as well. Like? No.

"Well, he's different with you than with anyone else I've seen," she said softly. "Not that I've spent much time around him. And no, he didn't turn me. Kylan has never turned anyone."

My lips parted. "Ever?"

"Never," she repeated. "Turning a human creates a link between maker and progeny, something Kylan would never allow. He's a loner, relying only on himself and never anyone else. It's what makes him a formidable leader. His loyalties only go so deep. Betray him, and pay the price. That's what everyone says about him, anyway."

Her comment about him never allowing a link to another had me almost tripping over myself.

But he's linked to me.

At least temporarily.

Was that why he felt so strongly about severing the connection between us? Because he couldn't afford to let me be so close to him?

It provided a fresh perspective.

What had he said the other night? That none of this was his intention and it just sort of happened?

I frowned. Did he mean that?

I assumed he'd planned it with all those comments about wanting to possess me entirely. But what if it'd been on accident?

"Yeah, so, life as a vampire, not as glamorous as you'd think," she mumbled, her focus shifting to the night sky. "There's no how-to guide, and my maker isn't exactly a great mentor. So I've learned to rely on my instincts to survive."

"You seem to be doing well so far."

She shrugged. "Yeah. I was worried Kylan might kill me last week for telling him about Tremayne, but I couldn't stop myself even if I tried. The whole—" Something started singing in her pocket. She pulled out the slender device and frowned at the screen. It displayed a long number with no name. "Speaking of makers," she grumbled. "I need to take this."

"Okay." I forced a smile. "I'll just be here."

She nodded, looking grateful. "Thank you," she mouthed before answering the phone. "Vilheim." She walked back toward the manor, leaving me to my musings and the clear night above.

Peaceful.

Beautiful.

Lonely.

Was that why Kylan enjoyed it out here? Why he preferred the secret lake in the woods? *Are you there now?* I whispered, knowing he wouldn't hear me.

I closed my eyes, wallowing in the cool breeze.

I wish you would talk to me, Kylan.

He could at least explain this bond to me and what it meant. Or maybe I didn't want to know since he intended to break it.

"Raelyn?" Mikael's voice floated over me, pulling my lips up in the first smile I'd experienced in what felt like years. He sauntered toward me in a pair of jeans and a sweater, his expression somewhat reserved, but his eyes grinning.

I threw my arms around his neck, more than a little relieved to see him again.

"You're okay," I whispered, tears pricking my eyes. I knew he would be fine, but seeing him brought home the emotions of the last few days. "Goddess, I'm so glad you're okay."

He patted my back and gave me a wry smile. "You missed me?"

"You have no idea. Kylan is a lot of work to handle alone."

He chuckled. "Tell me about it."

I almost accepted his rhetorical statement as an invitation. I wanted to talk to someone so badly, but instincts held me back. Some sort of warning that Kylan wouldn't approve, and as much as I wanted to ignore it, I couldn't.

So instead I released him with a smile. "I really am glad you're okay. I was worried."

He kissed me on the cheek. "I like you, Rae."

My cheeks heated. "I like you too, Mikael."

"I know." He put his arm around my shoulders, guiding me on a walk through the yard. "That's why this is so hard."

"What do you mean?"

"Life." He sighed, gazing up at the night. "You know Kylan bought me eleven years ago this month? Seems like a lifetime ago. He's given me a lot. I should be grateful, but he's so…"

"Mercurial?" I suggested, recalling the time I called him that to his face.

"Yes, and overindulgent, too." He shook his head, sighing. "He makes you want things that he'll never completely give. He gets you addicted to him. Forces you to love him. But he never loves you back."

His words were nails to my heart. "I know," I whispered.

"He'll destroy you, Rae," he whispered. "I don't want him to wreck you."

I bit my lip. *Too late for that.*

"It's really my only choice," he continued softly. "You understand that, right?"

My brow furrowed. "Only choice?"

"Yes." He turned me to face him, his gaze sad. "What we're doing, it's the only way to protect you."

"I don't…" I swallowed. "What are you saying?"

"That he's sorry," a feminine voice said from the left. Zelda emerged from the tree line, her slender shoulders straight, her head high. I'd never seen her exude such confidence.

Mikael went to her, wrapping his arm around her and kissing her temple. "Yes, exactly that. I'm sorry."

I frowned at him. "For…?" I trailed off, thinking about everything he'd said. About Kylan being addictive, his penchant for manipulating humans into caring for him, Mikael's desire to protect me *from* Kylan.

No.

He couldn't mean—

Zelda twirled a blade between her fingers.

My eyes rounded. "You…" I couldn't finish the statement. But wasn't Mikael with Kylan when the harem died? "But how…?"

"It's complicated," he murmured, taking a step toward me as I took two steps back. "You have to see this as a gift, Rae. He'll only bring you misery. Trust us, we know."

"I'd prefer that over being killed," I snapped, shocked by the ludicrousness of their actions. "Have you both lost your minds?"

He chuckled. "Probably. Kylan has fucked with mine long enough." He sounded so sad, so broken by that. "Please don't fight, Rae. I can make it quick."

My brows shot up. "Quick?" He was completely insane. "Kylan will kill you when he finds out."

"He'll be too busy dealing with other things," Zelda said. "Like the fallout from murdering yet another harem member. It's perfect timing. Right before his big event and after showboating you around the city. Everyone expects to see his precious Raelyn again. But where did she go?" Zelda tapped her chin with the knife. "Oh, that's right. Kylan killed her for sport, just like all the others. And yet, he punished Tremayne for doing the very same thing. Not looking good, is it?"

I gaped at her, seeing beyond her meek chef's presence for the first time. "Who are you?"

Her lips curled. "This is so much bigger than you, Rae. You're just a victim of circumstance and the last nail in Kylan's coffin."

That was not an answer at all, just further proof of her madness.

Mikael pounced, his hand snagging my bicep before I could jump away. His gaze held mine, a note of indecision blinking down at me. "I'm sorry," he whispered, real pain entering his expression. "I really do like you."

I almost laughed, but the glint of Zelda's blade had my brain taking over.

They're going to kill me.

I struggled, yanking myself away from him, only to have Zelda catch me from behind. She locked my arms together in a practiced way, immobilizing me.

Trapped.

My shoulders ached as I tried to shift, to dislodge her from behind, but I couldn't move.

This can't be happening.

My heart pounded in my ears.

Why had I stood here talking to them? I should have run. But shock and confusion had trapped me before them.

"We can't delay any longer," Zelda said, her voice sounding far away despite being right behind me. "Prove yourself, Mikael."

He compressed his lips into a fine line, a glimmer of irritation flashing in his eyes. "Compassion goes a long way, Zelda."

"Not when we're on a timeline. He'll only stall for so long."

He? He who? Kylan? No. That wasn't right.

"Fine." Mikael stepped forward, sending my pulse through the roof.

"Don't do this," I pleaded, trying futilely to escape Zelda's hold. "Please don't do this."

His light eyes radiated grief, but a hint of resolve flickered in his irises. "I'm granting you peace, Rae."

Oh Goddess, he really believes that.

"Mikael…" But there wasn't any hope. I could see it in the way he looked at me. He was going to do this—kill me and frame Kylan. Just like someone else—Zelda?—did with his harem.

Kylan! I shouted to him, needing him to hear me. *Kylan, please!*

But the door between us remained closed.

If he heard me, he didn't acknowledge it.

Kylan… I need you!

"I'm sorry," Mikael said again.

"Do—" My plea ended on a gargle, my neck radiating fire.

A blade.

From Mikael?

"Goodbye, Rae," he whispered, his hand dropping, fresh blood—*my blood*—dripping from his knife.

Time froze, my mind refusing to believe, to accept…

He did it.

He actually did it.

Warm liquid pooled in my throat, flooding my airway. Too fast. Too much.

Kylan, I whimpered. *Help me…*

Nothing.

Zelda and Mikael betrayed you, I told him, needing him to know.

A harsh gurgling sound filled my ears, suffocating my reality.

Kylan…

No reply.

Tears filled my eyes. He'd blocked our connection so thoroughly he couldn't hear me at all.

Because he never cared.

Discarded me.

Our bond.

I should have t-tried h-harder.

I should—

My side screamed in agony, something sharp digging inside of me, blackening my world, splitting it in half.

I—I can't…

Kylan… I can't breathe…

Drowning…

I blinked, my vision fading.

The snow was cold. Heavy.

Such failure. Mine. His.

My soul cried out, reaching through the bond, tugging on the only one who could save me now. *Kylan, please…*

The walls were too dark.

So lonely.

So bleak.

Abandoned.

He's not coming for me.

My heart stuttered.

I'm going to die here…

Alone.

Chapter Twenty-Six

KYLAN

I PUSHED MYSELF FASTER and harder over the ground, welcoming the intense exhaustion settling over my limbs. The tingling sensation was one I hadn't felt in a very long time. It consumed me, leaving me shaking as I returned to the house.

My mouth was dry, begging me for hydration—blood.

Fuck. I'd not been this spent in… I frowned. Forever? I only needed to feed once a month to maintain strength, and I indulged almost every day, had overindulged just the other night.

I opened the fridge, searching for a snack as a sense of unease washed over me.

Why am I so tired?

It'd been one hell of a run, but not *that* overbearing. I exercised often enough, even without needing to.

I rolled my neck, loosening my straining muscles, my energy depleting with each breath. Almost as if my life essence was being sucked out of me.

A spasm rolled through me, forcing me to grab the countertop for support.

What the fuck is that?

I closed my eyes, searching inside myself for a source. It hit me like a freight train.

Raelyn.

She was siphoning my immortality—absorbing it—consuming *me.*

I growled and searched for her mind, wanting to know how the hell that was even possible, and found nothing. No consciousness. Just an empty void.

Nonexistent.

"Raelyn!"

I spun around, searching for a scent, finding it lurking in the air. Sprinting up the stairs, I stopped in our room. Empty.

Her blood was up here. Weak, but present.

I followed the scent to Mikael's room, pausing.

If she chose to break this bond on her own by seeking him out for comfort…

My foot met the door, the wood flying open to slam against the wall. No sign of her or Mikael, but the shower running had me darting into the bathroom.

Zelda shrieked, jumping beyond a very naked and wet Mikael. Concern entered his gaze, flecked with guilt. "Y-your Highness?"

Raelyn's blood lingered here, but not heavily. Had she stopped by Mikael's room today? "Have you seen Raelyn?"

He swallowed and shook his head quickly. "N-no. Why?"

Zelda peeked out from behind him, her blue eyes wide. "I saw her heading outside with Angelica a little while ago, My Prince."

The reminder had me leaving them without a word.

Something was very wrong.

I couldn't sense Raelyn at all, apart from her drawing on my essence. My heart hammered at what that could mean.

I was outside in a blink, her blood much stronger.

Why had I come in through the front? I would have sensed her out here after my run had I gone through the back.

"Raelyn!" I called, phasing to where her scent was the strongest.

Angelica looked up at me from the ground, covered in blood, her dark eyes aghast. "Y-your H-highness… I… I…"

I threw her off of Raelyn, the cry of pain distant to my ears.

"Raelyn," I breathed, falling to my knees beside her. My hands floated above her, my mind not knowing where to start. "Oh, Raelyn…" She was ripped apart, her throat torn open, her chest littered with puncture marks, her icy eyes glassy and sightless.

My throat constricted.

I'd failed her.

She was dead.

How?

Why?

Who?

I raised my eyes to Angelica's quivering form near the tree line, her body bent in a bow I yearned to demolish.

"*You*," I growled, my instincts screaming at me to shred her alive the way she did Raelyn.

"I-I didn't do it!" she shouted, shaking on the ground. "I was trying to h-heal her," she added in a broken sob, lifting her wrist.

I phased to her, grabbing her arm and noting the fresh bite marks. Raelyn's scent was all over her. I squeezed, her yelp of pain suggesting I'd broken bone, but I didn't care.

"Don't move," I demanded, going back to Raelyn's side to slice my own wrist and hold it to her mouth.

A ridiculous idea.

She couldn't fucking swallow.

She was fucking dead!

I yelled in fury, agony ripping me apart from the inside.

Broken…

My heart thudded loudly, my fingers closing into fists against her chest, my body breaking over hers.

Dead…

Had she called for me in her final moments?

I'd never know because I closed her off. Blocked her from my mind. The one link that could have—should have—protected her.

Instead of going to her myself, I gave her to Angelica.

I'm a coward.

Unworthy.

I knew she was in danger and I left her alone, too arrogant in my own defenses to consider her at risk here.

She deserved better.

"Raelyn," I whispered, touching my temple to hers. "I'm so sorry."

My harem's massacre had hurt, but this…

I shook, my vision clouding, my mind rebelling, my soul…

My mate.

Sometimes you just know, I'd told her. *I knew* you, *Raelyn.*

My lungs contracted, my body shaking from fatigue.

Her death is killing me…

Would that be so bad? I wondered. I'd lived for so long, alone, just surviving to do what? Manage an empire? Enjoy the pleasures in life that I'd indulged in several times over already?

Raelyn had been the first exciting thing to enter my life in a very long time.

And she's gone.

No heartbeat.

No breath.

Her still-warm body motionless.

Death hadn't fully taken her yet.

I'd been so close. I should have been able to save her.

I failed.

And it fucking hurt.

Crushing my chest, destroying me from the inside out. The ceremony bound our souls, and hers was screaming—taking me under with her, tugging on my essence, as if trying to claw her way back to the surface.

I lifted, my eyes searching.

No signs of healing.

But she still feels alive.

Her mind was vacant, but there. Her soul still attached to mine.

If she was dead, I wouldn't sense her at all.

I recalled everything I knew about the ceremony, the stories, the expectations—*she's connected to my immortality.*

That's why I was so exhausted.

My essence was healing hers.

I lifted her into my arms, standing. How long would this take? Was there anything I could do to expedite it?

Darius would know.

I started toward the house and paused. Someone here had betrayed me. Likely Angelica, from the scene of evidence, but Raelyn's blood had been fresh in the house…

Something isn't right.

Until I knew the truth, I couldn't trust anyone. Except Judith. I'd seen her while out on my run, patrolling the perimeter herself. Which only confirmed that the culprit was already inside.

I balanced Raelyn against my naked chest with one arm and touched the device in my pocket, alerting my security team. It was a panic alarm of sorts that Judith had installed in my phone. They would be able to ping my whereabouts.

Judith appeared, her face filled with concern, her gun already drawn. Relief smoothed her features at finding me alert, then her brow furrowed at Raelyn's mutilated body.

"Oh…" She pressed a hand to her mouth, her reaction confirming she had nothing to do with this mess. I might have a traitor in my midst, but I could still read my people, and true shock shone in her eyes. "Kylan, My Prince, I—"

"I need you to take Angelica into custody. Withhold blood, but no other punishment until I return."

Judith blinked, finally noticing the crumpled vampire in the snow. I couldn't even look at her. Regardless of whether or not she did this to Raelyn, she'd failed me.

And she would be punished.

"Return?" Judith asked, her voice soft.

"I'll be in touch." I dropped my phone, not wanting to be tracked, and traced to the garage with Raelyn before Judith could argue.

Selecting the keys to my fastest car, I secured Raelyn in the passenger seat and flipped off the GPS locator.

If anyone fucked with me in this state, they'd die. Including the city guards.

I navigated the streets quickly, aware of all the icy patches from nearly two centuries of experience. Raelyn remained broken beside me with no signs of life aside from the tug of her soul against mine. Her limber form confirmed my suspicions as well, her body not quite taking on the final stages of death as her soul hung in limbo.

There had to be a way to expedite her healing, something I wasn't doing.

Heavens, the pain she must have experienced, all while I ignored her…

I flinched and grabbed her hand. "I'll never let you down again," I vowed. *Ever.*

The city lights appeared ahead, polluting the dark sky. I always hated this view, much preferring the solitude of my home, but tonight I craved those buildings and a certain vampire lurking inside.

You better be there, Darius.

I didn't know where else he would go, especially considering our ploy to make it look like I was playing with Juliet. Their bond was pure, true, created out of love. That much had become increasingly clear throughout dinner the other night in the little ways Darius catered to her. She smiled often, her dark eyes brimming with adoration every time she glanced at him.

Raelyn and I didn't have that. I'd created the connection by accident, then finalized it with the purpose of breaking it, because I couldn't stand the idea of someone touching her before me.

So selfish.

And yet, it was the only thing keeping her alive.

My heart skipped a beat, my breathing quickening. I'd inadvertently saved her life. How could I remove such a bond after this? I… I didn't want her to die. Ever.

The realization had my jaw tightening. How had this woman affixed herself so completely in my life? In my mind? In my heart? From the beginning, I'd been obsessed. An innate familiarity had stopped me before her on Blood Day, then her ice-blue eyes had captivated me. And when she bit me, I had to have her.

I expected the infatuation to die quickly, but it'd only grown into this all-consuming obsession. She was inside me.

And I want her to stay there.

I entered the tunnels, my lights off, my night vision and instincts guiding our way. The guards rarely patrolled down here, very few in the city knowing how to use them. My engineers had constructed a maze on purpose, providing me with the only real road map. Gates closed frequently, blocking paths, but I owned the remote to them all. Just a simple touch of a button and the underground became my playground.

Tonight it was a necessary escape.

I accelerated, the need for answers overwhelming me.

She's alive, I consoled myself. *Barely.*

But not breathing.

My hands tightened on the steering wheel, the exit I desired appearing quickly. The city streets were bustling with vampires, all out for midnight lunch.

Fortunately, most were walking on the sidewalks, not driving.

Minutes later, I was parked and had Raelyn in my arms.

My thumbprint called the elevator, the top floor not arriving fast enough.

She still had no heartbeat.

Come on, Raelyn. Where's my fighter?

Darius stood waiting, the call of the lift clearly having notified him of an imminent arrival. His black slacks and half-buttoned dress shirt suggested he'd readied himself quickly.

"I need you," I said by way of greeting, his gaze immediately falling to the bloodied woman in my arms.

His eyebrows rose. "Jesus Christ."

"There's a name I haven't heard in a while," I muttered, walking by him to lay Raelyn on the couch. "She's not breathing, but I can *feel* her." I met his alarmed gaze. "We completed the ceremony."

"Making her immortal," he inferred, his brow crinkling. "But she's not breathing."

"And has no heartbeat." I ran my fingers through my hair. "Help me. What am I not doing that she needs? I know she's there, but she's not… she's not healing."

Darius blew out a breath, nodding. "Right." He glanced sideways as Juliet entered wearing a pair of jeans and a sweater, her hair mussed, her cheeks red. They'd clearly been enjoying themselves. She walked to his side, her big eyes trained on Raelyn's mutilated form.

"How open is your connection?" he asked, his arm wrapping around his *Erosita.*

"At the moment?" I searched, uncertain. "It's hard to say since I can't hear her at all."

"But you feel her," he murmured. "Can you follow that path, push into her mind?"

"There's nothing there but an empty void." A growl underlined my words, born of frustration. The empty void was because I'd closed her off and not heard her cries.

How many times did you call for me, little lamb?

She must have felt so helpless and alone.

Because I deserted her, forced her away, blocked her mind.

"…deeper," Darius was saying. "When Juliet loses consciousness, I can still sense her. It just takes some navigating through the darkness. Don't look for thoughts so much as emotions."

"You can feel me when I'm unconscious?" Juliet asked softly.

"Yes," he replied without elaborating.

I knelt beside Raelyn, touching my forehead to hers. *All right, little lamb, where are you hiding?*

She didn't reply, not that I expected her to.

I slipped into her mind through our link, the absence of her awareness sending a chill down my spine. "Is it possible that her soul is hanging on, but her body is too damaged to recover?" I asked, fearing that her access to my immortality had trapped her in a place she could never escape from, an eternity in hell.

"The *Erosita* shares immortality with her mate. Could you recover from the wounds she suffered?"

"Yes, undoubtedly." It took a lot to kill a vampire, even more so for one of my age.

"Then she will too, but perhaps slower. I'm more concerned that she's shown no signs of healing yet. Even a freshling would be slowly regenerating by now."

"I know," I whispered, refocusing.

What am I missing?

The ceremony was complete. I felt everything snap into place, her being fusing with mine, our minds becoming one. It had scared the shit out of me, forcing me to build an impenetrable shield between us.

What if that had impacted our union?

No.

I was completely inside her now, her vacant essence surrounding me.

So alone.

Vapid.

Sad.

I frowned, tugging on that last sensation, following it.

Such pain.

Abandon.

A loss of a will to live.

Deep, deep sorrow.

He left me…

The three words were a breath in my ear, not solid, but clear.

Raelyn's illusions of betrayal pierced my heart, not just from my closing her off but from her innate devastation over what I'd done to her. I could *feel* her suffering, all because of what I'd done to her.

And she was wallowing in that self-destruction instead of fighting.

Because she didn't see a point in trying.

I'd given her no reason to come back to me, no cause to survive. If anything, I'd demolished her hope through my insensitivity.

My Raelyn. I tried to caress her soul, to comfort her being, but it was like stroking a ghost.

So fractured and lost and dejected.

Her psyche was refusing to let her heal.

I don't accept that, little lamb, I whispered to her. *You're coming back to me.*

She didn't react or reply, her spirit floating helplessly with little determination or fight left in her. I'd chased it all away without meaning to, having blamed the bond for my unusual fixation, but it was always her that drew me in. Not her blood, or even her body, but her soul.

You're mine, darling. Time didn't matter. I claimed her the moment I saw her. I just hadn't realized it yet.

I cupped her cheek, my mind still flirting with hers. *You can't hide from me. I'll find you, Raelyn.* Enemies called me relentless for a reason. I didn't give up when I desired something, and right now, I wanted her.

If it was strength she needed, I would give it all to her.

My immortality.

My soul.

My heart.

Take it, I encouraged. *Use me.*

My fingers curled around the back of her neck, resolved to force as much of me as I could into her. She would survive this. She would wake up. She would be mine in every way. Whatever the cost, I'd pay it.

Now, Raelyn, I demanded. *You're going to breathe again if it's the last thing I make you do.*

She was stubborn, but I was persistent.

I needed her, not just to know who did this to her, but because I felt empty without her. We were nowhere near done yet. Perhaps we never would be.

Eternity was a long time, but if I could enjoy it with anyone, it'd be Raelyn. She had the fire I desired, possessed an intelligence I admired, and the passion between us went deeper than all my experiences combined. That was why I marked her, why I gave her my blood. I'd never allowed—or even considered allowing—another consort to be close to me. I guaranteed their mutual satisfaction and nothing more.

I'd given Raelyn my blood because I wanted to. I'd bitten her because the heat of the moment required it. I rarely fed from anyone during the act for my own enjoyment, but I couldn't stop myself from tasting her.

She was my addiction.

My renewed purpose.

A reason to enjoy living again.

Breathe, damn it, I growled. *I need you with me.*

Raelyn was resilient. She would survive this. I refused to consider any other outcome, and I told her as much over and over and over again. She could ignore me all she wanted, but I would force her to heal.

All my energy—my being—flowed into her, my age, experience, everything. I pushed it all through our bond, holding nothing back.

Knowledge.

Power.

History.

My deepest, darkest secrets.

Exposed.

Hers.

Forever.

Because I couldn't break our connection now, not after granting her access to the deepest depths of my soul. She would always maintain an awareness of me unlike any other. And I would never repeat this again.

A dull thud snapped my focus.

Just a flicker of sound.

Followed by another distant thump.

I waited, my breath frozen in my lungs.

Seconds ticked by.

And then a third beat. A fourth. A fifth.

Tears filled my eyes, my forehead pressing into hers.

Raelyn.

The singing of her pulse had never sounded so beautiful. She still had a long road ahead of her, but she would recover. And I'd be waiting for her when she finally opened her eyes again.

Chapter Twenty-Seven

KYLAN

"HOW IS SHE?" Darius asked after knocking on the door, a coffee mug in his hand.

I stroked Raelyn's hair, her naked body pressed up against mine beneath the covers. "Still healing from the blood loss, but she's regenerating steadily."

He set the coffee on the nightstand beside me. "Good. Her skin looks healthy too."

Yes, her creamy complexion had returned earlier today. I'd bathed her again, removing the last of the blood from her body, leaving her clean and ready for rebirth. "Her thoughts are increasing as well."

"Any indication of who did this to her?"

"Not yet." I frowned and decided to go for honesty. "So far all her thoughts are about how much she hates me." Which sucked. Having her say it was one thing, hearing the truth behind the statement was entirely another. "I really have been an asshole to her."

Darius chuckled. "Well, I'm sure she'll be forgiving when she realizes you saved her life."

I snorted. "You don't know her like I do. She's going to give me hell." Something I was going to enjoy far more than I should.

Something akin to wonder crossed his features, his mouth opening, then closing.

"Say it," I encouraged.

He shook his head. "It's not important."

"I'm not going to retaliate, Darius. Just say it."

He leaned against the wall, hands in the pockets of his black trousers, legs crossed at the ankles. "She's changed you."

My lips twitched. "This world—Lilith's creation—takes all the fun out of life. Raelyn provided something I haven't experienced in ages. A challenge."

"So you're not a fan of the blood alliance," he surmised.

"I can respect certain aspects of the system, but overall? No, I'm not loving this new world." It was boring and too structured.

"I would have taken you as one of her biggest supporters."

"Who? Lilith?" I scoffed at that. "I hate that bitch. All this Goddess shit is just a glorified power trip."

"But she does have a lot of support."

"Unfortunately, she does. For now."

"For now?" he repeated, raising an eyebrow.

"If there's one thing I've learned in this life, it's that dictators only remain at the top for so long. Lilith is very good at pretending she cares, keeping all her royals and alphas in line by stroking their egos when required, but she'll eventually make a mistake. And not everyone adores her, regardless of the facades in place."

"You think there are those who want to overthrow her?"

"Of course." I ran my fingers through Raelyn's hair, holding his gaze. "They won't show their cards for a long while, as the best plans take time, but I imagine we'll see shifting in the ranks soon." Or perhaps we already had.

I eyed his carefully blank expression, searching for signs of his knowledge on the subject.

He didn't blink.

Didn't move.

Didn't even twitch.

Either Darius was an excellent actor or he truly knew nothing. My money was on the former. An old vampire suddenly taking an interest in politics while mating with a human female he clearly cared for? Those were two very intriguing life changes to take on at once. Almost as if he'd planned it.

But who was I to speculate?

I smiled. "Well, what do I know? I'm just the oldest royal in existence, assuming Cam is really dead."

Still as stoic as ever.

"You'll be a fantastic politician, Darius," I murmured. "I'm excited to see where your career takes you."

He finally grinned. "Thank you, Your Highness." He pushed off the wall, his stride confident, and paused just inside the door. "You could try suggesting scenes to her."

My brow furrowed. "To Raelyn?"

"Yes. Telegraph an image of her outside with Angelica, see if she leads you to the truth of what happened." His green eyes met mine. "She's suffered significant trauma. It's fresh in her mind somewhere. You just have to find it." He left without another word, leaving me to consider his suggestion.

Was the answer lurking behind her hatred for me?

Let's see, little lamb.

I caressed her thoughts, flinching when I came up against a wall of frustration engraved with my name.

All just a game. I meant nothing, just a temporary diversion until his new consorts arrive.

I chuckled. Oh, if that were true, I'd have visited the harem camps by now to see whom I wanted to select. Yet I hadn't even studied their files or monitored the videos sent to me from the instructors.

Because I didn't care.

I only wanted the consort beside me.

Not that she'd ever believe that.

He used me. Bonded me to him so he could master my mind and heart, and like an idiot, I let him. I hoped… No. Stop. It's ridiculous. What's the point? I never meant anything to him.

If this stream of conscious was in real time, I could correct her. Alas, her mind only repeated her most consistent thoughts, ones she'd considered again and again—the most important items in her psyche. All centered around me and how I'd failed her.

I sighed and pushed through the initial wall, curious to see what lay beyond it.

Images of a blonde female and Silas flickered in the distance. I followed the strand to a memory of them laughing, my view from Raelyn's point of view.

"His face," the woman said, her full lips pulling into a grin.

"Like Rae's performance was any better," Silas replied, shaking his head. "Goddess, I thought they'd all know she was faking it."

Raelyn's giggle pierced my heart—a sound she'd never made in my presence. "Anything to pass a course."

"Not going to move on to the next level, then?" Silas teased, winking.

"Dear Goddess, no. Sexual arts are not for me."

"Hope you don't end up in the harems, then," the blonde said. "Or worse, the breeding camps."

But that's where you went, Raelyn whispered, the memory morphing into a thought. *Fuck, Willow, I hope you're okay. I miss you.*

I pulled back, noting the name. She'd mentioned it once or twice, something about the woman being her friend. Seeing their interaction now from Raelyn's perspective, I believed that.

True friends.

All of them.

And society had ripped them apart.

I picked up my tablet, ignoring the coffee Darius had dropped off, and searched the records for an image of the female. Her breeding camp designation and pale blonde hair made her easy to find.

Still alive.

But the updated image of her made her look like she wished she wasn't.

Yes, that was not a favorable fate, especially for a female.

And what about Silas… I pulled the latest stats from the Immortal Cup. Only four left already, Silas among them. The winner would be declared soon, assuming any of them survived the final round. His sapphire eyes lacked the confidence I'd seen on Blood Day, his muscular stature fatigued, but the tightening of his mouth indicated his resolve.

He was a survivor.

Just like Raelyn.

I flipped back to Willow, zooming in on her bruised face. Her downcast gaze made it difficult to tell if she possessed the strong will of her friends, but something told me she was a formidable human too.

A topic to discuss with Raelyn at some point. After we solved our present issue.

I still wanted to know who tried to kill my consort. No, my *Erosita.*

The term warmed my heart, the realization of just *who* she was to me feeling more right than I could have ever imagined.

I set the tablet aside and slipped back into her head, bypassing the onslaught of repetitive phrases about my horrible character and searching for new threads. The idea Darius had mentioned trickled through the bond, but rather than imagine Angelica outside, Raelyn focused on the sky, a hint of wonder trickling through her.

My lips curled at her happiness.

She really did love the outdoors, the snow, the mountains. Her heart sang with it, radiating a pleasure I wished I alone could give her.

And then her joy sped up, Mikael's face appearing.

I growled, low and deep. Why did *he* make her happier than I did? Because I'd left them alone for a week to train?

Wait…

Relief emanated throughout her being.

"Goddess, I'm so glad you're okay."

"You missed me?"

I frowned at the exchange. When had that occurred? Mikael claimed he hadn't seen her, yet her vision showcased him leading her along the tree line outside. Without Angelica.

Was this a dream or a memory?

They kept walking, confusion seeping into her mind, the image blurring at the edges.

Keep going, I urged, squinting.

Everything kept darkening, as if she didn't want to think about what came next. It went black, then illuminated again, her heart pounding as Zelda appeared.

Betrayal sang through our bond.

Kylan. Help me…

My hands shook, the words not current but spoken in her memories. She'd called for me—just as I thought—and her soul had wept when I didn't reply.

…betrayed you.

A lump formed in my throat. Raelyn had… she'd spent her last seconds trying to warn me of the truth. Not cursing my name, but *warning* me.

"Oh, sweetheart," I whispered, pulling her closer. "But who, darling? Who betrayed me?"

I followed her thread of immense sadness to an image that had my heart stopping.

A vision of Mikael slicing the blade across her throat.

"Goodbye, Rae."

I froze.

Mikael?

No. No, that was impossible

He…

I…

The vision flashed again.

And again.

Repeating through my thoughts, fracturing my grasp on reality.

The swipe of the blade.

Raelyn gurgling.

Mikael's sad voice.

It all culminated inside me, ripping my heart in half. I'd trusted him. Loved him in my own way. My best friend…

This couldn't be right. *Why?* I demanded. *Why would he do this?*

"You have to see this as a gift, Rae. He'll only bring you misery. Trust us, we know." His words in her mind were accompanied with such grief, such suffering. Because of me? Because I hurt him? How? I did everything to take care of him. I protected him. I gave him things few humans ever experienced.

And he'd taken the one thing from me I adored.

The one speck of happiness on my horizon.

All to, what, save her from his own misery?

I was an asshole, but not *that* horrible. There were many out there who were much worse than me, but Mikael had never experienced their brands of "affection" because I'd protected him from it.

I held Raelyn tighter, my heart beating in time with hers. *You don't think I'm that horrible, right?* I asked her softly, hearing all her accusations again in response. *Right, you probably do.*

I sighed, Mikael's betrayal simmering between us, heating my blood.

I'd failed them all.

Her.

Him.

Not on purpose, just by habit.

But that didn't justify Mikael taking Raelyn's life.

My throat constricted, my heart hammering in my chest. How had it come to this? Why?

Mikael was with me during the massacre of the harem. He'd shed real tears, his agony tangible. I'd soothed him in the only way I knew how. But had he known the entire time? Had he been involved? Who helped him?

Trust us, we know, he'd said.

Who was "us"?

Raelyn's mind opened up again, the scene flickering back and forth, revealing bits and pieces. Mikael's light eyes held so much heartache, his regret tangible.

"He makes you want things that he'll never completely give. He gets you addicted to him. Forces you to love him. But he never loves you back."

"I know."

My heart faltered with the words, so fresh, so brutal. Was that what they thought? That I forced them to feel this way while refusing to reciprocate?

"Fuck," I whispered harshly.

The memory continued in jumbled order. Raelyn's shock mingled with my own, her fear heightened as…

"Zelda," I said, my jaw tightening.

I stopped listening, her knife captivating my attention.

She'd been a part of this, her taunts making Raelyn cringe. Mikael looked so resolved.

And that blade slit Raelyn's throat again.

And again.

And again.

"Fuck!" I shut it off, unable to see it anymore.

I couldn't…

This hadn't…

I buried my face in Raelyn's neck, my mind racing with conflicting needs.

Revenge.

Punishment.

Sorrow.

Loyalty.

Raelyn whimpered again in her mind, my name repeating over and over, followed by a deep sadness that I'd left her there to die alone.

Fuck, that hurt worst of all—her anguish.

She thought I didn't care.

That I'd abandoned her to her fate.

"No," I whispered, locking my arms around her. "No."

I wouldn't leave her again. Not now. Not ever.

Mikael…

I cursed against her hair.

He'd have to wait.
Everything had to wait.
Raelyn mattered most.
I'm here, I promised her. *I'm never leaving you again.*
Not even to seek vengeance.

Chapter Twenty-Eight

RAE

SOAP. My nose crinkled. *Minty. Masculine.*

Odd. The scent was everywhere. All over me. Inside me. Consuming me. And I was overly hot too, my clammy skin pressed against something equally warm—the source of the heat.

Kylan.

I blinked into the darkness of the room. No snowy mountains, just dark drapes like the ones in his penthouse.

My brow furrowed. Had he moved me while I slept? I blinked again. When had I slept? I couldn't remember, everything was foggy, the last few days a blur.

Kylan took me back to his home. We went for a hike. My heart stuttered, recalling what happened there. The subsequent days of pain. Angelica urging me to go outside. And—

I flew upward on a gasp, my hand at my throat.

Mikael.

Zelda.

Kylan abandoning me to my fate.

It hit me so hard I couldn't breathe, the pain of my death so sharp and vivid. They just kept stabbing me. Over and over and over, my body dying while my soul held on, feeling everything.

I touched my bare side, my breasts, my stomach.

No marks. No blood. Just smooth, warm skin.

How?

I touched my unmarred throat again, convinced this was a trick somehow. Humans didn't just magically heal.

Am I no longer mortal?

"No, you're mine," Kylan replied, his voice low, cautious, and underlined with a darker emotion.

I spun to face him and winced as my head whirled with it. Both my palms went to my temples, a shudder of pain ricocheting throughout my being. "Ow," I mouthed, my voice failing me.

"Here." He put something between my lips—a straw. "Sip this and swallow."

I almost refused, but I needed the liquid, my throat aching without it. Cool water touched my tongue, soothing the burn inside my mouth and downward. It felt good. Relieving. Calming. My eyes fell closed while I continued to drink, my muscles relaxing until all I wanted was to lie down again.

Kylan set the cup aside and pulled me into his arms, my head finding his shoulder. It felt right—comfortable—and so, so good.

I yawned, my body slowly falling—

"Raelyn," Kylan murmured, jolting me awake.

I'm in his arms.

How had I allowed him to lure me into this position? He abandoned me when I needed him, pushed me away, used me and broke me, and—

"Saved your life," he added softly. "Not that it forgives everything else, but your link to my immortality is why you're alive." He tightened his hold, his lips brushing my temple. "You wanted to give up and I wouldn't let you."

What? The last thing I remembered was screaming for him in my mind and receiving no reply.

"Ouch," he muttered, flinching. "Yeah, I deserve that."

Deserve what? I wondered to myself.

"The memory," he replied. "And the pain associated with it."

My lips curled down in confusion. *What is he…?* My thought trailed off as an image of my mutilated body floated through my mind, trailed by a rush of emotions.

Confusion.

Fury.

Distress.

Not my own, but Kylan's feelings.

Followed by an onslaught of words intertwined with his memories.

Raelyn! Where are you? What's happened?

She's dead…

I'll murder whoever did this, rip them apart, scatter their remains, burn everything.

I failed her.

The link…

She's fighting it.

Because of me.

Fuck, Raelyn, don't do this. Don't you dare let go.

That's it, little lamb. Breathe for me. I'm not leaving you until you're awake. Maybe not even then.

You're stuck with me now, princess.

I need you to tell me who did this to you. Who is behind all this?

That last one had me pulling away from him, his true motives finally shining. "Y-you…" I swallowed, my throat still sore even after the water. But I had to say this. "You only saved me to learn—"

"No." He pressed his finger to my lips, pushing me down onto the bed as he hovered over me. "Look deeper, Raelyn, and you'll know that's not true."

I stared into his near-black eyes, shrouded in thick, dark lashes. He didn't glance away, his gaze open, his mind mine to explore. More words rushed over me, all laced in fury and confusion, hints of lust, murmurs of devotion, regret, sadness, and utter devastation.

Mikael's name was the loudest among them.

And a restrained rage lurking in wait for Zelda.

Kylan had seen my memory when I first woke… *No*… He'd seen it in my nightmares while I was healing.

"You already knew," I breathed.

He nodded. "Yes."

"Yet you stayed here?"

He cupped my face. "I promised not to leave you again, Raelyn. I meant it."

My lips moved but no sound escaped. He stayed with me.

I reached for his thoughts again, needing more explanation. He remained patient, granting me full access to everything. All of him.

The ceremony made me his *Erosita*, like Juliet to Darius. And granted me access to Kylan's immortality.

That's how I survived, and his mental urging that I not give up hope.

His memories overwhelmed me, his anguish when he thought I was dead, his reaction when he realized my soul still flourished, him driving us here, cocooning me in his penthouse for nearly a week while I healed.

Promises.

Decisions.

He never truly wanted to break the bond—it infuriated him to even think about—but he had never meant to instill it either. And now he refused to destroy it. Yet a hint of uncertainty remained, his desire to let me choose, to not force the connection upon me.

"It can only be broken by another vampire fucking you," he said softly, naturally aware of my snooping through his head. Which meant he'd allowed it and was continuing to leave himself open to me.

"I remember that part," I grumbled, recalling his original intentions clearly.

A flurry of possessiveness overwhelmed me, restricting my ability to breathe. It pressed on my chest, agonizing my insides, setting my blood on fire, sending tears to my eyes.

And then it was gone in a blink, leaving me winded and slightly dizzy.

"That's a mere fraction of how I feel when I think about sharing you, Raelyn." He stared down at me, his dark eyes intense. "While my intention may have existed in the beginning, there's a reason I couldn't follow through with it and refuse to do so now."

I gaped at him, shocked by another blast of that covetous energy from his mind to mine. "How are you doing that?" I managed to say, my voice raspy.

"We're mated. I can share everything with you and vice versa, including intense emotions."

"And thoughts."

"Yes, and images." He traced my bottom lip with his thumb, his gaze dropping. "I can see your memories just as you can view mine. Our connection is wide open, making us able to push things to each other as well."

"Which can trigger us to remember certain things." *Like what happened outside.*

"Yes," he whispered. "I pictured you outside. You showed me the rest."

I shivered and caressed my throat again. "It-it was awful."

Kylan rolled to his side, pulling me with him, our heads sharing the same pillow, our gazes locked. He ran his fingers through my hair, brushing it back from my face.

"I should have been there, should have been listening for you. Instead I left you with Angelica and assumed she would protect you." His irritation at that last part hummed through our connection, causing me to frown.

"You blame her."

"Partly, yes. Mostly, I blame myself."

"But you blame her too." I could hear his lethal intentions for her, all because she left me unprotected. "Her maker called. That's why she walked away." I didn't fully understand the link between maker and progeny, but I imagined it made him her superior.

"Vilheim called her," Kylan repeated, a crease marring his forehead. "That's coincidental timing."

His comment triggered a memory. Something about a timeline…

"Not when we're on a timeline. He'll only stall for so long."

Zelda's words played through my head. I hadn't known whom she meant at the time, but what if—

"She meant Vilheim," Kylan finished for me. "He's the reason I employed her. Vilheim recommended Zelda to me." His body tensed around mine, his memories of their conversations flickering through our bond. He didn't hide a single detail, letting me see everything from his point of view. "That was two years ago."

Suggesting she was put in place by Vilheim with the intention of discrediting Kylan. I listened while he reasoned through the plots, considerations, and potential partnerships.

Vilheim isn't experienced enough to inherit the region.

But he could become a sovereign under another's rule.

So which royal promised him power in exchange for overthrowing me?

Names rolled through his mind, motives judged and assigned, until he had a firm list of suspects who could be trying to take over his land. As well as a list of bored royals and alphas who might be having a go at him for pure sport.

"Our dinner party next week should be fun," he murmured, a plan forming and taking hold in his thoughts.

So quick and thorough, and undeniably intelligent.

I stared at him in awe, loving this side of him—the complicated musings of a clever being with thousands of years of experience. His perceived cruelty was the result of insightful plotting. Kylan didn't thrive on pain. He punished others to make a statement, to keep everyone in line. And he bore the weight of the region on his shoulders alone, trusting no one to help him.

He slid his palm beneath my hair, wrapping around the back of my neck.

"I've never let anyone see this much of me, Raelyn." A hint of fear underlined his proclamation.

"You believe confiding in others is a weakness," I whispered, hearing the confirmation in his deliberations.

"Providing others with the opportunity to harm me is an innate fault, yes."

"But it can also make you stronger." I cupped his cheek, holding his gaze. "I only ever survived because I trusted Silas and Willow to have my back. They helped me when I was shortsighted, and I returned the favor. Sometimes having an ally can give you the leverage you need to succeed."

"There's a difference between having an ally and a confidant," he replied. "I have many allies—"

"Whom you don't trust," I interjected. "You didn't even tell Judith we were here." A thought I'd overheard when he was reviewing his revengeful plans for the party. "And she's done everything to earn it." According to everything he'd shown me, anyway. "You push away everyone who could help you, relying solely on yourself to survive. It's a stressful way to live."

"It's more stressful to worry about when someone might betray you," he countered. "People are cruel, Raelyn. I've learned that the only one I can trust in this life is myself."

He showered me in his experiences, showing the way others had harmed him throughout his very long existence. All minor incidents that collectively added up to one sound conclusion—he could only rely on himself.

"Yes, I agree; looking out for yourself guarantees the outcome to always be in your best interest. But that doesn't mean you can't trust others to help you, Kylan. You've let a handful of bad experiences dictate your approach to life." I pressed my palm to his face. "My entire life has been ruled by vampires and lycans, most of whom were cruel. Should I not trust you as a result of their behavior?"

"You don't trust me," he said softly. "I can see your indecision, Raelyn. You worry I'll hurt you."

"Yes, and I imagine I'll feel that way for a long time," I admitted. "But that doesn't mean I won't take a risk and give you a chance to prove me wrong." And I meant it. Even after everything he'd put me through, I still wanted to trust him. Part of it stemmed from my access to his mind, granting me the ability to understand his motives and methods, but a larger part of it was my soul's innate belief in Kylan being my destiny.

I couldn't begin to comprehend it, but I relied on the instinct.

What did I have to lose?

Absolutely nothing.

I was born into this life as a servant, and Kylan gave me the opportunity for more. It was the closest I'd ever be to immortality, to living an actual life.

"Those are not the best reasons to agree to this, little lamb," Kylan said, a touch of sadness in his tone. "But they are practical."

"What other reasons would you give me?" I asked softly, studying his features.

Yes, he'd spent the last week nursing me back to health, but the thing that saved me—our bond—was never planned. And if I understood everything correctly, to remain immortal required my fidelity, not his. What kind of relationship was that? A one-sided one where I benefited from his life energy while being forced to remain faithful for eternity whereas he could do whatever he wanted.

"You want commitment," he murmured, following my thoughts. He brushed his thumb over my eyebrow, his fingers skimming upward to run through my hair again. "I've never given that to anyone, Raelyn."

I nodded, having seen that in his thoughts as well. "I know."

"I've never bonded in this manner with anyone, either," he added. "I can't tell you what to expect because I don't know." He tilted his head to the side, his dark eyes simmering. "But I know I want you."

"For now."

"Yes, for now." He brushed his lips over mine, the movement slower and more tender than his usual embrace. "I think we both need time to figure this out."

Which he'd given me by extending my mortality. "Yes."

"And first, we need to deal with those trying to discredit me."

"We?" I repeated, my eyebrows lifting.

"Oh, yes." He nipped my lower lip before pulling away. "I have an idea and it very much involves you."

"I'm listening."

His lips curled. "Yes. Yes, you are."

Chapter Twenty-Nine

KYLAN

"LILITH, HOW LOVELY OF YOU TO JOIN US." I greeted the blonde vampire with a superficial hug after she descended the grand staircase. Her deep-red gown revealed everything, giving her a devilish appearance rather than a holy one. Very, very appropriate.

"Kylan," she murmured, brushing her lips against my cheek. "You know I never miss one of your parties, as rare as they are these days."

"Yes, it has been a while," I murmured, extending my elbow to escort her into the main room. "It's just so much to organize, and I never know who may or may not make an appearance." *And your late arrival means I can finally start the show,* I thought with an internal grin. *Let the countdown begin.*

"Well, from what I hear, most of society planned to attend."

I smiled. "It's almost as if they're expecting some sort of entertainment."

Her lips twitched deviously. "I believe they are."

Rumor of Raelyn's death had spread, something Jace helped circulate. He also suggested in casual conversation that it might be time for someone to step in temporarily as leader of Kylan Region.

The latter was why nearly all the royals and alphas were in attendance tonight.

Jace's offhanded remarks had grown into speculation as to whether or not he would challenge me tonight.

Exactly what we intended.

All these bored immortals wanted a show.

I'd be giving them one, just not the reveal they expected.

"I'm sure it'll be an enlightening evening, Kylan." Lilith winked as she left me to mingle with the others, her intrigue clear. There was a reason she'd ascended to the highest throne, her age and experience marking her as queen on the chessboard. Strategy was her version of foreplay, and she'd mastered the art long ago.

I both despised and admired her.

You're giving me heart palpitations, Raelyn whispered, making my lips curl.

I picked up a champagne flute from a passing waiter to hide my reaction behind the crystal glass. *Why? Because I'm destroying your perspective on religion, little lamb?*

You're destroying a lot of things.

I sipped the blood-laced liquid, amused. *Good. Remind me to show you a few religious texts at some point. I think you'll find some of the passages familiar but with slightly altered language.*

Her amusement fluttered through me, almost distracting me from the task at hand, but not quite. *You're all right, yes?*

I'm the same as I was when you asked me five minutes ago.

Can you blame me for worrying? Mikael and Zelda were in the same building as her, albeit completely unaware of her presence. The only ones who knew Raelyn was alive were Judith, Darius, Juliet, and Jace. *Judith is still with you, right?*

Her mental sigh almost had me smiling again. *Yes, Kylan.*

She better—

Not go anywhere, she finished for me. *Yes, we know. And I'll tell you if something is wrong, as I've promised a thousand times now.*

My lips twitched at her familiar fire. *Stop being defiant.*

Stop being mercurial.

"You appear in good spirits," a familiar voice purred, Robyn drawing her nails up my suit-clad biceps. "What has you grinning like that?"

"A man never reveals his secrets, darling. You know that." I kissed her cheek, causing Raelyn to growl in my head. *Calm down, little lamb. Robyn isn't my type.*

Would you like me kissing another man?

I almost shattered the flute in my hand. *Absolutely not.*

Then stop kissing other women.

It's part of my charade, love.

Her responding snort said how she felt about that.

Your possessiveness is actually quite endearing, Raelyn.

You won't find it endearing later when I bite you again. She sent me a graphic image of exactly what she intended to bite, causing me to laugh out loud.

At this point, love, even that small attention might make me come. It'd been nearly two weeks since I'd last been inside her, mostly because I'd wanted her fully healed and prepared for tonight. And partly as a result of my concern over

Raelyn's feelings toward our bond.

"Kylan?" Robyn snapped, pulling my attention back to her.

"I'm sorry, darling. Were you saying something?"

Her blue eyes widened. "What the hell has gotten into you?"

"I've had a very illuminating month," I replied. "And I'm not quite myself anymore."

True concern entered her expression. "Kylan—"

"Actually," I said loudly, deciding to begin the show. "Now that everyone is here, I'd like to say a few words." I set my drink on a nearby table and sauntered toward the middle of the room.

Ready, Raelyn?

Not like I have much choice now, she thought back at me, her mental voice amused. *Just say the word and I'm there.*

My resulting smile caused a few guests to take a step back. They all clearly thought me mad. This was going to be fun.

"Thank you all for joining me in Kylan City this evening. I know it's been a while since I hosted a gathering, and I just thought, with recent events, it might be a grand time to entertain you all." Several vampires chuckled at that, the implication clear. They all gathered here tonight because they expected a diversion, and I'd just confirmed that I intended to give them one.

"As you all have heard, I recently massacred my harem for sport and my latest consort met a similar fate. To be fair, she was a defiant little female from the beginning, as several of you observed, yes?"

Murmurs of agreement sounded throughout the room while Raelyn scoffed in my head. *Thanks for that.*

You're very welcome.

Smart-ass, she growled, entertaining me immensely. I adored that sound. It made me want to force it out of her in the bedroom, specifically in the form of my name.

Stop distracting me, little minx. I have a show to put on.

Then get on with it already.

I cleared my throat to disguise the laugh ready to burst out of me. Raelyn made this almost enjoyable, an emotion I would need, considering the tasks at hand.

"Oh, before I continue, may I introduce tonight's cuisine?" I snapped twice, indicating to Cherise that I was ready for her presentation.

The former reception manager had proven herself quite capable at organizing the dining rooms of K Hotel, so I'd opted to provide her with another opportunity to impress me—this time by catering tonight's event in the ballrooms of the hotel.

Maeve had helped as well with organizing all the guests' rooms and greeting everyone appropriately. The new hotel manager was in for a treat with acquiring them as staff. Another announcement for me to make this evening.

Humans dressed in varying degrees of lingerie filed out of the kitchen, their hands full of trays. It was typical for a host to offer blood. I asked Cherise to improvise by lacing popular hors d'oeuvres with blood, as well as to spice up the entertainment with revealing outfits.

Approval radiated throughout the room as the mortals were admired and fondled. The few lycans in attendance gravitated toward the meatier appetizers, while the vampires focused on the mortal offerings more than on the food options.

If anyone wished to take a human upstairs after the party, I couldn't deny them. Not without raising suspicion. Whether I approved or not, that was the nature of our world.

Zelda appeared in the mix, her expression confused, her eyes searching.

I'd purposely asked Cherise to add the woman to the lineup. She usually hid in the kitchens. Not tonight.

And finally, Mikael. I'd requested something very special for him.

He sauntered out in a tuxedo, flanked by two of my security guards—both items marking him as my equal, not my servant.

It was the first time I'd seen him since the night of Raelyn's murder, and it took considerable effort to force my lips upward in a welcoming smile.

"Ah, my favorite blood virgin," I murmured while silence fell over the room, the shock at my chosen attire for him evident in the way everyone stilled. "I haven't seen him in two weeks," I informed them all. "After what happened to my consort, I was afraid that a similar fate might befall my beloved Mikael and opted to keep him out of my reach for his personal safety."

A faint blush painted his cheeks as he made his way toward me, his lips curling. He'd interpreted my words the way I desired, as a subtle apology for abandoning him for so long. I wanted him to believe I'd meant to keep him safe while having everyone else assume I meant to protect him from my insanity. Dressing him as an equal only further proved my weakening mental state, at least to the casual observer.

He stopped at my side, his posture submissive while still holding an edge of confidence. It physically hurt not to react to his nearness.

He betrayed me. Framed me. Hurt Raelyn.

Yet, the bastard had the audacity to smile as if all was right in the world.

I gave him everything.

And I would leave him with nothing.

I pressed my palm to his lower back, a gesture of support that helped to hide the tension radiating up my arm.

Almost there, I told myself, retribution simmering in my blood.

The final feature of the flesh parade elicited several gasps from the crowd, including one from Lilith herself. She'd appeared unfazed so far, but her lips finally parted as Angelica stumbled forward beneath a layer of silver chains. Her emaciated form shivered, her dark eyes crazed from the lack of blood.

Kylan… Raelyn's discomfort cooled my nerves. While I'd mentioned this part of the plan, she'd not fully grasped what I intended until now.

Trust me, sweetheart, I whispered. *Let me focus.*

Okay, she replied, warming my heart. I expected her to hesitate, but she didn't. Not even a blink.

Thank you. I caressed her mind with mine, an intimate version of a hug.

Angelica stopped before me, her head bowed. The taller of the two security guards who escorted Mikael—Gavin—stepped forward to give her a shove, forcing her to her knees. She whimpered as she landed, the silver digging into her skin. Unlike lycans, vampires were immune to the precious metal, but the chains were thick and heavy, especially to one in such an emaciated state.

"Hmm, we're missing someone." I glanced around for show, knowing exactly where my weasel was standing. "Oh!" I caught the jackass's gaze and smiled theatrically. "Vilheim, this one belongs to you, yes?"

"Yes, My Prince," he replied, his eyebrows rising.

"Then you should join us." I punctuated the invitation with a grand wave of my hand, fully aware of how insane I appeared to the room. It was that or kill all the guilty parties without proper explanation, and I much preferred this route. Especially as I hoped it would produce the real player behind the scenes.

After much deliberation with Darius and Jace, we decided the culprit had to be someone merely desiring a bit of chaotic fun. Because all those who were eligible to inherit my territory were either uninterested in expansion or too far away to truly reap the rewards of my land. And while I had as many enemies as the next royal, proving me insane yielded very little reward in the long run and would only ensure my retaliation.

Which meant I had it narrowed down to a handful of candidates, and only two of those candidates had deigned to attend this evening.

Robyn and Walter. The old alpha was on his way out the door, old age forcing him to step down. He would enjoy one final row among the higher-ranking members of society, especially if it left him with a legacy to enjoy.

Of course, that didn't mean I discounted Robyn. She was equally as likely, especially considering her penchant for fucking with others.

"Vilheim," I greeted as he stopped beside us, his expression bored. "Now we can begin." I took in the silent crowd, pleased that everyone was more intrigued by me than by the half-naked humans on display throughout the room. Perfect. "How would you all feel about observing a vampire trial?"

"That depends on what you're accusing her of," Lilith replied, her face carefully blank.

"Murder." My single-worded reply inspired several murmurs and exchanged looks of confusion. "Right, maybe I should explain. There are certain rumors spreading of my mental state, of which I won't question, but the assumptions surrounding my harem is something I would like to address. You see, I didn't kill any of them."

The voices grew, several explanations of disbelief and a few chuckles littering the air.

"Oh, come now, Kylan. We all know you have a penchant for blood,"

Robyn said, her voice filled with humored surprise.

"Undoubtedly," I agreed. "But not reckless murder. I wasn't home when my harem was killed, and Raelyn's murder occurred while I was out for a run. I found Angelica standing over her body covered in my consort's blood. That's why I've kept her locked away and blood-starved for two weeks. Tonight I am putting her on trial for murdering my property."

A chorus of disbelief and outright annoyance answered my claim, several stating they couldn't believe I was mad enough to blame another. Others claiming that punishing a vampire for the murder of a mortal was ludicrous. And many more sighing that I'd officially lost my mind. Clearly.

"Enough." Lilith raised her hand, calming the crowd, her green eyes sharp with knowledge. "All right, Kylan. I'm intrigued. Proceed."

I smiled. She'd just agreed to a trial for not only Angelica's sins but mine as well. If this went the wrong way, she'd use the incident to claim me as mentally unstable. It's what I would do in her position.

"Thank you, Lilith." I inclined my head in mutual understanding and released Mikael to walk around the vampire dressed in chains, hands behind my back. She appeared so broken and fragile that I almost felt bad, then I remembered how she abandoned Raelyn. "You know the murder I'm accusing you of, Angelica. How do you plead?"

"I d-didn't d-do it," she whispered, shaking her head. "I-I d-didn't."

"That's fascinating considering I found you covered in her blood at the scene of the crime. Explain to me what happened."

"I… I was t-talking to V-Vilheim." She paused, shuddering violently. "I-I found her like that. I found her a-after I hung up the phone."

My eyebrows rose in mock surprise, my gaze going to Vilheim. "She's using you as an alibi. Can you believe that?"

He laughed, his execution flawless. "It's ridiculous. Why would I call her?"

"Y-you did!" She lifted her head, a fire in her gaze that bespoke of desperation and fury. "Y-you called me!"

He took a step forward, but I stopped him with a hand on his shoulder. "Shh, let's hear her out," I encouraged. "If anything, it'll amuse me."

He fixed his jacket, backing off, and nodded. "Yes. Fine. But I want the honor of killing her."

"Of course," I replied. "The honor will be all yours." I crouched in front of Angelica, meeting her infuriated gaze. Most would be sobbing in her condition, but she looked ready to commit murder. "What did he say when he called you?"

"He asked me what you had me doing," she growled. "He wanted to know about Rae." Her expression fell on that last word. "I sh-shouldn't have left her. But I d-didn't kill her. I swear it."

Vilheim snorted. "That wasn't even entertaining. Why would I care about a consort?"

I stood and smoothed my tie. "Yes, why indeed?"

Are you ready, Raelyn? I asked while feigning a thoughtful expression.

Yes. Her immediate response was laced with fire. She wanted to avenge Angelica despite barely knowing the woman. I admired that tenacity and sense of loyalty, even if I questioned it. *She's been punished, Kylan.*

Has she? I countered, gazing at the emaciated female. *I gave her a task and she failed.*

But she's not the one who attacked me.

You wouldn't have been attacked if she had done her job, I pointed out.

She sighed in my mind. *She's suffered enough.* A blast of guilt hit me, Raelyn unleashing her inner turmoil at seeing Angelica disciplined over something she felt was uncontrollable. *Please, Kylan.*

My command overrode everything else in this territory, something Angelica should have known before accepting that call. But soothing Raelyn's discomfort meant more to me than making an example out of Angelica.

All right, little lamb. It's time.

"I feel as if we need another witness," I said to the room, glancing around. "Someone who may be able to speak to Angelica's account of what happened." I pulled a device from my pocket and hit a button. "Judith, we're ready for you."

"Of course, My Prince," she replied over the speakerphone, playing her part as requested.

Mikael noticeably stiffened, but Vilheim remained unaffected. I couldn't wait to see his exterior shatter.

Hushes of speculation fluttered through the air, the majority of the guests quiet and intrigued while a few discussed my mental state in whispers. Jace met my gaze from across the room. He gave away nothing in that icy stare, but I knew he approved. This was exactly how he would handle it.

Heels clicked over the tile, causing several to look in the direction of the grand ballroom entrance.

My lips began to curl, ready to welcome my big surprise.

She appeared at the top of the staircase, her auburn strands piled high on her head to expose the delicate column of her throat. The red gown I'd chosen for her flowed to the floor and cut suggestively to her upper thighs while the opaque fabric clung to every inch of her skin without exposing it.

Gorgeous, I thought, smiling widely now. "May I introduce my *Erosita,* Raelyn."

Chapter Thirty

Rae

CHAOTIC CONVERSATION AND WHISPERS of disbelief trailed around me as I descended the stairs, my legs shaking from the effort to remain confident. Judith walked behind me, her presence helping to ground me in the moment.

I could feel their gazes on me.

The hunger.

The shock.

The general lethality lurking in the room.

Lycans and vampires, most of status, all waiting for me to join them as the star witness.

Just breathe, little lamb, Kylan whispered, his mind brushing mine. *I'm waiting for you at the bottom.*

I couldn't see him, my eyes averted in a display of subservience necessitated by my role. Knowing he was there helped me move faster, my heels clacking over the marble stairs, my dress shifting with my movements.

"Hello, little lamb," Kylan greeted, his hand wrapping around the back of my neck to draw me in for a kiss as I reached the bottom. "You look delicious."

"Thank you, My Prince." The words were whispered against his lips, my heart pounding in my ears.

I have you, love, he promised. *Trust me.*

Warmth flooded my thoughts and my blood. *I know.*

He took a step back and extended his arm. "Now, let's see about getting some proper answers."

Some of the heat fled my body as Kylan led me closer to Mikael. Gavin stood behind him, his stance protective as he held Mikael's biceps. Others would think he meant to guard the blood virgin, and perhaps that was even what Kylan told him. But I knew the truth, as did Mikael. His light eyes met mine, horror mingling with sorrow radiating from him.

Because he felt bad about what he did to me?

Or because he pitied his situation?

If he was sorry about what he did to you, there would be at least a spec of relief inside him. I sense none. The last three words were a growl in my head, Kylan's displeasure raising the hairs along my arms. He had expected—hoped—Mikael would show some semblance of care regarding my being alive, but his pulse rang of fear more than anything else. Proving to Kylan that Mikael only ever cared about himself.

Deep sadness crept through our connection, Kylan truly distraught over having failed his blood virgin.

But you didn't, I told him, certain. *You treated Mikael better than anyone else ever had or ever would.*

Yes, however, he always desired more from me. Something I never could give. He opened the line of thought, showing me what he meant.

Mikael taking care of Kylan through small acts such as bringing him evening breakfast, coffee, serving him wine—doing whatever was asked of him even when it clearly hurt.

He never said no.

He always obeyed.

And he never stopped looking at Kylan as if he were the sole purpose for living. His desire evident in every glance, his body bending to whatever will was bestowed upon him, and his heart always there for the taking.

Love, I realized. *He wanted your love.*

"All right, where were we?" he asked out loud instead of replying to me.

Glancing at Mikael's broken features, a confirmation wasn't needed. His sorrow stemmed in knowing he'd failed Kylan, that he would never have him again. That he'd lost the love of his life forever. And everyone would know after today.

"Oh, right, Angelica said she had to take a call and that's why she left Raelyn alone. I'm curious to hear my *Erosita's* side of the tale, since she lived through it after all." He turned me toward him, his fingers tilting my chin up to meet his gaze. "Speak." A hint of mischief followed that word through the bond, his way of trying to lighten our dark situation by reminding me of our first time together.

I narrowed my gaze. *I'm not a dog, Kylan.*

Yes, of that I am very much aware, pet. "Now, Raelyn."

"Angelica and I were outside when her phone rang. She said it was Vilheim, her maker, and she had to take the call. Mikael found me shortly after." I paused to glance sideways at him, his light eyes rimmed with tears. My heart stuttered, uncertainty filling me inside.

What will you do to him?

"What happened next, Raelyn?" Kylan demanded. *I'm sorry, love, but I need you to say it.*

But what will you do to him? I asked, my focus still on Mikael, watching him fracture beside us. He knew what was coming. He knew his fate. I should have been thrilled by the prospect of revenge, but all I felt was immense sadness for our situation. Of the lengths at which he'd gone to keep Kylan to himself, all at the expense of his own life.

I don't know what I'll do yet, Kylan admitted softly. *But I need you to finish the story.*

The unease and expectations of the crowd were closing in on us, their eagerness at what I had to say overwhelming me. I swallowed, shuddering, and closed my eyes, unable to stand the sight of Mikael's tears any longer.

I took a deep breath, steadying myself. "Mikael walked with me for a bit, saying he liked me and apologizing, but I didn't understand why. Then Zelda appeared with a knife, said something about my death being the final nail in your coffin, and told Mikael to prove himself by killing me. So he slit my throat before stabbing me."

I flinched at the memory of the sharp edge piercing my rib cage, my chest, the sensation of drowning in my own blood—

Kylan wrapped his hand around my neck suddenly, squeezing. My eyes flew open to meet his heated gaze, his expression yanking me back into the present faster than a command.

"Sounds like your humans need a lesson in discipline," a female remarked from the crowd.

Kylan's attention slowly shifted toward the woman—Robyn, I realized—and narrowed. "Are you suggesting mortals are intelligent enough to craft a plan like this on their own?"

"Well, I didn't hear mention of a vampire in the mix, so yes."

His lips curled as he released my neck, pulling me to his side to face her. "Fascinating that you mention that. See, from the memory I've pulled from my *Erosita's* head, I can confirm Angelica did in fact receive a call from Vilheim, because the image of the phone number is in Raelyn's head. What's more is the phrase Zelda said about being on a timeline and only stalling for so long."

He snapped his fingers to his left, where Judith appeared with a tear-streaked Zelda in her arms. I'd not even noticed the captive female, but seeing her now had my blood heating for retribution.

My eyes narrowed. *You.*

"I'm going to kill you, Zelda," Kylan said flatly. "The question at this time becomes whether or not I make that a quick death or a long, excruciating one. Care to elaborate on your words to Raelyn?"

She blanched, her focus going over my shoulder with a pleading stare.

Kylan followed her gaze, turning as he went. A dark-haired vampire with ashen features stared back at us, his expression unreadable.

"Oh, right," Kylan said. "Yes, for those unaware, Vilheim used to be Zelda's owner, but he gifted her to me after I expressed gratitude over one of her desserts." He shifted again to face her. "I'm starting to think that wasn't a coincidence, Zelda. I suggest you start talking because he can't help you, and trust me, I'm itching to punish someone for what was done to my property."

The choice of words stung until I felt the purpose behind them. Kylan couldn't risk anyone knowing that I actually meant something to him. He needed to appear strong and infallible, not weakened by emotion.

"I…I…" She began to sob in earnest, her legs giving out beneath her, sending her to the ground.

"Vilheim told her to do it," Mikael said quietly. His heart was in his eyes as he looked only at Kylan. "I figured out that she let him in to destroy the girls, your harem, while we were gone. When—"

"You figured it out?" Kylan repeated.

"Yes. I found a bloody shirt in her room, and when I asked her about it, she broke down and told me what happened. I was going to tell you, but she called Vilheim. And…" Mikael trailed off with a wince, his expression breaking all over again. "H-he said if I helped them discredit you, he would make sure I ended up with you in exile. Rae was my task." His blue-green eyes met mine, apology radiating in them before he refocused on Kylan. "I'm sor—"

"Don't," Kylan growled, pain splintering our bond. He couldn't stand to hear it, not now, not while hiding his emotional frailty. "Is there anything you'd like to say, Vilheim?" He slowly turned to face the shorter male, releasing me in the process. While Kylan's exterior radiated calm, his fury burned between us. He wanted to kill.

"Would you like me to speak for you?" Kylan pressed, his eyebrows rising. "Because if I were to guess, I'd say you wanted to discredit my mental state so someone else would take over my territory and grant you more power. I mean, we both know you're nowhere near the appropriate age to inherit a region yourself, so that leaves having a new ruler as your only option. And that begs the question: which royal did you have in mind?"

"That's a hefty allegation," the Goddess said, moving to stand beside Kylan. "However, I find myself curious as well, Vilheim. And as you know, conspiring against a royal, let alone *your* royal, is punishable by proper death. I'm sure Kylan will want to extend that sentence as long as possible." She raised a blonde brow at him.

"Absolutely," Kylan confirmed.

She nodded. "As I thought. Vilheim, I suggest you speak quickly before Kylan removes your tongue for sport."

The gruesome image formed in my head, compliments of Kylan. His hand caught mine before I could wince, his touch forcing me to remain calm.

"He's insane," Vilheim said. "Surely you see that."

The Goddess's brows rose. "Thirty minutes ago, perhaps I would have considered that, but after everything I've seen tonight? It's quite clear to me that Kylan is very much alive and well." She placed her manicured hand on Kylan's arm and turned to him. "I mean, turning a consort into an *Erosita* just to catch the culprit? That's brilliant."

My blood ran cold at the insinuation. That couldn't—

"It worked marvelously, as you can see," he murmured, prickling my insides.

No. He established the connection by accident, not to fortify me as bait.

Kylan, tell me that isn't why you did this.

He ignored me, his eyes and focus completely on the Goddess.

She shook her head. "Really, Kylan, sometimes I think you play this game better than I do."

He gave her an indulgent smile. "Oh, come now, darling, you'll always be the queen on the chessboard."

She blushed, her lips curling. "I've forgotten how much fun you can be. I need to visit more often."

"You do," he agreed. "But first, Vilheim?"

My heartbeat was in my ears, rushing through my bloodstream. *Please tell—*

I need to focus, Raelyn, he replied, his mental voice brisk and to the point.

I swallowed. *Of course.*

Once this finished, we could talk. Then he would confirm that he hadn't just forged this bond between us to keep me alive for tonight. He'd opened his mind to me. I would have seen that, right?

Unless he knew how to hide it.

I frowned. Could he conceal details from me? No. He gave me unfettered access to his memories, his being, and I still had the ability to enter, except, it seemed cloudier now, as if he was indeed trying to keep something from me.

The truth of our bonding?

"I have nothing to say." Vilheim appeared unfazed by the threat of the two oldest vampires in existence standing before him.

"Nothing?" Kylan repeated. "Well, that's fascinating because we both know you didn't contrive this plan all on your own. You're not intelligent enough for that, which is why I never promoted you. So that leaves me wondering who put you up to it." He tapped his chin and glanced around the room, searching.

The Goddess eyed him speculatively, as one would an opponent.

Her bright green eyes flicked to mine, causing me to freeze. *Oh*… I wasn't even supposed to be watching. But now I couldn't move, my mind frozen. She tilted her head to the side, curiosity brightening her features. As if she hadn't seen a human in years.

So ancient.

So cold.

So… not a Goddess.

The instinct hit me suddenly, nearly knocking me to the floor. I'd feared this being since my first breath, but now I saw beneath the veneer.

She was just another vampire. Albeit an incredibly old one like Kylan, but nothing ethereal or Goddess-like about her.

"Robyn," Kylan called. "You know how much I adore watching you in action, darling. Would you mind helping me break Vilheim?"

The Goddess—*no, Lilith*—slowly shifted her focus to the crowd.

"Oh, sweetheart, I think you're far more advanced than little old me," the blonde royal replied. "And I much prefer to observe your work."

"Nonsense." He released my hand and held it out to her, his smile so enticing my heart stopped. The male was much too beautiful, and that look only made it worse. "Please. Join us. I insist." His tone held an edge that no one could dare defy, not even me.

Robyn set her drink aside and started through the crowd. "Well, I can't say no to that."

"Excellent. So I was thinking that, rather than removing his tongue, we could bleed him and feed his blood to the humans in the room for fun." Kylan glanced at Lilith. "Such a degrading act should force an old vampire like Vilheim to open up, yes?"

"To waste such precious blood on mortals?" She sounded outright disgusted. "Yes, absolutely. But we'll have to kill the humans afterward, you realize."

"Of course." Kylan waved a hand at that. "I assumed that was the after-party."

Lilith nodded. "Then yes, please, proceed."

Several members of the crowd stepped back as Kylan removed his suit jacket. He handed it to me without a word and began rolling his shirtsleeves. "Have a go, darling. I'll join you in a minute."

Robyn brushed her palms over her dress and stepped toward Vilheim. His gaze noticeably narrowed at her, the first crack in his exterior. She swiped her nails across his jacket, sending the buttons to the floor, and roughly pushed the fabric from his shoulders. He opened his mouth, and she slapped it shut so fast and hard that blood pooled on his lip.

Kylan, I warned.

I see it. But he pretended not to, his gaze on his sleeve.

Vilheim made to speak again, only to be hit even harder, Robyn's nails ripping the skin from his face.

I flinched from the brutality, shocked that a hand could cause that kind of damage. Everyone taking several steps back suddenly made sense, especially as Robyn went full force—on his face.

Lilith placed a hand on Kylan's bicep, her stance tense. She nodded once, some sort of exchange between them.

Vilheim started to fight back, his arms up in front of his face as he struck back at the crazed female.

It was all too fast for my mortal eyes, their movements quick, and words began to pour from the male's mouth in a foreign hiss.

I didn't understand any of it, the scene unfolding at a rate my brain couldn't comprehend.

Air whooshed around me, my head spinning as I collided with something hard. Cement circled me, unforgiving, my lips parting on a scream that was silenced by Kylan's lips. Brief. Enough to ground me, and then I was staring at his back.

What just happened?

My breath stuttered, my heart racing in my chest. I grabbed Kylan's sides, needing my balance, as he growled deep. "Did you just attack my *Erosita*, Robyn?" he demanded.

"What?" She sounded winded, but I couldn't see her. "No, of course not. She clearly moved in my path. You all saw it."

"No, what I saw was you going after another royal's property," Lilith replied, her voice cool. "It also appears as if you are trying to maim Vilheim to a point of incoherence."

"Sh-she iss," the male slurred. "Sh-she s-set me up."

Shocked whispers shattered the silence in the room, sending a chill down my spine. Now what?

I glanced around and found Zelda on the ground in a bow of supplication. Mikael stood beside her, flanked by two of Judith's guards while she stood watch over the quivering Zelda.

Kylan slowly pulled me around to his side, his jacket sprawled out on the ground and smattered in blood. I'd dropped it in the shuffle, not that he seemed all that saddened by it.

"Why, Robyn?" he demanded. "Why orchestrate all this?"

The blonde straightened, her lip bloody, her dress ruined. And she smiled. The look so unnervingly delusional that I questioned whether she'd truly gone mad.

"Oh, come on, Kylan. It wasn't that big of a deal. All I did was tell Vilheim that Jace would inherit your territory and promote him to sovereign—under my suggestion, of course. And really, he did most of the rest. The only thing I had to do was get someone on your plane to send those emails, which was easy after involving your little blood whore." She waved a theatrical hand at Mikael, who flinched as if she'd touched him.

"You attempted to discredit another royal out of boredom?" Lilith asked, her tone incredulous.

"Why not?" Robyn shrugged. "Honestly, it wasn't even that entertaining."

"Not that entertaining," Kylan replied. "You slaughtered my harem, Robyn, and nearly killed my *Erosita*."

She shrugged. "Humans are replaceable. You know that better than anyone. Don't be angry, love. It was all just for fun, and you figured me out. Easy."

"Don't be angry," he repeated as if tasting the words. "You tried to discredit my sanity, and you want me to be okay with it. Lilith, I think Robyn is the one here suffering from age insanity."

"It would appear that way," she agreed, her tone thoughtful. "I can't let this go unpunished, Robyn."

"Of course." The blonde shrugged. "Do your worst."

Her nonchalance sent a spear of rage through my gut. The woman didn't even care that she'd been caught and didn't fear retribution.

Because royals were rarely ever killed. The last one to face the punishment of death was Cam, for challenging the Goddess herself, and from what Kylan had implied, Cam might actually still be alive.

So no wonder Robyn wasn't afraid.

She knew they wouldn't hurt her permanently.

Lilith clasped her hands. "Robyn, you are hereby excommunicated from all events—including Blood Day—for a decade. That marks you ineligible to purchase or acquire new humans at any point until after your expulsion is complete."

The blonde royal's face went white. "A decade?"

"Hmm, yes, that does seem a bit short." Lilith turned to Kylan. "How long did it take your *Erosita* to recover from her injuries?"

"Seven days," he replied flatly.

"Yes, a much better number. Your term of excommunication will be seven decades, Robyn. Might I suggest you treat your current harem and house staff decently in the interim? It will be a while before you have a chance to replace them, and most will die of old age prior to that point."

Robyn sputtered, her full lips making soundless words of disagreement.

"Would you prefer a longer sentence?" Lilith asked, arching a brow.

"I… No, no, My Queen." Robyn bowed, her legs shaking beneath her. "I… I accept. Of course, I accept."

"Excellent. Then I suggest you leave, as this is a social event and you are no longer welcome here."

Robyn stilled, her body frozen in her curtsy.

"Now," Lilith snapped.

"Yes, of course." Robyn erected her spine, her blue eyes filled with mingling emotions—shock, hurt, fury. She flashed a look at Kylan too fast for me to read and disappeared by phasing out of the room.

"Well, this has been a fascinating evening," Lilith said, turning to Kylan, a bejeweled blade in her hand. "Shall I do the honors or would you like to?"

"Oh, allow me." He held out his palm. "Please."

"He is yours and has harmed your property." She gave him the knife and turned to address the crowd. "Vilheim has been accused of conspiring against his royal. While, yes, Robyn played him, he should have gone to Kylan to report the activity rather than playing along."

She paused as if waiting for questions.

No one uttered a word or a sound.

"Is there anyone here who objects to Vilheim, Vampire of Kylan Region, receiving the required punishment for this crime?"

Silence.

"Hearing no objections, you may proceed, Kylan."

"Thank you." He stepped away from my side to approach Vilheim, who was kneeling on the floor, two unnamed vampires on either side holding him there.

"Asshole," he grumbled.

"Is that your final word?" Kylan asked. "Because I'm not all that impressed."

Vilheim chanted something in a foreign language that had Kylan chuckling and shaking his head. "You were never worthy, Vilheim. And you never will be." He drove the blade into the man's chest quickly and efficiently, a collective hiss following the noise.

Proper death, I realized, shocked.

I'd never seen a vampire die. Didn't even know how they could die. And here Kylan had murdered the male in a room full of his brethren and lycans.

The body disintegrated into ash, littering the floor. Kylan used Mikael's jacket to wipe the razor edge clean before handing the item back to Lilith.

Was she the only one with that weapon?

Was it laced in a special substance or crafted specifically for this purpose?

"Excellent." She hid the weapon somewhere in her dress, the metal disappearing in a blink. "Now, I imagine you'll be handling your human problem, yes?"

"Well, there is one matter that remains unresolved."

She arched a brow. "Oh?"

"Yes. I'm officially one short in my region, a consequence not of my own making but of another royal's. And given the headache all of this has caused with my harem and the false implications against my character, I feel I'm entitled to a new resource."

I didn't quite follow what he meant, but the whispers in the room suggested everyone else did.

"I see," Lilith murmured, her gaze narrowing. "We have rules for a reason, and I'm not sure this incident provides justification to break them, Kylan."

"A life for a life," someone said from the audience. "It does seem justified in this scenario. Vilheim is dead. Kylan requires a new recruit to uphold the balance in his territory. Even numbers and all that."

Lilith glanced in the direction of the speaker. "Are you seconding his request, Jace?"

"I am. I agree that it's only fair given everything he's been through these last few months." Jace stepped forward with a champagne flute of blood, his hand tucked in his pocket, the picture of nonchalance. "I may not care for the man, but I'm inclined to agree with him on this."

More whispers sounded, the room filling with noise and speculation.

"He's right." The low growl in the voice suggested the words were from a lycan.

"Walter?" Lilith appeared astonished. "You agree as well?"

"I do. It's what I would require if in his shoes."

"Me too," another said.

Several more began to speak up, all agreeing to the terms, and continued until the chatter reached a level Lilith could no longer bear.

"Enough," she said, her command silencing the room.

Kylan stood before her, his expression blank, his mind even blanker. I had no idea what he was thinking because he'd blocked me again. Not entirely, but just enough to keep me from hearing his plans.

I'd been so overwhelmed by my surroundings and the chaos that I hadn't noticed. My heart gave a subtle pang at being pushed away, but I had to believe it was for him to better focus. He'd probably been too inundated with my concerns and confusion to focus.

Yes, that has to be it.

Lilith sighed. "The Immortal Cup is coming to a close, Kylan. I can't give you any of those recruits, as we're already down to two, but given the outcry of support, I could make a concession for next year."

My heart stopped. *Already down to two? Was Silas one of them?*

"Actually, I already have a human in mind," Kylan said smoothly, distracting me from my thoughts.

"You do?" Lilith asked, raising a brow. "Dare I ask which one?"

He smiled. "Yes." He held out a hand for me. "Raelyn."

Chapter Thirty-One

RAE

KYLAN'S HAND WAVERED BEFORE MY EYES.

Had he just suggested…?

No.

I'd misunderstood.

There was no way he meant—

"Your *Erosita*?" Lilith asked, sounding even more shocked than I felt. "No, absolutely not."

"Why not?" he countered, dropping his hand to his side. "She was one of the top twelve candidates designated for the Immortal Cup. Her test scores are phenomenal. She's gorgeous, intelligent, and played her part in my game perfectly to catch my betrayers. I cannot imagine a more suitable candidate for immortality."

"She's defiant," Lilith said, glancing at me. "Even now, she's staring directly at me."

"Because she was born not to be a human but to be a vampire. My vampire."

The murmurs started again, several of them rising in assent, while my heart thudded loudly in my ears.

Kylan, I breathed.

But he remained closed, his attention solely on Lilith.

"Darius," Jace murmured, his focus on the drink in his hand as he swirled the contents. "You became rather familiar with Raelyn over the last week or two, yes?"

The vampire in question smirked. "I did. Kylan failed to remark on her oral abilities in the bedroom, which are a solid ten, for anyone who might be curious."

"So good enough to join our ranks?" Jace asked.

Darius shrugged. "She could use a little refining around the edges, but I imagine Kylan is up to the task. He worked wonders on my Juliet."

All lies. We spent the last week relaxing. Darius's relationship with Juliet was unlike one I'd ever witnessed, his adoration for her obvious. And Kylan hadn't laid a hand on her, too busy plotting for tonight and making sure I was comfortable.

But we never reviewed this part of the plan.

Several around the room voiced their consent, one of them even saying to give Kylan what he wanted because he'd earned it.

Lilith took my measure again, the curl in her lip suggesting she found me lacking.

She would never approve.

And I didn't even know if I wanted her to, not anymore.

Wouldn't becoming a vampire mean giving up my bond to Kylan?

It hit me then, the reason he was doing this.

You're giving me a way out. The gift of immortality without tying me to him forever. *Kylan…*

"She will be my responsibility, and I promise you'll be impressed by the next Blood Day."

She tore her gaze away from me and lifted her eyebrows. "You're proposing to make her yourself?"

"I am."

"Your first progeny," she said, sounding flabbergasted. "I never thought I'd see the day, Kylan, let alone see you waste it on someone so unworthy."

"You forget that I can see inside her mind through the bond. Trust me when I say there is no one worthier of this honor than Raelyn." The veracity of his proclamation sang through our connection, his pride in me shattering the temporary barriers he'd put up before.

He was not only giving me a way out but also providing us with the opportunity to be with each other out of desire, not necessity.

Because I wouldn't rely on him for immortality.

Which meant he'd have to work to keep my interest.

And he wanted to work for it.

How had he kept this from me? Looking in his mind now, I knew this was always part of his plan—to demand compensation for his loss in the form of my eternal life.

I didn't know what to say.

All I could do was gape at him.

"All right," Lilith murmured. "If that is your request, consider it granted."

"Thank you." He inclined his head.

"But I expect to see considerable improvement the next time I see her."

"Of course," he replied. "Disciplining Raelyn is one of my favorite pastimes." His amusement rolled over me, but I was still too shocked to respond or even mentally roll my eyes.

He wants to turn me.

To become my maker.

"Now, there is the small matter of what to do with the rest of you," he said, facing Angelica first. He crouched to remove some of the chains from her naked body. "You are badly in need of some blood."

Her hollow eyes glared up at him. "You knew," she growled.

"I did, but you still failed me, Angelica. I told you to guard Raelyn, and you left her." He ripped more of the chains off of her, his strength showing in each pull as he freed her from the restraints. "When I tell you to do something, it carries weight over everyone else. Do you understand?"

She swallowed, her body shuddering as he removed the last of the metal by snapping the shackles off her ankles with his bare hands. "Y-yes, Your Highness."

"Good. Then consider your punishment complete." He looked up at Mikael, his expression cruel. "Can I offer you a drink, Angelica?"

Mikael's lips parted, his eyes tearing up again. He wore the look of a broken man, a lover abandoned and destroyed.

My heart ached for him.

Even after everything he'd done to me, I couldn't help the catch in my breath.

All he ever wanted was Kylan.

And he'd never have him.

"Kneel," Kylan demanded.

Mikael dropped to the ground, his head falling. He wasn't even going to beg. He just knew.

A pang shot through me, the source of it Kylan. His struggle hurt my heart more, his mind not knowing what to do. To kill him quickly, to extend the pain, to slaughter him for the room… to let him live.

"Give her your wrist." His voice never wavered, but inside, the act was killing him.

You don't have to kill him, I whispered. *Not to avenge me.*

What would I do with him? he asked softly. *Lock him up until he dies?*

Can you give him to someone?

He deserves a worse fate, Raelyn.

I know, but he did it because he loves you.

Mikael whimpered as Angelica pierced his vein, her ravenous mouth sucking and pulling for the sustenance her young vampire body required to survive. She was half-starved and faced with a blood virgin. His essence was addictive to even the oldest of vampires. Against her, he stood no chance. She'd devour him unless Kylan stopped her, and Mikael knew it.

Kylan stood, ignoring the scene despite his aching heart, and focused on Zelda with a sadistic smile. "Cherise," he called.

"Your Highness," she replied, practically running forward to meet him, hope in her gaze. "You've pleased me greatly with your improvement. We'll discuss promotional opportunities later, but for now, I need you to handle that one for me." He pointed to Zelda. "She's a former chef. Perhaps she can help you create something featuring her blood."

My stomach rolled at the notion. *Kylan…*

She deserves worse. Be thankful I won't be the one killing her.

"Of course, My Prince," Cherise replied, her lips curling. "I'll be happy to handle that for you."

"Thank you. Be sure to drain her completely. I no longer have use for her, and she's unemployable in this region."

"I understand." Cherise bowed and grabbed Zelda by the hair. "Come along, former chef."

He looked at Judith and his security team before finally returning to a fading Mikael. His mind rioted between right and wrong, finishing it and allowing forgiveness.

He really did care about Mikael.

I could see it inside his soul. It wasn't love, but a deep friendship established over a decade.

His mental sigh was heavy and tired. "Enough, Angelica," he said, pulling her away from Mikael. She only fought for a second before realizing who had tugged her away, and she scrambled backward, wiping her bloody mouth. "Judith, please take Mikael to my quarters. I'll finish this on my own time."

"I'll prepare him for you, My Prince." She stepped forward and lifted him with ease.

Kylan nodded and glanced around the party. "Well, I hope I've provided an eventful evening for you all."

A few chuckles answered him, as well as a shake of the head from Lilith. "Never a dull moment in your company, Kylan."

"It's the only way to live." He smiled at everyone, but inside, his heart was fracturing at the task he had before him, and it hurt me to hear his pain. "Everyone, enjoy yourselves. Eat. Drink. Be merry. And of course, revel in my hospitality. It might be the last party I host for a while." He held up his hands, taking a theatrical bow. "I have a few things to see to, including an *Erosita* to fuck one last time, so I'll leave you all to it."

Lilith raised her glass, as did Jace and Darius.

Kylan took my hand and pulled me past them, his steps slow as he murmured farewells to guests who shifted into our path. When we finally ascended the stairs and entered the elevator, he blew out a long breath and brushed his fingers through his hair.

"Just give me a minute before you say anything," he said, hitting the down button to take us to the reception area.

Rather than reply or point out that I still didn't know what to say, I wrapped my arms around him.

He didn't move at first, his surprise slipping through the bond. Then he returned the hug, his face falling to my neck to bury against my skin.

I'm here, I whispered. *You're not alone.*

He shuddered and tightened his hold. *What was my life before you?*

Boring? I suggested. *Complacent? Easier?*

He chuckled in my mind. *Boring sounds right.* He kissed my pulse and released me as the doors opened. Maeve stood waiting for us in the lobby, handing Kylan his keys. "Excellent. Thank you. I have a final task for you, if you don't mind."

"Of course, My Prince."

"Inform everyone that I've promoted you and Cherise to Tremayne's old position. One of you can maintain K Hotel here, while the other can take over Tremayne Tower, but just be sure to rename it. I'll maintain the property in Lilith City. And feel free to split the other properties appropriately between yourselves."

Her mouth fell open. "B-but, Your Highness—"

"You didn't apply, I know. But I am tired of promoting old vampires to positions of power they bear no respect for. It makes much more sense to hire someone who actually understands and appreciates the business, which clearly you and Cherise do. She just needed a subtle reminder, is all."

Tears filled the woman's eyes, her lips curling into a breathtaking smile. "I don't know what to say."

"Start by saying you won't disappoint me, and we'll go from there."

"I won't disappoint you," she promised, her exhilaration palpable. "Thank you, Your Highness. Thank you."

He nodded, his palm going to my lower back. "Be sure to tell the others for me, including Cherise, and let me know who is going where."

"Of course. Yes." She actually bounced on her heels. "Forgive me, I'm—"

"Excited, I know. Enjoy your evening, Maeve. You've earned this." He pushed me forward, his steps quick as we passed several humans bowing in the reception area.

After situating ourselves in the car, I turned to him. "That was very kind of you."

He pulled out onto the street. "It was practical, Raelyn."

"It was nice," I corrected. "You're not nearly as formidable and cruel as you long for everyone to believe, you know."

He snorted. "Don't let anyone else hear you say that."

"Don't worry." I patted his thigh and relaxed in my seat. "It'll be our little secret."

He glanced at me sideways. "I think we're going to share a lot of those, Raelyn."

Chapter Thirty-Two

KYLAN

"ARE YOU SURE THIS IS WHAT YOU WANT TO DO?" Jace asked, his expression unreadable. He'd left the party early with Darius and Juliet and met me at my estate, just as I requested.

I nodded. "Yes, I'm sure." There was no other alternative.

"He doesn't deserve your kindness," Darius said, leaning against the doorway to my office.

"Is it really kind?" I asked as I signed the last of the documents.

He shrugged. "It would be to some."

Perhaps. I picked up the file, eyeing them both. "I can't kill him," I admitted. "As much as I know I should…"

"You care," Jace finished. "Our kind is obsessed with calling it a weakness, but it's not. It's what links us to humanity and keeps us sane."

"I suppose that's one way to look at it," I murmured, handing the file to Jace. "See that he's taken care of properly, please."

My royal counterpart nodded. "Luka will make sure he lives out his days untouched."

"In lycan territory," I said, still confused by his suggested placement.

"Maybe you should visit sometime," Jace murmured cryptically. "You may find something interesting there."

"Why do I feel like I'm being initiated into something?" I asked, wary.

"Because you are," Jace replied, holding out his hand. "You're not alone in your suspicions, Kylan."

I pressed my palm to his. "Regarding?"

"Everything." We shook once, then he released me. "I'll be in touch soon with more details. Until then, I'll handle your blood virgin problem the way you've requested."

"Unharmed," I repeated.

"I've already given you my word. He'll be fine. Just lonely." Jace started toward the door but paused. "Are you really going to turn Raelyn?"

"If that's what she wants, yes."

"Is it what you want?" he asked as he stepped through the threshold. "Be honest with her, Kylan. I hear that's what relationships are founded upon."

Darius snorted. "As if he knows a damn thing about women."

"He seems pretty familiar with them." Jace usually surrounded himself with them, always indulging. Though, the last few trips, he'd been alone. Odd for him.

"Not when it comes to feelings of the heart," Darius replied, following his superior. "Good luck with Raelyn. Follow your instincts. You might find your heart."

He disappeared while I gaped after him.

What horrible advice. My instincts when it came to Raelyn were to lock her in my room and never let anyone see her again.

Which was exactly where I left her—to shower off the evening's affairs and relax.

I hit Send on the email to my constituents, confirming Tremayne's replacements, and closed my tablet.

This was the night that never ends, which would continue if Raelyn took me up on my proposal.

She sat waiting for me on the bed in a towel, her damp hair falling over her exposed skin. Her blue eyes met mine, emotion swirling in their depths. "I heard what you did to Mikael."

I paused in front of her, suddenly concerned that she might not approve. "He couldn't stay here."

"I know."

"And I couldn't kill him." Even if he did deserve it. I just couldn't bring myself to finish it, not after our last eleven years together. He'd loved me, which was his own fault, but also kind of mine. Subjecting him to a life of loneliness seemed punishment enough.

Raelyn's lips curled into a sad smile. "You made the right choice, Kylan. As hard as it was for you, I get it."

"So you're not mad at me?"

She snorted, climbing to her knees to place herself at eye level with me, and grabbed my shoulders. "I can't fault you for showing compassion." She brushed her lips over mine, her willing kiss the best reward. We'd been chastely intimate over the last week due to her healing, the complete opposite of what my body craved, but what hers required.

I traced the seam of her mouth with my tongue, requesting entry, and pushed inside. She accepted the invasion with a moan, her arms sliding around my neck. I palmed her ass, pulling her up against me, needing more.

It'd been a long fucking night.

I needed to lose myself just for a moment, to let the sensations take over, to just enjoy Raelyn. Her hypnotic touch. Her citrusy scent. The caress of her mind against mine. The feel of her bare skin. Her taste.

"Fuck," I whispered, unable to stop myself from taking more of her. I deepened our kiss, taking her the way I craved, mapping every inch of her mouth with my tongue. So fucking addictive. So gorgeous. So *mine*.

I threaded my fingers in her damp strands, holding her to me as if she might disappear. Once I turned her, she could. But I needed her to have that option, to be my equal in every way except age, or this relationship would always be one-sided. I wanted her to choose me.

My heart hammered in my chest.

Just one more time.

As mine.

That's all I needed. Then I could set her free if that's what she decided.

But for tonight, I would have her completely.

"Raelyn," I whispered. "I need—"

"Yes," she replied, already seeing my thoughts. "A thousand times yes, Kylan. Take me. Keep me. *Fuck* me."

I shuddered against her, my cock already hard.

She unbuckled my pants without asking, her touch knowing, her skill impressive. I tossed her towel to the floor, my lips falling to her neck and lower to her gorgeous breasts. Ripe and beautiful with perky little nipples. I sucked one into my mouth, causing her to arch her back on a moan while she unzipped my trousers.

I switched to her other rosy bud, licking and nipping.

"You're perfect, Raelyn," I praised. "Everything about you is just so damn perfect." I meant what I said to Lilith earlier. I couldn't imagine a more qualified candidate for immortality.

She pushed the fabric down my hips and started on my dress shirt. By the third button, her patience was gone and she ripped the rest of them off by tugging on the fabric. I shrugged out of the remains, leaving me shirtless before her.

"Pants. Off." They were stuck around my thighs.

I smirked. "Are you commanding me?"

"Yes, I am."

I chuckled while obeying her. "Lie on the bed, princess. Legs spread. I want to see how wet you are for me."

She groaned, her muscles clenching in response. The sweet aroma of her arousal welcomed me home, my body aching to join with hers.

No one had ever made me feel this way—so complete. As if I could lose myself forever in her arms.

I never wanted it to end.

Never wanted to say goodbye.

My clothing disappeared to the floor as she positioned herself the way I desired, her pussy glistening in wait. I kissed her damp lips, needing to taste her. My tongue dipped inside her, coating my taste buds with her unique flavor.

"Fuck, Raelyn. You have the prettiest cunt." I nibbled her clit and nuzzled the soft red curls on her mound. She'd stopped shaving at my request but continued to keep herself groomed. I kissed her everywhere, worshiping her, cherishing every inch, and memorizing her intimately.

"Kylan," she growled, her fingers in my hair, pulling. "I need more."

"Oh, so do I," I whispered. "So do I."

A night.

A month.

A year.

A decade.

An eternity.

It would never be enough.

I gave up trying to understand it. Stopped trying to fight it. And just embraced it.

Because fuck if I had the energy to continue disputing these feelings. It was never about the bond, but about Raelyn.

It was always her.

That fire.

Her spirit.

Her heart.

I kissed a path up her body, adoring every inch, and ignoring my cock's urge to flip her over and fuck her from behind.

This had to be different. Special. *Real.*

I wanted to make love to her. Something I'd never done with anyone, had never seen the point of doing, but with Raelyn, she deserved it and so much more. And I wanted to experience that with her. To honor her in a manner unlike any other, to revere her and love her.

"Raelyn," I breathed against her lips, my hips settling between hers. "You've changed me irrevocably." I slid inside her, my dick begging me to take her hard while my heart compelled me to keep it slow.

She pushed up against me, forcing me deeper. "You've destroyed me for anyone else," she whispered. "You've taken every part of me and made it yours."

"Ah, but, Raelyn, I haven't." After all the taunts of doing otherwise, it was never her mind or her heart or her soul that I captured. "It's you who owns me, sweetheart. Every piece of me exists inside you and no one else."

I kissed her softly, rocking into her oh-so slowly, savoring the feel of her, the way her walls clamped down around my shaft, the way she moaned every time I finished a thrust.

"Kylan." Her icy blue eyes glistened, her cheeks flushed. "Will it hurt?"

"Turning?" I asked, my lips tracing hers. "No, sweetheart." It'd been ages since my rebirth, but I showed her the pieces I remembered. The deep sleep, waking to new sensations, the initial thirst.

"Will we lose this connection?" she breathed, her body arched beneath mine as she sought the pleasure she craved.

I kissed her jaw, her neck, nibbling a path to her ear, and told her the truth. "I don't know what will happen." My maker had died shortly after my rebirth. "We'll still be linked, but differently."

"Will I still be yours, Kylan?" she asked softly, her nails digging into my shoulders. "Tell me I'll still be yours."

"A demand?" I teased, nipping her pulse and shoving my cock deep inside her. She moaned in response, her pussy clenching around me. "Mmm, keep doing that and I might accept forever."

"Kylan," she growled, scratching my back, marking me in the most delicious fashion.

"Again."

"Agree to stay with me," she countered, her legs tightening around my waist. "Tell me I'll be yours."

I pushed into her again, hard and fast, and smiled when she gasped my name. "I love that sound." I kissed her as I repeated the action, limbs trembling, her orgasm mounting. It wouldn't take long.

I swiveled my hips in a way I knew she'd enjoy, her responding cry confirming it.

My name left her lips on a curse, her mind rebelling as her body begged for more. She wanted a response almost as badly as she wanted to come.

"You're soaking my cock," I whispered. "Possessing every inch of me with your pretty cunt." I grabbed her hips, angling her upward to go even deeper and drive her wild. Her heels dug into my back, her skin vibrating with need. "Scream my name, Raelyn. I want everyone to hear you claiming me as yours."

The words sent her over the edge, her mouth obeying my command.

With each syllable, repeated over and over again, I felt her ownership over me solidify and grow, consuming me from the inside out.

She might be mine, but I was most definitely hers.

In all ways.

My climax hit, spilling into her with an impact I felt down to my very soul. It almost hurt, so intense, so complete, so fucking amazing. She milked me dry, squeezing out every last drop as I shook above her.

I'd never felt this empty, this replete, and yet full, in my entire life.

Love.

Devotion.

Energy.

Flowing openly, cocooning us in this private moment meant only for mates. My heart belonged to her. My spirit. My mind. I didn't hold anything back, allowing her to feel the full weight of everything I owned and giving it to her for safekeeping.

"Now," she whispered, melting into me. "I want to do it now."

"The turning?"

"Yes. Make me yours. Your equal. Your proper mate. Please, Kylan. It's what I want, what I *need*." Her thoughts confirmed it, her decision made. But not because she desired freedom or a way to escape me.

Raelyn desired immortality to be with me always as my partner.

I couldn't imagine a more deserving female.

She truly wanted this, always had.

And I wanted it for her.

It was the one gift I could give her, the one way to reward her for everything she'd given me.

My Raelyn.

My heart.

My mate.

I kissed a path to her neck, my incisors already aching for one last feed. It wouldn't be the same when she turned; it would be better. Sinking deep, I began to drink, her essence coating my throat as she moaned beneath me, coming again from the impact.

Fuck, it felt good around my cock, still lodged within her.

"Kylan," she chanted, her nails embedded in my skin. "Oh, Kylan."

Keep moaning my name like that and I'll be forced to stop and fuck you again.

She groaned, her mental voice nearly incoherent from the onslaught of pleasure I was unleashing on her bloodstream.

I continued drinking, monitoring her heart rate, waiting for the right moment.

Her connection to my immortality prolonged it, her soul already pulling on mine while she continued to squirm.

But eventually, it dimmed.

Her screams quieting to moans.

Whimpers.

Raelyn's skin cooled, her heart slowing.

I pulled away to see her partly conscious, her eyes drooping. This was the crucial moment where the soul began to slip away from a mortal, dancing with death.

I bit my wrist, placing it at her mouth, forcing my life essence over her tongue.

She didn't react at first, her sleep-induced mind fogged from understanding what was needed. But her body began to take over, her instincts rushing to the surface as she latched onto the life-reviving liquid, taking her fill.

Seconds turned into minutes, my body nearly hollow. I took my wrist away,

Raelyn's cry of disappointment making me chuckle darkly. "You'll have more later, baby. But for now…" I kissed her softly, hating what I had to do next.

This was the part that might hurt a little.

Temporarily.

I covered her mouth completely and pinched her nose.

Some preferred a bullet. Others strangulation. The occasional broken neck.

But I couldn't do any of those things, not with her.

I closed my eyes, my body shaking with the effort of having to suffocate her. To stop her heart completely.

It's okay, she whispered.

It's not, I replied. *But it will be.*

I trust you.

Those three words brought tears to my eyes, because she did. She really did. And I trusted her too. Something I never thought would be possible with another, but it was with her.

She drew her palm over my lower back, a final brush before letting it fall to her side. A tear fell from my eye as she began to convulse, her body fighting despite her mind's acceptance.

Panic began to well within her, the last stage of her death where reason no longer existed.

And then she went still.

Her heartbeat slowing.

Slowing.

Silent.

I gave it a final moment before releasing her, my forehead against hers. "Sweet dreams, Raelyn."

Chapter Thirty-Three

RAE

DARKNESS ENGULFED ME, leaving me blind. Trapped. Alone.

Was this a dream?

A nightmare?

Reality?

I pushed against the hard surface beneath me, beside me, in front of me. It didn't budge.

Kylan? I could feel him nearby, his thoughts amused. *Kylan, what's going on?*

You can do better than that, princess. Unless you're still a lamb?

His taunt had my lips curling downward. *What are you talking about?*

Shuffling had me looking left, the sound close. Feet crunching over snow. Kylan's steps. His pants stretched as he crouched above, providing me with the perfect image of where to find him, just not how.

What is this?

A coffin. Push it open.

It won't move.

"Because you've barely tried. Give it another go," he encouraged out loud, his voice close.

I placed my palms on the wood above me and gave it a shove. The door creaked open, revealing a sliver of moonlight. Another push opened the casket completely, allowing snow and dirt inside.

I jumped out of it, my bare feet hitting the cold earth with far more ease than I anticipated.

Kylan's eyebrows popped up, his expression one of surprise. "Well, that was impressive for a newbie." He stood, in his arms clothing and shoes. "As much as it pains me to say it, would you like something to wear?"

I spun around, the shifting of a paw alerting me to our audience.

Wolves.

Six of them.

All lounging by the frozen pond, observing us.

"Why am I outside?" I asked, eyeing the glistening ice dangling from the frozen trees. The frosty bite to the wind. And wow, the moon practically glittered.

This was amazing.

I knelt, my fingers raking through the crystallized water on the ground. *Snow*, I marveled, as if seeing it for the first time all over again. *Wow…*

Kylan's amusement warmed my cooling skin, his enjoyment at watching me react to my new senses palpable.

Wait… "I can still hear you," I said, standing again, my feet barely acknowledging the cold. "And feel you."

"Yes," he murmured, moving toward me. "I'm not aware of anyone having that ability between maker and progeny but suspect it's related to our mated souls. I could sense you throughout your rebirth as if it were happening to me."

I tried to recall how I'd felt, my mind hazy. "It's all so… obscure." He bit me. Suffocated me, maybe. His blood in my mouth. I shook my head, the entire experience a blur. "I don't really remember."

"That's typical. You'll find aspects of your mortal life fading as well, as you are officially transcended to your immortal life." He handed me pants that I pulled on and a sweater, then socks and boots. I only dressed out of habit, not really feeling the need despite the cold weather.

"But why am I outside?" I asked again, still confused by that part.

"The final stage of the process is being one with the earth." He pulled a hat over my head and kissed my nose. "I thought you might prefer to wake here, and I already had a nook in the ground anyway."

I raised my brows. "Why?"

He shrugged. "Every vampire has hiding places, Raelyn. Now you can share this one with me because no one knows it exists." He closed the box, the top covered in grass, and brushed snow over the area to blend it with the surrounding landscape.

I recognized the log behind it, my lips parting. "That's where we first…"

"Yes." His lips twitched. "All the more fitting for your resurrection site, in my opinion."

I smiled and shook my head. "You have so many layers, Kylan."

"Do I?" He stalked over to me and grabbed my hips, pulling me against him. "You must be starved, love."

My brow furrowed. "Actually, I don't feel hungry at all."

"Really? Most freshlings wake up starved." He brushed his lips over mine. "Let's head back to the house. Maybe the scent of blood will trigger your appetite."

I scrunched my nose, the image of biting a human not appealing. But of course, that's how I would feed. I just hadn't really considered the reality of it until now.

"Okay," I replied, another realization settling over me and sending a blast of adrenaline through my blood. "I'll race you."

He chuckled. "Raelyn, you're a baby vampire. Let's take this one step at a time."

My eyebrows rose. "Are you saying I can't keep up?"

"I'm over five thousand years old. I know you can't."

"Then you won't mind racing me." I took a step back, feeling more energized than, well, ever. "Unless you're afraid."

"The only fear I have is of you hurting yourself, princess. You're immortal, not unbreakable. Not yet, anyway."

"I feel pretty durable." Strong, even. And fast. A part of me wanted to sprint just to see what I could do. I'd never felt so alive, so free, so exultant.

"Most vampires wake up weak and starving for blood." He tilted his head, his gaze curious. "I don't sense any hunger in you."

"Because I'm not hungry." At all. I just wanted to run, to feel the elements against my skin, to fly.

"All right, darling. I'll race you, only to see if it inspires your appetite and because I can feel your eagerness." He nipped my bottom lip hard enough to bleed and lapped at the wound. "Still delicious."

I narrowed my gaze. "I can do that back now."

"You can try," he taunted. "Catch me and I'll let you." He released me. "I'll even give you a head start." He gestured to the path. "You know the way."

Pure cocky male gazed at me, his eyebrow arched in challenge.

"Can I bite you wherever I want when I win?"

He smirked, his expression all confidence. "Sure, princess. And when you lose, I'll bite you wherever I want."

I shivered, liking the sound of that. "Okay."

"Go."

I blew him a kiss and started running, my legs carrying me over the snow with ease—unlike the first time I tried this.

You'll have to do a lot better than that. His taunt radiated through me, urging me to push myself harder. *Remember, love. You're not human anymore.*

He opened up his mind, pushing experience and knowledge through our bond. It set my blood on fire, exciting my nerves and my very being.

So much power. Strength. Agility.

And I possessed all of those traits now.

His blood was my blood.

His soul married to mine.

Our hearts beating as one.

I closed my eyes as I moved, my senses taking over, my body shifting and moving down the path on muscle memory alone—*his* muscle memory.

It was exhilarating.

Staggering.

Beautiful.

My hand found the back door mere seconds before Kylan appeared, his expression one of wonder.

"You phased," he breathed, looking me over. "You actually fucking phased."

I stared up at him, confused. "Uh, yeah." I supposed I did. It felt incredible, as if I were flying over the land but without my feet touching the ground. "Let's do it again."

He grabbed my shoulders before I could take off, his eyes holding mine. "Raelyn, only the oldest vampires can phase. It took me almost two thousand years to acquire that ability."

My lips parted. "What?"

"Exactly." He took my measure in full, his thoughts running through a myriad of scenarios at once. I followed them all, taking in every detail without blinking. "Our bond seems to be giving you my level of ability," he summarized out loud. "I've never heard of anything like this, but it's the only conclusion that makes sense."

"No one has ever turned their *Erosita* before?"

"Not that I'm aware of, no." He cupped my cheek. "You're one of a kind, Raelyn."

"Rae," I corrected, smiling. "Now that I'm a vampire, I can choose my name."

His gaze glittered in response, darkness brewing inside him. Possession, adoration, domination, all poured out of him, swathing me in a mental blanket that was all Kylan. "You will forever be my Raelyn, but if you prefer others to call you Rae, that is your choice."

I went onto my toes to press my lips to his. "I'll always be your Raelyn," I agreed. "But to everyone else, I'll be Rae." It felt intimate to grant him sole use of the name—the one he gifted me—while regulating everyone else to the shortened version. "I'm still yours, Kylan. For as long as you'll have me."

"Careful, sweetheart," he whispered against my mouth. "Because I'll keep you forever if you allow me."

"I hope you do." And I meant it. "But only if I get to keep you too."

"Oh, Raelyn, when will you understand?" He pressed me up against the door, his mouth capturing mine in a domineering kiss that took my breath away. "You already own me, love. Always. Forever. Completely."

I shuddered against him, his words searing my being.

"You're inside me, Raelyn. You've been there since the moment I first saw you, that first defiant bite solidifying my fate." Both his hands were on my face, holding me to him, his hips pinning mine against the hard surface behind me. "My soul chose you, my mate, my partner, and my blood married yours. I'll never desire another, not when it'll jeopardize what we share, not when I have you in my bed every night. What would be the point?"

The sincerity in his voice rivaled the words in his mind, the promises he left unsaid, the emotions he reserved only for us. He gifted me immortality to grant me freedom, the ability to choose, because he wanted a partner at his side in life, not a servant. That was his biggest secret of all, the one he would never admit to the world because it wasn't necessary. I knew and that's all that mattered.

Kylan never desired a lamb.

He craved a fighter.

Me.

And he'd do everything in his power to prove himself worthy of my love. Like granting me immortality even while knowing it provided me the tools to escape him.

Not that I ever would.

"You're inside me too," I whispered. "I want this—you—Kylan."

He kissed me, his lips worshiping mine, his tongue a familiar presence in my mouth. I never wanted this to end, and it didn't have to.

We'd battle the new world together.

With me by his side.

As an equal.

His mate.

"For eternity," he vowed.

"Yes." I wrapped my legs around his waist as he lifted me into the air. "Make me yours again, Kylan."

"Oh, Raelyn." He nibbled my lip, his nose touching mine. "Now that's a command I'll accept."

Amusement warmed my chest. "Good. Expect it often."

"Only if you anticipate mine in return." He carried me inside, directly up to our room. "I want these clothes off and you on the bed. Now."

"Still as dominant as ever."

"That part will never change." He nipped my bottom lip. "Now obey before I start disrobing you myself."

"You still owe me a bite," I reminded him, my feet touching the floor.

"I do. You can bite me when you're naked."

I smiled. "Still making the rules." Not that I would have it any other way.

"Always, little lamb."

"I'm not a lamb anymore."

He tossed off my hat and threaded his fingers through my hair, yanking me to him. "No, sweetheart, you're not. You're my Raelyn."

"Then you're my Kylan."

"'Til death do us part," he teased. "Or so the vows go."

"Which means you're stuck with me for a very long time." I started unbuttoning my pants while he held me before him. "I should warn you: I'm rather defiant."

"Yeah?"

"Yeah." I grabbed his sides, leaving my jeans loose at my waist.

"Prove it."

I lifted to press my mouth to his while holding his gaze. And tugged his bottom lip between my teeth.

Biting down.

Hard.

Claiming him.

My mate.

My royal vampire.

My Kylan.

Epilogue

Rae

One Month Later...

KYLAN HAD A SURPRISE FOR ME, something he kept hidden in his mind behind a carefully crafted wall. He refused to give me any details other than to say all would be revealed at tonight's event.

A month of coaching and I still wasn't prepared for this.

I constantly wanted to drop my gaze.

To hide.

To stand in a corner.

To be invisible.

But on Kylan's arm, none of those actions were an option. He introduced me to everyone as Rae, his new progeny and lover, and they all greeted me with unfettered curiosity in their gazes.

Kylan had declined to take a harem this year, stating he didn't require any new members. That only added to everyone's interest.

A royal with no harem, just a vampire mate.

Very few in his position lived such an existence, the alpha of Majestic Clan being one of them. I'd met Luka and his mate, Mira, earlier this evening. We were at some sort of lycan bonding ceremony. The Clemente Clan Alpha, Walter, was officially stepping down and handing the reins to his son, Edon.

"May I present my progeny, Rae," Kylan said, introducing me to yet another alpha. Niko of the Ernest Clan. Two females flanked him, one I recognized as his mate, the other a female with dark eyes and dark hair that matched his own.

"Lovely to meet you, Rae," Niko murmured, taking my hand and kissing it a little too suggestively.

Isn't that his mate? I asked.

Cora, yes. He's not known for being faithful.

Clearly. I forced a smile while carefully removing my palm from his and threading my arm through Kylan's. "Nice to meet you as well."

"My mate, Cora, and our daughter, Luna," he said gesturing to the female behind him.

Luna has been promised to Edon, Kylan murmured.

She doesn't look very thrilled about that.

An alpha female promised to an alpha male? No. It's a match made in hell, but she has no choice. "I assume you're looking forward to the festivities this evening," Kylan said out loud.

"Yes, very much. The Clementes have agreed to take Luna tonight to help acquaint her with their customs."

Luna flinched with her father's casual words, her lips curling downward even more.

She's a lycan, though. Doesn't she have certain rights?

Oh, sweetheart, there is so much about this world you don't yet know. "When is the actual mating ceremony?" he asked, feigning interest.

"Next full moon." Niko sounded proud. His daughter appeared ready to throw up. Cora grabbed Luna's hand and gave it a squeeze, whether in reprimand or support, I couldn't tell. The mated female wore an unreadable expression.

"Perhaps we'll attend," Kylan murmured. "I'm introducing Rae to all aspects of society. She may find that particular ritual fascinating."

Niko's lips curled, his brown eyes darkening with lust. "Yes, it can be quite arousing."

That sounds like an affair I'd rather skip, I noted dryly.

You may change your mind in about five minutes. "Speaking of arousing, I'm in need of a proper drink. Walter mentioned a feeding room?"

"Yes, in the main quarters, I believe." Niko gestured to the oversized lodge beside us, the one where most of the guests were staying.

The Clemente Clan estate was very different from our home. Still surrounded by trees, but a lot warmer, and all the homes had a woodsy feel rather than the clean, sharp architecture of Kylan City.

"Ah, yes, thank you." Kylan shook Niko's hand. "I'm sure we'll see you again very soon."

I really hope not, I thought while saying, "Nice to meet you all."

Luna gave me a cynical look while her mother merely nodded once, expressionless. Niko, however, appeared very pleased to have met me. A little too pleased.

He kept his hands to himself this time, mostly because Kylan steered me away from his reach, and we murmured our goodbyes.

Yeah, so I don't like him.

No, I imagine you wouldn't, Kylan replied. *I believe he would have chosen you for his harem, if given the chance.*

I gagged in my mind, causing Kylan to chuckle. *I remember a time you felt that way about me.*

No, I always found you attractive, even when I hated you.

He kissed my temple as he opened the door, escorting me inside. "Do you hate me now, Raelyn?"

"Only sometimes."

He chuckled and led me through another entryway. "Well, perhaps this will encourage you to like me more."

I glanced around, seeing nothing. "What will?"

"You'll see." He released me, taking a step back. "I'll be back in a moment. Don't go anywhere."

I frowned as he disappeared, the door closing softly behind him. *What are you doing?*

It's a surprise. Enjoy.

Another perusal of the small bedroom revealed nothing. *Kylan*?

No reply.

The curtains in the corner rustled as someone slid open the glass doors from the outside. This couldn't have been part of Kylan's plan. I started toward the door, hand on the knob to leave when a familiar voice breathed my name.

I spun, meeting a pair of dark blue eyes I never expected to see again. "Silas."

He smiled and bounded toward me with open arms. I jumped on him, hugging him back fiercely, his broad shoulders accepting my vampire strength with ease.

"You're alive," I whispered. Which I already knew. Kylan had told me Silas won the Cup, but seeing him—here—made it so much more real.

He buried his face in my hair, inhaling. "God, you reek of vampire," he chuckled. "And Kylan."

I laughed. "Um, yeah, he sort of—"

"Turned you," he finished for me. "Yes, I've heard—everyone's heard—and I also saw you with him outside, but I couldn't approach."

I pulled away to study his face. "What? Why?"

"Oh, Rae, you really don't know?" He chuckled, releasing me to brush back his sandy hair. "Hierarchy, sweets. You're on the arm of a royal, while I'm just a newbie lycan. They consider me a baby. Talking to an alpha, let alone a royal, yeah, I'm lucky to even be given a job at this party. Clemente

Clan has delegated me to security duty."

"You're not allowed to talk to me?" I asked, flabbergasted.

"It's not customary, no," Kylan said as he entered the room.

Silas took a step back, his eyes dropping. "Your Highness."

"Silas," Kylan murmured, his palm sliding to my lower back.

"I apologize for the intrusion. This was all me. Rae did nothing wrong."

Kylan remained silent for a moment while I stared between them, shocked by Silas's submission and words.

When mortals were granted immortality, they acquired rights.

But Silas appeared as nothing more than a human in this moment, not a brand-new lycan.

And I *knew* that Silas wasn't a submissive, could see it in the way his hands curled even now while he deferred to another male.

"You're a good friend to her," Kylan finally said. "Which is how I knew you'd scent her out when I left her alone."

My gift, I realized.

Yes, was his single-word reply. "I don't mind you two keeping in touch. Just be discreet."

Silas lifted his gaze warily, his brow furrowed. "You're giving us permission to socialize?"

"You're Raelyn's friend. I accept that." He brushed his lips against my temple. "That doesn't mean Walter or Edon will, but I've never been very fond of the rules. Just ask my consort." He winked at me and turned to leave. "Five more minutes, love. Then we're needed back outside."

He closed the door behind him, giving us privacy once more.

Silas stared openmouthed after Kylan, making me giggle. "You look shocked," I teased.

"That's Kylan?" he asked, gesturing. "The formidable, sadistic royal we read about in university?"

"He has quite the reputation, yes, but he's not all bad. Sometimes I like him." I knew he could hear me, and felt his humor in my mind. "But enough about me, what about you? A lycan, huh?"

Silas grimaced. "Yeah, Walter had first pick since he's retiring. His son is actually the one who turned me, much to Edon's chagrin."

"He didn't want to turn you?"

He snorted. "No. I'm his first, and probably his last given the experience. It's all part of the alpha trials. His ascension will conclude at the next full moon."

"I thought tonight was the ascension."

"Oh, no, tonight is just the initial ceremony." He palmed the back of his neck, sighing. "It's going to be a bloody month."

"How so?"

He just shook his head. "A lot of it is clan ritual, secret, and all that."

"But you'll be okay, right?" I pressed.

"Pfft, how long have you known me, Rae?" He nudged my shoulder. "I'm a survivor, same as you."

I smiled, somewhat reassured. "Yeah, we are."

"And Willow too, somewhere," he said softly.

My heart broke a little. "Yeah, she's surviving too." *I hope.*

"Well, I better get back before someone notices I'm missing. But I'm glad you're okay, Rae."

"You too, Silas." I hugged him again—hard—and watched as he disappeared through the sliding doors with a backward wave.

Kylan joined me again, his arms sliding around me from behind. "You want to see him again next month?"

"At the full-moon ceremony?" I guessed.

He nodded against my shoulder.

"Yes."

"I thought so." He kissed my neck. "Shall we return to the party or make an early exit?"

I twisted to face him, my blood heating as I took in his sinful tuxedo. "I'm all for an early exit."

"A woman after my own heart," he murmured, kissing me softly.

"No, I already own it," I reminded him. "It's your cock I want."

"Raelyn," he growled. "What am I going to do with that mouth of yours?"

I gave him my best innocent look. "Punish it?"

"I'll be doing more than that." Another kiss, this one harder. "Always so defiant."

"You love it."

"No, I love you," he whispered.

I smiled. "I love you, too."

Regally Bitten

Book Three

SILAS

TWENTY-TWO YEARS of promises wrapped up in lies.

Win the Immortal Cup, they'd said. *And join us in immortality.* The images that had followed were ones of wealth, excitement, and a life of indulgence.

Those images depicted the worst kind of deception.

As I writhed on the ground, growling in pain through my "welcome" to immortality, I couldn't help but wish I'd died instead.

Because what lay ahead was a fate worse than death.

Edon—my torturer—crouched before me, his expression bored. "It'll pass." The crowd around us chuckled.

His father, Alpha Walter, snorted. "This year's crop was shit."

"Clearly," Edon agreed, standing. "Can we finish this now?"

It's not done yet? Fuck.

"Part of the fun is seeing how long the new ones last in limbo," the alpha replied, his tone filled with disgust. "But clearly he's not long for this world."

"An omega," someone else jeered.

I wanted to snarl at the word, prove him wrong, but the pain had me groaning instead. Too many weeks without food, battling for my life, had weakened me to this degraded state where I could hardly move.

But I'd won.

And for what?

Torture.

Edon sighed. "He had a lot of promise." He ran his fingers through my matted hair, down my jaw, the touch surprisingly intimate from a male. "Shall I end him or finish it?"

"Up to you, son. These are the decisions an alpha must make for the clan." He whistled, the sound piercing my skull and shooting stars off behind my eyes. And then he howled. Others joined in, including Edon, and energy shimmered through the air.

Shifting.

I felt the magic crawl over my skin, enticing me to follow suit, but something blocked my ability, causing me to growl low and feral.

Edon's brows rose. "Well, well." He tilted his head, still in human form as his clan circled and sniffed, their muzzles terrifyingly large. "Perhaps there's hope for you yet, Silas."

My lips curled, a defensive instinct shuddering down my spine.

Edon's palm circled my throat, his obsidian pupils ringed with inky embers. "Challenging the son of an alpha is a dangerous move. And ballsy as fuck." He squeezed, but I didn't give an inch.

If he wanted to kill me, fine. I'd been through hell and back, only to find out I'd fought for a life that didn't exist. Not here. Not with the Clemente Clan.

The excitement rose in the crowd, the decision of my life weighing in the palm of their future alpha.

And then he struck.

His fangs sank deep into my neck, the power rippling over my skin and connecting to his earlier bite.

My moan turned into something deeper, starker, more animalistic, as my bones shifted into something *other.*

Edon watched, his palm shifting to my nape, his gaze cold and merciless.

I hated him.

Feared him.

Wanted to *be* him.

All in the span of seconds as my body transitioned into its new form.

More howls.

My own joining the fray.

My instincts heightened.

Scents and sights I never knew existed.

And then strong human fingers ran through my stark white fur, Edon's forehead pressing to mine. "Welcome to Clemente Clan, Silas."

Several Weeks Later…

BE USEFUL, THEY TOLD ME. *Guard the perimeter.*

In other words, they didn't want me to disturb the precious mating ceremony between my sire—the alpha heir—and his intended from Ernest Clan.

Fine.

I'd prowl around out here, memorize the scents, listen to the secrets from afar, and plan. Because I couldn't continue on as the pariah in the Clemente Clan. The only turned wolf in over two decades. A half-blood to them all.

No.

I didn't survive all this bullshit just to be exiled.

Nothing in this world was what they promised us. *Nothing.*

I hated it here. Loathed my new life as a lycan. And while I respected that it could be a hell of a lot worse, it could also be better. There had to be something else out there, some other way for us all to live in harmony.

A low growl had my ears twitching toward the woods that bordered the party, my eyes finding a tall female with elfin features standing near the forest edge.

Her clenched fists displayed her discomfort, her focus on a male towering over her.

"You will behave," the alpha wolf snarled. "Yield to him, Luna. Or else."

With those tender words, he entered the festivities, leaving her snarling in his wake.

The alpha's intended, I realized. Her stature depicted her strength and defiance, marking her as distinctly different from all the other females I'd seen around her. I also recognized her name as the one whispered amongst the Clemente Clan, their curiosity at what she would look like a hot topic among the males.

Beautiful, I thought. *Beautiful and pissed.*

It intrigued me. I clearly wasn't the only one dissatisfied with my circumstances.

Her focus shifted to me, sensing my presence in the woods. I held her gaze, my instincts refusing to bow to another.

She snorted in reply, the sound carrying along the breeze.

Rather than come after me as most alpha wolves would be inclined to do, she flipped her long dark hair over her shoulder and returned to the party, deigning me as insignificant.

Just like everyone else.

My fur ruffled in irritation.

Someday these wolves would take me seriously.

I just had to figure out my place in this new world. Because one thing I knew for certain—I didn't belong at the bottom.

Chapter One

LUNA

FUCK. THIS. SHIT.

I couldn't decide whom I wanted to punch more—my father or the Clemente Clan Alpha, Walter.

Probably both.

My mother squeezed my hand. Again. A polite reminder to keep my mouth shut and accept my fate. Just like she did all those years ago. And wasn't she a happy pup?

I almost snorted. All of this was complete and utter bullshit. I wanted to pick my future mate, not have one assigned to me. Especially not a prick like Edon. He looked just like his father, with those sinfully dark eyes, nearly black hair, and arrogant smirk.

Walter had quite a reputation for fucking his harem to death. His poor *mate* was usually forced to watch or participate. And she appeared just as broken as many of the females in this clan.

My future, I growled to myself. *Not fucking happening.* I'd break Edon's dick before he touched me with it. And I let him see that with a glance.

His eyebrow arched, intrigue flashing in his pupils.

Of course he wanted to play.

All males did.

But I had a plan, one that guaranteed he'd deny me tonight. Then I'd be on my way back to Ernest Clan. Oh, my father would be pissed. He'd probably try to sell me off to the highest bidder. I would deal with that when the time came, just as I planned to handle tonight's little ritual.

Alphas were possessive.

And I intended to use that to my advantage.

My father introduced me to some royal vampire and his new toy. I barely listened. The politics in this world sucked. It was all most people knew, but my mentor growing up spoke of an old time, one where females had more rights. Where we chose our own mates. Where we hid from vampires and humans.

What I wouldn't give to have been born in *that* century.

Alas, no. I was stuck here with these assholes who expected me to bow, curtsy, and maintain polite conversation, as if I weren't an alpha female. Forcing me to deny all my instincts, to accept my place as beneath the males of the pack even though I could easily slaughter most of them.

It churned my stomach.

Conversation flowed around me. Formalities shoved down my throat. Until, finally, the ceremony began.

I couldn't wait to get this over with.

And from the looks of it, neither could my intended mate. Only, he was looking forward to something very different from what I had in mind, something that would not be happening once he realized my secret.

Hums of approval haunted the air, the wolves eager for the show to start. Only a handful of royal vampires remained, mostly the ones intrigued by the lycan rituals. I wasn't surprised to see Jace among them. He was notorious for taking wolves to bed. A dangerous proposition for a bloodsucker, but he struck me as someone who could handle himself.

He stood with two other royals, their eyes glittering in the night.

I ignored them in preference for the surrounding alphas, their expressions hungry and expectant as they formed a crescent near the altar beneath the full moon.

Next month when this happened, it would be to complete the mating bond.

But I wouldn't be here to see it. Because I had no intention of seeing this through.

Edon stepped to the front, his black button-down shirt undone at the collar. Unlike me, he was permitted to wear clothing for this event. I would be expected to approach him naked, to show him everything I had to offer.

Because all alpha males cared about was fucking.

And he would want to make sure I met his physical needs.

My lips curled. *Oh, won't you be shocked.*

Chants began, my parents taking their position on either side of the aisle. Wolves and vampires alike dotted the audience, everyone in human form.

I stood at the end, allowing my mother to remove my dress and heels.

No undergarments—not because of any requirements, but because I preferred it that way. Easier to shift when I wore minimal clothes.

I rolled my shoulders, confident in my appearance. Our clan undressed in front of each other all the time; some didn't even bother with clothes. But it was a little weird to walk down along the path between foreign lycans.

Clemente Clan had a different vibe. The air here was different, too, the texture resembling a sultry kiss against my pale skin. I rather preferred the icy planes back home. *Former-day Russia*, my advisor once called it. Clemente Clan was in the southern United States. All foreign terms in this new world, but I knew all about the old one. Something that would infuriate my parents if they knew, which was why it'd been my little secret with Claudette and my brother, Logan.

"May I present Luna of Ernest Clan," my father said, his tone filled with pride as we approached the Alpha of Clemente Clan and his heir apparent.

Yes, I hope you're so proud of yourself for forcing me to mate a man I don't know, I thought. *Such excellent parenting.*

Edon met my gaze and held it, the challenge in his dark depths clear. He expected me to bow. I narrowed my eyes instead.

I bow to no one.

My mother's nails bit into my forearm, causing me to flinch.

My father cleared his throat.

I could practically hear Logan scolding me as well. *Don't be an idiot, Luna,* he would say. *Play it cool.*

He was probably the only one I'd ever listen to, his advice usually sound.

Fine, I thought to them all. *Fine.*

I would bow. Only because this would be our first and last meeting.

My knees bent, my head lowering. It felt so wrong. So ridiculous. And I couldn't help peeking up at him as I did it, which earned me a surprised look from the alpha heir.

"You're going to have your hands full with this one, son," Walter commented.

"I can see that," he replied dryly.

Pricks, I thought, righting myself after my half-assed attempt at a curtsy or whatever the fuck that'd been.

Edon stepped forward, his eyes roaming over me as if he were appraising a piece of meat. Which, I supposed, was accurate considering our predicament.

My parents moved to allow him to circle me. An inspection. If he approved, we would become betrothed. If he didn't, I'd be sent home with a very angry alpha father.

But I'd been on the receiving end of his wrath many times.

I knew what he would do.

And I didn't fucking care.

A life as a rogue lycan would be better than a forced mating to a monster inside the Clemente Clan.

Edon drew his finger down my arm, the heat of his chest caressing my back. "What's wrong, little wolf?" he breathed into my ear. "Afraid?"

"No," I replied, turning to face him, much to the shock of the audience.

Intended mates were meant to remain absolutely still during the alpha male's inspection. My mother had gone over the rules a thousand times, and her sigh behind me said how she felt about my disobedience.

Anger colored the familial bonds, my father's annoyance palpable.

It gave me pause only because I knew it wouldn't be me he punished later for this, but my mother. I felt it writhing in his intentions, distorting the air with a violent promise that had my eyes dropping to the sliver of tan skin peeking at me from Edon's unfastened collar.

He hadn't moved, perhaps unsure of how to handle my outright rudeness. Should he castigate me before the masses? Or should he allow it to slide since I wasn't yet his to throttle?

A hint of unease trickled down my spine. He merely continued to stare, as if waiting for me to do something else.

When I didn't, he continued his perusal, his touch tracing along my skin. No one spoke. The audience waiting for his decision. This could take minutes or hours. He could choose to fuck me right here, just to test the merchandise. He could send me to my knees. He could ask me anything he wanted to know and I had to answer.

It was all so one-sided.

Whatever the alpha male wanted, he received. Fuck what the female wanted.

Edon's palm slid up to my nape, the act a gesture of dominance that prickled goose bumps along my arms. I hated him. Wanted to snarl at him, to fight him, to tell him to back the fuck off, but I felt my father's tension through the bond. One more outburst and my mother would pay. Severely.

Then he really wasn't going to like what was coming next.

I'd already done the unthinkable. He just didn't know it yet.

But Edon suspected it. I could tell by the way his nostrils flared, the way his pupils tapered into points as I boldly met his gaze again.

His lip curled. Not necessarily into a snarl, but into a smirk.

He leaned in to brush his mouth over mine in a chaste kiss, one that resulted in growls of approval from the audience.

They wanted a show.

They wanted him to mount me.

I could feel it in the wind. In the way the hairs along my neck danced in warning. This pack was cruel. They didn't believe in equality.

But then again, none of the clans did. Not anymore.

Edon's nose ran along my cheek to my ear and down the column of my throat. Scenting. Searching for the anomaly I knew his wolf senses had picked up on. He continued to trek downward between the valley of my breasts, along my flat stomach, to the apex between my thighs.

He looked up at me from his knees, the obsidian pools of his irises swirling with warning. He most likely knew now. Surely he smelled the evidence of the male I allowed to fuck me this morning.

His growl confirmed he did.

Only, it wasn't the menacing sound I expected but one underlined in heat and hunger. The kind of sound a wolf made when he desired his mate.

This is wrong, I thought, confusion settling over me.

Alpha males were possessive. And the rituals required my virginity. Something I'd given away not even twenty-four hours ago, wanting to be certain he knew.

And he did.

I saw it in the way he watched me.

His tongue slid from his lips, tasting me deeply, leaving me absolutely no doubt of his knowledge. Because I had purposely not showered afterward. I *wanted* him to know.

Another lick had my knees going weak.

This can't be happening.

He should be raging. Ranting. Threatening to kill whoever defiled my body. Demanding my parents take me away at once. Not—

Teeth met my flesh, causing me to cry out in surprise. The lycans in the audience rumbled in excitement, enjoying the very primal display of ownership.

The bastard had just *marked* me.

Right on the damn thigh.

And the way he gazed up at me showed his pleasure at doing so. He slowly stood, his well-over-six-foot height dwarfing my five-foot-five frame. His fingers clasped my chin, holding me in place as he brushed his bloody lips over mine. I fought the urge to growl, not in warning but in need.

Then his tongue slid inside, forcing me to experience the intoxicating mix of my own arousal tinged with coppery sweetness.

Bastard, I thought at him.

He smiled against my mouth. "Welcome to Clemente Clan, little mate," he said, loud enough for everyone to hear.

A spiritual cuff wrapped itself around my neck, banding my heart, as the reality of his actions and words settled into the air.

He'd bitten me and claimed me vocally.

The ceremony was already complete, the betrothed bonds well enforced.

He'd severed my ties to Ernest Clan with that bite against my thigh, and I'd been so shocked I'd not even felt my familial ties shatter.

But I did now.

Especially as I looked at my mother, noting the slight mist in her gaze. And then my brother. He stood in the front row, his hair the same color as mine, his eyes a bright blue. He appeared as unfazed as everyone else in the audience, but sadness radiated from him, a sadness I felt deep in my heart.

Goodbye, he was saying. A word he already spoke to me last night when leaving me with his final bit of advice to behave and to keep my head high.

"You may be his, but you're still an alpha female, Luna. Never forget it."

His parting statement wrapped around my soul, attempting to ground me as despair threatened to rip me apart.

I was no longer one of Ernest Clan, but the betrothed alpha to the Clemente heir.

Astonishment mingled with horror inside me. I'd been so certain this wouldn't happen. No alpha in his right mind would accept damaged goods.

My head swung in his direction, his fingers still lightly tracing my jaw. I gaped openly at him as the howls thundered around us, the next phase of tonight's rituals expected to commence.

Edon smiled, his lips dipping to my ear. "I prefer my women experienced, little mate. Makes fucking all the more exciting."

My heart leapt into my throat. My defilement had the opposite impact of what I'd anticipated. It'd made me even more desirable in his eyes.

And now…

Now his pack expected us to go consummate the bond. For him to fuck me all night. Either before them all or in the privacy of his quarters. It was his choice, not mine.

Wolves weren't shy. We were primal beings. But the idea of being intimate with him in front of all his pack had my head swimming with doubt.

I wasn't really experienced.

This morning's stupid affair had only lasted a few minutes.

And I'd hated it.

But being with Edon? That would be so much worse. He'd bite me again, only much harder than before. He'd take me any way he wanted, over and over again, even if I cried. Fuck, he might even *want* me to cry.

This wasn't supposed to happen at all.

His eyes tracked every thought as they spun through my mind, his lips curling deviously. So much intrigue. So much desire.

This is going to hurt.

I really *fucked this up.*

Chapter Two

Edon

LUNA OF ERNEST CLAN was not what I expected. Not in the slightest.

The females of Clemente were always willing, sometimes a little too willing. But Luna, she reeked of defiance. And I found the harsh scent intoxicating.

She'd even gone as far as to fuck another wolf this morning.

Clever and deceitful, little mate.

If I hadn't been buried deep inside another pussy just last night, I might have cared more. However, it struck me as a double standard to expect my intended to come to me as a virgin. And I meant what I said—I preferred my partners experienced.

I also preferred them to be excited participants in the act. Fucking an unwilling female held no value to me whatsoever. While I adored the chase, I wanted my prey to *desire* her eventual capture.

Ah, but Luna, she possessed no yearning to be here at all. It was written in the defiant lines of her shoulders, the fury highlighting her honey-brown eyes, and the overall air of resistance that permeated her aura.

"Come," I demanded, my palm at her nape as I led her away from the chaos of the ceremony.

My father wouldn't be happy.

He intended me to fuck her publicly in front of the clan.

But as the rising alpha, I chose my actions. Not him. The bastard could indulge in his sick proclivities himself. I would not be sharing my mate the way he shared my mother and his other females—humans and otherwise.

Luna remained brittle beneath my touch, but her legs followed my direction.

The alpha female in her wanted to rebel. The woman in her knew better. Because if she tried, I'd put her in her place so fast her head would spin. And I really didn't want to do that. Not here.

In the privacy of my quarters, maybe.

Two sentries stepped out of my way as I approached, their heads bowed in reverence.

I ignored them, guiding Luna through the front house, into the royal courtyards, and up to the log cabin I called my own. It was smaller than my father's, which sat on the opposite acre of this massive property. Ample woods separated our estates, a necessity due to our conflicting natures.

He was the current alpha.

I was the one destined to take his place.

That sometimes led to complications—complications that I always won of late, much to his obvious chagrin.

Luna glanced at the weeping willows outside my home, causing me to pause.

We were completely alone out here, no one daring enough to enter my property without sufficient permission or cause. And the majority of the clan was busy celebrating anyway.

Alpha transitions happened once every three hundred years or so, making the next month a rare time for lycans. It was also the first one to occur for Clemente Clan in the new world.

Things felt new.

Fresh.

Exciting.

Which meant they were all too busy enjoying themselves to bother with us. They expected me to fuck my betrothed. As most of them had seen me in the throes of passion before, it wouldn't intrigue them much now.

My father had wanted me to break her in front of the masses, but he'd just have to deal with my choice to do so privately. Figuratively speaking, anyway.

Luna swallowed, her tension palpable.

I released her and took a step back, giving her the space she clearly desired. "We're alone here."

She blinked, confusion marring her pretty face.

No, not pretty.

Beautiful.

Unmated alpha females weren't allowed to attend political events, like Blood Day or the Immortal Cup ceremonies. Those were reserved for clan alphas and their respective mates. But I'd anticipated her features after meeting her parents several years ago. She had her mother's caramel-colored eyes and her father's brown hair. Her alabaster skin matched them both—a trademark from her region of the world—but her curves were all her own.

Lithe, athletic legs.

Supple waist.

Fantastic tits.

And a scowl that made my heart race.

Oh, this was going to be fun.

"Why?" she demanded, seeming to have found her confidence once more.

"Why what?" I countered, knowing exactly what she meant but desiring her to say it. To admit that she purposely fucked another male this morning just to piss me off.

Luna growled, the sound primal and sexy as hell. "I'm not a virgin."

I smiled. "Neither am I, sweetheart."

"Being a virgin is a requirement for potential female mates."

"Perhaps I don't care about the *requirements*," I countered, meaning it. If I wanted a docile wolf, I'd have taken one of the omegas in our clan as a mate. No, I preferred an alpha female, someone who could fight me when I needed it, and this one more than fit the bill.

There were three others in existence as backups, should I require one.

But my father and Niko were old friends. This pact between our two clans was created the day of her birth.

She'd always been mine.

Just as I'd always been hers.

No amount of fucking around was going to belittle that point.

Her pupils flared in the moonlight, her stance defensive. "I won't yield to you."

I tilted my head forward, deeply amused. "Oh, you will. And you'll beg me to fuck you, too."

She snorted. "Not a chance in hell."

I laughed outright and shook my head. "All right, little mate. Let's play." I unbuttoned my shirt, not wanting to ruin it in the dirt, folded it, and placed it on the doorstep. Her nostrils flared as I unfastened my trousers.

She thought I meant to fuck her.

Poor darling wolf was in for one hell of a shock.

I kicked my shoes and socks off with my pants, leaving me as naked as her. "Do your worst," I invited her.

Her gaze snapped upward from my package, her cheeks flushing. "*What?*"

"Attack me, little mate. Show me what you can do." The pack wanted me to deflower her. Well, that was already done. So I'd taste her in other ways. Starting with her ability to keep up.

"I…" She licked her lips, her confusion adorable. "What?"

"If you don't want to fight, then we'll fuck," I replied, trying to goad her. "It's one or the other. Lady's choice."

"You want me to fight you?"

"Yes. You claim you won't yield. Prove it." I arched a brow. "Unless this is you already yielding, in which case, I'd prefer to take you from behind." She had a delectable ass that would feel perfect against my groin as I thrust into her—

Luna's fist narrowly missed my face, her punch astonishingly accurate and powerful. I felt it in the air that whistled by my cheek as I dodged her.

Impressive.

She followed up with another hook that almost landed in my gut.

I hadn't expected to have to work hard to avoid her hits, but she proved to be quite the little boxer as she came at me full force, making me sidestep and jump to evade being hit.

At this rate, she'd be exhausted in minutes.

But I rather enjoyed watching her tits bounce with each move.

And I always did enjoy a little physical sparring before fucking.

I caught her next throw, deftly twirling her in my arms to bring her back to my front, and clamped my opposite arm around her. "Boxing is fun, but can you wrestle?" I wondered aloud.

She responded by dropping into a leg sweep that nearly sent me to my ass, and followed it with a kick to my shin.

I growled, turned on and furious at the same time.

Most would heed that as a warning.

Not Luna.

She came at me again, not even winded, and I realized this little thing might actually make me work for it.

This time when she tried to punch me in the face, I caught her wrist and twisted it, putting her on the ground. She yelped in response, cradling her arm as I stood over her. "I'm impressed," I admitted. "But I'm the alpha of this clan, not you."

I took a step back and startled as she leapt at me like a wild cat, tackling me to the ground. Her hands tried to find my throat, her nails turning into claws. The scent of blood tinged the air as she drew those sharp talons across my skin, her intention to maim clear.

Fuck.

Protective instincts overcame me, forcing me to fight back. I grabbed her forearms, using a pressure point to loosen her grip, and grappled over the ground in an effort to restrain her. But she thwarted several of my moves deftly, confirming that she wasn't just smart, but also fast. And strong, too.

It took far too many minutes to finally get her on her back in a position she couldn't escape from. My hips and thighs pinned hers, one of my hands holding her wrists above her head while the other clamped down hard around her throat. "*Yield*," I demanded, the snarl in my tone one I rarely had to use with my wolves.

"Fuck you," she snapped, not even fazed by her inferior position.

"Poor choice of words," I said, pressing my very aroused cock into her slick folds. Not inside. Just against. Enough to demonstrate my dominance and warn her of my intent should she push me too far.

She bit her lower lip, her cheeks flushed in glorious fury. And when I tried to hold her gaze, she looked away.

The first sign of submission.

And a very telling one.

While her body might be wet and willing beneath mine, her mind was nowhere near ready. If I took her now, I would only confirm to her that I was a monster. As we had several centuries ahead of us, I preferred not to start off on the wrong paw.

I sighed, shaking my head. "I really hope you enjoyed whatever pup you allowed between your legs, little mate, because it's the last time someone other than me will ever please you." I released her and leapt off her before she could get another swipe in.

She sprung expertly to her feet, assuming the fighting position. "I didn't yield."

I grinned, amused by her determination. "No. Not with your words, anyway. But your body definitely did." I glanced pointedly at my slick cock, and then back at her. "I should make you suck it off. Just to prove my point."

Although, I strongly suspected she'd bite me instead. Her clenching jaw verified that to be an accurate assessment. It should have pissed me off. Instead, all it did was please me greatly.

I'd definitely chosen right with this one.

The wolves of my experience were just so damn submissive. I desired a female with fight. One who wasn't afraid to challenge me.

Like Luna did now with her eyes.

I grabbed her chin and wrapped my opposite arm around her back when she tried to strike me again. I'd gone easy on her, and I allowed her to feel that in the way I held her now. She couldn't squirm, could barely even breathe. That was how hard I held her as I took in every detail of her beautiful face.

"No one will touch you here," I said softly. "Not when they all know you're mine." It served as a warning while also confirming her security in the pack. Because she didn't need to fear anyone. But she also couldn't fuck anyone but me.

"Let go of me," she demanded, a note of fear finally tinging that sweet voice of hers.

I ignored her request while making her hold my gaze. "Don't worry, little mate. I'll never force you, and there is plenty of willing pussy on these grounds."

I allowed that to sink in, compelling her to see the truth of my statement. Then I released her with a shove, sending her back several steps so she couldn't physically retaliate.

"I strongly suggest you consider our circumstances, Luna. You're here because I require an heir. And I will have one." Because I had no doubt she would one day succumb to me. They always did. "What you have to decide is whether you want to end up alone after fulfilling your purpose or be by my side.

Because I mean it. None of my wolves will touch you. Ever."

"While you can fuck whoever you want," she replied, giving a harsh laugh. "Yes, I'm very aware of society's rules, *Alpha*."

So disrespectful. So fucking hot.

My cock pulsed, eager to put her on her back again. But I refrained, instead staring her down with one of my infamous *alpha* glares. "Keep me satisfied and maybe I won't desire anyone else." Cruel words, but true. Lycan society encouraged the males to take a harem, even when mated. But the females, no. Once mated, they were to remain faithful.

Those who weren't died. Badly.

Luna had to know that.

She laughed, but it lacked humor. And she slowly shook her head. "Go fuck whoever you want, *Alpha*."

I narrowed my gaze, displeased with her easy dismissal. Most in my position would have already mounted her and forced her submission. I offered to play first.

Still, she denied me.

Even with her body ripe and willing.

"Fine," I replied. "This is my house. Pick whatever bed you want. Just not mine. I may have company later."

I didn't wait for a reply, my inner wolf raging at me to either fuck or run. And I chose the latter.

Her arousal was even more potent as I shifted, my nose picking up the trace of liquid heat rolling down her inner thighs. It took considerable effort to back away and not pounce on the one my wolf recognized as his intended.

She didn't want me. Not yet.

I darted toward the tree line, a growl vibrating in my throat.

The bolder females of the pack would track me down, demand I allow them to satisfy the lust burning inside me.

And maybe I'd let them.

I wasn't mated yet. Nor did I have a mate who wanted me. So why shouldn't I indulge in another?

Luna's snarl gave me pause just inside the tree line, her dark head bowing as she fell to her knees.

"*Fuck*," she growled. "Fuck. Fuck. Fuck!"

My lips pulled back at her display of rage. It seemed my intended did care. She cared *very* much. But there was also a note of cunning in her scent, a plan taking root in that mind of hers. A mind I very much wanted to get to know.

What are you thinking, little mate? I wondered, an image of her trying to escape our grounds flashing behind my eyes. Was that telegraphed through our subtle link? Or something else entirely?

Regardless, it intrigued me.

I rather hoped she would try to run.

Because I always did enjoy a good chase.

Chapter Three

Silas

THIS TASK IS BULLSHIT, I thought, kicking a stone with my paw.

Every day, they sent me out here to "guard" the perimeter. Right. Because the nearest territory was hundreds of miles away in each direction, which meant there were other patrols out there doing the same thing and stopping anything that could get this close.

They'll probably send me there next. The only reason I'd been allowed to stay this close to the heart of the pack was because of my supposed need for training. Not that anyone had bothered to explain a damn thing to me.

No.

All they did was tell me to patrol. Like maybe I could learn something by sniffing grass and dirt in wolf form. I snorted. *Right.*

The only scent I continued to pick up out here was a sweet orange blossom aroma that belonged to Edon's intended mate. She seemed to enjoy running the perimeter. Alone.

Everyone stayed clear of her, including me. But I couldn't help wondering what she was up to out here.

I trailed her scent along the creek, following at a distance. As we were on the boundaries, it still qualified as me doing my job. It just gave me something a little more exciting to do.

Something about her intrigued me. She smelled different from the pack, but my interest went deeper than that. Her presence boasted a hint of pride that the other women around here seemed to lack. Perhaps because Luna was an alpha—a rare designation for female lycans.

Hmm, no, it was the way she moved so gracefully through the bayou, her long legs dancing across the ground with liquid ease.

I nearly approached her twice this week, just to make myself known, but I sensed that would break a myriad of rules.

For one, I was the omega of the pack. A new wolf. A weakling.

At least in the eyes of everyone else.

But I certainly didn't feel all that *weak*. If anything, I felt restless. Like I needed to be doing something more important than wandering—

Death.

My nose twitched.

Another breeze ruffled my fur with the foul stench, stirring my instincts to high alert.

Where is it coming from?

I tracked a pungent tendril through the creek and to the other side. These lands still belonged to Clemente Clan but were just outside of the primary grounds housing the pack hierarchy.

And something was very off.

My lips pulled back in a low snarl, the reek of violence unsettling my insides. Something or someone had died out here in the worst kind of way.

Torture.

Innards.

Blood.

I lifted my muzzle, scenting for the source.

There. I bounded through the moss-covered trees, my pads silent over the grass-covered stones below.

A corpse lay demolished in the grass.

The head rested a few feet away, leaving a nasty stump of a neck behind.

Vampire.

Pack scent rioted with the stench of decay, naming the clear murderer as someone from Clemente Clan. But who would do this? It broke one of the most sacred laws among the Blood Alliance—no exterminating of immortal life without higher order.

And this vampire's death clearly wasn't sanctioned.

Unless Walter approved it.

Or whomever this vampire belonged to.

But then again a whole ceremony would have been performed.

No. Definitely an unsanctioned kill.

I lifted my head back in a howl to alert my fellow sentries, uncertain of how else to proceed since no one had actually given me details on proper protocol.

What is it? a deep voice asked in my head, causing me to stumble on my four legs.

What the hell? I thought, glancing this way and that. No one in Clemente Clan had telepathic abilities that I knew of. Or maybe they did. Because how the fuck would I know? No one told me shit.

Silas, the voice growled. *Report.*

Who is this? I demanded, spinning again, confused as fuck and slightly paranoid that I might be hearing things.

Edon, your alpha, came the voice, a hint of irritation underlining his now recognizably arrogant tone. *Report.*

How are you in my head? I asked. *Wait, can all of us do this?*

Oh, fuck. That would be bad. Very, very bad. I didn't want anyone in my head. A lot of private and very rebellious thoughts formed up there, thoughts that, if voiced out loud, could get me killed.

Like my interest in Luna's exquisite scent.

And my overall hatred for this new life.

A long-suffering sigh that didn't belong to me—in my own fucking head—caused my fur to stand on end.

Calm down, Silas. I made you. It's the link between a sire and his progeny. It exists within the pack psyche but can only be accessed by us. Now can you tell me what the fuck is going on over there?

It was the most the alpha heir had said to me since he turned me all those weeks ago. And yet this link had existed the entire time?

Fuck.

And what the hell is a pack psyche?

Silas, he growled. *Focus before I come out there myself.*

The threat in his tone had me swallowing a whimper. I did not want to see him out here. Or really at all. Especially after the hell he inflicted on me during the change.

Edon was not a kind lycan. That, I knew for certain. Even if he seemed to be allowing his mate to roam freely over the grounds.

Silas! You are severely testing my patience, something I strongly encourage you not to do.

I sat several feet away from the corpse, grimacing even in wolf form. *There's a dead vampire on the outskirts of the property, and it reeks of pack.*

Silence.

Edon? I wasn't sure if he heard me or not.

I'm on my way. Don't let anyone fucking touch the scene, or I'll have your hide.

I growled in response to the threat, hating him even more. But as the sounds of paws approaching tickled my ears, I took guard as he demanded. I shifted back into my human form, something that hurt the first several times I'd done it, but now felt second nature, and stood with my arms crossed.

Three wolves with silky white coats appeared, all males, all purebreds in the pack—meaning they were born as lycans. As long as one parent had a wolf gene, the child was born a lycan. Hence the need for the breeding farms.

Where Willow is being held, I thought, flinching. She'd been part of my class, one of my best friends. On Blood Day, the Magistrate sent her to the breeding farms to create either more humans or more lycans.

I really hoped it was the former.

At least Rae is okay, I consoled myself, thinking of my other best friend. It'd been a welcome shock seeing her at the alpha ceremonies. When I heard Kylan, the infamous harem-slaying royal, had taken her as a mate, I'd worried about her well-being. But she'd seemed fine. Happy, even.

Well, that makes one of us, I thought as the approaching wolves shifted into human form.

"What'd you do?" the stockiest of them demanded. What was his name? Edwin? Ethan? Goliath?

Fuck if I knew.

None of them wanted to be friends with the human turned lycan, so I'd returned the favor.

"I asked you a question, mutt," Goliath—he looked like a Goliath, anyway—growled.

"I found a dead vampire," I drawled, stating the obvious.

Three matching unamused expressions stared back at me.

"Edon says not to touch him until he gets here," I added.

That seemed to grab their interest.

"Edon, huh?" The redheaded one scratched the stubble along his jaw. "Do we take orders from Edon yet, Barry?"

"No, we don't, Glenn," the third—Barry—replied, his lanky body the least threatening of the trio.

"Didn't think so." Glenn smiled, the expression one of evil intent.

This is going to end badly, I sighed to myself. "He may not be your alpha yet, but he's the heir. Best to do what he says."

Glenn's gaze lit up with wicked determination. "Nah, I didn't hear any orders, mutt. I think we'll do whatever the fuck we want. Isn't that right, boys?"

"Yep," the minions beside him said in unison.

Part of me wanted to welcome them to their funeral with open arms and allow them to do whatever the hell they wanted. But the obedient part of me—one beat into me over years of submission in the university—caused me to fold my arms and stand my ground in front of the corpse. "No."

I didn't elaborate.

Didn't lay down a threat.

Just merely enforced the fact that they would not be fucking with this vampire corpse until Edon gave his approval.

Barry chuckled, shaking his head. "Allow me."

I saw his punch as it formed, noted the way his body angled for a fight before he even took a step. And I deftly dodged the throw while landing one of my own against the flat planes of his abdomen.

"Oomph," he breathed, hunching over from the strike I knew would leave him winded for at least thirty seconds.

Unfortunately, my instinctual reaction caused his buddies to charge me at once.

I caught Glenn's fist, twisted his arm, and sent him to his knees. Which left my right side open for Goliath's brutal attack.

One crack to my ribs, the other to my back, in quick succession, sent me tumbling back. But I'd endured much, much worse. I'd survived the fucking Immortal Cup. I knew how this worked, and I used his temporary victory to my advantage.

Because he didn't try to hit me again.

He merely stood there smirking like a dumbass, assuming I wouldn't get back up.

The disbelief in his gaze was a gorgeous sight as I kicked out my legs not even seconds later, landing on my feet, and sent my palm into his nose.

Crunch.

My other hand slammed into his sternum.

Snap.

And my knee sailed into his side.

Pop.

His howl as he fell to the ground was music to my ears.

Movement in my peripheral vision had me kicking out sideways into Glenn's abdomen, then my fist crashed into his skull with a deafening blow. He whimpered, falling on top of his friend, as Barry stood and held out his hands in defeat.

I narrowed my gaze at him. "Are we done?"

"Yes," a low voice snarled from the woods.

Edon.

He strode forward on two feet, shirtless, and in a pair of jeans that slung low across his hips. An indication that the bastard had jogged here on two legs instead of shifting into the faster form of four.

In other words, the jackass had taken his time on purpose.

"What happened?" he demanded, taking in the scene of his two wounded wolves and Barry's contrite stance.

"Just fucking around, boss," the idiot said.

Yeah, fucking around, my ass, I thought.

Edon arched a brow at me. *Care to say that out loud.*

I folded my arms instead, staring him down.

A beat of silence passed.

Snitching wasn't my thing. Besides, it was pretty damn obvious what happened. They attacked; I defended. *No one touched the body,* I added mentally. *Your Highness.*

Edon snorted. "Barry, get the jackass twins back to central. I'll deal with you all later. Silas, you stay."

Woof woof, I thought. Oh, it was entirely stupid to challenge an alpha. I knew that. But I had nothing to lose other than my life, and that could only be taken with due cause. Edon would sooner throw me to the rogues of the world, a place where I suspected I might actually be happier.

Maybe then I could find an old bed to sleep on instead of curling up under a random tree on the ground.

Although, likely not.

But a wolf could dream.

Dumb, Dumber, and Dipshit all took their leave, hobbling away under the careful eye of their future alpha. When he glanced back at me, I said nothing. If he thought I intended to apologize for putting those assholes in their places, then he had another think coming.

"They threatened to touch the corpse, didn't they?" he asked once they were too far to hear.

I didn't confirm or deny it, just continued to stare at him.

"Defying an alpha is a dangerous game," he warned.

"Try telling those three idiots that," I suggested.

"Those three idiots, as you call them, are purebreds and far higher in the pack than you."

Like I didn't know that. It was why they lived on the main grounds. Why they had a roof over their heads when I didn't. Why they could talk to someone of Edon's status while I was expected to bow and grovel.

Well, fuck that.

Edon took my measure, his smoldering irises running over each exposed inch of my skin. Nudity never bothered me. I'd spent many, many years being appraised by immortals, evaluated for my looks, my agility, my intelligence. I knew where I stood on every measure. My becoming a lycan just heightened all those attributes. Whereas wolves like the idiot trio never had to fight for anything in their lives. They were born into their positions. Just like Edon.

I *made* mine.

I fought for it.

And I would continue fighting until my dying breath.

Edon smirked. "You held your own, mutt. Earned a little respect. Try to hold on to it, yeah?" His focus shifted to the dead vamp, his amusement dying as he took in the severely abused torso, bite marks, and twisted ligaments.

He began to prowl in earnest while his words replayed through my mind.

He saw the fight.

Why else would he comment on me holding my own? Unless he determined it from the broken pile of males he stumbled across.

But no.

I suspected he'd watched the whole damn thing unfold as some sort of fucked-up test.

"You told me to guard the body on purpose," I said out loud.

"Of course I did," he replied, crouching by the shaved head of the former bloodsucker. "You're my only progeny. I had to see if I could trust you." His knowing gaze flicked upward, a hint of respect in his depths. "Your loyalty may one day be rewarded. Something to keep in mind."

I swallowed the dubious sound threatening to crawl out of my throat.

"What do you smell?" he asked, his attention again on the scene.

"Dead vampire and pack."

Edon shook his head. "I mean, do you smell anything else? Anything that can help us determine who engaged in this unsanctioned kill?"

I scented the air again, frowning. "All I smell is collective pack, but I've not learned everyone's signature traits yet."

"It smells like collective pack to me, too," he agreed, frowning. "Which means someone purposely covered their tracks." He grabbed the chin of the vampire, tilted it to the side this way and that. "He's one of Silvano's. A higher-ranking official, but not a sovereign or a regent. Just an upper-level wannabe diplomat."

Edon stood, glancing around, his nostrils flaring.

"I need you to bury the body," he continued. "Maybe near one of the bordering creeks."

My brow furrowed. *What?* "Shouldn't we tell someone?" This seemed like something the Goddess would want to know about. The royal vampire, Silvano, would probably appreciate a heads-up as well.

He faced me. "And if we did, what would happen?" His tone lacked his usual arrogance and instead infused a note of curiosity.

Another test, I realized.

I considered the query carefully, recalling all my years of political study.

And frowned.

"They'd demand an eye for an eye." Edon neither confirmed nor denied it, his mostly black eyes holding mine, waiting for me to continue. "Which you'd be forced to accept," I added, thinking out loud. "And the omega member of the pack would be sacrificed—me."

"So I suggest you bury the body, *Omega*," Edon replied.

I scowled. There was the pompous prick I loved to hate.

But he was right.

Because what else could I do?

My lips nearly parted on a reply of acceptance, when the hint of orange blossoms teased my nose. *Luna.*

Her light brown eyes flashed from the trees a few yards away, her white coat a stark difference from the moss and ivy decorating the landscape.

If Edon noticed her presence, he didn't show it. She studied the scene openly, not at all afraid of me for catching her in the act.

Did she realize I followed her as well?

That I adored the way her paws—

"Silas?" Edon interjected.

Right. Alpha demand. Not the best idea to lust after his female either.

I cleared my throat. "I'll, uh, get to work." I glanced at the tree line once more, but Luna was already gone. *What are you up to?* I wondered, not for the first time today.

Edon smirked, his hand falling to his jeans as he unbuttoned them. "I have a little wolf to catch, so I'm going for a run," he murmured, sliding the fabric down his toned legs. "Hold on to these for me," he added, handing them to me. "I'll be back for them."

I wanted to growl an unsavory reply, but the magic of his shift held my tongue captive in my suddenly dry mouth.

It was beautiful. Graceful. The most amazingly perfect shift I'd ever seen, and I'd observed several over the last few weeks on these grounds. He was just so liquid, so practiced, so fucking smooth.

Would I one day look like that? Doubtful. My bones still crunched. His just seemed to slide into their natural place as if he should always exist in this giant wolf form.

Edon shook out his coat, stretching.

No, *preening.*

He knew I was admiring him.

And he liked it.

I could tell by the cocky twinkle in his gaze.

He nudged me then with his nose, pushing me not so gently toward the body at my side. His nip to my arm seemed to be a warning.

Hurry up, he said into my head. *I'll be back in an hour.*

And with that, he took off through the woods—in the direction of Luna's orange-blossom scent.

Chapter Four

LUNA

SHIT. SHIT. SHIT. TOO CLOSE.

I ran across the grounds, trying to put as much distance as possible between me and Edon. The progeny noticing me was fine. The alpha, not so much. I'd avoided him for the better part of a week, and I wanted to keep it that way.

Ugh.

My damn nose always got me into trouble. However, the scent had drawn me toward the perimeter, where I'd watched in shock as the new lycan took on three full-blooded males while Edon watched from the sidelines. I'd thought for sure that the alpha would intervene and beat the young wolf into submission.

He didn't.

Instead, he leaned against a tree and watched in amusement.

The others were too caught up in their own testosterone to see him. But I caught the sexy tilt of his mouth as it quirked up at the show.

Then it was gone just as fast as it had appeared when he stepped forward. The three purebreds cowered. The young one did not. And that only drew me into the action more, my curiosity forcing me to step forward to hear every word.

The newbie's cocksure attitude shocked me, but not nearly as much as Edon's reaction. He'd *allowed* it.

My father never would have tolerated that kind of lip. He'd have flogged the fur right off the disobedient wolf.

A nip at my heel had me whirling midstride, a snarl on my lips that died as Edon towered over me.

Oh, dear forest above, he's fast.

And stealthy, too, because I hadn't even felt him gaining on me, much less being close enough to bite.

I swallowed, uncertain. Was he angry with me for spying? I wasn't officially pack yet, shouldn't be privy to any political matters. But his stature seemed calm, not aggressive. If anything, he appeared agreeable.

We hadn't spoken since that first night, and I'd pretty much been doing my own thing ever since. He began to circle me, appraising every inch of my wolf form. It was hard not to cower to his much bigger size.

If anyone questioned his alpha status, they just needed to ask this guy to shift, because *wow.*

Even I could admire the breadth of his shoulders, his strong thighs, and sleek, white coat. Perfection in wolf form. And the low rumble coming from his chest said he felt the same about me.

Another nip to my hind leg had me spinning again, a growl catching in my throat. He jumped to follow, his teeth snagging my rump—not hard, but playfully.

I didn't understand what he was doing.

We just kept dancing in circles, his teeth touching my coat, my legs whirling me around, until finally I lunged at him. I didn't like this dizzy game.

His masculine growl had my blood running cold until he tried to pin me with his jaw against my nape.

Oh. Hell. No.

I leapt away from him, only to find my much smaller form beneath his, grappling for purchase on the ground. I had half a mind to shift just to demand him to explain himself, but his muzzle against my neck forced me to fight back.

Round and round we went, sparring in wolf form beneath the willow trees.

He never snarled.

But I sure as hell did.

Especially when I pinned him with my jaws around his scruff. Only, he flipped me off him with a shake and pounced again.

It was ridiculous.

And… admittedly fun.

He's playing, I realized with a shock that landed me on my rump beneath him again.

His mouth closed over my flank, sending me skidding away once more, this time at a dead run through the underbrush. He gave chase, his strides longer, more knowing, but I refused to give up.

I ran with everything inside me.

Fast.

Hard.

Sprinting over the earth at breakneck speeds.

It felt amazing. Free. Exciting.

And every time his teeth skimmed my hide, I pushed myself to pick up the pace even more.

Edon's paws were silent, his presence behind me so invisible I thought I'd lost him.

Until he landed on me once more.

We tumbled and rolled from the impact, cascading us down a hill to the bank of a nearby river. Edon clamped down on my scruff to keep me from falling over the ledge, then gently pulled me back.

I blinked several times, dazed.

Then something soft and soothing ran over my muzzle. Edon's tongue.

I made to back away, but a growl from him held me captive as he licked me again. It stung a little, telling me I'd scraped my nose on something—likely during the tumbleweed fall down that hill—and Edon was *cleaning* the wound.

I flinched at the sensation of his tongue slicking across my fur. It didn't feel bad, just intimate. And I didn't want to be intimate with him.

Except the wolf inside me had very different feelings on that front. She was practically preening beneath his touch, urging me to lean into his side to beg for more.

Disagreeing with my animalistic soul went against my instincts, stirring a discomfort inside that I wanted to relieve.

But I refused to give in to Edon or any other alpha.

I wanted to be in charge of my life. To be free to make my own fucking choices. Not have to submit to an alpha for direction.

Edon rumbled, the sound one of pleasure and happiness, and my damn wolf almost purred in response.

I needed to shift back into my human form where *my* brain ruled. But I couldn't. *She* refused to budge.

Gah. Damn alpha hormones!

I swore he chuckled, as though he knew all about my internal struggle. And maybe he did. The mark on my thigh denoted me as his regardless of how my heart or mind felt. That meant our mating bond had begun. It would only be a matter of time before he owned every piece of me.

While I would own exactly none of him.

As was proven by his behavior this past week. I had no idea where he slept, but it wasn't in his bed. Not that I cared. If anything, it'd been a relief.

But it certainly painted a picture of what life here would become.

Me—alone—raising a pup while he fucked and played and ruled.

Edon nuzzled my nose, his obsidian eyes glowing with curiosity. Maybe he wasn't as entrenched in my head as I feared. He rolled into me, his warmth a blanket of security that set my fur on edge.

I didn't need his protection.

His adoration.

His attention.

I didn't *want* any of it.

Except my wolf seemed quite content to accept it all. She bathed in his energy, reveling in the power he possessed, his strength, his agility.

The water flowed before us, rippling over the rocks, flowing toward the ocean south of us. I'd studied the geography extensively prior to arriving, had spent the last week pacing the grounds to acquaint myself with the perimeters.

I'd originally pegged the newbie as the weakest link. After watching his performance today, I wasn't so sure.

But I could take him.

He wasn't an alpha, just a male. My training and strength and years as a wolf far outnumbered his. It wouldn't be hard. I just had to find the right time to catch him off guard, subdue him, and run.

Given how much freedom this pack had allowed me, it'd probably take at least a day for them to realize I was gone.

Edon even longer if he continued to avoid his home at night.

He stood and stretched beside me, drawing my gaze to the athletic lines of his form, the sexy masculinity of his coat, and the breadth of his shoulders.

He was a big wolf. In every way.

The image of him nude in human form flashed behind my eyes unbidden, reminding me of his muscular build and the way his abdomen tapered into an impressive V at the waist. Which seemed to point to his most masculine part. And yeah, I could begrudgingly admit it was well proportioned.

He nudged me with his nose, causing my eyes to lift to his. Amusement and hunger shone brightly in those ebony orbs—a promise of passion to come.

"And you'll beg me to fuck you, too."

His words seemed to hum across the air, engraving themselves in the moment and vowing to come to fruition.

Such arrogance.

But he was an alpha lycan. They were *all* arrogant.

And if it were up to my wolf, he'd probably win.

I laid my head back down, my way of displaying boredom and disinterest. It earned me a low sound in response, one brought on by the back of his throat. A growl of intention.

Not happening, I thought, conveying it with my body posture, refusing to look at him.

Silence fell between us.

My fur danced in anticipation, waiting for him to pounce again, to engage me in another game. But seconds rolled by into minutes. Until finally I looked back to find him gone.

He'd left me without a word.

An act I saw fitting because I intended to do the same to him. And soon.

Chapter Five

Edon

WELL, AT LEAST LUNA'S WOLF LIKED ME.

The woman beneath, however, clearly did not.

That was fine. After that beautiful display of speed, I could wait. Because winning her over would be worth the chase.

Someone above had crafted my ideal female. Feisty, sexy, athletic, and fierce. Just sensing her had heated my blood. And then her shock at my wanting to play had amused me deeply.

Did the Ernest Clan not engage in such affairs? Because we Clementes enjoyed our sparring. Well, we used to, anyway.

My father's way of ruling our people was more self-serving than caring. From what my grandfather told me, it wasn't always like this. And it didn't have to stay this way unless I wanted it to. Which remained to be seen.

I trotted along the grounds, scenting for anything suspicious along the way. The Alpha Trials were well underway, and my father seemed hell-bent on putting me through the wringer. If I failed, he would continue to rule for another year until we could restart the process.

Some alphas required almost a decade to complete the ascension.

I planned to do it in one.

This year.

So I welcomed whatever damage he wanted to send my way. Even if it came in the form of a dead vampire.

It had to be a test to see how I chose to handle the situation.

As far as I could tell, I only had one option. Pack first. Always. And fuck bullshit politics. I would not sacrifice my only progeny over a corpse. Especially as he was proving to be useful.

Most of my kind looked down upon the mutts, claiming them to be half-breeds since they weren't born lycan. But I saw it from a different angle—Silas grew up fighting for his life. That did something to a man. It strengthened his resolve, made him harder, faster, and smarter. Nothing was given to him on a golden platter, unlike the idiots who questioned my authority earlier. They were all pompous pack royals, sitting neatly beneath the alpha line and awaiting their futures in glorified enforcer roles.

While Silas, he had no role.

He was one of a kind since all the previous mortals turned lycans were dead in our clan. Mostly because my father had sired them. The last one in our territory was turned just over two decades ago. I'd been a wee pup, but old enough to witness what happened to the female who won the Immortal Cup that year.

My father turned her.

Then gave her to his buddies as a present.

The next time I saw her was during the burial my grandfather organized in her honor. He'd forced me to attend, saying I needed to know how to properly respect the dead. When I asked after my father, wondering at his lack of attendance, I was told that times had changed.

"Your father leads in a different time and manner than I once did," he'd said that day. "That's evidenced now by this poor girl's treatment."

I thought of her as I came upon Silas sitting naked on a log with my pants folded neatly at his side. The stench of death had lessened, but I pinpointed the grave several yards away. Silas had probably shifted to dig the hole in his wolf form. Which explained his now wet hair—he'd gone for a wash in the creek after.

Because he didn't have a home.

Or a shower.

No one would provide him with shelter here, yet his presence was required on the grounds. I suspected my father intended to use him somehow in the Alpha Trials.

Let's go for a run, I told Silas, meeting his wary gaze. I'd grab my pants later. *Shift.*

I didn't wait for him to comply, just jumped over the log he sat on and took a path away from the main grounds, deeper into the marshlands beyond. Wolves didn't live out here, mostly because we preferred to be together.

But there were times when some of us needed an escape—especially me. I'd actually spent the last few nights out here, away from the expectations of the pack to clear my head. That was how I'd been so close to Silas when he'd howled in alarm.

I just needed space.

From my packmates.

From my father.

From the trials ahead.

From Luna.

There were certain demands that I'd yet to meet, much to my father's fury. When he found out that I'd left Luna alone after the mating ritual, he'd struck me. Hard. But I wasn't like him. I wouldn't force an unwilling female into bed. And rather than hit him back, I'd walked away telling him to mind his position. Because we both knew that in a fight, he'd lose, the traditions be damned.

My grandfather had met me around the back of the house, where he'd suggested I take a few days away. Given the growing anxieties of the pack and Luna's chilly welcome, I'd agreed.

Silas's scent grew stronger as he caught up to me, his transition to wolf form taking longer than it should. *Have you been eating and sleeping regularly?* I wondered.

He didn't answer right away, but his mind did with a series of images outlined in his memories.

His first nights—cold and alone.

Sleeping under a tree in wolf form.

Learning to hunt on his own after several days without real food.

Bathing in the creek when he realized he wouldn't be given access to normal showers.

Stealing a roll from the mating ceremony, then throwing it up when the rich quality hit his stomach.

I sighed. *I've severely neglected you.* Mostly to protect him. My father wanted me to kill Silas, not turn him. I'd considered it after observing Silas's initial transition, but the fight in his gaze when he glowered at me that night had me making another choice. Watching him today confirmed my decision as the right one.

But if I'd showed him any favors before the pack, they'd definitely use Silas against me in the trials.

So we would have to be very discreet.

I'm fine, Silas said after a beat, unwilling to voice the real thought in his head. Which I translated to be, *No shit,* based on the firing images of his fist meeting my jaw.

If I were in human form, I would have smirked in amusement. I liked this newbie. He had an impressive set of balls on him. His fighting style wasn't half-bad either.

The trials are a difficult time for an alpha heir. With my father leading them, I suspect they'll be close to unbearable. I picked up our pace to a slight run that Silas held with ease. At least his athleticism had remained in spite of the poor nourishment. Definitely a fighter. *I think the vampire was the first test.*

Silas followed me in silence, his mind racing with images of the body and the surroundings. He'd taken stock of every detail, every scent, and all the potential clues.

With each passing second, this male amazed me more.

Most of the wolves my age were like Glenn and his idiot minions. Silas was different, his approach thorough and not impulsive.

My grandfather would probably like him.

If it's a test, then you failed, Silas said, surprising me. *The Blood Alliance favors order, and you broke the Goddess's cardinal rule by covering up the murder.*

My ears flicked in irritation. *You think I should have reported it?*

Yes. He glanced at me. *I mean, I'm thankful you didn't. But I won't be surprised if the dead vamp resurfaces in the next few weeks, thereby forcing your hand.*

Then maybe we need to hide it better, I thought.

The river would carry the remains to the ocean, where the body will eventually decompose in the waves.

A solid plan, one that would distort the evidence. It would also make it impossible for anyone in the pack to stumble across the remains. I should have suggested it earlier rather than tell him to bury it, but I'd been distracted by Luna's lingering scent. My desire to chase had overridden reason.

I'll handle it, I told him.

Silas tripped beside me, his shock evident in the tense lines of his limbs. He'd obviously expected me to demand he do it, but I had another task in mind for him.

I need you to keep an eye on things for me, report back anything and everything that piques your curiosity. If something doesn't feel right, I want to know about it. If you see pack members acting suspiciously, tell me. I slowed my run and ducked beneath a low willow tree toward a path no one but me ever traveled.

We were over a mile from the outskirts of the pack's central zone. Very few bothered to venture this far, the home grounds spanning thirty miles of well-kept acres of land. This area was a pit in comparison.

But it held a secret.

One my grandfather had gifted me a decade ago.

An escape.

Sure, Silas replied, sounding about as thrilled as a pup getting his first bath.

It's not a task to take lightly, Omega. There could be great reward in it for you if you perform well. Having the respect of the clan alpha carried a lot of weight. And considering I planned a complete overhaul of my father's staff, it would be wise for Silas to remain on my good side.

Of course, I hadn't exactly given the newbie cause to trust me.

Nor did I really trust him.

Our sire link, however, provided a unique opportunity. One I intended to exploit for my benefit.

It's not like I have anything better to do, Silas muttered, his tone edging the line of disrespectful.

My father would put him in his place with a harsh bite to the nape. Or worse. He believed in ruling with an iron fist, his preference for cruelty well known in

Clemente Clan. His advisors approved, as did the elder families of the pack.

Families like the one Glenn came from.

Those were the males my father forced me to befriend, the ones he wanted to influence my upbringing and opinions.

My grandfather had other ideas.

He taught me about the old ways, customs long dead, thanks to societal laws today. He taught me the value of respect.

If my father ever found out, he'd oust my grandfather and force him to live with the rogues in no man's land.

Fortunately, my father was too busy lording over his kingdom to notice. If anything, he seemed thrilled to not have to deal with me.

Until now.

The rules forced him to interact with me for the Alpha Trials.

And he'd been very clear about his disappointment thus far.

I think Luna is up to something, Silas said, startling me once more.

What do you mean?

She keeps scouting the boundaries, like she's considering the best escape route. Silas sounded nervous. *I've watched her cross over a few times just to see if anyone would stop her.*

I snorted. *Of course she is.* I suspected it after the mating ceremony, and even more so today when I found her creeping near the perimeter.

She's an alpha female, I added. *Independence is ingrained in her. I'm actually surprised she hasn't run yet.*

You're not mad. Not a question, but a statement.

No. I'm intrigued. I hope she runs. Because then I could catch her. And that would be so incredibly fun. *Keep an eye on her. If she makes a break for it, let me know.*

And then what?

I slowed to a walk, transforming into my human form as I moved. My bones lengthened, the magic of my lycan soul giving way to the male within. And then I rolled my shoulders, cracking my neck and popping my joints into place. "And then I'll chase her," I replied out loud, eyeing the property ahead.

Silas remained in his wolf form, likely because shifting took too much out of him and he didn't want me to see just how weak he'd become from all his transformations today.

Smart wolf.

Showing weakness to the alpha was the fastest way to being dominated.

"This cabin is mine," I told him, nodding to the small wooden lodge ahead. "It's a bit archaic and uses solar technology to keep the utilities fresh, but I keep it well stocked with supplies." I looked down at him. "And there's an extra bed inside that's rarely used."

A hopeful note graced the air, one I only caught because I'd been waiting for it. Silas hid it in the next breath, his stance becoming bored as he searched the area with his nose.

"You can crash here, but don't tell anyone." Not that I expected anyone to notice. My nose never picked up on any pack out here. It was why I used it as a refuge. Only my grandfather seemed to know about it. "Whatever you find inside is fair game. Including the food." Which I'd try to keep as refreshed for him as I could. If he was going to help me, then I needed him in top shape.

I also sort of wanted to see what kind of lycan he'd become under the right circumstances, because he was already proving to be stronger and faster than half the purebreds back at the main camp.

Why are you doing this? he asked, sounding hesitant.

Because it's the right thing to do, I admitted. *Also, I need an ally, and no one will suspect me of working with you in the Alpha Trials.* The clan all thought I'd left Silas to fend for himself, just like my father would have done.

And, in truth, I had. Not necessarily because I didn't care, but because I'd been a little preoccupied with the upcoming ascension.

That changed today.

How do you know you can trust me to help? he asked, his tone incredulous.

"I don't," I replied out loud.

Seems like a risk.

"It is," I agreed.

He remained quiet for a beat, then stood and shook out his fur. *Is there a shower in there?*

"Yes."

All right, he replied. *A favor for a favor.*

If that was the way he wanted to look at it, then that worked for me. "Then I'll let you get acquainted while I go retrieve my pants and handle our headless friend." I didn't bother with a goodbye. If Silas needed me, he could tap into my head.

Although, I suspected he wouldn't.

Silas struck me as a wolf who relied only on himself to survive. It was something we had in common.

Because while I desired his assistance, I wouldn't depend on it.

The only one who could win these trials was me. But I'd use every advantage I could to pass, including the sire bond to Silas.

Chapter Six

Luna

I COULDN'T ESCAPE EDON'S SCENT. He returned to his home two days ago—a few hours after our frolic—and only left twice to handle pack business.

I hated it.

His presence overwhelmed me, taunted my lady bits, and left me in a writhing pile of need in my sheets.

And the bastard knew, too.

It was written all over his amused expression as I entered the living room. He sat lounging in a pair of jeans that he wore like a king, his chest bare, his abs defined, his package—

Stop, I demanded, focusing on the kitchen and not the very virile wolf on the leather couch.

"There's coffee in the pot," he called. "Just brewed it."

Of course he did. Because he sensed me waking up from the dream his nearness caused.

Or, more likely, my fantasies came from his unwanted bite the other night. I healed almost instantly, but his claim thrived inside me, heating my veins and forcing me to walk down the path of fate. My wolf was attuned to him, curious, hungry, and intrigued.

I forced her to heel every time he walked into the room. But we all knew he'd win me over eventually. Probably around the time I went into heat.

He stood behind me now, his stealthy moves barely perceptible to my senses, but I *felt* his warmth. Like a liquid caress down my spine that culminated between my thighs.

"Do you want to go for a run?" he asked, his voice deep, seductive, and far too dominant.

I pointedly poured a cup of coffee—something I meant to do upon entering but couldn't because my hormones held me frozen in the middle of the room like a damn idiot.

Hatred at being here rippled through me, the ire overriding my need.

My family hadn't even said goodbye after the ceremony. Not that I expected them to. I was raised for this purpose and this purpose alone. It was my brother who had taught me how to fight, who had made sure I was prepared for the trials that lay ahead. Unlike my father, Logan actually cared if I survived. My mother, she would probably care, too, if my father hadn't degraded her to omega status.

I saw similar notes of that treatment here in Clemente Clan. Edon's mother barely looked up from the ground, the alpha female so sickeningly submissive to Walter that I could hardly stand looking at her.

And the other females were either omegas or betas, all with their tails between their legs when it came to the males of the grounds.

It was wrong and yet far too common. Our society saw men as the betters and women as serving a single-minded purpose—to provide pleasure and pups.

Well, I wouldn't be doing either of those things if I had my way.

Edon could kiss my alpha ass.

As if he heard me, he pressed his groin into my ass as he grasped my hips, his lips falling to my ear. "You realize fighting me only makes me want you more, right?"

A growl rumbled in my chest. I tried to swallow the noise around a mouthful of scalding coffee, but it was already too late. We both heard it.

He chuckled and pressed a kiss to my neck—the gesture both seductive and holding a hint of command that I loathed. "Run with me later."

So we'd escalated from a request stage to a demand stage. I set my cup down and turned in his arms. Big mistake because it put my back to the counter and gave him an opportunity to cage me between his impressively muscled arms. He gripped the counter on either side, his body angling over mine, crowding me.

"It's a run," he said before I could even comment. "I'm not asking you to fuck, even though we both know you want to. I just want—"

"I do not want to fuck you," I bit out.

His lips curled. "No?" He leaned in to run his nose along my cheekbone and then down my neck, the light caress scattering goose bumps down my arms. I shivered, and not because I was cold. "Mmm, your scent determines that to be a lie."

"It's my wolf." My voice came out gravely, underlined in both frustration and yearning, and I hated the sultry quality to it. "You forced the mating bond. My wolf is responding."

"Forced?" he repeated, drawing back slightly, his eyebrow arching. "I forced nothing."

"Oh?" I feigned a look of surprise. "So you didn't bite me the other night in a claiming ceremony? Huh. Didn't realize I dreamed that." I tried to return to my coffee, but his knee lodging between mine held me before him, captive.

"You were mine whether I bit you or not. Be thankful I didn't do more." The threat in his tone had my hackles rising.

"Thankful. Right." I snorted. "Okay. Thank you, Edon, for not raping me. *Yet.*"

His obsidian gaze narrowed. "Most wolves beg me to fuck them."

"I'm not most wolves."

"No, you're not. You're my intended. But something you seem to be ignoring, little mate, is that I had no choice in this either."

"You had more of one than I did," I argued. "*You* could have denied me."

"And what? Subjected you to whatever punishment Niko desired? You realize he would have killed you, right?"

"He would have been pissed, but not enough to kill me."

"No?" He laughed, but it lacked humor. "You really don't know how our politics work if you believe that for a second. My father would have demanded your life for such disrespect, and Niko would have given it to honor the clan ties. Because he would have had no use for you after my rejection."

I opened my mouth to argue that point, then closed it. I knew my father would have beat me for defying his orders. That wouldn't have been anything new. It was Edon's comment about Walter that gave me pause. I'd never considered his reaction or what he'd demand, and given what little I'd observed of him over the last week in Clemente territory, I was inclined to believe Edon's summarization.

Oh, I would have fought it, but with that many angry wolves? I wouldn't have stood a chance.

"Ah, you see it, don't you?" Edon taunted, his tone holding a hint of menace. "You thought fucking another wolf would save you from a life by my side, but all it did was guarantee it." He leaned in so close that his breath fanned my lips as he added, "You're not the only one who enjoys defiance, little mate."

I shuddered beneath him, conflicted.

He wasn't anything like I envisioned. Alpha, yes. But he didn't demand my compliance the way my father would command it from my mother. Instead, Edon seemed to want to coax it from me, like we were playing some sort of game. Only, I didn't understand the rules of this battle between us.

"You weren't the only one forced during the ceremony," he continued, his mouth brushing mine with each word. "Yes, I could have rejected you and chosen to do this all over again in a year with another intended mate. But my pack needs a regime change. I will not fail them."

His words surprised me almost as much as the desire pooling in my belly. His nearness, his touch, and his lips so close to mine were all fucking with my head.

I needed space.

To breathe.

To *run.*

He nipped my lower lip, not harshly, just a sweet little taste. A taunt. A promise of what could be, if I allowed it.

Only my wolf was already possessed by his claiming bite. It would never truly be consensual when I submitted, and we both knew it.

I swallowed and closed my eyes.

What did he mean by his pack needing a regime change? Did Edon plan to rule them differently? I wanted to ask, to request he clarify his intentions, but my jaw wouldn't loosen. If I gave in to those queries, I risked giving in to him. And I refused. I'd rather live a life as a rogue than as a glorified alpha pet.

"Edon?" a feminine voice called from the entryway, disturbing the moment.

"Mmm, since you don't seem to want to run, then I guess I'll go play." He pressed a quick kiss to my lips before he pushed away to meet the intruder in the hallway. "Bianca," he greeted, the licentious tone in his voice causing my stomach to clench. There was no question as to what those two intended to do.

And as she came into view, I could see why.

The blonde, curvy beta oozed sex.

"Bianca, have you met Luna yet?" The way he asked it told me he knew we hadn't met yet. He was escalating the stakes of our game by introducing me to one of his mistresses—because I had no doubt there were several throughout the clan. All alphas had a harem of humans and wolves. Edon would be no different.

It was part of the psychological madness that broke alpha females. We were a possessive breed, and to share our mates with others went against our natural instincts.

I didn't even claim Edon as mine yet, and my wolf already wanted to shred Bianca to pieces. Especially as her arm slid around his waist in a knowing caress that spoke of their intimate familiarity. That he leaned down to kiss her on her perfect blonde head only infuriated me more.

"I've seen her exploring," Bianca replied, a note of disinterest in her tone. "She's not very friendly," she added in a loud whisper.

Edon chuckled. "No. She's really not."

Fuck you both, I thought, turning around to dump my coffee in the sink.

If Edon wanted to taunt me, so be it. He wouldn't win.

I turned around with a serene smile, meeting his gaze without hesitation. "I'll give you both some privacy and go for a run." I pulled my shirt over my head, unfastened my shorts, and shimmied out of them while focusing solely on him.

His smile died at the sight of my naked breasts, his eyes traveling lower to the well-groomed thatch of hair between my thighs.

He would be able to smell my arousal, the way my body naturally responded to his. Maybe it would fuel his time with *Bianca.*

I refused to even think about it.

"You two have fun now," I added, smirking at his conflicted expression.

His arm blocked my exit, his hand curling around my hip to tug me into him as his mouth descended over mine.

Bianca growled in annoyance, which, for some reason, only made me want to kiss him back to piss her off more.

I didn't even know the female, and I hated her on sight.

Mostly because she had the audacity to walk into Edon's house without knocking, knowing that he had me here. Her boldness spoke of her confidence, of her desire to throw our mating bond off balance, and I found myself wanting to return the favor in kind.

Because even if Edon entertained a harem, it would never compare to what we would have together.

So I allowed his tongue to slide inside my mouth to explore and pressed my body into his at the same time. He rumbled low in his throat in approval, his hips angling toward mine as he deepened the kiss.

It wasn't my first time embracing a male like this, but it was the first time I *reacted* to it.

What began as a hint of fun and revenge turned into something primal. Hot. Overwhelming.

My wolf stretched inside me, roaring to life and taking over my instincts. I slid my arms around his neck, pressing my breasts flush to his bare chest. He growled in response, his groin hot against mine.

Fuck. This was far too arousing, far too *right.* I'd meant to play with him, but now I couldn't release him. I wanted more. To feel his prowess, his dominance, his skill in the bedroom.

He kissed me with the same vigor, his tongue skillfully mastering mine into submission as his palm spanned my lower back.

I wanted to climb him like a tree, find out what else he could offer me.

Until his lips left mine to travel to my ear. "Thank you, Luna. Bianca will handle the rest. I wouldn't want to *force* you, after all."

My blood went cold, my arms freezing around his neck.

His amused chuckle soured my stomach.

Bastard, I thought, livid.

My nails bit into his nape, drawing blood, marking him as *mine,* before I released him completely. His nostrils flared, his amusement dying.

"Enjoy your playtime," I said, hating myself for the yearning in my voice.

Bianca practically purred beside him, her fingers trailing over his chest—a chest I'd just vacated—all the way down to his belt.

I refused to stay here to observe what happened next, to hear him fuck her in the home we were destined to share.

But it gave me a nice dose of reality regarding my new life, one I would not accept.

I'd spent the last several days testing the boundaries. I knew where to go. How to run. And it seemed Bianca had just provided me with the distraction I needed to keep Edon off my tail.

He wanted to fuck her? Fine. I hoped he enjoyed it. Because I wouldn't be returning to find out.

I shifted in front of him and bolted from the house.

No more Clemente Clan.

No more Edon.

No more fate.

I chose my rules, my life, my destiny. Not anyone else.

Fuck all of you.

Chapter Seven

Silas

IT TOOK ME SEVERAL MINUTES to orient myself as I stirred to awareness.

A mattress, not leaves, cushioned my back. Instead of tree branches, wood beams decorated the ceiling above me. And an open window beside me graced my senses with fresh forest air.

My eyes stung with an emotion I didn't want to acknowledge. *Relief.*

Fuck, I couldn't remember the last time I slept in a bed. Intellectually, I understood it'd only been a few months since my time at the university. But that all felt like several lifetimes ago, between the fight for immortality and my transition to Clemente Clan life.

Everything inside me ached. Not from physical strain, just from the pain of existing. I had killed so many people, all in a game meant to entertain others. My reward? Being turned into a lycan and essentially exiled from the pack just for being alive.

You could be Willow, my subconscious whispered, causing me to flinch.

Being forced to fuck humans or lycans for the rest of my brief life was definitely worse. As were several dozen other avenues available to humans in this world. Hell, I could have been picked for a moon chase.

I groaned at the thought, digging my palms into my eyes.

Fuck. I'd be expected to participate in a moon chase one of these days.

Would I be able to hunt and kill my old kind? Doubtful.

I rolled to my side, my stomach churning from both the motion and the thoughts running rampant through my mind.

Eating a full meal last night had not been a wise decision. I'd barely kept half of it down afterward. Everything was so rich. So crisp. Not at all like the food from my previous life, or even my new one.

Raw fish from the streams hadn't been my favorite, either, but at least they mostly stayed down. The meat from Edon's fridge was too flavorful for my taste buds.

Yet the wolf in me craved more.

It was so fucked up having this creature inside me dictating my wants and needs above my common sense.

With a deep growl, I forced myself out of the soft bed. I had no idea what time it was, nor did I really care. But it felt like I'd been sleeping for days, not hours.

I frowned at my appearance in the mirror. *Maybe I did sleep for days.* Because I looked a hell of a lot better than I did last night, or whenever I'd lain down.

The hollows beneath my eyes were gone.

My hair still resembled a blond mop of locks, the shaggy strands hitting just below my ears. *I really need a haircut.*

There are scissors in the kitchen, a cool male voice replied, giving me pause.

Are you always in my head? I demanded, feeling slightly violated by this whole sire-progeny bond bullshit.

Yes. He didn't elaborate. Not that I expected him to. The alpha hadn't proven to be all that chatty, just authoritative.

And maybe a tiny bit sympathetic—a trait that left me conflicted. I didn't want to like him. However, I couldn't deny feeling a hint of gratitude for giving me a place to rest.

I blew out a breath and consoled myself with a hot shower. The water beat against my back, giving me a brief glimpse of heaven.

I'd practically lost myself the first time I stepped into this marble enclosure, my body so thankful for a proper cleanse. Now I just indulged in it because I wasn't sure if I'd be allowed to take another again. Who knew when Edon would change his mind about the arrangements? They were definitely temporary.

He wanted me to keep an eye out for him.

Fine.

I'd do it because there was nothing else to do out here. And also because I appreciated the shower.

It took effort to leave the soap and water behind, but I managed in favor of the scissors Edon mentioned. Then I stared at my reflection once more. I had no idea where to start or how I would reach the back.

"Fuck it," I said, giving it my best shot. It wasn't like I had anyone to impress.

Thirty minutes later, I appeared almost human again. Minus the feral glint in my blue eyes where the wolf peeked out. I'd seen my reflection in the water numerous times, knew what I looked like, but it seemed even more real now as I stood here before the mirror.

You've missed two days of rounds, Omega, Edon said, intruding on my thoughts once more. *There are whispers about it floating around. Go make an appearance to shut them up before someone tells me to look for you.*

Two days?

You needed the sleep was his reply.

Shit. No wonder I felt better.

Pushing away from the sink, I ventured into the kitchen to snag another piece of the too-savory meat. It nearly made me gag as I chewed and swallowed, but the wolf in me grinned. I chugged some sweet orange liquid after it, grimacing the entire time, and wandered out into the midafternoon sun.

The solar panels Edon mentioned were high up in the trees, their wires looping down the trunk like a vine to feed into the cabin. From what I gathered, the water came from a nearby well. Something about the system pumped it into the home and through a filter. I actually liked the taste of it.

Closing my eyes, I focused on calling my wolf to the surface—something that came to me surprisingly naturally now. The transition shifted over me, reforming my bones and lowering me to the ground onto four paws. It wasn't as sleek as Edon's. Not even close. But it felt right for me, and that was all that mattered.

With a shake of my fur, I bounded off in the direction of the main grounds. Hopefully, an appearance was all they needed. If anyone demanded an explanation, I'd just tell them I fell asleep out in the marshlands.

But something told me no one would care enough to ask.

I was the pack omega. The newbie. The grunt.

I only existed because of a game that left me on the clan's doorstep.

Most would say I was lucky to be alive.

Today, for the first time, I sort of agreed.

A rusty scent caught my nose, causing me to pause mid-run. Vampire. But that didn't make any sense. We were hundreds of miles from the nearest vampire territories. I knew my geography, understood Clemente Clan's position on the globe, including the heart of the capital. Vampires shouldn't be anywhere near here.

So why did a dead one appear the other day?

And now this one?

I sniffed, tracking the source. Unlike the first visitor, this one permeated the air with life. His scent didn't match any of the visitors from the mating ritual, and the blood lacked the rich quality of a royal.

Was it a rogue of some kind? A vampire without a liege?

The trail took me deeper into the marshlands, away from Edon's cabin and the clan headquarters. All that existed out here was swamp and wildlife. Why would he choose to muck through—

A bolt of white in my peripheral vision caused me to spin on my haunches.

My instincts triggered the chase before I could register that I was running, my paws bounding over the earth toward whatever had caught my eye.

Several yards later, the scent of orange blossoms hit my nostrils, causing them to flare. *Luna.*

I knew that little she-wolf was going to make a run for it!

By the looks of it, she was heading south, likely with the ocean in mind. Where she intended to go from there was anyone's guess. But I didn't plan to let her get that far.

My predator drive honed in on her sprinting form, pushing me to a speed that sent shivers of delight down my legs. It felt good to run this fast. Really good.

Luna was quick.

But my strides were longer.

I caught her back leg with my jaws, yanking her to the side. She whirled on a snarl, her jaws going for my throat without preamble.

Fuck.

I dodged her, then found myself in a ball of rolling fluff as my wolf took over my reactions. Subduing her became my primary objective, the inclination laced tightly with survival.

She was wild.

Fierce.

Furious.

But no matter how agilely or swiftly she moved, she couldn't get a hold on my throat. I refused. And when I saw an opening to go for *her* neck, I took it, slamming her into the ground beneath me.

It happened in a matter of seconds that felt like minutes.

She stilled on a growl, her defeat written into the lines of her form.

And then she began to shift.

I jumped backward, confused.

Until she attacked me again—on two legs.

The woman was fucking crazy!

But then I realized why she'd done it.

If I left a mark on her with my teeth, Edon would have my balls in a vise.

Damn. I was almost impressed by her wit. Except I was more focused on turning human as well, something that happened faster than ever before.

She took off in a dead run instead of hitting me while I was vulnerable.

And I gave chase.

Two legs felt natural to me, my athleticism in this form superior to my performance on four paws. I caught her in seconds, tackling her to the grass once more.

She pushed and shoved, sending us sprawling until I seized her around the waist and yanked her under me.

Her resulting snarl vibrated against my chest as her fist sailed toward my jaw. I captured it just in time, pushing it to the ground, then did the same with her other hand. Which left her writhing beneath me in an effort to throw me off her.

"Stop," I growled.

She didn't.

Her legs squirmed, trying to gain the upper hand, and I knew exactly what she intended, so I pressed my groin into her sex, belatedly realizing how bad an idea that was. I'd just wanted to stop her from kneeing me in the jewels.

Instead, I'd aligned my hardening length right against her slick folds.

She immediately stilled.

I took a moment just to breathe, my heart racing in my chest.

Her light brown eyes held mine, her pupils enlarged in a mixture of fright and something else. Something darker.

"Do it," she said. "Dominate me to completion."

It was a dare that held a touch of a plea that I didn't understand.

"I don't…" I swallowed, my blood running far too hot for my liking. This position stirred chaos in my mind. A primal part of me—the wolf—wanted to fuck her. *Hard.* While my human side knew that would be wrong.

And yet I couldn't let her up.

She'd just run again. I could see it in the stubborn set of her jaw.

"Coward," she taunted.

My eyebrows rose. "You're calling me a coward for not raping you? That's charming."

Her teeth sank into my lower lip before I realized she'd moved, her bite deep and drawing blood.

"*Fuck.*" I yanked my mouth away from hers, cursing again at the resulting sting of the open wound.

She grinned up at me, my blood tainting her lips.

"You're insane," I accused, half-crazed myself by the feral sight of her. *What is wrong with me?* It was the wolf inside. Instincts overriding reasons. I pushed it back down, needing my head clear.

But Luna rubbed her soaked pussy against my length, a low mewl of yearning emanating from her chest.

"You don't even know my name," I marveled.

"Silas," she hissed. "Newbie. Dominant. Male."

The broken speech confused me. Then I realized the wolf had completely stolen her senses. Because it was a pair of black irises that stared up at me now, not light brown. "Luna…"

"Take me," she begged, pressing against me once more.

"No." I rolled off of her, then jumped up onto my heels as she came after me in a haze of brown hair and white skin.

Her nails slashed across my chest, her knees came at my groin, and her fist attempted another hit at my face. I caught her and whirled her into my arms, forcing her back to my front. She tried to stomp on my foot and kicked back at my calves.

It fucking hurt.

"Stop this, Luna."

"Never." She completely lost it in my arms, fighting for her life—and clearly coming for mine.

Her one goal seemed to be to kill me, leaving me no choice but to defend myself once more. I blocked hits and kicks, dodged her claws, and tried to find a way to subdue her that didn't end up with us on the ground again.

Hurting her would be a mistake. On some base level, I understood that. But years and years of fighting for my life came to the forefront, taking over my vision and painting it in red.

I hadn't survived this long to be taken down by an angry little alpha wolf.

And I'd killed men twice her size in battle several times over.

"Luna," I snarled, demanding her submission, demanding she cease this before I *really* fought her.

She didn't heed the warning, her lithe form dancing around me in a wave of violence that called to my inner animal.

"Yield, little alpha," I demanded, giving her one last chance to do the right thing.

"Fuck you," she seethed, her claws swiping across my cheek and leaving a burn in their wake.

Primal need vibrated through my veins, stirring a reaction from within I couldn't repress. I had her on her back in a second flat, her hands clasped above her head, my other palm at her throat. "*Yield*," my wolf roared.

And she did.

Oh, how she did.

Her nostrils flared, her eyes resembling obsidian pools of lust, her mouth glowing with traces of my blood.

I licked it off on instinct, earning me a growl of approval from the female beneath me. Her lips parted, her tongue touching mine.

My chest rumbled. *More.*

Part of me acknowledged how utterly fucked up this was, but the sensation of pliant female wolf overrode my sanity.

I needed to *taste* her.

To dominate her.

To *win* her.

My mouth sealed over hers, the kiss brutal in its damnation and perfection. She hungrily met me move for move, her arousal sweetening her natural orange scent as we devoured one another.

Blood.

Growls.

Bites.

Licks.

It went on, the embrace one of the most erotic experiences of my life, and we weren't even fucking yet. Not in earnest. Just our mouths mating in a forbidden kiss.

I released her hands, needing and wanting to feel every inch of her.

Her fingers clawed into my hair, holding me to her as she returned the passion, her other hand raking nails down my back, marking me.

It was so fucking primal.

So fucking wrong.

Yet so fucking right.

"We can't do this," some weak part of me managed to say. But for the life of me, I couldn't remember why.

"We can do whatever we want," Luna replied, the sultry quality of her voice sending me cascading over the edge into a world of sensation and alpha female.

She had me by the balls.

Whatever she wanted, I'd do, if it meant I could continue tasting the heaven she offered. The bliss. The alluring escape from reality.

I wanted it all.

And I found it in the form of a wolf who wasn't mine…

Chapter Eight

Edon

I COULDN'T TAKE MY EYES OFF the sight before me, my lips parted in absolute awe.

Primal energy radiated off Luna and Silas, their erotic aroma seducing my senses and stroking the ire burning inside. An intoxicating combination that left me frozen beside a nearby tree.

Silas had shouted Luna's name repeatedly in his mind, sending me running here to find them engaged in a battle between their wolves—in human form.

I didn't catch all of it, but the predatory nature of their duel told me everything I needed to know.

Neither of them was thinking with their heads. Only their instincts.

Silas had caught Luna.

Now she wanted to submit to the stronger wolf, to feel him dominate her in the most basic way—through the art of fucking.

It was why I had wanted to chase her. I'd wanted to be the wolf on top of her. But Silas had beaten me to it.

Yet something held him back.

And rather than take advantage of the moment to subdue them both, I leaned against the tree stump and watched him fuck her mouth with his tongue.

I should have been furious.

I wasn't.

Well, no, I *was*.

But this was also really fucking *hot*.

They were both naked, sweaty, and tainted with Silas's blood. How far would my progeny go with this? All the way? Or would that hesitation get the best of him?

Luna had all but lost herself to her wolf, her body writhing up against him, her long, sexy legs wrapping around his waist in an effort to move him along. Yet Silas didn't give her what she craved. He controlled the kiss, his hands roaming over her in tantalizing strokes that only seemed to turn her on more.

His mind told me how badly he wanted this, how he longed to sink inside her slick heat and propel himself into oblivion. Deep down he knew it was wrong; I sensed it in his thoughts. But his wolf refused to acknowledge it, too eager to rut against the willing female beneath him.

Silas showed remarkable strength in pushing the urge down, satisfying himself with licking Luna instead. He started at her neck, pausing to circle her thundering pulse before continuing a path downward to her breasts.

Her fingers threaded through his thick blond hair, holding her to him as she mewled in pleasure beneath his wicked mouth. An image of him doing the same to me flashed behind my eyes, giving me pause.

And as he trailed his mouth along her abdomen, I imagined it was my body he caressed with his tongue.

Holy fuck, I thought to myself, my balls squeezing tight at the exquisite fantasy. Which only deepened as I added Luna—placing her at this tree—watching Silas licking and sucking all the way down to my cock. Her little fingers would disappear between her thighs, pumping in and out in response, her moans music to our ears.

Moans that I heard now as Silas licked her deep, in the place only meant for me.

And still I couldn't move, too fascinated by the show in the field and the strange ideas populating my mind.

Silas on his knees before me, taking my cock deep into his throat before passing me to Luna, who sat eagerly waiting for me to fuck her mouth.

Just as that vision ended, a new one of me inside Luna appeared, pumping her sweet cunt full of my cream—cream that Silas licked from her like he licked her now, before she returned the favor by sucking him off to completion.

I shuddered, my dick harder than it'd ever been.

Luna's cries of satisfaction blended with Silas's groans, his face soaked by her eager pussy. The entire scene played out before my eyes, her climax a scream that echoed off the trees, causing the birds to fly.

And she soared with them, her body vibrating beautifully beneath Silas.

Another man.

One I created.

One who *owed* me his life.

Yet he defiled that partnership by taking *my* female. And he continued to do so with abandon, bringing her to another earth-shattering orgasm I felt to my very bones.

I wanted to destroy them both. To rip them limb from limb. But, at the same time, I wanted to fuck them.

It didn't make any sense, this riot of sensation, this anger, this *need.* I couldn't tell what I craved more—retribution or Silas's mouth around my cock. And Luna, oh, darling Luna, I wanted to mount her more than I'd ever desired mounting another woman.

It'd been over a week since her arrival, and we'd barely spent a moment together other than the first night and our little run the other day. I'd avoided her, spending time with my grandfather instead. I needed to prepare for the trials. He was the only one willing to help me.

But now I regretted more than ever not going to her, not forcing her to yield the way she did for Silas now.

It was his name leaving her mouth as she screamed a third time.

I growled in response. A low, feral sound, one that had her stilling beneath Silas. He lifted his head, looking for the source. Rather than let him see me, I ducked behind the tree, not ready yet to discipline them for their actions.

Because I'd end up either killing them or fucking them both.

I ran a hand over my face, my cock straining at my zipper. *What the hell is wrong with me?* It shouldn't even be a decision. Silas needed to die for betraying me—his sire—in such a way. And Luna, she needed to be brought to heel.

Yet I still couldn't move.

My blood hummed hot, desire tightening my groin, my base urge telling me to run out there and *join* them, not punish them.

I shook my head. Dazed. Confused. Way too turned on for my own good.

I should have taken Bianca up on her offer to fuck this afternoon, should have let her go to her knees like a good little wolf and take my cock between those plump fuck-me lips.

But I couldn't.

It felt wrong.

Oh, goading Luna had been fun. At least until she ran off. Not that I blamed her. I'd been an ass, but her comments about rape and forcing the bond had truly pissed me off.

Women usually adored me, but Luna acted as if it would be a hardship, even when her body clearly desired mine.

It infuriated me, left me frustrated, and some twisted part of me had wanted to hurt her right back.

Which obviously fucking backfired because I'd left her all hot and bothered with a desire to run. And now all my threats of her not finding a wolf to fuck her were blown out the window by my own damn progeny.

How did this happen?

No, better question.

Why did I let this happen?

I stole a deep breath, needing this insanity to end. Whether I fucked them or killed them remained to be seen. I couldn't just stand here like a pansy ass and allow this to continue.

But when I finally stepped into the clearing, they were both gone.

Silas's scent led back to the home I generously lent to him, while Luna's went toward the main properties.

They'd split up, leaving me with a choice of whom to follow first.

It was easier than I expected. I chose Silas. Because I owned him. And he was about to find out what it meant to demolish the trust between progeny and sire.

Maybe after I dealt with him, this urge to chase Luna down and fuck her into submission would subside.

Maybe, but not likely.

I was the alpha here. Not her. Not Silas. *Me.*

It was time for both of them to realize that.

It was time for them to *kneel.*

Chapter Nine

Silas

FUCK. What did I just do? How could I let that happen?

I paced the interior of the cabin—lost.

Edon knew.

I *felt* his knowledge deep inside, the fiery energy burning and coming right for me. But I was helpless to run. Like he'd placed a shackle on my leg, forcing me to stay here, to wait for him.

I was a dead wolf. I knew it in every fiber of my being. There was no excuse in the world that would save me now. Not that I even had one.

Fighting had left me aroused.

And Luna. *Fuck.* I couldn't say no, didn't want to deny her. Part of me wondered if it was her intention all along to put me in this position, to distract her very irate intended mate.

But I caught the fear in her gaze when his growl echoed over us. She ran faster than I did, her terror leaving a pungent scent behind.

What would he do to her? Was he there right now? Punishing her?

No.

No, he wasn't.

Because I could feel him here.

Could sense him lurking in the shadows of the room, debating my fate.

I shivered, uncertain of what to do. Should I try to fight? To plead my case?

He surrounded me with his dominance, his power a palpable presence that weighed on my spine, demanding submission. Yet my legs locked in rebellion, my abdomen tightening beneath the intensity.

"You touched something that didn't belong to you," he said, his voice low, a rasp of sound that sent a chill down my spine.

I swallowed. "I know." Not the right response. I should have apologized, should have promised it wouldn't happen again.

But both statements would have been lies.

I neither regretted it nor could vow not to repeat it. Because something had happened between Luna and me, some sort of intense pull, and it was far from done. I wanted to taste her again. To fuck her. To *own* her.

It was completely insane.

I barely knew her.

Yet my wolf desired her. Not as a mate, but as a prize. And he refused to be denied.

Edon circled me, the shadows of the room keeping his presence concealed. However, I *felt* him moving, eyeing me as one did its prey.

The setting sun outside seemed to be an omen of what was to come—the end of a day, the end of a life.

"How did she taste?" Edon asked softly, the words holding a lethal edge to them. Almost as if he were daring me to reply.

If I was going to die, I'd go out with my spine intact. "Like oranges."

"Mmm." Edon stood behind me now, his hum a vibration against the back of my neck. "And did you enjoy it?"

"Yes."

I waited for the blow to come, waited for a threat, *something.*

Silence fell between us. If the warmth of his skin didn't bathe my own, I'd have thought he left. Awareness teased my senses, a new scent arising.

No. It'd been there since Edon arrived.

A dark, addictive flavor. The cologne of the forest, a predator in his prime, evaluating his target—me.

Only, it wasn't violence radiating from him, but something harsher. *Savage need.*

My heart skipped a beat, then sent my pulse racing, pumping blood to the one part of me I couldn't allow to react.

But something about Edon's masculinity appealed to me. His dominance was a trait to be revered. Respected. Acknowledged.

It took significant effort to keep my head upright when all I wanted to do was bow. To go to my knees before him. To acknowledge him as the bigger wolf.

"You clearly took oral training in university." His words were a breath against my ear, his chest a threatening flame brushing my back.

My mouth went dry, my body reacting to his nearness in a way I never would have anticipated.

It's because of the fight and subsequent fuckery, I told myself. *You're aroused because of Luna.*

Are you? Edon's voice taunted. "Did you only learn how to please females in your classes?" he asked, his hand gripping my hip. "Or did you learn how to pleasure males as well?"

Oh, fuck. I wasn't the only one aroused. No wonder he radiated heat. His cock was just as hard as mine and touching the cleft of my ass.

I licked my lips, the words stuck in my throat.

Silas, he growled into my mind. *My patience will only go so far.*

Yes, I admitted with a tremble. *Yes, I learned how to pleasure males in addition to women.* I wanted to be completely prepared for whatever life threw at me.

Never in my wildest dreams did I expect it to be an aroused alpha lycan.

Nor would I have guessed my instinctual reaction to that predicament to be a favorable one.

But my dick stood proud, my skin tight with yearning, my stomach clenched with a readiness that required satisfaction.

Luna might have started it. But some sick and twisted part of me wanted Edon to finish it.

"Kneel," he demanded.

A war battled inside me, my pride telling me to remain upright while my wolf *begged* me to obey.

I gave in to my wolf, my knees buckling.

Edon placed his palm on my head, his fingers lightly running through my hair as he circled to stand before me.

I'd been in this position before—being presented with a lycan's cock to suck. Humans learned all manner of *skills* at the universities. Oral sex was one I perfected and achieved high marks in, on both males and females.

His grasp in my hair tightened, pulling my scalp and forcing me to look up at him.

A black whirlpool of fury mingled with arousal stared down at me.

I couldn't tell if he wanted to fuck me or kill me, as he seemed to be walking a fine ledge between the two.

He tensed his grip even more, his opposite hand going to my throat. "I should kill you for your blatant disrespect."

My throat bobbed beneath his palm, causing him to squeeze a little harder. I could still breathe, but barely. And while it should have scared the shit out of me, all I felt was a tingle deep inside. A yearning building between my legs.

It was so fucking messed up.

How could I be attracted to this asshole?

I never had a preference either way when it came to sex, but I never saw myself being into a power-exchange situation.

"I should kill you," he repeated. "But I find myself more intrigued by your oral skills. Luna seemed to enjoy them. And now I wonder how I'll feel about them. Do you think you'll please me enough to change my mind about your life, Silas? Or will it just make me want to kill you more?"

His words should have sickened me, should have left me feeling fearful of my future. But all they evoked was a sense of challenge, a desire to prove myself to him, to blow his fucking mind. Because this? This I could do. And I would do it well. "Fuck my mouth and find out."

Edon's resulting smile was all wolf. Hungry, wild, and barely restrained. "Open up, Silas."

The dare in his voice had me grasping his hips and tugging him forward.

He wanted to dominate me? He'd have to work harder.

Because I knew how to bring a man to his knees. I'd done it before, and I would do it again now.

I took him deep, the way I liked it, and groaned at the masculine taste of him. Fuck, my wolf senses intensified this just like they did with Luna, providing me with a new experience despite my years of training.

He reminded me of the forest, the fresh leaves mingled with life. So different from Luna's oranges, yet their combination of flavors created the perfect mix on my tongue. I wanted more. Much, much more.

And so I took it, swallowing him to the back of my throat while sucking at the same time.

"*Fuck*," Edon breathed, his grip tightening in my hair to a painful degree.

I dug my nails into his flesh in response, forcing him to stay in place as I devoured him with my mouth. His thighs tensed, the power in his body rippling around me in a violent wave. My balls ached, my body primed from what felt like hours of foreplay with Luna, and now Edon.

It was overwhelming to the point of pain.

But the taste of him drove me onward, his cock threatening my gag reflex as he attempted to control the rhythm.

It wasn't kind.

It wasn't easy.

It was an intoxicating blend of alpha brutality, unadulterated lust, and anger, all wrapped up in a culmination of grunts and merciless thrusts.

I slid one hand to cup his sack, squeezing it in warning as he forced himself even deeper, trying to make me take his well-endowed cock all the way to the end.

My silent reprimand only intensified his energy, his need to put me severely beneath him taking over. But I held my ground, accepting only what I could while also driving him mad with my tongue.

His harsh exhales and pants told me I was winning, that he couldn't hold out on me much longer.

He wanted this almost as much as I did, perhaps even more.

"Swallow it," he growled, the words heating my veins and causing my cock to weep with want, begging to be touched.

But I focused on him.

His shaft.

The salty pre-cum teasing my tongue.

His guttural sounds as he drew closer to the climax he craved.

Each primal shift of his hips, lodging him to the point where I could no longer breathe.

I accepted it all, fighting back with my mouth in the only way I knew how—by forcing him closer to that edge with each suck, nip, and lick.

He cursed, his face contorting into beautiful lines of aroused agony. He didn't want to like this, didn't want to need it, but he couldn't seem to help himself. His dick pulsed, signaling his pending release, and then exploded down my throat.

"Silas," he hissed, his nails clawing at my scalp, his opposite hand around my nape, forcing me to take every inch as he came over and over again.

My own grip tightened, indicating to him that I couldn't breathe.

But he didn't seem to care, too lost in his oblivion to notice.

Or maybe it was on purpose.

Maybe he wanted me to die like this, on my knees, with his cock buried in my throat.

The idea of it angered me, had me forcing him backward with a shove that seemed to stun him from his orgasmic bliss.

He released me long enough to catch a breath, then wrapped a hand around my throat, dragged me up to my feet, and pushed me up against a wall. I gasped at the sudden move, my back protesting the savage treatment.

His eyes resembled smoldering black orbs, his jaw so tight I thought it might break. But then his mouth landed on mine. Not gracefully. Not kindly. But ruthlessly. As if he didn't want to kiss me but couldn't stop himself.

And my tongue responded in kind.

Because I didn't want to kiss him either. Didn't want to be anywhere near him. And yet my fucking dick practically begged me to touch him, to stroke him once more, to do *something.*

As if he heard the plea, he aligned his groin with mine, his damp skin—from my mouth—heaven against my aching flesh.

I couldn't stop myself from pressing into him, seeking friction, heat, *relief.*

His teeth sank into my lower lip, drawing blood.

I bit him right back, earning me a snarl from the beast.

My hands grasped him just as cruelly, my nails digging in just as much as his, my need to fight him harsh and apparent. And still we kissed as if we were old, angry lovers fighting through a haze of violence.

I hated him.

Wanted him.

Loathed him.

Desired him.

And his responding growls told me he felt the same.

It wasn't unheard of for alphas and royals to pick harem members of the same sex—most enjoying a good degradation.

But this went deeper.

This wasn't about Edon needing to humiliate or tame me. I sensed it in his movements, his mind, his snarls, his strokes, his kiss, his general handling, that this went beyond societal platitudes and games.

We were connected on a bizarre level, his turning me into a wolf binding us in a forbidden dance that left us starved.

"Jack yourself off," he said, his hand moving to my throat. "Do it now."

Fuck off, I wanted to say, but I couldn't, my palm already moving toward my swollen flesh. I hissed at the first pump, my back bowing off the wall and directly into the wall of male before me.

He didn't kiss me again but watched each of my strokes with a hungry gleam that only turned me on more.

I'd never felt anything like this, all my previous experiences almost clinical in comparison. We weren't allowed to engage in sexual activities outside of classes, not that I'd ever desired anyone enough to try. Rae and Willow were my best friends, not my fuck buddies. And none of the men in my courses ever intrigued me, despite the sexual things we had to do to each other in our classes.

But Edon… he made my blood *burn.*

And Luna, fuck, her scent drove me crazy.

It had to be my wolf, all the new sensations stirring a riot of insatiable yearning.

The pressure built in my gut, causing me to strengthen my grip and increase my movements. If he told me to stop, I'd kill him. Or worse, I would disobey him.

I needed this, earned it, fucking *required* it.

My sack practically twisted in its fury to find release, my lower abdomen threatening to explode beneath the onslaught of the exquisite eroticism of the moment.

Edon's gaze lifted to mine, holding me captive, his grasp squeezing, endangering my airway.

And forcing me to erupt.

My groan vibrated beneath his palm, coming out as a choked sound that left me panting against the wall in a cold sweat. Ropes of semen decorated his abdomen, my arousal marking him in a way it shouldn't.

However, it gave me a brief moment of joy to claim something that didn't belong to me. To name the alpha as *mine.*

He must have known, must have seen the glimmer of pleasure in my eyes, because he mercilessly propelled me to my knees with a single demand. "Lick me clean."

A shudder of annoyance rocked my spine. Not because of the task—which was indeed degrading—but the idea of removing my scent from his skin.

This is so fucked up. He couldn't be mine, nor did I *want* him to be mine.

Ever.

And I proved it to myself by doing exactly what he dictated, laving every inch of his torso to remove the evidence of my arousal from his skin.

He remained in a towering position above me for so long I thought he might command me to suck him off again. His cock strained toward my mouth as if in agreement. His body hot and hard and clearly in need.

I didn't dare meet his gaze. If I did, we'd repeat this entire dance. And I wasn't sure I'd survive another throat fucking from him today. Anger radiated heavily from him, mingled with a lethal intent.

He wanted me dead for touching Luna.

I couldn't blame him. Alphas were possessive.

But he also seemed to be struggling with something deeper—this bizarre connection between us.

In the end, it was the connection that won.

He released me without a word or a strike and left as quietly as he'd arrived.

I remained motionless on my knees in his wake, unable to speak or move.

Because my fate still hung in the balance.

He'd merely spared it for another day, to be handled whenever he saw fit.

Somehow, that was almost worse.

Chapter Ten

LUNA

EDON'S HOUSE REEKED OF BETA BITCH. My jaw clenched in response, any and all residual guilt riding my wolf gone in an instant.

I shouldn't have submitted to Silas. It was stupid. Really, *really* fucking stupid. Not that I had much choice. He was a hell of a lot stronger than I expected, his prowess very uncommon for a newbie. Most humans resembled pups after a change, at least from what I'd heard. I'd not met any, as it was extremely rare, but Silas struck me as far more extraordinary than usual.

Unfortunately, he was now a dead wolf walking, thanks to me, and was probably being punished right now, hence Edon's prolonged absence.

Fuck.

Okay, maybe some guilt remained.

I buried my head in my hands, hiding in my room and dreading Edon's return.

He *knew.* His growl shook the ground beneath me out in the marsh, heightening the sensations in my core to a dangerous level.

Because I'd thrived from the chase, my body reacting unspeakably to the adrenaline that coursed through my system. That, coupled with Edon's assaulting kiss not even an hour before, and I'd been hopeless to my need.

Oh, and Silas's tongue. Holy hell, that man's tongue could win wars. He had me coming faster than my hands ever had, leaving me hot and needy and screaming for more.

Until Edon's growl rumbled the earth.

It sounded an awful lot like the one echoing through the home now.

I swallowed. *Shit.* He was back. I felt his anger in the air, thick and intoxicating and overwhelming.

He didn't knock on my door. He opened it.

I nearly drowned in the furious dark pools of his eyes.

"Did you enjoy your run?" he asked, his voice deceptively calm.

"Did you enjoy your playtime?" I countered, noting his healthy glow.

His lips curled. "Oh, you have no idea. Best head of my life. You'll have a lot to live up to."

A growl built in my throat, my blood heating while my stomach constricted. How could he be so blatant about fucking another woman's mouth?

I nearly snorted. As if I had the right to be pissed. I just ran back from having another wolf's tongue between my thighs.

And Edon had just come from delivering punishment. I smelled Silas all over him. Whatever punishment he'd received, it wasn't good. It was also all my fault.

My shoulders fell, leaving behind a defeated feeling. It was a sensation I hated. A weakness. But I couldn't help it. My actions had led to the death sentence of another wolf, someone who, for all intents and purposes, didn't deserve that fate.

"What? No offer to prove me wrong?" Edon taunted.

"You look pretty well satisfied," I muttered, nodding at his well-endowed, yet clearly appeased, groin. "If you need more, then go fuck yourself."

A feral sound came from his chest, sending a shiver down my spine. "Careful, Luna. Or next time I'll make *you* watch while I fuck someone else."

I swallowed. The way he said it made it sound like a promise, not a potential situation. My father forced my mother to observe his activities over the years, each one breaking her more.

"What? No fiery comeback?" He waited. "Don't tell me your defiance is gone already."

I said nothing. He wanted my submission. Instead, I gave him my silence.

"Your ground privileges are officially revoked. The next time you want to run, you'll have to ask. If I catch you outside the boundaries of the village without my express permission, I will punish you. Do you understand?"

I met his gaze. Did I understand? "Yes." Would I comply? Fuck no.

The tilt of his lips said he knew, too.

And that he would enjoy administering whatever punishment he had in mind.

Fine.

It didn't scare me.

He had no idea what sorts of punishments I grew up enduring. I was so incredibly well versed in the art that he would have to be extremely creative to even consider impressing me.

So good luck to him.

Edon left without another comment, the air thick with promise and sex in his wake.

I wanted to vomit.

Today, I tried and failed to escape.

Tomorrow, I would try again.

And the next day.

And the day after.

Until I either died trying or succeeded.

Edon thought I'd given up? Hardly. I was just getting started.

* * *

I WOKE TO BLISSFUL SILENCE.

Either Edon stupidly expected me to obey his command or he had a trap waiting for me.

Regardless, I was going for a run. No one grounded me. Especially not him.

Pulling on a pair of jeans and a tank top, I decided to take a walk through home base first and see what they were saying. Because if Edon informed them of my little house arrest, then I needed to know whom to evade.

It would also give me a cover if he asked where I went today. *Oh, you know, around.*

Only, the second I set foot on the main property of Clemente Clan's headquarters, I regretted it.

Bianca stood with a group of friends, her face positively glowing as she spoke—loudly—about the things Edon did to her last night.

You went to her? Again? I thought, irritated beyond measure. It was so illogical, so completely unfair given that I'd shared an erotic session with his progeny, but to know he went to this bitch in his aggression-filled hormonal state pissed me off to no end.

Which was how I justified my fist meeting her face.

Twice.

It all happened so fast, my reaction to hearing her gloating—in front of me—about fucking *my* mate, that I couldn't pull my wolf back in time before striking out.

That she smelled like Edon only made it worse.

Mine, my wolf growled, sending my fist into the bitch's jaw a third time.

"*Enough,*" a male voice snapped, one underlined in authority.

One that belonged to an alpha.

Walter.

My knees bent without preamble, my head bowing in a submission I felt down to my very bones. *Survival,* my wolf whispered. Something that didn't happen with Edon. Because somewhere deep down I knew he wouldn't hurt me, unlike the alpha approaching me now.

Walter would gladly flog me, rape me, beat me to a pulp. I felt it in his intentions with every step, his interest in breaking whom he saw as the strongest female in his pack—a female who needed to learn how to properly heel.

The back of his hand met the side of my head, the strike sending me to the ground on a whimper. "You do not have authority here, Luna of Ernest Clan," he said in a deceptively calm voice.

His foot connected with my midsection next, causing me to curl in on myself in protection, years of my father's similar treatment flashing behind my eyes.

I can do this.

It only hurts for a little while.

Go to the happy place.

Think about sparring with Logan.

Don't—

His next strike came to my back, shooting pain up my spine.

"Gentlemen, who wants to help me teach the little wolf a lesson?" he asked, the licentious notes in his voice sending ice through my veins.

Because I knew what he was proposing.

I'd seen my father do the same to my mother for misbehaving, had to watch her gang rape firsthand. It wasn't meant for her pleasure but my father's. And as he oversaw the treatment, he didn't care about those seeking their own ecstasy through the use of her body.

He'd even fucked another woman beside her just to prove his point.

It'd made me so sick, stunned me so harshly, that Logan had to hold me all night to keep me warm. He promised that when he took over, things would be different, that he wouldn't treat our people with such disrespect.

But now that I wasn't there, who knew what vile things my father would implant in Logan's mind?

A crowd formed, hungry male testosterone filling the air.

Violence seemed to rain down upon me in the form of jabs, kicks, touches I didn't want to feel.

It all blended together, the chaos a cloud in my mind.

This can't break me, I pleaded with myself. *You've been beaten before. You've been drowned. You've lived outside in subzero elements for days. You can do this. You can do this. You can—*

A furious growl rumbled the ground, one that seemed to shake the foundations of my heart and broke through the cruel fog circling my aching body.

"*Mine,*" the voice said. "You will not touch what is *mine.*"

"She's a disobedient little bitch who needs to be taught a lesson," Walter replied, a belt in his hand that appeared to be tinged with blood.

My blood.

I didn't remember him hitting me, couldn't even feel the remnants of any slash, but I felt certain he'd struck me more than once.

"And you will not be the one delivering that lesson."

"Like hell I won't," the alpha growled.

Edon caught his father's rising wrist, twisting it so harshly the bone threatened to snap. "You have no authority over my mate. If I want her beaten, she will be beaten. If I want her raped, she will be raped. But you will not dictate the punishment. *I* will."

He shoved the alpha back with a force that elicited gasps from the crowd. So much power. So much command.

An alpha in his prime.

The rising heir.

I saw it now in his stance, in the way his muscles bunched across his bare back. Even in nothing but a pair of jeans—no shoes—he stood with an authority few others would ever possess.

This male *required* dominance.

And if I wasn't already on the ground, I'd be kneeling at his feet beneath the aura of superiority rolling off him in waves.

Edon turned, his eyes pools of black that brought the majority of the crowd to their knees with a single glance.

No one would challenge him.

Not here.

Not ever.

"Luna is *mine*," he said, his tone carrying across the village, and probably into the surrounding areas as well. "If anyone would like to fight me for the right to touch my property, I stand well prepared." He stared down every male in attendance who remained standing until each of them bowed their heads. And then he returned to Walter, who had stood with an ambience of fury that chilled the atmosphere around us. "Your days are numbered, Alpha Incumbent. I bow to you no longer. Do not touch Luna again without my permission, or I will make you regret it, *old man*."

Edon didn't wait for a response; he scooped me off the ground and carried me through the throng of bowing wolves.

No one stopped us.

No one said a word.

Not even the furious alpha in our wake.

I buried my head against Edon's neck, my face wet with tears I hadn't realized I'd shed. Just the fear of those men touching me had destroyed my confidence, the helpless realization of my fate, and the knowledge that I couldn't fight them all off.

They wouldn't have killed me.

They would have subdued me and made it hurt so much worse.

Edon brushed a finger along my spine, his touch burning through the fabric of my shirt. Just a tender stroke, a notion of comfort, that somehow hurt even more.

I'd lost my shit over a female for bragging about him, for fucking him when he didn't truly belong to me. I couldn't even imagine what he had done to Silas.

The jealousy inside me had burned so hot, forcing my wolf to the surface. And this was just the beginning.

Edon would always take other females, likely even in front of me. How would I stomach it if I couldn't even handle it now?

The scent of his home drew my eyes upward to the familiar beams above, his legs having moved so quickly that I didn't even realize we were here until he slammed the door shut with his heel.

I expected him to drop me in my room or on the couch, but instead he took me to his bedroom.

Punishment, I realized. He had to do something, to put me in my place for behaving the way I did, and this was where he planned to do it.

Would he make me blow him? Fuck him? Use a belt against my skin the way his father had? Strangle me? Burn me?

Lycans healed quickly, especially purebreds like me. Which meant I could withstand all sorts of torture before passing out, and I'd almost always wake up as good as new without scars.

I opened my mouth to explain, to voice an apology, to say *something*, but my throat refused me. It was too tight. I could barely even breathe.

He set me on the mattress. "Lift your arms," he demanded.

I complied only because I didn't know what else to do, and I whimpered as he peeled off the remains of my bloody shirt. He guided me downward onto my side, and my legs automatically curled into my abdomen.

This was going to hurt.

I needed to find my happy place, to think of the few moments I enjoyed in my childhood, to think about Logan and Claudette and all our lessons together about the old world. To pretend I lived there. With them. In harmony. Without tyranny. In a place—

Agony sliced through my ribs, causing me to cry out.

Edon held me down, his fingers prodding my tender skin, his expression livid.

It took me a moment to realize he wasn't inflicting pain on purpose but was trying to assess my wounds.

"I'm going to fucking kill him," he gritted out, slowly rolling me to my other side to better examine my back. It hurt like a son of a bitch, my entire body tingling beneath his touch. He cursed, the sound harsh enough to make me flinch. "Don't move."

As if I could.

My body ached from the two kicks. Wait, hadn't there been more than two? *Yes.* Walter had a bloody belt. But I couldn't remember what he'd done with it. I'd retreated into—

Ice stabbed my arm, forcing a scream from my throat, but a stern hand forced me to stay put. The room began to spin a little, painting my vision in a drunk-like sensation. I tried to shake it off, tried to focus on the shifting wall, but couldn't.

Was this Edon's punishment?

To make me delirious?

To fuck with my mind?

"I'm not going to punish you, Luna," he said softly, a warm cloth sliding over my back and causing me to hiss.

"*Fuck…*" It stung. No, it *burned.*

And, wait, had I said something out loud? Or had he read my mind?

"Shh." He combed my hair away from my face, his palm sliding to the back of my neck. "The pain medicine will kick in soon to provide some relief. It won't last long with how rapidly our bodies consume drugs, but it should give you a little bit of comfort while your insides heal."

Another swipe of the cloth had me clenching the bedsheets, my lips parting on a groan that turned into a plea for him to stop.

I hated this show of weakness.

Hated more how I craved his touch.

"I need to clean the wounds," he explained, his cloth returning. Or maybe it was a new one. I couldn't tell. The stench of antibiotics made my stomach heave, my skin screaming beneath the healing salve.

Until another wave of dizziness hit me.

I blinked rapidly, trying to clear the dots from my vision.

"Pain medicine." The two words were a breath near my ear, his touch turning into a caress against my back. My eyes drooped closed, the sensation easing me into a cocoon of warmth I longed to live in forever.

Then a second prick had my eyes flashing open in concern, only to be soothed by a low growl from Edon.

Mate, my wolf acknowledged, at peace with his touch, the way he took care of me, the manner in which he protected me from others.

His warm body curled around mine in the bed, pulling me gently back into him. *Sleep*, my mind whispered.

Or maybe that was Edon.

Mmm, but I didn't want to sleep just yet.

My tongue felt too funny. Thick. Dry. Like I'd licked a lot of sandpaper.

Odd.

I twitched my nose, the scents swirling around us confusing me.

I smelled only Edon.

And another masculine scent, one that reminded me of cypress trees. I rather liked the calming nature of it but didn't know where it came from.

"My grandfather," Edon whispered, either due to somehow reading my mind or possibly because he'd deciphered my sniffing. "That's where I was last night, little mate. Bianca was showboating because I turned her down. She's jealous of you."

I frowned. He might have turned her down last night, but he definitely spent yesterday with her.

"Did I?" he asked softly, his lips caressing my neck. "I said someone sucked me off, but I didn't say it was her."

I didn't understand.

I also didn't know how he was in my head, how he heard my thoughts. Unless I was voicing them out loud? I did feel pretty weird. Dizzy. Like I was on the verge of a dream without sleeping.

"It's the medication." He kissed my temple, his arm draping across my chest while his other slid beneath my head. "Rest, little mate. You'll wake up as good as new. I promise."

Why is he being so nice to me? I wondered, suspicious. This wasn't how alphas treated their mates. Not in a very long time, anyway.

Claudette whispered of a different time, one where females and males chose each other for life, their faithfulness to one another the heart of the mating bond.

Now males were encouraged to cheat and females demanded to endure.

Logan once said he preferred the world Claudette spoke of in our studies.

I did, too.

But I wouldn't be able to find that here. Or anywhere, really. The old world no longer existed. Only this new society controlled by the Blood Alliance.

I closed my eyes, Claudette's words a low murmur in my mind. *"Everyone deserves a choice. Everyone deserves their very own Jolene Mason."*

She loved once.

A male named Jolene. Claudette spoke of him often, about how choices matter. In the end, his heart went with another, but hers always belonged to him. Which was why she never mated.

"What did you say?" Edon asked, his breath a warmth against my skin.

I shook my head, not sure what he meant. I hadn't said a word. Or maybe I had. But what would it matter at this point?

Dreams didn't exist here.

And love was a figment of the old world.

"Give me a chance, Luna," Edon murmured. "I just may surprise you."

"You already have." The words slurred in my mouth, sounding drunk with sleep.

He nuzzled my throat, the gesture far more alleviating than I wanted to admit.

But it lulled me into a false sense of safety.

One that followed me into my dreams, where I envisioned a world that didn't exist. A fantasy future based on a past I didn't know but wished I did.

Chapter Eleven

EDON

LUNA SLEPT SOUNDLY IN MY BED, her lithe form curled around one of my pillows. She hadn't moved much in the last two days, but her body appeared to be fully healed. *Finally.*

I swept her hair back to place a kiss against her temple and ventured into my living room, where Silas stood waiting.

I'd called him here through the sire link, much to his annoyance.

He was dressed similarly to me in a pair of jeans, his blond hair damp from his run, his skin glistening with a sheen of sweat that seemed to define his muscles even more.

Silas arched a brow, his skepticism written in that single expression alone. But I also heard it in his thoughts, his uncertainty underlined with a begrudging satisfaction at my demanding his presence.

Is he going to kill me? Or fuck me? he wondered, causing my lips to quirk.

"I haven't decided yet." A lie, of course. If I wanted to kill him, he'd already be dead. It was the fucking-him part I hadn't quite figured out. Because I wanted to. I just didn't think it would be right.

Of course, I'd already taken advantage of his mouth. Why not push him all the way?

"I hate that you're always in my head," he said flatly.

"Better get used to it." I would always be there unless one of us died. And if he looked deep enough, he'd realize the link went both ways. "I need you to watch Luna for me."

His lips parted, drawing my attention to his mouth.

Which reminded me of the other night and how skillfully he took my cock.

Mmm, yes, I wanted to do that again.

"*What?*" He gave a laugh. "You're fucking with me."

"Not even close," I said, taking a step toward him. He held his ground, something that only intrigued me more. "You're the only one I can trust with Luna." Because I had a permanent link to him that I could access regardless of the distance. "Just don't touch her."

Without my permission, I wanted to add, surprising myself. An image of Silas going down on Luna flashed behind my eyes, causing my blood to boil—in a good way. I shook it off, forcing myself to focus on the task at hand.

"Can you do that, Silas? Can you watch without touching?"

His nostrils flared, challenge written into his features. "You're setting me up for failure before I've even begun."

"This isn't a test."

"Everything in this fucking world is a test," he retorted, his anger warm and hot. I wanted to play in it, to stoke it higher, to see how far I could press before he exploded.

If it wasn't, he'd have an actual friend do this, Silas added, speaking to himself.

"I don't have friends." Nor did I need them. "My last *friend*—a term I use loosely—died just after my thirteenth birthday. My father called him a distraction. Said I didn't need one of those and sliced the kid in half in front of the clan. Didn't have a whole lot of offers for friendship after that."

Silas's eyes widened a fraction, the only indication that my words had alarmed him.

"Look, I need to go speak to my grandfather," I continued, uncertain of why I felt the need to explain myself, but did so anyway. "And I need someone I can trust—someone I *own*—to guard Luna. You are that someone, Silas. I'm not asking you for a favor. I'm not testing you. I'm giving you a task as your alpha and sire. You will stay here and protect my mate until I return. Should anyone disturb my home or you or Luna, you will alert me. Do you understand?"

He lifted a shoulder. "Fine."

Oh, his defiance goaded my inner wolf. I wanted to bend him over and fuck him into submission. But I didn't have time.

And it would wake up Luna.

"We're going to have a chat later about obedience," I said, stepping away from him. "And it'll probably end with you on your knees again."

Hunger flashed in his gaze before he could conceal it. "You're the alpha."

"And you're my omega," I returned, amused. "Behave."

Silas barked into my mind as I left, causing me to chuckle as I took off at a jog toward my grandfather's estate.

The insanity of what had happened to Luna left me feeling on edge, but a few minutes with Silas had cooled me off enough to run the grounds without trying to kill anyone. That would change if anyone stepped in my way. Especially if it was one of the jackasses who joined my father in his little circle of punishment the other day.

One of the older members of the clan, Barry's father, had found me in the woods and alerted me of my father's intentions. I'd taken off running before he finished, arriving just as two of the wolves—Glenn and his idiot of a brother—started taking off their pants.

It didn't take a genius to understand their plan.

They were going to gang-rape Luna into submission.

Over my dead body, I thought, my bare feet pounding over the earth, my blood pumping full of rage yet again.

If that had been another of my father's little tests, I'd failed, and I didn't give a fuck. Luna was mine. No one touched her except me. The others might crave a broken female in the bedroom, but I did not. Her fire was one of my favorite traits about her, and the pack had snuffed it out, leaving her cold and disturbingly distant in my arms.

Luna had clearly been abused before, as she knew how to retreat into her mind.

I'd seen that look so many times on my mother's face. These days, she wore it permanently. She didn't even acknowledge my presence when I visited her now, so broken and alone.

That would not happen to Luna.

I refused to allow it.

Silas's uncertainty trickled through our connection, causing my run to slow to a jog as I navigated through his thoughts for the cause.

Hunger. He'd been about to eat when I called him to the house. Not wanting to sprint on a full stomach, he'd returned the items to the fridge and took off toward his fate. Which, apparently, he thought would include his very public death.

The man sure did hide his fear well, because I hadn't caught an inkling of it on him, just cocky, irritated male. But his mind painted a very different scene.

Help yourself to whatever food you need, I thought at him. *And I want to know when Luna is awake.*

Annoyance darkened our link. *Sure.*

I smirked. *Don't sound too thankful, Silas, or I may be inclined to do something ungracious in the future.*

Like fuck my mouth? he drawled. *Or should I consider that a gracious act?*

Oh, the pair of balls on that man nearly rivaled my own. *Keep talking, progeny. I'm considering this foreplay.*

Probably best you don't flirt with me too much, Sire. *There's a gorgeous alpha female in the other room.*

I stopped jogging.

Like, flat-out froze.

And he must have sensed my sudden pause, because he added, *I'm not going to touch her.*

You better not. Except my earlier intrigue returned, causing me to wonder what would happen if I walked in on another sexual interlude between them. My blood heated once more, the idea arousing as fuck.

Hurry back, Silas said, sounding bored. *Or I'm eating all of your food.*

I snorted. *Go for it.* He needed it more than I did. His lean, muscular form could use a hint of bulk, something I knew he had more of prior to the Immortal Cup and recruitment into Clemente Clan.

He'd get it back.

I returned to my run and smiled when I found my grandfather waiting on his old porch, his shoulder braced against a pole at the top of the stairs. "Trouble in paradise?" he drawled, likely having sensed my hesitation about a mile ago when talking to Silas.

"Errant progeny," I replied, walking up the stairs and past him into the house.

"I can't wait to meet him."

"I know." I'd already told my grandfather a few things about Silas, mostly in regard to his fighting skills and defiance. "I'm pretty sure you're going to disown me for him."

My grandfather chuckled and shut the door behind us before collapsing into his favorite recliner. "It's about time you had some competition for my affection."

I snorted and took over the couch. "Are you kidding? I can't wait to be rid of you, old man."

"Yeah, yeah. That's why you've been to see me practically every day since your mate arrived, right?" He gave me a knowing look. "What'd she do now?"

Nothing like cutting directly to the point of my visit. "She attacked Bianca." And, according to Barry's father, the bitch deserved it for goading an alpha female so publicly. Luna's possessive reaction should have pleased me, but the violent aftermath of the incident severely tainted my pleasure. "My father attempted to beat Luna into submission as a result."

My grandfather whistled. "A ballsy move to touch another alpha's female."

"I think we both know he has no respect for me or my pending claim to his territory." Things had been tense with my father for years, and I strongly suspected he wanted me dead. Fortunately, he wasn't strong enough to do it. Nor could he face the political repercussions of assassinating his only heir.

"You need allies," my grandfather said for the thousandth time. "Walter did one hell of a job alienating you, to the point where it's almost a sure thing you're going to fail these trials."

"Gee, thanks for the vote of confidence," I drawled, irritated.

"You need Luna on your side. And that boy Silas. And anyone else you can get to help you. Because whatever Walter has planned, it's going to be bad."

"It already is bad," I corrected him, thinking of the vampire I had to cut up into pieces before depositing him in the ocean. My grandfather had confirmed it was definitely the start of my Alpha Trials and that Silas's idea to get rid of the evidence was a sound one.

"He's only just begun."

I know, I thought, leaning forward with my elbows on my knees. "I didn't come here to discuss the trials, Gramps. I need to ask you about something else."

"Yeah?" He cocked his head in that curious way he favored, the one that made him look like a young pup despite being close to seven hundred years old with white hair and wrinkled skin. He was one of the oldest lycans in existence, most dying around the six- or seven-hundred-year mark. But not my grandfather. He was a stubborn old bastard, much to my father's chagrin.

The pack gave him his space out of respect, while my father avoided him entirely.

"Well?" my grandfather prompted. "I'm not getting any younger over here."

My lips quirked. He always seemed to know what I was thinking. But I doubted he could anticipate what I wanted to know now. "Who's Claudette?"

Luna had murmured about the woman in her drug-induced daze, saying something about her lessons and the history of the world. Most of it I already knew, having learned much from my grandfather about the old times, but then Luna said something utterly fascinating.

"Everyone deserves a choice," I repeated her words now, my eyes narrowing at him. "Everyone deserves their very own Jolene Mason."

Strange words from a woman who had never met my grandfather.

Even stranger for her to use his full given name, not the pack alpha designation he'd gone by for the last few centuries.

And the mist that entered his gaze told me I'd struck a chord.

There was a story here.

A long one.

Chapter Twelve

Silas

EGGS AND SPINACH.

Two items I grew up eating that somehow managed to taste far too rich now.

My lycan palate was too intense for my stomach. I couldn't seem to eat anything without it churning inside me. Even now, my breakfast threatened to expel itself all over Edon's granite counters.

So much for my promise to eat all his food.

I force-fed myself another bite, grimacing as I swallowed. "Ugh," I groaned, setting my fork down and bowing my head. "I fucking hate this."

The hairs along the back of my neck flickered to life, alerting me of an approaching presence. But I relaxed as I scented the familiar orange blossoms of Luna's scent.

She's awake, I told Edon, since he demanded I inform him.

Good. No touching.

I rolled my eyes and didn't bother with a reply. Instead, I glanced over my shoulder and admired her sleepy approach. She'd thrown on a shirt too big for her frame, one that hit her at her knees. *She's wearing your shirt,* I thought at Edon, then paused in confusion as to why I felt the need to share that detail.

Yeah? How does she look in it?

Hot, I admitted, once more surprised by my easy candor with the alpha male.

It was probably a result of having his cock shoved down my throat. Sort of erased any and all formalities between us. That I kind of wanted to do it again, well, I didn't quite know how to feel about that yet.

"You're alive," Luna whispered, her eyes widening a fraction.

"For now," I replied, standing. "Do you want any eggs? I made too many." Not true. I just didn't want to eat any more.

The way her nostrils flared in disgust told me her answer before she voiced it. "No. I'll make something more appetizing."

I frowned. "It's eggs and spinach. A staple."

"It's bland and boring," she countered, going through the cabinets with the ease of someone who knew her way around the kitchen. Specifically, *this* kitchen.

Which, yeah, made sense. She was Edon's mate.

What is she doing? Edon asked.

Get your ass back here and find out, I thought back at him.

His amusement touched my mind, leaving behind a caress that heated my blood. *Oh, Silas. You're an expert in respecting your betters, aren't you?*

I snorted. *You seemed pretty satisfied with my* respect *the other night.*

He growled, the sound hungry and aroused. *Are you flirting with me?*

No. I'm stating a fact. We both know you enjoyed it. Don't deny it.

I wouldn't dream of it, he replied, his voice silky and warm and deep. *Careful or I'll demand a repeat.*

I hope you do. I regretted the thought immediately, my hands gripping the countertop as I closed my mind. He wasn't supposed to hear that, but his resulting silence told me he had. *Fuck. Ignore me. I'm just irritated.* Understatement of the fucking century. I wasn't just irritated but also frustrated, and confused by the riot raging in my head.

I pressed my forehead to the cool marble, trying to thwart the headache.

And failing because Edon was back in my mind again.

Don't touch Luna until I return. His command only pissed me off more.

"I already said I wouldn't," I grumbled out loud and in my head.

"Wouldn't what?" Luna asked, drawing my attention to her curvy ass. She'd bent over to retrieve something in the fridge, presenting me with her delicious backside. The shirt had ridden up to the bottom of her rounded cheeks.

No underwear.

Fuck.

Edon said something back to me, but I ignored him in favor of the female before me. "Edon won't leave me alone," I said in an effort to explain my show of mental insanity. "It's this damn sire bond."

"Ah, the psyche. I assume you're the only one he can access other than me right now, not that he's tried opening our door. Which means he's probably smarter than I give him credit for." She finally stood up again, in her arms an array of items that had my brow furrowing. "It's not a common bond, you know. Your sire bond, I mean. Most lycans are born, not made." Her light brown eyes met mine. "It's not something I'll ever be allowed to experience."

"Trust me, you should be grateful. Edon is a pain in the ass."

Her lips curled. "You're not afraid of him at all, are you?"

Was I? "Not really." I couldn't exactly say why. Maybe because I trusted him on a naïve level, thanks to the sire bond. Or perhaps because he'd never been particularly cruel to me. Even on the day of my turning, he gave me relief by not extending the pain. Much to his father's disapproval—a stark emotion I'd sensed, more than witnessed, in the air that day.

"I'm not either," she replied as she broke an egg into a mixing bowl. She added several more while chewing on her lower lip. "I should fear him," she continued softly. "He's more powerful than Walter. I can feel it in his aura, the way he takes charge, but some part of me refuses to retreat the way I should."

"Maybe because you're his mate." I folded my arms on the counter, leaning forward a bit on my stool to observe her choices in ingredients. "He can't hurt you."

She snorted. "Clearly, you've not been around a lot of alpha pairings. I mean, you've seen Walter's mate, right? She's utterly broken. It's what Edon has grown up around, what he likely intends to do to me. Yet…" She trailed off, her brown eyes lifting to mine. "He saved me from Walter the other night. Or I think it was the other night. Honestly, the drugs Edon gave me sort of fucked with my concept of time."

"What are you talking about?" I asked, confused. "What happened?"

"You weren't there?" she countered, then shook her head. "Right. You're probably not allowed in the main village as a newbie." She cocked her head. "Wait, how are you here right now?"

"Edon told me to guard you," I admitted. "He's worried about packmates using you against him in the Alpha Trials." Which, I suspected, had something to do with whatever she'd just mentioned about Walter. What had happened to her while I was out wandering the boundaries?

"And he chose you to protect me?" She sounded so surprised that I growled, my earlier irritation returning in spades.

"I may be a *newbie*, but I'm not weak, Luna." Something she knew firsthand. "I kicked your ass just the other day, didn't I?"

She bristled, her wolf prowling beneath the surface. "First of all, yes, you did. And I want a rematch. Secondly, that wasn't what I meant, jackass." She flipped her long hair over her shoulder and returned to her odd mixture of flour, eggs, and milk. The addition of cinnamon had my nostrils flaring.

When she didn't continue, I prompted her with, "What did you mean?"

"That it isn't common for an alpha to talk to a newbie, let alone to interact with one. And asking you over to his house? Especially after the other day? Yeah, that's definitely not normal. You should be dead for touching me, not sitting calmly in the alpha's kitchen watching over me while I make pancakes."

"You sound disappointed," I drawled, cocking my head. "Wishing he would have killed me?" I wondered out loud, grinning. "Should I remind you that you begged me to fuck you and not the other way around?"

I didn't know why I said it. Maybe because I wanted to talk about what the hell happened between us. Or maybe because a dark part of me wanted to know how she felt about it all. To find out if she wanted to explore the forbidden dance we'd started and not come close to finishing.

A dangerous topic.

One I should divert us away from.

And yet, I didn't. Instead, I waited and watched as she stopped stirring her mixture.

"I did not beg you," she said, her soft voice underlined in steel.

"You did."

"I did not," she said through gritted teeth. "I was… the fight… my wolf… I did not *beg*."

I chuckled. "Whatever you say, little moon." The nickname fell from my lips unbidden, a whisper from the animal prowling beneath my skin. Once said, I couldn't retract it. Nor did I want to. It suited her, and it served as the first nickname I'd ever given a person.

"*Little moon*?" she repeated, a growl in her tone. "Really?"

"Says the one calling me *newbie*," I pointed out.

"That's not an endearment, *Silas*. It's a title. It's who you *are*."

I smiled. "*Luna*." I drew her name out across my tongue, teasing her. "Means 'moon,' yeah? And you're smaller than me. So I could argue it's what you are as well."

"It's not appropriate for anyone to give the alpha's mate a pet name."

"Should have thought about that before begging me to fuck you." I really should stop baiting her, but the resulting snarl from her lips humored me greatly. It'd been far too long since I had someone to verbally spar with, and Edon didn't count. He didn't *spar*; he commanded.

Very unlike Rae and Willow, who fired back insults at me without even flinching. They were the reason I survived my university years. But, somehow, bickering with Luna felt different. More intimate.

Not because of the oral sex.

I knew Rae just as well as I knew Luna in that department, having tasted them both between their thighs. Although, my experience with Rae was purely clinical in a university class setting, and she faked her enthusiasm. While Luna, well, that had been a moment of heat and passion and unlike anything I'd ever expected. So perhaps that added the heated flare to our sparring, the one buzzing through my blood as she growled in response to my taunting.

A splatter of goop hit me on the forehead, drawing me from my thoughts. "What the hell?"

"That's for saying I *begged* when we both know I didn't," Luna replied, already refocused on her disgusting-looking batter. "I commanded it. There's a difference."

I reached across the counter to snag a towel and used it to wipe off my head.

"Seriously? A food fight?" I snorted. "No wonder I bested you so easily."

"I'll have you know that I'd just sprinted about fifteen miles, and I was tired."

"Whatever helps you feel better." We both knew I would dominate her even fully rested. She was smaller, faster, and definitely athletic, but I had the drive and determination to survive instilled in me from years of fighting for my life. Luna, for all intents and purposes, had lived a pampered existence in comparison. As evidenced by the ease with which she started assembling her pancakes on the griddle.

She hummed a little melody under her breath as she worked, forgetting all about me at the bar behind her.

It was oddly relaxing. I barely knew the female, but something about the homey element of the moment placated my inner wolf. Provided me with an insight into what life could be like as a lycan.

Not with her, but with a wolf of my own.

If I was ever allowed such an experience. If ones even existed here.

I had to get out from under Edon first. Along with a million other tasks, like figuring out where the fuck I belonged in this clan.

"Your stress is ruining my usually peaceful cooking experience," Luna said softly as she flipped a round pancake onto the growing stack. "Is it because of what happened the other day?"

I cleared my throat. "No. That was fine. I'm—"

"Fine?" she repeated, glancing back at me with an arched brow. "I was more than *fine,* thank you."

My lips twitched. "As I recall, you didn't perform at all. So I wouldn't know, would I?"

She set her spatula down and faced me fully, planting her palms on the counter. "You want another taste, newbie? Is that what has your fur in a twist over there?"

"Maybe I do," I replied, teasing her a little. Edon would probably have my balls if he knew, but hey, he wanted me to watch without touching. He said nothing about goading her or engaging in a little healthy banter.

Besides, this was the most conversation I'd indulged in with anyone in months.

Fuck if I was going to stop now.

Luna's gaze narrowed. "You must have a death wish, wolf."

"Or nothing to lose." I shrugged. "I have no family. No friends." Minus Rae and Willow, but they weren't exactly here. And I wasn't sure if Willow was even still alive. Just the thought spoiled the moment, darkening my spirit and forcing the rest from my lips without thought. "I have no real clan. I'm just a mutt without a home, the property of an alpha who only needs me until he's done with his trials, and then I'll be on my own again. Back to the status quo without any regard for my feelings or needs. Just a new lycan struggling to survive in this hell."

Whatever amusement I'd felt from my banter with Luna died a withering death at the end of my summarization. It really was quite depressing. And the glimmer in her eyes said she agreed.

"It didn't use to be like this," Luna whispered, her voice low, cautious. "Lycans used to value family. Pack hierarchy was about respect, not dictatorship. Alpha females could choose, and mates were revered, not treated as toys to be used and tossed aside." She swallowed, her gaze lowering. "We're all in hell, Silas. Only those at the top seem to benefit in this new world."

"New world," I repeated, confused. "It's year one hundred seventeen." I knew because I'd competed in the one hundred seventeenth Immortal Cup.

"Yes. Year one hundred seventeen of the new world," she explained. "I mean, you know the vampires and lycans are far older, right?"

"Of course." Some of the royals, like Rae's mate, Kylan, were over three thousand years old. "But I've never heard it called the 'new world' before."

"Haven't you ever wondered what the world was like one hundred and eighteen years ago? What about two hundred years ago?"

I frowned. "Everyone knows what it was like—plague and famine. The Blood Alliance cured the nations of their violent wars and instilled rule and order."

Her smile was sad. "That's the university talking, the society you were forced to accept. But tell me, is lycan life what you dreamed of, Silas? Is this everything you wanted and more?"

I almost laughed but couldn't, my throat constricting with emotion. She'd hit a somewhat sensitive subject for me. "No. Everything they promised me was a lie."

"Exactly," she replied. "They indoctrinate humans in society's ideology, feed them false expectations to keep them controlled, all for the false honor of winning the Immortal Cup. But as you see now, it's not all that fulfilling, is it? And you, Silas, have it better than most."

I swallowed, considering her words, and watched as she turned to check on her food.

Here I sat at the counter in an alpha's kitchen, somewhat healthy and well fed, which, according to Luna, was rare. Yet I'd never felt more alone than I did lately, lying by myself at night, wondering what I had to live for next.

It was always about the Immortal Cup, to achieve immortality. And now that I had, I didn't know what to dream of anymore.

Because all those dreams of the future? They were littered with lies.

Yet, as Luna said, I had it better than most.

"Do you know how Yao is faring?" I wondered aloud, speaking of the male who came in second at the Immortal Cup. He went to Jace Region to become a vampire.

Every year, the vampires and lycans took turns taking the final two candidates and gifting them immortality. My year had been Walter's and Jace's turn.

Walter had first pick and chose me.

"I don't." She sounded apologetic. "Most winners disappear after the Immortal Cup, the majority of them not making it through their first year. Especially in lycan clans." She turned off the burner with a sigh. "But he's probably okay. Vampires like adding to their ranks, while lycans can do so the old-fashioned way. Mutts—no offense—tend to be more expendable as a result."

And that was exactly how I felt. *Expendable.* "Well, as you said, I have it better than most."

"I think we both do," Luna replied, placing a plate piled high with pancakes in front of me. "Edon's not…"

"Like the others?" I offered.

"So it seems," she murmured, reaching into the fridge again. "I mean, he let you live."

"For now."

She smiled as she returned with a bottle of maple syrup. "There's nothing temporary about it if he let you stay here alone with me."

"Maybe." I palmed the back of my neck, blowing out a breath. "Honestly, I struggle to understand him."

"Me, too." She picked up my uneaten food and scraped it into the trash. "All right, enough about Edon. How about a lesson in being a wolf?"

I cocked a brow. "Pretty sure I have the wolf thing down now, but thanks."

She laughed. "Sweets, you're not even close to mastering the lycan thing. Trust me."

"Did I or did I not kick your ass the other day?" I countered. "And *sweets*?"

"Do you prefer 'big wolf'?" She blinked her eyes innocently at me. "'Cause I can improvise on the whole nickname front. And maybe you won because I wanted you to."

"You tried to kill me."

She shrugged. "And now I want to feed you. Are you interested in the lesson or not?"

Considering no one else wanted to teach me anything, I wasn't about to say no. "I'm all ears, little moon."

She smirked. "Good. Lesson number one on being a lycan? You need to please your taste buds. And when we're done, I'm fixing your hair—that'll be lesson number two. Now open up, Silas."

Her words heated my blood with the memory of Edon saying those exact same words to me for an entirely different reason.

I swallowed thickly, unable to deny her despite the sickness I knew would follow. Because I wanted to give in to her, to experience, just for a few moments, what it might feel like to be taken care of by another. Especially one as beautiful as Luna.

No, she wasn't mine. But just for a moment, I allowed myself to pretend and parted my lips for her.

Chapter Thirteen

Edon

SILAS'S SATISFACTION WARMED the sire bond. *What are you doing?* I wondered.

Eating a pancake, he replied. *And it's fucking decadent.*

You made pancakes?

Luna made pancakes.

I grinned. *She cooks?* That news caused my lips to quirk up at the corners.

"Silas?" my grandfather asked, his gaze knowing.

"Luna made him pancakes." It should have bothered me that she cooked for him and not for me, but oddly, it didn't. I actually liked the idea of them taking care of each other.

"Claudette probably taught her," my grandfather mused, smiling. "She used to be a wicked chef before, well, everything."

"And now she's a mentor in Ernest Clan," I replied, recalling the details my grandfather had just given me. "Whose primary purpose is to train and ready the future leadership for an uprising." Only, according to my grandfather, Claudette's primary objective was Luna's brother, Logan. But it seemed she'd educated them both. "And your job is to mentor me," I added, arching a brow. "That about sum it up?"

"It's not like I provided all those history lessons for fun, kid," he said, smiling.

"I never thought you did," I admitted. I just hadn't realized the full extent of it until now. He provided me with historical contexts to persuade me to the revolutionary side. To enlighten me about another way of life. To recruit me into a new alliance among those who desired change. "You were just waiting for me to ascend before you explained every detail."

"And I still am," he admitted. "We've only just begun, but the plans have been in the making for over a century."

"Why wait so long? Why not rebel at the beginning?"

"Several did. And they all died." He paused to let that sink in. "We suspect those in power now planned their takeover for many, many years."

"And now you're doing the same." Through the art of "mentoring" the incoming leadership, at least in select clans. That wouldn't be as easy to accomplish in vampire society since they didn't procreate or die. Lycans, however, required regime changes because we constantly aged. I was on the rise as the new alpha, and my future son would replace me in a few hundred years.

"Yes. We're moving all the pieces into play but still have at least another decade before we truly begin."

I whistled low, shaking my head. "What about the vampires?" I wondered out loud.

"There are those in power today on our side."

"Which ones?"

He smiled. "Can't give you that information just yet, son."

I narrowed my gaze. "Don't trust me, old man?" I knew he did, or he wouldn't have spent the last two decades advising me in this way. I just enjoyed ribbing him.

"Nah, just not my place to elaborate. But you'll find out soon enough." He crossed one ankle over his opposite knee. "There will always be diversity in the class systems amongst vampires and lycans, but I'm not alone in my belief that our superiority also comes with great responsibility. We have a duty to protect those beneath us."

"You mean humans."

"I mean everyone. Take your Luna, for example. You protected her against your father, and you're doing so again now by having Silas stand sentry at your home."

"That's different." And I highly doubted Luna would appreciate my grandfather claiming her to be beneath me, even if it was true.

"Is it? She's in your care as your mate, and you've chosen to fulfill your duty of offering protection. Without it, she'd probably be in a bed somewhere having her dignity and alpha tendencies fucked right out of her."

The stark words caused me to flinch.

Which resulted in a smile from my grandfather. "You're the alpha this clan needs, Edon. Your reaction just now proves it. Because your father? He'd have smirked with enthusiasm at the very idea of breaking that girl's pride. You grimaced."

"Because it's wrong."

"Exactly. Alpha females are a prized species and very rare. Without them, alpha males can't be conceived. But rather than respect what few remain, lycans like your father have chosen to destroy their morale and disrespect the sanctity of the mating bond. You've seen what that does to a wolf, Edon. Your mother is Luna's future, if you choose to follow in your father's footsteps."

Just the idea of it turned my stomach. "I won't do that to Luna." Oh, I'd bring her to heel, yes. But not like that. Never like that.

"I know. But others will try to demand you do it anyway because that's the world we live in now." His smile was sad. "Your grandmother was one love of my existence. What we had was very special. Unique, too. And deeply revered. Something we'll talk more about someday soon. But I'll tell you now, if another wolf even looked at me the wrong way, your grandmama would have dealt with the problem swiftly and efficiently."

"Like Luna did with Bianca," I mused.

"Yes. Alpha females are as possessive as their males, or they used to be."

"I don't understand why that changed." Or why males would want to break such pride in their females. Luna's fire was what drew me to her, what made her irresistible to my wolf. Her defiance resembled foreplay.

My grandfather rubbed the silver stubble dotting his jaw. "Breaking the sacred mating bonds essentially disrupts wolf loyalty and restructures all the pack dynamics. If the alpha isn't being true to his mate, then the betas feel they need to follow suit with their own mates, and so on."

"Right, but why?" I interjected. "Why would lycans choose to do that to begin with?"

"They didn't choose to, Silas. Those in power did. The alphas making up the Blood Alliance today—or the majority, anyway—created this new way of life to stir dissension among the packs. To break the loyalties that used to be part of our core foundation."

"Okay, but why the hell would anyone want that?" I pressed, flabbergasted.

"Control," he answered simply. "We're pack animals. We fight for our own. But if you disable that mentality, destroy the bonds that tie us together, we begin to fight for ourselves, not as a unit. So you give the wolves someone to protect and cherish—an alpha—and that alpha reaps all the rewards and benefits. But to maintain that absolute power? He has to ensure that he always remains on top, number one, with no ties or loyalties to anyone else. Otherwise, what happens?"

"Events like the other day happen," I said, following his train of thought.

"Yes. You chose your mate over the orders of the current pack alpha."

"So he's probably furious." Which I'd felt, of course. I just didn't give a shit. Luna had been my only concern. "I failed his loyalty trial."

"In his eyes? Absolutely. In mine? You passed with flying colors."

"Except it's not you I need to be impressing," I pointed out, running my fingers through my hair. The more I pissed off my father, the harder my trials were going to be. "He's definitely going to use Luna against me."

"Which is why you need to bring that girl to your side sooner rather than later."

I snorted. "Easier said than done."

"Stubborn?"

"You have no idea." But I adored that trait about her.

"Well, you better figure her out soon because your father is definitely not going by the book with his tests, and I wouldn't put anything past him at this point. Including potentially having you killed just so he can remain in power for another century or so."

I scoffed at that. "Not even he is that stupid." It would be a clear violation of lycan politics. "The pack would riot."

"Would they?" he countered. "Because from what I've seen, he's created an heir and isolated him from everyone else, thereby ensuring that pack loyalty falls in his favor." He shrugged, the gesture far too nonchalant. "Just an observation."

His words sounded more like a warning, one underlined in a bad omen.

Because he was right.

My father had always treated me as an outsider, pretty much scaring off anyone and everyone who thought to ally with me.

Which meant Silas was in far more danger than I originally realized because our sire bond practically guaranteed his loyalty.

And I'd left him at my house with my only other liability—Luna.

I stood. "I have to go."

"You're a good man, Edon," my grandfather called after me.

"We'll see," I muttered, jogging down the stairs.

Tapping into my link to Silas, I asked, *Everything okay?*

Yeah, he replied, but his voice sounded off.

What are you two doing? I wondered, taking off at a sprint toward my house.

She's, uh, cutting my hair.

My eyebrows rose. Luna had already fed him, and now she was grooming him? Who knew the alpha female could be so maternal? *I'm on my way back.*

Okay.

Don't let your guard down.

His sardonic snort came back at me, the male essentially telling me to fuck off. Because yeah, he'd probably spent his entire life on alert. Humans were not treated well in this world. However, my grandfather said it wasn't always this way.

The more I learned from him, the more I questioned our ridiculous customs. Particularly surrounding the Alpha Trials. It was clear to everyone, including my father, that I was the strongest wolf in the clan. Why the fuck did I need to prove myself?

I entered the village, seeing it with a fresh perspective. The luxury of the cabins, the males lounging about like kings rather than hardworking lycans, and wondered what the peripheries of my region looked like right now. Oh, I'd visited them, but only with my father's entourage. And something told me the outsiders put on a show for him.

A show I wanted to see through.

A show I wanted to end.

My time was nearing. I just had to survive the next few weeks, then I could enact change. I would start by replacing everyone in this village. These lycans weren't my friends or allies; they belonged to my father's pack. And he had made it clear from the beginning that I didn't belong. Had killed the only male strong enough to befriend me. Then the others gave me a wide berth, afraid to contradict the alpha incumbent.

That was a mistake.

One I would rectify very, very soon.

Chapter Fourteen

LUNA

"SIT STILL," I demanded, my scissors poised far too close to Silas's forehead for him to be squirming like that.

"I can shave myself," he muttered.

"Yeah?" His caveman look said otherwise. "Your haircut and facial scruff remind me of a shaggy dog, Silas."

He scoffed low in his throat. "I just trimmed them."

"I know." I could see the frayed, uneven ends all over his damn head. "Stop moving." I straddled his thigh, needing to get a closer look at his "trim."

"Do you even know what you're doing?" he demanded.

"Better than you do, apparently." I'd already lathered his hair with water from the bathroom sink. Now I just needed him to sit on the stool beside it like a good little wolf and let me work.

However, he wasn't very little.

No, Silas was all man at well over six feet with a muscular build that dwarfed most purebred wolves. Except maybe Edon. I suspected they were close to even, with Edon having just a little more bulk on him due to his upbringing. But Silas would catch up to him if he ate properly.

And wouldn't that be a sight to behold? Two sexy-as-fuck males with alpha tendencies.

Silas might be the youngest, the newbie, but I smelled the dominance in him.

It was almost as strong as Edon's.

"Look at me," I said softly, needing to judge the hair length on either side of his head.

Bright blue eyes met mine. *So beautiful*, I thought, lost for a moment in his stare.

I cleared my throat, forcing myself to refocus on the task at hand.

Admiring Silas's physique and handsome face could only earn me trouble, and we'd already gotten into enough together. Not that I wouldn't turn down a repeat if our situation was different. Because that wolf's tongue…

My thighs threatened to clench, which was a problem given my position.

Stop thinking about it.

Only, I couldn't. It was all I had thought about since finding him in the kitchen. Pancakes didn't help, and neither, it seemed, did this distraction.

If anything, I'd only made it worse.

"Luna," he murmured, arching a brow.

"Uh…" I licked my lips. "Yeah, looks even." Or at least I hoped it did, because my focus was shot.

Fix the chin scruff next, I told myself. *That'll help.*

It didn't.

If anything, being that close to his mouth only heightened my arousal, something he had to smell. He was a wolf, after all, and my legs were spread not two feet away from his face.

Fortunately, he didn't tease me. He just sat ramrod straight with his hands fisted at his sides.

But I felt the heat coming off him.

He wasn't completely immune either.

Maybe we both should have put on more clothes—him a shirt, and me, well, I should have put on some pants. Because I was bare under Edon's shirt, something Silas had to know since I was straddling his jean-clad thigh.

Just finish it, I coached myself. *Quickly.*

I turned to grab one of the blades I had found in Edon's bathroom, my balance wavering. Silas caught my hips, holding me steady as I righted myself. "Sorry," I said. "Sink was farther away than I thought."

"No problem." He sounded gruff, if a bit hoarse. No sign of the teasing male from the kitchen. This one was holding on to his control with everything he owned, and my nearness only made it worse.

"I'm almost done," I said in an effort to console us both. His jaw didn't need much, just a subtle smoothing. He must have been using a jagged knife to do this before, because it left his chin fuzz rather uneven.

"Sure." He released me, his touch leaving behind a burn I wanted to explore but couldn't.

The forbidden nature of touching him was almost like a drug, my fingers moving to places they shouldn't, all under the guise of fixing his hair and scruff. He knew, too. I could see it in his eyes, the irises turning to liquid fire, and in the way his muscles seemed to clench and tense beneath every stroke.

"What was that the other day?" he finally asked, a touch of hesitation in his voice. "I know we shouldn't talk about it, but…"

I need to know were the final words of that statement. I understood because I felt the same way.

"My wolf was in fight-or-flight mode. You won her over. She submitted." Pretty standard in the lycan community, but it had never happened to me before. None of the males in Ernest Clan desired me, my fate promised to another at birth. The only reason Volk had done the deed when I asked was because of our friendship, but neither of us had enjoyed it.

My experience with Silas was different.

He actually made me come.

And would have again had Edon not interfered.

"Is it always like that?" Silas cleared his throat. "I mean, the submission and wanting-to-fuck thing."

At least he'd stopped claiming I begged him. But I almost preferred the prior teasing to this serious discussion.

Because thinking about it clearly, without humor, stirred a craving inside me to do it again. To finish what we started.

"It happens," I replied, referring to his submission and fucking clarification. "But the wolves have to be mutually attracted to one another."

He frowned, making it difficult for me to shave around the edges of his full lips. Not that talking helped all that much either.

"But our wolves had just met," he said, those bright eyes lifting to mine.

"We've been sniffing around each other quite a bit, Silas." I pressed a thumb to his mouth to keep him from replying and focused on trimming the hairs just above and below his lips. "I know you followed me around. I could smell your curiosity." It hadn't bothered me, just put a damper on my escape plans. "I knew we would fight. Actually, I chose you as the weak link because of your newbie status." My eyes found his once more. "Obviously, I underestimated you."

An understatement.

He'd defeated me without breaking a sweat. And all while taking care not to harm me.

"You impressed me," I admitted softly, finishing the job along his jaw and releasing his mouth. "You impressed my wolf."

"It… it was intense."

"Yes." I smiled. "That part is normal, from what I hear. But you were the first to ever, well, taste me like that." I grimaced a little at how innocent I sounded. It wasn't like orgasms were unfamiliar territory for me. Just the whole receiving-one-from-someone-else thing—that was new. "You're, uh, talented."

He chuckled, the sound low and tempting. "Talented, huh?"

I swallowed. "Yeah. You, uh, yeah." I shook my head, my skin heating. "We shouldn't talk about it anymore." Or I was going to give in to the urge to experience it all over again, and wouldn't that be a catastrophe in the making.

"Oh, I don't know; I find it a fascinating conversation," a male voice drawled from the hallway. "Please continue, little mate. Tell us all about how Silas made you feel beneath his tongue."

My hands froze against Silas's chin, my heart leaping into my throat.

Silas didn't appear surprised at all. Either he'd sensed the alpha's arrival or he didn't care. I couldn't tell. But probably the former.

I hadn't heard or scented Edon's approach, something I attributed to his stealthy alpha ways and the fact that his cologne was a permanent fixture inside his house.

He stepped into the entryway to lean against the door frame. "Well, Luna? Tell us about his talent. Or would you prefer my summary? I did watch it all unfold, after all."

"Edon…" My throat resembled sandpaper, his name rough on the air. No amount of swallowing or coughing would clear it, the sensation latching on and refusing to let go. And all the while, he stood there with an eyebrow arched, his expression otherwise unreadable, as he no doubt smelled the arousal permeating the small room.

I couldn't hide it.

And neither could Silas.

"I was just cutting his hair," I said, explaining our proximity. I set the blade down, nearly finished anyway. "He looked like a shaggy dog."

"A shaggy dog with a talented tongue," Edon returned, evidently not letting that part go. "Which isn't at all what I asked about, little mate. I want to hear about what you did then and how he made you feel. If you're really descriptive, maybe I'll allow him to do it again, something I know you're both craving. Right, Silas?"

Silas didn't appear nearly as rattled as me, his gaze meeting the fuming alpha's without even blinking. "Yes."

His lack of a denial shocked the hell out of me.

As did the growl in his chest while he stared Edon down.

"Mmm," the alpha murmured. "Your turn, Luna. Tell me how it felt. Tell me if you want to experience it again." He didn't break his focus from Silas as he spoke, but his tone resembled a demand, not a request.

I couldn't speak, the violent intensity in the room too thick for me to form a coherent thought, let alone a sentence. The palpable energy raised the hairs along the back of my neck and tightened my belly. Something was happening, a war of dominance, a claim, but I couldn't define the prize.

It wasn't me, exactly. But it revolved around me, tantalizing my every nerve and lighting my bloodstream on fire.

You're stronger than this, I whispered to myself. *Don't let him dominate you.*

Except that wasn't my problem at all. I could stand up to Edon every day of the week. But right now?

Yeah, right now, I didn't *want* to defy him.

And that was a very telling problem.

"I don't think she wants a repeat performance, Silas," Edon said slowly, his eyes narrowing. "But I know you do. So what should we do about that?"

He pushed off the doorjamb to join us in the small space. It was a decent-sized guest bath with a full tub and double sinks, but two virile males and little old me made for quite the crowded area.

I took a step back, hoping to put some distance between us, but Silas's palms landed on my hips and held me in place over his thigh. He hadn't stopped looking at Edon, the two of them seeming to communicate on an entirely different level.

The sire bond, I realized, swallowing. I'd never actually witnessed a proper one before. My father inherited a winner from the Immortal Cup when I was a little girl. I never met her because the woman didn't survive her turning.

But Silas had more than survived his own.

"Hmm, still so quiet," Edon mused. "I suppose we can rely on your body to tell us what you want, little mate." He moved even closer, placing his bare chest a hairsbreadth away from my arm and effectively trapping me between him and Silas.

I felt captured.

Overwhelmed.

And really fucking *hot*.

Both males exuded heat like it was their job, and I seemed to be absorbing it through every pore. I nearly panted in response, my body on fire beneath Silas's hands. His thumbs were drawing little circles against the shirt, as if to provide a semblance of calm.

It did nothing to slow my racing heart.

Or to quell to the growing need slicking my thighs.

They can smell it.

They know.

And Edon's grin confirmed it.

"I want to know how wet she is," he murmured. "Silas?"

The warmth on my hip shifted south as Silas drew his touch down my thigh and then upward beneath the shirt. His blue eyes slid to mine as he slipped a finger through my damp folds. I shuddered, my hands going to his shoulders to keep myself upright.

This was all so unexpected. So insane. And so undeniably arousing.

Why was Edon okay with this?

How could he allow another male—his own progeny—to touch me this way?

Was it all a ploy? Would he turn on us in the next moment? Punish Silas for touching me? Punish me for allowing it? What—

Oh, fuck… That little brush against my clit nearly had my knees buckling.

"She's practically weeping," Silas replied, his voice low and steady and grounding me in the moment. Only to be derailed by two of his fingers penetrating me deep without warning.

I moaned, my nails biting into his bare skin.

Again, I nearly demanded.

And as if he heard me, he repeated the action.

"She smells fucking amazing." Edon's voice was so close, drawing me back to them both, confusing my senses, and sending waves of hot and cold shocks up and down my body. "I want to taste her."

Silas withdrew his touch, eliciting a whimper from my throat.

And then he lifted his hand for Edon.

My lips parted as Edon took Silas's fingers into his mouth—deep—and sucked my arousal right off the other man's skin.

Oh.

My.

God.

That had to be the hottest thing I'd ever seen.

And the groan they both released?

Holy fuck. I squeezed my legs, seeking friction, only to be thwarted by Silas's muscular thigh.

"Delicious," Edon murmured.

"I know," Silas agreed, his blue eyes inflamed with need as he studied my expression. "She screams beautifully, too."

This was surreal.

Two males and me in a bathroom filled with testosterone and *need.*

"Kiss her for me, Silas," Edon whispered. "Fuck her mouth with your tongue."

Silas grinned. "Gladly."

I wasn't given time to agree.

Wasn't given time to even comprehend.

Silas's fingers were already in my hair, pulling me to him with a ferocity that left me no choice but to obey.

And I melted into him.

Because that tongue was so fucking wicked. The man excelled in kissing. I already knew this from my first experience, but this time blew my mind all over again. The way he nibbled my lower lip, the way he took charge, the way he tugged on my hair to angle my head to where he desired me most.

I moaned, the sound one I couldn't swallow even if I tried.

And then I felt Edon behind me.

His warmth a brand against my back as he drew his fingers lightly down my sides to the hem of my shirt. I shivered as he began to lift it, exposing my body to them both inch by inch.

Silas released me, allowing Edon to tug the fabric over my head, and then his mouth was back on mine again. The movements so seamless I knew they were communicating mentally, but I couldn't bring myself to feel left out. Not when Edon dropped a kiss to my shoulder, then on the back of my neck, while

Silas owned my lips.

I'm going to die, I thought. *And I'm okay with that if this is how I go out.*

Because holy *wow,* this was the most intense experience of my very short life.

Two hot, dominant males touching, stroking, licking, and nipping.

And then I was kissing Edon.

It all happened so quickly, his fingers replacing Silas's to tug my head back toward him. My neck protested the sharp shift, but my body wept in gratitude, especially as Silas began to lick a path down my breasts.

Oh…

He pulled my nipple into his mouth, igniting my bloodstream with another heady flood of lust. I needed more. I needed him to go lower. I needed *friction.*

A plea broke from my lips, one Edon swallowed before dominating me with his mouth.

So much harsher than Silas.

The hint of violence in Edon's kiss blended with the soft nibbles against my breasts, the light strokes along my thighs.

Edon was definitely the alpha.

But Silas… he held his own. Those nips against my skin as he kissed along my chest weren't kind; they were markings of his own.

I shivered, overheated, overstimulated, overwhelmed, by them both.

Until Edon released me.

His mouth hovering over mine.

His grip tight in my hair.

"I know Silas can suck cock, but can you?" Edon's words were a whisper against my lips, and they shook me to my core.

He couldn't mean…? When he mentioned receiving the best head of his life, he wasn't talking about…?

I blinked several times.

And Edon smiled in response. "You enjoyed his oral ministrations so much that I decided to try them for myself. He's quite skilled." He canted his head, those obsidian pools holding so many secrets—including the one he'd just given me. "I want to see you on your knees, Luna. I want to watch you please Silas as he pleased me. Will you kneel for us, little mate? Will you take his cock between those beautiful lips and swallow his seed?"

Oh, fuck…

Just the notion of the two of them together had me nearly coming on the spot. And the idea that Edon wanted to watch me suck Silas off?

Dear God Almighty.

Silas swirled his tongue against my nipple, drawing my focus to where he gazed up at me from my breasts. Yearning tinged with understanding in his beautiful eyes.

We both knew Edon was the one in charge.

We were both at his mercy.

But that wouldn't stop us from *enjoying* the alpha's demands.

"Luna?" Edon whispered, his lips brushing my ear. "You enjoyed his tongue between your thighs, didn't you?"

I nodded, my voice still nonexistent despite all the moans that seemed to be leaving my mouth.

"Don't you want to taste him? To feel him come down your pretty little throat?"

My legs tensed, another groan working its way past my lips.

Silas leaned back away from my chest in response, one blond eyebrow arching. "Now's your chance to prove you're more than fine, little moon."

I couldn't believe this was happening.

That Edon seemed to be okay with it.

But of course he was. He'd just admitted that Silas had sucked him off the other day. And while I would have killed Bianca for admitting such a thing, the image of Silas going down on Edon provoked a completely different response from me. Still lethal, still violent, but in an entirely erotic kind of way.

My only regret was not having been there to fucking watch.

Because these two together? They would set the bedroom on fucking fire.

I knew because the entire bathroom felt as if it'd gone up in flames.

My hands met Silas's chest, his hard muscles flexing beneath my palms. I'd never gone down on a male—my chastity something my father required these last twenty-two years of my life—but I knew the general idea of how to perform the act.

And something told me Silas would be a hell of a lot more patient than Edon.

As if sensing my thought, Edon nipped the pulse of my neck, then laved the tender skin with his tongue. "Such a good little mate," he praised. "Mmm, I just may reward you. If you please us enough."

His words should have pissed me off, but instead they provided the opposite impact. I took them as a challenge. I wanted to blow both their minds not to earn a reward but to earn their mutual respect.

I was an alpha female for a reason.

I didn't bend over and take it.

I fought.

And I won.

My fingers traced the lines of Silas's rigid abdomen as I went to my knees before him. The look in his eyes encouraged me to proceed, telling me without words that he wanted this, too. I allowed him to see the alpha inside me, the wolf who was about to destroy his world in the best way.

Arousal deepened his gaze to an oceanic blue. "Keep looking at me like that, Luna. And don't stop. Not even when I hit the back of your throat."

That wouldn't be a problem.

Because I wanted to watch him fall apart, to gain the upper hand, and to dominate *him*.

The curl of his lips said he knew it, too. And what's more, he approved.

"Now, little mate," Edon said, applying pressure to my shoulders. "Taste him. Suck him. Fuck him with that pretty mouth. And swallow."

Chapter Fifteen

Silas

DON'T HURT HER, Edon warned.

I met his burning gaze. *Says the male forcing her to suck me off.*

Does she look forced to you? he asked, a taunting note to his words. *You can smell her arousal as well as I can. She wants this.*

She wants to eat me alive, I replied, noting the challenge in her eyes. *Topping from the bottom.*

An alpha female through and through, he agreed, running his fingers through her hair.

I swallowed as Luna slowly drew my zipper down, her body perfectly positioned between my sprawled legs. She licked her lips, her expression hungry, and tugged down my jeans. My dick sprung forward, eager to meet her mouth. She wasted no time, her tongue memorizing my shaft in a way that had my balls aching for another stroke, another taste, another *lick*.

"Fuck," I breathed, my head falling back on a wave of euphoria. Luna put all my previous experience to shame, and she'd barely even started. It helped that I actually desired this.

My courses at the university were all forced. Rae typically volunteered to be my partner, mostly because she knew I'd go easy on her. Unlike in my male-on-male studies, which tended to be a bit more violent.

And still had nothing on Edon.

Lust pooled in his obsidian depths, his cheeks flushing as he watched Luna move her mouth up and down over my cock. Her eyes were all mine, her focus on my face incredibly alluring as she fought to take even more of me into her throat.

I was gone to her and her ministrations, unable to focus on anything else.

Until Edon's mouth settled over mine.

He'd moved so silently, so quickly, that I hadn't sensed him coming for me until he thrust his tongue between my lips.

My muscles tightened.

My hands curling into fists.

I didn't know what to do beneath all the sensations. Fire burned deep inside me, stirring a maelstrom in my groin that hardened my dick even more. It almost hurt. I could barely breathe, my brain fracturing beneath the onslaught.

Mmm, I can feel your pleasure through our sire bond, Edon whispered in my thoughts. *It's making me so fucking hard.*

One of his hands cupped the back of my neck while the other remained on Luna's head, urging her to go deeper. Always in charge. Always dominant. And at the moment, I didn't care. I would do whatever he wanted so long as this didn't stop.

My spine tingled, my thighs flexing, just the thought of him demanding that Luna release me leaving me cold and restless.

What if that was the purpose?

What if—

Shh, he murmured, cutting off my concerns. *I wouldn't dream of allowing this to end too soon.*

Why are you doing this? I asked, my body strung tight as a bow ready to release.

"Because I can," he growled against my mouth. "Because I want to. Because I enjoy seeing Luna down on her knees." He glanced at her, his cheek brushing mine. "Look at her, Silas. Look how beautiful she is with your cock in her mouth."

I shuddered, his words, coupled with the sight, nearly undoing me. Her pupils were blown wide, her cheeks flushed with excitement.

"Did you enjoy watching me kiss him, little mate?" Edon continued, his voice low. He stroked his fingers through her hair, his opposite palm still against the back of my neck.

She swallowed around my shaft, sending a jolt of electricity through my veins. And then she moaned in approval—a moan I rivaled with my own groan. The intensity of her mouth and Edon's warm tones heightened my senses, destroying my ability to move, to think, to inhale, to *be.*

Molten energy caressed my veins, rocking me to the core of my existence. Luna's little noises didn't help, nor did her slight gags as she took me too far. But she didn't stop. If anything, it urged her onward, and all the while, she held my gaze, that look in her eyes enough to demolish a saint's resolve.

I cupped her jaw, my fingers grazing the side of her head near Edon's palm.

He brushed the tips of my blunt nails, the touch sending a shock through my system.

This was an experience I never could have anticipated.

Two alpha lycans, both watching me with predatory gleams.

Luna hungry for my cum.

Edon desiring my submission.

I couldn't resist the pull, couldn't back down from the way they made me feel.

"I'm close." My voice was hoarse.

"Good," Edon whispered. Between Luna's mouth and Edon's lips brushing my ear, I could hardly see straight. "Come for us, Silas. Come hard."

"*Fuck*." The demand shoved me off the cliff, my orgasm a harsh assault that jolted me from my head to my toes. I nearly fell, but Edon was there, his hard body cradling my back, his hands on my shoulders.

And Luna.

Fuck, Luna.

She stared up at me with such heat, such vigor, as she accepted my seed down her pretty little throat. Every. Single. Drop. And her greedy mouth sucked for more, her fingers digging into my thighs.

I quivered, my pulse racing, my vision coming in and out as I panted between them.

Edon massaged my tensing muscles, his hands a brand against my bare skin. And then he gripped my chin, forced my head back, and took my mouth once more.

His snarl shook my very spirit, the possession in that sound one I didn't understand. He drew blood, his teeth skating across my lips before devouring me with his tongue.

I couldn't react fast enough, my moves one step behind. It left me bewildered, hot, and ready to fuck all over again.

Luna seemed eager to oblige, her lips moving up and down, her hands growing bolder and exploring my torso, my hips, the tops of my thighs.

Edon smiled against my mouth, the expression tinged with cruelty. "That's enough, Luna." He reached over me to grab a fistful of her hair and tugged her away from my groin.

She made a noise of protest, her pupils so enlarged I couldn't see the light brown of her irises. Long lashes fluttered as she blinked.

"Watching that made me thirsty," Edon murmured, his voice low. "Luna, clean up the mess you made of my guest bath. When you're done, you can join us in the kitchen. If you want."

Confusion settled over her features. A confusion I shared.

Trust me, Edon whispered into my mind. *She needs this lesson.*

"Now, Silas," he said out loud, releasing me.

He stepped toward the door, his expression expectant.

Clearing my throat, I stood, uncertain of what else to do. Luna gazed up at me, a flurry of emotions traversing her beautiful face. Shock. Hurt. Annoyance.

I didn't like any of them, but a growl from Edon had me taking a step toward him.

What was I supposed to do? Demand we pleasure his mate? Demand another orgasm? Push Luna onto all fours and fuck her the way I craved?

"Silas," Edon hissed, the alpha in him yanking at the sire bond.

I left the room without looking back at Luna, but I *felt* her disappointment, her fury, and most importantly, her unfulfilled need.

Why did you do that? I demanded, following him down the hall while I buttoned up my jeans.

He led me to the kitchen, silent until he opened the fridge. *She left you in the same position earlier this week, did she not?*

Because you showed up, I pointed out.

Maybe. He retrieved two bottles and set them on the counter. *But she still left you hard as a rock and unfulfilled. Now she knows how it feels.*

I snorted and took a seat on one of the three barstools surrounding his kitchen island. *So you're teaching her a lesson in delayed gratification?*

No, her lesson is about behavior. She's an alpha female. If she wants more, she can demand it. And when she does, she'll learn that I'm more than happy to reciprocate.

I considered his objective as he found a bottle opener from the drawer. *You're giving her control.*

To an extent, yes.

This male was nothing like the alphas I had read about in my studies. They all took what they wanted, everyone else be damned. But Edon wanted his mate to have a choice, and for whatever reason, he'd included me in that choice.

"What? No argument to the contrary?" he taunted, passing me one of the drinks.

"Not sure I can argue," I admitted, sniffing the pungent liquid. *Beer.* Not something I'd ever indulged in, but I was aware of the substance. Lycans enjoyed alcohol, especially when playing with humans.

"And here I thought you'd always have a comeback," he mused, leaning on the marble slab of the kitchen island. "Still think this is all a test?"

"Yes." I just couldn't figure out if I'd passed or failed.

He nursed his beer for a long moment, clasping the neck between two strong fingers, then set it to the side. "My father doesn't want me to ascend, and the way I see it, I have two liabilities." He arched a brow. "Care to guess who those liabilities are?"

Wasn't hard to follow that implication, but it didn't make much sense. "Why would he consider me a liability? I'm just a mutt."

His gaze narrowed. "Maybe, but you're *my* mutt. And I protect those that rely on me."

"I don't rely on you," I countered, narrowing my gaze right back at him. "I rely only on myself."

"Which I can admire, but you're out of your depth here, Silas. It's why you're going to stay at my house—*this* house—until further notice." He picked up his beer again, eyeing me as he took a swig. *And drink that. It's not cheap,* he added mentally.

It smells foul, I muttered, forcing myself to sip from the rim. *Tastes like shit, too.*

"Fine." He focused on the hallway. "Luna!"

A feminine snarl rumbled, preceding her entry. "*What*?" she demanded, hands on her hips. She'd thrown on Edon's shirt again, but it didn't hide her nipples protruding through the fabric.

She was all pissed-off, aroused female, and fuck if that didn't make me rock hard again.

"Finish Silas's beer," he said, gesturing at the drink. "I don't want to waste it."

"Why don't you finish it?" she countered. "Try tasting it, Edon. Suck it all up and swallow. I hear it's fun." With that flippant remark, she stalked off, leaving him smirking in her wake.

"Oh, I adore her." He finished his beer and picked up mine. "If neither of you is going to accept my gift, then I'll enjoy it myself." He licked the rim, his gaze holding mine. "You're staying here."

"I didn't argue to the contrary, did I?" Turning down shelter and protection seemed like a pretty stupid thing to argue about, even if it did infringe on my independence. But I could still look out for myself under his roof.

"No, you didn't." He sounded satisfied, a tone that oddly provided a sense of relief. I liked knowing I'd pleased him. Which was strange because I usually didn't care about anyone other than myself and those closest to me. I supposed he qualified for the latter, being my maker and all.

His throat worked as he swallowed, drawing my attention to the thick cords of muscle along his neck and shoulders. While we were roughly the same height, he definitely outweighed me. That explained why the jeans I found in his room were just a little too big for me in the thighs and waist. I still wore them today because they were in better condition than my sole pair. If Edon had noticed, he didn't seem to care. He had told me I could help myself to anything in his cabin. It seemed he'd meant it.

"I don't want you to run alone either," he said after a bout of silence. "That applies to you both, I mean. I'd rather you both sort of stick together."

"Is that why you had her acquaint her mouth with my cock?" I wondered out loud, arching a brow. "To help us *bond*?"

He chuckled. "No. That was purely for my enjoyment." He set the half-finished bottle to the side and placed his palms on the countertop, leaning forward. "Watching her suck you off was hot as fuck. Maybe next time you can watch her do it to me, or maybe she'll watch as I come down your throat. What do you prefer, Silas?" His gaze dropped to my lips. "Because I'm eager to try both."

And I was hard again.

Really, *really* hard.

Because both those scenarios? Yeah, they both aroused me. Which was so utterly fucked up, but here we were.

Luna chose that moment to join us, fury and lust riding the air around her. "The bathroom is swept up," she said, her tone as cold as ice. Yet it did nothing to alter the temperature of the room, the heat brewing between me and Edon resembling a churning tornado of temptation waiting to suck us all down to hell. "Anything else you need me to do, Your Royal Fucking Highness?" she asked.

I couldn't look at her, Edon's gaze captivating mine, but I suspected she was glowering at him.

"Yes," he said, his tone laced with command. "I'm famished, Silas. You?"

Catching the innuendo underlying those words, I smiled. It seemed we were moving on to the next stage of his *lesson*. "I could eat."

Edon broke our connection to glance at Luna. "Come feed us, little mate."

Her cheeks blossomed into the most delectable shades of red. "Are you fucking serious?" She glanced between us in utter disbelief, her fury seductive as hell. "Yeah, you both can go fuck yourselves."

She turned on her heel, only to freeze at Edon's growl. It was low and menacing and reverberated through the room in a way only an alpha could.

"Get over here," he demanded. "Now."

Luna bristled but didn't move a step in either direction.

"You can run if you want, but we'll catch you," he warned. "And you know what will happen when we pounce." He waited a beat, watched as she stole a calming breath, and smiled. "What's it going to be, Luna? Are you going to behave for us or make us work for it?"

Chapter Sixteen

LUNA

TRAPPED.

That was how I felt.

Both males watched me with predatory expressions, awaiting my decision. And something told me that, regardless of what choice I made, I was about to be devoured—by both of them.

I'd been so pissed after Edon and Silas left me in that bathroom all hot and bothered. My first time going down on a male, and he couldn't even say *Thank you.* No, instead he left with the alpha who'd commanded me to my knees.

I wasn't a toy but a lycan. An *alpha* lycan. And Edon was treating me like some omega bitch in heat.

Probably because I was acting like one.

But hell, these two males were messing with my head. I couldn't think straight around so much testosterone. There was something acutely unfulfilled between me and Silas—a dominance that had yet to be established.

And Edon… So much between us was definitely unfinished.

The alpha in question lifted one arrogant brow. "Luna?"

Run or play chef.

Except something told me it wasn't food they wanted to eat, but me. Which meant he was giving me the choice to accept it or play hard to get.

After the hell he just put me through in the bathroom? There was only one real option. "Come get me."

The words were tossed over my shoulder, my legs already moving.

Growls sounded behind me—Silas and Edon leaping from the kitchen to give chase.

The shirt flew over my head as I fell into a shift, my wolf ready and waiting, and bolted from the house into the surrounding courtyard.

I knew exactly where I wanted to go—the river's edge where Edon had chased me before. It was secluded and peaceful. And perfect for the activity I had in mind.

Because I was done playing submissive to these two males.

They wanted me to suck their cocks? Fine. But they were going to fucking return the favor.

My paws pounded over the earth, the silence behind me unnerving. I knew they were close, could feel the presence of their dominance gliding across my fur, but they moved with a precision and skill that seduced me even more.

Especially Silas.

Not only should I be able to best him in a race, but I should also be able to sense him. However, he was just as stealthy as his maker.

It sent a thrill down my spine, had my wolf preening in response. No one in Ernest Clan had ever appealed to me like this, not even Volk. And he'd been the only one I could stomach touching me before.

But now… *now* I desired a lot more than touching.

I blamed the mating bond. It had changed me on a level, exciting my hormones into a frenzy only the alpha could tame. Except that didn't quite explain Silas.

Mmm, maybe it was the sire bond confusing my wolf, forcing me to yearn for them both.

Or perhaps I'd finally found two males worthy of my attention.

One of them nipped my back leg. I responded by pushing myself even harder, my need to reach the river a palpable presence in my mind.

They could have me there.

But only if they agreed to my terms.

A low growl vibrated my spine, teeth clamping on my scruff to pull me to the ground. I rolled with it, allowing the much bigger body to nearly pin me—and used my back paws to kick him off.

Only to have a second, even larger male on top of me.

I squirmed, then whined, my goal of reaching the riverbank so close yet so far.

Edon merely tilted his head above me, his muzzle so much bigger than my own. He nudged my head, forcing me to reveal my neck.

Surrender, he was saying.

I wanted to, but not here. I wanted the water. The tranquility. The peace.

And somehow he knew, because he let me go with a soft growl of patience. It said he knew I was his, that I could run wherever I wanted and he'd still have me, so if I wanted to play, he'd play.

I was on my feet in a second, sprinting again.

This time he allowed me to hear his presence as he ran alongside Silas, their pursuit a wave of heat at my back.

They had me and they knew it. This run represented foreplay, a way of drawing out my eventual capture. Anticipation heightened, our pants music in the wind, and finally I reached my desired location.

Edon circled me one way while Silas moved in the opposite direction, their prowls sexy as fuck. No wonder they were drawn to each other. Sexual energy oozed from them both, leaving me in a puddle of need between them.

I shifted back into human form, my thighs already soaked with my expectation. Acceptance formed on my lips, a plea to have them both, when howls sounded in the distance, causing Edon to still.

He listened intently, as did Silas, as a wave of warnings littered the air.

Ice drizzled through my veins, severely damaging my aroused state.

That was the sound of a furious alpha male—Edon's father. It was underlined in a demand for blood. For retribution.

Edon and Silas seemed to be communicating, their eyes locked on one another.

And then the alpha heir took off, leaving us by the stream.

Silas shifted, his expression grim. "He told us to stay here."

"I gathered that by his departure," I replied, noting Edon's speed. "He's fast." Like, really, really fast. He'd clearly been toying with me and indulging in my pace, because holy fuck, that wolf could run.

"Yeah, he is." Silas palmed the back of his neck. "Luna…"

I swallowed, meeting his wary gaze. "Yeah?"

"Something's wrong," he said, his voice hoarse. "Like, really fucking wrong."

The hairs along my arms danced, my stomach churning.

He wasn't talking about us or what had been about to happen. No. He meant with the pack.

"I know," I whispered. "I feel it, too." A depraved sickness, a calling for death.

And I suspected one of us was the target of that call.

Chapter Seventeen

Edon

BIANCA.

Her vacant blue eyes stared up at the tree above, while the rest of her body lay several feet away.

Someone had *chewed* through her neck. A horrible way to die that required strength and skill to accomplish.

And Luna's scent was all over the scene.

My teeth clenched as I stayed just out of sight, careful to keep my scent from the others. Not even my father had sensed me yet—a testament to my growing gifts and his weakening ones.

Fury emanated from the pack, words being exchanged that made my blood boil. They'd already taken a vote, not giving a damn that their alpha heir—me—wasn't in attendance. If I had any question as to pack loyalty before, I had my answers now. Everyone standing in this clearing was allied to my father. And it would be in my best interest to remember that.

"Where's your son?" one of them demanded.

My father howled again, the call meant for my ears.

But I didn't move, too furious to take a step.

This was a fucking setup. But I couldn't say a damn word because I was Luna's alibi. Not exactly a winning case, even with Silas on my side. Because everyone would see it as me protecting my mate and progeny. And going against a pack vote would render my relationships irreparable, which was the last thing I needed right now.

The pack demands retribution, I told Silas after describing the scene.

But she's innocent.

That's not the point, I replied. *My father's making me choose between the pack decision and my mate. It's his fucked-up way of forcing me to prove my loyalty to Clemente Clan.*

Failure was not an option here. If I chose Luna, the pack might very well try to kill me.

And you can't choose Luna? Silas asked, his mental voice holding a note of incredulity.

I sighed. The male might be an impressive wolf, but he was still so new to pack politics. Luna would at least understand this. I hoped she would, anyway.

The pack has already voted, I explained. *If I ignore the vote, I risk a mutiny.* Which, I suspected, was my father's goal.

That doesn't make any sense, he growled. *We know she didn't do this.*

I palmed the back of my neck, eyeing the restless wolves a few yards away from me. If I didn't make an appearance soon, they'd go looking for me. Or worse, they might accuse me of being an accomplice to the crime. I wouldn't put it past my father to try.

Let me explain this another way, I said, focusing on both Silas and the antsy wolves. *Luna's new. She has no allies here. However, Bianca had several. Those who knew her want revenge, and they don't care about innocence, not after witnessing Luna punch her the other day.*

So they won't even bother figuring out who did this.

In their minds, Luna is already guilty. And my saying otherwise will just make me look like a male protecting his mate. This trial was designed to hurt one of my perceived weaknesses—Luna. My grandfather had warned me that this would happen. I just never expected it to be so blatantly obvious.

I don't have a choice, Silas, I whispered, stepping into the clearing with a bored expression. I'd already phased back into human form, leaving me naked. But anyone who mistook my nudity for vulnerability would have one hell of a wake-up call.

"Seems my female has been busy," I said, eyeing the remains with disinterest. "I suppose Bianca shouldn't have run her mouth with falsehoods." Because the last time I'd touched her—aside from the casual hug or in taunting Luna—was well before the mating ceremony.

"Are you implying Bianca deserved her fate?" my father demanded.

I lifted a shoulder. "I'm saying it's probably not wise to provoke an alpha female in the middle of a mating moon. The same could be said about a mating alpha male." Except I seemed rather at ease in sharing my intended with Silas. But that was a matter for another day.

Some of the pack members growled. I ignored them, feigning nonchalance.

"That said, I suppose I need to have a word with Luna." I folded my arms. "Unless you question my ability to punish my mate?"

"Considering you interrupted my last one? Yes, son. Yes, I do." My father looked around at his buddies, who all grunted in agreement. "You'll punish her publicly or I'll kill her myself."

I snorted. "You can't kill my mate."

"Can't I?" he countered. "It'll delay your ascension by a decade or two, but I'm sure more alpha females will be available soon. We can always ask Ernest Clan to produce another as well. I'm certain Niko would happily oblige after we inform him of his daughter's shortcomings."

Yeah, and he would most certainly take out his frustrations on his wife in the interim as well. *No, thanks.* "I'm not interested in waiting, old man." I chose the words with care, making sure he heard my growl on the final two. His time was at an end whether he acknowledged it or not.

"We don't need to rush this, Edon. I'm more than fit to continue running things," he replied, sounding as nonchalant as I had moments ago. "Pretty sure the pack would agree, too."

Of course they would. Because he'd made sure of it.

Which meant I had no choice.

I either punished Luna publicly or risked her death and my standing in the pack. Neither consequence was negotiable on my part.

The sooner I took over this hell, the sooner I improved it.

And Luna didn't deserve to die for something she'd clearly not done.

But looking at the lycans surrounding Bianca, I knew with all my being that no one would believe her innocence. Not even if Silas vouched for her whereabouts as well. If anything, it'd probably result in his death in addition to Luna's.

I fucking hate you, I told my father with a glance. It was too brief for anyone else to see, but his lips quirked up in response.

This was another of his damn trials.

A test.

And I only had one option.

"Fine." It took considerable effort not to growl that single word. "Prepare the ring. I'll find Luna."

I didn't give my father a chance to argue, my feet already moving. *Silas, I need you for another task…*

Chapter Eighteen

Silas

"ABSOLUTELY NOT," I growled, the second Edon appeared. He'd thrown on a pair of jeans, leaving me and Luna stark naked before him. Not that I cared. I was too focused on the insane plan he'd spoke into my head not even ten minutes ago.

"It wasn't a request, Silas." He didn't even look at me, his dark gaze on Luna. "They're calling for your blood."

"I know," she replied, her arms wrapped around herself. She hadn't stopped shaking since the howls began, her mind already processing what the pack wanted before I even had a chance to speak.

Still, I'd relayed every word from Edon, including the *task* he'd given me. A task I'd snorted at in my head and refused, but the alpha chose not to hear me.

"I won't do it," I said again, standing my ground. I could handle a lot. Not this.

Edon turned on me then, his palm around my throat in a flash as he shoved me up against a tree. "The alternative is far worse, Silas. If you care about her at all, you'll do as I say."

"Bullshit," I retorted, livid and not at all frightened by the stronger wolf before me. "She's innocent. I'm not going to fucking—"

"It's fine," Luna cut in, her breath shuddering out of her in defeat. "I accept the punishment." She captured Edon's gaze, a hint of a fighter lurking in her caramel-colored depths. "But I *am* innocent."

"I know," he replied, his grip on my throat lessening in severity without releasing me. "But I still have to do this."

She nodded, her arms still tightly folded around herself as though she were cold.

I gaped back and forth between them. "Why the hell are you just accepting this?" Lycans and vampires were supposed to have rights. They were the superior species. This punishment shit was for humans and humans alone.

"There's still so much about our society you need to learn." Edon's palm flexed, his expression intensifying. "You will do what I say, Silas, or things will get very bad for you both."

I scoffed at the threat. "I can take a punishment." Or several. I'd more than held my own in my twenty-two years of life. This would be no different.

"Perhaps you can, but what about Luna?" Edon snapped. "If you refuse, someone else will take your place. Perhaps more. And then how will you feel, Silas? Because they'll make you watch as they shred her apart, and you'll know all along that you could have helped prevent her mutilation by completing this one fucking task."

"What you're asking me to do—"

"No, what I'm *telling* you to do, Silas. This isn't a fucking request. I need you to help me protect what dignity Luna will have left after this." He released me with a shove. "This is happening. Otherwise, she dies."

Luna shuddered visibly.

And Edon grabbed her arm. "Let's go."

I stared after them, my jaw on the ground.

For two decades, I learned all about the glamorous lives of lycans and vampires. Especially those of the alphas and royals. Yet never once did anyone talk about this—the thirst for punishments, for keeping fellow lycans in line, for brutalizing each other into submission.

Because that was what this was at the core: a way to break Luna's psyche and force her to bow to her male betters.

The alpha heir didn't want to do this.

However, he was going to anyway.

Because his world required it.

There is no better life, I realized, gazing up at the trees above me. *It was all a lie.*

We have a chance to change it, Edon said softly. *But I can't do anything until I ascend.*

Which required him to have a proper mate—Luna.

And it seemed his father was hell-bent on removing that requirement, leading me to wonder, *Do you think he orchestrated Bianca's death and framed Luna?*

Of course he did, he replied. *This is all a fucked-up test, and if I don't punish Luna, he'll kill her and delay my trials. I need to beat him at his own game.*

I swallowed, my fists clenching at my sides. *So you need me.*

Yes.

No elaboration. Just that single-word reply. It served as a concession of sorts. Edon could command me all he wanted, but at the end of the day, he required my acquiescence for this to work. Denying his demands only made his job harder. It would also end up hurting Luna even more.

"Fuck," I muttered, running my fingers through my hair. "*Fuck.*" It would be so easy to run, to hide from what was about to happen, but I couldn't. Some stupid part of me felt an obligation to stay, not just for Edon but also for Luna.

Loyalty. A dangerous emotion. Which was crazy because I barely knew them, yet some inherent part of me felt indebted to them both. No, not necessarily indebted, but something else. Something stronger.

It reminded me of how I regarded Rae and Willow, only even more intense.

My wolf. I blinked. *It's my wolf.*

You have less than five minutes to make a decision, Edon warned. *As soon as we reach the ring, I'm calling for you.*

He didn't mean mentally, but in a howl. And if I ignored that command, I'd be hunted. That much I understood. Running, I supposed, was never truly an option. To ignore the call of an alpha went against the grain, something I felt deep inside. My wolf would never allow it.

And Edon knew it.

I sensed it through our bond, his assurance that I wouldn't let him down.

Whatever this was between us seemed to grow by the second, leashing me to him in a way I both craved and loathed. I fought him because I could, but some part of me would always enjoy submitting, too.

It confused me.

Enthralled me.

Anchored me.

There was never a choice.

I would do as he demanded because he commanded it. And what I hated most of all was that I'd probably enjoy it because my compliance would please him.

"So fucked up," I grumbled to myself, my feet already moving toward the main camp. I could feel Edon's tug, his need for me to obey, to do what he required, and my body responded in kind.

But it wasn't just about Edon.

I felt Luna, too.

She'd somehow found a link to my veins, heating my blood in a way no one else ever had. I shook my head, refusing the connection. Except it fired again, drawing me nearer, forcing me to submit to them both.

Two alphas.

And me—a mutt.

I didn't know what we were doing, had just sort of gone along for the run earlier when Edon chased Luna. Not because he told me to, but because I wanted to. And that only baffled me more. It was as if my inner wolf, not my mind, drove my instincts, leaving me with no alternative but to follow along.

A howl pierced the night.

Not from Edon, but from Luna. It was agonized and sounded all wrong. Pained. Destroyed. Followed by cries of approval and excitement. *The pack.*

Chaos thrived through the sire bond.

What's wrong? I demanded.

No response.

My walk turned into a sprint as I pounded barefoot over the earth, unfazed by the rocks and dirt beneath my heels. Branches scratched my arms, my sides, my exposed thighs—I had left my jeans at Edon's house before our little run through the woods.

What's happening? I asked again, running as fast as my legs allowed. I was just outside of the main village, the snarls of the pack growing louder with each step. They were near the location where the initial mating ceremony took place. That seemed to be where all official pack matters happened, right in the heart of the territory, surrounded by the cabins owned by Clemente Clan elite.

Edon, I said as I neared one of the larger lodges.

No response.

I ignored the call from my wolf, suppressing the urge to shift. It would take too much time and energy, and I needed to be ready for—

I froze just outside the punishment ring.

Luna lay curled in a ball in the middle of violence, while Edon stood just off to the side and watched as the pack descended upon her. He didn't pay me a glance, his expression bored, his body language nonchalant. But I *felt* his anger through the bond.

Why aren't you stopping them? They're going to kill her!

She's fine, he replied, his mental voice a low growl. But he held up his hand, causing a few of the wolves to still. A warning rumble from his throat caught the attention of the others and earned him a death glare from his father.

"You prefer her death?" Walter asked from across the crowd. "Because I'll happily arrange it." He took a step forward, only for Edon to shake his head.

"No. I merely wish to propose an alternative." There wasn't a hint of anger or annoyance in his tone, even though I felt it raging through our connection. If Edon could, I suspected he'd kill his father right now. Instead, he said, "One of Luna's biggest flaws is her inability to heel."

"A flaw I attempted to remedy the other night before you stopped me," his father replied. "One your pack is willing to solve for you right now if you allow them to continue." He gestured to the salivating males, their lewd stares on Luna's petite frame.

Walter must have orchestrated this harsh reception at the main camp. Because it hadn't been part of Edon's preliminary plan at all, a fact I somehow just understood as if I were connected to my sire's mind.

He hadn't stopped the initial attack, because he knew it would make him appear weak. He also knew his wolves needed to expunge some of their anger to feel satisfied. Which would allow him to better recommend and facilitate Luna's punishment.

I blinked, startled by all that knowledge. Whether he pushed it into me or if I'd stumbled upon it in error, I didn't know. But I felt the veracity of it in my bones.

Edon had a plan.

Everything he did was done with a purpose in mind. Just like this.

"I don't think your method will break her penchant for dominance," Edon said, tucking his hands into his pockets. "But I have one that might." He let that hang in the air, piquing the curiosity of his pack as they glanced between the alpha incumbent and the alpha heir.

Walter folded his burly arms over his bare chest and smiled. "And what, *Alpha Heir*, do you suggest?" he asked, the incredulity in his tone a clear insult.

"Make the mutt fuck her." Edon waved a hand in my direction. "I can't imagine anything more degrading than allowing a mutt's cock inside me. Wouldn't you agree, Father?"

It took significant strength to force my gaze to lower as the focus of the pack fell upon me. I wanted to stare them all down in challenge, to dare them to consider me beneath them, but my defiance would only make this worse. And I understood what Edon was doing. He wanted to belittle Luna's position in the pack by having a newbie defile her.

"Are you sure he can even perform?" Walter drawled.

The hairs along the back of my neck sprung up as the urge to attack hit me square in the gut.

Easy, Edon whispered into my mind. *They assume you're weak. I want them to hold on to that assumption until the time is right.*

I fought the urge to frown, his words not at all what I expected to hear.

"There's only one way to find out," he said out loud, addressing his father's concerns regarding my ability to fuck. "Even if he can't, I imagine submitting to the mutt will put Luna firmly in her place."

His father stroked his chin, a movement I caught in my periphery, as I hadn't yet lifted my gaze from the ground out of fear that I might accidentally challenge one of these jackasses with a glower. The pack collectively would be impossible to beat. But some of these idiots without backup? Yeah, I'd hold my own just fine. And I'd enjoy it, too.

"I can smell her fear," one of the lycans said, a grin in his voice. "I say we make the mutt put on a show, see what he can do."

"I bet he can't last more than ten seconds in that pussy," another said.

Someone snorted. "Nah, I'd give it at least thirty."

"Really? I'm going for a minute. He's not even hard yet."

And then the betting began.

The need for blood had morphed into a pit of ribbing and lecherous expectations surrounding my sexual prowess.

"Don't the humans study this shit, though?" an intelligent male questioned. "What were his scores?"

"Fuck if I know" was the response.

Edon remained silent, but I felt his relief through the connection. A relief I did not share. He wasn't the one who had to perform for these assholes. They weren't just asking me to fuck, but to essentially rape Luna. She knew, of course. Had already told me it would be fine.

"I mean, it's not like we weren't going to… you know…" had been her quiet statement shortly before Edon arrived.

That didn't make it right.

That didn't make it *okay* either.

She remained tucked in her little ball, her body trembling, her face hidden. There were scratches along her back from where some of the pack had clawed her and a few marks on her sides that likely came from shoes or maybe fists.

This is so fucking wrong, I thought, not for the first time.

There's no alternative was Edon's reply.

The conversation continued to flow around me, the pack growing more eager by the second as they entertained themselves with the thought of my taking Luna. Most voted in the low minutes. Others in the seconds.

If I was going to do this, I'd go long just so none of those assholes won.

Except then I'd be prolonging Luna's torment.

I resisted the urge to grab my hair and tug on it, my attention still fixed on the ground. The lycans had started circling me, taking my measure, weighing my abilities based on my appearance.

It was ludicrous.

I couldn't believe I'd fought in the Immortal Cup just to endure such treatment. They considered me a lesser being solely because I was not born a lycan. But the trials of my life placed me far above them all. And one day, I'd prove it.

"All right, son. We'll try it your way," Walter said, his tone holding a begrudging lilt.

It was then that I realized why Edon had chosen this method—he knew the pack would approve. He essentially used his father's techniques against him by exploiting the clan's thirst for degradation.

Because it wasn't just Luna they were embarrassing, but also me.

"But I want him to fuck her ass," Walter added, causing the world to still around me. "He doesn't deserve to experience alpha pussy."

Luna seemed to freeze, her tension palpable.

What Walter demanded was even more invasive somehow; it was also something I'd never done. And I suspected Luna was the same.

"No," Edon growled, the sound charging the energy in the air. "I've not taken her ass yet. It's mine. He'll take her pussy instead."

His father smiled. "Taking her virgin ass would be an even better punishment."

"As I stated the other day, she's my mate and I decide how best to punish her, and this is my decision." His attention fell to me. "If you touch her ass, I'll kill you."

"Noted," I whispered, my throat dry from the war of wills happening before me.

How Edon expected me to perform under these conditions was beyond me. And the resulting snickers from the crowd said they all agreed. Some even went as far as to comment on my lack of arousal. Apparently, they didn't understand why raping a female might not appeal to me.

Luna will prefer you to anyone else in this pack, Edon murmured, his mental voice different from the harsh tone he'd used only seconds ago when threatening my life. *Remember that when you slide inside her sweet heat. Remember the chase, how she drew us down to that stream with the intent to have us both. The way she submitted to you in the field. Her wolf desires you, Silas.*

"On your knees, Luna," Edon said, the command in his voice a slap against my senses. "It seems the mutt needs some motivation to perform. Use your mouth to help him out."

Chapter Nineteen

EDON

IT'D TAKEN PHYSICAL RESTRAINT not to react when the pack had assaulted Luna upon arrival, and it took even more restraint not to react now as she struggled to rise.

Any hint of concern or soft treatment on my part would only worsen this experience. My father's eyes were on me, his irritation over my taking control of the situation evident in the harsh lines of his mouth.

But there were little things I could do—like grab a fistful of Luna's hair to yank her upright. To the audience, it looked like I'd grown impatient. In reality, I was lending her my strength as I positioned myself behind her. She stiffened when her back hit my legs, a reaction that pleased the crowd.

I gently drew my thumb along the sensitive skin behind her ear, my fingers still woven into her hair in what hopefully resembled a painful grip. She didn't outwardly relax, but her weight sank into my thighs as she used the support I offered.

That inherent trust went straight to my cock. She understood what I was trying to do without my having to voice it, and it seemed Silas did as well. His approval warmed the bond, his mind not missing a single detail despite his focus being on the ground.

Ignore everyone around us and focus solely on her mouth, I whispered to him. It was my job to protect them, to allow them a hint of peace under the guise of punishment. And I would succeed if Silas let me, if he followed my words and just gave in to the pleasure of the moment.

I circled Luna's throat with the hand not in her hair, making a show of my dominance while secretly angling her in a way that could obscure the motions of my thumb. Her pulse thundered beneath my touch, something I sought to ease with slow, hypnotic circles.

I hoped she felt the similarities of this moment to the one we'd shared earlier when I stood behind her while she sucked Silas off. I needed to bring her back to that experience, to remind her of the chase, and remove everyone around us.

A difficult feat.

Fortunately, I had her wolf on my side. A wolf I'd left unsatisfied earlier with the promise for more. And now I would give it to her.

In the form of Silas's cock.

"Motivate him, Luna," I demanded, my voice far more cruel than my touch. "Show everyone here how eager you are to submit to your better."

She growled even as she complied, her tongue drawing a path along Silas's growing erection as she boldly met his gaze.

Something passed between them.

An understanding.

One I felt connected to even as I stood on the outside.

"That doesn't look very submissive to me," my father pointed out.

I didn't stop tracing her pulse, my touch light even as I infused a harsh edge into my response. "She's on her knees before a mutt with his cock pressed up against her lips. I wouldn't necessarily call that very alpha-like."

"More whore-like," Glenn put in helpfully.

"We need a new pack slut with Bianca gone," Barry added. "Should we consider this an audition?"

"Are you kidding? I won't want her mouth anywhere near my dick after this."

The ribbing continued, derogatory statements about Luna's actions and Silas's position within the pack blending into a haze of disgust around us. I felt my little mate's tension and sensed my progeny's annoyance, providing me with a much bigger task of helping them both perform under less-than-welcome conditions.

Because if Silas couldn't get it up and fuck Luna, my father would intervene. Something I sensed he was eager to do, even now.

Tell me about her tongue, I said to Silas. *Tell me how it feels.*

Forced, he growled back at me.

You accused me of that earlier today, but as I recall, she quite eagerly sucked you off. I hummed into his mind, the sound low and soothing. *Tell me how it felt to come down her throat. To feel her swallow around your dick as it pulsed inside her mouth.*

He groaned, out loud and through the link. *Edon…*

Just think how good her pussy is going to feel clamped down around you, Silas. Pure heaven and something I've not even felt yet. God, I want every detail. Every fucking sensation.

And why did even thinking about that turn me on? Hearing about Silas's pleasure as he fucked the woman destined to be mine should piss me off, not cause my dick to harden painfully in my pants.

But fuck, I wanted to watch him.

I wanted to hear their shared pants, smell their arousal, and connect with my progeny as he took my mate's sweet, hot cunt from behind.

Silas must have heard me, because he groaned again, his shaft fully engorged and parting Luna's beautiful lips. He thrust deep inside just as he'd done in my home only hours before. She flinched at the intrusion, but a swipe of my thumb against her pulse seemed to reassure her once more, and she swallowed him to the best of her ability—which was fucking impressive and a skill destined to be admired.

Shit. I could feel him beneath my hand, his head lodged so fucking deep that I doubted she could breathe. His hands flexed at his sides, uncertain, his abdominal muscles clenching with restraint. The wolves around us thought he was about to come already, their jeers threatening to spoil the moment.

But I understood his tension.

He wasn't about to explode.

No. Silas craved dominance. He wanted to grab Luna and force his cock even deeper into her pretty little throat, but my hands were in his way. And while he might feel comfortable dominating her, he couldn't challenge me.

I nearly smiled.

The two of them were perfection, their unspoken battle for command a fucking aphrodisiac to my senses.

I yanked Luna backward, my gaze meeting Silas's briefly as his lips curled into the faintest hint of a snarl that he forcibly swallowed.

"Present your cunt for the mutt," I demanded, pushing Luna to the ground onto all fours. Everyone else would have seen it as a shove, but my hand around her throat helped ease her into the fall, giving her the notice she needed to catch herself on her palms.

My father was too busy laughing at what someone had said to notice my movements, something I'd taken full advantage of in the moment.

I smacked Luna's ass, my hand positioned in a way to make a loud sound without causing much pain. "Spread" was all I said.

And she did.

She spread those beautiful thighs, not just for me but for Silas as well. And fuck if that wasn't burning me up inside in the best way.

Every detail, I reminded him as he knelt behind her. "Don't touch her ass," I made sure to say out loud. It was for my father's benefit after his outrageous demand. I hadn't protected her for myself, which she had to know since I'd yet to take her in any manner. But I wasn't sure how she felt about anal and refused to find out in front of these jackasses.

"Understood," Silas replied, his voice thick with a variety of emotions—emotions I felt through our sire link.

Anger.
Excitement.
Challenge.
Annoyance.
Lust.

Is she wet? I asked softly, watching as he positioned himself near her entrance.

Yes, he admitted, his throat working as he swallowed. *Fuck. Yes.*

Good. It seemed my positioning tactics had worked. Or maybe exhibitionism appealed to my little wolf. Perhaps it was a mixture of both. *Slide in slowly. Pretend you're nervous.*

Another swallow. *I won't hurt her.*

I know. That was why I'd chosen him for this task.

And maybe, just maybe, I'd also wanted this. Why else would I have allowed him to chase her with me this afternoon? It wasn't so I could just fuck her in front of him.

No. We'd been in that together. The three of us. Dancing some sort of erotic dance. One I intended to continue now.

Shit, she's tight, Edon. My head barely fits. Sweat beaded across his brow, his teeth snagging his lip. Around us, the wolves tittered, expecting him to blow his load in a single thrust. I tuned them out to the best of my ability, focusing on my mate and progeny and on their joining below.

A mental groan through the link had my balls tightening, Silas losing himself to the sensation of her constricting sheath. His words all jammed together as he described the intensity, the heat, the overwhelming urge to shove his hips forward to fuck her to the hilt. And then he gave in, bottoming out against her on a growl that I felt to my very bones.

Fuck, she's perfect, he told me.

Those three words should have spiked envy within me, and they did to an extent, but not for the reasons they should. I wanted to join them, to lick Luna's sweet cunt while Silas drove into her, and then force him to return the favor. I wanted to fuck her ass while he took her pussy, to kiss him while he moaned, to drag my teeth along her neck and truly claim her as mine before allowing him to lap up the wound with his skilled tongue.

My blood heated with every passing second, a thousand ideas slamming into me one after another, and not all of them were mine.

Because I wasn't the only one who wanted to play.

Silas's yearnings grew hotter by the second, his mouth craving my cock, his ass flexing as if expecting me to join, and I felt the stirrings of both of their arousals warming my insides.

How does she feel? I asked him.

Slick. Hot. She's squeezing me so, so good. He thrust deep, hitting a spot that made her gasp. Not in pain, but in pleasant surprise, although I doubted many of my brethren knew the difference. *Fuck…*

Silas started thinking about his university courses, angling himself in a manner that maximized the experience for them both while also helping him last longer. I nearly smiled, but something about his calculative mind only excited me more.

How would it feel to be inside him and hear his thoughts? To listen as Luna joined us on her knees, taking him into her mouth, sucking him to completion and then licking him clean.

My dick throbbed against my zipper, begging me to join them, to give in to the urges and ignore everyone else.

But they were relying on me to keep them safe, to protect them from the masses. Which meant I had a role to play in this fucked-up trial. Hmm, although maybe I could find a way to indulge both roles—alpha and lover.

I circled them and pretended to evaluate the discipline of my mate. Luna's face was hidden beneath her hair, adding to the effect of her humiliation. I crouched before her, threaded my fingers through her gorgeous strands, and tilted her head upward to study her features.

Ruby-red lips—swollen from Silas's cock.

Pink cheeks.

Blown-out pupils.

Stunning.

"You seem to be enjoying yourself," I murmured, my voice meant only for her.

But of course, my father heard it. "Then how is this effective?" he demanded.

His comment caused some of the amusement among the crowd to die.

But I had them all right where I wanted them.

"I can't imagine a more degrading experience than to not only allow a mutt to fuck me but to enjoy it, too." I stroked my thumb across her lips. "Make her come, Omega. Assuming you can last that long."

That uplifted all the spirits, everyone laughing at my dry tone and cruel suggestions. Shame colored Luna's expression just long enough for everyone to see, leaving them all with the belief that my method of belittling her was working.

Silas, however, took my words as a challenge, his determination thriving through the bond. He read between the lines and understood that I didn't desire Luna's pleasure for the enjoyment of the pack.

Providing Luna with relief allowed us to give her a semblance of strength, a way for her to hold on to the moment and choose to give in to the sensations Silas stirred now with his skilled penetrations.

I released her and stood, taking on my assessing role once more. Arousal stirred in the air, not just from the couple rutting on the ground but from the others in attendance. My father was among them, his eyes falling hungrily on Luna as she moaned.

A myriad of crude comments followed.

They called her a whore.

A slut.

Belittled her place in the pack.

Claimed she loved the feel of lesser males filling her and said she didn't deserve the status of alpha female.

I watched each slur slap my darling mate across her pretty face, Silas's job becoming more difficult by the second. But it was the commentary regarding what came next that forced my hand. The wolves were getting too carried away, making assumptions about who might taste her after Silas finished, and it left me no choice but to intervene. I had to bring Luna back and help her ignore everything around us before I lost the feisty female inside of her.

And most importantly, I had to make sure no one else could touch her afterward.

I could share her with Silas. Everyone else? Not a fucking chance.

"Mmm, I love you like this, Luna." I knelt before her again, blocking her face from the view of others and traced her mouth with the tip of my finger. "On all fours, being fucked by another wolf of my choosing," I continued. "It's making me want to see how well you multitask." I pinched her chin between my fingers, forcing her gaze upward. "I want your mouth."

Those words were met with collective sounds of entertainment, but I ignored them all, my focus on the beautiful alpha before me.

Trust me, I told her with my eyes. *Let me help guide you through this, to give you an act of power.*

I needed her to understand what I was giving her. So many males used oral sex as a way to dominate their women, but I always understood the power in bringing a female to her knees. Feeding her my cock gave her all the control, and the flare of her nostrils said she knew it.

Oh, I would benefit.

But she'd thrive in the moment of it, knowing she'd brought an alpha male to his knees with a flick of her tongue.

I witnessed the fire in her gaze when she sucked Silas off, the way she was hell-bent on destroying his sense of being. And I was telling her with my gaze now that I'd give her the same opportunity.

Silas groaned, his cock lodged deep inside her, his fingers working that sweet little bundle of nerves between her legs as he stroked that spot deep within her. *She's clenching around me. Fuck, Edon, I won't last if she keeps that up.*

Don't you dare come, I warned. *Keep fucking her until I say otherwise.*

He cursed, my demand hitting him in a place he couldn't ignore.

I arched a brow at Luna, asking her without words for permission. If she said no, I'd laugh it off with a harsh comment and find another way to exhaust her. It wouldn't be easy, but I refused to allow anyone else inside her.

Her nostrils flared, her cheeks darkening to a deep rose.

And she parted her lips. "Yes." Barely audible, spoken on a breath, but enough for me to continue.

I drew down my zipper, the top button of my jeans already undone, and hissed as my dick fell within inches of that beautiful mouth. Her tongue licked the head, her eyes holding mine, and I nearly came from that look alone.

No fear.

No mortification.

Just pure feminine lust.

I wrapped one hand around the back of her neck, the other sliding into her hair to position her where I wanted. Her honey-brown irises seemed to pulse, her desire a palpable presence that ate through the last vestiges of doubt in my mind.

Do it, she seemed to be saying. *I dare you.*

Careful who you taunt, I thought back at her, my lips curling.

I'm not afraid of you, her look said, and fuck if that didn't make me even harder.

Silas shifted his grip on her hip, angling his thrusts in a manner that stirred little mewling sounds from her throat that I quickly silenced by thrusting into the damp cavern of her mouth. She swallowed around me, a growl rumbling in my chest in response, one Silas mimicked on a groan.

This wasn't my first time sharing a female with another male. Yet it *felt* like the first time. The intensity shrouded our surroundings in a haze of sound and musk, the lycans eager to join in, but I kept them all at bay.

Silas and Luna were mine. They just didn't know it yet.

Edon, Silas groaned. *Fuck… Luna…* His broken thoughts joined my own as the luscious woman in question ran her teeth along my shaft.

I know, I agreed. *I know.*

She was a goddess, her body seemingly made for us both, and wow, could she multitask. I watched her push back against Silas, urging him to fuck her harder as she punished me with her mouth.

So good.

So perfect.

So… fuck…

Silas's thoughts melded with mine, our heightened need an intoxicating mix that drove us both to the edge that much faster and seemed to spur Luna on as well. Her body tightened, her eyes glazing over on the verge of oblivion as a scream vibrated my dick.

Luna came apart between us, her face glowing on the wave of her orgasm. Silas growled low in his throat, his torso pulled taut as he fought the urge to follow her. I hadn't given permission yet, and that small part of him that I owned forced him to submit, to wait for my command.

Now, I told him. *And don't hold back.*

I wanted to see all of him, to witness his explosion, to *feel* it as if it were my own.

He didn't disappoint, his snarl a feral sound that sang to my wolf, forcing me to pick up my own pace between Luna's lips. She received me eagerly, her hooded gaze holding mine with a lazy ease as she sucked and nipped and licked.

Whoever taught her to suck cock deserved a medal.

Because the woman knew exactly how I liked it, drove me to the near edge of madness while milking Silas's seed with her hot little cunt.

He was still coming, his forehead pressed against my hand in her hair, placing him in a submissive position that appealed to my wolf. The positions of their heads so close to my groin inspired an entirely new idea, one where I took turns fucking each of their mouths as they waited enthusiastically on their knees to see who would receive my seed first.

But I had to finish the current trial before I could engage in such a fantasy.

And so Luna won this round, my ecstasy erupting down her slender throat on a final pump of my hips. She drank me eagerly, her eyes closing as if indulging in a sweet treat.

Silas groaned again, my rapture cascading hot energy through our connection and coercing a final shudder from him. My name intertwined with Luna's in his mind, his bliss complete.

Until the sounds of expectation chilled the air around us.

My father was already preparing, his fucked-up mind twisting Luna's punishment into something so much worse.

No. I refuse.

I tightened my grip on Luna's neck, guiding myself between her lips to a dangerous point near the back of her throat.

Round eyes flashed up to mine, the mist of her oblivion bleeding into uncertainty as I stared down at her.

She'd finished swallowing.

I should be pulling back.

Instead, I pushed in even more while pretending to shudder through a second climax. She gagged, her pupils dilating, her hands lifting to my thighs as if to push me off her.

Trust me, I wanted to say.

What are you doing? Silas demanded, noting the tension along her spine. He started to shift, but a mental command from me froze him in place. *Why?*

I need to knock her out, I explained, my grasp turning to cement as Luna tried in earnest to shove me away. *Don't let her move.*

Silas clearly didn't approve, but he obeyed.

Claws pierced my skin, Luna trying to fight her way out from between us as terror took hold of her. I hated doing this to her, hated the look of fury mingled with betrayal that she gave me now, but I held her anyway.

Some wolves might want to play with an unconscious female.

Most—my father included—wouldn't.

I supposed they could always wait for her to wake up, but she'd be gone before that happened.

Luna's choked whimper hurt my heart, her eyes growing glassy from the lack of oxygen. Until, finally, she went limp. I gave it another few seconds to make sure she wasn't faking it, listened for her pulse to slow, and shook off my pretend orgasmic state with a low growl of relief.

And then I let her go.

She collapsed, unmoving.

Silas shifted back onto his knees, his spent cock heavy against his thigh. He didn't look up, his gaze on Luna.

I stood to zip up my pants, ignoring the urge to check on my mate. Already her pulse had returned to normal, telling me she was fine. Which, unfortunately, meant I didn't have a lot of time to finish this act. If she stirred too soon, the pack would descend upon her.

And then I would be forced to defend her.

Rolling my shoulders, I glanced down at Luna and Silas with a detached expression and shrugged. "She's an excellent multitasker." I glanced at my father. "Better than Bianca, too."

He narrowed his gaze. "It's cruel to speak ill of the dead."

While I agreed, it took considerable effort not to retort, *It's also cruel to kill a lycan for the sake of a trial.* Which was exactly what had happened here.

I had no idea how my father managed to coat Bianca's remains in Luna's scent, but he clearly orchestrated all of this. Some of the pack members knew, too. I could see it in the satisfaction gleaming from their gazes. They hadn't cared about Bianca at all, just wanted a reason to incite retribution to see how I fared with the challenge.

Or maybe they didn't know and they just enjoyed the show anyway.

The fact that I couldn't tell the difference bothered me.

"Take my mate back to my cabin, Omega," I demanded, not looking at Silas but at my father. *Wait for me there*, I added mentally to my progeny.

Silas bent to scoop her up into his arms and paused at my father's growled, "We're not done."

"On the contrary, we're very done." I glanced at Silas. "Why are you still here? You obey me, not him." *Take her quickly. I'll handle this.*

My father snarled low and menacing. "You're forgetting your place, *son*."

"No, I'm ascending to my place, *old man*," I replied, aware of Silas doing exactly as I commanded. He moved quickly, lifting Luna and bolting from the ring.

No one stopped him, all of their focus on the two alphas squaring off in the ring.

I captured and held my father's gaze, refusing to give an inch. If he wanted to throw down, I was ready. The pack might back him, or maybe they wouldn't. I'd satisfied the punishment requirements, degraded my female, just as they necessitated. I'd done everything right and won their favor in the process. At least mostly.

And the look on my father's face said he understood that, too.

I smiled. "You'll have to do better than that to break me, Father."

His jaw ticked, his mind working through his options. All of them pointed to walking away, and we both knew it. But I couldn't deny the hint of relief that slithered down my spine as he gave a subtle nod of consent before leaving the circle.

Several of my packmates patted me on the back, their pride a sickness I wouldn't allow to infect me. That they felt fulfilled by my actions against Luna said so much.

This was not a world I wanted to indulge. It was one I wanted to change. And soon, *very* soon, I would be in a position to do so.

Chapter Twenty

LUNA

DEEP MALE VOICES FILTERED in and out of my conscious. I couldn't understand them, my mind blinking in and out of awareness.

Something warm slid between my legs, sending tingles up and down my spine. Lips caressed my neck. More words. A damp cloth against my back. Another kiss to my jaw. Someone combing fingers through my hair.

It all provided the most intensely sensual dream of my existence—surrounded by heat, alpha wolf, and protective strokes.

I sighed into the male wall behind me, stretching against him, and smiled as he kissed my temple. "You're safe," he whispered.

I know.

Yet, a memory nagged at me. One where I wasn't safe at all, but horrified. I chased the image in my mind, trying to find the source and truth of it, and gasped, my hand flying to my throat.

"It's okay, Luna." I recognized that low voice, that scent, that *male.*

Edon.

My eyes flew open to find him lying beside me, his dark eyes glimmering in the low lighting of his bedroom. I glanced over my shoulder and found Silas to be the source of heat at my back, his palm a brand against my hip. He'd been the one to claim I was safe.

Liar.

Edon had suffocated me with his cock, leaving me vulnerable and alone and so fucking cold. I clutched my neck, surprised my throat didn't ache from him nearly killing me.

"*Why*?" I demanded, my voice coming out in a growl that vibrated my chest as I met the alpha's gaze.

"To keep the others away from you," he replied, lifting his palm to my hand and gently peeling it away from my skin. "I could feel my father planning to prolong your punishment at my expense. So I took away the object of his desire. *You.*"

I blinked, surprised not only by his explanation but also by his lack of hesitation in explaining himself. My fingers curled into a fist, the memory too fresh beneath his touch, even while my mind reasoned that he'd done the right thing.

Well, no. The *right* thing would have been to declare my innocence and not allow any of that bullshit to occur. But sometimes circumstances prevent even the most moral of people from completing the appropriate action.

And I knew what would have happened if Edon refused to punish me. *He* would have received a correction far worse, likely in the form of my death—an act that would allow his father to prolong the ascension process.

My shoulders sagged as I huffed out a breath, hating this life more than ever.

Except Edon hadn't reacted at all how a normal alpha usually would. For one, he'd attempted to protect me. Most would have thrown his mate to the wolves—literally—and just stood around to make sure no one killed her. Instead, Edon had Silas defile me, which would appear horrible to the onlookers. But to me… I looked over my shoulder again, meeting those bright blue eyes.

Yeah, I, uh, hadn't exactly minded.

"Are you all right?" he asked softly, his thumb tracing my hip bone.

Edon leaned in to kiss my neck again, his nose skimming my jaw.

"Y-yes," I stammered, swallowing. *What's happening? Why are they—*

I jolted as Edon nipped my pulse, drawing my focus back to him. He was only an inch or so away, with one arm tucked under his head and his opposite hand resting along his side. "Tell Silas you don't hate him."

My brow furrowed. "What?"

"He's worried you hate him for fucking you. Tell him you don't."

"Maybe I do." I didn't, but that wasn't the point.

Edon's lips curled. "Please, little mate. Put Silas out of his misery. He's giving me a headache." The growl behind me only seemed to amuse Edon more. Damn alpha male.

"The only person I should hate in this situation is you," I replied, trying to knock that arrogant smirk off his too-alluring mouth. Alas, my words only worsened it, his teeth flashing now as he full-on smiled at me.

"Would an apology fix it?" The teasing quality of his voice told me he wasn't exactly offering, but playing.

"You choked me."

"I did."

"And you don't feel bad about that?" I pressed.

He lifted a bare shoulder—because yes, he was naked. Of course he was fucking naked. And it seemed Silas was, too.

"Choking you beat the alternative," the alpha replied, his tone as unapologetic as ever. He lifted his hand to draw his finger down my throat, to my sternum, and lower to my belly button. "Do you want us to make you feel better, little mate?" His gaze darkened with the words. "I think Silas would like that."

"Silas has his own voice," the male behind me replied.

"Then why don't you use it?" Edon countered, looking over my shoulder at his progeny. "Talk to Luna. She's awake and very alert." He punctuated his words by drawing his thumb upward to my breast. Electricity hummed in my veins as a result of that touch, my body hyperaware of being sandwiched between two virile male wolves. They practically radiated heat, their scents commingling with mine and bathing me in lust and sex.

I shivered, which invited him to stroke me again. Only, this time he pinched my nipple. I hissed, arching into Silas, and then gasped as Edon lowered his mouth to kiss my abused breast.

Fuck… This… I don't…

I closed my eyes, then opened them again, conflicted.

"I'm sorry," Silas whispered, his lips against my ear. "I didn't… I hope I didn't hurt you."

Hurt me? I nearly laughed. Except nothing about it was remotely humorous. I'd only been with one other wolf, and he'd lasted all of a few minutes. Mostly because we were on a timeline, but I certainly hadn't enjoyed the experience.

Silas, however, made me feel things. Tingly things. Sexy things. He'd helped me forget the pack and their cruelty, had erased the reason for our joining, and had given me pleasure.

Because Edon had told him to.

Oh…

"You didn't want…" I swallowed, closing my eyes.

"Of course I didn't," he replied. "Who could possibly desire a situation like that?"

Shit. The punishment had been just as horrible for him, perhaps even worse with all the things his pack had said about him, the way they'd betted on his sexual prowess, the degrading comments about mutt cock, and the way Edon had forced him to perform by using the sire bond. I understood why he did, had oddly been a bit thankful for the consideration, but I hadn't taken Silas's wants or desires into account.

Actually, I hadn't thought much about his desires at all. Not when I demanded he fuck me out in that field, or again when I went to my knees in the bathroom. I'd just assumed he wanted it.

"I should be apologizing to you," I realized out loud, rotating to my back to stare up at him. He was perched on one elbow, his other hand following my motion to stay on my hip. "I'm sorry, Silas. I haven't taken your feelings into account at all, too caught up in my own shit to pay attention to much else. Which isn't an excuse. It's, well, the truth."

His brow furrowed. "Why the hell are you apologizing to me? I just raped you on Edon's command."

The alpha growled a low warning. "Careful."

"What? At least admit what we did to her." Silas narrowed his gaze at the alpha male. "None of that was consensual."

"Nothing in this world is ever fucking consensual," Edon countered. "It's all manufactured and organized by those in control."

Silas snorted. "Says the future Alpha of the Clemente Clan."

"You say that like it was my choice."

"And you think being the omega of a lycan clan was mine? That I wanted to go into the Immortal Cup and kill all those people? Some of whom I've known all my life?"

I gaped back and forth between them, shocked by Silas's fury and the ease with which he expelled those words at the alpha who had created him. But what startled me more was Edon's reaction. My father would have lashed out and put the newbie in his place, perhaps even killed him.

But not Edon.

No. He merely sighed and shook his head. "No, Silas. I don't. Just as turning you into a lycan wasn't my choice. But here we are. So either we fight about it—a fight you will lose—or we work together and see what we can do about building a more positive future in the clan."

Silas gaped at him. "How?"

"By listening to our elders," Edon replied cryptically. His gaze fell to me then, the ebony in his irises swirling with dark brown flecks. "Was all of it nonconsensual? Did we rape you, Luna?"

My throat went dry as I slowly shook my head. Because no, it wasn't rape. Was Silas technically forced to fuck me? Yes. But I'd wanted him already, and it wasn't exactly a hardship to receive him. And Edon had offered me a choice with his gaze, asking if he could take my mouth. I'd understood he was trying to give me back a semblance of power by offering me a distraction.

"Your father would have killed me," I added out loud. "I much preferred your method."

"That doesn't exactly make it right," Silas muttered.

"No, it doesn't," I agreed, lifting my hand to palm his cheek. "But as far as punishments go, I didn't mind this one. I… It wasn't nonconsensual. At least not on my part. It would have happened down by the water. Right?"

Except I didn't know if Silas participated in that chase voluntarily or because Edon had made him. I didn't even know if he was here now because he desired it or if he was following orders.

I frowned. "Did you not…? I mean, do you not…?" I couldn't find the words. So I looked at Edon. "Are you forcing him?"

A startled laugh came from the alpha, the sound low and sexy and causing the hairs along my arms to dance on end. "No, little mate. I may have a bit of sway, but his reactions are all his own."

From what I'd observed, I wasn't so sure about that. "You made him fuck me."

He glanced between us, a frown forming between his eyes. "Are you looking for an apology? Because I don't have one to give. Would I have preferred this all happened under other circumstances? Yes. Do I regret how it all has gone down? Also yes. But what alternative did we have? Oh, I mean, I suppose I could have let the pack continue beating you, Luna, before fucking you." He narrowed his gaze at Silas. "Which, by the way, Silas, would have been rape because she wouldn't have wanted it. Unlike how she felt about you."

Edon paused, his expression hardening.

I wasn't quite sure how to respond to that, and by Silas's silence, I suspected he wasn't either. Fortunately—or perhaps, unfortunately—Edon wasn't finished.

"You both can talk to me all night about choices, or lack thereof. Because I get it. Trust me. I have a father who is hell-bent on making me fail these Alpha Trials, and I suspect he won't shy away from killing me. But rather than complain about it, I'm facing it, because that's the only way we can enact change in this world." He gazed down at me with a knowing gleam. "Surely you understand, Luna. What with Claudette's teachings and all."

My lips parted. "You know about Claudette?" *How?* And why wasn't he livid? She preached about the old times, constantly telling me not to give up the fight and giving me every reason to live. All words that could have gotten her killed if my father had overheard them.

"Yes."

"How?" I demanded. Had I mentioned her in my sleep? After the drugs the other night? In passing and just forgotten?

And then a more disturbing thought hit me. *What if there are spies in Ernest Clan? Has something—*

"Jolene Mason," Edon said, confusing me even more.

"What about him?" I asked, my throat as dry as sandpaper. Jolene wasn't a man I knew personally, but I knew all about him from Claudette. He was a legend among lycans, the male she once loved who ended up with another, and he was one of the strongest alphas in history. At least until the new world.

A fire lit in Edon's gaze, one I recognized as pride. "Jolene's my grandfather."

Chapter Twenty-One

Silas

I HAD CLEARLY MISSED some sort of history lesson, because I had no idea who they were talking about. But whatever Edon had just revealed seemed to shock the hell out of Luna. My hand instinctively tightened on her hip, my need to protect her an overwhelming urge I didn't quite know how to dispel.

Claudette was her mentor at Ernest Clan, Edon explained, taking pity on my confusion. *She's a very old friend of my grandfather's. From before the new world.*

What does that mean? I asked, confused by his phrasing.

"They remember what the world was like before Blood Day ever existed. When the Alpha Trials were a time of pride between father and son, when mating actually meant something, and when humans had certain rights." Edon met my gaze. "It's illegal to speak of such things, Silas. But my grandfather has taught me all about the prior world, and I believe Claudette has bestowed the same lessons upon Luna."

"She did," Luna whispered. "Every night. To me and Logan."

Edon nodded. "Well. Then maybe you know me better than you think."

Respect shone bright in her gaze, her lips curling. "That's why you treat Silas as you do. You respect the old customs of the sire bond."

He snorted. "I'm trying, but he's not making it easy on me."

My eyebrows shot up. "Lying right here."

"Trust me, we know." His dark eyes captured mine. "But are you here because I demanded it or because you want to be?"

"You know why I'm here."

"But Luna doesn't." He gestured with his chin. "She seems to think I'm forcing you to lie there. Am I?"

He already knew the answer, so I looked at Luna as I said, "No. I demanded he let me stay so I could check on you and make sure you were all right." I cupped her cheek, needing her to see my sincerity. "I want to be here, Luna."

"But he made you…?" She trailed off, biting her lip.

Yeah. That. "As he said, there wasn't a better alternative." I ran my thumb over her bottom lip, tugging it from her teeth. "I would have chosen a much different setting for the experience, but it happened. And now, I just need to know you're okay."

She swallowed. "I'm okay."

"Good." I bent to brush my mouth against hers. "Next time, I promise it'll be better."

"Next time?" Luna repeated, sounding hopeful.

I smiled against her lips. "Assuming Edon allows it."

The wolf in question wrapped his palm around the back of my neck and squeezed. I lifted my gaze to his, not at all apologetic. While I respected that she was his mate, he'd brought me into this fucked-up game, and I wouldn't turn down another chance to play with her. Nor would I allow her to go on thinking Edon had forced me to touch her. As if I could ever consider such an activity a hardship.

Edon grinned and pulled me into him, his mouth capturing mine. I jolted in surprise, then melted into the embrace. Because fuck, the man knew how to kiss. He oozed dominance, skill, and pure masculine need. It was so different from the femininity of Luna's touch, so much more virile, but equally addictive.

His tongue owned my own, demanding I submit. But I didn't. I kissed him right back, matching his pace, and threaded my fingers through his hair to hold on. Luna squirmed between us, her little gasp an intoxicating addition to the experience. And when her arousal scented the air, we both broke apart to stare down at her, hungry for a taste.

"Mmm, I think she likes watching us," Edon murmured, stretching out beside her on his elbow, his opposite hand sliding down my arm to my hand. "But I want to focus on her. Silas?" He placed my palm on the top of her thigh, his gaze on her face.

"I think she's more than earned our joint attention, yes," I agreed, mimicking Edon's pose on her other side and staring down at her.

Indulging the two of them came so naturally, my movements instinctual and so very, very right. I leaned down to kiss her again, this time sliding my tongue between her lips.

She clutched my shoulder as if needing to hold on for the ride, and maybe she did. Because as soon as I finished kissing her, Edon took over and told me through the sire bond to cup the wet space between her thighs. She jerked beneath my touch and then moaned long and loud into Edon's mouth.

A rush of wetness met my exploring fingers, making it easy to slip through her slick folds to her entrance and dip inside. She squeezed me in the same way she had my cock, and fuck if the sensual memory of that alone wasn't enough to make me come again.

But this wasn't about me.

This was about Luna.

And for once, I was in complete agreement with Edon's intentions. He drew his lips down her neck to her breasts, allowing me the opportunity to kiss her again. I set a lazy rhythm with my tongue against hers, reveling in the sensation and addictive flavor that was all Luna. "I could do this for hours," I admitted on a breath.

She hadn't let go of my shoulder, her other hand in Edon's hair as he continued suckling her rosy peaks. Mutual appreciation permeated the air, the three of us exuding our own erotic scents that seemed to intermingle and bond to one another. It created the most enthralling mixture, one I wanted to roll in and wear on my coat for the rest of my days.

Edon growled in approval.

Luna sighed.

And I gave in to the urge to kiss her harder, to heighten her arousing perfume for my personal gratification.

She satisfied my craving in spades, as did Edon. I groaned, so fucking hard for them both that I could hardly see straight. But the thought of pleasing her grounded me, two of my fingers lodged deep inside her and stroking that place I knew females enjoyed. Her hips rose in response, little mewling sounds of excitement pouring from her mouth to mine as she crested the edge of an orgasm that wasn't quite ready to rise.

Luna quivered, sweat breaking out across her skin. I nuzzled her cheek and throat, adoring her scent and the racing pulse at her neck.

"More," she whispered. "Please. More."

"Needy little thing," Edon teased, kissing a path down her abdomen to where my hand played below. I shifted to allow him access to her sweet bundle of nerves and smiled as her back bowed off the bed.

My lips captured her scream as her world unraveled. Her slick channel tightened so hard around my fingers I thought she might break them. The memory of her doing that to my shaft had me moaning into her mouth.

Fuck, you're killing me, Edon whispered. *I want this to be about her.*

I do, too, I replied. *But fuck. Her pussy is like liquid heaven, Edon.*

Mmm, I know. I want to lick every inch of her. He punctuated the point by drawing his tongue down to my fingers and back up again, his groan of approval an intensely palpable sound.

Luna's nails dug into my neck, her teeth skimming my lip in a silent demand to strengthen our embrace. *Still topping from the bottom,* I mused, giving in to her because I wanted to. And maybe because I enjoyed her dominance just a little.

Edon's amusement trickled through the bond, his mind focused on the task of making her scream again. I removed my hand and allowed him to take over, my palm skimming a damp trail up her abdomen to her tits. I drew a pattern against each of her nipples, saturating her skin in her arousal, and then lowered my head to lick her clean.

She didn't release my nape, her razor-like claws digging into the base of my scalp and keeping me right where she desired. I growled a low warning in reply, my wolf rising to the surface to take on her sexual challenge.

And my teeth sank into her breast.

"Fuck," she breathed, arching beautifully beneath me.

Did you just mark my mate? Edon asked, a hint of something dark in his tone.

I stilled. *I… yes.* It'd been such a natural move, my inner beast responding to the supple female beneath my mouth. Luna shuddered, her chest rising and falling in quick succession, her lithe form shaking in ecstasy and not distress.

My canines were lodged in her, unmoving. Because I'd frozen in place beneath Edon's comment. Tension lined our link, the alpha rising.

Had I pushed him too far?

I tried to apologize, but the words wouldn't form, not even in a thought.

Because I had *wanted* to bite her. And her response said she'd enjoyed it. But maybe she was too lost to the sensations to realize the gravity of what I'd just done?

Edon lifted his head, eliciting a complaint from Luna's parted lips.

Until she caught the dark gleam of his gaze.

It took considerable effort for me to release her, to shift backward enough to yield. My eyes just automatically dropped, my wolf bowing to his superior.

I swallowed, uncertain and still unable to voice the words I needed to say.

"Edon," Luna whispered, her hand still on my nape.

He said nothing, his superiority a heavy presence between us. Seconds ticked by, my heart threatening to halt in my chest. I didn't know if I should run, roll over, or beg for forgiveness. Yet all I could fucking do was lie here with my palm splayed against Luna's abdomen and my head angled a few inches away from her chest.

Edon leaned down to taste the holes I'd created on her breast, his mouth closing over her skin.

Luna practically came off the bed, a surprised scream parting her lips as he slid his canines into the same bite. I didn't move, too conflicted and aroused by the sight. Edon rose once more, grabbed me by the throat, and yanked me to him on a snarl.

I jerked as his teeth sank into my lower lip, the bite a punishment and a claim. My blood heated, my lower abdomen tightening. *Fuck.*

Mine, he groaned into my mind. *Both of you are mine.*

Chapter Twenty-Two

LUNA

I COULDN'T HEAR A DAMN THING over the pounding in my ears. The way Edon held Silas now, I couldn't tell if he wanted to kill him, eat him, or fuck him.

It had taken me a moment in my lust-dazed mind to realize what had happened—Silas had bitten me. He'd demanded my submission the way an alpha male did a mate, something Edon had to take as a challenge.

This whole thing was so fucking confusing. Especially the way I *felt* after Silas sank his teeth into my skin. Peace, safety, and a healthy dose of desire had knocked me into a cloud of intense yearning. I'd wanted to give in to him, my wolf already submitting before the true alpha in the room growled. Then my wolf had gone weak in the knees, leaving me breathless between both males.

Were they going to fight or fuck?

I still didn't know.

Not even as Edon bit Silas, eliciting a sharp sound from them both.

And then they were kissing almost violently, their tongues sparring with each other in a war for dominance. Edon won, his teeth drawing blood—blood that he licked up and swallowed before going in for more.

It was so damn intense, yet sensual, and incredibly arousing.

I released Silas, my hand dipping between my thighs while my other palmed my breast. This was too much. I needed relief. And I needed it now.

Only, both my wrists were pinned above my head in a second as Edon stared down at me. I whimpered and then moaned as Silas's tongue slid through my damp heat.

Oh, wow…

How did they do that? They moved so fast, and— *Fuck!* Silas's mouth sealed over my clit so intensely I couldn't hold back my scream.

Edon took my mouth, his kiss not nearly as harsh as the one he'd given Silas. But still showcasing his control. "Tell us what you want, little mate," he whispered. "Our hands? Our mouths? Our cocks? Tell us how to please you."

Energy hummed through my veins, setting my spirit on fire with an intense *need* that only these men could satisfy. How had I ended up here? A mewling, squirming mess beneath two virile males. I never even wanted to join Clemente Clan, and now I had two reasons to stay.

"Luna," Edon pressed, his lips whispering over mine. "What do you want, sweetheart?"

Everything.

Pleasure.

Fucking.

My hips lifted to meet Silas's mouth, my nipples tightening into impossibly hard peaks. Never had I felt this way, not even beneath my own touch. And I'd already come twice today. These two played my body with an ease that was as unsettling as it was addictive.

Edon growled, the sound a low warning, the alpha demanding a response.

But I had none to give.

I didn't know how to articulate my desire. It was all too new, too overwhelming, for me to wrap my head around. My wolf preened, soaking up the sexual tension and bathing in the heat.

Teeth snagged my lower lip, biting gently in reprimand for ignoring the alpha above me. His dark eyes held mine as Silas slid two fingers into me, scissoring in a way that sent a shudder down my limbs.

Somehow, I was even more turned on than moments ago. My body shook with a craving I couldn't vocalize. Couldn't—

"How many lovers have you taken?" Edon asked softly, his palm circling my throat. "Where have you taken them?"

I swallowed, my vision blinking in and out of focus beneath the onslaught of Silas's tongue and strokes deep inside. Edon's pupils engulfed his irises, his handsome face so close to mine. He wanted to know about my experience, but I didn't know why. Maybe to make sure he didn't push me too far? No. Alphas didn't care about such things. They pillaged and raped without thought.

But not this one, my wolf whispered.

Mmm, Edon was proving to be an anomaly. I just wasn't sure how to trust him after everything I'd learned. Except he had a similar mentor, it seemed.

"Luna." He nipped me again, clearing my vision enough to see the stern lines of his forehead, the knowing gleam in his eyes, and the slight smirk playing over his lips as he pulled back to study me. "I need to know what we can do to you, little mate."

Permission, I translated, somewhat stunned by the realization. The alpha wanted me to lay down the rules so they could play within the boundaries I created.

"You're not at all what I expected," I admitted, palming his cheek and pulling him down for another kiss—one he allowed me to take more than he actually gave. "My experience is limited. But I'm open to, um, exploring."

Another kiss. This one deeper. Domineering. Laced with excitement. "I need more, Luna. How many have been inside you? And where?"

I swallowed, my breath shortening as Silas did something particularly sinful with his tongue. If he kept that up, I would—

He stopped, his exhale hot against my damp skin. "Answer him," he said, whether because he wanted the answer as well or because Edon demanded it through the link, I didn't know. But hearing the command in his tone, coupled with the look from the alpha, I could hardly refuse them.

"Only two, including Silas," I whispered. "And the first was only once—the day of our ceremony."

A glimmer of amusement brightened Edon's gaze. "To deter me from taking you."

"Y-yes."

"And how did that work out for you?" he mused as Silas chuckled against my heated flesh. I gasped as his teeth skimmed my clit and then latched on with a renewed vigor that cascaded waves of pleasure through my being.

"Fuck," I breathed, grabbing the bedsheets on one side while my opposite hand curled around Edon's neck. "So good…" I tried to pull him down to kiss me, but he remained there, observing me.

"Does that mean you don't disapprove of my choice in keeping you?" he wondered aloud, a dark smile in his eyes. "Or would you still prefer I send you home? To be punished by your father?"

"Edon…"

"No. I want an answer, little mate. Tell me how you feel right now, with Silas tonguing your sweet cunt and my palm upon your breast. Would you give it all up? Do you long for another? For the one who fucked you first?"

I nearly laughed at the notion of desiring Volk over Edon and Silas, but I caught the predatory gleam in my alpha mate's gaze. His wolf drove these questions more than the man did, his need to know where my desire lay a key detail to satisfy the lycan alpha hovering above me.

My nails bit into his neck, my eyes narrowing. "Fuck me and I'll tell you who I prefer."

That earned me a growl. "Oh, Luna, you're playing a dangerous game."

"Afraid you won't measure up to the challenge?" I asked, feeling far bolder than I should. Especially when beneath a powerful alpha male. But I couldn't help provoking him, my need to battle one I refused to suppress.

Silas slid his caress to my lower abdomen and kissed a path up to my breast before settling at my side. His blue eyes glowed with approval, his lips—glistening with my arousal—curled at the sides. "Your penchant for topping from the bottom is admirable, little moon." He kissed my cheek and lifted his gaze to the alpha. "She's ready."

"Little moon?" Edon repeated, leaning in to capture Silas's mouth in a long, devastating kiss. "Mmm, you taste amazing."

"I taste like Luna."

"I know." He kissed him again, causing my heart to skip several beats. They were so close, their joined arousals intoxicating and elevating my own to incredible heights. I squeezed my thighs, seeking friction, only to have them parted as Edon positioned himself between them. The head of his cock nudged my entrance and slid inside with expert ease without breaking his embrace with Silas. Their tongues dueled, Edon's cock elongated, and my pussy wept with unrestrained *need.*

I tightened my hold on Edon's neck, my other arm going around Silas, in this odd embrace of ecstasy. Edon grasped my hips, anchoring himself deep inside me, his size overwhelming and so very *alpha.*

I groaned, my head falling back as I strove to accommodate him, and then gasped as he began to move.

Really, *really* move.

Hard.

Harsh.

Thrusts.

His grip turned bruising, forcing me to take him, as his mouth dropped to my neck. Silas's mouth moved to mine, kissing me soundly, swallowing my whimpers as Edon set a brutal pace.

Mating, I realized. *A male wolf taking his mate.*

I had no choice but to accept it.

And worse, I *wanted* to.

My hips rose to meet his, my instincts taking over, and my kiss with Silas melted from soothing to something feral. He palmed my breast, tweaked my nipple, and palmed me again. And then Edon was kissing me, his tongue dominating and forceful, reminding me of his cock below. Silas moved, his mouth sliding along my shoulder, to Edon and back.

So much sensation.

Intense.

Hot.

Erotic as hell.

Silas kissed me again, then Edon captured my mouth, and then Silas claimed my lips once more. And all the while, an inferno built inside my lower abdomen that begged to be unleashed.

Their touches turned molten, Edon's shaft a brand, his body shifting in a way that stroked my clit even as he met that aching spot deep inside.

And Silas.

Fuck, he was everywhere. His hands, fingers, tongue, and lips. I swore he kissed Edon, too. Licked him. Nipped him. Adding to the insanity of the moment, blending it all together into a tornado of *feeling*.

This… I never could have anticipated *this*.

Teeth scraped my skin, growls rent the air, and heat unlike anything I'd ever felt singed the atmosphere around us.

I moaned both of their names, uncertain of whom I touched, but knew I held them both.

And then I was kissing Silas again, his mouth grounding me as Edon took me to new heights below. God, he could move. So much strength and power, his wolf inching along the surface as he dominated me in the oldest of manners.

I raked my nails down his back, claiming him.

"More," I demanded, arching into him and teetering on the brink of an explosion that would likely destroy me. But I didn't care. I wanted this—wanted them—even if just for tonight.

Or maybe longer.

Something to evaluate later.

Because holy wow, they were kissing again.

My orgasm erupted, shrouding my vision in black and stirring a loud, erotic sound from my throat. I shook beneath the onslaught, my limbs tensing and vibrating, my breaths coming in pants, and through it all, I felt them licking and sucking and stroking.

Edon shifted his weight, leaving me empty, and then Silas was there.

I arched beneath him, groaning as he set a slightly softer pace, easing me through the pleasure and kissing me soundly. Edon knelt beside us, stroking himself lazily with one hand while drawing his opposite palm down Silas's spine.

My breath hitched as I realized his intent.

Silas grinned, glancing up at Edon. "I'm not afraid of you."

"You should be," the alpha replied.

"Maybe," he agreed. "But I'm not."

"Mmm. Another challenge." He tsked. "What am I going to do with the two of you?"

"Fuck us?" I suggested, my voice raspy and well used.

"Oh, that I will definitely be doing. And soon, little mate, it'll be you in the middle. But as Silas is the one with more experience, I'll take his ass first." He punctuated his statement by doing something that made Silas jolt above me.

Readying him, I suspected. *Oh, sweet mother of lycans…*

I'd seen this done before, but never for pleasure. Males did this to harm. Yet Silas seemed accepting, his expression expectant in a hungry way, not a scared one.

His mouth sealed over mine, drawing me back to him, to his cock, to his movements, to his expert touch. I quivered, my body still reeling from the oblivion of moments ago. There was no way I could come again—or so I thought—but his knowing strokes fought to prove me wrong.

Fuck.

This was insane.

How could I possibly fall apart again? Wolves were known for their stamina and sexual prowess, but this was too much.

Although, I'd witnessed it countless times. Not necessarily in the females, but definitely in the males. They were insatiable, their drives overwhelming and unstoppable.

Yet I'd been the one to come multiple times. Not Edon. He'd only orgasmed once down my throat earlier, then faked a second.

Silas groaned as Edon positioned himself behind him, the two of them joining in a way I couldn't see but felt beneath their weight.

"Fuck," Silas whispered, his head dropping to my neck. As the sound that followed wasn't one of agony, I assumed Edon had used some form of lubricant. But he certainly wasn't gentle. He drove in hard, Silas receiving him with a grunt, his own cock pistoning into me at the same time.

I marveled at the intimate dance, the way our bodies locked together in such a unique fashion that guaranteed all our pleasure.

Edon's words replayed in my mind.

And soon, little mate, it'll be you in the middle.

"Ohhh," I moaned out loud, the idea of it heating me from head to toe.

Because yes. Yes, I wanted to experience that. And if the expression on Silas's face was anything to go by, I'd enjoy it immensely. He kissed me again, unleashing all his emotions with his tongue and forcing me to swallow each one.

Edon chose our pace, somehow angling himself in a way that didn't crush Silas into me even as he gave in to his more violent urges. Growls, groans, and words of approval spiraled between the three of us.

So different from what I'd observed in the past.

This wasn't about dominance—not entirely, anyway—but about mutual gratification. Edon whispered his lips across Silas's neck, his gaze capturing and holding mine. I reached up to brush my knuckles across his cheek, then returned Silas's kiss and lost myself again in the rapture of the moment.

Silas groaned, the intensity seeming to rip him in two as Edon propelled us into a frenzy. I lifted my hips, touched them both, nipped at Silas, watched Edon's expressions, and felt the ball of liquid fire churning once more. Until I couldn't see or think or move.

And I was falling.

Falling over a cliff into dark, all-consuming waters of ecstasy.

I felt Silas stiffen, heard his sounds of approval as he followed me. His teeth punctured my neck. Or maybe it was Edon who bit me. I really couldn't tell, too overwhelmed and engrossed in my liquid heaven. But I *felt* Edon come, his roar one I was sure everyone in the territory heard. It vibrated through Silas and directly to my heart, shadowing me in a protective layer I accepted without thought.

Everything just felt so right.

Complete.

Whole.

I refused to fight. Refused to think.

Instead, I closed my eyes, drunk on the sensations floating through my body, the tingling of my limbs, and the overall satisfaction warming my insides.

This was a life I could enjoy. At least for a little while.

I allowed it to follow me into my dreams. To ease me into a state of being I'd never before felt.

A state of happiness.

Of peace.

Of harmony.

Of home.

Chapter Twenty-Three

Edon

LUNA SLEPT PEACEFULLY BESIDE ME, her cheeks flushed, her hair tousled, and her lips swollen. Silas rested on her other side, his palm on her hip and his chest pressed up against her back.

Protection radiated from him, his eyes closed but his body alert.

I'd never spent much time with a human turned lycan. Most were too weak to survive. Silas, however, proved all the odds wrong. He thrived in his new form, already rivaling the strength of those three times his age. A natural-born enforcer, at least according to my instincts.

And he was mine.

Everyone in the pack assumed him to be a regular mutt without much skill. I wanted to keep it that way, at least for now. Not only would it give me a playing card for the right moment, but it would allow him to continue to grow and master his skills.

It also provided me with additional security for Luna.

Whatever was happening here between the three of us defied the natural order. Alphas mated other alphas. Yet somehow Silas had inserted himself in the bonds meant for Luna and me alone. I sensed his presence deep inside, his earlier bite a mark that claimed Luna as his even though I'd already identified her as mine.

And when I'd bitten him, something additional snapped into place beyond our sire bond.

I needed to go to my grandfather, to ask him what the hell was happening. Not just between the three of us, but with the pack in general.

Like how my father had framed Luna for Bianca's murder.

That shouldn't be possible.

"What about the vampire?" Silas asked softly, his eyes still closed but his mind clearly attuned to mine. It seemed he'd finally realized the bond went both ways. Or maybe I'd telegraphed loudly. Either way, he was awake and listening and thinking. "The vampire we found smelled only of pack, not a specific culprit. Did your father orchestrate that as well?"

Light blue irises flickered at me as he lazily lifted his lids, his expression one of serene comfort from our fuck fest over an hour ago.

When I told him I wanted to take his ass, he hadn't even flinched. His studies had included such activities, but I knew from his mind that I'd taken the most care I could with him despite my harsher thrusts. I'd actually made it enjoyable—something that had shocked us both.

Because the whole experience was new for me.

I'd fucked females in a variety of ways, but never a male, and I doubted I'd ever desire another in such a manner. However, Silas? Yeah, I intended to do that again. And again. And again.

And eventually, I'd take Luna, too.

"You'll need to warm her up a bit more before that can happen," Silas mused, proving to be inside my head. His lips curled. "And what a fascinating place your head is."

I snorted. "I can block you." Mental walls were something my grandfather had taught me how to build. He said they would be necessary for when I gained access to the pack psyche—which would happen as a result of my ascension. No one would be able to just pop into my head, though. Not like Silas, anyway. Or Luna when we completed the bond. Those connections would always be unique.

"Maybe, but you won't," Silas replied, referring to my threat to block him.

"But I could."

He smiled. "Sure."

His arrogance should have irritated me. Instead, it merely amused me. Probably because I was much too relaxed to be annoyed. "Regarding the vampire, I think you're right," I said, returning to the topic I'd been mulling over before my brain fled downward to my dick.

"Did I tell you I smelled more the other day?" Silas asked, his brow furrowing. "Or I smelled something. It was before I caught Luna running. She distracted me from it."

"No, you didn't mention it." I frowned. "Where was it?"

"Out near the border, in the marsh."

Meaning it was in Clemente territory, just outside of where the elite members of our pack resided. There were hundreds of wolves within our borders, but only a handful of carefully selected lycans lived at headquarters. Everyone else resided outside of the marsh areas in run-down towns or other patches of wilderness. "Have you smelled them anywhere else?"

"Prior to the dead one? No. But I haven't been out there recently."

Luna began to stir between us, her lips parting on an adorable little protest that said her body wasn't ready to wake yet. Given the events of today, I wasn't surprised. She'd already recovered from the beating—mostly because the pack hadn't been given enough time to do any severe damage. But sexually, Silas and I had exhausted her.

Something I would not apologize for.

Not when she wore the results of our affection so fucking well.

We should run the borders in the morning, Silas said, switching to our link.

I need to see my grandfather first.

Jolene. He seemed to be pondering the name, having clearly recalled it from earlier. *Why haven't I seen him?*

He doesn't socialize with my father's circle often. However, he lives nearby. I'll introduce you soon.

Surprise sparked in Silas's gaze. He didn't comment out loud, but I sensed his quiet pleasure at the potential opportunity. Nothing we were doing here was considered normal. Me—the alpha heir—introducing a newbie mutt to a former pack alpha? Yeah, that didn't happen in our society.

Yet something told me my grandfather would more than approve of my breaking that unspoken rule.

Can you stay with Luna tomorrow while I visit with my grandfather? I asked.

Silas grinned at me. *A request instead of a task? I need to let you fuck me more often.*

I scoffed at that. *I don't need you to let me do anything. A simple demand and you'll go down on all fours like a good little wolf.*

He arched a brow. *Yeah? Now who's acting arrogant?*

I nearly laughed. *We both know it's true. Just as we both know you'll guard our* little moon *tomorrow.*

"She's *my* little moon," he whispered, his arm sliding around her possessively. "And your little mate."

"And what nicknames shall we give each other?" I wondered out loud, pitching my voice low so as not to disturb the sleeping beauty between us.

Alpha, he taunted.

Omega, I returned.

Not the most original of names. But then again, maybe we didn't need any.

"Maybe Luna and I can run the border tomorrow together, see what we can find, while you meet with Jolene," he suggested quietly, proving to me his worth as a potential enforcer.

Silas's ability to focus appealed to me, his mind sharp and on task even during intimate moments. I supposed he had to be constantly analyzing situations given everything he'd survived over the years.

"I could bring her up to speed," he added. "Help us all prepare for whatever trial is next."

I nodded. "Yes." We were approaching the upcoming full moon. Whatever task my father meant to throw at me next would be the harshest. Because he was running out of time to incapacitate me. So either it'd be something to take me out of the running, or—

"He's going to try to kill Luna," Silas finished for me.

Because I couldn't ascend without a mate.

And my father had made it pretty clear these last few days that he saw her as expendable.

"It's not going to happen," I said.

"I know," Silas agreed.

I held his gaze for a long moment, noted the possession flaring in his pupils, and nodded again. "I know," I repeated. "Because he'll have to get through both of us." Something my father would never anticipate.

Oh, he might try to take me down.

But Silas? He'd never even consider it.

And that would be his ultimate failure.

Get some sleep, Silas whispered. *You need it more than I do. I'll keep watch.*

It seemed odd to rely on another, having spent my entire existence looking out for myself at every turn. However, for once, I obeyed another, and allowed my eyes to close.

Because he was right—I needed rest.

Good night, Edon.

Good night, Silas.

Chapter Twenty-Four

LUNA

WARM. I snuggled into the source of my happiness, content with the heat blanketing my skin. A chuckle graced the air, deep and low and deliciously amused, followed by a kiss against my forehead.

"You appear well rested, little moon," Silas mused, his hand drifting up and down my spine.

I stretched against him on a sigh. "Mm-hmm."

Light peeked in through the drapes, illuminating Silas's features as I opened my eyes. He grinned down at me, the picture of ease. "Good morning, beautiful." He glanced at the window, his smile growing. "Well, afternoon."

"What time is it?" I wondered out loud, searching for a clock.

"Time for lunch and a run," he replied, nuzzling my cheek. "Edon wants us to check the borders."

"For what?"

"Odd scents," he replied, sliding out from under me. "I'll explain over lunch."

I grabbed his nape and pulled him back to me for a long, indulgent kiss. Mmm, he tasted like peppermint and smelled of soap. His wet hair confirmed he'd taken a shower while I slept, but he hadn't bothered to put on any clothes. Something my hands were very grateful for as I explored his warm, muscular torso.

Fuck food.

I wanted to lick and taste him instead.

My wolf came alive with the idea, her fur smoothing out beneath my skin as I gave in to the urge to sink my nails into his nape while my opposite hand slid downward.

Silas smiled against my mouth.

"Careful or Edon will be jealous," he warned as my touch went south to his growing arousal.

Firm. Hot. Smooth. Perfection.

"Where is he?" I wondered aloud, referring to the alpha male who had awoken all these forbidden ideas inside my head. If this was all just a way to prime me as his mate, it'd more than worked. Because I wanted more. *So much more.*

"Edon's meeting with his grandfather," Silas replied, stretching out on top of me. "He left an hour ago."

I ran my tongue across his lower lip, my legs parting around his shifting hips. "Does he know we're awake?"

"He does."

"Are you talking to him right now?" I asked, my damp folds embracing Silas's hard cock and sliding against him in invitation.

He groaned, his forehead falling to mine. "I am."

"Mmm." I kissed him again, sighing as he entered me slowly all the way to the hilt. I didn't even need foreplay, my body already strung tight just from waking up beside him. Which was insane after everything that happened last night, all the orgasms ripped from my body.

But wow. I was addicted now. And I refused to stop.

Silas kissed me deeply, his hips setting a lazy rhythm that teased my senses. I squeezed him with my walls and wrapped my legs around his waist to encourage him to go faster—*harder*—but he maintained the same pace. Almost as if he was trying to taunt me.

I scratched my nails down his back, eliciting a hiss from him. He bit my lower lip in reprimand, then smiled. "Eager, little moon."

"Fuck me."

"I am."

I nearly growled. "You're playing."

"Yes," he agreed. "But still technically fucking you." He punctuated the point by thrusting deep. My back bowed off the bed in response, earning me a chuckle from him.

"Does Edon know you're inside me?" I asked, grasping his shoulders as he repeated the motion.

"Yes." He nibbled my jaw and pressed a kiss to my throat. "He says to make you earn it." His tongue traced a path up to my ear, his teeth snagging on the lobe. "And to remind you that he has a task for us to complete."

"Tell him I don't follow orders well," I panted, tightening my thighs around

Silas's waist.

"Oh, he knows," Silas replied, his words a whisper against my ear. "But he doesn't mind, darling Luna. Do you want to know why?"

The dark provocation in his tone sent a delicious shiver down my spine. "Yes," I admitted, swallowing.

"Because he enjoys sensual punishment." Silas pulled out abruptly, forcing my legs to unwind, and flipped me before I could even begin to react.

So fast.

So strong.

So—oh, dear wolf—mine.

He slammed back inside me so harshly that I screamed and then moaned beneath the onslaught of pleasure that followed. "*Fuck*," I breathed, shocked and incredibly *hot*.

"That's what you want, right?" He growled the words against the back of my neck, his body covering mine as he drove into me with far more force than he did last night. His wolf clearly craved dominance. And mine appeared to adore submission, something I would have claimed to be impossible just a week ago.

"Silas," I hissed, shaking beneath him, my body torn between torment and ecstasy. *This* was a punishment on its own, and one hell of a way to wake up.

"Edon says to tell you that he plans to take your ass later," he murmured, his words warm against my sensitive nape. "He wants you writhing and wet and begging between us. Which is why he's telling me to stop, Luna. To leave you panting and wanting. Should I listen, little moon? Or should I play rebel, too?"

He didn't pause but picked up the pace.

"Don't," I said, referring to his threat to halt. "Keep going." I didn't care at all that I sounded desperate, because I was. Shit, the way his cock hit my insides, I thought I might combust, and I would if he withdrew again. "Silas…" His name tumbled out of me on a moan, eliciting a deep sound of approval from him.

"Yeah, that's what I thought," he replied, threading his fingers through my hair and twisting my head back at an angle that nearly hurt. And kissed me. Hard. His dominance complete as he seated himself inside me over and over, his tongue matching the thrusts below.

Domineering, all-encompassing, addicting.

I no longer recognized myself.

Didn't understand who I was becoming.

But I lived for this moment alone.

The stirring ache tightening my insides, sending liquid lava through my veins, and shooting off stars behind my eyes.

My orgasm crested but didn't peak.

My legs quivered.

My breaths turned to gasps.

So, so close.

Right there.

"Ohh," I groaned, shattering on a wave of intensity that shook me to my very soul.

Silas followed on a snarl, his teeth sharp against my neck, puncturing in a bite neither of us should indulge in. And yet, I accepted it. My wolf bowed down, acknowledging the stronger male and preening from his claim.

It left me shaking beneath him, my body a mess of rapturous quakes and agonized bliss.

"Fuck." The word was a puff of air against my neck from Silas, his heavy mass trembling in time with mine.

I nearly laughed, the puzzle we'd created with our limbs one that would take some careful untangling. We'd come together in a frenzy, the wolves taking over in the last few moments and driving our coupling.

Just like last night.

Only slightly less overwhelming without Edon.

But still far more amazing than anything I could have expected.

What are we doing? I wanted to ask. Except Silas probably didn't know. Just as I doubted Edon did either.

This was uncharted territory.

Alphas were destined to mate other alphas. One male and one female. Not a trio. Yet that didn't feel right. Edon and Silas were too connected, too *something*. I couldn't identify exactly what, but the idea of taking one over the other felt wrong.

Maybe time would fix it.

Although, I doubted that.

If anything, time would only deepen this strange link between the three of us.

Silas twisted and yanked me into him, kissing me thoroughly while gathering me in his arms. "Time for a shower, little moon. We can play more later. With Edon."

I shivered as he stood and effortlessly lifted me with him. "Is he mad?"

He smiled. "Scared?"

"No."

"Neither am I." He carried me into the oversized marble bathroom and set me on the counter, his arms blocking me in as he gripped the stone on either side of my thighs. "But he's amused, not angry. He knew we'd defy him. And now he's eager to punish us both. So thanks for that."

I smirked. "Not my fault."

"Oh, it was entirely your fault. I was ready for lunch and a run, but now I have to shower again." He pushed away to turn on the water, then glanced over his shoulder. "Now get your ass in here so I can fuck you again before we eat."

"My fault, huh?" I repeated, laughing. "Seems you're just as *hungry* as I am."

"Or maybe I'm just making sure the experience is worth my while." He waggled his brows and gave me a playful smile that warmed my insides.

This was a new side of Silas, a relaxed one.

I rather liked it.

"Fucking, food, and a run," I contemplated aloud. "My kind of day." Not that I had a lot of experience with the fucking part. But between Edon and Silas, I'd be well educated very, very soon.

* * *

I SORT OF EXPECTED EDON to come barging in at any moment and demand to join us, but he never did. Instead, he remained in mental contact with Silas throughout our shower and spurred us on with a few dark promises of what he intended to do to us later. By the time we finished, we were ready to go again, but Silas insisted on eating and going for a run.

Once he explained why, I agreed.

I made us a few quick sandwiches—to replenish our depleted energy reserves—and then led the way to the outside boundaries to see what my nose could detect.

We went in wolf form because it was faster, and my sense of smell improved on all fours.

Silas trailed behind me, his much bigger size impressive for a human turned lycan. *Mutt* seemed too degrading a term for him. And *newbie* was too soft.

Maybe *changeling* would work.

My nose twitched, drawing me from my musings. Silas joined me, his focus already following the direction of the scent. He must have sensed it before me.

Another sign of his abnormal strength as a changeling.

He took off toward the scent with me on his heels, the stench of death growing with each step as we hit the boundary crossing.

I half expected to find another dead body, like they had last week.

But there was nothing.

Silas did a circle, his muzzle in the air, and snorted.

We'd found the strongest point, but there was no sign of a vampire.

He took a few steps out into the field, then turned and went the other direction, only to snort again and look at me.

I shook out my coat, giving him a negative on tracking, and started along the boundary in the opposite direction. But the scent lessened until it disappeared, sending me back the other way to the same spot.

This doesn't make any sense.

I began the shift, which triggered Silas to follow. When he was standing before me in full human form—something that took him slightly longer than it did me—I repeated my words out loud. "Someone, somehow, is fucking with pack and vampire scents," I added.

"Like they did with yours at Bianca's death site." He glanced around, his palm holding the back of his neck. "And the body we found reeked of pack, not a single culprit."

"It has to be his father, or someone high up. But I don't know how they're doing it."

"Neither does Edon," he replied, his lips flat. "He was supposed to ask his grandfather about it. Hopefully, he's learning something useful, because he's been silent for about an hour now."

I frowned. "Silent?"

"Yeah."

"Is that normal?"

He lifted a shoulder. "Edon only talks to me when he has something to say, which is more often than not, but I imagine he's busy right now."

Fair enough. I studied the field and then the terrain back to the main camp and pinched my lips to the side. "Why would a vampire play this close to the heart of the clan territory? If we were near the Silvano or Lilith Region borders, I'd understand it. But we're several hundreds of miles from the closest vampire stronghold. Hanging out here is an invitation for trouble."

Vampires and lycans played nice for the Blood Alliance, but they weren't exactly allies. They merely split everything fifty-fifty and ruled in their own ways within the boundaries of international law. Beyond that, they were not required to be friends or business partners. Instead, the vampires tended to make business arrangements with their fellow undead, while lycans stuck to pack trades.

"It's odd," Silas agreed, walking along the border. "Let me show you where we found the body. Maybe you'll pick up on something we didn't."

Doubtful, but I agreed anyway.

We jogged in human form to the spot about two miles away, but the scents were all clear of death.

"Edon disposed of the remains," Silas explained.

"He did a good job, because I can't pick up even a trace of it."

Silas nodded. "Yeah. He made sure of that."

We hunted around and found nothing.

I finally shook my head. "Everything seems fine here. Normal, even."

"Yeah." He blew out a breath. "I guess we'll—"

His knees buckled beneath him, sending him crashing to the ground on an agonized cry that rang harshly in my ears.

"Silas!" I collapsed with him, my hands going to his shoulders as my eyes roamed over him, searching for the source of his pain. But he appeared unmarred, his skin as tan and taut as moments ago.

But he held his heart as if someone had shot him there and fell to his side, his legs tucking into the fetal position.

"*Fuck…*," he wheezed, tears leaking from the edges of his eyes. "Edon," he finally managed, his voice hoarse, his body shuddering violently. "Something's… wrong… with Edon…"

Chapter Twenty-Five

Silas

IT TOOK FAR TOO LONG to shake off the initial burn in my chest.

And then I was running on all fours.

My body ached, my ears vibrated from the intense beating of my heart, and my vision blurred. But I had to get to him, to help him, to save—

No! he shouted through my mind.

I ignored him, my instincts pushing me over the earth with Luna hot on my tail. Our paws raced in sequence, her lithe form a strong presence at my back as we hit the outskirts of the main village.

They'll kill you, Silas, Edon barked into my thoughts. *Stop!*

I shook him off, but something in that command made me trip just behind one of the lodges. Luna landed on top of me, winded and dazed from my misstep.

It's another trial, Edon said quickly. *If you or Luna interferes, they'll use it as an excuse to kill you both. This is about allies. I can't… have… allies.*

The way he broke off at the end had my heart racing all over again. He'd clearly exerted significant effort into yelling at me. Which meant I needed to *hear* him.

"What is it?" Luna asked, already in human form again.

I forced myself to shift, my breaths coming in pants from the harsh run and forced swiftness with which I changed back and forth between wolf and man.

Edon's link wavered, his consciousness coming in and out.

"He doesn't want us to interfere," I whispered, swallowing. "Says it's a test about allies."

"What sort of…?" Luna glanced sharply at the trees, taking a defensive position at my side.

My brow furrowed, my senses on alert, seeking whatever had captured her interest. *There*, my wolf spotted. A slight flicker of movement in the trees.

Luna growled low, the sound far more ominous than anything I'd ever heard from her.

And the intruder responded with a chuckle. "Claudette certainly outdid herself," a deep voice said as a male with silver hair and dark eyes stepped silently onto the path. "And Edon is right, Silas. This is about allies. If you go to him right now, they'll expect you to join. Or worse, they'll see how long you can last."

"Until what?" I demanded. I didn't need to demand his identity. His resemblance to my sire told me his identity—Edon's grandfather.

"A strength test," Luna said, her voice hoarse.

"Yes," the old man confirmed.

"What the hell is a strength test?" I mean, I understood the gist of it by the name. "What does it entail?"

"They beat the alpha until he's unconscious, just to see how much he can take," Luna whispered.

The elderly lycan nodded. "And knowing my son, he'll add both of you to the mix, just for fun."

"To remove all of Edon's allies from the board," Luna added. "Perhaps permanently." She canted her head, her gaze astute. "You're Jolene."

The elderly male smiled. "No one has called me by that name in many moons, child. But yes, I am." He glanced sharply to his left, all traces of amusement dying. "You must go before they find you."

Luna followed his gaze, her face whitening. "They'll hunt me."

"Silas knows a place." He arched a brow at me. "Don't you?"

The cabin, I realized. "But what about Edon?"

"Don't let my looks fool you, boy." His grin was all teeth, resembling the wolf beneath the skin. "I'm still an alpha, and that's my grandson in there."

Howls from the heart of the village sounded, sending Luna back two paces. "They're coming."

"Go," Jolene urged. "I'll distract them."

He unbuttoned his shirt, revealing a torso that displayed his strength, and dropped his trousers to begin his shift.

Luna grabbed my arm before I could watch the transformation, power flooding the air.

Holy shit.

"Silas!" Luna hissed, tugging on me. "If they find me—"

Another howl sounded, this one far too close.

And it didn't come from Jolene.

I fell to my knees, transitioning as fast as my body allowed. But it wasn't quick enough. Three wolves stepped around the corner, their gazes hungry as they locked on Luna midshift. She snarled, her hackles rising, and then Jolene stepped in front of her with a growl, his large size a startling sight.

His low growl forced the other wolves to heel, their gazes dropping from the clear alpha before them.

I stood captivated by the show of dominance.

This is Edon's future. What he's capable of even now.

And yet his pack was beating him to a pulp. To what? Test his endurance?

I could *feel* his agony through the bond, his pain a visceral force of nature that called to me to find him and help him. But I also felt his reluctance, the warning in his mind to stay away. To protect Luna at all costs. To let him endure this trial alone.

Because if we came for him, his father would beat us, too.

And unlike Edon, we wouldn't survive.

A nip to my ear forced my attention to the side where Luna stared at me with an imploring expression. Fear radiated from her, more howls assaulting the air as someone announced our position to the pack.

Living as a lycan was no better than being a human.

They were animals, thriving on the pain of others and demanding submission in the cruelest of ways.

Even the strongest among them was punished just for his position. Beat down by his brethren to prove his place at the top.

Why the fuck would anyone allow that?

For the same reason I fought in the Immortal Cup. Edon endured their bullshit to secure his place at the top, to ascend to the only position where he could effect change.

These tests went so far beyond his fate. This was about restructuring the Clemente Clan. And if Edon had to, he'd put that above everyone else in his life—including me and Luna.

That was why he needed us to run.

He couldn't protect us tonight. We were on our own. But he'd left me with the keys to our safety. Such a clever male, always one step ahead.

My heart warmed with a respect I never expected to feel, one that had me meeting Luna's gaze and tilting my head in a *follow me* gesture.

Her relief was palpable as I took off into the woods, my paws pounding over the earth in a pattern meant to confuse anyone following us. Because no way was I leading them to Edon's refuge.

Edon's approval sang in my blood, his mind filled with gratitude even as his anguish violated our link. *Don't let those bastards kill you,* I said.

It'll take more than a beating, Omega, he whispered, his mental voice disturbingly soft.

I mean it, Alpha. We're not done yet.

Amusement met my words, but he no longer spoke. He seemed to be reserving his energy. As long as I felt him, I wouldn't worry.

Over an hour later, I finally led us to the small cabin outside the borders. Luna panted heavily behind me, her eyes alight with life and wonder and awe. She'd obviously enjoyed the run, or perhaps the adrenaline born from the escape.

I shifted near the door and opened it for her. "It's not as nice as his main place, but it's comfortable."

Oddly, the familiar surroundings held a hint of nostalgia for me. I'd barely spent any time here, nor had it been long since my last visit. Yet so much had occurred over the last few days that it felt like ages since I last set foot in this place.

However, the kitchen was still well stocked, and all the amenities worked.

Luna ventured into the main bedroom, likely trailing Edon's scent, and came out a few minutes later wearing an old T-shirt. She tossed me a pair of shorts that I put on while she rummaged through the cupboards.

Then she stilled, her shoulders tightening.

"Luna?" I slowly walked up behind her, placing my palm against her back. She trembled beneath my touch and turned into me. Whatever excitement she'd felt from the run had died a swift death. Now she stood before me with a posture that radiated defeat.

"We ran," she whispered.

"Yes."

She swallowed, looking up at me. "We ran like cowards."

"No, we did what Edon wanted us to do." I palmed her cheek. "They would have hurt us, Luna."

"We could have fought," she argued. "But we didn't even try. Fuck, I didn't even think to try. I just… fled." She blinked. "I… What if…?"

I folded my arms around her, tucking her head beneath my chin. "It's not our time to fight." *Yet*, I added mentally. Because one day—a day I suspect would be soon—we would fight. But not tonight. "We helped Edon by not being there." At least that was what I gathered from the bond.

"But what if he's wrong?" She pulled back to stare up at me. "What if his father takes it too far?"

"Then we have to rely on Jolene to help him," I said, unnerved by the notion of relying on anyone other than myself.

"Can…?" She paused, her throat working. She cleared it twice before continuing. "Can you feel him?"

"Yes." My connection to Edon thrived even beneath the pain. "He's conserving his strength." A plan had formed in the alpha's mind, one I couldn't quite define. But I knew he was okay. "I think the wolves are searching for us." Because there appeared to be a lull in the trial, some sort of waiting game that Edon was using to his advantage to heal.

She straightened her spine, a flash of challenge overtaking the uncertainty in her gaze. "I'll fight them if they find us."

"They won't find us here." I was certain of it, not just because of my evasiveness on the run, but because I trusted Edon. He kept this place for a reason. A safe house for times when he needed to hide—and now was one of those times. "But we should prepare just in case."

She nodded, slipping free of my arms. "Traps."

"Traps?" I repeated.

Another nod. "Yes. We'll smell them, but if we set alarms out in the fields, we'll hear them, too. And it'll give us enough time to ready ourselves."

Sounded like a good use of our time. "Okay. I'll help."

"No." She glanced at me. "You need to gather medical supplies. Edon is going to need us to nurse him back to health. So keep in touch with him, then bring him here when he's ready. Meanwhile, I'll prep the grounds."

I nearly smiled at her bossiness, intrigued by the alpha female coming out to play. But an amused reply wouldn't be all that appropriate considering our situation. So I settled on saying, "Okay. I'll keep talking to him."

"Good." She seemed a little more herself now that she'd found a measure of control. "Tell him we're waiting for him."

"I will."

"And that we're not going down without a fight."

"He knows that, Luna."

"He doesn't," she replied, meeting my gaze. "But he will." Something appeared to snap inside her, a resolve of sorts, one she didn't quite have before. I hadn't noticed it was missing because I didn't know to look, but I caught it now.

She no longer wanted to run.

Luna had finally accepted her mate.

And she would do whatever she needed to do to keep him.

My heart panged a little at the realization, my place firmly on the outside of their strengthening bond. Alas, now wasn't the time to worry about myself or my irrational feelings.

I had a sire to save. And for whatever reason, he'd put me in charge of the well-being of his mate. I wouldn't let him or Luna down.

I know, he whispered, the words a stroke against my heart. *I'll see you soon.*

Chapter Twenty-Six

LUNA

I KICKED A PILE OF DIRT and snorted as it sent dust flying everywhere. This vegetation was so different from my homeland. A lot warmer, for one. And dry.

Although, I suspected the latter was due to a lack of rain.

Not that I cared about the weather.

Or even about the lack of water.

No, my mind was on Edon and the fact that I had run. It'd been second nature, my terror at being thrown into a circle with him overriding my senses.

And turning me into a fucking coward.

I growled low in my throat. It wasn't like me to flee. I always fought. Even strutting into the damn mating ceremony, I'd fought in my own way.

But the notion of having my strength tested by Walter and his men had locked me up in a manner I wasn't accustomed to. Visions of how they assaulted me after I punched Bianca, and the comments and licentious desires voiced during the punishment ring… I shuddered again just thinking about it all.

Was it really any wonder I'd wanted to escape?

Hadn't that been my goal since Edon marked me as his?

Yet arriving at the safe house with Silas had awoken a whole new field of thought. I'd run to save myself, something a week ago I would have respected.

But leaving Edon to suffer now felt wrong. I'd seen too much of the male beneath the alpha veneer and had heard the whisper of his true intentions in the way he spoke about the past and future.

He reminded me of Logan.

And I would never leave Logan behind.

Another snarl worked its way out of my muzzle, the sound far more ferocious than I felt.

Everything had changed so quickly. My initial thoughts of running to rogue territories where I could fend for myself were gone in an instant. And behind, I felt a connection to a male I was born to hate.

All my life, I'd been promised to a future alpha with two primary purposes in mind—to mate an alpha female and force her to carry his offspring.

End of discussion.

No choice.

My life over before it even began.

Yet Edon wasn't the male I expected. He didn't force me to do anything. Not really, anyway. He minded my wants and needs, didn't push me outside of my boundaries, and clearly valued my protection.

Hence, Silas.

Oh, but that added a whole new layer of complexity to this entire situation. Because I liked Silas just as much as I liked Edon, but in an entirely different manner.

Both were dominant. No question. They desired my submission and would do what they had to do to acquire it. With Edon, I expected that. Silas, however, was a surprise. My alpha inclinations and purebred genetics should make it easy to best him. Yet, not only did he put up one hell of a fight against me but he also *won*.

And it wasn't a result of my weakness.

I could take on wolves twice my size.

No, Silas had a strength to him that few others possessed. And I suspected it was born of years and years of having to fight to survive. It marked him as similar, but different, to Edon.

Silas also had a softness to him that Edon lacked. He was slightly more intuitive and constantly analyzing his surroundings and choices. Edon, too, contemplated his actions, but he never wavered in a decision and his word was law. Rather than debate it, Silas seemed to cave, deferring to the stronger of the pair rather than trying to rebuke him.

The dynamic between them was intoxicating and hot as hell.

It left me wanting them both equally, unable to choose, and that stirred a whole world of problems. Because, eventually, whatever game Edon was playing would die. He'd told me from the beginning that none of his wolves would ever fuck me. Yet Silas had done so more than once now without consequence.

Sure, Edon had allowed it. Twice. But there was no way he'd continue to accept it. Unless he shared me to help tame his possessive instincts? It was frowned upon for alphas to display proprietorial tendencies. Maybe Edon was just preparing himself for future social requirements involving mate sharing?

I frowned.

No. This went deeper. I could feel it in my bones, and Edon didn't seem all that eager to comply with societal requirements. He'd kept the other wolves from touching me more than once now. Except for Silas, whom he appeared quite eager to have join our nest.

Maybe *too* eager.

What if Edon prefers Silas? I stopped in my tracks, the moon bright overhead. *Didn't Edon say Silas gave him the best head of his life?* I performed for him just last night, and he'd said nothing, had even faked a second orgasm down my throat.

Because I wasn't as good?

It'd been my second time—Silas being the first—so of course it wasn't as good.

I shivered. Competition always heated my blood, but in this case, it chilled me. Because I didn't want to compete with Silas for Edon's affection. If he were anyone else, hell yes, I'd fight to the end. But not Silas.

Shaking out my coat, I continued walking, needing a new train of thought. This had just gotten too deep and confusing. I should be concerned about Edon's well-being, wondering if he would even survive that death trap, not thinking about my sexual skills—or lack thereof—and comparing myself to Silas.

Selfish, I thought to myself. *And stupid.*

Just like running.

Ugh. Part of me wanted to sprint back to camp to find Edon, but I knew it would be a death sentence. He was likely too hurt at this point to fight, and it'd be me against a pack of bloodthirsty wolves.

Who were beating the shit out of their future leader.

Why was this even acceptable behavior?

So degrading and—

My ears twitched, the sound of a branch snapping alerting me to the presence of another. Someone strong. His aura blasted mine, something that, I realized a second too late, had been done on purpose to grab my attention.

Jolene stood about ten feet away holding an unconscious Edon in his arms.

I startled, shocked that he'd managed to get so close to me in human form without my noticing. But then again, he was an alpha male for a reason. And he'd lived a very, very long life.

"He's breathing, but barely," he said, his voice grim. "Walter was going to kill him."

Had I been in human form, my lips would have parted. Murdering an alpha heir wasn't unheard of, but it was rare. Most alphas didn't want to give up their place to their offspring, yet our circle of life required it.

Walter must have thought he could just make another male. Given the mental state of his current mate, however, I suspected that would be impossible. Unless he found another alpha female to fuck.

Someone like... me. My eyes rounded. Oh. Fuck. No.

The expression on Jolene's face suggested he'd just read my mind. "Come," he demanded. "He needs the kind of healing only a mate can provide."

Claudette had spoken of this, the rare connection between lycans where strength could be given and borrowed for healing. I suspected Edon tapped into it the other night to help me after Walter and his men had beat me.

And now he needed the same from me.

No. He required a whole hell of a lot more.

Which is why he didn't want us at the ring, I realized as I followed Jolene. *Edon knew he'd need me for this.*

However, I had to be willing. So it went far deeper than preserving his only vitality source. Edon relying on me to help him in a time of need required significant trust. I could so easily walk away now and let him die. But he'd put his faith in me not to. And somehow, knowing that only made me move faster.

I didn't want to prove him wrong.

I wanted to make him proud.

To assist in the only way I could.

By being his mate in every fashion of the word.

"They demanded he reveal your location," Jolene informed me as we approached the cabin. "But he refused. Walter claimed he'd chosen you over his loyalty to the pack, and they annihilated him for it." He shook his head, a low growl coming from his chest. "My son has twisted this clan into a pack of asinine heathens."

I snorted my agreement even while my heart skipped a beat. Oh, he'd hidden me from Walter to protect himself just as much as me. I understood that. But this was the third time he'd safeguarded me from the horror of his pack.

Silas met us at the door, aware of our approach, his expression grim as I shifted back into human form. He handed me the shirt I'd abandoned on the front stoop and looked at the male beside me. "Edon says to thank you for intervening."

Jolene looked surprised for half a beat before moving directly to Edon's bedroom. "You can still hear him." Not a question, but a statement.

"Yes," he confirmed, causing me to breathe a sigh of relief.

"Then he's not as bad as I feared," he said, laying Edon out on the bed.

"He's surviving on energy reserves." Silas swallowed. "I, uh, can feel it."

Jolene seemed impressed. "Your sire bond is unusually deep."

Silas cleared his throat. "Yeah. Maybe." He started toward the bathroom. "I prepared some supplies that will help. I'll grab them."

I shared a glance with Jolene. "It doesn't bother you?" he asked. "Whatever's happenin' between the two of them?"

"Why would it bother me?" I asked, not really in the mood to play this game or discuss relationships right now.

"Why indeed," he drawled, a twinkle of amusement in his gaze. "Well, I suspect you know what to do."

I nodded.

"Good." He intercepted Silas as he returned, taking the supplies and handing them to me. "Silas is gonna help me find a cot to sleep on for the night. You get to work on my boy."

Silas gave me a look as if to ask, *Are you okay?*

I nodded again. *I've got this.*

And I did.

There was no other choice. Either I nursed Edon back to life or I well and truly ran… for the rest of my days. Because bowing to Walter—assuming that was his plan—would never happen. I'd die first.

Silas and Jolene left me alone, their voices turning to a low murmur as Jolene explained what I needed to do. Normally, it would have shocked me to hear an alpha be so patient and willing to explain to a new lycan, yet it didn't. Oddly, it only solidified what I had to do.

Jolene had taught Edon to be the man he was today, and clearly the elderly wolf's principles were deeply instilled in the male I now claimed as my mate.

I brushed Edon's thick hair away from his bruised face and bent to brush my lips over his. "I'm here," I whispered. "Take whatever you need."

Closing my eyes, I focused on his scent and breathed him in. Deep, luscious pulls filled with forest and male and underlined with a hint of spice that seemed to be all Edon.

I accepted him.

Acknowledged his claim.

And allowed him access to my wolf.

Nothing happened, the air cool, his exhales shallow.

I picked up one of the towels, already warm and damp, and used it to wipe the blood away from his mouth, his cheeks, his forehead, then kissed him again.

His lips tingled beneath mine but didn't move, his breath still weak.

I repeated the action with the towel, cleaning up his torso and arms, his strong thighs and calves. It took nearly an hour of wiping him down, swapping towels in the bathroom and moving him this way and that to wash him thoroughly. He'd still need a shower, but at least his wounds were accessible.

Using the ointment Silas prepped, I swabbed each gash and wrapped up the deepest of the wounds. Throughout each ministration, I ran my lips over him, kissing his jaw, his temple, his mouth, his neck, and allowed him to feel my consent in each touch.

We hadn't truly finalized our mating. That wouldn't happen until the next full moon. He'd only claimed me. But now I was claiming him, assenting to our relationship, and granting him access to my soul.

His wolf seemed to yawn beneath his skin, the beating leaving him depleted and alone, but I knew he sensed me, could feel him sniffing the connection with interest.

I stretched out beside him, my palm on his abdomen, my other hand propping up my head, and began humming to him. A haunting melody, one Claudette taught me long ago, but it always made me feel better.

His breathing had evened out, his healing well underway, but he appeared to be reluctant to use me. "Edon," I whispered, sliding my palm up his torso to rest over his heart. "I know I ran, but I'm not weak. You can take what you need."

Still nothing.

Stubborn wolf.

But I felt his interest. I pictured him prowling around me, scenting me, his growl low and filled with intrigue. My wolf didn't move, her posture one of strength, not submission. He needed an equal right now. A female worthy of his needs.

This time his growl wasn't just in my head or a figment of my imagination, but a real sound—a broken one from his tormented throat.

I leaned into him, running my nose up his neck and pressed my mouth to his ear. "Are you intimidated?" I whispered. "Is that why you won't take what you need?" I nibbled on his lobe, then bit down hard enough to draw blood. "I'm not afraid of you, Alpha."

A snarl came from his chest, the wolf threatening to break free.

"Take what you want," I told him, my voice a low purr. "I'm here."

He fell silent again, the pacing resuming—at least in my mind.

I sighed against his neck. "This is going to be a very long night if you continue on like this."

No reply.

"Good thing I'm stubborn, too," I said, kissing his steady pulse. "A battle of wills it is."

Chapter Twenty-Seven

EDON

GLENN.

Barry.

Oscar.

George.

My father.

A growl warmed my chest, the sound a vow of retribution designated for those swimming in my mind. I had a very long list of lycans I wanted to kill.

They'd taken the strength trial too far.

And my father demanding the location of my mate? Yeah, that was the icing on the cake. I knew why he wanted her, and it had nothing to do with pack loyalty.

My mother was barren after all the trials she'd endured beneath his rule. She barely even opened her eyes anymore. Making a new heir would be impossible. But with Luna? Oh, he could create one.

Fucking monster.

I spent so many years of my life trying to gain his favor, only to fail. Well, that was done. I no longer craved his acceptance or advice. I would become the alpha I intended to be at the next full moon, and my poor excuse for a father would be the first lycan I banned. His cronies would be next.

My entire body ached, especially my rib cage where my bones slowly mended back together. They'd shattered my insides beneath thousands of kicks; it was honestly a wonder I'd survived.

No.

Not a wonder.

My grandfather had stepped in, threatening to go to the Blood Alliance about my father's behavior. Killing an heir unjustly was frowned upon, and my father couldn't use a strength exercise as an excuse. Not unless I tried to fight back, which I hadn't. I'd taken their beating, as the alpha ritual required, and he had chosen to take it too far.

Well, he and my fucking packmates who had far too eagerly participated.

Hence, my list.

Another growl vibrated my chest, my anger thriving through my veins. I wanted to smash their—

My senses piqued as someone responded to my sound of ire.

Not vocally, but with another growl. A sexier one.

Luna.

Her supple form was stretched out beside me, her palm a pleasant weight over my heart. It took significant effort to peel my eyes open, but I was thankful for trying because I found a gorgeous sight staring down at me—waves of brown hair tousled over one shoulder, head resting on her opposite hand, and honey-brown irises gazing at me with a fierceness that caused my breath to hitch.

"About fucking time," she said, causing my eyebrows to lift.

My lips parted on a reply that lacked sound. Not that it mattered, though. Because her mouth settled over mine before I could even try again.

Shock coursed through me, followed swiftly by heat and intense longing.

Shit. Luna was kissing me. Eagerly. Dominantly. It took half a beat for me to register why she acted so impulsively. She wanted me to activate our mating link and absorb her strength.

Not happening.

I refused to use her in that manner. Nor did I need the boost. My energy reserves were healing me just fine.

But her company?

Yeah, now that I'd accept.

Except I couldn't move without flinching. Nor was my mouth working right.

She palmed my jaw, causing me to wince. "It's broken," she whispered, her nose nuzzling mine. "Let me help you, Edon. Please." Another kiss, this one followed by a nip to my lower lip when I didn't do as she requested. "Why are you fighting me?"

Oh, the ways I could answer that if my mouth worked. I would tell her: *You fought me first, sweetheart. Maybe I consider it foreplay. Delayed gratification, little mate.*

However, the truth of it was, I didn't want to hurt her. I also didn't know her true intent. While I appreciated her being here for me, I also knew it was her obligation—one society had demanded of her. And I refused to force her. Especially when I didn't need her strength to heal. Would it restore me to full health faster? Yes. But she deserved better than me sucking the life from her like some vampire.

Luna pulled back, her gaze shadowing over. "Why are you rejecting me?"

My eyes actually widened. *What?* This wasn't about rejection.

"Is it… I mean, do you…?" She bit her lip, glancing away, then back at me again with a sadness that hurt far more than my fractured rib cage. "Do you want me to get Silas?" she asked softly, her expression radiating an emotion I couldn't name. Not quite sadness, but definitely spasmed with pain. "I don't know if the sire bond can help, but if you prefer him, I'll understand. And I'll get him for you."

Where are you? I asked Silas through the bond.

Doing a perimeter check with Jolene before he goes to sleep, he replied. *Why? Is something wrong?*

Yeah. Luna seems to think I'd prefer you playing nursemaid instead of her. While I wouldn't mind Silas lying beside me now, I didn't exactly favor him over Luna. *Something tells me her touch will be a bit more tender and what I need right now.*

He snorted in my head. *You don't strike me as the kind of guy who enjoys tender, Edon.*

I wouldn't mind it from a certain female wolf, I thought, gazing up at her. *Except she seems pretty upset.*

Because she thinks you would prefer me there? He sounded as confused as I felt. *What did you say to her?*

Nothing. My jaw is broken.

Still? I could almost see him scratching his head. *Jolene said you would heal faster because of your mating bond with Luna.*

Yeah, only if I take energy from her, but I'm not.

Why the hell not?

Because I don't want to force her.

You don't want…? He started laughing, causing me to frown.

That wasn't meant to be funny, Omega.

Oh, but it's rich, Alpha, he returned. *You'll command me to fuck her, but you won't accept the bond she's offering now? Really?*

Seriously? We're going there again? You can't tell me you didn't enjoy—

"Edon?" Luna whispered, the earlier annoyance in her tone completely gone now and replaced by something akin to disappointment. "I know you probably can't speak, but can you at least nod?"

I lifted my chin an inch, testing my neck movement. It hurt like a son of a bitch, but it worked.

If you would let the woman in and absorb some of her strength, maybe it wouldn't hurt, Silas taunted in my head.

Fuck off.

I swore the jackass blew me kisses in reply, his amusement palpable. But the look on Luna's face ruined my inclination to smile.

"Do you want me to get Silas for you?" she asked softly.

I didn't nod.

Her brow furrowed. "I don't… I don't know what you want, Edon. I'm trying to help, but you don't want me. Clearly. So I'm going to get Silas, okay? Maybe you'll let him help, or, I don't know." She shook her head, but I saw it in her eyes before she shuttered them.

Rejection, I realized. *She thinks I'm rejecting our mating.*

Because you are rejecting it, Silas replied.

No, I'm not. I'm just not sucking on her life source, I thought back at him, irritated.

But does she know that?

Apparently not, I said, noting the way her lower lip wobbled before she sucked it in. *Ah, little mate…*

She'd been so strong, lying beside me, wanting me to take from her. The lack of blood on my skin told me she'd bathed me, too.

She's accepting her place by your side, Silas murmured. *I saw it in her earlier.*

And I felt it now.

Luna started to roll off the bed, causing me to reach for her. Which ended in a grimace and a groan that had her looking back at me in alarm.

"Sorry, I didn't mean to hurt you more. I was just trying to, uh, move." She cringed. "You need some pain medicine or something."

No, what I needed was a brand-new body. One that I could use to kill my father and his idiotic cronies.

"Look, with you rejecting me, I obviously can't help you," she said, some of her spine seeming to return. "So I'm going to get up real fast and find Silas. Since you and he are, well, closer."

Shit. That wasn't it at all.

I growled because it seemed to be the only response I could make, and it caused her to freeze in place.

Then she narrowed her eyes at me. "Did you just growl at me?"

This time, I nodded.

"Why?" she demanded.

Because you just accused me of rejecting our mating bond, I thought at her.

Of course, it was Silas who replied. *Then maybe you should do whatever it is you need to do to accept her.*

You make it sound easy, Omega.

Because it is, Alpha.

I wanted to argue that point, but I couldn't. Because I'd clearly accepted the sire bond to him without hesitation. But Luna was a bit more complex. I'd already initiated our mating against her will. If I took from her now, it would finalize our destinies.

Of course, she didn't have a choice regardless. And neither, really, did I.

Luna released a noise of frustration. "You're a stubborn wolf, you know that?"

My lips threatened to twitch—which hurt and sort of ruined the moment.

Her eyes narrowed. "You're amused?"

My chin tilted in the affirmative, which only had her glowering more.

"Rejecting me entertains you?" She scoffed, the mood between us chilling in a heartbeat. "Wow. Okay. I get that I wasn't exactly favorable to our mateship in the beginning, but I thought last night changed things. Which was really naïve of me, and I see that now."

Whoa, hold on. That's not—

"God, you know, I was actually worried about you?" She laughed, but the sound was tinged with sadness. "Never mind. I'll leave you here to your *amusement.* Because hell if I'm going to sit and enjoy it with you at my own personal expense."

She rolled off the bed, leaving me snarling at her back.

How *dare* she run off when I had no voice to defend myself!

Get back here, I demanded.

But she couldn't hear me, nor did she adhere to the command radiating from my chest. She kept moving, her spine straight even as her dejection soured the air.

Alpha female through and through, refusing to allow others to see her pain. But her scent belied her bravado.

When she reached the door, something inside me snapped.

No way in hell was I allowing her to walk away from me like this.

She staggered beneath the weight of our sudden connection, her breath puffing out of her in a gasp as I dug my mental claws into her and coerced her to stay. My wolf didn't want to play; it wanted to dominate.

This female belonged to me.

And she thought I meant to reject her?

Fuck. That.

Every wall constructed between us came tumbling down as I yanked forcefully on the mating link—the connection that began to form the first time I bit her. Neither of us had explored the bond, mostly because it was more of a formality than a desire. But now? Now I wanted to know everything about it.

Because if she believed for one second that I didn't want her, she had another think coming.

You. Are. My. Mate. The words were from my mental wolf, a growl into her heart and mind at the same time as he circled her like prey. *You will not walk away from me.*

She turned and swallowed, her eyes wide. "I… I…"

Get back here, I told her. *Now.*

But she didn't. Instead, the impudent little female glared at me. "No. You were laughing at me, Edon. Just because you engaged the bond now does not mean I have to accept it."

And she did the unthinkable, her mind swiftly rebuilding the blocks I'd just knocked down.

It was bad enough that our bond wasn't complete and I only had a one-way ticket into her mind. With the connection open, I could push things at her—like words and feelings—and take whatever she willingly offered, but that was it.

And now she wanted to shove me out completely?

Not fucking happening.

I wasn't laughing at you, Luna, I said quickly, needing her to hear me before she finished reconstructing that wall of hers. *I was amused by you calling me stubborn. And I didn't reject our mating bond. I just didn't want to use you.*

She stilled, her lips curling downward. "Explain."

Rather than explain, I recapped the entire conversation from my point of view. I even clued her in on my discussion with Silas by providing an overview. Once I finished, her frown no longer existed.

"That's the dumbest thing I've ever heard," she accused. "The whole point of a mating bond is to help each other, Edon. You're not the only one with reserves of strength, and frankly, I'm insulted that you don't think I can handle a little vampirism. I'm not an omega or beta wolf, but a born alpha. It's in my blood, you dick."

My eyebrows rose. *Careful, little mate. You might be alpha born, but I'm still* your *alpha.*

"Are you?" she taunted. "Because all I see is a broken wolf who has refused to do what he needs to do under some misguided attempt to protect his female. A female, mind you, who can more than hold her own." Those beautiful eyes narrowed once more. "How would you feel if I rejected your strength? If I assumed you to be too weak to help me?"

That's not—

"No, that's *exactly* what this is, so don't try to play it another way. You don't think I'm strong enough to help you." She folded her arms, my shirt hitting her at her thighs. It was a very sexy look on her. Not that this was the time to consider it. "Why did you mate me, Edon? To make pups? To fuck your progeny? What purpose do I serve for you if you don't find my strength worthy to suit an alpha?"

My blood heated at her accusations, my heart racing in my chest. *Get. Over. Here.*

"No."

Now who is being stubborn? I asked, irritated as fuck. *You want to prove you're strong enough? Then march that sweet ass back to this bed and lie down.*

"I don't have to lie—" She gripped the wall for support as her knees buckled beneath my wolf's hungry demand. One pull on her reserves had my rib cage sighing in relief and the rest of me begging for more, but I only meant for it to be a demonstration, not an actual solution.

Yet, now I didn't want to stop.

Now, Luna, I demanded, holding off on my desire to take more from her. *Unless you're suddenly too scared?*

An unflattering noise came from her throat, one that told me exactly how she felt about that. "I fucking hate you," she said as she moved toward the bed.

Liar, I whispered.

She scoffed but stretched out beside me again. "This doesn't mean I forgive you."

I indulged myself in another taste of her vitality, my wolf stretching in contentment beneath her beautiful warmth. She sighed beside me, her pleasure heating our link and encouraging me to take more. So I did, allowing her energy to tingle through my veins, down my limbs, into my bones, and to my very soul.

Fuck, but it was arousing and incredibly intimate. Like my own personal pain-relieving drug, only in a feminine, supple form with curves for days.

I needed to get hurt more often if this was my reward.

"Don't you dare," she said, either because I spoke those words through the bond or she picked them up, I wasn't sure.

Thank you, little mate, I murmured, meaning it.

She said nothing for a while, her focus on the ceiling, but eventually, she rolled onto her side to face me. "You're welcome."

Chapter Twenty-Eight

LUNA

MY BODY TINGLED FROM EDON'S INTRUSION. Not in a bad way, but a good one, leaving me a little breathless beside him. And needy.

He remained utterly still, his eyes closed as if in slumber, but I felt his alertness. Our bond wasn't yet complete, but I felt it lingering, the call from his wolf to mine to finish our link at the next full moon.

All it would take was a single bite—of my teeth into his skin.

Not all alphas required it, their initial claim enough to force a female into the mating link. But I knew Edon wanted more, could hear it now that he'd opened the gate and allowed me inside.

Every part of him was free for me to explore, while my own emotions and thoughts remained locked up behind a wall of steel that he couldn't access without the completion of our bond.

But his mind was now mine, and what a fascinating place to be.

I could sense Silas there, his sire bond strong and thriving.

I also picked up notes of his confused feelings, how he desired us both on a painfully equal level. Edon questioned it, wondering how to make it work, and my overreaction only added to his overall confusion.

He thought I was jealous of Silas. And maybe, to an extent, I was, but not entirely. When I thought he preferred his progeny, I felt left out more than anything else. Worthless, too, as if my entire purpose to him was soiled and wrong.

Then he'd explained his intentions.

Such a waste of time and energy.

In roughly thirty minutes, his body appeared healed—at least on the outside—because of our link. *So take that, stubborn wolf. Thinking I couldn't handle it, or didn't want to help. Idiot.*

His lips curled. "I may not be able to hear you, Luna, but I can sense your emotions." His voice sounded clear, his throat and jaw fully mended. And when he glanced at me, I noticed the lack of swelling in his facial features, his handsome face completely unmarred. "You're feeling smug."

"With good reason." I lifted my head onto my palm while remaining on my side and facing him without touching. "How are you feeling, Edon?"

"Relaxed." He rotated his head on the pillow, his eyes holding mine. "Warm."

We stared at each other like that for a long moment, peace floating between us. Everything just felt so right. The way my vitality hummed through my veins to his in effortless silence, lulling us into a state of perpetual tranquility.

"Kiss me," he whispered.

Not a request so much as a demand.

He was an alpha, after all.

I smiled. "You want me? Come get me."

His pupils flared with interest. "You going to make me run, little mate?"

I nearly laughed. "Another day, maybe. Right now, I'll settle for you shifting off your back." Seemed like a good place to start since he hadn't moved in what felt like hours.

"Are you doubting my ability to fuck you, Luna?" he asked, one eyebrow lifting. "Because I assure you, that won't be a problem."

"Who said anything about fucking? All you wanted was a kiss."

"If you're going to make me work for it, then I'll return the favor in kind." He moved before I could reply, his big body stationary one second and on top of me the next.

A breath pushed from my lungs in surprise not only at his show of strength but also at the speed with which he reacted. "*Fuck*," I breathed.

"Yeah, that's the idea," he murmured, his hips settling between my splayed thighs. "Now kiss me, little mate."

His lips were a hairsbreadth from mine, his body radiating heat and bathing me in a sea of lust I couldn't deny.

So I didn't.

I kissed him. Not sweetly, not quietly, but passionately, and adored the growl he gave me in return. It rumbled from his chest to mine, a possessive sound that immediately soaked my inner thighs in my readiness.

My wolf submitted on instinct, the much stronger alpha taking control of my mouth with his tongue. I moaned, the wanton rush of lust flooding my every thought.

I was so lost to him.

To his touch.

To his presence.

To his very existence.

The forced fate I'd dwelled on most of my life gave way to a fervor unlike anything I could have anticipated.

I wanted Edon. *Badly.*

And I allowed him to feel that by pressing my aching heat into his hard shaft. He groaned, the sound coming from deep in his abdomen and exciting my need. "Edon," I whispered, arching into him again.

"I thought you just wanted a kiss," he teased, nipping my lower lip and kissing a path to my ear. "Aren't you worried I can't perform?"

"The throbbing cock pressing into my pussy says you'll be just fine," I replied, swallowing thickly.

"Mmm, I don't know." He licked the column of my neck, tasting the perspiration dotting my skin and leaving me shaking beneath him. "Maybe you should be on top, little mate."

I shuddered, the image of mounting him in my own way destroying my ability to think or respond.

Because yes. *Fuck* yes. I wanted that more than I wanted to breathe.

And somehow he knew.

He rolled onto his back, taking me with him, his hands on my hips. I straddled him on impulse, keeping my sex against his, my body trembling with unrestrained desire.

"Take me," he encouraged, his fingers tugging on the shirt I still wore. "But remove this. I want to watch every move as you fuck me, Luna. Every moan, every bounce, every pant will be mine."

Oh, dear wolf, he's going to destroy me.

I slowly removed his old shirt from my body, tossing it to the floor below, and licked my lips. His predatory grin had me quivering, the promise in his gaze one I intended to fulfill.

"Scared?" he taunted.

"Terrified," I whispered. It wasn't a lie. Because this feeling stirring in my chest? Yeah, that scared me. But I couldn't stop myself from lifting and taking him inside me, from rocking my hips against his and growling his name low and long from my throat.

This was a gift.

One I cherished more than he would ever know.

The offering of freedom, to express my alpha instincts and take what I wanted from the strong male below.

Most females in my position were never offered such an experience, the males preferring to dominate in every form of the word. But Edon remained still, his body strung tight with the effort of allowing another to dictate the pace and ride him.

A tear slipped from the edge of my eye, one he caught with his thumb before wrapping his palm around the back of my neck and bringing me down for a knowing kiss. Maybe he did understand the gravity of what he offered, which only endeared him to me more.

"Edon," I whispered.

"Shh." He licked the seam of my mouth. "Devour me, little mate. Make me yours."

And I did; with every lick, nip, and kiss, I claimed him. *Mine.* The only thing I didn't do was bite—an act I would save for the next full moon, when it truly counted.

My stomach burned, my thighs shaking.

An orgasm hovered on the horizon, the kind that would demolish my ability to think and, likely, my inclination to breathe.

But I chased it anyway, rising and falling onto him, driving him deeper, and moaning every time my clit rubbed him the right way.

Oh, how I needed more.

I picked up the pace, sweat dripping from us both, but it wasn't enough. I whimpered, collapsing against him, my lips kissing his jaw. My body convulsed almost painfully, the hint of rapture so close yet so far.

Edon threaded his fingers through my hair, bringing me back for a kiss, his opposite hand flattening on my lower back. His bottom half bucked into mine, causing me to gasp against his mouth. Fuck, not even full strength and the man could move.

I caved to his prowess, luxuriating in his skill.

Being on top provided me with the confidence associated with control, but with each stroke upward, he redefined the meaning of *alpha.* So much poise, so much power, so much *perfection.*

One of his palms remained on the back of my head while the other slid from my spine to my side and then to my stomach and downward.

The rough pad of his finger flicked my swollen nub, exactly how I needed it, and sent me cascading over the falls into a whirlpool of ecstasy. His name careened from my mouth, only to be swallowed by his as he caressed me through the intense waves of pleasure. Each one rippled over me, driving me to the edge of the earth and back again. I panted, whined, gasped, each noise consumed by Edon as his tongue fucked my mouth with expert skill.

I barely noticed my back hitting the mattress, or the male driving into the apex between my thighs.

All I could think was, *This is heaven.* With Edon blanketing me in his primal heat, I never wanted to move again. Except my hips still rose to meet his thrusts, my limbs vibrating beneath the onslaught of increased pressure in my lower abdomen, as another spiral of oblivion overwhelmed my senses and covered me in goose bumps.

Fuck…

It wasn't even my orgasm that had hit me, but Edon's. He'd left the link open, showering me in his sensations and pulling me into the euphoric black hole with him. And shit, it was hot. Sensual. Amazing.

He gave me everything.

His excitement.

His dominance.

His overwhelming urge to take me all over again as soon as he finished shaking.

His craving for darker pleasures.

I shivered, intrigued by the ideas flooding his thoughts—ideas he didn't hide from me. He wanted to take me in every way, mark me as his so no one else could touch me.

Except Silas.

I saw him in those fantasies, too. Edon liked the three of us together. No, he more than liked it. He *yearned* for it. Even now I could sense him communicating to Silas, but I couldn't hear them. Their link remained separate from the one I shared with Edon. However, I sensed Silas humming words into the alpha's thoughts—words Edon seemed to be returning.

"What is he saying?" I asked, my thighs still pillowing Edon's waist.

"That he wants to sleep on the couch," Edon replied, his lips against my neck. He lifted onto his elbows, his gaze warm as he studied my face. "He seems to think you'll be uncomfortable if he joins us, so he's ignoring my command."

Part of me wanted to grin at the latter part of that sentence, but the former captivated my interest. "Why would I be uncomfortable?"

"You tell me, little mate." He combed his fingers through my hair. "Are you okay with Silas joining us?"

"What would you do if I said no?" I wondered out loud. "Would you deny him?"

He swallowed, his eyes flicking to the headboard before slowly returning to my face. "If it is the desire of my mate, yes. I think I would have to."

My eyebrows actually rose. "You would choose me over him?" For some reason, that didn't elate me the way I had expected it to. Actually, it had the opposite impact. "You can't do that to Silas."

He chuckled. "I didn't say I wanted to, Luna. I won't lie to you. I want him as badly as I want you, but your comfort is important to me. Just as it is to him. If you don't desire him in our bed, then he wouldn't want to join us. Which leaves me little choice but to respect both of your wishes."

I blinked. "You're not at all who I expected you to be."

"Considering you were anticipating a male like my father or your father, I'm going to take that as a compliment." He drew his thumb along my jaw, his eyes tracing the movement. "What should I tell Silas?"

"To get his ass in here," I replied without hesitation. "Why the hell would he sleep on the couch?"

His lips curled. "It's as if you can read my mind, darling Luna. Because I said the exact same thing to him." He kissed me deeply, his cock slowly sliding from my body. "Mmm, fucking you might be my new favorite activity, but Silas needs some relief."

"I'm fine," he replied from the side of the room, his lithe form leaning against the doorjamb in a pair of jeans. Water beaded across his naked torso, his hair damp from what I assumed was a recent shower. He must have taken one after his run of the perimeter.

"Prove it," Edon murmured, slipping off of me to the side. He gathered my body against him, spooning me with his chest to my back so we both faced the entryway. Edon lifted himself onto his elbow while his opposite palm ran over my stomach and downward to the evidence of our fucking. "Come here, Silas."

The other male narrowed his gaze but walked into the room and shut the door with his heel. He must have said something to Edon, because the alpha chuckled behind me. The vibration coupled with the finger gliding through my folds had my throat drying too much for me to speak.

Not that I knew what to say.

A moan seemed more appropriate, especially with the way Silas's gaze tracked Edon's movements. He gripped my thigh and guided my limb backward to rest over his legs, thereby spreading me wide for Silas's view.

"Doesn't she have a gorgeous pussy?" the alpha asked softly, his lips near my ear as his hand returned to my center.

Silas visibly swallowed. "Yes."

"But you're *fine*, right?" Edon dipped two fingers into me, penetrating me deep. "Take off your jeans, Silas. Show us how *fine* you are."

His glower deepened, those blue eyes darkening to a midnight-blue shade as he unbuttoned and unzipped his pants.

Both males were equally endowed and beautiful in their own rights, but Silas's shaft was slimmer and longer, while Edon's was thicker and almost harsher. Somehow, both cocks were appropriate to each man.

And I found myself thirsting for them both despite having just gotten off with Edon inside me.

Silas kicked his jeans off to the side, his hands on his hips. "Satisfied?"

"Me? Very." Edon circled my clit with his thumb, his entire hand seeming to explore the dampness between my thighs. "But you look uncomfortable, Silas. Maybe we can help with that. Unless you're still *fine*."

I squirmed as Silas knelt on the bed, his heat and presence an aphrodisiac to my senses. *Yes, please,* my wolf whispered.

"Lie down beside Luna," Edon instructed him, the authority in his voice leaving no room for argument. It was as if he hadn't just survived a near-life-threatening beating at all, like he wasn't still in the process of healing. Although, I felt him pulling on my reserves, just a little, to foster his recovery. He might be in charge again, but he wasn't at full strength. He was just an alpha with a hell of a lot of ego.

For good reason, I thought, smiling as Silas lay down beside me. "Hi," I whispered.

"Hi," he replied, giving me a much softer look than the one he'd given

Edon. I sighed as he leaned in to kiss me, his lips soft and warm and coaxing against mine. Never rushed, just all Silas—tasting and mesmerizing.

Edon removed his touch, eliciting a whimper from me that Silas overpowered on a growl.

"*Fuck*, Edon," he groaned, arching in a way that removed his mouth from mine.

And I could see why.

Edon had grabbed Silas's shaft and was stroking him—using the combined juices of our arousal for lubrication.

That was why he'd touched me so completely, to coat his palm in the aftermath of our lovemaking and paint Silas's cock with it.

My thighs tensed, heat pooling in my lower abdomen. Because wow, that was hot. And Silas seemed to approve as well, his eyes closing on a guttural sound as Edon twisted his grip over the head.

Who knew watching a male jack off another man could be so damn arousing?

Or maybe it was just watching these two interact, while sandwiched in the middle, that turned my blood to boiling lava.

Didn't matter.

I was lost to the moment, my eyes glued to Edon's hand and the rhythm he set. Not harsh or fast, but firm and knowing. Silas's muscles tensed, his abdomen a riddle of ridges I wanted to explore with my tongue.

"He's close, little mate," Edon murmured against my ear. "Do you want to slide down so he can come in your mouth? Or should I let him come all over your sweet cunt and have him lick you clean?"

Silas responded with an unintelligible noise, his eyes fluttering as his body began to convulse.

"Hmm, seems he decided for you." Edon nibbled my neck, his warmth a blanket against my back as Silas erupted against my folds, coating me in his seed. "Isn't he beautiful?"

I nodded. "Yes." He truly was, with his golden hair falling in waves to his ears, his neck straining from his tensed jaw, and his athletic form bulging with strength.

But it was the growl coming from him I adored most of all. So primal and masculine and utterly fascinating. Mmm, I wanted to hear him do that against my ear.

His eyelids lifted to reveal gorgeous blue irises, slightly unfocused from pleasure. "Fuck, Luna, keep looking at me like that and I'll come again."

Edon chuckled, his lips caressing my throat. "I think you should clean her up first. With your tongue."

Silas shuddered, then leaned in to brush his mouth against mine, his palm falling to my hip. "Did we make a mess, little moon?" He nuzzled my nose, his breath hot against my parted lips. "Do you want me to lick it all up? Or should I massage it into your flesh and mark you as ours?"

Bold words.

But they were met with approval from the male behind me. I *felt* it through our mating bond. He liked Silas laying claim to me. Just as he enjoyed sharing us both.

"Tell him what you want," Edon encouraged, his voice deep. "Tell *us* how to serve you, little mate."

He kissed my neck while Silas took my mouth, leaving me unable to reply between them. Not that I knew what I desired. I couldn't choose. I wanted both.

And when I finally had an opportunity to voice that out loud, both males chuckled. Edon's palm dipped between my legs, his fingers sliding through my folds and mixing our arousals together as one, then brought his hand up for both Silas and me to lick.

No words were exchanged.

Just feelings.

Our bodies moving as one—a joining of instinct alone.

I lost track of who touched whom, whose mouth belonged to whom, and just indulged in the sensations. All the while, I felt Edon's gentle tug against my strength, his body still healing despite his outward prowess.

And eventually, after much petting and pleasure, the three of us fell into a slumber.

Where I dreamt of a future about a trio of wolves who lived happily ever after.

Only to be eaten alive by society's rules…

Chapter Twenty-Nine

Silas

THE GUESTS ARE ARRIVING, I told Edon as I observed from the perimeter.

Car after car traveled down the gravel path toward the heart of the Clemente Clan territory. Inside were a mix of elite wolves and vampires, all here to witness tonight's full-moon ceremony.

Electricity danced across my fur coat, every part of me vigilant.

Tonight was Walter's last chance to stop Edon's ascension.

And the last two and a half weeks had been far too quiet for my liking.

His father had to be planning something because no way did he just give up after the strength test. Not after everything he'd pulled. Instead, he'd left the three of us on high alert waiting for an attack that never came.

Which meant we were all exhausted.

Something I suspected was the point.

Anything out of the ordinary? Edon asked.

Other than the fact that I'm the only one guarding the perimeter right now? Not really, no.

Edon was silent for a long moment before saying, *They're up to something.*

I know. Because last month, there were twenty of us on perimeter duty. Tonight? None. I wasn't even technically assigned to be out here. But my loyalty to Edon and Luna put me right where I needed to be.

We have an hour before we begin. I want you nearby when it all starts.

I'll be there. The confirmation really wasn't necessary, and neither was his demand, but they added to the formality of today.

We'd fallen into a dangerous rhythm these last few weeks, one where I'd begun to hold a much more powerful place in Edon's life. Tonight, however, he had reverted me to my place as his progeny.

No, actually, that wasn't quite right. I'd played the part of progeny at last month's full-moon ceremony. No one had spoken to me or acknowledged me, apart from my old friend Rae, whom I'd secretly spoken to during the opening reception. And Edon had treated me as if I didn't exist.

Nothing about tonight compared to my last experience.

Because I had Edon in my head. In my blood. In my very soul.

He'd also put me on protection duty not just for him but for Luna, too.

So no, this was nothing like the first ritual.

I had much more to lose this time.

And yet, I would be losing everything tonight regardless. Because Luna and Edon were about to finalize their mating bond. Once Luna bit him beneath the moon, he would become hers irrevocably, thereby sealing the connection he created a month ago.

Leaving me on the outside looking in.

Again.

My tail twitched, my ears flattening. Part of me wanted to celebrate with them, while the other part of me felt incredibly alone. I knew this was all meant to be temporary, but the last few weeks had been among the best of my life. Which was saying something beneath the shroud of stress.

I enjoyed being with Luna and Edon. A lot. And not just in a sexual sense. They just felt right, like they could be my home.

Which was crazy.

I had no home.

Only temporary beds.

I just happened to favor the one I'd slept in last night most of all. With Luna's head on my shoulder and Edon's arm around her waist, it'd been heaven. Only, I'd awoken this morning to reality shining down on me in the face of a coming moon.

Edon had provided a temporary distraction by having Luna go down on me while he fucked her from behind. He hadn't taken her ass yet—neither of us had—but I knew he would soon. After learning about her lack of real experience, he decided to ease her into it with my help. And while I loved being involved, something told me I wouldn't be there for the eventual climax.

Just an instinct.

A whisper of fate.

In the shape of a full-blown orb over my head.

I gazed up at it, my nose twitching at the growing stench of the undead descending upon our property. Rather than brooding, I should be checking the other boundaries, searching for anything untoward.

Luna and Edon were counting on me, and I refused to let them down.

The problem was, I had no idea what to look for. With all these foreign scents and the heightening energy in—

My instincts flared, the distinct sound of a branch snapping to my left drawing my focus. One of the vehicles had stopped, pulling to the side of the road while all the others had continued onward. It left only me and the unknown entity inside alone on the perimeter.

Something that couldn't be a coincidence.

My suspicions were confirmed the second the door opened and a male in a black suit stepped onto the gravel path.

Dark eyes flashed beneath the pale moon, zeroing in on my location within the trees. "Silas," the royal vampire said, his voice easily carrying to my ears.

I shivered.

That he recognized me in wolf form after only one previous meeting spoke of his intense power. Not that I ever doubted it.

Kylan was notorious, after all.

Violent. Ruthless. Cruel.

And mated to one of my only friends.

He stepped aside, holding the door to his black car open, and arched a brow. Apparently, he considered that an invitation. Rae popped her head out with a frown. "Where is he?" she asked.

My lips curled. I missed that voice. Hell, I missed *her*.

And Willow.

We used to be so close, but it felt like a lifetime ago. A memory consisting of false dreams and hopes that were all slaughtered by the reality we now resided in.

Kylan nodded up in my direction. "He's playing in wolf form at the moment. Shall we bark at him? Maybe that'll encourage him to move faster."

I snorted. *Asshole.*

Excuse me? Edon replied.

That was meant for Kylan, not you.

Kylan? he repeated. *As in the most lethal vampire in the world?*

I shifted while saying, *The very one. He's summoning me.*

What? His concern radiated through our link as I looked around for the pants I'd purposely carried here in case I needed to be in human form. Although, this wasn't one of the scenarios I'd originally anticipated. Not that I minded.

It's fine. I told him about how Kylan arranged for Rae and me to speak during the last full moon, and felt Edon's shock through our link.

For once, the alpha was speechless. Good thing, too. I only had enough room to handle one dominant personality, and I needed all of my focus to approach the royal standing by the car.

He wore a suit—something that I assumed was standard issue for all vampires. While his relaxed position against the car appeared unthreatening, I knew better.

Rae peered out at me as I approached, her beautiful face lighting up in relief. She practically leapt out of the car and directly into my arms. If it bothered the royal, he didn't show it. He merely observed with a stoic expression, his boredom palpable.

"You're okay," Rae whispered, her hands running over my bare arms like a mother checking her child. She checked every inch of my torso as if needing to convince herself that I wasn't hurt.

I chuckled. "You've gotten rather handsy, Rae. That professor from our socialization course would be so thrilled."

She startled, then laughed. "Hey, I aced that course."

"With my help," I reminded her.

"Yeah, yeah." She scoffed, then smiled. "I've missed you."

"Likewise." I hugged her again, this time without all the petting, and sighed against her hair. "It's good to see you." I had no idea how much I needed this embrace—how much I longed for my friend—until she arrived.

Emotions welled up inside me.

Abandonment.

Confusion.

Loyalty.

Adoration.

Loneliness.

"What's wrong?" Rae whispered, pulling back to study my face. She palmed my cheek, her gaze flickering between my eyes. "What have they done to you?"

"Might I suggest we return to the car?" Kylan said, his focus on the empty road ahead. "I would rather we not draw undue attention."

A soft beam of light appeared on the tail end of those words, indicating another approaching vehicle.

Rae slid back inside first.

Kylan gestured for me to follow.

My neck hummed with awareness as I adhered to his unspoken command, then my blood chilled as he joined us inside the stretched-out car. There were two benches—Rae and Kylan took one, while I took the seat across from them.

A tap on the roof sent the car into drive, navigating us toward the heart of the territory.

"Arriving with you is going to inspire questions," I noted dryly.

I must have telegraphed that to Edon, because he immediately replied with, *Oh, I have several for you.*

Later, I replied. *For when I'm not sitting across from a royal vampire.*

Apprehensiveness tingled through the bond, Edon's worry for my safety a warmth I rather liked.

I promise I'm fine, I told him. *Focus on Luna and the ceremony.*

"Are you talking to your new alpha?" Kylan asked, interest coloring his features as he wrapped an arm around Rae's shoulders. His fingers danced over the strap of her red dress—a color that matched her striking auburn hair.

I met his knowing gaze and decided lying to him would not go over well. "Yes. I am."

He nodded, his approval palpable. "That's an intriguing development. It's not common for an alpha to care about his progeny. At least, not anymore."

"What do you mean?" Rae interjected.

"In the old society, alphas took exquisite care of their made lycans. But in today's world, those in power are no longer expected to care for the young. And lycans, especially, prefer to create offspring through fucking rather than gifting immortality to an adult mortal."

He spoke with such stoicism, as if his words meant nothing at all. And maybe they didn't—*to him*. But they meant everything to me.

"Edon's not common," I said, realizing the error in my statement the second it left my lips. "What I mean is, he's a decent alpha. And he was checking in with me on security." Not exactly a lie. It just happened to be my personal security he was worried about more than the perimeter.

Kylan smirked. "Sure." His gaze glittered beneath the dim light overhead. "He seems to be taking excellent care of you. Based on your increased muscle mass and general health, I mean."

I swallowed. His astuteness and candor unnerved me. And I didn't know how to respond.

Fortunately, Rae did. "Shouldn't he look healthier? He's a lycan now."

"Most don't survive the turning these days," Kylan replied, his eyes not leaving mine. "Nor are they cared for afterward."

She snorted. "Why am I not surprised?"

Kylan grinned down at her—finally giving me a reprieve—and stroked her pulse with his thumb. "Because you're learning, Raelyn." He kissed her before she could reply, the move a strike that had my hands curling into fists.

Too fast.

Too harsh.

And fuck, I didn't want to smell my friend's responding arousal. But I was trapped in this very small space while he devoured her as if I wasn't seated across from them.

She squirmed, a protest sliding from her lips as he kissed a path down her neck and slid his fangs into her flesh. "Kylan…" His name came out on a chastising groan that had me swallowing across from them.

I'd seen Rae fake pleasure countless times in class.

This wasn't fake. At all.

My stomach churned, my heart skipping a beat. This was not how I wanted to see my childhood friend. Ever.

You have a lot of explaining to do, Edon growled into my head.

Yeah, I suspected I did. Although, it wasn't like my past came up much in conversation. He was more focused on the present and future, not my years at the university.

Kylan released Rae with a dark chuckle, leaving her winded and gazing up at him in confusion. "That should buy you about twenty minutes of privacy," he said, nuzzling her chin before nipping her bottom lip.

"Wh-what?" she asked, her chest heaving as she blinked several times.

He focused on me, his hand going to the door beside me. "Twenty minutes, Silas. Then I'm coming back for my consort. Be advised, allowing her to stay in a confined space with another male isn't something I enjoy. I suggest you not give me any reason to be even more uncomfortable. Understand?"

The car rolled to a stop beside yet another royal vampire—Jace. And beside him was a dark-haired female wearing what appeared to be a lingerie-style gown.

"Silence does not appease me, Silas," Kylan pressed. "Shall I repeat my concerns?"

"She's one of my best friends," I bit back, my irritation getting the best of me. "Your Highness," I added, hoping to temper my statement at least a little.

He grinned. "Edon looks good on you, young wolf. As does Luna." He twisted the handle before I could reply, then glanced back at Rae. "Pull yourself back together and meet me outside." The chill in his tone whipped through the car, but he winked at her before stepping out into the night. He slammed the door behind him and pulled a handkerchief from his pocket to dab his mouth before addressing the royal standing outside. "She's a work in progress."

"I see that," Jace replied, his lips going to the neck of the beauty beside him. "As is Juliet. Isn't that right, sweetheart?"

She didn't lift her eyes from her shoes but nodded stiffly. "Yes, Your Highness."

"Does her presence here mean Darius is nearby?" Kylan asked as the pair began walking.

"Yes, he's mingling with Luka and Mira somewhere."

"Ah, of course he is," Kylan murmured, his voice still strong in my ears despite his growing distance.

One perk of being a wolf? Fantastic hearing.

Just as I could hear Rae's heart beating a mile a minute in her chest. "Are you all right?" I asked.

She swallowed and nodded. "Yeah. Just. Yeah." She cleared her throat. "He's just… Kylan."

"And he's treating you okay?" I looked pointedly at the wound on her neck. "Because that looks like it hurts."

She laughed. "Trust me, it doesn't. He just got me all hot and, well, anyway. Biting is fine. It was his way of giving me a cover story for my absence so we could talk, and we're wasting time. How are you really?"

"I could ask you the same question. That's one hell of a cover story, Rae."

"As I said, he's Kylan. The only thing he's guilty of is making me crave more, which, I suspect, was the point. He's a territorial asshole like that, and you're sort of a button for him."

"Me?" I almost laughed. "A button? How?"

"He knows we used to, you know, for class. And for a while, he used your fate over my head because he thought I loved you as more than a friend."

My eyebrows shot up. "*What?*"

"It's neither here nor there, and you're deflecting," she accused. "Talk to me, Silas. What's going on?"

I blew out a breath and rubbed my palm over my face, shaking my head. "There's not enough time for me to tell you everything."

"So summarize it."

"It's really nothing. I'm just glad to see you, Rae. That's all."

Her icy blue eyes narrowed. "I can smell your lie. I can also smell Edon and Luna on you."

"Really?" My brow furrowed. *Since when could vampires scent lies?* "I thought baby vampires could hardly sense anything at all. And how do you know it's Edon and Luna?"

"Because my link to Kylan isn't, uh, typical."

I knew the circumstances surrounding her turning weren't exactly normal, but I thought that had more to do with politics than with the physical change. "How so?"

"We're not talking about me right now, Silas. We're talking about you. Why do you smell like the alpha heir and his new mate? And what's with the morose energy you were oozing earlier? It's not like you."

Ah, typical Rae, refusing to let me off easy. I sighed again. Deflecting her questions would only make her more suspicious and fight harder for an answer. And I didn't have the energy to fend her off. Besides, if I could talk to anyone, it was Rae. She knew me better than most, with the exception of maybe Willow.

My heart gave a pang at the memory of our lost friend. She was either already dead or wishing for death. I preferred to think of her as the former; it was less painful than the alternative.

Giving my head another shake, I met Rae's gaze and told her a short version of everything that had happened since my turning. If anything, it would be nice to have another ally on our side, someone to keep an eye on the surroundings and maybe clue me in on anything her new vampiric senses picked up on.

She remained eerily still while I spoke, her expression giving nothing away even as I explained my recent sleeping arrangements—with two alphas. I didn't give her specifics, but she read between the lines.

And I ended with a summary of Walter's exploits.

That reddened her cheeks. "What a dick," she said.

I laughed out loud. "Oh, Rae, I've missed your version of a filter."

"What? He sounds like an ass."

"You're not wrong," I admitted. "But it's left us all a little on edge for tonight."

She nodded thoughtfully. "And you're not on edge at all about the fact that the two wolves you've fallen for are mating each other—without you."

I blinked. "That's not, I mean, I care about them, sure, but they're supposed to be together. Whatever is happening with me is temporary."

"What you described doesn't sound all that temporary to me." She cocked her head. "I'm pretty sure Kylan would tell you it's downright uncommon."

"Same could be said about a harem member being turned into a vampire consort."

"Touché, but again, we're talking about you, not me." Some of her fiery personality surfaced with that comment. "You can admit to me how you feel, Silas. I won't judge you."

"I'm not afraid of you judging me, Rae. It's just a fact of life I have to accept. Edon and Luna are alpha mates. That doesn't involve me at all."

"Except you were roaming the perimeter and searching for threats—to protect them."

"As is my job as his progeny."

"And their lover," she added. "Don't discount what you are just because there's not a proper term for it." Her smile was sad. "I might be a vampire now, but I still know you, Silas. You've always been amazing at hiding your feelings. That small slip in your facade tells me just how exhausted you are. You never slip."

I allowed my head to fall back onto the headrest behind me, my throat tightening. "It's been an enlightening few weeks, Rae."

"Months," she corrected. "And I agree."

"It was all bullshit," I continued, allowing some of my anger to slip free. "All of it. The grandeur, the promises of immortality—it was all *bullshit.*" Fuck, how many people did I kill in the Immortal Cup? Six? And the problem was, I would have killed them all for the future I thought waited for me on the other side. People I knew. And how messed up was that? "It makes me so angry, Rae. So fucking angry."

She reached across to grab my hand and gave it a squeeze. "I know how you feel."

"Do you?" I asked, laughing humorously. "I suppose you do. Kylan, huh?"

Her lips quirked up. "He's not as bad as you think."

I snorted. "That wound on your neck says otherwise."

"Don't worry. I'll bite him back later."

"How does that work?" I wondered out loud. "You're both vampires. Don't you need human blood?"

Some of her amusement faded into a secretive expression. "Like I said, my turning wasn't exactly common."

I opened my mouth to press that comment, when an approaching scent tickled my nose. *Death.* Not the same perfume Kylan and Rae wore, but one similar to the putrid stench I kept picking up near the borders over the last month.

Except we were nowhere near the border now.

No, we were in the heart of Clemente Clan territory.

I glanced out the windows, searching for the source, everything falling silent in the car. Rae must have picked up on my alertness, because she didn't say anything but instead glanced around, too.

"Vampires," she whispered. "A lot of them."

"Yeah," I agreed, searching the darkness with my wolf vision.

The door flew open, causing me to scramble back as Kylan appeared. "Come, Raelyn." He held out a hand. "Now."

She didn't hesitate, a palpable energy shifting between them.

"Warn your alpha heir, Silas," Kylan said, his voice laced with command. "A war is coming your way. And it seems the Silvano Clan is out for blood."

Chapter Thirty

LUNA

EVERYTHING FELT WRONG. The moon. The air. This ridiculous dress my mother brought me to wear. The way Edon wouldn't stop pacing. The hairs dancing along the back of my neck.

The fact that Silas isn't here… I swallowed, my eyes closing. *He should be here with us.*

No one could hear me but myself, and yet I knew Edon felt the same, could hear my thought echoing in his own.

Since opening the link between us a few weeks ago, neither of us had sought to close it. If anything, he'd only widened the entrance, allowing me unfettered access to his mind at all times. It was Edon's method of establishing trust, something I very much appreciated because I never had to guess at his intentions.

Annoyance radiated off him in waves, coupled with concern and a slight hint of fear.

Not for us, but for Silas.

Rae—the infamous harem member turned vampire—was apparently an old friend of his. Something he'd failed to mention to me and Edon.

Which had me questioning how much Silas trusted us.

A ridiculous thought, really. I knew how he felt, could sense it in his every touch. And Edon could *sense* his emotions.

No, it wasn't about trust at all. Silas just hadn't mentioned it, or really much about his past. We were all so focused on the present, on what Walter would do next.

I opened my eyes to find Edon watching me, his expression sheltered. "Almost time," he said softly.

"I know." The moon's energy slithered across my skin, making me thankful Edon chose this location to prepare. We were very alone here on his grandfather's private porch, hiding us from the flurry of activity in town. Jolene had gone on ahead saying he wanted to have a word with an old friend. We suspected he meant a member of the quiet resistance, but we were too concerned with our own fates to press it.

Edon cupped my cheek, his opposite hand falling to my hip, where his thumb stroked the silk fabric of my gown. "After tonight, we can begin anew."

I leaned into his touch. "Yes." I just wish I knew what that would entail. Everything had seemed so right these last few weeks with Edon and Silas, but tonight would change everything. The foreboding nature of it weighed against my spine, leaving me unnerved.

"You feel it, too," he whispered. "That something's missing."

"Silas," I said.

He nodded. "Yeah."

"He should be here."

Another nod. "Do you want me to call him?"

"I don't know." Would it make it better? Or would it feel like goodbye? Because I wasn't ready for that. Somehow, in some way, that wolf had gotten under my skin nearly as deeply as Edon had. Almost as if that bite he'd bestowed upon me was a claiming. Except I knew that was impossible. Only bites beneath the full moon ended in a mating.

Edon brushed a kiss against my lips before pressing his forehead to mine. "This isn't the end, little mate."

"Then why does it feel that way?" I asked, swallowing. "Why do I feel like everything's about to change?"

He sighed, his minty breath mingling with mine. "Because it is. But that doesn't mean it's an end so much as a new beginning."

"Without Silas."

"We don't know that."

"No. I think we both know exactly that," I argued, pulling back to stare up at him. "My bite will connect us irrevocably. Forever. It'll override your sire bond."

"But not delete it."

True. "It'll supersede it," I clarified. "Which isn't fair to Silas."

On that, he didn't have an argument. I saw it in his gaze.

"Forcing him to remain with us will be cruel," I added, swallowing. "You know that as well as I do. He'll never be an equal."

"He was never meant to be our equal, Luna." He lifted his touch from my hip to my cheek, cradling my face between his palms. "We're alphas. We're meant to mate. Silas…" He trailed off, his expression pained.

"He's not an omega," I whispered.

"I know."

"But he's not an alpha either," I admitted, my stomach churning. "Staying with him… Edon, it'll hurt him."

"I know," he repeated, his gaze falling.

"I don't want to hurt him."

He pressed his lips to mine again, this time the kiss lingering as if he needed a moment to gather his thoughts. But as he met my gaze once more, I knew what he planned to say.

We need to let him go.

It's for his own good.

Even if it kills us to do it.

However, none of those comments left his mouth. Instead, he froze, his hands going rigid against my skin.

And then I smelled it.

The rancid stench of death. Everywhere.

I couldn't look over his shoulder to survey our surroundings because he held me too tightly. Yet I *felt* the incoming wave of power.

This was more than a few royal vampires and their sovereigns.

An army approached.

Edon shoved me through the door of his grandfather's home, causing me to stumble into a nearby chair on a curse. And then he was shifting.

Snarls ripped from Edon's mouth as he charged toward the tree line that led to the main camp, leaving a command behind in my skull. *Stay.*

Fuck that, I thought back at him. Not that he could hear me. Not that anyone could hear anything over the sound of war in the backyard.

I took off after him, my gown disappearing in my wake as I called to my wolf.

My paws sprinted over the earth, my senses heightening with each growing second.

So many vampires. Rage. Blood. The need for a fight.

It shivered down my spine, stirring a pool of dread in my lower belly.

This was the final test—the one Walter had set up for Edon to fail. I felt it in every bone of my being, knew what he desired.

My mate's death.

Not on my watch, I thought, pushing myself faster than ever before as I followed Edon's trail.

War cries littered the air, followed by howls.

I paused on the outskirts, my eyes going wide at the onslaught of chaos.

Hundreds of vampires had encircled the camp, their attack imminent.

Walter stood in the middle of them, squaring off against their leader—Silvano—an old-as-fuck vampire known for his temper.

Shit…

"I've sanctioned no such activities," Walter growled, his words echoing off the surrounding lodges. Wolves paced around him, but they were well outnumbered by the army of undead.

Edon joined him, walking into the circle on two legs while pulling up a pair of jeans he'd retrieved from somewhere. I crept up to the side of one of the houses to watch, my coat shivering beneath the wave of violent energy stirring in the air.

"What the fuck is going on?" Edon demanded.

"Silvano thinks we've been hunting and slaying vampires on our land," Walter said, folding his arms. "Something we all know I'd never sanction."

Oh, shit…

This all tied back to the first trial.

The one with the dead vampire body.

The body Edon had disposed of.

"I see." Silvano gestured for two of his suit-clad vampires to step forward, one of whom held a bag. He dumped the contents onto the lawn—a collection of heads. "These say otherwise, Walter. Go ahead, take a whiff. They reek of your mutts."

My ears flattened, shock coursing through my system.

Edon merely folded his arms, mimicking his father's stance. "Then we have a problem in our clan, one I'll solve as soon as I ascend."

His father snorted a laugh. "How quaint." He turned to his son, eyes narrowing. "And so very coincidental."

"Took the words right out of my mouth," Edon replied, not looking the least bit ruffled. "If I didn't know better, I'd say this is all part of your fucked-up alpha trials. Well, you're too late, old man. I'm ready and I'm ascending, with or without your approval."

"So, what? You orchestrated all this to belittle my legacy? To taint my reputation?"

Edon's lips twitched. "We both know I don't have the support in this clan to pull off something like that."

"Oh, no?" Walter feigned surprise. "Maybe we should put that theory to the test." He glanced around while Silvano observed in stoic silence, his vampires all poised and ready for battle. One signal from him and chaos would begin, but he held off.

Because this was all for show.

The realization hit me as soon as Walter asked, "Who among you had a hand in this?" He glanced around, his gaze astute. "My guess is my son promised you something in return for framing me in this madness. That'll be hard for him to accomplish if he doesn't ascend this year. I implore you to step forward with the truth now, or risk an uncertain future, as my son has."

Bastard.

He planned all of this.

And that thought was confirmed as two males gingerly slunk forward, eyes averted.

"Forgive us, sir," one of them said, his voice low. "But E-Edon said it was sanctioned, that w-we were paying back a debt."

"H-he claimed it was done with Si-Silvano's approval," the other whispered.

Silence fell.

A hum of anger stroked my fur.

And then Edon laughed. "I can't believe you've let him manipulate you this way." He shook his head, still grinning. "You're both imbeciles."

Walter was an expert in the art of faking astonishment. "You just couldn't ascend normally, could you? Had to try to tarnish my reputation in the process." He shook his head, sighing. Then met Silvano's gaze. "He's been trouble from the beginning, but I've tried. It's hard, though, when his mother is so completely useless."

The female in question was nowhere to be seen.

But the words ignited a flame in Edon's gaze. "And why is she useless?" he demanded. "Oh, right, because you've broken her." He snorted and looked to Silvano. "I've neither sanctioned nor plotted against your territory in any way. What the hell would I have to gain from it?"

"A great deal," Walter argued. "Framing me and tarnishing my reputation would only prove to the pack that I was unfit to lead, and allow you to become their savior. Something we both know you very much need, as you're not all that respected by your peers."

He opened his hands for the wolves around him, most of whom snorted in agreement.

Walter sighed, the sound dramatic as he refocused on Silvano. "Tell me how to make this up to you, old friend. Tell me what you want."

"My death, I presume," Edon drawled. "Fascinating. I mean, you've been trying to accomplish that throughout the trials. Right?"

He pressed a palm to his chest. "Me? All I've done is try to make you stronger." He again looked to the pack for approval, which they of course gave because they were all fucking sheep.

"Is that why you framed my mate for murder?" Edon asked. "Why you took it upon yourself to punish her—in an attempt to gang-rape her? Why you beat me to within an inch of my life in your so-called strength test?" He smiled. "Sure, *Dad.* I'm certain that was all done for my benefit."

"You've grown too close to her, and that mutt of yours, to think clearly, son. It's something I warned you against." He sounded so contrite and sad that I almost wanted to applaud him for the act.

The problem was, it seemed everyone around him believed this bullshit.

Several alphas had joined the ring, watching from the sidelines, including my parents. And a handful of royal vampires, too. They all wore matching expressions of indifference. But I sensed their acceptance.

They were going to let Walter kill his son.

To make it up to Silvano and—

"There's only one problem with your accusation," a deep voice said from behind the masses, startling me. Silas pushed through the ring in a pair of jeans and stepped up to his sire's side. The lack of surprise in Edon's features was either a result of anticipating Silas's arrival or very good acting.

"I was the one who found the dead vampire body," Silas said, eliciting a few expressions of surprise from the circle. "And those two idiots were right on my tail. When I reached out to Edon, he was just as shocked by the corpse as I was."

Walter snorted. "That proves nothing. You're just a mutt without any standing in this community."

Silas smiled. "And yet, it's my sire you're accusing. As I have access to his mind, I'd argue my input is worthwhile in this discussion."

"While I'd argue it's inadmissible due to influence," Walter replied without missing a beat. "Just as his bitch of a mate would be deemed worthless in this trial. Yet, I don't see her here trying to defend you, Edon. How interesting."

"You'd like that, wouldn't you?" Edon said, his lips thinning. "Because then you could claim her beneath the moon as your own. After my death, of course."

"Well, I'll need a new heir. Might as well use the only alpha female in the territory who can deliver the kind of son I require." Walter shrugged. "Although, I'll have to break her in a little. Since you've failed so spectacularly."

My blood chilled.

Over my dead body, I thought, a growl threatening my throat. But I swallowed it before I let it slip.

"You can try," Edon replied, canting his head to the side. "Something tells me it'll be harder than you think."

Silas snorted. "More like impossible." He folded his arms. "You know, I am curious about something."

Walter arched a brow. "And I should care why?"

Silas lifted a shoulder. "Because you're the alpha incumbent. I'm one of your wolves. Oh, and your son is my sire."

Brave words, I thought, my tail twitching.

But that wasn't it at all.

He was stalling.

I just didn't know why.

"None of those are reasons for me to acknowledge or even listen to a mutt." Walter focused on his son. "What on earth have you been doing with this trash to give him such confidence?"

Edon's smile was wolfish. "Bonding."

"This has all been mildly entertaining," Silvano interjected. "Alas, I'm no longer amused by this family quarrel. Clemente Clan crossed the borders without permission and murdered several of my brethren. I seek retribution for the lives lost, of which I count twelve. An alpha heir is only one. I require eleven more."

"Don't you find it odd that you were able to cross the boundaries so easily with this many vampires?" Silas asked, his tone remarkably calm considering he was addressing a royal vampire. That he held the male's gaze spoke volumes. "I was the only one patrolling tonight, while there were almost two dozen of us on the last full moon. Seems a bit, I don't know, arranged?"

"Are you suggesting I'm working with Walter? To have my own men killed?" Silvano asked, his white eyebrow meeting his equally white hairline.

"I'm suggesting your arrival was anticipated. And also, Edon doesn't yet have the authority to command the wolves to leave the borders." Silas's arms fell to his sides. "Make of that what you will."

A setup.

Which I already figured out.

But now I wondered if Walter and Silvano were working together, if perhaps the vampire knew all along that the alpha wanted to remain in charge.

Maybe he had a few minions to sacrifice.

Wouldn't be unheard of to discard a few immortals in such a way—made the paperwork easier.

What if they had an agreement drawn up among themselves? Walter helped Silvano get rid of a few unruly vampires while Silvano helped Walter maintain his position. As they shared a boundary, it would be within their best interests to remain loyal to each other.

"That is intriguing," Kylan agreed from the sidelines.

"Yes," Jace concurred beside him. "I wondered why the wolves weren't on the border. Care to elaborate, Walter?"

The alpha chuckled. "Well, we were supposed to be having a ceremony tonight. I suspect my wolves were interested in observing."

"You had one last month and relegated many of them to border patrol," Silas said. "Including me."

"Because you're a mutt unworthy of attending," Walter growled, his veneer slipping slightly. "You're lucky we even let you into the heart of the territory—something I'll be rectifying quickly once this mess is over."

"But that still doesn't explain the others," Jace pressed. "Why force them to guard one ritual but not another?"

"Tonight's a bigger ceremony with the ascension of their new alpha," Walter replied, his gaze narrowing at the royal. "What are you really accusing me of, Jace?"

"Me?" He touched his chest, his dark brows lifting. "Nothing. I'm merely curious, old friend."

Typical politics. No one meant what they were saying, and yet everyone was tossing around accusations—in silence.

"Regardless of who allowed what, I am owed my retribution," Silvano declared, his voice ringing through the night.

Simple words.

Followed by a gesture of his hand that had my heart dropping to my stomach.

A shot rang through the air, piercing my ears and shooting my pulse into overdrive.

It wasn't sanctioned.

The discussion wasn't done.

But Silvano had clearly decided to finish it, with Edon as the target.

A scream rent the air, telling me the bullet was silver—a lycan's one nemesis other than time. And to my absolute horror, I watched as Silas fell.

He'd leapt in front of the gun, the barrel still pointed at Edon.

Chaos erupted in the wake of the gunfire, starting with Edon lunging at the attacker and twisting the man's head at an angle it would take several days to return from. While Silas writhed in the middle of the field, blood pooling from his wound.

I shrieked, my shift reverting on instinct and forcing me to run to him on two legs.

But someone else reached him first. A vampire in a suit. His name not registering. My mind fracturing beneath the insanity of the moment.

I tried to chase him, to call after Silas, but cement arms clamped down around my waist, yanking me backward.

"There you are," a deep voice said against my ear.

I shivered, the menacing energy coupled with the feel of his chest against my back twisted my heart. "Walter," I breathed.

"I prefer *sir*," he replied. "But we'll work on that, little slut. We'll be working on a lot of things."

Chapter Thirty-One

EDON

SILAS! I roared, my body twisting this way and that as I fought blow after blow from the vampires descending upon the field. *You better not fucking die on me, Silas. Or I swear, I will crawl into the afterlife just to beat you myself.*

No reply.

Fuck!

I told him not to intervene.

I told him to stay put.

I told him not to speak.

Did he listen to me at all? No. And how the fuck did he move so damn fast? I hadn't even seen the gun, but I heard it just before the bullet sailed into Silas's chest. Now I had no idea where he even went or who took him. He just disappeared before I had a chance to react.

My fist met the face of another bloodsucker, my instinct to shift overwhelming my thoughts. But I couldn't afford the few seconds required to take on my beast form. There were too many damn vampires and not enough lycans fighting.

I growled, snapping my elbow back into another assailant and my knee into the asshole in front of me. He collapsed on a grunt, his weapon falling to the ground. I snatched it up in a flash and used the dagger to slice the throat of the male behind me.

Then moved on to the next.

All the while calling to Silas.

Without a reply.

I could feel his life energy seeping from this plane, the silver taking him from me far too soon. And all I could feel was rage.

Walter would pay for this.

All his fucking cronies, too.

A howl parted my lips as I demanded the pack to assemble, to fight, and to my surprise, several answered the call.

About. Fucking. Time.

And those who hid? Well, they'd be first on my cull list. Because no way was I letting an army of vampires take me down.

Not today.

Not for something I didn't do.

My father disappeared, leaving me to fend for myself. *Coward.* Silvano stayed, but not to fight. He merely supervised, as if enjoying the carnage.

Killing vampires took a lot of effort.

Lycans were easier, as we lacked the immortal gene. But that didn't make us weak. I proved that by taking down three more of his men while he observed in stoic silence.

Where the hell was my grandfather? He could put an end to this madness.

And Luna… I'd felt her moments ago. Where had she run off to?

A smack against my side had me focusing on the idiot who'd just thought to strike me. I put him down with a fist to his chin before whirling on the vampire approaching behind me.

They were all so young, maybe a hundred years at best.

Which meant Silvano had brought his D-team to the fight.

Poor choice. But hey, it worked in my favor, so I wasn't about to complain.

Silas, I tried again.

Static. Quiet. Nothing.

My heart ached, my soul crying out at the injustice of his fall. Why had he jumped before that bullet? How—

Stars flickered behind my eyes as something hard slammed into the back of my skull. I blinked, shook my head, and danced around to fight, but my vision began to bleed into spots of light.

No. I wasn't giving up. Not yet. Not when… *What is that?* The sharp cry echoed in my ears, kick-starting my heart. *Luna!*

Chapter Thirty-Two

LUNA

"FUCK YOU," I snarled, my arms straining as I tried futilely to loosen Walter's hold. He'd yanked me behind one of the houses, one hand encircling my neck while the opposite held both of my wrists.

"As soon as Edon dies, I'll grant your wish," he growled, his lips far too close to my neck for my liking.

His goal wasn't lost on me. My ties to Edon would die with him, allowing Walter to stake his claim beneath the moon.

And then I'd be well and truly fucked. Both figuratively and literally.

Not going to happen.

I kicked back against him, and he responded by shoving me into the log exterior of the home, causing me to cry out in pain. Because *fuck,* that hurt.

My father stood close by with a look of disgust on his face. Not at Walter, no. But at *me.*

And my mother—her eyes shone with tears.

Logan, however, appeared ready to commit murder. He'd already tried to intervene once, which resulted in the black eye now blossoming on his handsome face.

Our father was a fucking dick.

But my brother appeared ready to try again. His hands fisted at his sides, his blue eyes locking on mine as he tried to convey some sort of plan. He looked pointedly at my wrists gripped tightly behind my back. And then he cocked his chin sharply.

I didn't understand his goal until he charged forward—his focus on Walter. I jerked my hands just as he crashed into the shocked alpha behind me, thereby breaking his grip.

However, the one on my neck squeezed harshly.

I hacked, my airway crushing beneath his grip, but was suddenly freed as Logan slammed a fist into Walter's jaw.

My father roared in fury, charging forward, only to be slammed off his path by my mother. "Run!" she shouted at me. Just before my father yanked her to the ground on a yelp.

I didn't want to listen.

I didn't want to run.

But I wasn't about to let their rebellion be all for nothing.

My legs took off, my body aching from the places Walter had manhandled me. If I could hide until sunrise, I'd be safe for another month. I just had to get away, to—

A hand clamped over my mouth, yanking me backward into a hard body that smelled of death. Another arm clamped around my middle as I tried to fight, furious that I'd escaped only to fall captive yet again.

What the fuck?!

I'm not this woman.

I am not weak.

Let me go!

I fought with everything I owned, earning me a curse and a grunt from my new captor. And then he slammed me harshly into an ungiving surface.

Another damn house.

I growled, fed up with being manhandled and treated like a damsel. This wasn't—

He spun me around, his forearm at my throat, and piercing blue eyes met mine. The color of ice. "I'm all for a feisty wolf, darling, but right now, we need your help to understand something."

My lips parted. *Jace.*

And who the hell was *we*?

He pushed me through the door of the home and shut it behind him with a kick. "We don't have a lot of time, so I suggest you be a good little wolf and play along."

"I told you, it's too soon," another male said, his stance casual as he leaned against the wall. "We need more time before we show our cards."

"So we let Edon die and try to start over?" Jolene replied, hands in his pockets. "Can't guarantee I'll be alive long enough to see it through, gentlemen. I've given that boy everything I've got, and he's exactly what we need in this region."

"And what about Silvano?" the dark-haired vampire asked, his tone as nonchalant as his pose. "It's going to raise a hell of a lot of questions, especially so soon after what happened to Robyn."

"That wasn't even related," a fourth voice put in with a sardonic snort. *Luka.*

Shit. What had Jace just pulled me into the middle of?

"Whether it was or wasn't isn't the point. All this unrest is going to alarm Lilith." The dark-haired one pushed off the wall. "I'm not discounting the fact that you've put a lot of effort into this, Jolene. I'm merely pointing out the paperwork that will be involved should we intervene. It may set us back years, as we'll be forced to maintain a low profile."

"If we don't intervene, we lose two clans," Jace replied softly. "Which sets us back several decades."

"Two?" Luka asked.

"Logan just assaulted Walter." Jace looked at me. "To save his sister."

I swallowed. Was this where he wanted my input? Because I didn't know what to say.

"Well, shit." Luka rubbed a hand down his face, shaking his head. "Niko isn't going to like that."

"No, I suspect not." Jace was still looking at me. "Tell us about your relationship with Edon and Silas."

My eyebrows rose. "Excuse me?"

"You're fucking them both. Is it because Edon's making you?" His flat tone didn't match the severity of his question.

"Fuck you," I growled. "And fuck your assumption."

His lips quirked upward. "Oh, Claudette has raised you perfectly, I see." He glanced at Luka. "There's hope for your precious daughter yet if Logan's anything like this one."

"Considering he just attacked Walter, I'll say he's a perfect candidate."

Jace lifted a shoulder. "True." His focus locked on me again. "Your relationship with Edon and Silas isn't accepted by current social conditions. How do you feel about that?"

"Like my relationship with Edon and Silas is none of your damn business," I replied flatly. "What the hell is this? There's a war going on outside, and you're all gossiping with me about who I'm fucking? Talking about my brother like he's some pawn in your game of chess? Fuck that. You're wasting my time." I took a step, only to find the dark-haired male suddenly at my back.

Power vibrated off him in waves, causing goose bumps to flare across my limbs and reminding me that I was very much naked in a room full of dominant males.

Not good.

Especially considering Jace's penchant to play with wolves.

I swallowed. "Look, Edon's innocent. He didn't attack Silvano's vampires or issue any sort of edict telling his wolves to go on the hunt. His father just wants to maintain his power." I looked imploringly at Jolene. "Tell them."

"They already know, sweetheart," he replied, sliding off his jacket and handing it to me. "They're trying to figure out if they should intervene."

"Well, if you ask me, I say you should," a new voice declared as Kylan entered from the back of the house. "I mean, what's a revolution without a little kickoff party?"

The only indication that they were surprised by his appearance was the slight stiffening in Luka's shoulders.

"You know, I missed my invitation to the party," Kylan drawled, his expression one of stark amusement. "But I've sensed your intentions for some time now. What are we all waiting for? I vote we take out Silvano. He's one of the reasons we're all in this mess. I promise he won't be missed by those who count."

Silence met his statement.

But the tick in Jace's jaw said the male had struck a nerve.

"I can do it," Kylan continued. "I mean, I already have a knack for pissing off Lilith. Maybe she'll put me wherever she hid Cam."

All the males exchanged a glance.

"Oh, come on. I can't be the only one who suspects he's still alive." He looked at Luka. "His Erosita lives with your clan, right?" He sighed at their continued silence. "I see. Well. If my services are requested for whatever the fuck this is, you know where to find me."

Jace stopped him with a hand on his shoulder, their gazes locking in a long, silent duel while the cries of wolves and vampires bled through the night air outside.

My chest ached for them all, especially Edon. The only thing that kept me upright was the strength radiating through his mating bond.

He was alive and fighting and mourning Silas.

Whom he couldn't feel anymore.

A tear slipped from the edge of my eye, my nails grasping my jacket even tighter around myself. "We can't just stand here," I whispered. "I don't know why you're all standing around debating a timeline when you could be helping. But I do know this: not intervening when you can just makes you all a bunch of cowards." I looked pointedly at Jolene. "Your grandson is fighting for his life out there. I'm going to join him with or without your help."

I thrust my elbow backward, expecting to strike the dark-haired one, but only met air. He stood by the door with an amused expression. "We should introduce her to Juliet," he said, glancing at Jace. "See if we can't instill some of that feisty energy."

"Trust me, D. Mira is already working on it," Luka put in.

D smiled. "Brilliant." And then he opened the door. "After you, little wolf."

Little wolf.

Little mate.

Little moon.

I was really, *really* tired of everyone calling me *little.*

I was not short.

I was not weak.

I just happened to be less muscled and tinier than the others around me. But I possessed an alpha bloodline for a reason. And they were all about to find out why.

Chapter Thirty-Three

EDON

RED.

Everything around me was stained in *red.* The vampires. The wolves. Silvano and his fucking smirk. The moon. The grass. The male trying to bite me.

All. Fucking. Red.

I couldn't hear Silas. I couldn't find Luna. I couldn't focus on anything other than the assholes who kept trying to take me down.

I would not fall. Not like this. Not until I knew Silas's and Luna's fates.

A growl ripped from my throat as I took down yet another bloodsucker. They just kept *coming.* Fortunately, it seemed most of them were without weapons.

So what happened to the gun? I wondered for the thousandth time. Someone had one. Yet he'd fled, leaving only vampires with knives in his wake.

Which led me to believe it wasn't a vampire who tried to shoot me, but a wolf.

How did Silas know?

No. No time for that now. I'd analyze later.

Silvano. He was the key to ending this all. If I could just fucking get close enough to incapacitate him, his minions would—

Shit!

A sharp edge struck my rib cage, sending me to my knees and rolling away from the source as fire licked through my veins.

Another damn knife.

Better than a gun.

I whirled on the ground, ignoring the pain shooting up my side, and lashed out at my attacker. Only, the air fled my lungs and refused to replenish.

He punctured my lung.

Okay, so worse than a scrape.

A cringe rendered me useless for half a second—long enough for my assailant to jump on top of me and aim the blade at my throat.

I caught his wrist, twisting it, but spots danced before my vision, leaving me woozy. He pressed down, his strength matching mine because of his superior position.

Sadism radiated from the male's face, contorting his lips into a wicked sneer.

Not good. Not good at all.

I grasped his throat with my opposite hand while trying to break his wrist with my other palm. Anything to deter him from placing that deadly weapon at my neck once more.

But he inched closer.

And closer.

Until a ball of white knocked him off me with a violent snarl.

Luna.

Relief flooded me at the sight of her svelte form destroying the vampire's face while he screamed in agony, his knife long forgotten. I grabbed it, then gave myself a second to recover before jumping to my feet. It hurt like a son of a bitch, but newfound adrenaline surged inside me.

My mate was alive.

She was here.

And the woman fought like a damn goddess.

She took down two more vampires with her jaws alone, ripping out their throats before returning to my side, her sleek coat painted in blood.

Gorgeous.

If we weren't in the middle of a fight for our lives, I would have grabbed her, forced her to turn, and fucked her on this very field.

But I had another horde of vampires appearing from the tree line as if Silvano had a whole army of reserves just waiting to attack. He must have deployed them in waves. It explained why he hadn't acted sooner during my argument with Walter.

What are your real intentions? I wondered. Because he wouldn't waste this many resources just to take me down for an old friend. This had to be a double cross, a way to weaken the Clemente Clan and take more land.

And my idiot of a father had fallen for it by opening the borders.

Come right in.

Destroy my wolves.

As long as I keep my throne, I don't care.

When I survived this insanity, my father would pay.

With my lungs barely recovered—thanks to my lycan healing—more vampires poured onto the grounds, their orders clear. *Kill on sight.*

The newcomers were refreshed.

I was not.

My wolf ached to come out to play, but there wasn't time. I twirled the knives in my hands—ones I'd stolen from the vampires who came before them.

"Welcome to the Clemente Clan," I greeted them, narrowing my eyes. "Allow me to properly introduce myself."

Luna growled and acquainted them with her teeth while I carved my initials into their skin.

I was mid-design on Vampire Three when a hush fell over the crowd. And all the bloodsuckers collectively fell to their knees.

My eyes tracked across the field to the cause.

Kylan.

He stood casually in the middle of the bloody field wearing a pristine suit. And unceremoniously dropped Silvano's head on the ground.

"I'm sorry. Did I interrupt?" he asked, his tone nonchalant as he wiped his hand off with a handkerchief.

"I think you destroyed their fun," Jace replied as he joined him.

"Pity." Kylan folded the soiled fabric and returned it to his pocket, then took in the crowd. "Well, I see our societal laws are working splendidly. Would someone like to call Lilith? I'm sure she'll be thrilled."

Silence.

Of course no one wanted to report this to the Blood Alliance.

Luna shifted beside me, her pale skin glowing with blood as she stood proud at my side. I brushed my lips along her neck, then skimmed my nose across her cheek, taking in her alluring scent. "Thank you," I whispered.

"You're my mate," she replied softly, her gaze finding mine. "Silas?"

I shook my head, my heart stuttering in my chest. *I can't sense him*, I admitted into her mind. *I can't sense him at all.*

And it left me feeling so fucking empty.

Hurt.

Lost.

Alone.

Guilty.

Luna cupped my cheek and kissed me tenderly, even as her eyes filled with tears. "You're not—"

"Where's Walter?" Jace demanded, shattering our moment.

I pressed my forehead to hers briefly, allowing myself the second of grief before righting my spine and focusing on the royal. It was on the tip of my tongue to claim my place as alpha when my father's gruff voice sounded from behind one of the lodges.

"Here." The asshole appeared with a handful of alphas, including Luna's father. All of them appeared pissed off, but my gaze was for the bastard leading them.

It was still a full moon.

And I had a hell of a lot of aggression to work out.

For myself.

For Luna.

For Silas.

"Fight me," I demanded before anyone else could speak. Politics be damned, I wanted this bullshit done. "End this once and for all."

His resulting laugh lacked humor. "Now isn't the time for your antics, boy."

I smiled. "On the contrary, now is the perfect fucking time. We're all here, right? It's still a full moon. My birthright defines tonight as my ascension. And I'm calling it. You want to keep your place as clan alpha? Earn it and fight me for it. Maybe you'll even have a leg up since I've been out here battling with the clan while you tucked your tail and ran."

A few of the exhausted wolves around me snorted their disgust, but for once, it was directed at my father and not me.

I tossed my blades onto the ground beside two of the kneeling vampires and stepped forward. "Fight. Me." I allowed the demand to permeate my growl, vibrating the field around us. "Or bow and acknowledge me as your alpha."

My father bristled. "I don't have to do or acknowledge anything."

"Actually, you do," my grandfather interjected. He strolled up to the field with Luka beside him, the two males standing at equal height. Energy radiated off them, denoting their bloodlines. But it was my grandfather who seemed to be the more powerful of the duo. "It's the right of any alpha heir to challenge the alpha incumbent during any full-moon ritual after the heir's twenty-second birthday. Which, for Edon, occurred three months ago."

Several wolves murmured their agreement, including two of the alphas at Walter's side.

I cocked a brow. "Scared?"

My father spit at the ground, his eyes narrowing. "Of you?" He let out another of those humorless laughs. "Hardly."

"Good." Because I intended to destroy him and I wanted him aware of every fucking minute. "Wolf or man form?"

He seemed to consider—whether it was my question or his chances of talking his way out of this, I wasn't sure.

I didn't care.

I just wanted to annihilate him.

"I want a second," he declared, referring not to time but to his desire for a partner.

Whispers hushed through the crowd, the alpha's demand not a common one. Usually, two wolves fought to the death—alone.

But I immediately understood why my father chose this route.

He didn't think I had anyone to fight at my side, and he was banking on it being a two-on-one fight.

Asshole.

His lips curled. "Unless there's no one you trust to stand at your side?" he taunted.

Luna bristled. "I'll fucking stand at his side."

Fuck. That wasn't going to work for me. If she tried to fight my father, I'd lose my focus. I trusted her, knew she could fight, but no way could I allow my father to touch a hair on her head.

And his responding grin said he knew. "Well, this should—"

"I'll fight with him," my grandfather announced.

Murmurs littered the night, all shocked at the pronouncement. Except my father merely chuckled. "We both know that's against the rules, Jolene."

Jolene. Never *Father.* Or *Dad.* Always *Jolene.*

"Some would say provoking a war in order to maintain power is also against the rules," my grandfather replied casually.

Disbelief colored the alpha incumbent's features. "Don't tell me you believe the bullshit my son is spouting about me."

"Unfortunately, there's no way to confirm or deny the cause, what with all the witnesses being dead and all." He glanced pointedly at Silvano's head on the ground before looking at Kylan—who shrugged—and then took in the carnage of slain lycans throughout the field. Barry and Glenn were among them.

How sad.

"Do you believe this?" My father glanced at Niko. "The old alpha is accusing me of orchestrating this carnage. All to deflect away from the rules that say a former alpha is not permitted to play in the challenge ring. At least, not as a second."

"And here I thought you would welcome the chance to fight me," my grandfather drawled. "A shame you're such a coward."

I smirked. The old man knew how to play with words—a talent I'd picked up from him.

"Unlike you, Jolene, I merely wish to follow the rules, and as Luna spoke up first, I'm going to allow the bitch to serve as his second instead." His smile was all teeth. "Unless she's backing down from the challenge?"

I grimaced, knowing full well she wouldn't.

But a deeper voice responded instead. One that halted my heart.

"As his progeny, I volunteer to be his second."

Chapter Thirty-Four

Silas

THE CROWD PARTED AROUND ME, expressions of surprise on their faces.

Yeah, look all you want, pansy asses, I thought as I moved with Rae at my side. I was in a bit of a mood, thanks to the silver bullet that nearly pierced my heart.

When Rae told me what was happening, I hadn't even needed to think about my decision. Edon needed a second, and I was the only one he could trust apart from Luna. And while she could more than hold her own, I knew she'd also serve as a distraction. His protective instincts would require him to intervene, thereby skewing his focus.

With me, he should be able to do his thing. I hoped, anyway.

Jolene gave me a subtle nod from across the courtyard as I caught his eye. Rae had mentioned he was stalling, and Kylan told her it was because of me. They wanted me to fight at Edon's side. I didn't need their support, but I appreciated the vote of confidence.

The royal in question intercepted me, his midnight irises dropping to my chest and noting the dry blood and healed wound. He smirked.

You're welcome, his eyes seemed to say, leaving me uneasy. I didn't want to owe him a debt, but I did. Except it wasn't like I'd asked for his help. He was the one who sliced his wrist open and forced me to drink from him.

He held out an arm for Rae. "Consort."

"Sire," she returned, settling into his side.

"Good luck, wolf," he murmured, moving out of my way.

Luck. Yeah. Seemed a bit frivolous.

Because I didn't need it.

His blood had left me feeling oddly energetic. Revitalized. All of my senses were heightened, as if I'd been reborn as something decidedly other. I could *hear* Edon's heart beating despite him being several yards away.

Fuck, I could hear *everyone.*

"Silas," Luna breathed, tears shining brightly in the depths of her eyes.

That look erased my thoughts and sent me walking swiftly in her direction. I caught her as she threw her arms around my neck. Edon met my gaze over her shoulder, his dark gaze sparkling with a multitude of questions.

Likely because he couldn't access my mind.

We'd have to figure out why later.

For now, he needed to get his head in the game and not worry about things we had no control over.

"Surprise isn't a good look on you, Alpha," I said, a warning lacing my tone. "I much prefer you enraged and craving vengeance." If we were going to fight his father, I needed his focus.

"You're okay," Luna whispered, not receiving the same memo.

And the broken quality in her words derailed me once more.

Fuck propriety. These idiots can wait another minute.

I cupped Luna's cheek and kissed her softly while ignoring the sounds of surprise rising from the crowd. She shivered against me, her arms winding around my neck. "You were shot." Her words were so soft I doubted anyone other than me and Edon heard her, even with their enhanced hearing. "With silver," she added.

"I healed." I brushed my lips over hers once more before pressing my mouth to her ear. "I'll explain later, little moon. I promise."

She nodded, her throat bobbing. "Right. Yeah." She seemed to be remembering our surroundings, a mask falling over her features. "Right," she repeated.

Edon stood motionless beside us, his ears picking up every word, his expression still rimmed with queries.

"You ready to ascend?" I asked him as I released Luna with a final kiss to her temple.

He looked me over, his gaze pausing on my chest and roaming downward before returning to my face. "Can you fight?"

I smiled. "I'm not bleeding, am I?"

"You look remarkably well healed for someone shot with silver," he apprised, narrowing his eyes. "Do I want to know how that's possible?"

"Not right now, no." I flicked my gaze to his father and squared my shoulders. "As I said, I volunteer as his second."

Walter chuckled, the sound cruel. "I think you've been *volunteering* to serve my son in more ways than one lately." He glanced at Jolene. "I suppose triads do run in the family, right?"

Triads? That wasn't a term I'd heard before, but I could guess at what it meant.

"Well, I accept your choice, Edon," Walter continued, his voice a low drawl. "I'll just take a piece out of Luna after I win."

Edon grinned. "So confident."

"I am," he replied. "Because I pick Niko as my second."

Gasps littered the courtyard, echoing off the surrounding lodges and trees. Edon and I shared a glance.

"That has to be against the rules," Luna said, taking the words right out of my mouth. "If Edon can't fight with Jolene, you can't fight with the alpha of another clan."

"Your daughter's manners are severely lacking," Walter informed Niko conversationally. "I'm starting to question how you raised your children in Ernest Clan."

Niko snorted. "Trust me, I'll be having a long chat with Claudette when I return." He glowered at Luna. "And the rules state Walter can pick anyone tied to his pack, of which I am, thanks to your union with his son. It may not be a common choice, but it's an acceptable one. As I have an heir who is almost of age, I am eligible to compete. Not that it matters, as I have no intention of losing."

Walter chuckled. "Neither do I."

"You're forgetting a key detail—the alpha heir must accept your terms," Jolene said. "And as they are ridiculous, I suggest—"

"Oh, I accept," Edon announced. "I was just waiting for the two of them to finish showboating." He sounded so poised and at ease by the prospect of taking down two alphas. No, not just alphas. But two *experienced* alphas.

With me by his side.

A newbie.

An omega.

"Are you sure about this?" I asked him softly. Because I sure as fuck wasn't. One of the other wolves in the clan? Yeah, sure. But another alpha? That was an entirely different situation.

"Definitely," he replied.

"Edon," Luna whispered, her hand circling his arm. "You don't know my father like I do. This isn't a good idea."

"Have some faith." He kissed her on the cheek and stepped forward. "What form do you choose, Walter?"

His choice of using his father's first name wasn't lost on me. He was detaching himself from family obligations and preparing himself for what had to be done.

He was readying himself for the inevitable kill.

"Wolf," his father replied, his eyes on me. "That won't be a problem for your new progeny, will it?"

Ass, I thought. He knew I'd be weaker in my animal form since it was all still so new to me.

But of course, Edon didn't take that into account. He merely said, "Wolf it is. I just need a minute with my second and we can begin."

"Sure," his father agreed, sounding smug.

Edon turned to me, his palm finding my nape as he tugged me close. "Why can't I hear you?" he demanded, the words a whisper meant for my ears alone. Luna didn't even seem to pick up on the question, because her brow furrowed as if she couldn't figure out what he was doing.

"I don't know," I admitted. "But I think it's related to Kylan."

"Kylan?"

"Yeah." I pitched my voice even lower, ensuring that absolutely no one—not even Luna—overheard. "He gave me his blood."

Edon's eyebrows shot up. "*What*?"

"What is it?" Luna asked, her concern palpable. "What are you two talking about?"

Edon held my gaze for a long moment, then released me and bent to speak directly into her ear. Despite the soft tenor, I heard every word—thanks to my enhanced senses. "Silas drank Kylan's blood."

She gasped, her pupils widening. "That's—"

"Forbidden," Edon finished for her. "Yes."

"It's not like the royal gave me a choice," I said through my teeth, my gaze slipping to the vampire in question. He winked at me from his position near the edge, completely unperturbed. "Why is it forbidden?"

"Because it enhances your senses and strengths," Edon whispered. "Which happens to be perfect for our current situation, apart from Kylan's energy blocking my access to your mind."

Luna frowned. "Walter must not realize Silas was shot."

"And I see no point to educate him otherwise," Edon replied, glancing at his father. "He more than earned a little surprise, don't you think?"

I rolled my shoulders, my neck popping along the way. "Yeah. I'd say he does."

He glanced down at my jeans and then back up. "Those mine?"

"Yeah."

"Good." He gripped my neck again and yanked me forward until our chests touched. "His blood might be running through your system right now, but you're still fucking mine. You feel me?"

His mouth sealed over mine, making it impossible to reply.

Holy. Fuck.

Edon was claiming me.

In front of the entire fucking pack.

And not just as his progeny.

The sheer possession in his kiss left me breathless and kick-started my heart.

Until a growl from his father halted the moment.

Edon ended our embrace with a nip to my lower lip, his dark eyes glowing with intent. "This isn't over."

"I know."

"No holding back, Omega."

"Right back at you, Alpha."

"Then let's kick some ass." He grabbed Luna and kissed her tenderly before spinning her into my arms. "That wasn't goodbye, little mate. Just a promise."

"I know," she breathed, her focus sliding from him to me. "You'll protect each other."

"Always," I vowed, bending my head to run my lips over her freshly kissed ones. "Be prepared to run should anything happen," I breathed against her ear.

I released her before she could reply and moved to Edon's side.

Walter stood scowling at his son from several yards away. "You disgust me."

"Good," he replied. "That means I'm doing something right."

His father opened his mouth to speak again, only to be cut off by Jace. "I'm growing bored by all the chitchat. Are you going to fight? Or shall I go have a drink and come back later?"

Walter chuckled. "Always so eager to watch wolves rip each other apart, aren't you, old friend?"

"I do enjoy a little blood, yes," the vampire drawled. "Maybe I'll sample some of your wolves when this is all done."

Walter shrugged. "You're my guest."

"Only for the moment," Edon put in. "Soon he'll be my guest, and there will be no sampling of anything without consent."

Walter shook his head. "I should have killed you when you were a pup."

Edon grinned. "Stop stalling, old man. Let's finish this."

"Gladly." Walter shrugged out of his jacket and shirt, revealing a muscular torso dotted in fine brown hairs. Niko followed suit, his body slightly less broad but equally lean and athletic.

"We need a strategy," I whispered.

"We have one." Edon popped the button on his jeans, sliding down the zipper. "Kill."

Yeah, excellent strategy, I thought, removing my pants. *Really glad I asked.*

I don't see the problem, wolf. Did you not assassinate the majority of your opponents during the Immortal Cup?

I jerked upright, my gaze honing in on Kylan. He studiously ignored me, his gaze on Rae. *Get out of my head.*

He tsked. *Now, now. I'm only here to help, then I'll release you back to your alpha.*

I don't want your help, I snarled, kicking my jeans away from my feet and calling my inner wolf.

If you die, Raelyn will be upset. Therefore, you will tolerate my assistance and strength just as you accepted my blood.

Had my lips not been in the process of elongating into a snout, I would have cursed. Kylan wanted to help? Fine. *Just don't distract me.*

On the contrary, wolf. I intend to guide you. Walter thinks you're weak in your animal form; it's why he chose it. And now that he's seen his son's affection for you, he's going to use both to his advantage by having Niko attack Edon while Walter tries to kill you. It's a classic move, one that he'll hope to use to distract his son and thereby weaken you both.

Thanks for the tip, I thought at him and shook out my coat.

That wasn't my tip, Silas. My suggestion is you hold your own against Walter until Edon is done with Niko.

Hold my own against a three-hundred-year-old alpha. Got it.

Three hundred twenty-two, but that's just semantics. Use my blood. I gave you more than enough. It's powerful. Don't waste it.

If I knew how to use it, I would.

Instinct, wolf. Follow your instincts.

Jolene stepped into the field, his expression stoic as he took in the four wolves in the courtyard. "Give them a wide berth," he advised, sending the crowd backward to create a giant ring—one that reminded me of a much larger version of the punishment circle.

Edon sat beside me, his wolf form slightly bigger than mine. He seemed perfectly at ease, as though we hadn't signed up to fight to the death.

Niko and Walter paced in expectation, their sizes rivaling Edon's.

Leaving me as the smallest.

The omega.

Great.

With that spirit, you'll die in two minutes, Kylan chastised. *And that will upset my consort. You do not want that to happen, Silas. Trust me.*

Threats don't really work in this situation, I informed him.

Did you really survive all this torment just to die at the hand of an alpha you loathe? he countered. *Because that would be a damn shame.*

It's not like I want to die.

Yeah? How about you prove it, wolf? Think about what that sadistic ass is going to do to your precious Luna. Think about what he's already done. Channel it and use my strength. Don't make me regret lending it to you.

His commentary overrode whatever Jolene was saying. Something about the parameters, which I summed up to be a fight to the death or until someone submitted.

As I was standing in a ring with three alpha males, I highly doubted the latter would occur.

Jolene listed a few ritual rules, stating no one from the audience could interfere—which caused Kylan to snort into my head—and reiterated the terms Edon agreed to with Walter.

"Whoever wins claims Clemente Clan as his own. If the alpha incumbent of Ernest Clan falls, his successor takes charge. Are there any objections before we begin?"

Silence.

"Then I hereby declare this challenge valid. You may—"

Walter lunged, and I reacted by dodging to my left. *Fuck!* I didn't realize we would immediately start. The damn alpha hadn't even waited for Jolene to finish. And if the snarls I heard to my right were anything to go by, Niko hadn't either.

A whirl of white fur raced past me just before Walter charged again.

I dodged him, eliciting a growl from him and several gasps from the crowd. Why it shocked them, I had no idea. Nor did I have time to consider it as my attacker leapt toward me.

Another skip away, followed by a roll and a prance to the side, had him snarling furiously.

Apparently, he wasn't a fan of my playing hard to get.

Too bad for him.

Because I wasn't about to stop.

All I had going for me was speed and agility. If he caught me, I was fucked. My strength didn't match his, and we both knew it. That was why he kept trying to catch me and why I kept just out of reach.

Shock permeated the air, followed by the pungent stench of fear.

I couldn't look to find out what caused it, my gaze firmly on the raging alpha coming after my tail.

His claws swiped a little too close for comfort as I danced just out of reach again.

If Kylan was talking, I didn't hear him, one hundred percent of my focus on the field and my opponent. I just needed to—

Something smacked into my back, sending me flying over the earth and directly into Walter's path. He slammed into me at full force, his claws ripping through my side in a sharp stab of agony.

Fuck!

Fight! a voice demanded. I didn't know whom it belonged to and didn't hang around to find out.

I struck out at Walter with one of my paws, faster and harder than ever before, and grunted when I hit solid fur. Fighting in animal form was new to me, something I had no experience with, so I gave myself over to my wolf and let him drive my motions.

Snap.

Swipe.

Duck.

Roll.

So fast.

Repeat.

Pain sliced up my back, nails digging into my flesh as I bit down on a mouthful of white fluff. And skin. Oh, yeah. I tasted blood. A lot of it. And I wanted *more*.

Walter was bigger and stronger, but I had speed on my side and I used it to my advantage, returning his strikes with a vengeance. Yet it still wasn't enough. He had me pinned, his teeth searching for purchase against my throat.

I refused to yield, scrunching my shoulders and protecting my neck while squirming beneath him and seeking for a weakness. Anything to shove him off me, to—

Cheers sailed into the night, and suddenly Walter was gone. Edon pinned him, their forms evenly matched, and then they began to spar over the ground in a whirl of bloody fur I couldn't track.

I heaved a breath, climbed to my paws, and shook out my coat. Niko's headless form lay on the ground a few yards away, his wolf form having melted back into his human one upon death.

Edon won.

Not yet, a voice replied. *And he's wounded. So stop fucking around and go help him.*

I didn't think; I acted, running after the blur of white and knocking into Walter's side. He yelped as Edon caught his limb, his teeth shredding the leg to the bone and crushing it beneath his jaws.

I bit Walter's flank, forcing him to heel as Edon switched to the opposite thigh and bit down.

Only, Walter didn't want to stay still.

The bastard bellowed from his throat and rolled with a force I didn't expect, crushing me beneath him and leaving Edon somehow on top. Canines met my throat, pushing downward into my windpipe, crushing the vital—

Edon ripped him off me with a growl and clamped down on Walter's neck.

The sounds that came from them both would haunt me for eternity.

And yet, I couldn't stop watching, fascinated by the sight of Walter *bleeding.* I wanted to lap it up in victory, to bathe in his torment, but the damn wolf slammed a paw on the ground, causing Edon to freeze.

I didn't understand at first.

I thought something was wrong.

And then it registered.

Walter. Had. Fucking. Yielded.

Oh, hell no! That bastard deserved his death and worse, not to be let off and allowed to live.

But Edon stepped away, his lips curled to reveal his razor-sharp teeth as he watched Walter shift back into his human form with two very broken legs. He collapsed into the fetal position, like a fucking baby, and shivered.

"It's a fight to the death or until one of them yields," Jolene announced, his voice grim. "The Clemente Clan alpha incumbent has yielded."

Insults littered the air from all sides.

"At least Niko died with honor," one said.

"All for a sorry excuse for an alpha," another added.

"Pathetic."

"Weak."

"Kill him. He's not worthy of life."

Edon returned to his human form, a variety of gashes and deep wounds marring his athletic form, and stood. He narrowed his gaze at the male quivering on the ground. "Submit," he growled. "Call me your alpha."

Walter trembled, his shoulders shaking, but his lips remained closed.

Edon grabbed his nape and yanked him around to shout into his face. "Submit!"

"Y-you're the alpha," he whispered.

"Not good enough, old man." Edon tossed him back onto the ground. "Not. Fucking. Good. Enough." He kicked him in the side, causing Walter to cry out in pain. "I want to hear it from your fucking lips, you old piece of shit. I want every fucking confession, too. Or I'll end you right now, right here."

Walter's resulting grin was bloody and malicious. "You don't have the balls to kill me, kid."

Edon's eyebrows rose. "No?" He glanced at me and then to Luna. "We all know you didn't kill Bianca, that my father somehow placed your scent all around the scene of the crime. How badly do you want to hear his admission?"

"It's not needed," Jolene said, stepping onto the field with a sword. "Your father's been tapping into the pack psyche. I've suspected it for years, and tonight confirmed it. He compelled his own wolves to ignite a war and then hid like a coward while they all fought for their lives." He shook his head and glanced down at the pathetic male on the ground. "You've literally driven yourself mad, just like I once advised would happen if you abused the power of being alpha."

"Fuck you," Walter spat, interrupting my mental reply. "You know nothing of true power. You're just a weak old man too afraid to do what's necessary to keep the pack alive."

"And it took me far too long to realize you felt that way, my son," he replied, handing Edon the sword. "I warned you the pack psyche isn't a place to meddle, but you've been playing in the minds of your wolves for too long."

Pack psyche, I thought, frowning. Luna mentioned that once, but I didn't really understand it. *Is it like a hive mind?*

Yes, Kylan replied. *I'm not a wolf, but from what I understand, the pack psyche is a mental plane of existence that can only be reached by the alpha of a clan. It gives him the ability to check in with every member under his protection, to monitor them, and to reach out as needed. Similar to your sire link to Edon, only it requires a significant amount of focus to intrude, while your bond is far more natural.*

From Edon's expression, he already understood all of this. He gave a humorless laugh and shook his head. "Fuck, I should have known. Of course you invaded the pack psyche. I never even considered that as a cause, but it makes so much sense. You turned everyone in this pack against me for your own gain—through brainwashing. And used them all—*their scents*—to frame others for crimes you committed."

Like the vampire, I translated, understanding. *That's why it smelled like pack. But how did he taint Bianca's body with Luna's scent?*

By altering the senses of those at the scene, Kylan replied. *Best guess, anyway. I assume her body was removed immediately?*

I honestly didn't know. But it was likely.

Walter snorted. "Trust me, the brainwashing wasn't required." He spit out a mouthful of blood and glowered up at his son. "Everyone knows you're a pathetic excuse for an alpha. They'll never follow you."

"Not the ones you kept close, no," Jolene interjected. "But you're forgetting all the other wolves who reside within our boundaries. Wolves who you've kept out of the inner circle. Wolves you denied for far too long. Wolves you've left to starve."

"They weren't worthy of my resources," Walter replied. "And they seem to be doing fine on their own."

"Because I guided them," Jolene growled. "I ensured they survived long enough for Edon's new reign."

Edon twirled the sword, his gaze narrowing. "Which begins now."

Walter began to speak, but Edon didn't give him a chance.

The blade sliced through the air so fast I almost missed the beautiful connection to Walter's stocky neck. Which would have been a shame because seeing him beheaded was one of the most magnificent sights of my existence.

Almost as good as watching his head roll across the ground to the chorus of gasps.

Luna stepped forward and spit on the old man's corpse. "Bastard."

I would have smiled, but that would have looked more like a snarl in my current form.

"I'd say that's a fair judgment," Jace announced conversationally. "I mean, the man did provoke a war with Silvano through his antics."

"Oh, they were working together," Kylan replied. "Did I fail to mention that when I dropped his head on the ground? My bad."

"A royal and an alpha leading their people to unnecessary harm?" another mused, causing conversation to boom through the air and leaving me with an insane headache of noise.

All to be ended by a screech of sound that came from an unknown source near the lodges.

Such agony and pain, and holy Goddess…

Lilith.

Chapter Thirty-Five

EDON

WELL, SHIT. This isn't going to go over well.

Lilith entered the circle of death with wide green eyes, her stiletto heels sinking into the earth and her pristine blonde hair frizzing from the heat. This was not her terrain and it showed.

She took in the dead bodies of Niko and Walter, the sword in my hand, and then the field of death around us. Some of the vampires and lycans were beginning to stir, their supernatural genetics allowing them to heal—at least the ones who still had heads.

Only silver to the heart or a beheading could keep a wolf down indefinitely.

Which reminded me… *What happened to the gun used against Silas? And who fired it?*

None of the other vampires had fought with silver, telling me they were trying to minimize the damage. A fact that further proved my father and Silvano had been working together.

Except the attack went far beyond the means necessary to stage a coup.

So what had Silvano wanted to gain, exactly? He couldn't take over the territory if it still thrived with wolves, and as only a handful were truly dead, he stood no chance in owning Clemente Clan.

"Why?" Lilith demanded, her eyes on Silvano's head. "Who took his life?"

"I did," Kylan replied, his stance relaxed. "It was the only way to stop the fighting. Once I held his extinguished life in my hands, his vampires fell to my control. And I commanded them to cease their violent nonsense."

Lilith gaped at him. Then glanced around again, taking in their audience—wolves, vampires, royals, alphas, mates. She shook her head as if to clear it, her face far more pale than usual beneath the moon.

There were over a hundred gathered in this field. Most of whom were naked and covered in blood.

She studied Walter's remains, then narrowed her gaze at me. "I assume you're now in charge here?"

"Unofficially," I replied, straightening my spine. "We never had a chance to finish the rituals given the unexpected attack led by Silvano."

While I was technically the Clemente Alpha now, I hadn't ascended properly, so I didn't have access to the pack psyche yet. However, that wouldn't stop me from handling any challenges thrown my way. I might not have the mental power, but I did possess the physical means to stand my ground.

"Find us a meeting location, preferably out of the mud," she said, her voice ringing with an authority that ruffled the fur of my inner wolf. "I want all royals and alphas in attendance to report at once for an emergency council meeting."

Of course she did.

"Meanwhile, everyone else—clean yourselves up. We are not animals," she seethed, turning on her heel before I could correct that statement. I had no idea where she thought she was going. Maybe back to her car, or just to the gravel road to clean off her ruined shoes.

"We can use the main lodge," I called after her and added some directions for her to follow.

She didn't acknowledge me but did turn the way I suggested. With a shake of my head, I turned to address my wolves.

"Gather the dead," I instructed. "We'll mourn them properly tomorrow. Move anyone who is healing and not yet awake to a safe location." I took in the still vampires, then focused on Kylan, as he'd claimed to be in charge of them now. "Silvano's vampires are welcome to collect their dead however they desire. My wolves won't interfere." I added that last part with a sharp glance toward the lycans in question. "We are at peace."

"For now," a vampire put in, his dark hair blending into the night. He approached Kylan, his casual attire of jeans and a T-shirt vastly different from all the royals in attendance. And were those tattoos peeking out beneath the hem, on his bicep? How strange. He almost appeared more wolfish than vampy.

"I will not bow to you," he announced flatly, his focus on Kylan.

"An unwise decision, but one I can respect," the royal replied. "*For now.*"

"As Silvano's oldest vampire on site, I will attend the council meeting in representation of his lands," the male added, ignoring the lingering threat in Kylan's tone. These two clearly had a history of some kind.

"Of course. We look forward to your explanation of what happened here." Kylan grinned. "I'm sure it's quite a tale." He pointedly turned his back on the ballsy vamp and addressed the crowd. "You heard Lilith—clean yourselves up. And if anyone draws a weapon or instigates another fight in our absence, I will dispense with you as I did Silvano."

A shudder seemed to traverse the crowd, Kylan's reputation for cruelty working strongly in his favor. No one wanted to go against the supposedly mad royal.

Not even me.

And his blood ran through my progeny's system.

Fuck.

I turned to Luna, my palm finding her nape as I tugged her in for a kiss that she reciprocated on a sigh. "Stay close to Silas. I don't know how this is going to go."

She nodded and cupped my cheek. "We'll be waiting for you."

"I know," I whispered, running my tongue across her bottom lip. "You owe me a bite, little mate." Something I would request right now—while we still had a full moon above our heads—if I couldn't feel everyone's eyes on me. Alas, duty called.

It was time to play alpha.

I released Luna with another brush of my mouth against hers, then grabbed Silas and captured his lips with my own.

Shock rippled through his body like it had the last time I kissed him, as if he couldn't believe I was showing him affection in front of everyone. We would be discussing that later because if he thought I meant to hide this, he had another think coming. I wanted them both, and fuck anyone who thought ill of me for it.

"Guard Luna," I told him.

"With my life," he vowed.

I let go of him and found my grandfather's gaze across the yard. There was a wistfulness to it that I didn't understand, but pride lurked in its depths. "I'll help out here while you tend to Lilith," he said, the words traveling across the space with ease, thanks to my wolf hearing.

I nodded. "Thank you."

"Just doing my job," he replied, grinning. "Take Logan with you. He'll represent Ernest Clan."

I frowned and looked around. "Where is he?" I hadn't seen him at all, not even during the fight.

My grandfather nodded his chin toward one of the cabins. Logan stood beside it with his arm around a badly beaten Cora. Luna followed the line of sight with a gasp and took off toward her mother, with Silas hot on her tail.

Fucking Niko.

If he were still alive, I'd kill him again. Because those blemishes on the alpha female's form had the dead alpha's mark all over them.

Logan released her to Luna, one of his eyes badly bruised and screwed shut—likely from his father's fist. Had he tried to join the fight to help

Clemente Clan? And his father stopped him?

No, it had to be something worse for Cora to be given such a beating.

"We stood up to Walter when he tried to take Luna," Logan explained, sensing my confusion.

My eyebrows rose. "Walter *what*?"

"It doesn't matter," Luna said, her arm around Cora's waist. "He's dead. They are all dead. Go to the council; we'll be here when you get back." Alpha female underlined those words, causing my lips to twitch. Luna wore her dominance with pride, and I very much approved.

"Yes, ma'am," I replied, winking at her.

Silas snorted. "So you'll bow to her command, but not to mine."

"She's an alpha. You're just an omega." It was more of a taunt than the truth.

Another snort. "An omega who fought by your side in a death ring. For which you're welcome, by the way."

I clasped his shoulder and gave it a squeeze. "Yeah, you're right. You'll make a fine enforcer." Logan's brows lifted in surprise. He knew what that term meant, as did everyone standing close enough to hear. "Keep everyone in line while I'm gone."

I didn't wait for him to reply to my orders and instead led the way toward the main lodge with Logan at my side. We stopped by one of the cabins so I could grab a pair of jeans—they were a bit tight, but worked—and continued on in silence.

Everyone was waiting for us when we arrived, Lilith's expression holding a touch of impatience that I ignored as I settled into a position against the wall.

I knew there were a lot of alphas and royals in attendance tonight, but there hadn't been a chance for me to take stock of who was actually here. Most were among the usual crowd.

Claude, Lajos, Cormac, Jace—all vampires with a penchant for playing with lycans.

Kylan was the only uncommon attendee. His arrival last month had surprised me. All the royals were invited to these events, but only a handful usually appeared, and Kylan was notorious for keeping to himself. Now that I knew about his connection to Silas—whatever that was—his appearance made sense.

The ballsy vamp stood in Silvano's place with his arms crossed. Something about him struck me as not right. Power lurked beneath his skin—a power he seemed to be hiding. When he caught me staring, he arched a dark brow in challenge.

Yeah, I didn't want to fuck with him. He struck me as much harder and harsher than Silvano. Like he was used to handling wolves in addition to vampires.

No, thanks.

As for the lycan portion of the council, we had all our neighbors on this side of the globe, as well as a few from the areas surrounding Ernest Clan. All wolves enjoyed a good ascension, as it was part of our pack nature.

Luka from Majestic Clan.

Brandt from Calgary Clan.

Vlad from Vladik Clan.

Miko from Maykel Clan.

Dimka from Kostenka Clan.

All varying ages of leadership, but averaging around two hundred years or so. Which meant the majority were long-standing friends of my father, something that would likely hurt me after my ascension.

Oh well.

Those who opposed could kiss my fluffy ass.

"Now that we're all here, we can begin," Lilith announced, her focus on me—a subtle chastisement for making her wait. As if I would apologize for organizing my clan before attending a political meeting. My wolves would always come first.

Lilith launched into a diatribe about her disappointment in the council for not acting sooner, how only one of them had bothered to call for her, and how fortunate it was that she was already en route when she received that call.

A bunch of stately bullshit. What would she have done? Clapped her freshly manicured hands together and screeched for everyone to halt?

Yeah, that would have been a lovely sight.

She asked for an explanation of how it all began, which Vlad provided as an observing party. When he reached the part about accusations of Silvano and Walter orchestrating the battle, all eyes fell to the ballsy vamp.

"What do you have to say about this, Ryder?" Lilith demanded.

He lifted a shoulder. "Sounds like classic Silvano to me. That asshole only ever thought of himself." He paused before adding, "May he rest in peace."

Lilith clearly did not appreciate that response. Her eyes narrowed. "That's all you have to say?"

"You act as though I knew what was happening," he replied. "A bunch of vampires passed through my lands on their way to the border, and I followed because it piqued my curiosity. I didn't even play in the mess. I'm only standing here as a result of my age and birthright. From what I observed, Silvano orchestrated one hell of an attack with the expectation of taking over Clemente Clan afterward. Best guess, he agreed to Walter's terms with the intention of double-crossing the alpha. Didn't work in either of their favors, though."

For once, the esteemed Goddess appeared speechless.

Okay, I might like this Ryder guy.

"But if I were you, I'd seek out Catalina," he added, his tone as bored as his stance. "She ran off after shooting the Clemente Clan's newest addition with silver. I guess she didn't want to face the consequences of that with the new alpha since he was her original target."

Kylan smirked. "Good thing Jace knocked her out and tied her up in one of the lodges."

"Seemed strange she was in such a hurry to flee when her brethren were all so eager to fight," Jace put in conversationally.

"Indeed," Kylan agreed. "Shall we fetch her for you, my lady?"

"As if I trust you not to kill her without a trial," Lilith seethed.

Kylan's brows rose. "I wasn't aware I required a trial under such situations. Would you have preferred we allowed them to continue fighting like animals?" He cocked his head to the side. "Or do we need to discuss the requirements dictated by our bloodlines? Because last I checked, I'm the oldest of vampire kind, and I would say that affords me a semblance of responsibility. But maybe I'm wrong. Perhaps I need a larger title to assert such power."

Several members of the council shared glances at the very clear challenge issued by Kylan. Everyone knew his birthright superseded Lilith's, but he never laid claim to her position. Likely because he didn't desire the headache that came from being in charge and preferred maintaining his own territory.

But his actions of late seemed to be pushing some of her boundaries.

Testing the waters.

Subtle provocations to her place at the top of the hierarchy.

"I want to talk to Catalina," she replied, her head held high, her gaze on Kylan alone. "All of you"—she glanced around quickly before focusing on the royal again—"will remain here while I investigate this mess and determine a proper recourse."

"You want us to stay in the Clemente Clan lands?" That came from Brandt. "For how long?"

"For as long as it takes me to make a decision," she snapped.

"I'm not some dog you can command, vampire queen," Dimka drawled. "We have responsibilities back home."

She narrowed her gaze at the ash-blond alpha. "You will stay until I give you permission to leave. Unless you'd prefer we relocate to Lilith City?"

Several of the alphas bristled at the threat. None of us wanted to go to the heart of vampire territory. Especially not *her* territory.

"Five days," Luka suggested. "We'll agree to remain here for five days while you investigate. That should be more than enough time, and it's a blink of an eye for most of us."

"Most of ye evidence will be washed away with'na week," Cormac agreed, his voice heavily accented. Scottish, I thought, if my geography of the old lands was right. "I cannae agree to longer, lass."

Several concurred with nods and words of assent, leaving Lilith no choice but to cave to their demands. "Fine. I will begin immediately."

I nearly scoffed. As if she would have waited a few hours.

"Jace, come with me. And, Edon? Make appropriate accommodations," she demanded. "Oh, and congratulations on your ascension." The latter was nearly a sneer, but she tacked on a polite smile before exiting the room with a flourish.

"I'll stay at Walter's," Jace said as he passed me. "Your mother and I are old acquaintances."

It was on the tip of my tongue to argue, but he left before I could comment.

And then everyone else in the room started adding their own accommodation requirements at once.

Shit. It's going to be a long damn week.

"Welcome to leadership, kid," Kylan said, clapping me on the shoulder.

Yeah. A great fucking welcome.

Chapter Thirty-Six

LUNA

"YOU WENT TO UNIVERSITY TOGETHER?" My eyes widened. "Wow. What are the odds?"

Silas and Rae shared a look. "Not great," they both replied at the same time.

I nodded, pretending to understand. These two clearly had a history together, one that left me feeling a little miffed because *I* wanted to be the one Silas shared glances like that with. But we were nowhere near that level despite our time together, and I had no way of knowing if we would ever reach that place.

If Kylan shared my jealousy, he didn't show it. He lounged beside Rae on Edon's couch, his arm stretched out along the back and his fingertips idly brushing the woman's shoulder. Silas sat catty-corner in a chair, while I relaxed on the ottoman next to him.

My mother and Logan were making up one of the guest rooms for themselves. Apparently, Rae and Kylan would be taking the area I'd originally claimed for myself, leaving me firmly in Edon's quarters until these new living arrangements were over.

Not that I minded.

I just hoped Silas would join us, too.

I cleared my throat. "When did you say Edon would be back?" I asked Kylan.

From what I understood, Edon was busy finding sleeping arrangements for all of our apparent guests. Most of the royals and alphas had only intended to attend the ceremony and return to their jets, but the Goddess demanded everyone stay until she sorted through the mess Edon's father had created.

"I didn't," Kylan replied. "He seemed hell-bent on removing Jace and Darius from Walter's home, a fight I really don't think he'll win. So it may be a while."

"Why would he care?" Silas asked.

"Because Jace has a penchant for seducing wolves, and there's a broken one living in that home who means a great deal to young Edon," Kylan explained, his lips curling. "Little does he realize, the two share quite a history."

"He won't hurt her," my mother said softly as she entered the room, her gaze downcast.

So utterly submissive for an alpha female. But at least she wasn't near catatonic like Edon's mom. No, mine actually stood up for herself on occasion. Like tonight.

And now she would never have to fend for herself again, unless my brother bargained her to another alpha. She was still young and pretty enough for others to show interest, at least in making her a concubine. However, I didn't see Logan ever agreeing to a deal, not if his protective stance beside her was anything to go by.

"I never said he would, Cora," Kylan replied. "I merely stated his penchant and their history."

My mother's lips twitched. "History is something Jace has with many."

I narrowed my gaze, but Edon stalked inside before I could question her. He took one look at the living area and growled.

"Hi to you, too," Silas greeted, grinning.

"It's been a long fucking night." Edon went straight to the kitchen and came back with a beer that he rolled across his forehead. "I don't recall inviting you over, Kylan."

"That's all right, young alpha. I took it upon myself to do that for you," he replied.

Edon grunted. "I'm too exhausted to argue."

Kylan grinned. "No, I imagine the others put you through the wringer well enough." He stood and held out a hand to Rae. "Shall we retire and allow his triad to soothe him?"

Triad. Silas and I had asked Jolene to explain what that meant earlier tonight while we were cleaning up the courtyard. He'd answered vaguely about it being a rare relationship between three lycans, before being called away to help reset the shoulder of a recovering wolf. We didn't see him again after that.

"Why does everyone keep talking about triads?" Logan asked, his brow furrowing.

"Because your sister is in the heart of a blossoming one," Kylan replied as he pulled Rae up beside him. "Current society frowns upon them because it's an unbreakable bond that supersedes any and all other relationships within a pack, but denying fate is like trying to challenge a royal vampire—a very bad idea." He brushed his lips against Rae's mouth and smiled. "Unless you're Raelyn. Then you can challenge a royal vampire all you like."

She narrowed her gaze. "You're just trying to seduce me."

"Is it working?"

"Maybe." She nipped at his jaw, some unspoken message passing between their gazes—one that had Kylan grinning and tugging her out of the room on a whisper of sound.

"He's changed," my mother said, her brow furrowing as she studied the empty hallway in their wake.

Logan ignored her, his blue irises flitting from me to Silas to Edon and back to me again. "Wait… The three of you are…?" His eyes narrowed at Edon. "You're *sharing* my sister with *him*?"

Edon caught my brother's fist before it came near his face and shoved him backward. "I've had a really long fucking night, Logan. We'll do this tomorrow."

Silas jumped off the chair and intercepted Logan as he went for Edon again. "Back off."

"It's fine," I interjected, standing up and joining Silas. "*I'm* fine."

Logan blinked. "This is messed up." He ran his fingers through his hair and blew out a breath. "Fuck, this entire night is fucking messed up."

"No shit," Edon muttered. "And the week isn't going to be any better."

Logan shook his head and turned away from us without a word, leaving us for the bedroom down the hall.

"I'll talk to him," my mother whispered, reaching out to squeeze my hand. "Once he realizes Claudette's history in her own triad with Jolene, he'll come around."

"*What*?" I gaped at her. "What history with Claudette?"

She frowned. "You mean he hasn't mentioned it?"

"No," all three of us said in unison.

"Explain," Edon added in his alpha tone.

"Oh, I don't think it's my place," my mother said, taking a step back. "Maybe you should talk to your grandfather about it. I didn't realize… I just thought…" Another step away from us. "Ask Jolene."

She fled on those words, causing my forehead to crinkle.

Edon muttered a curse and cracked open his beer. "Fuck it. Fuck it all. I'm done trying to solve puzzles tonight. I just want to escape for, like, an hour and not fucking think."

Silas glanced down at me before turning to face Edon. "We can help with that."

I smiled, rotating as well. "Yeah. We can totally help with that." Silas and I had showered together earlier while everyone else was cleaning off and changing.

But Edon was still filthy.

Bloody.

And wearing a pair of jeans that clearly didn't fit.

I tugged on the button, loosening the waistline. "Come with us, Alpha."

Silas took the beer from Edon, saying, "Yeah, come with us, Alpha," and led the way.

"I earned that," Edon grumbled, his cheeks flushing.

"And you'll be drinking it," Silas replied with a glance over his shoulder. "You said you didn't want to think. So let us do it for you." He held open the door to the master bedroom. "Trust us."

I moved past Edon and Silas and tugged my shirt over my head, letting it flutter to the floor. Then batted my eyes back at them. "I'll be in the shower while you two work this out."

Their growls followed me into the bathroom, where I lost my jeans and turned on the water.

Silas and I hadn't spoken much during our shower earlier, just helped each other wash off and kissed a few times before joining the others in the living area. It hadn't felt right without Edon. Like we were missing a piece of ourselves. It was one of those mutually understood things that didn't require words. A feeling I noted in Silas's gaze likely as easily as he did in mine.

And as he entered the bathroom now, I knew he understood and shared my intent.

He set the bottle down, pulled off his shirt and jeans, and smiled as Edon kicked off his own pants.

With a jerk of his head, Silas indicated where he wanted Edon to go.

The alpha's jaw ticked—unaccustomed to following orders—but he eventually caved and joined me beneath the warm spray.

I rewarded him by wrapping my arms around his neck and kissing him.

His hands fell to my hips as he pinned me against the wall, his arousal growing against my stomach and shooting heat into my veins. Silas joined us and stepped up behind the alpha, his palms sliding over Edon's back.

Soap—crisp and clean—tickled my nose and told me what he was doing.

Cleaning the alpha.

While I distracted him with my tongue.

Mmm, Edon could kiss so damn well. So dominant and overpowering and utterly perfect. I moaned, arching into him and allowing him to deepen our embrace while Silas worked on Edon's legs, ass, and arms.

Soon it would be my turn to soap down the front of him while they fucked each other's mouths, and just the idea of it had my thighs clenching with unsuppressed need.

Edon growled at whatever Silas did to his backside and ripped his lips away from mine to kiss his progeny into submission. From the way their mouths dueled, it seemed to be a battle for dominance—a mesmerizing one.

I loved when they embraced.

It was so primal and hot and arousing. The way Edon reached around to grip Silas by the neck set my blood on fire.

I took the soap from Silas's palm to run it over the alpha's abdomen, lathering across every inch of his torso before moving down to grip his straining cock. His chest vibrated in response, the thick member pulsing in my hand as I slid my grip lower to cup his balls.

"*Fuck*," he breathed.

"Mmm, that's the idea," Silas replied, his lips trailing a path down Edon's neck to his shoulder.

It was almost always me or Silas in the middle, never Edon, and we were all enjoying the change. Even the alpha, who seemed a bit flustered by his progeny seizing control.

Silas captured my gaze and gestured downward with his chin, telling me what to do.

I smiled and slid down the wall to my knees before Edon, the water trickling over his abdomen to his thick thighs and washing the suds away. "Allow me to distract you, Alpha," I said, staring up at him. "Please."

His head fell back on a groan, the thick bulb jutting out toward my lips in implied welcome. I licked him, loving the salty essence on the tip, and then took him deep into my mouth. Silas kissed him again, making Edon jerk violently against my tongue.

My thighs clenched, my need growing by the second as they devoured each other.

Edon's fingers threaded through my hair, his opposite palm still holding Silas's nape as he guided him down and around to join me on the ground.

"My turn, little moon," Silas murmured, taking over. His cheeks hollowed as he sucked the alpha's cock to the back of his throat and visibly swallowed.

Edon's forearm slammed into the wall to better brace himself, his opposite hand shifting between my head and Silas's as we rotated his shaft between our mouths. His moans turned to a dark, guttural sound that caused a gush of heat to slick down between my thighs.

Such a sexy fucking noise.

I wanted to hear it again.

I wanted to *feel* it against my pussy as he lapped me clean.

I wanted him to growl like that into my ear while he fucked me to completion.

I must have whimpered, because his fingers were suddenly in my hair, yanking me up off the ground and into him. In seconds, he had me pinned against the tile wall, his dick deep inside me on a single thrust and my thighs wrapped around his waist.

"Edon," I breathed, arching into him.

And then my mouth was occupied.

Not by Edon, but by Silas, his tongue hot and penetrating and so fucking addicting. I held on to Edon with one arm and wrapped my other around Silas, my claws digging into his scalp.

Someone palmed my breast.

Edon.

Another tweaked my opposite nipple.

Silas.

His lips descended to lick the peak while Edon claimed my mouth.

Thought escaped me, replaced firmly by feelings and sensation. A hot palm met my ass, the finger sliding through the crease to find my other hole. I didn't jerk or cringe, used to this game of Edon's, the preparation he continued to bestow upon my body.

Two digits slid inside, the double penetration eliciting a low whine from my mouth. Not because it hurt, but because I wanted *more.*

He must have known, because he added a third, which sent me whirling over the edge into an explosive climax I hadn't even felt coming. I screamed, my walls clamping down around him on both sides and forcing him to join me in oblivion.

Silas's head fell to my shoulder, his pants mingling with ours. Edon slid out of me, his grip trading with his progeny.

And then I was full again, this time with Silas's long, hard perfection.

My head hit the tiles, my body sore and tingling and way too tight, and yet burning all over again. Edon was there, his mouth on my neck, his palm returning to my ass. Silas drove into me sharply, his movements urgent, causing Edon's knuckles to slam into the wall. But that didn't stop him from gliding those fingers back inside and scissoring them in a way that made me squirm.

"Come, Omega," Edon growled. "Come so we can lick her clean together."

Oh, fuck…

My body shook, my limbs tightening.

Everything seemed to center in my lower abdomen.

So. Damn. Constricting.

Silas seemed to go deeper, searching for that spot I loved, and hit it with the force I needed to shatter all over again.

Black.

That was all I could see.

Pure. Bliss.

They'd literally fucked me into another realm of being, a blank state, my mind just completely shutting off.

And I didn't care, too blitzed out to breathe. But I felt them licking me clean, heard Silas chuckle as he retrieved the beer and told Edon to drink the liquid as he poured it over me. And drink he did.

Every single drop.

His tongue memorizing my flesh.

His mouth trailing kisses over my body as they laid me in the cloud of Edon's bed.

Both of them nurturing me, worshiping me, loving me.

I sighed and nuzzled into one of their chests while the other spooned me from behind.

Heaven, I decided. *This is my heaven.* And I refused to let anyone force me to leave.

Chapter Thirty-Seven

Silas

"IT'S SURREAL TO SEE YOU LIKE THIS," I said as I found Rae curled up on the couch with a steaming mug of what smelled like chocolate. Kylan stood in the kitchen with Luna, the two of them conversing softly about breakfast.

Okay. *That* was even more surreal.

At least the bastard was out of my head. It only took two fucking days.

I just want to make sure we're on the same page, he kept saying. *And I may need to use you to protect my Raelyn.*

It did not escape me that the only reason he saved my life was to appease his consort. That if we weren't old friends, he would have let me die without a second thought. So having him in my head for so long really sucked. Especially as he kept reminding me that he could make me his puppet.

I don't care much for him either, Edon muttered into my head.

I was so happy to have him back that I didn't even bother to remark on him reading my mind without permission. Instead, I asked, *Where are you?*

Checking up on my mother.

Again?

Jace is living at her house, he growled.

I frowned. *I thought you said they were just playing chess?*

During his visit yesterday, he'd found the two of them on the porch engaged in a serious game. It had unnerved the alpha so much that he'd returned with a bewildered expression, stating he'd never seen his mother so lively. Which, I supposed, was saying a lot since all she was doing was sitting in a chair while moving game pieces around on a chessboard.

Edon grumbled something incoherent back at me, causing me to chuckle. It sounded a lot like, *Fucking royal bloodsucking jackhole.*

Try not to get killed by that royal jackhole, yeah?

The alpha's responding snort vibrated in my head. *I brought Logan with me. We can take him.*

Uh-huh, I thought back at him, collapsing in the recliner chair beside Rae. *Glad you two are getting along now.* It'd been tense at first, but Luna's continued promise that she was fine seemed to appease her brother a bit. Although, that didn't stop him from having a stern word with me and Edon about what would happen should we hurt her. As if we'd ever let that happen.

"Edon?" Rae asked, a smile in her light blue eyes.

"Yeah." I ran my fingers through my hair—it was getting shaggy again. "He's really not happy about Jace staying with Aurora."

"Jace has a way of maintaining a reputation without actually fulfilling it," Kylan said cryptically as he joined Rae on the couch.

"Hmm, that sounds oddly familiar," Rae replied, tapping her chin thoughtfully. "No idea why…"

Kylan nipped her pulse and nuzzled her neck, the gesture inexplicably playful. And so not what I would ever expect from someone so notoriously known for his sadism. "Mmm, seems there are many playing with reputations lately," he murmured against her throat. "Such as the wolves approaching the door."

I picked up on the scent a second after he said it, but it was Luna who went sprinting toward the foyer. She threw open the door. "Where the hell have you been?" she demanded. "I have questions for you."

Jolene chuckled. "Hello, darling. I assume Cora's been talking?" He stepped into the house with Luka at his back, his astute gaze roaming over the living area. "Where's my grandson?"

"Checking up on Aurora," I said, standing. "He's not keen on Jace staying with her."

Luka grunted. "Good luck to Edon. Jace is a force of nature."

"You mated Claudette?" Luna interjected, her entire focus on Jolene. "And never thought to tell us about it?"

He narrowed his gaze at her. "Careful with your tone, young lady. I'll be needin' a long nap before we go muckin' through my past. Not that it's any of your business, mind."

She popped her hands onto her hips, undeterred. "You being in a triad with my mentor isn't any of my business? Fascinating. I'd say it's pretty pertinent, don't you, Silas?"

Oh, I knew better than to disagree with my little moon. "I think he owes us an explanation of what a triad is and how it applies to our situation, yeah. But I also think we should wait until Edon is here to hear it."

The latter earned me a brief grin from Jolene. "We should probably discuss what Luka and I have overheard first, but I think we should wait for my grandson. Tell him to come back and to bring Jace and Darius with him."

"Does this mean I finally get to play?" Kylan drawled, cocking his head to the side. "Or are we still pretending I don't know what you all are up to?"

Luka narrowed his blue eyes at the royal. "For the record, I voted against bringing you on board."

"On board what?" Luna asked.

"But Jace and Darius seem to think you could be an ally," Luka continued, ignoring my little moon.

"In what?" I demanded, not pleased to see her dismissed so callously.

Luka looked me up and down, taking my measure. I hadn't actually met the alpha male yet, but I knew of him. Leader of the Majestic Clan, mated to Mira, and overall not all that memorable. "You must have a mighty big sack to stand up to a two-hundred-year-old alpha, boy."

"Told you he was special," Jolene drawled, clapping me on the shoulder. "Luna, too. Their little triad is going to prove invaluable." He glanced around. "Logan, too, wherever he's run off to. At least according to my Claudette."

"Still want to know what the hell you all are talking about," Luna replied, a low growl permeating her tone. "And more information about this *triad* everyone keeps mentioning."

Kylan sighed. "It's a rare relationship bond between three lycans. You, Silas, and Edon are clearly in a triad. Why is this so difficult and cryptic?"

"Because a ritual must be performed to solidify it," Jolene replied. "But I'm not sayin' more until the others are here. Meanwhile, I'll be makin' myself some coffee."

Your grandfather is being cryptic and rude to Luna, I growled. *Okay, not rude. But he won't explain the triad until you're back, and he wants you to bring Jace and Darius with you.*

"Tell him to bring Aurora, too. It'd be good to see her." That came from Luka.

I relayed the message to Edon.

What am I, a fucking errand boy? he demanded.

Guess that makes me a glorified messenger, I replied.

Edon snorted. *I'll sort my granddad out when I get there. Give Luna a kiss for me.*

Will do.

With tongue, he added.

I smiled. *The tasks you assign me are so cumbersome.* I grabbed Luna on her way to the kitchen and tugged her into me, my lips capturing hers before she had a chance to speak. "That's from Edon," I whispered after a moment. "And this is from me." I deepened the embrace, leaving her breathless and panting in my arms while everyone observed.

Mine, I thought at them, my instinct to protect her overwhelming. Maybe because there were too many dominant males in the house. Or just because I felt like it. Either way, I claimed her with a nip and caught her resulting grin with my tongue.

Ours, Edon corrected.

Ours, I agreed. *Hurry back.*

Chapter Thirty-Eight

EDON

TOO MANY FUCKING VISITORS IN MY HOUSE, I thought as I settled into my favorite chair. The couch beside me was littered with vampires—Jace, Darius, Kylan, and Rae. Darius's blood virgin, Juliet, sat primly in a chair pulled in from the kitchen area.

Luka was on the ottoman.

Jolene took my other recliner.

Logan lounged on the floor.

Cora, Mira, and my mother were in the dining room, drinking tea. Which was a really weird experience since my mom never left her house willingly to socialize. I couldn't even remember the last time she lifted her head, let alone spoke.

Yet Walter's death seemed to have loosened her up just a little, or maybe it was the royal she seemed so fond of. She had actually kissed Jace on the cheek before taking a seat across from Mira.

Like, what the fuck was that about?

Focus, Silas chastised. He stood behind me with his arms folded across the top cushion of my recliner, while Luna snuggled in beside me.

You're lucky I'm distracted, I told him as I kissed the top of my little mate's head.

And yet, you being distracted is what I'm trying to fix, he drawled.

I snorted and looked up at him. *Tired of being the omega? Want to play in the alpha's shoes?*

What I want are answers, he replied flatly.

Well, I couldn't argue with him there. "Where have you been?" I asked my grandfather. "We tried to find you."

"Luna mentioned that," he replied conversationally. "I was with Luka, eavesdropping on Lilith's interrogation of Catalina."

As far as excuses went, that was a good one.

"At the airfield?" Lilith had refused to stay in Clemente Clan headquarters, stating her private jet would suffice. And she'd taken Silvano's sovereign with her.

"Yeah. It wasn't easy," he replied, scowling.

I imagined not. There weren't many trees out there.

Huh. Who knew my grandfather still had it in him to play spy? I knew he was revered in his day as one of the strongest alphas of his time, but his age showed. Most lycans lived to be around six to seven hundred years old, and he was pushing the upper end of that range.

"And?" Kylan prompted, sounding bored. "What did the good sovereign have to say about her royal's behavior?"

"That he had tasked her with taking out Edon and Walter in a double cross." Luka lifted his ankle to rest on his opposite knee. "Catalina also confirmed that Silvano was using Walter to take care of some unruly vampires. He handed them off to the Clemente Clan for disposal."

Meaning the wolves shredded the bloodsuckers apart. "And my father had agreed to it." I didn't phrase it as a question but as a statement. Walter was an even bigger asshole than I gave him credit for.

"From what Catalina confirmed, yes. The lycans made a sport of it, like the moon chase, only hunting down crippled vampires instead." My grandfather sounded sickened by the admission.

"That explains all the scents without the bodies," Silas put in, referring to the stench he kept picking up on near the headquarters' perimeter.

I nodded. "Yeah, it does. So why double-cross Walter?" I rarely used my father's given name, but it felt more natural now. As if he no longer deserved the endearment of *dad.*

"Catalina said Silvano's goal was to gain more territory, especially around the old border between Texas and Louisiana. Where the blood farms and breeding camps are housed in this region," Luka said.

"He thought by weakening the pack, he could expand," Jace clarified. "And as the blood farms and breeding camps carry financial incentives, he could benefit from taking that over from the Clemente Clan."

"And charge our wolves a higher rate to procreate," I translated. "Something the clan would be willing to pay if they lost their leadership and needed to start over." I didn't know what kind of blood types the camps housed at the moment, but if there were traces of alpha in any of the humans, they'd be fucked nearly to death to create a new lineage.

You can create alpha lines from humans? Silas asked.

Yeah. I suspect you have traces of it, I admitted. *It's all about dominant tendencies, something I'd say you carry in spades.* Which was why I intended to make him my enforcer.

So an alpha doesn't need to be lycan born? He sounded confused. I couldn't really blame him. Genetics was complicated.

If a lycan sires a child with a mortal, then turns that mortal into a lycan during the pregnancy, the child will be born a lycan.

That sounds too easy, he said, looking down at me.

I met his gaze as I replied, *There's a ninety-nine percent fatality rate. The transition while a female is pregnant is typically lethal to the mother and the child. Only the strongest of mortals survive.*

Ah, and the strongest are usually alphas, he translated.

Not usually, *but* always. *Most humans are killed in the process.* "Which explains why he wanted the breeding camps. Brilliant bastard," I marveled out loud, interrupting whatever Jace had been saying to Kylan.

They both looked at me with arched eyebrows, obviously not pleased with my interruption, and desiring an explanation.

I cleared my throat. "I was just explaining the alpha creation process to Silas."

"Between lycans and humans," Silas clarified. "I didn't know that was how it worked. At the camps, I mean."

"Depends on the goal of the breeder," Jace said, his focus on me. "And what conclusion did you draw, Edon?"

"If Silvano destroyed the alpha bloodline in Clemente Clan, the lycans left behind would have been desperate to create a new ruling family. Which would either require involvement from other clans—an unlikely choice given how few alpha females remain in our world—or they would try the breeding farms."

"And pay top price for each host," my grandfather added. "That's the motive Luka and I determined as well." Pride lit his gaze as he added that last line—the emotion directed at me, not himself.

"What about Lilith?" I wondered out loud. "Has she drawn the same conclusion?"

Both of the alphas shook their heads. "She called in Ryder," my grandfather replied. "Seems to think he knows more than he's sayin'."

"I'm certain he does," Kylan replied, amused. "But it won't be about Silvano."

"Who is Ryder?" I asked. "He's not part of Silvano's hierarchy. Or I would have met him." Yet the other day in the field was the first time I'd ever seen the vampire. Age and power had wafted off him like a dark cloud, and he hadn't fought at all. "Why is he even here?"

"He lives near the camps," Luka explained. "On the Silvano side. He keeps to himself, refuses to play the political game, and only came along 'cause Silvano walked the army through his property."

"Yeah, he was asking Lilith to excuse him, saying he only volunteered to represent Silvano for the initial meeting and had no intention of staying." My grandfather snorted. "She refused, of course. Said with Catalina in custody, she needed an elder around to keep all Silvano's vamps in line."

Kylan smirked. "Bet he's thrilled he volunteered."

"Do you think he knew what Silvano intended?" I asked. "Was he working with him?"

Kylan laughed outright. "Hell no. He hated that bastard."

"Silvano marched the vampires through Ryder's lands," Luka said.

"I'm sure he did," Kylan replied. "It was the best way to provoke the old recluse to come out and play, and Ryder fell for it."

"But why provoke him at all?" I wondered aloud. "Why bring him into it?"

"Maybe to act as a scapegoat, should he need it. Or because it was the easiest route." Kylan shrugged. "Regardless, I'm certain Ryder isn't involved. He might be old and senile, but he's not suicidal."

"I'm inclined to agree with Kylan that Ryder would never work with Silvano on this." Jace's tone rang with confidence. "But that's the real problem. The question remains: How will Lilith react to the news?"

"You mean, will she punish me for taking Silvano's life?" Kylan grinned. "She can try."

Jace smirked. "She can, yes. Meanwhile, Edon and Logan should be all right, as Walter was the one who accepted the challenge and requested to fight with Niko at his side. No major hiccups, but I imagine she'll be watching them closely as a result."

"It was all within pack law," I added. "She can't fault us for following it." But Kylan, yeah, he might have an issue or two.

"Indeed." Darius scratched the dark scruff dotting his jaw. "Still, I think we all need to lie low for a few months while the dust settles. Too many upsets so close together is going to put the alliance on edge, and we can't afford to be noticed."

"Killing Silvano to stop the vampires and wolves from killing each other is hardly going to be seen as a revolutionary move," Kylan pointed out. "I'm the mad royal, remember? I do crazy shit all the time." He punctuated that with a kiss against Rae's neck. "Right, consort?"

She just shook her head, but the hum of energy between them suggested she was in his head. *How fascinating.* I wasn't aware vampire sires could communicate like that with their progeny. I always thought it was a wolf thing.

He turned her after he made her his Erosita, Silas explained softly. *She told me it altered her transformation.*

Fascinating, I repeated.

"It's true. All the rebellious acts of late have somehow involved Kylan. If anyone is at risk of censure, it's him." Luka glanced at the royal. "Which is why I didn't want to bring you on board. You're a danger to our plans."

"Are you suggesting I might tattle on you all to save myself?" Kylan asked, his lips curling. "What happened to good old-fashioned trust, wolf? Can't you smell my loyalty?"

I snorted at that. "You smell old and powerful to me." Just like Jace and Darius. They were at least two or three thousand years old.

Logan grunted. "They smell old to me, too. But I'd like to know what all this revolution shit is about while we're on the topic."

Jace smiled. "You're sitting in the middle of it."

And so began an hour-long conversation about those who sought to take down the Blood Alliance Council.

Four of the founding members were in this room—Jace, Darius, Luka, and Jolene. But there were several others across the globe, all living in quiet and waiting for their cue to rise up. It was something they hadn't planned to do for several more years, perhaps even decades, but events over the last two months had escalated their timeline.

This week, in particular, punted them way into the future.

Because Logan and I were groomed with a purpose—to lead our clans toward rebellion. However, it had to be subtle. Little things like getting rid of the moon chase might not be noticed, especially as it only happened a few times a year.

Another would be to allow relationships to form, to encourage matings rather than degrade them.

It just had to be quiet. Unnoticeable by the other packs.

"With Silvano out of the picture, we might have an opportunity," Darius put in. "Jaxon is one of the oldest in the territory."

"But not in a leadership position," Jace replied.

"Neither was I." Darius grinned. "Yet, here we are."

"Because of my place at the top." The royal winked at Darius's blood virgin. "It's nice to see your eyes, sweetheart."

She blushed but didn't drop her gaze. Clearly, she was in on all of this, because from what I understood, blood virgins were bred to be submissive to a fault. Yet she seemed rather confident and poised beside Darius, as if she had every right to sit in this circle.

And maybe she did.

"How many other young lycans are being trained for your rebellion?" Luna asked, her eyes on Luka. "Your daughter? For Logan?"

His expression darkened. "Just because Niko decided to retire early does not mean my daughter is to be wed next month."

Well, that wasn't at all what Luna had asked. But it seemed to be a sore subject for the alpha lycan.

"So my pack is to go without leadership until you decide she's ready?" Logan asked, his eyebrow inching upward. "You know I can't ascend without a mate."

"It's a topic we'll continue to discuss," Jolene put in with a sharp look at Luka. "And to answer your question, Luna, there are a handful of mentors in place to help guide the mentalities of younger lycans, yes. However, you, Edon, and Logan were our primary objectives for this wave. As we mentioned earlier, we thought we had more time. But it seems our pawns are falling into place earlier than anticipated."

"Much earlier," Darius agreed. "We'll need to reevaluate several avenues, but it seems others have opened up for us to navigate."

"You're welcome," Kylan interjected.

Darius ignored him. "I think it would be wise for Edon to engage in his triad, as it will set an immediate relationship precedent for the pack. Just as I would advise Luka to reconsider his stance on his daughter's nuptials. Ernest Clan will require unity to rebuild, and Logan can't do that alone."

Luka growled, but I jumped in before he could reply. "You know what would be wise? For someone to explain what the fuck a triad is before asking me to do it," I suggested, not so politely.

All eyes fell to my grandfather.

He sighed in resignation. "It's what I had with your grandmama and Claudette."

Luna stiffened beside me. "And what does that mean, exactly?" she demanded.

"Yeah, what she said," Logan agreed.

I didn't comment since I wondered the same thing.

But I was the one my grandfather addressed. "The three of us were very much a unit, similar to the one you, Silas, and Luna are forming." Sadness swirled in the depths of his dark eyes. "Your grandmama was the alpha female and Claudette was a human turned lycan. During my initial alpha rituals, I turned her, then claimed Yazmine beneath the moon a few weeks later."

As was the custom for an alpha ascension.

I understood that.

"And?" I prompted.

"And unlike your pairing to Luna, Yazmine was mine by choice. Meaning we went into our initial claiming with love already in our hearts. As you know, the male bites first. Then the female bites during the next full moon. But something happened between me and Claudette in the interim, and that something spread to my Yazy. We didn't understand it at first; the physical connection was just incredibly intense."

Sounds familiar, I thought.

"And by the next full moon, the three of us were too engaged for Yazmine and me to go through with our pairing alone. We invited Claudette to join us and performed a triad bonding instead, much to the surprise of our pack. Then we lived together as a trio for nearly five hundred years, three hundred of which I ruled Clemente Clan. We didn't split until the new world order, and to this day, I believe that split is what killed my Yazy." He swallowed, his eyes falling. "Triads are not meant to be separated."

"What he's telling you is a warning," my mother added softly from the living area, her voice surprising us all. “You can’t enter a triad lightly. All three of you have to be committed and be prepared to fight for it.”

Chapter Thirty-Nine

LUNA

TWO DAYS LATER AND LILITH still hadn't reconvened the council. Apparently, she wasn't in a hurry to deliver a verdict.

Which left wolves and vampires all over Clemente Clan headquarters.

And specifically, in Edon's house.

I stretched my legs, limbering up for a much-needed run as Silas joined me outside. "Human or wolf?" he asked.

"Human." Because I wanted to talk to him about all this triad business. We'd avoided the Jolene bombshell for long enough. While I could sense how Edon felt, I had no idea what Silas thought about it all.

Fucking around temporarily as a trio was fine.

Committing to one for eternity? Yeah, entirely different scenario. Even if it broke my heart to see Silas go, I'd let him if that was what he wanted.

And therein lies the problem—I can't read him. Just as he can't read me.

Supposedly, that problem would be fixed if we accepted each other under the next full moon, but I wasn't willing to do that until I knew he desired the same things I did.

"Human it is." He left to slip on a pair of socks and shoes and returned without a shirt. Something my eyes more than appreciated. "Ready?"

"Yep."

He grinned. "Lead the way."

"You just want to check out my ass," I said, taking off at a jog for the tree line.

"Those shorts are awfully short, little moon. Can't blame me for admiring the view."

I snorted and picked up the pace because I could. "You just saw me naked, like, an hour ago." He'd joined me in the shower not to fool around but for company. Which was nice. I liked the way he washed my hair.

Of course, I'd need another thorough cleansing after this run.

Maybe Edon would be back by then and the three of us could have some fun. I supposed it depended on how Edon's chat with his grandfather went. They were reviewing the list of packmates Jolene recommended for promotion to headquarters. Apparently, he'd been keeping tabs on everyone over the last ten years, preparing for the moment his grandson ascended.

A slap to my ass had me jumping a step. "Hey!"

"I thought we were going for a run. This is more like a lazy stroll."

I glanced over my shoulder at the cocky male. "You want to race, newbie?"

"What happened to *big wolf*?" he teased, referring to that day in the kitchen.

"You haven't earned it yet," I tossed back at him. "Beat me to the creek and maybe I'll reconsider."

I took off at full speed, not giving him a chance to reply or react. His chuckle followed me, the sound far too close for my comfort. So I pushed myself harder, my inner wolf growling in jealousy of my two legs. She wanted to be free to run, to smell the trees, and to feel the air currents against her coat.

Later, I promised.

I wanted to talk to Silas in our clothes because I didn't trust myself to engage him naked. We'd end up in a pile of limbs. Especially after an adrenaline-filled sprint through the woods.

His shoulder brushed mine, his long legs carrying him faster.

On four paws, I held my own because of my experience. But it seemed he had me beat in human form.

With every inch he put between us, I grew more and more agitated.

And equally aroused.

Because the man was sleek, lean muscle streaking through the trees and dodging branches like a professional. I wanted to lick that trail of sweat beading down his spine, nip the back of his neck, and pin him to the ground.

Only to have him wrestling me beneath him, something I knew he would do. And then he'd slide right into my waiting heat.

This is why we're wearing clothes.

Except my tank top suddenly felt sticky and far too heavy.

My shorts were too thick.

My shoes suffocating.

I wanted to *breathe*.

No.

I had to talk to him first, and we were almost to the creek—the same spot in which I'd played with Edon all those weeks ago. So much had changed since then.

A revolution? Who would have ever thought that was possible? But hell yes, I was in. Edon and Silas, too. The question was, would we fight together as a triad or as friendly packmates?

Silas reached the water's edge first, his triumphant smile drawing me to him all the more. It took serious effort not to jump him and wrap my legs around his waist. But I stopped just barely at his side, hands on my hips as I panted in much-needed breath.

He'd pushed me to my limit. I could still go another few miles, but damn. My legs felt a little like jelly.

"Did I earn my nickname?" he asked, much less winded than me. Something told me he could have gone harder, and would have, had it been Edon racing him.

I would need to work harder to keep up with those two. *Lucky male genetics.*

Silas cupped my cheek and brushed his mouth against mine. "I prefer *sweets* to *big wolf.*"

"Yeah?" I licked his lower lip. "What if I prefer *big wolf*?"

"You could nickname me *furball* and I'd still answer to you, Luna," he whispered, kissing me again.

And damn, he tasted so good. Like sex and wolf and man all wrapped up in a Silas package. Mmm, but I needed to talk to him first. That was the whole—*oh, that feels good*—point of this—

I arched into him, groaning as his tongue did something decidedly wicked with mine.

Hello, hardness, I thought, feeling his excitement beneath his jeans. He must have enjoyed that run as much as I did, even though we only went a mile or so.

His palm wrapped around the back of my neck, his opposite hand falling to my hip, and he devoured me with his mouth.

We kissed a little in the shower, but it was more nips and fun. Silas had meant to play then. Now? Yeah, now he seemed hungry. No, *starved.* And I was his next meal.

"Silas," I breathed, my pulse racing as it always did when he touched me. "I want—" His tongue silenced me and scattered my thoughts.

I shivered, my wolf bowing to his.

Hmm, no, I need… "Triad," I managed to force out, the word sounding much sultrier than I anticipated.

But it caught his attention. "Triad?" he repeated, pulling back just far enough to stare down at me with his blown-out pupils.

Oh, dear moon, the hunger in his gaze…

Focus! I chastised myself.

I cleared my throat, trying to remember what I wanted to say. But I couldn't. Not with him so near, his blue irises hypnotizing me, his full lips taunting me for another kiss. I wanted him, and not just physically. I wanted *Silas.* All of him.

"I want the triad," I whispered. "I want to be with you. With Edon. With *us*. I want to hear your mind. To know your soul. To touch your heart. I want to know what it would be like to be loved by you. To love you in return. To be your mate, your everything. To connect all three of us. Forever. But I won't make you, even if it's all I can think about, all I've ever truly wanted for myself in this life. Because you have a right to choose. And I would never take that away from you."

"Hey, hey," he said softly, his thumb brushing away the tears that had fallen unknowingly from my eyes.

Goddess, I was crying.

But the thought of him not wanting me in return broke something inside me.

I hadn't realized just how important this was to me until this second, this very breath. If he rejected me, rejected *us*, I… I wouldn't be able to breathe right again.

I already love him, I realized. *I already love them both.*

I pressed my hand to my mouth, shock riveting my system. How had I let this happen? Or was there never a choice?

My wolf submitted to them both on instinct.

She *knew* her mates even when my human half didn't.

"Luna," Silas murmured, his thumb stroking over my cheekbone again. "Sweet little moon, look at me."

I had let my gaze drop without realizing it, my mortification at falling so deeply threatening to destroy me.

"I-I can't," I admitted. Not a response to the command to look at him, but to the very real heartache ripping me apart. Never in my life had I felt like this, so terrified by the potential of someone's response.

I hated not being able to sense him or his thoughts. *How does he feel?*

It would be so easy to assume, but forever was a long time. This relationship circumvented so many of society's standards. Nothing about being a triad was considered typical. None of us truly understood what it meant beyond what Jolene had said.

But I wanted it so badly that my chest ached with the emptiness of incompletion. It hurt to breathe, bringing more tears to my eyes.

This wasn't about him rejecting us but about us denying the bond.

Now that I'd allowed myself to consider the triad, I could sense what the incompletion was doing to me. "I feel so empty, Silas."

"I know. I feel it, too," he whispered, his lips against my forehead. "It's agony without you inside me, little moon. Edon's there—I feel him every day—but you… I miss you even when you're standing right in front of me. I want that connection to you, too. That bond, to call you truly mine, to claim you both. I already do in my heart, Luna. You're already mine."

I swallowed, my eyes glassing over again. "You do?"

"Every day," he promised. "You're my little moon. My Luna. On the next full moon, I'll prove it to the world. To you and Edon both. I wouldn't be anywhere else."

I grabbed him and kissed him, my tears falling between us as I let all my inhibitions go. All my doubts. All my fears. Everything. I gave him all I had, kissing him until I couldn't even breathe and not stopping to refill my lungs.

He owned me.

Edon, too.

My neck prickled with awareness, a familiar warmth approaching from behind. How he found us, how he *knew,* I didn't care. Because as I felt Edon's lips on my shoulder, I collapsed, allowing both males to cradle me between them.

"I want it, too," he whispered into my ear. "I've wanted you both since the beginning. You're mine, little mate. And Silas is mine, too."

My clothes disappeared into a pile on the rocks. Silas's following suit. And Edon had arrived naked, likely in his wolf form.

I turned in his arms, kissing him as I did Silas, pouring all my emotions, my *heart,* into my tongue as it stroked against his. *I love you,* I thought at him. *I love you so much it hurts.*

He couldn't hear me, our mating bond incomplete.

And it sliced me wide open.

I didn't want to wait until the full moon, but we didn't have a choice.

Four more weeks… I'd have to survive all that time without him hearing me, without connecting to Silas.

"Don't cry, little mate." Edon licked the tear from my cheek. "We'll fix this soon."

"I want you to hear me," I said. "I want you both to *hear* me."

"Then scream for us, sweetheart," Edon said. "Scream for everyone to hear, to tell the world who owns you."

Silas nibbled my shoulder, his hot body pressed to my back. "Let us take care of you. Let us show you how we feel about you, how we feel about each other. Join us together, Luna. Mate us both. At the same time."

I shuddered, my heart slamming against my lungs. "Yes." I swallowed. "Yes."

If we couldn't have each other mentally, then we would do this physically.

Both of them inside me at once.

Sensing everything I had to offer.

"Yes," I said for a third time, my head falling back against Silas's chest as Edon licked up the column of my throat. His palm pressed into my abdomen, sliding downward to the ache between my legs.

"So wet," he hissed, his fingers slipping easily inside.

I moaned, my hips rising up against his touch, begging him to go deeper.

But he had something else in mind.

He removed his hand, then guided it around to my backside. Silas shifted to allow him room to move, but I felt his cock pressed into the alpha's wrist.

Heat slithered through my veins, lighting my body on fire as Edon penetrated my puckered hole.

Silas yanked my head back for a kiss, distracting me with his tongue. But the pressure built inside me as Edon worked to lubricate both sides, readying me to take them both.

It would destroy me.

Cripple my ability to think of anyone but them.

And I was okay with that. Because Silas and Edon made me feel whole. They were my pack, my past, present, and future, and I would only ever desire them.

"She's ready," Edon whispered seconds, or maybe minutes, later. I didn't know, my body strung too tight with anticipation to comprehend time.

He captured my mouth, his tongue fucking me thoroughly as he guided the three of us to the ground. Leaves pillowed my bare legs, pleasing my inner wolf immensely. Silas lay on his back beside me, his handsome features melting my heart. "Hop on, little moon," he invited.

His arousal beckoned me with a pulse that made my pussy clench in expectation. *Yes, please.* I crawled over him, straddling his hips and wrapping his shaft in my damp folds.

"*Fuck…*" He grabbed my hips, shifting me to where he wanted me—with his head at my entrance. "Slide down."

I did.

Because that demand? It demolished my ability to rebel, to fight, to do anything other than accept. My lower abdomen quivered, the feel of his thick, hot length inside me a growing addiction in my blood. I seated myself on him, locking us so deeply that he groaned in approval.

Edon grabbed my hip, his teeth skimming my shoulder. "Bend down and kiss him, little mate."

My heart fluttered, my wolf preening beneath the alpha's command.

I leaned into Silas, embracing him with my mouth and sighing as he wrapped his palm around my nape.

Mine, he was saying.

Yours, I agreed.

This was what I needed, our bodies connecting and confirming we belonged together. "More," I begged, no, *ordered.* It wasn't a request but a requirement. I needed *more.*

Edon stroked down my spine, eliciting goose bumps in his wake. It left me feeling light and cherished. More gentle touches, his tongue gliding along my lower back as he gripped my ass and spread me wide.

I half expected to feel his mouth *there.* Instead, he shifted, and something much harder and larger pressed against my opening.

I swallowed, suddenly unsure.

But a nip from Silas reminded me of my task, his lips moving beneath mine. Wicked. Smooth. Perfection. Urging me to return his kiss. And I did, losing myself to him as an intense pressure began to fill me from behind.

Slowly.

Carefully.

In and out, one inch at a time.

It hurt.

Yet it also did all sorts of sinful things to my insides.

I groaned into Silas's mouth, my lower half throbbing in both pain and pleasure, the two males joining with me in a way that left me spellbound.

"How do you feel, Luna?" Edon asked, his breath slightly more labored than before, as if he were pacing himself in this task.

"Hot," I whispered, swallowing. "*Full.*"

He chuckled. "Not full yet, little mate." He thrust in a little more, causing me to both flinch and moan.

"I can feel you," Silas said, his jaw clenching. "Fuck, I can *feel* you."

"Wait until I start to move," Edon replied, his hands running up and down my sides. "Just a little more, Luna. Almost there."

Something unintelligible left my mouth as he forced me to take him to the hilt.

Something that sounded a lot like a growl mingled with a scream.

Something that was reminiscent of his name and a curse.

He dropped his head to my back as he allowed me to adjust to them both. I couldn't move, pinned between two strong males, their hands and lips tracing along my skin as they each praised me for taking them both. For accepting our bond. For allowing us to join so completely.

And that was exactly how I felt—*complete.*

These were my two mates. My males. My lovers. My future.

"Fuck me," I said, needing to feel them move. "I need you to *fuck* me."

Silas chuckled, his lips ghosting over my cheek. "You heard the woman, Edon."

"Still topping from the bottom," he mused out loud.

"As if you would have it any other way," Silas replied.

"I wouldn't." Edon slid almost all the way out of me and rammed back in, causing me to cry out.

Fuck.

I expected that to hurt. It didn't. Instead, it left me winded in the best way. "*Please,*" I said, unsure of what I wanted to beg for more. Another thrust? Harder? Softer? Faster? I just felt so full. So absolute. So alive.

His hips snapped into mine again. "Is this what you want, little mate?" he asked against my ear. "To feel me taking your virgin ass and making it mine?"

Silas arched beneath me, his cock pulsing inside me. "Again," he breathed.

Edon complied, leaving me breathless and *hot* between them. I was wrapped up in delicious masculine muscles all moving in time with my body, sealing me in a cocoon of feral sex.

Both of them found a rhythm, one I tried to maintain, but each pump left me seeing stars. I'd never felt so utterly dominated. Completely mastered. Owned. Yet worshiped.

They were kissing me, touching me, making sure I loved it every bit as much as they did. And that care alone sent me cascading into a well of oblivion so deep that I fought to resurface.

A pinch to my clit brought me back, teeth against my neck, a palm squeezing my breast, and a stark demand to "Come again."

Edon. He wanted my pleasure, to split me in half for everyone to hear.

And my body craved to give it to him.

Both males moved sharply, in and out, hitting me in places I never knew were orgasmic points. It left me shaking between them, my pleasure mounting again, only this time was far more intense. Liquid lava poured through my system, culminating in my lower belly, threatening to burst.

"Edon," I whimpered. "Silas." I didn't know whom to beg, whom to cry out to, but as the fire escalated inside, I began to sweat. To vibrate. To scream.

It was ripping me in two. Half of me claimed by Silas, the other half by Edon. And their names poured from my mouth, just as they desired.

"Fucking beautiful," Edon praised, his cock so deep in my ass that I couldn't move, could only convulse as pleasure continued to ripple through me.

"Perfection," Silas agreed, his back bowing off the ground as he came inside me on a roar that echoed off the trees and blasted my senses apart.

Edon followed us both, his seed pumping deep inside me as if to find Silas's essence.

A sudden peace settled over me.

Joined.

We were finally together. All three of us, in mind, body, and spirit.

With Silas beneath me and Edon at my back, we were finally mated in a harmony of bliss.

Mine, my wolf whispered. *These males are mine.*

Just as I was theirs.

We didn't need a ceremony to complete us.

We were already complete.

As one.

The ritual next month would just be a formality. Because I felt it in my blood that our souls were already bound. Promised for eternity.

A triad.

Forever.

Chapter Forty

EDON

LILITH PACED THE MAIN LODGE ROOM, her gown fluttering around her in a ridiculous wave of red. She looked ready to attend a damn ball, not address an agitated crowd of alphas and royals.

Tonight was her deadline of five days since the incident. And she'd waited until the very last second to call her "emergency council meeting." Talk about a power trip.

I folded my arms and leaned against the wall, watching as she paced the wooden floor in her five-inch stilettos. One would think this bitch would be eager to run on back home. Alas, no.

"I have reviewed the evidence," she announced, pausing in the center beneath the brightest light. It gave her pale hair an ugly yellow glow. Fitting for her personality, it seemed.

It's starting, I told Silas. He was back at my house with Rae, Luna, Darius, and Juliet.

If something happened tonight, they were under strict orders to run to Jace Region. But I suspected the escape act wouldn't be needed. Lilith would have brought an army with her if that were the case, and yet only two minions stood off to the side—both young vampires Kylan and Jace could take out with a second's notice.

This revolutionary team was certainly proving handy.

Lilith cleared her throat and stared down Kylan. "I cannot allow a precedent to be set where royals or alphas decide to take the life of another just to soothe a situation. We're immortals. There are ways to incapacitate us without ending a life."

The royal smiled. "Duly noted. I'll remember that going forward."

"Why didn't you just shoot him? Or break his neck? Why remove his head?" she demanded.

"Because I didn't like the prick," Kylan replied. "And he put my life in danger by instigating a war. Why are we not analyzing his guilt, Lilith? How many lives were lost unnecessarily due to his meddling?"

"How do you know he's guilty?" she countered.

"Is it not obvious?" he asked, his eyebrows rising. "I thought you concluded your evidence research. If you've not ascertained that Silvano double-crossed Walter with the intent of hurting Clemente Clan for his own financial gain, then perhaps you need another five days in that fancy jet of yours."

That royal had balls. Big ones.

And Lilith appeared ready to murder him for it. Blood stained her porcelain cheeks, painting her skin in a cherry-red tone. "You ascertained all that before killing him?"

He narrowed his gaze. "I am over five thousand years old, Lilith. Nearly twice your age. That's granted me experience unlike anything you could ever fathom. And a double cross such as Silvano's is not an uncommon occurrence throughout my very long history. So yes, *young one*, I did. And I delivered the justice he deserved."

He took a step forward, his height advantage clear as he looked down at her.

"My only regret is not taking the wolf's head, too, as he certainly deserved it for plotting such a ludicrous political move. Had it been me, I would have been much slyer about it. But again, that kind of knowledge comes with experience. Something I have in spades."

She swallowed but didn't otherwise move. "Are you threatening me, Kylan?"

"No, sweetheart," he replied, smiling. "Why on earth would I desire your seat at the top? I live with enough targets on my back."

Silence fell over the room.

The sound of hearts beating echoing off the walls.

Everyone waited for her verdict and Kylan's reaction.

Your friend Rae might be one of the bravest people I've ever met, I murmured to Silas.

Why?

Because she lives with Kylan. That royal is fucking terrifying. He didn't appear fazed at all, his stance intimidating yet relaxed at the same time.

Something told me he would have no problem winning a fight against Lilith. Especially with this crowd. She might have a few supporters in attendance, but there were also several against her.

Except we couldn't go after her yet. I'd asked, and Jace explained that they needed her alive because she was the only one in existence who could help them find Cam, the former vampire king. He was believed to be dead. His *Erosita*—who lived with Majestic Clan, apparently—proved otherwise. Because if Cam was dead, she would be, too.

I'd absorbed all that information with a shocked expression.

Silas, however, had just shrugged and said, *"Nothing in this world is what it seems."*

If only we could all be that laid-back and accepting about it.

"No additions to your harem," Lilith declared. "No Blood Day attendance. No social outings of any kind. You are hereby confined to Kylan Region until I say otherwise. Is that understood?"

"Is this supposed to be my punishment?" he asked, cocking his head. "Sounds like a vacation."

"Then I'll consider adding blood rationings to the list," she seethed. "Get back in line or I *will* threaten your position at the top as royal."

His lips curled. "You could try. But I wouldn't recommend it."

Her jaw ticked as he stepped back to his place in our makeshift circle.

It'd been part of our plan for him to take control of the show, and he'd acted splendidly. I just hoped he didn't end up with any repercussions from it. But at least all the spotlight would remain on him as a potential rebel, and not on any of us.

"Edon and Logan are granted permission to ascend," she continued with a flourish, pointedly turning her back on Kylan. "Edon acted within his right of the challenge, and I see no reason for him to be punished. Logan was an innocent bystander whom I'm grateful to have coming of age. Unfortunately, he cannot ascend for eleven more moons, which poses a leadership problem in his clan."

"I have a suggestion," Luka cut in. "If I may."

She waved a hand. "I'm all ears, Alpha."

He cleared his throat and stepped forward. "After Edon's ascension, send Jolene to Ernest Clan to act as a leader while Logan completes his final year of training. The former alpha may be old, but he's still a force of nature. As was evidenced the other night when he took on the ceremonial role for Edon's challenge. I feel he would be more than fit to administer the alpha trials next year."

She considered him for a long moment. "Are there any objections to the notion?" she asked, addressing the other alphas in the room. Her gaze fell on me. "Edon?"

"I agree with Luka's suggestion. Jolene might be old, but he's still an alpha." I purposely used his given name, not my endearment for him. The more detached she believed me to be, the more likely she would agree. As much as I would miss him, I knew this was his desire—to return to his Claudette.

"And I have no objections either," Logan added. "There are no elder alphas in my clan, and I would be grateful for the leadership of one so experienced."

A few others nodded in agreement, no one speaking out about the clearly obvious path.

"Very well," Lilith said. "Edon, please advise Jolene of his new placement after we finish here."

"I will," I agreed. Not that I had a choice. She may have used the word *please,* but she meant it as an order.

She nodded. "The last item for us to handle is Silvano Region. Sovereign Catalina confessed to her involvement in his nefarious plans to instigate a war for the benefit of gaining land." She glanced at Kylan, a subtle edge to her tone. "Which means I can't trust his political choices in that region and need to conduct a full investigation personally. So I will temporarily be taking over as the royal of the territory until an appropriate candidate can be found."

"Or you could allow me to serve temporarily and save yourself multiple trips," Ryder drawled, causing several heads to turn his way. "I mean, I meet all the royal qualifications, and I already live in the region. Seems a more suitable answer."

Well, that's unexpected.

What is? Silas replied.

Ryder just volunteered to be the temporary royal of Silvano Region. And from the look on Lilith's face, she was *not* happy about it.

"You were offered a royalship a century ago and turned it down," she snapped, her temper showing. "Why now?"

"Because you said it would only be temporary." He smiled. "Temporary royalty, I'll accept. Permanent royalty? In this new world? No."

She bristled. "You are not suitable to lead."

"Why?" he countered. "Because I turned down your precious offer a century ago?" he snorted. "We both know I'm more than qualified, Lilith. And if I wanted to, I could demand the position permanently."

We could have heard a pin drop—it was that silent.

The other royals in the room seemed to be in agreement, their gazes riveted on Lilith, waiting for her decision.

But Ryder wasn't done.

"I've *chosen* to mind my own business, but Silvano changed that when he led an army of idiots through my yard. I don't know what he's been teaching vampires in his region, or why. What I do know is they need a makeover, one only I can provide." He arched a brow. "Unless you're doubting my sanity, too?"

Kylan smirked.

Ryder did not.

"We both know Texas isn't your playground, Lil," Ryder added. "Let me wrangle 'em up for you, teach 'em a lesson, while you find a fitting candidate to take my place. Although, as payment, I want freedom to go back to not giving a fuck and minding my own business. Understood?"

Damn, he was giving Kylan stiff competition in the balls department.

Because fuck. He'd just essentially commanded her decision, acting as though she'd already agreed.

And maybe she had.

Because she just kept staring at him, visibly speechless.

"Seems a sound arrangement, lass," Cormac said. "He's worthy and offering. Cannae get better than that, if ye ask me."

Lajos nodded. "It will take time to find a suitable candidate, Lilith. Managing both territories in the interim would be a hefty task. Give it to Ryder; just keep the bastard on a leash."

Ryder snorted. "Keep your bedroom fetishes out of this discussion, Lajos."

Lilith raised her hand between them before Lajos could reply. "Enough." She lowered her arm and pressed an index finger to her temple to massage it. "Fine. Ryder can take over as *temporary* royal. Until I come up with a better solution."

Shit. She caved. I expected her to fight harder or outright deny him, but she suddenly appeared too exhausted to care.

Darius says it's a smart political move, Silas replied. *Ryder could claim royalty at any time and demand a territory. She really isn't in a place to deny him.*

Really?

That's what Darius says.

Huh. Vampire politics was fucked up.

"I think that covers everything, then," Lilith continued. "The entire council will convene in Lilith City in two months' time. We will no longer be convening annually, but quarterly." She looked around the room, searching for an objection.

"Is that a social occasion I am not to attend?" Kylan asked, reminding me of an unruly child raising a petulant question.

It raised a smirk from Ryder across the room. "We could only be so lucky."

"*All* council members are to attend," Lilith replied, her tone laced with command. "Even Robyn."

All the good humor fled from Kylan's features. "It's as if you're daring me to kill another royal, Lilith."

She narrowed her gaze. "Given your recent track record, Kylan, I wouldn't recommend it."

"Why, darling, that almost sounds like a challenge," he murmured. "I assume we're all free to leave?"

Her jaw clenched. "Yes. You may go," she replied with a very tight smile.

"Excellent." He turned with a flourish, leaving without so much as a glance back.

Several followed but paused to thank me for my hospitality on their way out. A few even congratulated me, commenting that they would return for my official ascension. Jace was among the latter. Luka, too. Apparently, we would be having a party again in a little less than a month. Awesome.

Fortunately, Lilith said she wouldn't be able to make it.

Feigning my disappointment had not been easy.

Even Logan seemed to struggle as he waited beside me.

The rumble of cars starting outside was a welcome sound, causing me to sigh as the last of the council members disappeared, leaving me alone with Logan. We had a few matters to tend to, what with my grandfather moving to his territory.

"How would you feel about me bringing Claudette with me?" Logan asked. "To your ascension, I mean."

"I think my granddad would like that," I said, smiling. "Do you mind if I hold on to him for a few weeks? To sort out the chaos in Clemente Clan?"

He had sat through one of the meetings with my grandfather where we reviewed all the pack members, their skill sets, locations, and potential for advancement. So Logan knew what kind of shitstorm Walter had left for me to clean up.

"Yeah, I can manage for a few weeks without him." He smiled. "It'll give me a chance to sort a few members out on my own."

My own lips quirked up. "I hear that." There were several assholes around here I couldn't wait to remove. I clapped him on the back. "Keep in touch, yeah?"

"Pretty sure that's a given," he drawled. "Gotta make sure you don't hurt my big sister."

I laughed as we exited the lodge. "Trust me. Your sister can handle herself."

Pride lit up his blue eyes. "Yeah. She can."

I'm coming home, I told Silas. *Get Luna naked.*

Already a work in progress, he replied in a breathy tone. *We started as soon as the vampires left.*

I wouldn't have it any other way.

Chapter Forty-One

LUNA

THIS WAS MUCH DIFFERENT from my first mating ceremony.

For one, I didn't want to ruin it.

And for another, I wanted the alpha to smell my recent sexual experience for an entirely different reason.

The look in Edon's eyes as he kissed a path down my body before the pack made my efforts worth it. And as he met the apex between my thighs, he growled in hunger at scenting Silas's recent marking.

If the alpha sniffed around the back, he'd smell himself.

But he didn't.

Instead, he grinned and bit me where he originally did just over two months ago, reclaiming me for all to see. Only this time, Silas knelt and bit my opposite thigh.

I swallowed, the heat of their joint embrace lighting an ember inside me that refused to cool. If they didn't get up here quickly, I'd join them on the ground.

But slowly they stood, their matching grins so very wolfish.

"Do you accept us as your mates?" Edon asked, his eyes darker than midnight and yet glistening from the full moon above.

"I do." I wrapped my palm around the back of his neck and kissed him, then repeated the gesture with Silas. And knelt before them.

I ran my nose up and down their thighs, breathing in their rich masculine scents. These two virile males were all mine. For eternity. Mmm. The things we would do together. But first I had to claim them properly beneath the moon, in front of our peers and the pack, and all our ancestors above.

My teeth sank into Silas first, our connection snapping into place with a force that stole the breath from my lungs. All his emotions, his thoughts, his senses became mine. Just as he inherited the same from me, our link permanent and amazing and filling a void deep inside me.

Oh, but I needed Edon, too.

I wasted no time in biting him.

He groaned into my mind, two months of partial fulfillment slamming into me at once. Fuck, his desire to mate was potent. The happiness that followed nearly knocked me to the ground. And the overwhelming sense of love that flourished inside him, it melted my heart.

I jumped up into his arms, capturing his lips with mine and devoured him. Silas growled, his fingers threading in my hair as he tugged me away and covered my mouth with his own.

Mates, I breathed.

Yes, they replied in unison.

We kissed for so long that our audience grew restless. They wanted more. The three of us were naked, our arousal evident. But we weren't done yet.

Edon needed to establish a mating link to Silas and vice versa. It would go deeper than their sire-progeny bond and firmly solidify our triad.

After another long kiss with Edon, the males released me to focus on each other. "Before I do this, I have an announcement to make," my alpha mate said, his voice gruff and sexy as fuck. I loved his dominant tone. It was the one that made me go to my knees, but as I heard what he wanted to say in his mind, I didn't follow my instinct.

Instead, I smiled.

Yes, I told him. Not that he needed my approval, but I gave it nonetheless.

He gazed out at the crowd, his focus falling on several members of our clan—all new additions to headquarters after some careful selections these past few weeks. Such a different vibe from my first arrival. These lycans were curious, if a little wary. However, Edon would lead them into a new way of life, while Silas and I would help in any way he needed.

"It's very rare for a human turned lycan to survive. Even rarer for him to exude much strength in his new form. That said, I've noticed uncanny will and prowess in my progeny. So much so that I suspect he's of a rare alpha bloodline. Which would explain Luna's and my attraction to him." He paused to smile at Silas, a light hum telling me they were talking mind to mind.

Soon the three of us would possess that trait.

No walls.

No hiding.

All open intensity and love.

"So why am I telling you all this?" Edon continued, his amusement palpable from whatever Silas had said. Probably a comment about why Edon and I were enamored with him.

The only thing attractive about my blood is the way it fills my cock when you both want to fuck, Silas murmured into my mind. *That's what I told him.*

I bit my lip to keep from laughing and gave him a come-hither look instead. It earned me a low growl through our new connection.

Stop flirting, Edon chastised softly. *I'm making an important announcement.*

Out loud he said, "I'm telling you all this because I'm promoting Silas to the position of enforcer within the pack."

A wave of shock settled over the pack.

Followed by a clap.

Jolene stood, his eyes glittering with satisfaction, his hands loud as he applauded. And soon the others joined in, their focus and respect landing on Silas.

All signs of amusement had fled, his expression one of open astonishment. "Enforcer?"

"Consider it your new—official—nickname," Edon murmured, smiling as the sound of approval heightened. "You earned it."

I don't even know what it means, Silas whispered.

It means you're his right-hand man, I explained. *If Edon ever steps away on business, you're the acting alpha. It's extremely rare. Most alphas don't name an enforcer because it suggests he believes you're a contender for his position at the top. That you could be the Alpha of Clemente Clan.*

Silas gaped at Edon. "You can't be serious."

"You know I never do anything without purpose," he replied, wrapping his palm around the back of Silas's neck. "And now it's time to make you truly ours." He knelt while holding his new enforcer's gaze, adoration and esteem radiating from his expression. "Will you have us, Silas?"

"Yes." It came out choked, so he cleared his throat and said it again. "Yes." He reached for my hand, holding me close.

And Edon struck.

I shuddered, feeling the connections snapping, the energy sizzling between the three of us as the triad called for Silas to finish it.

The men switched places, Edon's arm sliding around my lower back as Silas knelt before us and kissed the alpha's lower abdomen. A taunting promise lit his blue gaze, sending a tremor through me for an entirely different reason.

Such a tease, I heard Edon chastise.

That I could sense him talking to Silas confirmed how close we were to completion. I whimpered, needing it to be done, to finalize our destiny.

I love you both, Silas murmured. *To the moon and back.*

To the moon and back, Edon agreed.

For eternity, I added.

Electricity wrapped around the three of us as Silas bit down, finishing the ritual.

Power snapped into place.

Voices.

Feelings.

Sensations.

Love.

All of it at once, leaving me overflowing with life—*three* lives.

I sighed, collapsing into the arms of my males, our lips all over each other at once. Not for sex. But for adoration. Worship. A vow for forever.

I barely registered the clapping, too caught up in the new connection to focus on much else. Silas's mouth whispered over mine. Edon caressed my neck. They were both in my head, but the alpha was louder.

Time to ascend, little mate, he murmured. *Join me?*

He didn't mean in the actual ascension—a female couldn't be alpha of a clan—but in the ceremony. *I wouldn't miss it.*

Enforcer? he asked.

I go where you go, Silas replied. *Always.*

You'll both be the ones who keep me grounded, he said softly. *There are trying times ahead.*

And we'll be with you every step of the way, I vowed.

Every step, Silas echoed.

I know, he whispered.

And he really did. I felt that surety radiating through him.

Just as I sensed his love.

Our love.

There might be a revolution brewing on the horizon, one that had the potential to end in disaster. But I wasn't scared. In fact, I welcomed anyone to try to take us down. Because as a unit, we were unstoppable.

Touch one of us, and we'll end you.

We're the Clemente Clan triad.

Tread carefully.

We bite.

Epilogue

SILAS

"BEAUTIFUL ASCENSION," Jace praised with a glance up at the moon.

"Thanks," I replied. "But it was Edon who ascended." And he was standing about ten yards to the right talking to Luka.

"Oh, I know. But I have something for you, wolf." Jace handed me an envelope. "It's from Kylan. As you know, he couldn't attend due to Lilith's little grounding punishment."

I frowned at the item. "He wrote me a letter?"

Jace shrugged. "Said it had information you would want. I didn't read it, so I have no idea what he meant."

"I see. Well, thanks."

He nodded and turned, then paused and rotated back around. "What does Edon plan to do with Walter's leftover harem? I assume he won't be using the slave girls in Aurora's basement?"

"I wasn't aware there were any," I replied, frowning. Edon and I had never discussed it. In fact, I'd never actually seen Walter's harem. I sort of assumed he'd killed them all.

Jace smiled. "Then Aurora did as I suggested. Clever girl."

"Which was what?"

"Ah, a gentleman doesn't kiss and tell, new wolf." He winked. "Consider that a lesson."

The royal wandered off with his hands in his pockets and a kick in his step, leaving me torn between demanding an explanation and reading the letter.

She gave them to Luka, Edon murmured. *There were only three, as Walter had a penchant for fucking his harem to death. It seems my mother tried to help the remaining females by feeding them when my poor excuse for a father wasn't looking.*

I grimaced. *That doesn't surprise me. But why didn't you say anything?* It seemed like something he'd mention.

Because I only just found out. The pack psyche is filled with information. Apparently, my grandfather helped her.

He's a lot scrappier than he lets on, I replied, eyeing the older male in the crowd.

He had an arm around a much smaller woman, her hair as white as his. But the way he held her reminded me of how I embraced my Luna. She stood beside them, the stars in her eyes. Happiness radiated from her, causing me to smile. *She really is beautiful, isn't she?*

Yeah, she is, Edon agreed softly. *Our little mate.*

Our little moon, I mused back at him.

You know I can hear you both, right? Luna put in. *Open connection now, boys. Behave.*

Never, Edon growled.

I could already see that fucking later would be fun. All of us in each other's heads? Yeah, that would be hot. Too bad we had another hour of mingling to do first. At least we were clothed again, because if I had to watch Edon and Luna prance around naked all night, I wouldn't last another five minutes.

So needy, Edon teased.

Says the male who is growing harder by the second, I tossed back at him as I opened the envelope. Might as well distract myself for a moment with Kylan's letter. I couldn't imagine what he had to say unless it was regarding Rae.

I unfolded the note, my eyes roaming over the words in a quick sweep that brought my heart to my throat.

Oh, fuck…

Willow.

Young Wolf,

My consort requested I send you my findings on an old friend. To fulfill her wishes, I'm drafting this correspondence.

After finally locating your friend's camp destination, I stumbled upon some troubling news. It seems she escaped four weeks ago and has yet to be found. Which leads me to believe she's now in Silvano Region. If only she'd chosen the opposite direction to run, you'd have her in your custody now, as she was being held in Clemente Clan's breeding camp.

I'll continue my search. However, for now, I've reached a dead end. Let's hope your friend has a fire similar to yours and my consort's. She'll need it to survive.

Regards,
—K

P.S. Congratulations on the triad.

THE STORY CONTINUES WITH REBEL BITTEN...

Rebel Bitten

Willow

Run, run, run!
They're chasing me, even into my dreams.

And when I awake, I see *him*. Striking blue eyes with a hint of the devil inside. He's my savior and my worst nightmare combined.

Because he owns me.
He found me.
He saved me.

But I don't want to be owned. I want to be free. Even if it kills me.

Ryder

I needed a diversion, a plaything, something to distract me from this perpetual boredom. And she appeared as if the Almighty above had heard my prayers.

Or, more accurately, the devil.

Because I'm not a good man. Humanity died inside me long ago. It was what I needed to survive.

But she's such a pretty little thing. I think I'll keep her and make her mine. At least for a little while. Humans are so fragile, after all.

Welcome to Ryder Region.
It might not be mine yet, but it will be soon.
For I haven't lived this long by playing nice.
I prefer to bite.

About The Author

USA Today Bestselling Author Lexi C. Foss loves to play in dark worlds, especially the ones that bite. She lives in Atlanta, Georgia with her husband and their furry children. When not writing, she's busy crossing items off her travel bucket list, or chasing eclipses around the globe. She's quirky, consumes way too much coffee, and loves to swim.

Also By Lexi C. Foss

Blood Alliance Series
Chastely Bitten
Royally Bitten
Regally Bitten

Dark Provenance Series
Daughter of Death
Son of Chaos

Elemental Fae Academy
Book One
Book Two
Book Three

Immortal Curse Series
Blood Laws
Forbidden Bonds
Blood Heart
Elder Bonds
Blood Bonds
Angel Bonds
Blood Seeker

Mershano Empire Series
The Prince's Game
The Charmer's Gambit
The Rebel's Redemption

Underworld Royals Series
Happily Ever Crowned

Standalone Novels
Scarlet Mark

www.ingramcontent.com/pod-product-compliance
Lightning Source LLC
Chambersburg PA
CBHW020534310726
48979CB00014B/2329/J

* 9 7 8 1 6 8 5 3 0 0 8 3 8 *